THIS SIDE OF PARADISE

人间天堂

（美）弗朗西斯·斯科特·基·菲茨杰拉德◎著
杨婵◎译

沈阳出版发行集团
沈阳出版社

图书在版编目（CIP）数据

人间天堂 /（美）弗朗西斯·斯科特·基·菲茨杰拉德著；杨婵译. -- 沈阳：沈阳出版社，2018.2
　　ISBN 978-7-5441-9123-4

Ⅰ.①人… Ⅱ.①弗… ②杨… Ⅲ.①长篇小说—美国—现代 Ⅳ.①I712.45

中国版本图书馆CIP数据核字(2018)第029256号

出版发行：	沈阳出版发行集团｜沈阳出版社
	（地址：沈阳市沈河区南翰林路10号 邮编：110011）
网　　址：	http://www.sycbs.com
印　　刷：	三河市海新印务有限公司
幅面尺寸：	150mm×215mm
印　　张：	8.5
字　　数：	280千字
出版时间：	2018年3月第1版
印刷时间：	2018年3月第1次印刷
责任编辑：	张　楠
封面设计：	白砚川
版式设计：	鼎夏图书
责任校对：	杨敏成
责任监印：	杨　旭

书　　号：ISBN 978-7-5441-9123-4
定　　价：50.00元

联系电话：024-24112447
E-mail：sy24112447@163.com

本书若有印装质量问题，影响阅读，请与出版社联系调换。

前言
PREFACE

《人间天堂》是美国二十世纪最伟大的作家之一——弗朗西斯·司各特·菲茨杰拉德迈向文学殿堂的处女作,也是一部划时代的作品,颇受文学大师托·斯·艾略特、乔伊斯、海明威等人的盛赞。除此之外,菲茨杰拉德的代表作《了不起的盖茨比》在外国文学畅销书排行榜上数年来始终名列前茅,之后他的长篇小说《夜色温柔》、短篇小说《重访巴比伦》《五一节》《富家子弟》等作品也陆续被众人熟知,并受到了广大读者的喜爱。

《人间天堂》是一部具有双重性质的小说,它不仅饱含强烈的自传性,而且也不乏纪实性。在小说主人公艾默里的身上,读者能看到作者菲茨杰拉德的影子,不管是艾默里的生活经历还是性格特点,都与作者有相似之处。与此同时,小说也描述了第一次世界大战前后美国真实的社会状态,尤其对美国中西部和东部中产阶级的生活状况更是做了详细的介绍,将青年学生的校园生活、思想情感的成长与波动都一一记录下来,揭露了他们的人生观、爱情观以及对于战争的看法等。有人称《人间天堂》为"爵士乐时代"的编年史,然而小说本身却超越了这个具体的年代和地区,从不同的方面讲述了青年学生经历的苦难与折磨、成功与失败,以及由此而引起的情绪上的变化。《人间天堂》对青年人探索人生意义以及追求人生目标具有十分普遍而重要的意义,这也是该部小说备受读者喜爱的原因之一。

除此之外，菲茨杰拉德在创作《人间天堂》时表现出了极大的激情与活力，小说中讲述的故事既浪漫又凄楚，着重描写了上世纪二十年代美国青年人的生活理念，以及对传统价值观念和道德标准的背叛精神，这些内容深深感染了读者，几乎成了年轻读者们领悟生活的重要秘籍。如此一来，自然也就不难理解为什么该书首次印刷的三千册，在三天之内就销售一空了。

虽然《人间天堂》描写的是与当代相距甚远的一代青年人的生活状态，但同时也像一面镜子一样反应出了当代人的生活，引人深思。

目录
Contents

1 第一卷 — 爱空想的自负者

第一章　艾默里——贝雅特丽丝的儿子 / 002

第二章　尖顶建筑和怪兽滴水嘴 / 036

第三章　自大的人开始反思 / 085

第四章　顾影自怜的美少年 / 113

插曲　一九一七年五月至一九一九年二月 / 146

2 第二卷 — 一个重要人物所受的教育

第一章　刚入社交圈的少女 / 154

第二章　康复实验 / 183

第三章　狂妄的嘲讽 / 206

第四章　鄙视一切的牺牲 / 229

第五章　自傲的人变得重要起来 / 239

第一卷

爱空想的自负者

第一章　艾默里——贝雅特丽丝的儿子

除了为数不多的几个孤零零却又难以言说的特色以外，艾默里·布莱恩继承了他母亲身上的属于她性格当中的每一个特色，因此他这个很好的儿子孕育而生了。他父亲原来就是个毫无用处的人，不擅长表达自己，但喜欢诵读拜伦的诗作，还常常在翻看《大英百科全书》的时候睡着，他因为在芝加哥做出一番事业的两个兄长接连死亡，而在三十岁时便成了一个富裕的人，就在他心里非常开心，感觉这世界都在自己手中的时候，他来到了旅游胜地巴尔港[1]，就是在这里，他和贝雅特丽丝·奥哈拉相逢了。于是，斯蒂芬·布莱恩把他接近六英尺的身高和到了最关键之时就会犹豫不决的个性遗传给了他的孩子，这两个特色在他的儿子艾默里的身上都可以看到。很长时间以来，他就在这样的家庭背景下徘徊生活，赫然是一个没有自信的人的形象，呆滞柔软的头发将他的半张脸都挡住了，他总是忙着"照顾"自己的妻子，但却因为不理解也无法理解她而感到厌烦。

但贝雅特丽丝·奥哈拉却完全不同！她是一个很棒的女人！从她很早的在属于她爸爸的威斯康星州日内瓦湖庄园里照的照片上，抑或是从她在罗马圣心女修道院拍的照片上——她年幼的时候，那些非常有钱的人家的女儿才拥有这种奢华的教育方式——都能够瞧出她容貌清秀，她的衣服制作精良、样式简单。她拥有过良好的教育——她的青年时期正处在在文艺复兴的强盛阶段，她对那些古老罗马家族的最近的传言都非常了解；就是红衣教主维多利亚和意大利女王玛格丽塔，以及必须要具备非常高的文化底蕴才能够听到的非常神秘的名人，都可以说出她的名字，知道她是一个极其有钱的美国女孩。她在英国学会了怎样选择威士忌并加上苏打水来喝而不喝葡萄酒，在维也纳居住了一个冬天，因此她闲谈的话题得到了拓展。总的来说，贝雅特丽丝享有了以后再也没有机会接受的教育；那是一种依照一个人或者蔑视或者喜欢的人和物的多少来权衡的

---

1. 这是位于迈阿密南面的一个海岛小城，乃避暑胜地。

第一章　艾默里—贝雅特丽丝的儿子

特殊指导；那是一种蕴含所有的艺术和传统，然而缺少任何思想的文化，就像一个优秀的园丁修剪了糟糕的玫瑰，使得一朵理想的花蕾绽放之后最后形成的文化。

她在不那么显耀的时候回到了美国，和斯蒂芬·布莱恩相逢，并同他结婚了——她作出这样的决断实在是由于她有一些厌烦，有一些难过。她怀上独生子的时候是在一个让人疲乏的季节，那是一八九六年的一个春天，他被带到了这个世界上。

等到艾默里五岁的时候，他早已是使她高兴的伙伴了。他是一个长着红褐色头发的小孩，有一对迟早会变得极其有吸引力的美丽的大眼睛，还有极其灵便并且充满想象力的头脑和在化装舞会上对于化妆服的独到的审美观。在他四岁到十岁的这些年当中，他和妈妈一起乘坐姥爷的私家车探险观光，一直从科罗纳多[1]往南到墨西哥城，但是在科罗纳多，他妈妈因为太过厌烦，最终在一家时尚人物光顾的酒店精神错乱，等到了墨西哥城时，居然感染了轻微、几近是流行性的结核病。但是感染这个病以后反倒使她开心起来，并且之后还利用这个病，将这个病当作是自己周围环境当中本来就有的组成部分——特别是在把几口使人惊慌失措的烈性酒喝下去之后。

就是如此，那些勉强算得上走运的富家公子在新港[2]海滩还在抱怨家庭女老师的管束，或挨揍、挨训、听父母念小说《敢作敢当》[3]抑或是《密西西比河上的弗兰克》[4]之时，艾默里却早已在纽约的沃尔多夫大酒店招惹默默听从的运行李的服务生了他，对于室内乐和交响乐早已失去了那种天生的厌恶，并从他妈妈那里得到了十分特殊的教导。

"艾默里。"

"哦，贝雅特丽丝。"（这般称呼他的妈妈有些奇怪，然而她一定要让他这么叫。）

---

1. 位于加利福尼亚西南的一座城市，位置和圣迪戈相近。
2. 这里是指罗得岛的一个避暑胜地。
3. 美国儿童文学作家小霍莱旭·阿尔杰（Horatio Alger,Jr, 1832—1899）著。小阿尔杰的小说多是围绕与贫困和诱惑作斗争的孩子最后获得财富和美名的故事。
4. 美国儿童文学作家查尔斯·奥斯汀·弗斯迪克（Charales Austin Fosdick, 1842—1915）写的冒险故事。

"亲爱的,现在别急着起床。我时常怀疑小时候就早起床会使得人心情烦躁。克洛蒂尔德会送上来你的早饭的。"

"那行吧。"

"艾默里,今天我觉得自己的年纪已经非常大了,"她说道,她那张面容就如同一幅生动形象的表现悲伤的浮雕,讲话的声音很小,但她的双手反而如同莎拉·伯恩哈特[1]的双手一般特别灵活。"我的心情十分焦虑暴躁。明天我们一定得远离这个令人害怕的地方,去追寻明净的阳光。"

听到妈妈的一番话,艾默里那灵活的绿眼睛就会透过他那乱糟糟的头发牢牢地看着他的妈妈。即便是在这个年纪,他对她也没有怀揣着奢望。

"艾默里。"

"啊,嗯。"

"你得用滚烫的热水洗一个澡——水一定要热,这样的话就会使你的心情放轻松。假如你想读书的话就躺在浴缸当中读。"

在他还不到十岁的时候,她就给他读《戏装游乐图》[2]的节选;等到十一岁他就可以口若悬河地高谈勃拉姆斯、莫扎特和贝多芬,即便这般讲让他有一些追忆的感觉。一天下午,他自己一个人待在温泉城[3]的酒店里,之后他喝了一点妈妈的杏子酒,因为杏子做的酒符合他的口味,他就多饮了几口,稍微有些不清醒了。这也仅仅是一时贪玩罢了,但是在非常高兴的状况下他会把香烟拿来吸,因为没有抵制住诱惑做出了恶俗、粗鲁的行为。虽然贝雅特丽丝在知道这件事以后觉得非常吓人,然而也使她感觉有些好玩,而且变为了后代人可能会说的她"乐趣"的组成部分。

"我的这个儿子,"某一天他听到她朝着满屋子非常震惊、一脸佩服的女客人讲,"非常成熟、十分惹人喜爱——然而有一些柔弱——我们全家都很柔弱;这个地方,你们了解。"她将光彩照人的手放在异常漂亮的胸口上;然后她压低声音悄悄地给她们讲了儿子喝杏子酒的事情。她们一个个都笑得很开心,因为她说起故事来绘声绘色的,但是那天晚上,晚间餐具柜可以上锁的都锁上了,

---

1. 法国著名的一位女伶。
2. 这是法国诗人、象征主义诗歌代表作家魏尔兰(Paul Verlaine,1844—1896)的一部诗集,他的诗都充满着音乐节奏。
3. 这里是指位于阿肯色州中部的一座城市。

就是为了避免出现意外,无论是男孩儿还是女孩儿……

这些家族内部在朝圣时一直是非常注重体面的:两个仆人,私家车,或许还有布莱恩先生,如果他能够叫过来的话,通常还得跟着一名医生。如果艾默里一直不停地咳嗽,就会有四个觉得非常讨厌的专职人员包围着他的床愤怒地看着他;在他感染上猩红热的时候,照顾的人包括医生和护士,数量就会达到十四个。但是,血液的浓度总是要比饭桌上的清汤浓度大,他的病情也好了。

布莱恩家族并不属于任意一个大城市。他们是日内瓦湖的布莱恩姓人;他们需要招呼的亲戚有很多,朋友反而有些少,并且从帕萨迪纳到科德角[1]享有使人羡慕的地位。然而贝雅特丽丝愈加对和刚认识的朋友交流感兴趣,由于她家里的一些事情,例如她自己的病史和很多新状况、关于她在国外经历的时光的回忆,她感觉这些都得定期再描述一次。就和弗洛伊德的梦一般,这些回忆都得讲出来,不然的话,过去的记忆就会快速蔓延,扰乱她的心情,让她心情烦躁。然而对于美国的女人来讲,贝雅特丽丝极其爱挑刺,尤其是讲到那些来自于西部的流动人口时,她更加说不出好话。

"她们讲起话来有非常重的口音,亲爱的,"她告诉艾默里,"她们的口音不是南方口音,也不是波士顿口音,哪里的口音都不是,就是有很重的口音"——她已经神志不清了。"她们口里讲的是不经意间学会的老式的、不流行的伦敦口音,也许不受欢迎,但总需要有人讲这种话。她们讲起话来仿佛一个在芝加哥的大歌剧团待过几年的英国男管家说话一样。"她此时讲话已经前后矛盾了——"就像——每个西部女人一生当中都会遇到那种时候——她感觉她的丈夫已经足够富有,因此她已经能够有——口音——她们想要给我们留下一个好印象,亲爱的——"

虽然她将自己的身体当作是一堆羸弱的肉体,但是她感觉她的灵魂也同样处于一种病态,所以这在她的生活当中处于一个十分重要的位置。以前她曾经是一个天主教徒,然而她发觉,当自己处在失去对于母教的信仰或者是再次将这种信仰找到的过程中时,那些神职人员往往会展现出比往常更大的关心,因此,她就采纳了一个令人喜爱的犹豫不决的做法。她经常哀叹美国的天主教神职人员品行粗鄙无能,坚信假如她生活在欧洲大陆大教堂的保护下,她的灵魂就仍

---

[1]帕萨迪纳地处美国太平洋海岸的加利福尼亚州,科德角位于美国大西洋海岸的马萨诸塞州,在文中意思是指整个美国。

然是罗马庞大圣坛上一点羸弱的火光。话虽这样讲，但除了医生以外，神职人员依然是她最喜欢与之交流的人。

"啊，威斯顿主教，"她会这样讲，"我不想交流自己的事情。我可以想象得到情绪异常兴奋的女人接连不断地向你的门口跑去，恳请你可以配合她们一些"——之后在和神职人员来往一段时间之后——"但是我的态度——依旧——非常古怪还是不相同。"

唯有对大主教和职位更高的神职人员，她才会将可以和他们述说的自己的恋爱袒露出来。她刚刚回国的时候，和一个没有宗教信仰的人相遇了，这个斯温伯恩[1]式的青年家住在阿什维尔，对于他那满是激情的亲吻和讲求实际的交谈，她明显非常热衷——他们从正反两个方面交流过这件事情，并且假仁假义的理智恋爱丝毫不掺杂在里面。最后她还是决定嫁给经济条件与自己相差无几的人，而那个阿什维尔的青年在遭受了一场精神危机后，加入了天主教会，他就是如今的——达西大人。

"的确，布莱恩夫人，他还是一个非常亲昵的朋友——那是红衣主教的能干的帮手。"

"艾默里跟随他的那一天总会到来的，我了解。"美丽的夫人小声说道，"达西大人对我非常了解，他同样会对他也非常了解的。"

艾默里已经十三岁了，长得瘦高瘦高的，愈加能够了解他那凯尔特人母亲的想法。间或他也接受家庭教师的教导——最基本的思想是要"赶得上"，把每一个他"没有做完的作业都完成"，但是因为家庭老师都没有发现他没有完成的作业，不清楚从哪里下手，所以他仍然觉得自己很棒。如此一来几年之后他会变成什么样的人还有待考察。但是，他同贝雅特丽丝坐船离开美国赶往意大利，离开港口才经过四个小时，他的阑尾炎就已经发作了。这或许是因为他经常在床上躺着吃饭的原因吧。于就在发了一连串的加急电报到欧洲和美国之后，一船的乘客都惊讶地发现，大轮船缓慢地改变航向又回到纽约，把艾默里送到了码头。如果不是关乎性命的大事，轮船掉头返回几乎难以实现。

艾默里做过阑尾手术之后，贝雅特丽丝精神崩溃，和震颤性谵妄的症状有

---

1. 斯温伯恩（Algemon Charles Swinbume,1837—1909），英国的一位诗人，同时也是文学评论家，他主张无神论。

些相像，因此艾默里就被送去了明尼阿波利斯[1]，暂时和他的姨妈、姨夫一块生活两年。等到了那个地方，西部文明自然、狂野的氛围第一次把他吸引住了——就好像是几近赤裸裸的接触。

献给艾默里的一个吻

瞥见这张纸的时候他的嘴角抽搐了一下。

"十二月十七日，周四，"纸条上面这样写着，"下午五点的时候，我将举办一个雪橇游晚会，如果你能到的话，我会非常开心的。

请回答

梅拉·圣·克莱尔"

他已经在明尼阿波利斯居住了两个月了，这里最令他不安的就是要尽力对别人隐瞒，不让学校里的同学知道他觉得自己有多么优秀，但是关于这种优越感的信念，是在移动的沙滩的基础上建立起来的，并没有多牢固。在某一天的法语课上（他被分在法语高级班），他展现了一下自己，艾默里极其瞧不上老师讲法语时发出的口音，搞得利尔顿老师特别窘迫，但班上的同学却都特别开心。在十年前，这位利尔顿老师曾在法国巴黎住过好几个星期，于是每次上课他都用法语的动词的词形变化来为难他。但是有一次，艾默里在历史课上也炫耀了一次，最终却丢尽了脸面，由于那些男生都和他同岁，在之后的一个星期里，他们相互之间讲起话来就怪里怪气地指桑骂槐：

"呀——我觉得，你们清楚吗，美国革命主要是中产阶级关心的事情，还讲什么华盛顿来自名门之家——非常有名的家族——我觉得。"

艾默里计上心头，有时有意把话说错，凭借这个找回一点面子。两年前他就开始诵读一本美国历史了，即使这本书只是讲到殖民战争，可他母亲却感觉写得非常好。

他在运动这一方面很不擅长，然而他在发现运动是测验你在学校实力和人缘的试金石以后，就开始坚持不懈地努力锻炼，努力获得在冬季运动会上的胜利，而且在脚踝肿痛、无论用什么方法都无法站起来的时候，他依旧很有勇气地坚持每天到洛莱溜冰场一圈一圈地锻炼，心里怀疑，他要多长时间才可以保持让冰球的球棍和冰鞋不会胡乱地纠缠在一起。

---

1. 位于明尼苏达州东南密西西比河河边的一座城市。

梅拉·圣·克莱尔小姐开展雪橇晚会的邀请信已经放在他的外套口袋中一个上午了,一块脏呼呼的花生薄脆糖紧紧地和它黏在一块。等到下午他才彻底地将纸条和糖弄开,松了一口气,于是他在心里好好想了一番,并且在科勒和丹尼尔合著的《基础拉丁读本》这本书的最后一页打了一个草稿,接着给她写了一个回信:

亲爱的圣·克莱尔小姐:

你很礼貌地邀请我参加你于下周四晚上进行的晚会的邀请函我今天早上收到了,我十分开心。能在下周四晚上参加晚会,我感到很荣幸。

满怀谢意

艾默里·布莱恩

因此,等到周四那天他满怀心事地在被铁锹弄平、非常容易滑倒的人行道上走着,而且瞧见了梅拉家的屋子,那时已经五点半了,他觉得他妈妈会非常赞同他晚到半个小时。他在门口的台阶上站着,双眼微微合上,故意表现出一副漠不关心的模样,打算一鼓作气走到里面去。然后走上前去,步履稳健地,和圣·克莱尔夫人见面,用非常标准的语调说道:

"亲爱的圣·克莱尔夫人,不好意思我迟到了,但是我的女仆"——讲到这个地方他停顿了一下,感觉自己简直如同背书一般——"但是我姨夫和我要去看望一个人——嗯,对了,我是在舞蹈学校碰到您那惹人喜爱的女儿的。"

接着他就会使用有些外国式的微微欠身的动作,去和那些神态有些拘束的小女人们握手,而且向站在一边的人点头,他们成群结队地互相依靠着对方,都站在那里一动不动地。

这时门被一个男管家(明尼阿波利斯三个男管家中的一个)打开了。艾默里走到里面,把帽子和外套脱下来。他没有听见隔壁房间传出来的叽里呱啦高声讲话的声音,就觉得有一些惊讶,认为这肯定是非常注重礼貌的原因。他对于这样的规则非常赞同——就和他赞同男管家的行为一样。

"梅拉小姐,"他讲道。

令他觉得震惊的是,男管家很吓人地张嘴笑着。

"嗯,非常正确,"他说,"她就在家里。"他没有感觉到他讲的含有伦敦口音的话已经拉低了自己的身份。艾默里神情冷淡地盯着他。

"但是,"男管家接着讲道,莫名其妙地把讲话的声音提高了,"只有她一个人待在家里。要参加晚会的人早已离开了。"

艾默里瞠目结舌了。

"什么？"

"她一直在等候着艾默里·布莱恩。就是你吧？她妈妈讲了，如果五点半钟你到了这里的话，你们两个就坐派克车[1]去赶他们。"

瞧见梅拉一个人走出了房间，艾默里感觉更加绝望，只见她身穿一件厚绒呢轻便大衣，一直包裹住了她的耳朵，很明显她是一脸的怒意，讲话的时候勉强带有一丝喜悦。

"你好，艾默里。"

"你好，梅拉。"他以前描述过自己充足的精力。

"呀——你总归到这里来了。"

"嗯——我得跟你说明一下。我觉得你还不知道我来的时候车子出了点问题，"他开始说谎，信口胡说。

梅拉瞪大了双眼。

"有谁受伤了吗？"

"嗯，"他接着胡说，"姨妈姨夫还有我。"

"有谁去世了吗？"

艾默里讲话停了一下，接着点了一下头。

"是你姨夫吗？"——非常惊讶。

"啊，不是的——仅仅是一匹马而已——仿佛是一匹灰色的马。"

听到这个部分，那个有着苏格兰高地口音的男管家悄悄地笑了。

"也许是汽车的引擎死了，"他说道。艾默里真心想肆无忌惮地教训他一下。

"现在我们就离开吧，"梅拉冷漠地说。"告诉你，艾默里，我们提前订了五人坐的大雪橇，并且大家都已经到了，因此我们不可以再耽误了——"

"哦，我也是没有办法的，对不对？"

"因此母亲让我等到五点半。我们必须在雪橇抵达明尼哈哈乡村俱乐部之前赶上他们，艾默里。"

艾默里脑海中的那些城镇此时已经不见了。他头脑里出现了一幅画面，就

---

1. 这是底特律派克汽车公司出产的豪华汽车，第一辆车在一八九八年生产，最后一辆在一九五八年生产。

见一群开心的人乘坐的雪橇发出叮叮当当的铃儿的响声在满是积雪的大街上奔走,此时气派的轿车到了,梅拉和他极其醒目地在三十几双眼睛中满是责备的人的面前抵达了,他对人们表达着歉意——这一次是真正的抱歉。他的嘴里吐出一声非常大的叹息声。

"出什么事了吗?"梅拉询问他。

"没事。我打了一个哈欠。咱俩一定可以在他们抵达那里之前赶上吗?"他恨不得还能有一丝希望,他们的汽车可能会偷偷地开进明尼哈哈乡村俱乐部,在那里和其他人碰面,他们或许能够找到一个寂静偏僻的地方,惬意地在暖和的炉火前面坐着,自然而然地将他失去的矜持再次找回来。

"哦,迈克有信心,我们肯定可以追上——我们快一些吧。"

他觉得胃里很难受。他们刚刚在汽车上坐好,他就着急地按照他自己已经考虑好的仿佛一个方格形的程序表的想法,讲出那稍微含有外交辞令类型的话来。那是他按照在舞蹈学校听见的几句"讨好的话"想出来的,那讨好的话的含义是说"非常美丽、和英国人有一些相似"。

"梅拉,"他压低声音,一字一句地说道,"我确实是很抱歉。你可不可以宽恕我呢?"

她神情庄重地观察着他,他的那双专注的绿眼睛,他的嘴巴,对她这个年仅十三岁的女孩子、热衷于时尚的审美眼光来讲,这的确是浪漫的表率。的确,梅拉很容易就宽恕他了。

"哦——呃——行。"

他又向她看了一眼,接着把双眼垂下来。他长着很长的眼睫毛。

"我觉得非常难过,"他情绪低落地说。"我和别人不一样。我不清楚我为什么会做出不符合规矩的事情来。我觉得,可能是我洒脱不羁的原因吧。"然后,他非常自然地讲了一句,"我抽烟抽得有点厉害。我的心脏被烟草残害了,心脏跳动不正常。"

梅拉脑海中浮现出一个没日没夜云山雾罩的场景来,就见艾默里脸色惨白,因为两只肺被尼古丁占满了,他整个人看起来都无精打采的。她轻声叫了一句。

"呀,艾默里,停止抽烟吧。这样会影响你的发育的!"

"我才不关心这个呢,"他满脸愁容,依旧坚持这般。"我必须得抽。早就已经习以为常了。我做的那么多的事情假如被家里知道了"——他踌躇了一下,

第一章　艾默里—贝雅特丽丝的儿子

没有再讲下去,给她一些时间想象阴森吓人的场景——"上周我去看滑稽歌舞杂剧[1]了。"

梅拉几乎要晕过去。他的绿眼睛又看向了她。

"你是我在这个城市唯一倾心的女孩儿,"他心情异常兴奋地讲道。"你非常惹人喜爱。"

梅拉自己也搞不懂她究竟是不是这样的人,这句话听上去很流行,虽然隐隐感觉总有些不对的地方。

外面浓厚的夜色已经开始弥漫;轿车忽然来了一个拐弯,将她甩到了他的身上;他们的手碰到了一块。

"你确实不应该吸烟,艾默里,"她低声讲道。"你不清楚吗?"

他摇了摇脑袋。

"有谁会关心吗?"

梅拉一时间有一些踌躇。

"我关心。"

艾默里心脏的频率忽然加快了。

"嗯,对,你关心!你和蛙喉帕克关系近着呢。我想那是每个人都知道的。"

"不是的,我们不是的,"她缓缓地把话讲了出来。

接着一阵沉默出现了,但是艾默里心里却非常开心。梅拉惬意地坐在车子里,和车外寒冷的空气分隔开,模样非常楚楚可人。梅拉把她的身子都包裹住,就好像很小的一包衣服,暴露在溜冰帽下面的是几撮卷曲的黄头发。

"由于我也有非常喜欢的人——"他停顿了一下,没有继续说下去,只因他听到一群孩子的笑声从远处传来,他在灯光照耀下的马路上通过已经结霜的轿车玻璃,模模糊糊地瞧见一群人坐在雪橇上。他一定得立刻做点什么。他使劲挣扎了一下,坐了起来,低下头把梅拉的手抓住了——准确地说,把她的一个大拇指抓在了手里。

"你让他继续开车,径直到明尼哈哈,"他小声地说。"我需要和你谈谈——必须要和你谈谈。"

梅拉看到了前面有一大堆人,而且马上就看见了她妈妈,接着——呃也

---

1. 滑稽歌舞杂剧包括脱衣舞、女演员半裸的粗俗歌舞等在内的诸多内容。

是因为礼貌吧——看了坐在旁边的人一眼。

"理查德，从这边的横马路转过去，径直到达明尼哈哈俱乐部！"她朝着话筒高声叫道。艾默里坐下来倒在靠垫上，长长地舒了一口气。

"我应当亲她一下，"他在心里说。"我打赌我行的。我打赌我行的。"

头顶上的天空有一半是明朗的，一半则是阴森森的，四周的夜色非常冰凉，紧张的氛围充斥着这里。道路从乡村俱乐部进口处的台阶开始一路延伸，仿佛皱巴巴的白床单上深颜色的褶皱；道路两边的巨大雪堆好像一排排高高的防波堤。他们在台阶上停留了片刻，抬起头看向假日的月光。

"仿佛一轮倾泻着银光的月光"——艾默里隐隐约约地做了一个手势——"使得人们被一层神秘感笼罩。你看起来和一个把帽子摘下、将一头乱糟糟的长发露出来的巫婆一样"——她伸手去弄她的头发——"呀，别弄它，这个样子很漂亮。"

他们迈上扶梯，梅拉在前面走着，走到他梦想中的小小的密室，密室内暖和的炉火在一张很大的长沙发前燃烧着。几年之后，这里将是属于艾默里的大舞台，将会是很多起情感危情的摇篮。此刻他们在这个地方交流了一下关于雪橇晚会的事情。

"常常会有一群非常害羞的人，"他发表着他的见解，"她们在雪橇的后面坐着，但是就是藏起来讲悄悄话还你推我搡。并且总是会碰到一个斗鸡眼的女孩子"——他仿照女孩子的模样做了一个非常可怕的动作——"好像她经常对和她一块出来参加晚会的人叽里咕噜说个不停。"

"你真的是一个非常风趣的人，"梅拉非常怀疑地讲道。

"你的话是什么意思？"艾默里马上警觉起来，他还是找回了自己可以掌控的节奏。

"嗯——老是说一些没有意思的事。你为什么明天不过来跟我和玛丽莲一起滑冰呢？"

"白天我对女孩子很不喜欢，"他立马接上她的话说道，接着感觉这样讲话非常不礼貌，又添了一句："但是我喜欢你。"他把喉咙清了一下。"我倾心于你，第一个，第二个，第三个全是你。"

梅拉双眼迷蒙，晕乎乎的。如果把这些讲给玛丽莲听那多么形象呀！这时和长得如此帅的男孩子坐在沙发上——暖和的火炉在面前摆着——想到此时就只有他们两个人独自坐在这栋大楼里——

第一章　艾默里—贝雅特丽丝的儿子

梅拉最终被攻陷了。此时氛围非常合适。

"我倾心的人前二十五位都是你,"她坦言说,声音有些打颤,"蛙喉帕克挨排在第二十六位。"

蛙喉在一个小时里后退了二十五名。他到现在甚至还没有留意到这一点。

但是艾默里就在她的身边耍尽了风头,他快速地在她的脸上亲了一下。他从前从未亲吻过女孩子,此时他非常新奇地努了努嘴,好像吃到了一种新尝到的水果一样。接着,好像野外新绽放的花儿在风中摇摆一般,他们的嘴唇不断地接触。

"我们这样很吓人的,",梅拉开心地,低声讲道。她将手放到他的手里,头抵着他的肩膀。一阵阵恶心的感觉忽然在艾默里的心里出现,他觉得讨厌,讨厌全部事情。他非常想要立即逃跑,再也不想和梅拉相逢,再也不想亲吻其余的人;他清楚地觉察到他和她的脸靠在一起,觉察到他们手牵着手,所以,他非常想要从她的身体中脱离出去,藏到一个看不到任何人的安全的处所,在他内心深处的一个犄角旮旯中。

"再亲我一下吧。"她的声音从一个广阔的宽敞的地方传过来。

"我不愿意,"他听见自己这样讲。然后话停了下来。

"我不愿意!"他用含有浓烈感情色彩的语调又讲了一遍。

梅拉蹭地蹦了起来,那受了打击的虚荣心使得她脸颊通红,脑袋后面的大蝴蝶结也随着跳动起来。

"我讨厌你!"她高声讲道。"你不要再觍着脸来和我讲话!"

"你什么意思?"艾默里磕磕巴巴地说。

"我要告诉我妈妈你亲吻我的嘴!我会如此说的!我会如此说的!假如我跟妈妈讲了,她就不会同意你和我玩了!"

艾默里站起身,无能为力地瞧着她,好像她是新发现的至今为止地球上从来没有听说过的一头野生动物一样。

忽然门被打开了,梅拉的妈妈在门口站着,一只手摆弄着她的长柄眼镜。

"啊呀,"她讲道,一边和蔼地调节眼镜,"接待处的那个男人对我说你们两个孩子在楼上——你好,艾默里。"

艾默里的眼睛看着梅拉,等着她发一通脾气——然而这些都没有发生。生气的模样不见了,脸上红彤彤的颜色消失了,梅拉回答她妈妈问题的时候语气和缓,仿佛夏天的湖面一样平静。

013

"呃。我们晚出门了一会儿，因此我想我们直接就——"

他听到楼下有尖尖细细的笑声传过来，安静地跟着母女俩下楼的时候还闻到了巧克力热饮和清淡茶点的香味。很多女孩哼唱的曲调和留声机放出的音乐交织在一起，他感觉脸颊上微微发烫，然后这热量布满了全身：

"凯西·琼斯——他登上火车头，

凯西·琼斯——工作指令手中拿。

凯西·琼斯——他登上火车头，

向着希望之乡招手告别满目含情。"[1]

自傲少年的快照

艾默里在明尼阿波利斯生活了接近两年的时间。在那里的第一个冬天，他脚上穿的是一双莫卡辛软帮鞋，鞋子新的时候颜色是黄的，然而在擦了很多次鞋油、又沾染了脏东西以后，颜色变得越发成熟，那是一种肮脏并且黄中夹杂着绿的褐色；身穿一件灰色麦基诺彩格厚呢双排纽扣束腰带的短大衣；脑袋上顶着一顶红色绒绒滑雪帽。因为他的一条叫做戴尔蒙伯爵的狗将他的红色绒绒滑雪帽叼走了，所以他的姨夫就把一顶灰色的给了他，这帽子拉下来就可以把他的整个脸遮挡住。但这顶帽子有一个不好的地方，戴了帽子呼出来的气会冻成冰；有一天这顶绒绒帽上结成的冰与他的脸粘在一块了。他抓了一把雪搓在脸上，然而冻伤的位置依旧变得青紫。

戴尔蒙伯爵把整整一盒蓝色漂白剂吃了下去，感觉没有什么问题。但是后来它就发起疯来，在马路上胡乱地跑着，朝着篱笆就撞了上去，在街沟里打着滚，躲避着艾默里，做着一些非常奇怪的动作。艾默里躺在床上痛哭。

"令人怜惜的小伯爵，"他吼道。"呀，令人怜惜的小伯爵！"

几个月过去了，他觉得伯爵非常会演戏。

艾默里和蛙喉帕克都觉得文学上最有名的台词是在《绅士大盗》[2]的第三部分出现的。

---

1. 凯西·琼斯是美国铁道史上的一位勇敢的火车司机，一九〇〇年四月，在伊利诺伊中部大铁道的一次撞车事故中，他让司炉工先跳车，自己英勇献身。之后有很多赞颂他的事迹的歌曲被创造出来，这里引用的就是其中一首的合唱。
2. 《绅士大盗》是法国作家莫里斯·勒勃朗（Mauric Leblanc, 1864—1941）创作的小说，后被改编为不同类型版本的剧本演出，这里指的应该是由作者本人与人合作改编的四幕剧，于一九〇八年十月二十八日在巴黎首次公开表演。

他们在星期三和星期六的白天演出的第一排坐着。这句台词是:

"如果你不能变成一位伟大的艺术家或是一位优秀的军人,那么,退一步来讲,不如变成一个大恶人。"

艾默里又有了新的恋情,而且写了一首诗。诗是这么写的:

"玛丽莲和赛莉,

两位女孩我仰慕已久。

玛丽莲的伶俐跃然纸上,

赛莉的温柔使人深浅难测。"

他的爱好非常宽泛:明尼苏达的麦戈文是不是会当选全美最优秀的橄榄球运动员或是获得亚军、如何变纸牌魔术、如何变硬币魔术、变色领带究竟为什么会变色、婴儿是如何降生的、三个手指的布朗作为棒球投手是不是比克里斯蒂·马修生还要厉害。

他念的书也非常繁杂,就像:《为学校争光》《小妇人》(两次)《普通法》《萨福》《危险的丹·麦克格鲁》《宽阔的公路》(三次)《阿什尔庄园的倒塌》《三周》《小长官的朋友玛丽·威尔》《营房谣》[1]《警察杂志》《Jim-Jam Jems》[2]杂志。

---

1. 《为学校争光》(1900),是由英国小说家拉尔夫·亨利·巴勃(Ralph Henry Barbour,1870—1944)创作的,书中详述了中学生的体育生活;《小妇人》(1868—1869),是由英国小说家露伊莎·梅·阿尔科特(Louisa May Alcott,1832—1888)创作;《普通法》(1881),英国法学家小奥利弗·温德尔·霍姆斯(Oliver Wendell Holmea,Jr,1841—1953)著;《萨福》(1884),法国小说家阿尔封斯·都德(Alfonse Daudet,1840—1897)创作;《危险的丹·麦克格鲁》(1907),是一首叙事短诗,由加拿大作家罗伯特·W.塞尔维斯(Robert W. Service,1874—1958)所著;《宽阔的公路》(1910)英国历史小说家杰弗里·法诺尔(Jeffery Farnol,1878—1952)创作;《阿什尔庄园的倒塌》(1840),是由英国作家艾伦·坡(Edgar Allan Poe,1809—1849)著;《三周》(1907),英国作家艾丽诺·格林(Elinor Glyn,1864—1943)所著;《小长官的朋友玛丽·威尔》(1908),是由安妮·菲洛斯·约翰斯顿(Annie Fellows Johnslon,1863—1931)创作;《营房谣》(1890),一首诗歌,由英国作家、诗人拉杰德·吉卜林(Rudyard Kipling,1865—1936)所著。
2. 这是美国二十世纪初山姆·克拉克在北达科伦州首府俾斯麦的一本杂志上出版的,是一本月刊书籍,每期共六十页,内容涵盖政治、经济、文化生活等各个方面,书中有插画,语言诙谐幽默,每期都用虚构作者"小吉姆·詹姆"的语气来书写。

至于历史，他将亨迪[1]的所有历史偏见收入囊中，他特别喜欢看玛丽·罗伯茨·莱恩哈特[2]的振奋人心的探索书刊。

上学反而使得他的法语被耽误了，也使得他变得对有威望的作家的作品失去了兴趣。他的老师们都觉得他慵懒、不值得信赖，还爱玩小诡计。

他从很多女孩子那里搜寻了一缕缕头发。有几个人的戒指在他的手上戴着。最终别人连戒指都不借给他了，只因他心情不好的时候有将戒指咬得变形的癖好。这个不好的习惯好像常常会使得其他的要借给他戒指的人提高警惕和产生猜疑。

在一整个夏天的那几个月的时间里，艾默里和蛙喉帕克每一周都要去专业剧团观看表演。观赏完表演以后，他们在八月晚上暖和的空气当中一块散步回家，顺着汉涅坪和尼克列大街，在欢乐的人群中穿行，毫无边际地想象。艾默里心里不清楚，人们怎么会留意不到他是一个以后要崭露头角的男孩子，而当人群里的人一个个地扭过头向他看的时候，在人们用意味不明的眼光看向他的时候，他就会把最浪漫的表情展露出来，好像双脚在沥青路上铺的气垫上踩着一样。

当他躺在床上之后，常常可以听见讲话的声音——隐隐约约、越来越小、令人魂牵梦萦——就像在他的窗外似的，而在他睡觉以前，他就会做一个他清醒的时候最爱做的梦，那是自己变成一个棒球前卫的梦，或许是梦到日本人入侵、自己被任命为世界上最年幼的将军并得到表扬。他梦到的总是自己处于改变的过程当中，而从来没有梦到过早已完成改变的情形。这一点也是和艾默里的性格特点相对应的。

自傲少年的行为规范

在妈妈让他回到日内瓦湖以前，即使他看上去非常内向，内心却信心满满，第一次穿上西装长裤，和紫色折叠式的领带搭配着，一个两边特别熨帖的"培尔蒙"领子，紫色的长筒袜子，在他的上衣胸口口袋里，一块镶嵌着紫色花边的手绢露出一角。然而他不仅仅是外表改变而已，他已经把自己的第一个哲学想法创立起来了，一个要遵守的行为守则，这个守则，尽量地讲得形象一些，

---

1. 亨迪（George Alfred Henty, 1832—1902），是英国的一名小说家、记者，擅长撰写历史冒险小说。
2. 玛丽·罗伯茨·莱恩哈特（Mary Roberts Rineheart, 1876—1958），美国的一位多产作家，素来享有美国的阿加莎·克里斯蒂的美誉。

那是一种势利的目空一切。

他已经了解到,他的最大好处已经和某一个有区别的、改变中的人的好处牢牢地绑在一起,这个人有一个称号,由于有了一个称号,他的过去总是能够与他关联在一起,这个称号就是艾默里·布莱恩。艾默里觉得自己是个幸运儿,有着无限开拓的才能,不管是好是坏。他觉得自己不是一个"意志坚定的人",反而是凭借的是他的能力(学习新鲜事物很快),凭借的是乐观的态度(查阅很多内容深奥的书籍)。他感觉非常骄傲的是,他肯定不会变成一个呆板的或是科学的天才。而登上其他的任意一座山峰他都会所向无敌。

身体方面——艾默里感觉他自己特别美丽。他的确是美丽。他感觉自己是一个很有发展前景的运动员,是一个体态轻盈的舞者。

社交方面——在这个方面,他的条件可能极其不安全。他知道自己有个性、有吸引力、有从容不迫的态度、有操纵所有同龄男生的能力、有令所有女生神魂颠倒的天分。

心理方面——彻底而毋庸置疑的优越感。

讲到这个地方,有一点是必须要赞同的。艾默里倒是有一个清教徒的善心。倒不是讲他彻底地受到良心的操纵——等到他后来的人生'他几乎完全将它移除——而是说在他十五岁的时候,他感觉自己要比其他的男孩子坏得多……冒失任性……好像在任意一方面都有控制别人的冲动,更甚至是不怀好意……掺杂着某些冷淡,也缺少感情,有时候甚至到达冷漠的地步——一种变幻莫测的荣誉感……一种罪恶的自私的想法……但凡和性相关的事情他都觉得好奇,呕心沥血,偷偷摸摸。

另外,在他的性格当中有一个怪异的特点……假如比他要大一些的男孩子(通常来说比他大一些的男孩子都对他非常厌恶)嘴里讲出一句尖酸刻薄的话,他听到后心里的平静就会打破,变得异常敏感,或是表现出胆小的愚蠢姿态……他会被自己的心情影响,虽然他有时候会感觉非常莽撞、毫无顾忌,然而他不但缺乏勇气,还缺少坚持的信心,也缺乏自尊。

虚荣,掺杂在一起的还有自我否定,即使不认为是自我了解,将人们看作是服从他自我意识的自动装置的看法,"超过"尽可能多的孩子、跨上模糊的世界高峰的心愿……就是在这样的心理背景下,艾默里随波逐流进入到青春期。

重要冒险之前的准备

火车携带着夏日的疲倦在日内瓦湖缓缓地停下脚步，艾默里瞧见妈妈在她停在车站砂石路上的电气汽车里坐着。那是一辆非常老旧的车子，是以前的车型，车身被刷成灰色。一瞧见她坐在车里的模样，以她为傲的自豪感在他心里情不自禁地产生了，就见她身材纤细挺拔，她的脸庞将外表的美和内在的自尊联合在一块并且消融了，随之而来的是模糊静思的微笑。他们见面之后冷漠地吻着，他在车里坐着，立马就感到了担心，就怕他已经把必要的魅力丢失了，令她觉得失望。

"亲爱的儿子——你的个子这么高了……你瞧一下车子后面，瞧瞧有没有车子跟着……"

她左右看看，小心谨慎地把车开到时速两公里的速度，她还让他担任警戒的任务；车子被开到一个车辆很多的十字路口，她把他叫下来，让他跑到前面像交警一样指挥着她开车。可以说贝雅特丽丝是一个小心驾驶的司机。

"你个子高了——但是你依旧那么帅气——早已度过了青春期初期，已经十六岁了吧，可能十四岁、十五岁，我总是记不住；但是你已经把这个年龄段度过了。"

"别吵我了，"艾默里嘀咕。

"但是，亲爱的儿子，你穿的衣服很古怪！身上穿的瞧上去仿佛是成套的，对吗？你的内衣也是紫色的吗？"

艾默里非常失礼地嘀咕出声。

"你需要到布鲁克兄弟服装专卖店去买几套确实漂亮的服装。嗯，我们今天晚上要好好谈谈，要不就明天晚上再去。我要和你聊聊你的心——也许你的心被你忽视了——你还不清楚。"

艾默里心里暗暗思忖他们这一代人的服装是多么的随便。只除去那细小的害羞以外，他感觉他和妈妈之间的原有的怀疑一点都没有消除。但是在最初回家的几天里，他在花园当中，在湖岸边毫无目的地闲逛，心里只觉得非常孤单，但是当在车库里和其中一个司机一块吸"公牛"牌香烟的时候，还会有一些心灰意懒的满足感浮现。

原来的和新建的避暑别墅群在六十英亩的土地上排列着，除此之外，还有很多喷水池，和忽然闯入眼帘的被茂盛的树叶丛遮挡住的白色的长凳。一大群数量还在不停地增加的白猫在众多的花坛当中寻找着,晚上它们在逐渐暗淡下来的树丛当中忽隐忽现。布莱恩先生和平常一样,一到晚上就藏在不允许其他人进去的书房中,就是在那个幽静黑暗的小路上,贝雅特丽萨终于找到了艾默里。就他为什么老躲着她的问题讲了几句之后,他和她在月亮的照射下进行了一次长时间的促膝长谈。他和她在一块总感觉非常奇怪,面对她的美丽容颜他感觉无颜以对,而正是由于她的美丽才孕育出他这般的帅气,他也没有办法面对这美丽的脖子和肩膀,一个属于三十岁的幸运女人的娇媚。

"艾默里,亲爱的,"她小声说道,"我和你分别后的生活非常古怪,简直无法想象。"

"是这样吗,贝雅特丽丝?"

"上一次我精神不正常以后"——她将这件事讲得仿佛一个勇猛、豪迈的英雄故事。

"医生们告诉我"——她换成了一种推心置腹、极度信赖的语气讲道——"如果世界上的任意一个男人像我一样喝酒,他的身体早就不行了,亲爱的,早就死翘翘了,躺进坟墓——早就躺进坟墓里了。"

艾默里脸部的肌肉颤抖了一下,心里怀疑,不清楚蛙喉帕克听到这话以后会做出什么反应。

"非常正确,"贝雅特丽丝用悲哀的口气继续讲,"我老是做梦——梦见令人惊讶的场景。"她用手把眼睛挡住。"我梦到大理石堆砌成的河岸被黄褐色的河水敲打着,梦到大鸟在天空中飞翔,毛色很杂,羽毛是彩虹色的。我还听到古怪的乐声,听到发狂一般吹响的喇叭的声音——到底为何呢?"

艾默里私底下感觉好笑。

"我的意思是再说下去,贝雅特丽丝。"

"说完了——这梦只是一再地重复——花园当中是鲜花争奇斗艳,五彩缤纷,对比起来,梦中的颜色就十分乏味了,月亮在旋转摆动,冬天的月亮都要比它明亮很多,但它又比秋天的月亮更加金黄——"

"现在你的感觉还好吧,贝雅特丽丝?"

"非常好——未来同样也会很好。谁都不明白我,艾默里。我清楚我讲的话你也不知道,艾默里,但是——谁都不理解我。"

艾默里被这样的场景感动着。他伸出手把他的妈妈抱住,他的头轻轻地在他妈妈的肩头动来动去。

"让人怜惜的贝雅特丽丝——让人怜惜的贝雅特丽丝。"

"咱们谈谈你自己吧,艾默里。这两年你的生活一定特别不好吧?"

艾默里原本准备和她撒个谎,接着他还是把这样的想法打消了。

"不是的,贝雅特丽丝。我生活得非常好。我自己去习惯中产阶级的日子。我变得碰到事情的话都要遵循旧有的规定。"他把这样的话讲出来的时候就连他自己都会感觉意外,他能够想到如果蛙喉帕克在的话,他一定会瞠目结舌的。

"贝雅特丽丝,"忽然他说出一句话来,"我想要在外面念书。在明尼阿波利斯,每个人都准备出去读书。"

贝雅特丽丝明显有些慌乱。

"但是你仅仅才十五岁。"

"嗯,但是别人都是十五岁的时候出去读书的,我也想要去外面,贝雅特丽丝。"

因为贝雅特丽丝不愿意再谈下去,所以在接下去的散步当中,这个问题就没有再被提到,然而过了一周以后,她使得他特别开心,只因她告诉他:

"艾默里,我的意思是还是让你依照你自己的想法进行吧。如果你还是不改变想法的话,你可以出去读书。"

"是真的吗?"

"去康涅狄格州的盛雷吉教会学校读书。"

听到这句话后,艾默里突然开心起来。

"一切都准备好了,"贝雅特丽丝接着讲道。"你还是出去读书比较好。以前我是觉得你应当去伊顿公学读书,接着进牛津大学基督堂学院,但是现在还不能够这样做——而现在上大学的问题还不需要思考,时间到了必然就会想到办法的。"

"那你准备怎样,贝雅特丽丝?"

"谁知道呢。我的生命仿佛是让我留在这个国家心情烦躁地度过我的岁月。对于成为一个美国人,我丝毫没有遗憾——事实上,我觉得遗憾那是平庸的人才有的懊恼,我一直坚信我们是一个前程远大的国家——但是"——她唉声叹气了一下,继续讲道——"我的一生应该是和一个更加远古、更加老练的文明一块消逝的,在一个哪里都是苍松翠柏、秋天一片金黄的国家里度过的。"

艾默里没有说话，因此他的妈妈接着讲道："让我感到惋惜的是你没有去过国外，然而我还是感觉，既然你是一个男子汉，你就应当在雄鹰的嘶鸣中长大——雄鹰的嘶鸣，我讲得对吗？"

艾默里表示同意。她对于日本人的入侵是不会感恩的。

"我什么时候可以出去读书？"

"下一个月吧。你必须提前出发朝东走，去参加考试。考试结束以后你有一周的时间休息，因此我要你顺着哈得逊河沿河而下去拜见一个人。"

"他是谁？"

"去拜见达西大人[1]，艾默里。他想要见你一面。他在英国的哈罗公学上过学，之后又去耶鲁大学上学——毕业后做了一名天主教徒。是我请他找你聊一聊的——我感觉他对你会有非常大的帮助的——"她轻柔地抚弄着他那一头褐色的头发。"亲爱的艾默里，亲爱的艾默里——"

"亲爱的贝雅特丽丝——"

因此，九月初，艾默里打包好行李，拿上"夏天穿的内衣六套，冬天穿的内衣六套，运动套衫，它也被叫做T恤衫一套，针织套衫一件，大衣一件，冬天的服装等衣服"，起身前去学校集结的地方，新英格兰。

那个地方有马萨诸塞州的安多佛高级中学、新罕布什尔州安塞特学校，都给人们留下已经失去的新英格兰的美好回忆——学校非常大，还有大学一般的民主管理制度；马萨诸塞州的圣马可学校、格罗顿学校、康涅狄格州的圣雷吉教会学校——他们都在波士顿和纽约人家庭招收学生；有着非常大的溜冰场的新罕布什尔州的圣保罗中学；康涅狄格州的庞弗雷特学校和罗德艾兰州的圣乔治学校，一派生机，气象万千；康涅狄格州的塔夫特学校和霍奇吉士学校，利用中西部的钱财为在耶鲁大学获得社会地位铺展道路；另外还有纽约州的三一珀林学校、康涅狄格州的威斯特敏斯特学校、科艾特学校、肯特学校，包括其他的上百所高级中学。所有的这些学校一年又一年的努力塑造了坚定、守旧、让人瞠目结舌的模式。对于他们精神的鼓舞就是大学的入学考试，他们模糊的目的在上百个报告里给解释明白了，就好比"赠送作为一名真诚的绅士所需要

---

1. 对于有职位的神职人员的敬称。

的完全的精神、道德和体育方面的锻炼,培养孩子正视他们的时代和他们那一代人的才能,使得他们在文理各科有着厚实的底子。

艾默里在圣雷吉士学校留了三天,用旁若无人的信心参与了各科的考试,接着原路返回,拜见他的学业监护人。除了早晨坐在哈得逊河的一条轮船上他瞧见白色高楼大厦时感受到了干净的感觉之外,这座几乎没有来过的大都会并未给予他什么其他的感觉。事实上,他的脑海中充斥着在学校里获得体育运动上的高超技艺的理想,他将这次的拜谒仅仅当成是重要冒险的非常令人厌烦的前奏而已。但是,到达那里以后他才明白,这次的拜谒并不是这么简单。

达西大人的房子是一座传统、排列杂乱的建筑,建在一座可以俯视哈得逊河的小山上,房子的主人除了出门走访他的罗马天主教世界以外,住在这里和一名被驱逐的斯图亚特王室的国王有些相似,等候着被召回,去治理他的国家。那时达西大人四十四岁,强壮——身材有一点矮胖,有些不均匀,头发好像金丝的色泽,性格聪明内向。当他进入到一个房间的时候,从上到下都是一身紫色的整齐的扮相,瞧上去和透纳[1]画的夕阳风景画很相像,令人又崇拜又关注。有两本小说是他写的:其中一本对天主教的反对很是强烈,那是他于入教之前写的,而在五年以后他又写了一本,在这本书当中,他尝试着把他对于天主教的一切有技巧的嘲讽,转化成对于美国新教圣公会的更加巧妙的拐弯抹角的抨击。他是一个非常崇拜礼教的人,富有热情,因为沉醉于信奉上帝的想法而决定不娶,而且对他的邻居很有好感。

孩子们对他非常崇拜,由于他的行为举止就像一个孩子一般;年轻人很喜欢和他在一块,由于他仍旧是一个青年,因此不会使得他们觉得惊讶。假如生逢其时,生逢其地,也许他就是一个黎塞留[2]——现在他是一个品行特别正派、对于宗教非常崇敬(即便不是非常虔敬)的神职人员,特别神秘地玩弄着那些幕后操纵的老旧的手法,愉悦地享受着生活带来的快乐,即便不完全是恣意地享受生活中的乐趣。

他同艾默里刚刚见面相互之间就留下了非常好的印象——一个是慈祥活

---

1. 透纳(Joseph Mallord Williarn Turner,1775—1851),是英国风景画画家,精于水彩画,注重追寻光和色的效果。
2. 黎塞留(Armand Jean du Plessis Richelieu,1585—1642),是法王路易十三时期的国务秘书,枢机主教,夺取政权稳固专治统治,他主张扩张法国版图。

第一章　艾默里—贝雅特丽丝的儿子

泼、让人敬佩的高级教士,能够在大使馆的舞会上风姿飒爽、使众人倾倒,一个是绿眼睛、神情专一的少年,这是艾莫里第一次穿着西装长裤,在还没有半个小时的交流中,他们的内心对于这种父与子的关系就已经接受了。

"亲爱的孩子,我已经等了你很多年了。你搬一张大椅子到这里来,我们坐下来谈谈。"

"我刚从学校过来——圣雷吉士学校,你清楚的。"

"你妈妈讲了——她是一个非常棒的女人。吸一支烟吧——我觉得你一定抽烟。呃,如果你同我很相像,那么你对于所有的理科和数学会很讨厌——"

艾默里用力地点点头。

"都很厌恶。对于英语和历史很感兴趣。"

"必然是这样。你在某一个时间段内还会对读书很厌烦,但是我很开心你要去圣雷吉士念书。"

"为什么这么讲呢?"

"只因为这是一所供君子读书的学校,民主不会这么早就在你的内心深处扎根。等到你上大学以后,你就会发觉到处都是民主。"

"我想要到普林斯顿大学上学,"艾默里说。"对于我选择普林斯顿的原因我也讲不清楚,我感觉哈佛大学的男生都有一些娘娘腔,和我以前很相像,但耶鲁大学的男生都穿着宽松的蓝色运动衫、抽烟斗。"

达西大人哈哈大笑。

"我就是当中的一个,你清楚。"

"嗯,你是特别的——在我的印象当中普林斯顿人不急不躁、美丽、高雅——你了解,就像春天一样。哈佛则有一点仿佛闭门谢客的感觉——"

"而耶鲁仿若十一月,清冽、充满生机。"达西归纳说。

"非常正确。"

他们清闲愉悦地说着话,慢慢地讲起悄悄话来,然后就一直沉溺在其中无法自拔。

"我曾经对美丽的王子查理[1]很倾慕,"艾默里宣告说。

---

1. 也就是查理·爱德华·斯图亚特(Charles Edward Stuart,1720—1788),垂涎英国王位者詹姆斯·斯图亚特之子,史书上称他为年轻的觊觎王位者,也被叫做美丽王子查理。他谋划了一七四五年至一七四六年的雅各宾派叛乱,后被驱逐回苏格兰,战败。

"你自然倾慕——还倾慕汉尼拔[1]——"

"对，还倾心南方联邦。"关于做一名爱尔兰爱国主义者，他抱着怀疑的看法——他怀疑做了爱尔兰人就是粗鄙不堪的表现——然而达西大人却明白地告诉他，爱尔兰是浪漫的一定会失败的事业，爱尔兰人民是非常讨人喜欢的，做一个爱尔兰人一定要变成他的主要喜爱之一。

他们那内容繁杂的交流进行了一个小时，而且之后又吸了几根烟，言谈之间达西大人了解到，艾默里竟然没有被培养成一个天主教徒，虽然这不会让他觉得特别反感，但仍感觉非常惊讶。说了一个小时的话之后，他说还有一个客人需要他的招待。原来这位客人是波士顿的桑顿·汉科克阁下，他是前驻海牙公使，也是一本内容博大精深的中世纪史的作者，同时还是一个声名远播、爱国、成绩斐然的家族的最后一个成员。

"他到这里来是想要歇息的，"达西大人将艾默里看作是同龄人，和他开诚布公地说。"我就仿佛是一个他躲避烦躁的不可知论的避难所，我感觉只有我了解他的呆板的想法，知道他的确已经像是在大海上迷失了航向一样，希望抓住如教会一般的牢固的圆木自救。"

艾默里在少年时期难以忘记的事情之一就是与他们一块享用的第一顿午餐。他的脸上流露着幸福的光芒，散发出独有的聪明和吸引力。达西大人借着提问赋予启示，将他认为自己学识最优异的一面表现了出来，而艾默里则在交流中智谋频出、满腹经纶，使人感觉他有千万个冲动、心愿、憎恨、信心、惊恐。他同达西大人交谈起来口若悬河，令人无法插嘴，一旁的长者因为接受能力有限，又缺乏接受新思想的心愿，但是态度又表现得不是那么冷淡，所以他好像问心无愧地只是倾耳细听，在他们两人之间布满的温暖阳光当中沐浴着。达西大人对于很多人来讲就是和煦的阳光；艾默里在年轻的时候也是阳光普照，但是随着他年纪的增长，在某种程度上，相互之间这样自然而然的感情流露那是再也不会出现了。

"他是一个很有前途的孩子，"桑顿·汉科克心里想，依照他的见闻他了解，

---

1. 汉尼拔（Hannibal，公元前247—前182），由迦太基率领，率次使得罗马人遭受重创，但始终没有攻占罗马城。

第一章　艾默里—贝雅特丽丝的儿子

毕竟他的足迹遍布两个大陆,他和巴涅尔[1]、格莱斯顿[2]、俾斯麦[3]都有过交流——事后他曾经对达西大人讲道:"然而他的教育不应当只托付给某一所中学或者大学来负责。"

但在以后的四年中,艾默里的聪颖智慧的精髓都汇集到了流行时尚之类的事情上,运用到大学错综复杂的社交关系中,用在比尔特摩酒店的茶点和温泉城高尔夫球场所代表的美国社会之中了。

总得来说,他经过了特别开心的一个星期,在这一个星期里,艾默里的想法得到了一个彻底的大检验,他对自己所抱有的成百个理论愈加信心百倍,他的生活兴趣让他变得斗志昂扬。他们的交流并不都是和他的学业有关系——希望不要和学业有关系!萧伯纳是干什么的,艾默里心中只是隐隐约约地了解——达西大人倒是高谈阔论着《可爱的流浪者》[4]和《奈杰尔骑士》[5],但是他特别留意,说得简单明了,不破坏艾默里的兴致。

然而和他自己站在同一时代的人的首次冲锋的号角已经在他的内心深处奏响。

"自然,你离开这个地方也不会觉得惋惜。对于我们这样的人来讲,我们的家就是我们不会觉得可惜的地方,"达西大人讲道。

"我确实感觉很可惜——"

"不对,你没有遗憾。世界没有谁对于你和我来说是不可缺少的。"

---

1. 巴涅尔(Charles Stewart Parnell,1846—1891),是一位爱尔兰民族主义者,英国下院议员,由于抵制格莱斯顿土地法被捕入狱,之后向政府妥协被释放。
2. 格莱斯顿(William Ewart Gladstone,1809—1898),是英国自由党领袖,四次担任首相,通过爱尔兰土地法案,对外施行殖民扩张政策。
3. 俾斯麦(Otto Eduard Leopold von Bismarck,1815—1898),德意志帝国宰相(1871—1890),经由王朝战争击溃法、奥,将德意志统一,史书上称他为"铁血宰相"。
4. 英国小说家威廉·J·洛克(William J Locke,1863—1930)于一九〇六年出版的长篇小说,写的是才华很高的青年建筑师为帮助心爱的姑娘的父亲还债,请求自己的情敌的帮助,但因为被心爱的人误会而失去了爱情,由此心情低落,更换姓名变成了一个流浪歌手。之后姑娘找到了他,但是他仍然选择和流浪儿做伴,过着自由自在的生活。
5. 著名侦探福尔摩斯的塑造者,英国小说家柯南·道尔(Arthur Conan Doyle,1859—1930)所创作的历史小说(1906),是下文说到的长篇历史著作《铁甲骑士队》(1891)的前撰,书写的是十四世纪后期英国历史上百年战争时期为英王爱德华三世效忠的奈杰尔骑士的故事。

"嗯——"

"拜拜。"

自傲者的辱没

　　艾默里在圣雷吉士学校的两年时间当中，虽然有痛苦的时候，但也有自鸣得意的时候，然而这对于他自己的日子来讲并没有多少意义，就像被踩在大学脚底下的美国"预科"学校，对于平常的美国生活并不存在多少意义一般。我们没有伊顿公学那般的学校，可以创建一个统治阶级拥有的自我感知；而我们仅仅有纯真正义、懦弱无能、无关大局的预科学校。

　　他一进入雷吉士学校就表现出了不好的一面，老师和同学通常都觉得他不但自负自大，而且不可一世，所以大都十分厌恶他。他打橄榄球非常狂野，在球场上既醉心于展现自己、非常鲁莽，又想保全自己，危险降临之时就逃得远远的，只求不违反规定。他在和一个体型和他一样大小的男孩子打架的时候，由于害怕而逃走了，周围的人对他的行为十分鄙视，但在一周以后被人逼得只得冒险，又同一个比他结实得多的男生打架，最终被打得鼻青脸肿，可是他反而觉得自豪。

　　他的心里对管他的所有老师都非常厌恶，再加上他对待作业慵懒、凑合，从而把学校里的老师们都惹恼了。他自己也失去了信心，感觉自己就像是一个被抛弃的人；开始藏在角落里赌气，熄灯之后才看起书来。因为害怕孤单，他结交了几个朋友，但是因为他们并不是学生中拔尖的人，所以他对于他们的利用也只是由于自己孤苦伶仃而已，在他作出对于他自己是非常重要的架势的时候，有人充当围观的人。他尝到了一种难以容忍的孤单的滋味，特别地不开心。

　　但是他也有过欣慰的时候。每当艾默里沉寂的时候，最后将他吞没的是他的虚荣心，因此，当学校里的耳聋的老勤杂工"哇啦哇啦"说着她从没有遇见过像他那么美丽的男孩的时候，他的心里依然可以产生让人欣慰的快乐。他对于自己是学校第一支橄榄球队里最机敏、最年轻的队员而觉得自豪；在结束了一场热烈的讨论的时候，杜格尔博士告诉他，如果他有这个心愿，他是有能力在全校获得最高分的，听到这话他又觉得很自得。然而杜格尔博士的观点是不对的。对于艾默里的天赋，他要在全校得到最高分是无论如何都做不到的。

　　懊恼，每天都关在学校里，老师不待见、与同学不合群——这就是艾默里第一个学期的状况。然而圣诞节的时候他回过明尼阿波利斯，他没有说关于学校的任何事情，并且非常不寻常的是，他还表现出特别开心的模样。

"呃，我最开始由于刚到那个地方，人生地不熟，"他用大人对小孩讲话的语气对蛙喉帕克讲，"但是没过多长时间我就熟悉了——我是球队里最灵活的队员。你也应当到外面读书，蛙喉。这是非常不错的事。"

热心老师的一件小事

在他第一个学期的最后一个晚上，资历很深的老师马格特逊先生传话到自习室，让艾默里九点钟到他的办公室一趟。艾默里心里怀疑，这是要跟他说大道理了，然而他已经下定决心，要对他谦逊恭敬一些，只因这个马格特逊先生对他非常和善。

传话的老师神情肃穆地招待了他，暗示他到一把椅子上坐下来。他咳咳嗓子哼了几声，好像一个知晓他必须小心看待要管理的事情的人一样，故意将友善的一面表现出来。

"艾默里，"他最终讲话了。"我让你来是为了个人的事情。"

"嗯，先生。"

"今年我一直在注意着你，我——我喜欢你。我感觉你身上有一种——一种非常优异的人的品质。"

"嗯，先生，"艾默里勉强讲出话来。他很厌恶被人议论，好像他是一个大家都知道的考试不及格的学生。

"然而我也留意到，"这位长者接着非常武断地讲道，"你跟男生玩不到一起去。"

"事实如此，先生。"艾默里把嘴唇舔了舔。

"嗯——我感觉你对他们不一定非常了解——呃——讨厌的是什么。我现在就讲给你听听，由于我觉得——嗯——一个男孩子清楚了他自己的问题所在，处理起来就简单一些了 就和别人所希望的一致起来了。"他带着小心翼翼的节制又"哼唧"了几声，然后接着说，"他们好像感觉你——嗯——有点太自以为是了——"

艾默里再也无法忍受了。他从椅子上站起来，讲话时几乎不能抑制住他的声音。

"我清楚——嗯，难道你认为我不清楚吗？"他的声音愈加大了。"我清楚你心里是怎么看的；你感觉你一定要把话跟我讲出来！"他顿了一下。"我要——我现在就得回去——希望我没有失礼——"

他慌张地离开了办公室。走在回教室的路上，在空气清凉的户外，他由于拒绝了别人的帮助而感到自鸣得意。

"这个可恶的老家伙！"他大声叫着。"就像我不清楚一样！"

但是，他已经计划好了，如此一来他那天晚上不到自习室去就有了一个非常好的理由，他就可以舒适地在床上躺着，一边嚼着巧克力华芙饼干，一边看完《铁甲骑士队》[1]这本小说。

可爱女孩的一件小事

二月里出现了一颗闪亮的星星。就在华盛顿生日的那天，纽约期待已久的盛世光辉让艾莫里大饱眼福。在他的眼中，纽约就是蔚蓝天空上的一道夺目的白光，在他心中藏着的是一幅雄伟壮阔的画面，能够和《天方夜谭》中的梦幻城市比肩；但是他这一次是借着电灯的灯光瞧见的，从百老汇一个连一个的招牌上和在阿斯特大饭店女人的双眼中，都透露出晶莹剔透的浪漫色彩，他与圣雷吉士学校的小帕斯克特就是在这里吃饭的。他们在剧院座位间的通道上走着，迎面传来了未调弦的小提琴仓促的拨弦声和不协调的声音，闻见了胭脂扑粉的浓烈的香气，这时候他已经在奢华享受的愉快的氛围中遨游了。四周的一切都让他沉醉。演出的音乐剧是由乔治·M科汉主演的《小百万富翁》[2]，他关注着舞台上一个特别美丽的黑发少女的舞蹈，双眼中蕴含着泪水，在那里坐着看得入了迷。

"啊——你——可爱的女孩，

你是一个多么可爱的女孩——"

---

1. 《铁甲骑士队》（The White Company）是由英国作家柯南·道尔于一八九一年发表的历史小说，书中描写的是铁甲骑士队弓箭手的冒险事迹。主人公阿莱恩·埃德利克逊因父亲与修道院院长的密切关系，从小就被寄养在修道院里，到二十岁时才离开，在外面四处流浪。后来他做了奈杰尔骑士的随从，来到了法国，成为了铁甲骑士队的一员，他骁勇善战，后来迎娶奈杰尔的女儿为妻，回到了英国，也成为了一名骑士。这本书中的人物性格聪明活泼，情节跌宕起伏。
2. 乔治·M·科汉（George M. Cohan,1878—1942），一位美国著名的喜剧演员、剧作家、导演、流行歌曲作曲家。二十世纪的前二十年里，科汉的轻喜剧风格在美国舞台独领风骚，他的歌曲在二十世纪的美国一直为人称颂。《小百万富翁》（1911）是他的引人入胜的剧作之一，一家三人在剧中扮演不同的角色。

男高音唱道，艾默里心里默默地，但是却饱含激情地，表示同意。

"你的——绝妙语言——字字

颤动着我的心——"

等到最后那个音符，小提琴声音变大了，而且加上了颤音，少女在舞台上跌倒，变成了一只折翼的蝴蝶，这时全场发出一阵热烈的掌声。啊，与这样一支有着温柔的旋律、使人沉醉的乐曲相伴着，在这样的氛围中谈情说爱，多么让人神往呀！

最后一个场景被安排在房顶花园里，大提琴的乐声对着月亮发出叹息声，而欢快的探险经历和如同泡沫那样流畅的喜剧则在银白色的月光下一遍遍经过。艾默里的心中满含热情，盼望做一个房顶花园的常客，去和一个女孩见面，她应当和那个女孩长得相像——最好就像那个女孩；她的头发在金色的月光中沐浴着，而在他的旁边，一个很难理解的侍从在不停地倒着葡萄酒。在幕布最后一次落下的时候，他发出长长的一声叹息，很长的叹息，在前排坐着的人都回过头来瞧着他，而且讲话的声音非常大，他听到：

"那男孩长得多漂亮呀！"

听见这句话，他就连这场音乐剧都抛之脑后了，他心里想着，在纽约人的眼中他是不是真的那么美丽。

他与帕斯克特沉默地走在去他们住的饭店的路上。是帕斯克特先讲话的。他那不平稳的十五岁孩子的嗓音，以郁闷的语气，将艾默里的思考打断了：

"今天晚上我就迎娶那个女孩。"

追问他上面所指的那个女孩是谁实在没有必要。

"我会非常骄傲地把她带回家，给我的家里人介绍她，"帕斯克特接着说道。

艾默里的确非常震撼。他真的期望是他讲了这句话而不是帕斯克特。这句话从他的嘴里讲出听起来会很成熟。

"我对于女演员有着很大的好奇心：她们都非常不好吗？"

"不可以这样讲，小弟，从外貌上是瞧不出来的，"老成圆滑的少年加重了些语气讲道，"但是我清楚那个女孩非常和善。可以看出来。"

他们向前走，在百老汇大街的人群里夹杂着，听着从咖啡馆里飘出来的乐声浮想联翩。一张张新面孔忽然浮现，转眼之间又消失了，就好像万家灯火一样，寡白的或是擦了胭脂的，乏了，但是又让人用那疲倦的开心支持着。艾默里专注地看着这群人。他在计划着他的人生。他准备在纽约定居,做每一家饭店和咖啡馆的常客,身穿燕尾服,一直从傍晚待到清早,他能够躺在床上酣睡,来将中午前那段呆板枯燥的时间度过去。

"嗯,那是真实的,我今晚就要迎娶那个女孩!"

满场喝彩的英雄

在圣雷吉士学校读书的第二年和最后一年的十月,是艾默里记忆当中最有意义的时光。和格罗顿中学的那场比赛从一个富有生机、鼓舞人心的午后,一直举行到了凉意满满的秋天的傍晚,艾默里担当四分卫,竭尽全力地高声叫着,将无法做到的擒抱做出来,叫喊着攻击套路的代号,声音削弱到沙哑、狂野的嘶鸣,然而依旧有心情去享受脑袋上绑着染血的绷带带给他的愉悦,在猛扑、身体碰撞和四肢难受的时刻,尽情享受着孤单而荣耀的英雄主义带来的快乐。在那样的时候,勇气就仿若十一月的傍晚流出的葡萄酒,绵延不绝,所以他就是永远的英雄,他就是古代站在挪威大木船船头的海盗,他就是罗兰,他就是贺雷修斯[1],他就是奈杰尔骑士,他就是泰德·科伊[2],经历过锤炼调整到最好的状态,接着借由自己的毅力,挺身而出,把进攻的势头给挡住了,听到了远方传来的欢呼声……最后鼻青脸肿、筋疲力竭,然而敌人依旧拿不住他,他躲过一个边卫,转身,调速,伸手抵挡……在格罗顿队守门员的身后扑倒了,两个人在他的腿上压着,那是这场比赛仅有的一个触地得分球。

老门槛哲理

艾默里从六年级那年的遭人嘲讽的自豪感和获得的成绩出发,夹杂着一种满不在乎的震惊回想上一年自己的境况。他已经彻底地改变了,如果艾默里·布莱恩会发生什么改变,此时也都发生了。艾默里加上贝雅特丽丝加上明尼阿波利斯生活的两年——这些性格上的特点和外界影响的印记就是他进入圣雷吉士时性格上的组成部分。然而在明尼阿波利斯生活的两年时光并没有形成很厚的覆盖物,遮挡不住一所寄宿学校里的探寻的眼神,去调查"艾默里加上贝雅特丽丝"这"双重夹层"的真相,所以圣雷吉士学校特别费力地将贝雅特丽丝这一夹层从他的身上挖掘出来,而且准备在艾默里这一基本组成之下铺设新的、

---

1. 罗兰是法国史诗《罗兰之歌》当中的主角,以拼搏、勇气、骑士精神闻名于世;贺雷修斯是罗马传说中"一夫当关,万夫莫开"的英雄人物。
2. 泰德·科伊在当时是美国著名的橄榄球运动员。

更加古老的巩固物。然而，不管是圣雷吉士学校还是艾默里自己都不清楚，艾默里这一基本组成自身并没有发生改变。他自己曾经饱受其害的那些性格特性，即他的喜怒不定，他的喜欢故作姿态，他的懒散，加上他的爱做蠢事，此时已经被当作是理所当然的了，被当做是一个优秀的四分卫、一个聪慧的男演员、《圣雷吉士闲谈》杂志主编所拥有的癖好：瞧见可塑性很高的小男生仿照虚荣傲娇的行为，在不久以前这种行为还是一种可卑的缺点，他就感觉迷惑不已。

橄榄球赛季之后，他的心情回到了模模糊糊的洋洋得意上来。节前的舞会之夜他一个人偷偷地溜出去，很早就躺在了床上，享受着倾听小提琴的音乐声在草地上飘过、闯进他窗户里来的乐趣。在很多个晚上他在床上躺着闭上双眼胡思乱想，梦到蒙马特高地[1]的隐秘的夜总会，在那个地区象牙白肤色的女人陪同着外交官和有钱的军人追寻浪漫的神秘，而一旁的乐队奏响匈牙利圆舞曲，氛围热闹，异国情调充斥着周围，充满了诱惑力、月光和探险感。春天时他依照老师的要求阅读了弥尔顿的诗篇《开心的人》，因此他的灵感被激发出来，才思泉涌，脑海中充斥着阿卡狄亚田园牧歌式的生活，以及希腊神话牲畜神潘的排箫。他移动了一下床，使得早晨的阳光可以在一早就把他叫醒，如此他就能够披上衣服，朝六年级教室旁边的苹果树上悬挂着的旧式秋千走去。他在秋千上坐着，越荡越高，越荡越高，直到有了一种好像荡向广阔的天空，好像荡到了森林之神和仙女赏玩的仙境的感觉，而仙女的脸庞又使他记起他在纽约街上瞧见的金发少女的面容，等秋千荡到最高处的时候，他好像瞧见那世外桃源的确就在一座小山的山梁后面，那褐色的路变得窄了，不见了，最后变成一个金色的小点。

那一年他刚刚十八岁，一整个春天他都在不断地读书：《印第安纳—绅士》《新天方夜谭》《马库斯·奥狄恩的道德标准》《名叫星期四的男人》，这本书他

---

1. 这是位于巴黎北区的蒙马特高地，因为山顶的白色圆顶的圣心教堂、周围的夜总会，还有建在这个地区的艺术家工作室闻名于世。

看不明白但依旧很喜欢；《斯多弗耶鲁求学记》[1]，这本书几乎被当成了教科书；《董贝父子》，他之所以看狄更斯的这本书是因为他感觉他的确应该看一些经典一些的书；罗伯特·钱伯[2]、大卫·格莱厄姆·菲利普斯[3]、全套E·菲利普斯[4]的侦探小说，分散的丁尼生和吉卜林的诗歌。至于说他要做完的全部作业，唯有《开心的人》和立体几何那某种特性的严谨透彻性还可以激发他那慵懒的兴致。

随着六月的到来，他感觉应该找人交流以便陈述自己的思想，但使他觉得出人意料的是，六年级的班长拉希尔倒是一个能够一块交流哲学的人。在非常多次的交流中，不管是在大路上，还是卧倒在棒球场边，或是夜晚点着香烟在黑暗里抽亮的时候，他们不断地探究学校教育的问题，而且就在那种状况下，"老门槛"[5]这个说法应运而生了。

"有烟吗？"某天晚上熄灯五分钟以后，拉希尔的头探进门里，低声问道。

"有呀。"

"我进去了。"

"拿两个枕头过来，就靠在窗台上，可以了。"

艾默里从床上坐起来，把一支烟点着，拉希尔也在窗台上躺下来，准备交流。拉希尔最热衷于谈的话题就是六年级两个人不同的前程，而艾默里抱着替他着想的态度不厌其烦地描述着他们的前程。

---

1. 《印第安第一绅士》（1899），美国作家布思·塔金顿（Booth Tarkington, 1869—1946）所写的长篇小说，书中写的是同政治腐败战斗到底的乡村编辑；《新天方夜谭》（1882），是出自英国作家史蒂文森（Robert Louis Stevenson, 1850—1894）的短篇小说集；《马库斯·奥狄恩的道德标准》（1905），是由英国作家威廉·J·洛克所写；《名叫星期四的男人》（1908），乃是由英国作家G·K·切斯特顿（G.K. Chesterton, 1873—1936）创作的侦探小说；《斯多弗耶鲁求学记》（1912），由美国作家欧文·约翰逊（Owen Johnson, 1878—1952）所写，讲的是主人公丁克·斯多弗二十世纪初在美国耶鲁大学与人际关系做斗争的故事。
2. 罗伯特·钱伯（Robert Chamers, 1802—1871），是苏格兰作家、杂志编辑、出版家。
3. 大卫·格莱厄姆·菲科普斯（David Graharn Phillips, 1867—1911），是一位美国新闻记者、小说家。
4. E·菲利普斯·奥本海姆（E. Phillips Oppenheim, 1866—1946），英国小说家。
5. 原文当中是"slicker"，在美国俗语当中有"耍滑、骗子"的意思，这里使用上海话里的"老门槛"一词翻译，即便这个说法现在的流行程度已大不如前了。（参看《上海俗语图说》，上海书店出版社，1999年6月第一版。）

"泰德·康弗斯？那好说。他考试会不合格，一整个夏天到哈斯特伦家补习功课，凭借大概四个优势进入谢菲尔德，接着在一年级中途的时候就因考试不合格退学。接下来他就返回西部老家，鼓捣了一段时间，最终被他爸爸叫去做油漆买卖。他就会结婚，接着会生四个小孩，都傻傻的。他将永远觉得是圣雷吉士学校断送了他的未来，因此他会将他的儿子都送去波特兰的私立走读学校上学。等到四十一岁他就会由于脊髓痨去世，他的媳妇将会给他做一个洗礼架，不用介意它的名字，送去长老会，上面还刻着他的姓名——"

"停止停止，艾默里。那也太悲惨了。讲讲你自己吧，你会如何？"

"我会进优等班。你也一样。我们都是哲学家。"

"我可不是这样。"

"你自然是哲学家。你的头脑多么聪慧呀。"然而艾默里也清楚，无论他讲得多么有道理，抽象的、理论的、笼统的物件都震撼不了拉希尔的心，除非他可以讲出这方面的详细内容、列举细节。

"这是哪儿的话，"拉希尔依旧坚定自己的说法。"我在这里都被别人牵住了，一点优势都不存在。我被当成了我朋友的牺牲品，真不好——帮助他们做作业，为他们解决难题，夏天还没趣地到他们家中去拜访，还要经常陪着他们的小妹妹玩耍。他们一个个都特别损人利己，我还要耐下心来，接着，他们感觉他们为我投一票，告诉我我就是圣雷吉士学校的'大师兄'，就算是对我的报答。我想要去每个人都可以自己做完自己的作业的地方去，我能够给人们一些引导。对于学校里的让人怜惜的家伙每一个都要巴结，这已经够让我讨厌了。"

"你不是个老门槛，"艾默里忽然讲出这样的话来。

"老什么？"

"老门槛。"

"这有什么含义？"

"嗯。它的意思是——就是——有非常多的含义。你不是一个老门槛，我也算不得，但是我比你要更像一些。"

"谁是呢？你为什么说你更像？"

艾默里思考一番。

"呃——嗯，在我看来，一个人沾点水将头发向后面梳得油光锃亮的，那就是老门槛的标志了。"

"就像卡尔斯代尔斯一样？"

"嗯——就是。他就是一个老门槛。"

他们俩用了两个晚上的时间做了一个明确的定义。老门槛的长相很是美丽，或者说是整理得整整齐齐，他头脑灵活，意思是说，有与人交往的能力，他用尽所有的方法在诚实的大路上一直向前，赢得人心，获取赞颂，从来不会惹出事情来。他衣冠齐楚，特别注意外表的干净整齐，可想而知，他的头发一定剪得非常短，中分，擦了很多水或是生发水，比对现在的流行发式，头发朝后梳得滑溜溜的，过去的老门槛架着玳瑁眼镜，用这个来当做他们的标志，有这一条就可以非常容易认出他们，因此艾默里和拉希尔从没有把人认错过。老门槛分布在学校的各个地方，头脑常常比同龄人聪敏一些，眼光独到一点，手下总是有几个可以使唤的人，然而他谨小慎微，将自己的聪敏隐藏得非常好，丝毫不会显露出来。

一直到念大学一年级的时候，艾默里都感觉老门槛这个分类非常有意义，到了大学里，他发觉老门槛的模样有些不清晰了，很难归类，所以要经过很多次的再分类，最终仅仅就是一个性格的特色罢了。艾默里的秘密梦想和做一个老门槛所具有的全部条件十分吻合，然而，除了这个，他缺乏勇气，不具备优秀的头脑和才智——艾默里也认为自己有一个和当一名纯正的老门槛格格不入的奇怪的性格。

这是第一次和学校传统所具备的虚伪性的真正决裂。老门槛是一个明确的成功人士，同预备学校的"大师兄"存在本质上的区别。

"老门槛"	"大师兄"
1. 有聪慧的社会价值思想。	1. 倾向于蠢笨，缺乏社交价值思想。
2. 着装考究。装作着装仅仅是外表——然而心里明白着装并不仅仅是外表。	2. 觉得着装是外表，所以常常不在乎穿的是什么。
3. 但凡可以展现自己的活动一定参加。	3. 万事尽职尽责，勤勤恳恳。
4. 考进大学，所以名利双收。	4. 考进大学，然而对前程怎样仍持有怀疑态度。由于周围少了原来的那些人而觉得沮丧，所以常常讲毕竟中学时期最开心。返回到母校作报告，大谈

	特谈圣雷吉士学校的学生时期的意义。
5. 头发梳得油光锃亮。	5. 头发不油亮。

艾默里已经明明白白地决定报考普林斯顿大学,即便那一届圣雷吉士学校就只有他一个人报考。在明尼阿波利斯盛行的说法,还有从当选过"骷髅会"[1]的圣雷吉士毕业生那里听说的故事来看,耶鲁大学有它的唯美色调和诱惑力,然而普林斯顿大学对他的吸引力最大。普林斯顿大学校园的氛围浓厚,色彩明丽,有着美国最适合陶冶情操的乡村俱乐部称号的醉人名声,大学入学考试就要到来,中学时期黯淡无光,早已成了历史。很多年以后他再回到圣雷吉士学校的时候,好像已经将六年级时的种种事迹遗忘了,只对自己是一个适应不了环境的孩子这一点印象深刻,他的脑海里呈现出急匆匆地走过走廊的场景,一边走一边受到脑海中塞满了人情事理的偏激的同龄人的讥讽。

---

[1] 耶鲁大学的秘密学生组织机构。每年五月的第二个星期四下午举行集会,从一年级生中选择十五人加入入会小组。这是一个神秘的机构,美国很多组织的首脑就曾经是这个机构的一员。

第二章　尖顶建筑和怪兽滴水嘴

原先艾默里仅仅注意到灿烂的阳光悄悄降临在大片绿蒙蒙的草地上，阳光在涂抹着铅的玻璃窗上一闪一闪，在房顶尖部、塔楼和雉堞上拂过。慢慢地他发现他确实是走在大学的路上，并且由于手里拿着箱子而吃惊不已，走路的姿势也变得不同以前，看到有人从对面走来，他就避开他们的目光。有几次他可以确定人们转过头用异样的眼光看着他。他心里不自觉地思考他的穿衣打扮是否有不妥之处，心里琢磨着那天早上要是在火车上把胡子刮一刮就好了。那些衣着白色法兰绒长裤、头上不戴帽子的青年要么是高年级学生，要么是低年级学生，看他们行为敏捷、走路胸有成竹的样子就能够判断出来。走在这些人的中间，他有种莫名的惶恐不安的感觉。

他发现大学路十二号曾经是一栋很大的常年搁置的破败不堪的大楼，现在很明显没人住在这里，可他知道不出意外的情况下，楼里会住十几个一年级新生。忙乱中与宿舍的女房东争论了几句以后，他便出去四处转悠看看这里，看看那里，可是还没有走出一排房子，他就惊恐地发现他是如此的独特，居然是城里唯一一个戴礼帽的人。他赶紧返回大学路十二号，摘下他的圆顶礼帽，露出脑袋再一次出门，在纳骚大街上徘徊不断，突然被一家商店的橱窗里的东西吸引了，进而停下脚步，认真端详着一批展示着的运动员的照片，一张橄榄球队长艾伦比的大照片位列其中，之后，一家甜品店橱窗上方的"冰激凌圣代"的标志让他有了念头。这个还可以，所以他一个步子就迈了进去，找了一个高凳子坐了下来。

"巧克力圣代。"他对一个黑人说。

"一杯双份巧克力圣代吗？还需要其他的吗？"

"嗯——没错。"

"腊肉小面包，好吗？"

"嗯——没错。"

第二章 尖顶建筑和怪兽滴水嘴

他饶有兴趣地吃了四个，很符合他的口味，所以又要了一杯双份巧克力圣代，这才得到了一丝满足。大概看了一遍枕套、皮锦衣以及墙上贴满的吉不森少女[1]画之后，他离开了甜品店，两只手放在裤子口袋里，接着在纳骚大街上漫无目的地溜达着。慢慢地，他试着去区分高年级和低年级学生，即便是还有一周，新生才会带上他们的专属帽子。那些过于明显、过于兴奋地感觉无拘无束的人就是一年级新生，由于每列火车都会载着一批新来的人，他们一到就混在了头上没帽子、脚上穿白鞋、手上抱着书本的人潮之中，这些人的使命似乎就是在大街上不停地在人群中穿梭，抽着刚入手的烟斗、从口中吐出阵阵浓烟。到了中午以后，艾默里发现到校的新生早已把他当做是高年级学生了，但他自己则极力装作是毫不在乎又放松开心，却也暴露出冷漠至极且特别挑剔的模样，这样的表现已然特别近距离地从他脸上的表情看出来了。

到了下午五点钟，他认为很需要听听他自己的声音，所以他返回到自己的住处，环顾四周看看是否有新来的人。他踏上左右摇摆不定的楼梯，一脸迫不得已的样子，把房间周围都看了一遍，心里念叨着除了班级旗子和合照以外，想要再摆放一些充满生机的东西是不大有可能了。就在此时外面传来了敲门声。

"请进！"

门口出现了一张消瘦的脸庞，一双灰色的大眼睛，脸上带着风趣的笑容。

"有锤子吗？"

"没有——对不起。十二号太太，记不清她叫什么了，或许她有你想要的东西。"

那个未曾谋面的人走进了房间。

"你也是被这所疯人院收留的人？"

艾默里表示了肯定。

"我们的租金那么贵，然而住的地方竟然是空无一物的像仓库一般的屋子？"

艾默里必须承认事实就是如此。

"我想去校园逛逛，"他说，"可是他们告诉我新生很少，如果去了很容

---

1. 吉布森是美国著名的插画家，在二十世纪的美国，他画的少女——以他的妻子为模特儿盛行了二十多年，画中少女的发式、衬衫领的裙子样式一度成为当时美国女性追求的对象，不管是枕套、桌布、杯垫、烟灰缸，还是其他广告礼品，都有吉布森的少女素描。

易迷失方向。所以我索性就在这里坐着好了，开动开动脑子来找点事情干。"

灰色眼睛的人开始做自我介绍。

"我姓贺拉狄。"

"我姓布莱恩。"

他们握手，与此同时用时新的动作身体忽然前冲。艾默里笑着露出了牙齿。

"你是哪一所预备学校的？"

"安多弗——你呢？"

"圣雷吉士。"

"哦，是吗？我有个表哥就在你那边上的学。"

他们开始具体地讨论起表哥来，之后贺拉狄说他想去看他的弟弟，六点钟一起吃饭。

"来和我们一起吃饭吧。"

"好的。"

在肯尼沃尔斯饭店，艾默里见到了伯恩·贺拉狄——那个灰眼睛的哥哥叫凯里——清汤，软乎乎的蔬菜，在老老实实吃饭的时候，他们的目光都放在其他一年级新生上，有稀稀拉拉的，特别不自然的模样，也有成群结队的，看上去落落大方，情绪很好。

"据说公共食堂非常不好。"艾默里说着。

"那只是别人瞎传的。不过你别无选择，只能去那里吃——不然一定要花点钱。"

"太倒霉了！"

"都是骗人的！"

"哦，到了普林斯顿，第一年你遇到所有的事情都要选择忍让。完全就是一所预备学校。"

艾默里表示同意。

"然而，什么都如预备学校一样，"他继续说。"哪怕是这样，我无论如何都不会去耶鲁上学。"

"我也是。"

"你在这里将要加入某个运动队吗？"艾默里向那个弟弟问道。

"我不参加——伯恩他要参加普林斯——《普林斯顿人报》，你知道。"

"嗯,我知道。"

"你准备加入什么活动吗?"

"哦——是啊。我可能会加入一年级生橄榄球队。"

"在圣雷吉士就是橄榄球运动队员吗?"

"还好还好,"艾默里谦虚地以肯定的语气说道,"可是我现在比那时瘦了好多。"

"你看起来不瘦。"

"哦,去年秋天我也是很健壮的。"

"啊!"

晚餐之后他们去了电影院,看电影时一个坐在他前面的人说起话来滔滔不绝,不停地在进行点评,引起了他的注意,以及那些好似疯了般的大喊大叫的声音,令他如痴如醉。

"呦呵!"

"啊,心肝宝贝——你这么大、这么健硕,然而又这么温婉!"

"抱一下!"

"啊,抱一下!"

"吻她,快,吻她一下,吻她!"

"噢噢噢——!"

一群人开始用口哨吹起《海滨》的调子,听见的人也有一句没一句地随声附和着。之后是一首歌词听起来有些模糊的歌,里面混淆着一片跺脚声,之后是一曲无穷无尽、前后没联系的哀歌。

"噢噢噢

她在果酱厂里上班

哎呀——那也没关系

但是你千万不可以捉弄我

因为我知道——清清——楚楚

她不是整夜做果酱、从不停歇!

噢噢噢!"

他们在人潮中艰难地挤出影院,向路人报以好奇又冰冷的眼神,别人也投来同样的眼光,此时艾默里胸有成竹地得出他喜欢电影的结论,希望如坐在前排的高年级同学那般去观赏电影,他们的两条胳膊全搭在椅背上,用盖尔语说一段露骨刻薄的评论,语气上既有严谨的智慧,有时又只是随便说说而已。

"要吃圣代——我是说要吃冰激凌圣代吗?"凯里问道。

"要吃的。"

他们用夜点心填饱了肚子,之后仍然在街上闲逛,不慌不忙地返回大学路十二号。

"愉快的夜晚。"

"真是太美妙了。"

"你们两个要打开箱子收拾东西吗?"

"是啊。走吧,伯恩。"

艾默里心想要在门口的台阶上休息一会儿,所以他和他们俩说了晚安。

随着夕阳西下,绿油油的树荫渐渐被黑影笼罩。早就升起来的明月在拱门上映出淡淡的青色光,在月光轻纱般的空隙间,传来一首歌,谱写了夜空,一首特别惆怅的歌,如白驹过隙,里面满满都是无尽的懊悔。

他记得九十年代毕业生向他介绍过布思·塔金顿[1]制造欢乐的方法:夜深人静的时候站在校园正中,举头看着天空,放开喉咙想即兴高歌一曲,却莫名刺激了倒在长沙发上、心情各不相同的本科生的欢笑与哀愁。

此刻,大学路远处模模糊糊的公路上,一群穿着白衣服的人影划破了夜的寂静,他们穿着白衬衫、白长裤,手拉着手,挺胸抬头向前看,前进的步调在马路上踩出鼓点般的节奏:

"回去啦——回去啦,

回去啦——回到——纳骚——楼[2],

回去啦——回去啦——

回到——最棒的——古老的——大楼。

回去啦——回去啦,

参加这场——俗世的——舞会——我们往回走,

---

1. 布思·塔金顿(Booth Tarkington,1869—1946)是美国的小说家、戏剧家。除此之外还是普林斯顿大学"三角俱乐部"积极分子、学生演员,《纳骚文学杂志》就是他编排的。
2. 普林斯顿大学距今最久(1754)的教学大楼,里面有有图书馆、教堂、师生住宅等。

我们——扫清——道路——回去啦——

回去啦——回到——纳骚——楼！"

渐渐地，这支朦朦胧胧的队伍向前靠近，艾默里把眼睛闭上了。调子很高，他们全都唱不到那个高度，唯独只有男高音，是他们让旋律平安地度过了危险的时刻，之后由优秀的男生合唱来完成。所以艾默里将眼睛睁开，但是心里有些不安，唯恐前面这些人会让他心中美丽如画的幻想破灭。

他在心中满怀憧憬地长长舒出一口气，这些人中走在最前面的是橄榄球队的队长艾伦比，消瘦的个子，目中无人，那神态都散发着光芒，被人看到好像今年全校的希望都落在他一个人身上似的，人们憧憬着他一百六十磅硕大的身躯灵活地左右躲闪，冲进深蓝与深红的界线，获得第一名。

艾默里深深地着迷于此景，他的目光从未离开过这支前进的队伍，每一排的人都手拉着手，身着马球衫，他们的脸模糊不清，歌声自然而然地变成胜利归来的四音节步伐——之后这一群人走过昏暗的凯普贝尔拱道，在校园里浩浩荡荡地向西面去了，歌声也渐渐消失殆尽。

时间不知不觉地飞速溜走，艾默里表现得特别的安静，坐在那里。一年级新生在晚上规定的时间里不允许到外面去，对于学校的这项规定，他感到有些可惜，毕竟他特别希望到那些静谧、花香四溢的羊肠小路上随意走走，在那里能够看到威瑟斯布恩楼，她宛如一位沉默的母亲，看着阁楼孩子辉阁楼与克里奥楼，那里还能够欣赏到黑乎乎、蛇一般的哥特式建筑蜿蜒而去，到了奎勒楼和帕顿楼，而这两栋房子又将神秘的气息带到了湖边分外宁静的坡地。

白天的普林斯顿渐渐地进入他的意识——威斯特学院与毕业生回校聚会，不禁让人联想起六十年代的大学生活；七十九大楼，红砖，威严耸立；上潘恩楼与下潘恩楼，就好像高贵典雅的维多利亚淑女，不情愿与商店经营者生活在一起；而充满着对明朗、湛蓝的渴望，能够高耸入云，屹立在这里所有大楼之上的，是霍尔德塔楼与克利夫兰塔楼那如美丽梦境般庞大的尖顶。

起初他就非常喜欢普林斯顿——它那疲乏困倦的美，它那令人捉摸不透的意义，联欢会那跨夜的纵情之乐，俊俏、幸运，搜寻着危险的大目标人群；而在这所有之下却是充满着我们全年级的斗争气氛。一年级新生一个个把眼睛睁得大大的，疲惫不堪，衣着贴身的运动衫在健身房中坐着，推举希尔学校毕业的人当班长，推举劳伦斯学校的一个名气不小的人当副班长，推举圣保罗学校的一个冰球明星作为秘书长，自从那天开始一直到毕业，这种气氛从未消失过，即，那让人近乎窒息的使人害怕和不解的"大师兄"社交体系，对"大师兄"的五体投地，可是这样的外号从来没有确切的名字、从来没有真正被接纳过。

最初这是预备学校的黑暗"传统"，而艾默里，由于只有他一个人来自圣雷吉士学校，所以他只能坐在观众席在一旁看着群体组合、扩大，再组合；圣保罗学校、希尔学校、庞弗雷特学校，他们都理所当然地在公共食堂的预留餐桌上吃饭，在健身房都有专门供他们换衣服的地方，无意中在他们四周建造了一道由名不副实却在社交上有着很大野心的人组成的屏障，来保卫他们自己，远离友好而又困惑不已的其他高中同学。自从艾默里开始发现社交屏障的那一刻起，他就很是不满，并把它当做是强者为了支持跟随他们的弱者，排斥其他强者的自私自利的行为。

他心意已定，决心也要做一个在年级中受人尊敬的人，所以报名参加了新生橄榄球训练，只过了两个星期，他就已经变成了球队四分卫，并且《普林斯顿人报》的一角对他进行了一段报道，但是他膝关节严重扭伤，赛季剩下的比赛就会缺席。他只能退出，谨慎思考这一状况。

大学路十二号里隐藏着十几个各不相同的问号。里面住着三四个不太引人注意并且受到了惊吓的劳伦斯学校毕业的男生，一所纽约私立学校的毕业狂人（凯里·贺拉狄把他们叫做"粗俗的酒鬼"），一位犹太青年，一样是从纽约来的，除此之外，还有贺拉狄兄弟俩。也可以当做是对艾默里进行弥补，面对这两个兄弟，他很自然地就喜欢上了这里。

听说，贺拉狄哥儿俩是孪生兄弟，但事实上黑色头发的那个，即凯里，比他的金发兄弟伯恩大一岁。凯里长得高，还有一双带喜感的灰色眼睛，会忽然散发出迷人的微笑他因此而马上就变成了这栋楼房里最闪亮的人，占据高处的麦穗收割者，对于自以为是的表现的监督者，直言不讳、诙谐的推销者。艾默里为他们长久的友谊做了充分的准备，相比于大学生活应该怎样度过而事实上又代表着什么这个问题，他已准备得万无一失。凯里因为性情的关系，现在并不知道要认真理解这个问题，所以他言语中委婉地指责出艾默里尽量别在这个尴尬的时机研究社交体系杂乱不堪的问题，然而他还是欣赏艾默里的，对他很是关心，也觉得非常开心。

伯恩满头金发，人特别内向，在学业上刻苦钻研，在这栋楼里总能看到他一个人终日忙碌的背影，晚上悄无声息地进来，早晨起床去图书馆钻研他的功课——他在争取《普林斯顿人报》的位置，竞选异常火爆，还有四十一个人都盼着这个冠军的位置。十二月的时候他患了白喉离开，让别人获得了位置，可到了二月里，他返回学校，再一次天不怕地不怕地报名竞赛力争人人羡慕的位置，毋庸置疑，艾默里和他的交集仅仅是在上下课来回的路上进行三分钟左右的交谈罢了，所以他并不能深入了解伯恩一心一意所喜欢的兴趣下面究竟隐藏着什么秘密。

艾默里不满足于这样马马虎虎的日子。他丢失了在圣雷吉士学校拼来的声望，那无人不知无人不晓，人人尊敬的名誉，可是，普林斯顿在激发他，以后还有很多东西能够刺激他那带着邪恶面孔，为了目的无所不用其极的心中沉睡的阴暗面，只需他能打进一个楔子。至于高年级俱乐部，在今年夏天他曾经碰到过一个只字不提的毕业生，缠着他吐露消息，从他那里得知的情况勾起了他的好奇心；小楼俱乐部，是由杰出的冒险家和衣着讲究的玩弄女性者组成的一大波混乱的人；老虎酒店俱乐部，虎背熊腰、力大无比，由于严格遵守入学前认真制定的规章制度而充满了活力；方帽与长袍俱乐部反对饮酒，暗地里是宗教虔诚的信徒，政治强大，之外还有浮夸的殖民主义俱乐部、文学正方形俱乐部，以及其他十几个俱乐部，年龄和地位各不相同。

将一个低年级的学生暴露在闪亮的灯光之下让他抛头露面的所有行为，都会被冠以"出风头"的恶名。因为有刺骨的点评，电影多次被搬上屏幕，可是做出点评的人一般都是在出风头，提起俱乐部就是出风头，特别强烈地支持某种做法，举个例子，举办狂欢酒会或是宣扬一定要禁酒，那就是出风头。总的来说，个人出头、吸引别人注意力，绝对是被唾弃的，而真正说话有分量的人是不承担义务的人，于是乎，到了二年级选举的时候，每个人都需要在以后的大学时光里捂紧嘴巴，不出风头。

艾默里发觉向《纳骚文学杂志》投稿总会石沉大海，可是若能在《普林斯顿人报》的编辑部担任职务，任何人都会取得非常大的成果。他要参加英语戏协会做不朽的表演的愿望也慢慢消失殆尽，因为他发觉最机智的人以及最有才能的人都汇集在三角俱乐部里，那是一个音乐戏剧组织，每年圣诞节都会组织一次大型的外出表演。此时此刻，在公共食堂觉得非常怪异的寂寞与烦躁不安，但心里却有新的期望与野心在莫名地敲打着自己，他的第一学期就这样在烦躁和嫉妒之间摇晃着过去了，他嫉妒萌芽状态的成就，他向凯里倾诉着困扰自己的问题与不解，为什么他们在年级杰出的人群中不被接纳。

不知过了多少个午后，他们懒散地倚在大学路十二号的窗台上，看着一个个同学们到公共食堂去，或是从公共食堂往回走，注意到那些追随者都紧紧跟随着那些更加出名的人身上，观察着那些形影相吊的人来去匆匆，两眼暗淡无光，羡慕那些以预科学校区分的人三五成群的欢快和安全。

"我们都是倒霉的中产阶级，问题就在这里！"有一天他对凯里抱怨道，当时他舒展四肢窝在沙发上，不断地抽着法拉马蒂牌香烟。

"哦，为什么不能是这样？我们进了普林斯顿，所以我们也能够用同样的方式对待那些没有名气的学院——比他们优越，更加胸有成竹，穿得更加讲究得体，出行更加光彩——"

"啊，我并不是由于这个原因才重视那些令人震惊的等级制度的，"艾默里认可道。"我认为身上穿辣猫品牌的衬衣很酷，可是，哎呀，凯里，我特别希望自己能成为一只辣猫。"

"然而在目前，艾默里，你仅仅是一个出气力的小市民罢了。"

艾默里窝在沙发那里沉默不语。

"我用不了——多久，"他最后说道。"但是我对凭借苦力来达到目的很反感。我希望能有自己的独特之处，你也了解。"

"得体的疤痕。"凯里忽然伸长脖子向窗外的马路看去。"朗格达克来了，你想不想看看他的样子——亨伯德就在他后面。"

艾默里猛地从沙发上站了起来，走到窗前。

"哦，"他说道，一面仔细端详着这些优秀人物，"亨伯德的模样看上去就像是一个特别杰出的人，可是这个朗格达克嘛——却是一个很粗鄙的人，是这样吗？我不相信这样的人。所有的钻石在加工之前都会显得很大。"

"哎，"激动过后的凯里说道，"你的文学天赋很高。看你的了。"

"我在想"——艾默里顿了顿——"我可能还真是个文学天才。实话实说，我有时候还真有这种感觉。这话听上去有些自命不凡，但是这话除了你，我不会再告诉第二个人。"

"唔——开动吧。把你的头发留长，如文学杂志上的这个丹维里埃一般作诗。"

第二章　尖顶建筑和怪兽滴水嘴

艾默里懒散地张开手去拿放在桌子上的一摞杂志。

"你看过他最近写的东西吗？"

"从未错过。很少见的。"

艾默里拿起一本看了起来。

"啊！"他震惊地说道，"他是一个新生吗？"

"是的。"

"你听这一首！我的上帝！"

"'一个女仆然后说道：

黑丝绒长裙的轻拂迎来黎明，

银烛台里插着白色的小蜡烛，

淡淡的火焰在飘动，就像是树影的婆娑，

皮雅，蓬皮雅，来吧——快来听——'"

"这，这写的是什么？"

"这是一首餐具室即景。"

"'她的脚趾僵硬像只白鹊一样飞起；

她在床上躺着，身下是洁白的床单，

双手像圣徒一般放在平静的胸口，

贝拉·库尼莎，快来透个气！'"

"我的天哪，凯里，这究竟是在写什么？我发誓我什么都没读出来，但是我也是一个文学爱好者。"

"难以判别，"凯里说道，"只不过你读的时候，脑子里要想着灵车以及馊牛奶。这一首比其他几首都要缺乏热情。"

艾默里把杂志随手扔到了桌子上。

"哎，"他叹了一口气，说道，"我简直是一头雾水，一点儿也看不懂。我明白自己并不是一个遵守规章制度的人，可是谁如果不遵守规章制度我就会很反感。我内心纠结到底是要陶冶情操，当一个大戏剧家，还是对《英语诗歌宝库》[1]不以为然，当一个普林斯顿的老门槛。"

"为什么要有一个固定的方向？"凯里提议道。"还是人云亦云的好，像

---

1. 英国著名文学批评家、诗人弗朗西斯·特纳·帕尔格莱弗整理的优秀英文抒情诗歌集，出版于一八一六年。

我一样。我打算通过伯恩的扶持，闻名于世界。"

"我不可以与世沉浮——我希望得到别人的关注。我要成为一个有名声的人，哪怕是为了别人的利益，抑或是做《普林斯顿人报》的编委主席，三角俱乐部的主席。我要成为一名被人敬仰的人，凯里。"

"你在自己身上花的心思太多了。"

艾默里因为这句话马上起身站了起来。

"我不仅花在自己身上的心思多，对你花的心思也很多。如果当一位目空一切的人很有意思，那我们融入到外面去，立刻和年级里的同学一起打闹嬉戏。比方说，六月份要举行年级舞会，我会找一个妓女过来，当然这件事我要处理得和风细雨，不然我不会找人来——把她介绍给所有喜欢玩弄女性的人，介绍给橄榄球队队长，以及那些四肢健壮、脑袋却只有一根筋的人。"

"艾默里，"凯里有些耐不住性子了，"你那是在胡闹乱忙。如果你真的要扬名立万，那就走出去，去斗争；假如你不想那样，那就放任自流吧。"他一脸想要睡觉的模样。"好了，把烟雾放出去。我们一起下去看橄榄球练习。"

艾默里也渐渐地认同了这一观点，打算到了次年秋季再进行他梦寐以求的扬名立万之路，现在则是蛰伏，欣赏着凯里在大学路二十二号畅游在自己的乐趣中。

他们用柠檬派在犹太青年的床上肆意涂抹 他们将艾默里房间里的灯弄灭，还弄得满满一栋楼都充满了煤气的味道，把十二号太太以及周围负责修理的管子工吓得手忙脚乱；他们将粗俗的酒鬼的东西——画、书本、家具——挪到了厕所里。这两个人从特伦顿喝得醉醺醺的回来了，迷迷糊糊地发现东西都变了位置，看到那幅景象后，一脸疑惑的样子，可是这两个酒鬼却把这件事当做打趣来看待，之后，艾默里他们觉得特别扫兴。他们吃过晚饭便开始玩牌，玩了一通宵，比大小、打二十一点、累积赌注。在某个同学生日的那天，他们说动了他买香槟祝贺生日，大家喝得尽兴。发现组织生日聚会的人喝酒不多，凯里和艾默里意外地将他扔下了两排楼梯，事情发生以后，感到后悔不已，羞愧自责，于是在那之后的满满一个星期里，他们都去校医院探望他。

"喂，这么多女人都是什么来路？"有一天凯里突然问道，质问艾默里怎么会有这么多信件。"我最近一直在关注信件上的邮戳——法尔明顿、多卜士、威斯托弗、达纳霍尔——什么情况？"

艾默里微微一笑。

"全都是从双子城[1]邮来的。"他将这些女孩一五一十地向他作着介绍。"一个是玛丽莲·德·威特——她很美丽，自己有车，有车就便捷了许多；一个是萨里·威瑟比——她越来越胖了；一个是梅拉·圣·克莱尔，我们早就认识了，可以非常轻松地吻她，如果你想的话——"

"你是怎么做到的？这么有办法？"凯里问道。"我几乎用遍了各种各样的方式，但是那些聪明人甚至都不恐惧我。"

"你是属于'乖孩子'一类的，"艾默里提醒道。

"你说得没错。我母亲总是认为无论哪个姑娘和我在一起一定都很安全。说实话，这样也很让人厌烦。如果我伸手去牵一个人的手，她们就会嘲笑我，不让我那么做，就如同这只手不是从她们身上长出来的一样。只要我牵起她们的一只手，她们就会立刻将我拉开。"

"你就闹脾气，"艾默里给他出主意说。"就对她们说你要抓狂了，她们来训斥你——回到家里马上装疯——过半个小时就回来——让她们害怕。"

凯里表示了否定。

"这招不好使。去年我给圣提摩西女子学校的一个姑娘写了一封特别煽情的信件。信中写到一个地方时，我激动得不知如何下笔，于是说：'我的上帝，我爱你！'她用一个修指甲的小剪刀将'我的上帝'这几个字抠掉，之后让全校的人传阅这封信。一点效果都没有，我就是一个'老好人凯里'，什么事都办不好。"

艾默里面带笑容，脑袋飞速运转着，尽力构想着'老好人艾默里'的场面。他甚至无法想象出这样一个场景。

二月里雨雪交加木曾停卜，连续不断的一年级学生期中考试结束了，大学路十二号的日子还是拥有那么多的欢乐，即便它算不上很有意义。艾默里依旧是一天一顿地去"乔家餐馆"吃三明治、玉米片、土豆丝，通常情况下都是由凯里或者亚历克·康尼奇陪同。亚历克毕业于霍奇吉士学校，他是一个寡言少语、孤傲的老门槛，住在隔壁房间，因为他们全班同学都考到了耶鲁大学，所以他迫不得已同艾默里一般做个独行侠，没有朋友。"乔家餐馆"店里的装饰丝毫

1.城指明尼阿波利斯和圣保罗两城。

没有任何亮点,并且还显得有些脏乱,可是食客能够毫无节度地赖账,这给了艾默里极大的便捷。他的父亲涉足矿业股票投资,所以,虽然他的工资每月都不会少,但却不会如他想象的那般阔绰。

"乔家餐馆"还有一个优点,因为地方比较偏僻,所以能够躲开高年级同学异样的目光,因此每天下午四点,或是由一个朋友伴随,抑或是一个人拿着一本书,艾默里总是要到这里吃上一顿饱饭。三月里的一天,他走进餐馆看到桌子上坐满了人,于是默默地走到最后面的一张桌子旁,在一个专心致志看着一本书的一年级学生的对面的椅子上坐了下来。两人相视一下,点点头,没有说活。二十分钟的时间里,艾默里一边吃着熏肉小圆面包,一边看《华伦太太的职业》(萧伯纳的书,是他在学年期中考试期间在图书馆翻阅书刊期间偶然发现的);对面那个一年级生一边吃着三合一巧克力麦乳糖,一边也心无旁骛地看他的书。

慢慢地,艾默里的目光从对面的人身上再移到书上。他从倒着的书上认出了书的作者以及书名——斯蒂芬·菲利普斯的《玛佩莎》[1]。然而,即便他看到了也没有什么意义,由于他在诗歌格律方面所懂得的知识仅仅限于比如"快到花园来,莫德"[2]这样的星期日经典曲目,还有不久前死记硬背的莎士比亚和弥尔顿那寥寥无几的几句诗。

他特别想和对面的人聊天,所以假装自己被手中的书吸引,然后不由自主地大声叫喊起来:

"哈!写得好!"

那个一年级生抬起头看着他,艾默里装作一脸尴尬的模样。

"你是在说你的熏肉小面包吗?"他那嘶哑、和蔼的声音与那副宽大厚重眼镜以及他给人的激烈的求知欲的感觉搭配得恰到好处。

"不,"艾默里回答道。"我是在说萧伯纳的剧本。"他顺手将书转向他,

---

1. 斯蒂芬,菲利普斯(Stephen Phillips, 1864—1915)是英国的诗人、剧作家,他所作的长诗《玛佩莎》(1897)是取自希腊神话依托里亚公主玛佩莎的爱情故事。下文所提到的大卫·格雷厄姆·菲利普斯是美国新闻记者和小说家。
2. 出自英国著名诗人阿尔弗莱德·丁尼生勋爵独白诗剧《莫德》,其中包括丁尼生最受欢迎的抒情诗之一《莫德》,其中一节:"快到花园来,莫德/因为黑蝙蝠,夜,已经飞走。/快到花园来,莫德/我独自赏花在花园门口;忍冬香气弥漫,四处飘散送,玫瑰幽香还要皓齿明眸。"在那时编成曲子被英国著名男高音歌唱家西姆斯·里弗斯所演唱。

嘴里补充道。

"萧伯纳的书我从来没有接触过。但我一直希望有机会能看一看。"这个孩子顿了顿，继续说道，"你有没有接触过斯蒂芬·菲利普斯的著作，你对诗歌感兴趣吗？"

"感兴趣，确实是，"艾默里做出了热情又肯定的回答。"但是，斯蒂芬·菲利普斯的诗歌我还是很陌生的。"（他仅仅知道已经离开人世的大卫·格雷厄姆·菲利普斯，还没听说过其他姓菲利普斯的人。）

"那也没什么关系，我认为。当然他是维多利亚时代的人。"于是他们开始谈论起诗歌来，并在讨论的过程中相互做了自我介绍，坐在艾默里对面的这个人正是那个在《文学杂志》上发表激情澎湃的爱情诗的知识渊博的托马斯·帕克·丹维里埃。他大概十九岁，双肩下垂，淡蓝色的眼睛，与艾默里从他的外表所了解到的那样，他对社会上激烈的战斗还有与其相似的让其他人很感兴趣的话题他都不大关注。但是，他热爱读书，好像艾默里已经好久没碰到过热爱读书的人了，只要隔壁餐桌上的圣保罗学校的那一伙人不认为他也是一个文学爱好者，今天的邂逅就会是非常有意思的。他们好像没有注意到这里，所以他可以毫不拘束地谈论起书来，一提就是几十本的书，他耳熟能详的书，他闻所未闻的书，他一知半解的书，如布兰塔诺书店[1]的店员一般一字不错非常顺畅地罗列出一大堆书名。丹维里埃被假象迷惑了——发现艾默里在认真倾听，一股愉悦之情油然而生。他质朴的性格让他几乎认为，普林斯顿的学生是由一部分平庸至极的人和一部分彻头彻尾埋头苦干的人组成的，可以找到一个人丝毫不结巴地吐出济慈的名字，但是又没有露出把柄，想到这儿，就会让人感觉很开心。

"奥斯卡·王尔德是否看过？"他对艾默里说。

"没有。谁写的？"

"这是人名——你不知道吗？"

"哦，想起来了。"艾默里的思绪飞速运转寻找着记忆的痕迹。"幽默歌剧《忍耐》[2]是他写的吗？"

"没错，就是这个人。我才看完他的《道林·格雷的画像》这本书，当然我也强烈推荐你也读一读这本书。你会喜欢的。要是你想看的话，我可以借给你。"

---

1. 在购物中心内。
2. 在伦敦于一八七一年上演的喜歌剧，讽刺王尔德和十九世纪七八十年代的唯美主义运动。

"噢，真是太感谢了，我一定会上瘾的。"

"你要不要来我的房间里坐坐？我那里还有几本别的书。"

艾默里犹豫了一下，看了一眼圣保罗学校的那群人——其中一个就是尊贵、完美的亨伯德——他在思量这个新认识的朋友是有多么坚毅。他向来没有走到过结交一个朋友又将他甩掉的境地——他还没有无情到做出这种事情来——所以他现在用玳瑁框眼镜后面盛气凌人的冷淡双眼观察着托马斯·帕克·丹维里埃的吸引人的地方和价值，因为他一直感觉隔壁桌子的人正在用漠视的眼神看着他们。

"去，我去。"

于是他翻出了《道林·格雷的画像》、《多洛雷斯》、《无情的美人》[1]；这使他在一个月里对什么都提不起兴趣。世界也变得昏暗、让人不得不关注，并且竭力用奥斯卡·王尔德和斯温伯恩的憨足的眼光来观察普林斯顿，他还以故作高雅的玩笑口吻称王尔德是"菲加尔·欧弗拉蒂"，称斯温伯恩是"阿尔杰农·查尔斯"[2]。他习惯性地每晚浏览书籍——萧伯纳、切斯特顿、巴里、皮内罗、叶芝、辛吉、厄内斯特·道森、亚瑟·西门斯、苏德曼、罗伯特·休·本森、萨弗伊喜歌剧[3]——杂七杂八、各种各样的书籍全都涉及到，由于他忽然发现自己这么多年来一本书都没有看过。

汤姆·丹维利埃刚开始仅仅是给了他一个托词，而并不是一个朋友。艾默里大概一个星期与他见一次面，他们一起把汤姆的天花板刷成金色，把在拍卖会上买的高仿挂毯挂在墙上，架起高架烛台，挂上提花窗帘。艾默里欣赏他机智，有书生气，可是没有软弱的性格，不造作。实际上，大概是艾默里在装作满腹诗书的样子，绞尽脑汁、尽力把每句话都说得好似名言警句。如果只有一个人沉浸于虚张声势的名言警句，很多的技巧就表现得更加独一

1.《多洛雷斯》（1866）是斯温伯恩作的长诗；《无情的美人》（1819）由济慈作。
2."菲加尔·欧弗拉蒂"和"阿尔杰农·查尔斯"分别代表这两位诗人的名字。
3. 巴里，英国小说家、剧作家详见175页注解；皮内罗（Arthur Wing Pinero, 1885—1934）英国演员、剧作家；辛吉（John Millington Synge, 1871—1909），英国剧作家、诗人；厄内斯特·道森，英国诗人、小说家，也是文艺颓废派人物；亚瑟·西门斯，英国诗人、批评家；济慈（John Keats, 1795—1821），英国著名浪漫主义诗人；苏德曼，德国戏剧家、小说家；罗伯特·休·本森，英国天主教神甫、作家；歌喜剧是在十九世纪末维多利亚时代的英国兴起的。

无二了。大学路十二号一片欢喜雀跃。凯里看了《道连·格雷》，装扮成亨利勋爵[1]，艾默里去哪里他就跟到那里，叫他"道林"这个称谓，假装煽动他有了邪恶的心理，以此来减少他疲惫厌倦的心情。到了公共食堂他依然用此种做法，其他进餐的人看见了都特别吃惊，艾默里雷霆大发，一副很尴尬的样子，自从那件事之后，名言警句仅仅在丹维里埃跟前才说，或者是对着刚好拿在手中的镜子中的自己说。

有一天，汤姆与艾默里尝试着按照凯里留声机的旋律来诵读他们自己作的诗歌与顿撒尼勋爵[2]的诗句。

"唱！"汤姆大喊道。"不会朗诵！是吟唱！"

此时正沉浸在其中的艾默里很是气愤，他说他想听一张没有太多钢琴音乐伴奏的唱片。凯里听到这话，一下子倒在地板上强忍着不笑出声。

"那就演唱《花儿与爱心》[3]吧！"他大声喊道。"啊，上帝，我的心焦躁慌乱。"

"把那破留声机关掉，"艾默里叫喊道，脸红得像火。"我不是在公演。"

在此期间，艾默里谨小慎微地极力要唤起丹维里埃对社交制度的认知，并且他也知道这位诗人的确比他要守旧得多，所以，只要头发上抹一点水，在一小部分人之间进行交流，一顶颜色更暗点儿的礼帽，就足够可以让他变得与常人一样。可是，身穿利文斯通领子的衣服、佩戴黑色领结的正式礼拜仪式他不理不睬；实际上，丹维里埃对他的不厌其烦有一丝抱怨；所以艾默里给自己规定一星期仅仅去见一次面，偶尔才带他到大学路十二号去一次。这保不齐会让其他一年级学生在暗地里嘲笑他们，他们把这两个人称作"约翰逊博士和鲍威斯尔"[4]。

另一个常客亚历克·康尼奇，大概是有些喜欢他，可是觉得他有些清高所以也有些怕他。凯里通过诗歌的胡说八道看到了他那值得信赖、值得尊敬的内心，感到特别有趣，所以一小时一小时地叫他朗诵，但自己则窝在艾默里的沙发上，

---

1. 《道连·格雷》中的人物，对生活中的美和感官享受情有独钟。
2. 即爱德华·普伦吉特，英国剧作家、诗人、小说家。
3. 歌曲《花儿与爱心》（西奥多·默西·托巴尼词、玛丽·D·布莱恩曲）于一八九九年发表，"花儿与爱心"在美国英语里经常用来表示多愁善感。
4. 约翰逊博士，英国大文豪，编写了第一部英语词典。鲍斯威尔编著的《约翰逊博士传》（1791）被好多人称赞。

紧闭双眼细细聆听着；

"她是沉睡还是苏醒？深深的吻

在她的玉颈上留下紫色的印痕

那是疼痛的血一番迟疑后的显现；

轻轻的吻也是轻轻的吮吸——比色痕更深……"[1]

"好听，"凯里轻轻地说。""这一节诗让大哥贺拉狄很是欢喜。我想这是一位大诗人。"汤姆看到他的朗诵得到了别人的赏识而喜出望外，所以就把《诗歌集》里的诗一首一首地朗诵，到最后凯里和艾默里几乎和他一样能够熟练地背诵了。

艾默里是在春天的午后着手写诗的，那是在离普林斯顿比较近的一个大庄园的花园里，人工湖中嬉戏的天鹅为他作诗营造了氛围，还有柳梢头缓缓飘动的美丽的云彩。五月天来得有些过早了，艾默里忽然感觉高墙早已困不住他的心了，他从来都是在校园里徘徊，不论是在美丽的夜空底下，还是在柔和的微风细雨中。

一个湿润的象征性插曲

夜晚雾气降临了。浓浓的雾从月亮那里袭来，在建筑物的尖顶和塔楼周围凝固，之后再从尖顶和塔楼坠落，于是沉浸在梦幻的建筑物的顶部依然对着漫漫长夜袒露着远大的理想。宛如蚂蚁一般装饰着白天的人影，此时就好似飘忽的鬼影一般在面前晃来晃去，擦肩而过。哥特式建筑的大楼与回廊在阴影中明晃晃地矗立着，许许多多灯光昏暗的淡淡的方块拼凑成每一栋大楼，渲染出无尽的神秘的氛围。不知道从何处传来了阵阵阴郁的钟声，预示着半点钟已到，艾默里在日晷前面驻足，张开四肢毫无顾忌地躺在了湿漉漉的草地上。阴森的冷空气模糊了他的双眼，延缓了时光的前进——在慵懒、无所事事的四月的午后悄无声息的流动的光阴，在悠长的春季的黄昏，好像令人十分难以捉摸。在一个个的黄昏，四年级学生的歌声中带有一丝忧郁的美，从校园中飘过，穿透他本科生顿悟的躯壳，展现出内心中炽烈、真诚的热爱，对灰色的墙、哥特式的屋顶并且对它们作为早已过去的年代的储存库所象征的所有事物的钟爱。

在他窗前能够清楚地看到的塔楼，直插云霄，组成了一个尖顶，并且依旧

---

1. 就是下文提到的斯温伯恩《诗歌集》中一首《维纳斯颂》的第一节。

期盼能够更高，直到尖顶的尽头在早晨看起来也是模糊不清的，这让他首次意识到校园人影的稍纵即逝和无足轻重，他们只是基督使徒传统薪火延续的接班人罢了，除了这个以外，没有任何别的意思。他喜欢这么理解，哥特式建筑，因为它的走向向上，与大学校园尤为般配，这早已融入他的大脑成为他自己的思想。大块安静的绿地，平静的教学大楼里时不时见到的深夜的灯光，都会在他的思绪上引起波澜，而大楼尖顶的高雅则变成他这种认识的代表。

"真是的，"他压着声音大声喊道，与此同时借用草地的湿气湿润了双手，之后抬起手摆弄着头发。"明年我要努力！"可是他心里清楚此刻建筑尖顶以及塔楼的精神能够使他不切实际地默许，可是明年他们就会让他落荒而逃。此刻他仅仅意识到自己的渺小无奈，可是努力了就会发觉自己的无能为力和技艺不精。

大学连续不断地做着梦——睁着眼睛做的梦。他心中一紧，感受到了一股激动，这或许就是大学的心脏慢慢的跳动。那好似一条小溪，站在小溪边的他掷出一粒石子，他刚刚把石子扔出去，细小的水波几乎就要消退了。时至今日他没有付出过一丝努力，当然也空手而归。

在夜里，他看到一个在柔软的小路上啪嗒啪嗒地走着的一年级生，他的油布雨衣吧嗒吧嗒传出很大的声音。不知道从哪个地方传来一声老旧的呼喊声，就在一个看不见的窗户底下，"把你的脑袋伸出来！"在大雾的覆盖下，一股水流的淙淙声可算是挤进了他的意识。

"啊，上帝！"在这个寂静的夜晚，他忽然呼喊出来，然后被他自己的叫声吓了一跳。雨还在时不时地下着。他在草地上安安静静地躺了一会儿，两只手用力地握着。之后他蹦了起来，伸出手打算抖抖他的衣服。

"水都渗到我的衣服里了！"他向日晷用力吼道。

历史事件

他一年级那一年的夏天，战争来临了。除了对德国人攻击巴黎有那么点兴趣以外，整体局势一点也没有让他感到丝毫不安，也没有让他想有更多的了解。他怀着看一场有意思的传奇剧那样的心情，盼望着这场仗能够打得更持久、更加残酷一些。如果战争没有像他预期得那样持久、残酷，他心里就如同观看买亏了的拳击比赛一般，没有激烈持久的比赛会令他很生气。

这就是他对这场战争所作出的整体反应。

"哈—哈奥尔唐斯"[1]

"行了,合唱队女演员!"

"赶紧的!"

"嗨,合唱队女演员,快放下赌博的骰子,过来扭扭屁股吧,你们意下如何?"

"嗨,合唱队女演员!"

指导教师百般无奈地发着火,三角俱乐部的主席的脸拉得像驴一般长,时而大声地教训,时而又闭口不言一副懒洋洋的样子,萎靡不振地坐在那里,内心思考着圣诞节来临时应该如何进行巡回演出。

"好吧,我们就练习海盗歌吧。"

合唱队演员们最后狠狠地吸了一口香烟,无精打采地到了各自的排练位置;扮演女主角的演员赶紧跑向前台,矫揉造作地将手和脚摆成营造氛围的姿势;指导老师手脚齐上,一边拍手一边跺脚,周而复始地敲打着,嘴上还不断地喊着拍子,他们终于排出了一场舞蹈。

三角俱乐部好似一个活力四射的大蚁冢。俱乐部每年都会表演一个音乐喜剧,带着演员、合唱队、乐队、布景,在整个圣诞节假日巡回表演。本科生包揽了剧本和音乐的所有作品,而俱乐部本身则是影响力最为广泛的机构,每年最少有三百人竞争参与。

艾默里在第一次二年级生的《普林斯顿人报》争夺赛中轻而易举就赢得了胜利,在演员表中有了一席之地,扮演"沸腾的油,海盗队长"。二年级的最后一个星期到来了,此刻他们每个晚上都会到卡西诺娱乐场去排练《哈—哈奥尔唐斯!》,从下午两点直到第二天早晨八点一直练习,困了的话就喝几乎不加牛奶的浓咖啡来保持清醒,上课简直就是睡觉时间,即便是课间也会一直睡过去。卡西诺娱乐场是一个特别神奇的地方,里面就如同一个谷仓一般的超大会堂,扮演女孩子的男生、扮演海盗的男生、扮演小男孩的男生都在里面;布景依然在按部就班地布置着;灯光人员正在有条不紊地调试着舞台的聚光灯,将一束束怪异的灯光映在带着怒火的眼睛上;耳朵里充斥着乐队不断地调音,以及三角俱乐部主旋律轻快、欢乐的节奏。为音乐喜剧填补歌词的男生在角落一旁叼着铅笔,皱着眉头,有二十分钟的时间来思考是否加演节目;业务经理

---

1. 奥尔唐斯,荷兰国王路易·波拿巴的妻子、法皇拿破仑三世的母亲。

与俱乐部干事正在讨论能够花多少钱置办"那些毫无章法的挤奶女工服装";九八年的俱乐部主席即老毕业生,坐在一个箱子上,回忆他们当年的事情比现在容易多了。

三角俱乐部的一次演出是怎么开始的一直以来都不被人所知,可是,无论如何,有杰出贡献的人可以在表链上挂一个黄金三角这件事却是一个闹得沸沸扬扬的谜。《哈—哈奥尔唐斯!》已经改了六次了,节目单子上罗列着九个合编者的名字。三角俱乐部所有的剧目,在起初撰写的时候都是"别样的内容——并不是普通的音乐喜剧",可一旦经过几个作者、俱乐部主席、指导老师以及委员会一起审核完毕后,就只剩下包含老掉牙的笑话的陈旧的三角俱乐部节目了。一个个重要的喜剧演员都没法一演到底,在巡回演出即将落幕的时候,不是被开除就是生病缺席或者找了其他借口,其中有一个是合唱队女演员芭蕾舞里的脸上长满胡子的人,他"强烈反对一天刮两次胡子",两个人把演出毁得面目全非!

《哈—哈奥尔唐斯!》剧中有一处特别精彩的地方。每当加入万众瞩目的"骷髅会"的耶鲁大学学生,一听到普林斯顿这个尊贵的名字,他一定要退场,这是普林斯顿的传统文化。还有一个传统文化是,"骷髅会"的成员在未来的生活中全都飞黄腾达,积累钱财,或者是积攒选票,积攒票证,喜欢积攒什么就积攒什么。所以,不管在什么时候,《哈—哈奥尔唐斯!》的演出中总有六个座位是不向外出售的,而是留给那些花钱请来的流氓无赖来坐,这些人本来就面目狰狞,三角俱乐部的化妆师竟然还给他们化妆打扮。演出进行到"狂热分子,海盗头子"用手指着他的黑旗帜说"我是一名耶鲁毕业生——请看我的骷髅标志!"——此时,那六个流氓无赖要按照先前的吩咐十分猥琐地从座位上站起来,表现出一副面带忧愁、失去自尊的样子,缓缓离开剧场。听说,请来艾力斯,有一次竟然将这样的情绪表现得淋漓尽致,怒发冲冠,不过这件事一直没有得到证实。

他们在圣诞节假日期间到八个城市的繁华地域去表演。艾默里钟爱路易斯维尔以及孟菲斯这两所城市,因为这两所城市的人知道如何招待来自外面的人、倾注非凡的激情、展示让人拍手叫绝的充满女性美的服饰。芝加哥他也颇为赞美,因为它充满生气,虽然那里的人们口音有些浓重——但是,这是一个崇尚耶鲁的城市,况且再过一周,这里还会迎来耶鲁欢乐俱乐部的演出,他们接待三角俱乐部的方式大概只是做做样子的问候罢了。到了巴尔的摩，普林斯顿就好像到了家乡一般，每个人都很喜欢。走到哪里都是人们喝着高度酒的豪爽场面，有个人向来都是喝得兴奋不已才上台表演，并称其喝烈酒是因为需要对饰演角色进行更深度的理解。私有车厢三节，但是，只有第三节车厢的人进入了梦乡，原因是第三节车厢是名副其实的"动物车厢"，那里是戴眼镜的群体以及名不副实的群体的聚集地。所有的事情都完成得那么匆忙，来不及令大家感到无聊，可是等他们抵达了费城，圣诞节假日即将结束，所有人都能够毫不费力地远离鲜花与油彩的浓重气氛，合唱队装扮成女演员的男演员忍受着腹部无以言表的疼痛，将紧身衣脱下，痛快地大口呼吸着。

等到巡回演出队伍刚宣布解散，艾默里便急切地想要赶紧回家，匆忙起身赶往明尼阿波利斯，因为萨莉·维瑟尔的表妹伊莎贝尔·伯尔赫在父母去国外度假期间要来明尼阿波利斯来过寒假。他只依稀记得伊莎贝尔还是一个小姑娘时的样子，他第一次去明尼阿波利斯的时候和她一起玩耍过。之后她去了巴尔的摩生活——可是从那时起，她到底过得如何，外人便无从知晓了。

艾默里扬起思绪的风帆，胸有成竹，兴高采烈。没有一丝迟疑地赶回明尼阿波利斯去见一个小时候就认识的姑娘，好像是一件有趣又不乏富有诗意的事情，所以他没有一丝愧疚之心地急忙给母亲发了封不要等他回家的电报……火车慢慢地向目的地行进着，而长达三十六个小时的时间里，他都沉浸在自己的思绪中，无法自拔。

"爱抚"

在三角俱乐部巡回演出的时候，艾默里持续不断地与当下很是火爆的美国现象，"爱抚晚会"有着接触。

墨守成规的母亲——当母亲的人都是墨守成规的——完全想不到她们的女儿是多么随意地让别人亲吻。"这是小保姆的专属表现，"哈斯顿·卡莫莱特太太向她天生丽质的女儿灌输着这样的思想。"先亲吻，后求婚。"

可是，天生丽质的女儿在她十六岁到二十岁的这六年里，每隔半年就要订一次婚，直到二十二岁的时候她将要与凯贝尔父子公司的小开汉姆贝尔结婚，那个汉姆贝尔还傻乎乎地觉得自己是她的初恋情人，但在每一次订婚后，天生丽质的女儿（舞会上有多此一举的规则，倡导适者生存，她就是在这种规则下被选中的）在月光下，抑或是炉火边，或者是在外面的黑暗地方，还与别人最后深情一吻。

艾默里看到过女孩子做出在他印象中觉得匪夷所思的事情来：三点钟舞会之后，在惊奇不已的咖啡馆中吃着夜宵，谈论着生活中的任何事情，神情时而严肃认真时而装模作样，但是却有种偷偷摸摸的激动，这在艾默里眼中绝对是名副其实的道德败坏。可是，在把纽约和芝加哥之间的城市当做是一个规模宏大的稚嫩的诡计之后，他才意识到这样的情景是很正常的。

大饭店的午后，冬季的暮色在外游荡，楼下带来了朦朦胧胧的鼓声……他们在大堂里不停地走来走去，内心焦躁不安，又端起一杯鸡尾酒，打扮得精巧细致，急躁地等待着。之后旋转门动了，三个被裘皮大衣捂得严严实实的人摇摆着步子慢慢地走了进来。于是，走进剧院，之后还有一张桌子，欣赏《午夜嬉戏》歌舞表演——固然母亲也会一起到场观看，可是如此一来，只会让事情变得更加闪烁其词、更加招摇，所有人都离开了，只剩她一个人孤寂地坐在那张桌子旁边，心里回味着这样的娱乐并没有像他们宣传的那样不堪，仅仅是太容易让人产生疲劳感罢了。但是天生丽质的女儿再一次坠入了爱河……这是不是太离谱？——虽然出租车里的空间很大，天生丽质的女儿和威廉斯学院的男生好像被挤了出去，他们顺势到了另外一辆车子。真奇怪！你是否发现天生丽质的女儿晚到了七分钟，她的小脸还红扑扑的？还好天生丽质的女儿"骗过了他们"。

"美女"已经变成了"调情者"，之后"调情者"又成为了"小骗子"。每天下午都会有六个人来找"美女"。假如天生丽质的女儿阴差阳错地被两个人找上了门，那么，那个没能与她约会的人肯定会很郁闷。"美女"在舞厅里，仅仅是在跳舞途中也会被十几个男人围住。在跳舞途中，想找到天生丽质的女儿，就想办法去找到她。

同一个姑娘……沉迷于丛林爵士乐与备受道德枷锁绑架的环境中。艾默里八岁之前碰到的任意一个天生丽质的姑娘，他都有可能在她们十二岁之前就亲吻人家，他认为这是一种容易让人沉迷的感觉。

"我们究竟因为什么要来这里？"那是一个晚上，在路易斯维尔的乡村俱乐部外面，他们在某一个人的气派汽车里坐着，那个手里拿着绿色梳子的女孩儿被他这样问道。

"我不明白。我是个玩心不改的人。"

"我们现在就说清楚吧——我们不可能再见面了。我现在将你约出来,是由于我认为你是我眼前最美丽的女孩子。你对是否还能见到我,就真的一点都无所谓吗?"

"对,我无所谓——但是你对待每一个姑娘都是如此吗?我到底做了什么要遭受如此恶劣的报应?"

"你跳舞不感到累吗?你不想抽根烟或是做一些你承诺过的什么事吗?你绝对是想要做——"

"哦,我们进去吧,"她终止了他的话,"如果你非要刨根问底的话,我们干脆就不要探讨这个话题了。"

如果手织无袖紧身运动衫是全新的款式,艾默里灵机一动,想了个别致的名称——"爱抚衫"。这个动听的名字传遍了每个大街小巷,常常被花花公子以及天生丽质的女儿们挂在嘴边。

客观的描述

艾默里现在十八岁,大概高六英尺的样子,很帅气,不是一般的帅气逼人。一张看似稚嫩的脸表露出天真无邪的样子,可是那双长而黑的睫毛以及能看穿一切的绿眼睛破坏了稚嫩的外表。他好像没有对异性的磁铁一般的吸引力,而这样的吸引力则一般都与男人或女人的美相辅相成;他的个性简直就是心理特点,相比于个性,他不能像自来水龙头一般开关自如。可是,人们一旦看到他的脸后,绝对会印象深刻,久久不能忘怀。

伊莎贝尔

她在楼梯顶上停了下来。站在跳板上的跳水运动员,第一场表演之夜的女主角,全国大学一年一度的橄榄球赛开始那天的高大、强壮的橄榄球队队员,当时他们内心的那种激动此时转移到了她的身上,像触电一般。她本来应该跟着一阵鼓声走下楼的,还有一种方法就是在《黛伊丝》[1]和《卡门》杂乱无章的主旋律中下楼。她对于她的出场历来没有这样充满兴趣过,她对于她的出场从没有那么心满意足。她的十六岁已然经过了半年。

"伊莎贝尔!"她的表姐萨莉在化妆间门口叫她。

"我准备好了。"她感觉一丝小小的紧张感不偏不倚地卡在她喉咙的位置。

---

1. 法国作曲家马斯内的三幕歌剧,一八九四年在巴黎加尔涅歌剧院进行了第一次演出。

"我要让人再取一双轻巧的舞鞋。等一会就行了。"

伊莎贝尔向化妆间走去,希望临开始前再照一眼镜子,可是突然想到了一件事,让她像瞬间凝固在了那里一般,眼睛直勾勾地看着明尼哈哈俱乐部的宽敞的楼梯。楼梯可望而不可及地向下绕着,她只能看到楼下大厅里露出两双男人的脚。穿着一样的无鞋带黑皮鞋,令人分辨不出是谁的脚,可是她急切地想要知道其中有没有艾默里·布莱恩的脚。这个年轻人直到现在都没有露面,可是他却占据了她一天中的大部分时光——从她来到这里的第一天里的大部分时间。从火车站乘坐汽车回来的途中,萨莉在连续不断地询问、说明、透露情况、还有夸夸其谈的时候,主动说道:"你记得艾默里,那是肯定的啰。哎呀,他就像着了魔一般想要再见到你。他在学校里多呆了一天,他今天晚上到。你嘛,他早就耳闻了许多许多——他说还能想起你的眼睛。"

这一句话令伊莎贝尔非常高兴。这就将他们两个人摆在一样的条件上了,虽然她自己的罗曼史她绝对有信心来自编自演,无论开始是否有烘托。可是因为等待已久而带来一阵幸福的颤抖后,她心里产生了怀疑,像泄了气的皮球一样沮丧,她忍不住要问:

"你说他了解过我很多事情,那究竟是什么意思?我的哪些事情?"

萨莉笑了。一时间她感觉自己像是成为了她那更加优秀的妹妹的经纪人。

"他知道你——人人都说你漂亮都说你"——她顿了顿——"我觉得他知道有人亲吻过你。"

听到这些话,伊莎贝尔裘皮盖毯下面的小手瞬间攥紧了。她对于别人说她那任意妄为的过去早就已经适应了,并且每次都会生气,但是——这个名号在其他城市还真是个不错的事情。她就是一颗"兴奋剂",哼——查就查还怕你们不成。

伊莎贝尔看着窗外,看到鹅毛大雪在寒风刺骨的清晨纷纷扬扬地飘着。相比于巴尔的摩,这里要冷得多,她已然忘记了,边门上的玻璃冻住了,窗玻璃上结了窗花,很是美丽,角落里满是积雪。她的心里却还在思考着一件事。他的穿衣打扮到底是不是那个男孩子那样?步伐稳健地走在那条繁华的商业街,脚上穿着那双软皮鞋,冬季狂欢节的那身行头也穿在身上,他会不会也是那样的打扮?像极了西部风格!然而那样的打扮不会是他,他是普林斯顿大学的学生,大概已经升到大学二年级了。事实上她对他了解得不多。很久以前拍的一张照片还夹在她的一本旧照相册里，他的大眼睛让她难以忘怀（现在他的大眼睛大概已经相当令人着迷了）。但是，当她下定决心要来萨莉那里去过寒假的时候，他已经表现出了一副能够被其他人着重看待的竞争者的样子。孩子是最聪明的活动规划者，他们用非常短的时间就能安排好他们的活动，并且萨莉则在表演一曲起联络作用的奏鸣曲，非常机智地触动了伊莎贝尔易于动怒的脾气，虽然是短暂的……

她们的汽车在一座距离堆满积雪的马路很远的、造型怪异的由白石堆砌的建筑物前面踩了刹车。威瑟比太太笑容满面地出来迎接她们，好几个不引人注意的很有礼貌的表妹也被叫出来认识。伊莎贝尔很是识趣地与她们一个个相互认识了。她兴趣盎然，与她所碰到的所有人都相互来往——除了年龄稍大的几个姑娘以及几个女人以外。她在她们面前的所有表现都是故意装出来的。那天早晨与她重新相互认识的六个姑娘都对她有很好的印象，首先是因为见到了她本人，其次是因为她的名气不小。艾默里不是一个隐秘的话题。他对于爱情的态度很明显有些草率、不专心，人缘既不能说好也算不上坏——那里的姑娘似乎都曾经与他相恋过，可是并没有一个人可以说出一些值得研究的信息。他要对她献出所有的爱……萨莉把这一情况告诉了她的小妹们，一见到伊莎贝尔她们也就尽快把消息都告知萨莉。伊莎贝尔心里暗自有了小心思，如果迫不得已，她就逼自己去爱这个人——这一切都是萨莉的功劳。如果她觉得非常失望怎么办？萨莉将他描绘得那么优秀——他非常帅气，"有些小名望，只要他想出人头地"，有一张能言善辩的嘴，并且非常花心。事实上，他身上有着她那个年龄和环境下所给她灌输的去追求的全部浪漫精神了。她心中疑惑，不清楚楼下柔软的地毯上跨踏地跳着狐步舞的双脚是不是就是他的舞鞋。

全部印象，其实还包括所有的想法，在伊莎贝尔的眼里都是不确定的。她的言谈举止散发出的是社交与艺术气质的怪异混搭，这两种性格特点通常出现在两种人身上，一种是出入社交场合的女人，一种是女演员。她从小受到的教育，准确地说，她的世故，是从那些被她的喜怒哀乐所影响的男孩身上学来的；她的机智成熟是她与生俱来的反应，如果她想有风流快活的样子也是易如反掌，只是会受到电话涉及的范围之内的有情人的多少的限制。她的黑褐色大眼睛暗送多少秋波，调情之意在她体态容貌的巨大诱惑下更是让人不由自主。

那天晚上，她就这样在楼梯上面等着派去的人送轻巧的舞鞋来。刚好在她

第二章 尖顶建筑和怪兽滴水嘴

等得心情急躁的时候,萨莉从化妆间走了出来,笑呵呵的,依然像往常一样笑容满面,很是愉快的样子,所以她们两个便一起下了楼,而这时伊莎贝尔心中来回搜索的探照灯照射的是两个想法:她很开心今天晚上她的小脸红扑扑的,她特别想知道他的舞是不是跳得非常棒。

下楼到了俱乐部的大舞厅中,一时间她被下午才认识的一群姑娘层层包围,之后是萨莉的声音,她嘴里念着一连串的名字,与此同时,她自己则向着六人一组黑白分明、特别拘束、好像在哪里见过的身影一步步靠近。她的直觉告诉自己布莱恩这个名字在她的脑海中出现过,可是刚开始她有些摸不着头脑,不知道他人在哪里。在那之后就是人来人往、很幼稚的一阵混乱,人们动作缓慢地向后退、互相碰撞,并且人人都发现自己是在和一个最不想说话的人脸对脸地站在一起。伊莎贝尔与哈佛大学的一年级生、原来一起玩过跳房子游戏的蛙喉帕克,一块冲出人群,好不容易在楼梯上有了一席之地,风趣地谈论着往事,这恰好是她所需要的。伊莎贝尔在社交场合能够专心致志地去做的事情是十分不可思议的。首先,她说话带有一丝南方口音,并且如痴如醉地用特别热情的女低音反复重复着;之后她再把刚说过的事情搁置在一边,让其他人去发表看法,而自己则微微一笑,仔细聆听着——那是她充满诱惑力的笑容;之后她改变方式继续说着同样的事,心里却好似在设计圈套,所有这一切名义上都是以相互交流的方式在进行着。蛙喉沉迷其中,丝毫没有发现她那样做并不是因为他,而是因为头发喷了水、梳理得十分光亮、眼睛里闪烁着绿光的人。他就站在距离她很近的地方,因为伊莎贝尔在这时就已经注意到他了。好似一个女演员,即使在自己魅力充分散发的时候,都会对坐在第一排的大部分人印象深刻,此时伊莎贝尔同样在观察着她的对手。首先,他有着褐色的头发,并且从她的神态中映射出的失望感来看,她明白她本来以为他有一头乌黑的头发,如广告中看到的那样修长的身躯……至于其他方面,只见他微红的脸颊,挺拔的身材,绝对是浪漫的形象;一套紧身的燕尾服,一件丝褶裥作为装饰的衬衣,和他的身材外貌特别般配,女人们依然喜欢男人们穿着这样的衬衫,但是男人们好像已经有些厌烦了。

正在伊莎贝尔这样从头到脚打量的时候,艾默里则在一旁安静地看着她。

"你不是这么认为吗?"她忽然转过身,朝他说道,眼里充满了天真无邪。

舞厅里一阵骚动,萨莉在前面带路来到她们的餐桌。艾默里好不容易才来到伊莎贝尔旁边，小声地对她说：

"你是我晚宴上的舞伴，你明白。我们练习的时候全是为彼此着想。"

伊莎贝尔呼出一口气——他们不谋而合。可是她仿佛感到一篇优秀的演讲稿从主角手里被抢走，交到了一位次要人物手中……她是千万不可以失去中心位置的。期间笑声接连不断，因为大家为寻找自己的位置而乱成一锅粥，充满好奇的眼光全都看向她，由于她坐了靠上手的位子。她心里洋洋得意地观看着下面的情形，而蛙喉帕克仅仅注意到她越来越红润的脸上增添的几分姿色，一时间竟然忘了把萨莉的椅子拽出来，脑袋一蒙，开始手忙脚乱了。艾默里坐在对面，信心满满，也非常得意，双眼注视着她，很明显一副特别着迷的样子。他斩钉截铁地说话，蛙喉也是如此。

"自从你开始扎头发的时候，我就听说了你的好多消息——"

"今天下午你觉得有趣不——"

两个人说到一半默契地停住了。伊莎贝尔害羞地向艾默里转过了脸庞。所有人从她的脸上都可以明明白白地看出答案，可是她依旧决定通过自己的语言来告知。

"怎么说——谁说的？"

"大家都说的——你离开之后已经好多年了。"她意料之中地红了脸颊。她右手边的蛙喉早已泄了气，失去了作战能力，虽然他自己还没有察觉。

"我来说说这些年我记忆中的你的事，"艾默里继续说。她向他那边靠了些，另一边有些羞涩地看着摆放在她眼前的芹菜。蛙喉默默地大呼一口气——他知晓艾默里，并且知道他那与生俱来就有控制局面的能力。他转过脸去跟萨莉说话，询问她明年是否到外面去上学。艾默里首先使用声东击西的方式去攻打。

"我发现了一个形容词很适合用在你身上。"这是他钟爱已久的发难方式之一——事实上他心里根本就不知道怎么说，可是这样说会让人产生好奇心，况且倘若他被逼到极点，他一定会将她们美言一番的。

"哦——是什么呢？"她满脸好奇的样子。

艾默里摇摇头。

"我还不是很了解你。"

"你会告诉我——了解我之后会吗？"她静悄悄地问道。

他点了点头。

"我们去外面坐坐吧。"

伊莎贝尔点点头。

"有没有人向你说过,你的眼睛很有洞察力?"她问。

艾默里想要让他的眼睛变得看上去更有洞察力一些。他思量着,可是还没有十足的把握,到底是不是她的脚在桌下触碰了他一下。可是也有可能是桌子脚碰的。难以分辨是什么。然而这一碰还是令他十分振奋。他此刻就在思考,不知道楼上的小屋到底能不能用。

林中的孩子

伊莎贝尔与艾默里很显然都不幼稚,可是也并不是特别的厚颜无耻。并且,外行的身份在他们玩的游戏中似乎没有任何可以利用的价值,这一场游戏在以后的许多年都会是她主要研究的一个难题。她和他一样,进行这个游戏都是由于精致的外表以及易于激动的性格激发的,其他则是轻而易举就可得到的通俗小说以及从稍微陈旧一些的小说选集里收集来的化妆间对话影响的结果。伊莎贝尔姿势造作地走路是在九点半钟,并且还是在她那明亮的大眼睛,最能说明她是一个初入社交的幼稚小姑娘的时候。相对而言,艾默里则没被外表所欺骗多少。他等待着伪装被褪去,并在这样的时刻不去解读她是否有带上面罩的权利。而对于她来说,他故意表现出的懂得人情世故的老练也没有将她打动。她生活在一个更大的城市,在交际范围上稍微比他好些。可是她接受他的自作聪明——这是在这种类似的事情上的十几个不值一提的行为标准之一。他也知道他现在是得到了特殊的待遇的,由于她早已有过训练了,他知道自己只是代表了她目前能看到的最好的目标,他一定要抓住机会,以免让自己失去自己的优势。所以他们就这样投入到了这场游戏中,手段非常狡猾,如果她的父母听说了这件事,那一定会是爆炸性的消息。

晚宴过后舞会开始……顺利开始。顺利吗?刚要跳几步,男孩子们就抢着和伊莎贝尔继续跳,并且还在角落里争论个喋喋不休,说:"你应该让我先跳的!""她也不希望这样——她向我提起过,下次我能够截舞。"这话完全正确——她对谁都这样说,就在跳完舞松手的时候,她还会用手按你一下,表达的意思就是:"要知道是因为你跟我跳舞才让我今晚这么开心。"

然而时间一点一点地过去了,转眼间就过去了两个小时,头脑笨拙的还想讨好别人的男孩子还是学学把看似激动的神情转移到别的地方吧,由于十一点钟的时候,伊莎贝尔和艾默里早已坐在楼上阅览室旁边的小房间里的长沙发上了。她觉得他们是光彩照人的一对,大概很明显就应该在隐蔽的角落里坐着,相反,那些黯淡无光的人则在楼下焦虑不已,吵吵闹闹。

刚好从门口路过的男孩子把头探进来,满脸嫉妒地伸着脖子向里望——从门口路过的女孩子仅仅是笑,仅仅是眉头紧锁,心里也明了。

此时他们已经到了非常明显的地步。他们相互诉说着自从上一次相见以来的变化,她聆听了很多她早就听过的话,他是一位大学二年级的学生,是《普林斯顿人报》编委会的成员,还有机会在四年级当上编委会主任。他也知道她在巴尔的摩交往过的男孩子中有几个"交了好运",表现出非常开心的样子来跳舞,他们的年龄基本在二十岁左右,开着引人注目的红色斯图泽轿车。其中将近一半的人好像都已从各个不同的高中和大学退学,然而有几个在运动上有些名气,这让他对她又有了新的认识。事实上,伊莎贝尔与大学同学的交集也是刚刚才开始。许多年轻学生和她都很面熟,他们认为她是一个"漂亮的小妞——他们多留意一些也是值得的"。可是伊莎贝尔将这些名字记成了胡里花哨的一堆,即便是维也纳的贵族听见了也会连连赞叹。这便是坐在长沙发上的稚嫩的女低音的本事。

他问她是否认为他有点目空一切。她回答说目空一切的人和自信满满的人是不一样的。她很欣赏男人的自信。

"蛙喉是你的好朋友吗?"她问。

"当然是——怎么啦?"

"他不会跳舞。"

艾默里露出了笑容。

"他跳舞的样子好像是女孩被他背在背上,而不是把手臂搭在肩上。"

她很喜欢这句话。

"你非常会评价一个人。"

艾默里极力否认。可是他以几个人为例子来评价给她看。之后他们开始讨论起手来。

"你的手很精致,"她说。"从你的手的样子来看,你似乎是弹钢琴的。我说得对吗?"

我早就说过,他们已经到了一个很是明确的地步——岂能用明确来概括,可以说是一个至关重要的阶段。艾默里多待了一天来见她,他的火车是在那天夜里十二点十八分开。他的皮包或提箱正在车站等候着他，口袋里的怀表开始愈发沉重起来。

"伊莎贝尔，"他忽然说道，"我想对你说一件事。"当时，他们都在很轻松地说"她眼睛里的有意思的表情"，伊莎贝尔根据他态度的改变就知道接下来会发生什么——事实上，他心里在想，要有多久才能发生。艾默里举起手，把电灯关了，此时，他们都处于伸手不见五指的黑暗中，仅仅剩下旁边阅览室照进来的微弱的红光。之后，他说道：

"我不确定你是否已经想到你——我要说的话。哎呀，伊莎贝尔——虽然听上去像是笑话，但是这并不是笑话。"

"我知道。"伊莎贝尔小声地回答道。

"或许我们不可能如同今日一样再见面了——有时候我的运气特别差。"他从她身旁移开，躺在了沙发另一边的扶手上，即便是在黑暗的环境中，她依然能够清晰地看见他明亮的双眼。

"你可以再见到我的——笨蛋。"这最后两个字有些语气强烈——所以听上去好像变成了一句亲切的话。他用他沙哑的喉咙接着说：

"我看上过许多人——女孩子——我想你也是看上过——男孩子，我是说，可是，实话实说，你——"他突然止住了没有继续说，弓着背向前，两手支颐，"哦，那又怎么样——你会走你的阳关路，而我呢，我也会走我的独木桥。"

一阵突如其来的沉默。伊莎贝尔心弦一动；她把手绢牢牢地缠绕成一个球，凭借着在她身上的微弱灯光可以看清，她故意把手绢缠绕的那个球扔在地上。他们的手瞬间触碰到了一起，可是两个人继续沉默下去。沉默不语的次数越来越多了，同时氛围也越来越美好了。小房间外面又有一对人摆脱了人群到了楼上，在旁边的房间里尝试着弹钢琴。在弹了一会儿一般是开头才弹的《筷子曲》以后，他们中的一个人演奏起了《林中的孩子》，轻柔的男高音将音乐送到了小房间：

"让我牵着你的手——

不必开口

我知道我们朝着梦乡走。"[1]

---

1. 这里的三句歌词和下文两句全出自音乐喜剧《好人艾秋》中的歌曲《林中的孩子》绥勒·格林词，杰罗姆·科恩词。不同的是原曲这里三句歌词系女生唱，男生唱歌词原文第二句不一样。

伊莎贝尔跟着旋律轻轻地唱着，浑身打颤，她忽然感觉到艾默里的手伸了过来握住了她的手。

"伊莎贝尔，"他小声说道。"你知道我深深地爱着你。你的确对我也有一点意思。"

"是的。"

"你到底有多在乎——你有没有非常喜爱的？"

"没有。"她的声音十分小，小得让他几乎什么都听不到，虽然他离她很近，以至于他脸上都能感受到她呼出的气息。

"伊莎贝尔，我准备回学校去，要在那里生活半年之久，我们为什么不应该——只要你在我心里有件事让我无法忘怀——"

"把门关上……"她的嘴唇好像只是稍微颤动了一下，声音小得可怜，他甚至都不敢确定她是否真的在说话。他把门带上以后，歌声就好像是在门外颤抖。

"月儿多明亮

吻我入梦乡。"

多么优美的歌呀，她心里想——今天晚上的所有事情都很美好，特别是这个小房间里的这一场浪漫的情景，他们十指相扣，难以抗拒的美妙一幕越来越近了。好似她未来的生活就如同当下这般无忧无虑、永无止境：在明亮的月光下，在朦朦胧胧的星光里，在豪华汽车的后座，在枝繁叶茂的绿树下停靠着的不高不矮却舒适无比的敞篷小客车中——仅仅是男孩子，可能不会永远是一个人，但是今晚这一个多么英俊。他轻轻攥住她的手。突然间他就把她的手拽了过去，紧紧扣住他的嘴唇，亲吻她的手心。

"伊莎贝尔！"他润物细无声般的语言融入到音乐中，好像与音乐声一起走得越来越近。她的呼吸越来越快了。"我能不能吻你，伊莎贝尔——伊莎贝尔？"她稍稍张开嘴巴，在漆黑的夜晚中转过头来面对着他。忽然间传来阵阵说话的声音，以及向楼梯上奔跑的时候，朝他们疯狂地袭来。艾默里瞬间伸手把电灯按亮，当房门开开时，三个男孩包括气喘吁吁、迫不及待地要跳舞的蛙喉冲进门来的时候，他早已镇定地坐在沙发上翻着桌子上的杂志了，而她则沉着冷静地坐在那里，没有一丝紧张感，不慌不忙的样子，甚至还向他们投以微笑。可是她的心仍在怦怦地跳个不停，她有一点似乎自己的一桩好事被他们破坏了的感觉。

第二章　尖顶建筑和怪兽滴水嘴

这件事很显然已经过去了。大家吵着要跳舞，他们两个人相互使了个眼色——在他这一边是无望，在她那一边是可惜，晚会依旧有条不紊地进行着，花花公子们没有了顾虑，所有的人都在不停地载歌载舞。

到了十二点一刻，艾默里被围在一小群聚集起来祝他一路顺风的人中间，很严肃地与她握手。忽然之间他变得不再沉着冷静，而她心里则有些不安，因为她听到有一个躲在后面爱说风凉话的人嘲讽道：

"把她带到外面去，艾默里！"他一把抓住她的手轻轻地捏了一下，她也做了回应，就好像那天晚上她给那二十多个人的手的回应一样——仅仅是这样罢了。

两点钟回到威瑟利家的时候，萨莉问道，她与艾默里待在小房间里的时候是不是干了"那个"。伊莎贝尔回头安静地看着她。她的眼睛里散发着的是空想主义者的光芒，如同圣女贞德那般有单纯梦想的梦想家。

"没有，"她对她说，"我不会再做那种事了，他有那方面的意思，可是被我拒绝了。"

她躺在床上的时候心里疑惑着，不清楚他明天的特别讲话会说些什么。他的嘴巴这么美丽——她会——？

"他们有十四个天使的守护[1]，"萨莉在旁边卧室里略带睡意唱道。

"该死！"伊莎贝尔不耐烦地埋怨道，一边把枕头拍打得隆起一个包，之后小心谨慎地钻进冰冷的被子里。"该死！"

狂欢

艾默里为了《普林斯顿人报》的事务返回了学校，那些无关紧要的势利小人，作为判断是否成功的精密寒暑表，伴随着俱乐部选举的即将进行，都开始对他献殷勤，所以，一群群高年级的同学都来膜拜他和汤姆，他们一个个脸上面带窘态，靠着桌子或者床沿，毫无章法地胡乱交谈着，完全避开了最重要的话题。艾默里发现有人在目不转睛地看着他，他觉得很有意思，如果前来拜访的人代表的是他一点都提不起兴趣的俱乐部，他就说几句另类的话语来吓走他们，这几天他从中感受到了很大的快乐。

"哦，让我想一想——"一天傍晚，他对一个瞠目结舌的俱乐部代表说道，

1.《林中孩子》里的一句歌词，参看第66页注。

"你们是哪一个俱乐部的代表?"

如果是常春藤俱乐部、小楼俱乐部和老虎俱乐部的人前来拜访,他就以一种"天真无邪,没有恶意的乖孩子"的形象,一副沉着冷静的样子,假装一点也不知道他们的目的。

三月刚开始,当那个成败在此一举的早晨来到,校园见证了奔放狂躁情绪迸发的时候,他与亚历克·康尼奇安静地悄然无息地进入了小楼俱乐部,一脸惊讶地看着他忽然就激动起来的同年级同学。

那里有内心摇摆不定的墙头草,从一个俱乐部跳到另一个俱乐部;那里存在着只能维持两三天友谊的朋友,他们泪流满面,高声叫喊,他们一定要加入同一个俱乐部,任何东西都不能够将他们分开;日积月累的怨恨,比如忽然出名的人时至今日依然对入学时候的怠慢记得非常清楚,现在全部公开批判,大声说出来;向来无声无息的人突然收到了渴盼已久的邀请马上声名大噪;有些自认为"万事俱备"的人居然被杀出的黑马打得措手不及,感觉自己被孤立、被人放弃,所以大放厥词,扬言要退学。

在他自己的那帮人中,艾默里看见有人被排挤在外,仅仅是由于戴了绿帽子,或者是由于"一个该死的成衣匠的人体模型",抑或是由于"天上有太大的吸引力",或是由于一天晚上喝得醉意朦胧,"我的上帝,不像一个正人君子",或者是由于反对票操纵者以外没有人知道的无法暴露在光天化日之下的理由。

这个很随意的社交活动在纳骚酒店的大型晚会上达到了巅峰,用大碗盛的潘趣酒[1]端过来给予每一个人,整栋楼下只能看见一张张脸,只听见一声声的叫喊,好像变成了疯狂的人潮拥挤的场面。

"嗨,狄比——恭喜!"

"好样的,汤姆,你在礼帽俱乐部有一帮能干的人。"

"喂,凯里——"

"啊,凯里——我听别人说你是带着所有举重运动员到老虎俱乐部的!"

"哦,我没有到小楼俱乐部去——那里全都是花花公子。"

"他们说欧弗顿收到常春藤俱乐部的邀请后直接晕过去了——他在第一天就加入了吗?"

---

1. 酒、果汁、牛奶等混和的饮料。

第二章　尖顶建筑和怪兽滴水嘴

"——啊，根本没有。他骑着一辆自行车朝穆雷—道奇大楼飞驰而去——特别担心弄错了。"

"你是怎么加入'礼帽'的——你这个老浪荡子？"

"恭喜！"

"恭喜你自己吧，不是说你有一大帮子人嘛。"

酒吧关门了，晚会也散了，参加晚会的人成群结队，手舞足蹈，一边唱一边飞奔在大雪覆盖的校园里，他们都有一个奇怪的幻想，心想势力范围与过度的紧张可算是过去了，在今后的两年中，他们终于可以自由自在地想做什么就做什么了。

过了很久之后，艾默里还把二年级的春季当作是这辈子最美妙的光阴。他的想法与现实生活很合拍；他唯一想的就是能够随波逐流，消磨时光，与十几个新认识的朋友一起度过四月的午后。

一天上午，亚历克·康尼奇进入他的房间，将还在睡觉的他叫醒，这时的太阳早已高高挂起，窗口闪烁着凯普贝尔大楼绝无仅有的光芒。

"起来，原罪，醒醒。过半个小时在伦维克咖啡馆门口等候。他们开着车。"他把五斗橱的罩子拿过来，以及罩子上放置的许多小摆设，小心谨慎地摆到床上。

"你到哪里弄来的车子？"艾默里嘲讽地问道。

"信任我就对了，不过言多必失，还是少说话为好，否则你就去不成了！"

"看这个样子，我还是睡觉吧，"艾默里平和地说道，他把被子重新盖好，另一只手到床边拿了支香烟。

"睡觉！"

"怎么！我十一点半还有一堂课。"

"真麻烦！当然喽，如果你不希望去海边的话——"

艾默里瞬间就跳了起来，从床上快速地下来，五斗橱罩子上放着的东西也撒在了地上。海边……他已经很久都没有去过海边了，上一次去，还是他和母亲一起出去旅游的时候。

"还有谁去？"他 边穿内衣一边问道。

"哦，狄克·亨伯德、凯里·贺拉狄、杰西·费伦还有——唔，差不多有五六个人，赶紧的吧，老弟！"

过了十分钟，艾默里就在伦维克咖啡馆里狼吞虎咽地吃着玉米片，喝着牛

069

奶了，才九点三十分，他们就已经兴高采烈地稳妥地驶出了城，向着狄耳海滨的沙滩开了过去。

"你瞧，"凯里说道，"这辆车是从那边弄来的。事实上，这辆车不知是谁从阿斯伯里里花园[1]偷来的，之后他们把车扔在了普林斯顿，人到西部去了。是亨伯德经过议会允许才搞来的。"

"谁身上带着钱呢？"在前排的菲伦比扭头说。

大家极具默契地同时回答没有。

"那就好玩了。"

"钱——什么钱？卖掉这辆车就有了。"

"可以当废品卖了，怎么都行。"

"如何去弄吃的？"艾默里问道。

"我实话实说，"凯里回答，眼神里带着怪罪他的目光，"活过短短三天这种小事，你怀疑我不能办到？有人持续好多年不吃东西都活过来了。读一读童子军月刊吧！"

"三天，"艾默里在思考着什么，"但是我的课怎么办。"

"安息日也包含在这几天中。"

"同样的，这一个半月里我只能再逃六节课。"

"如果我还能制造一个新词的话，艾默里，你是在没事找事。"

"你应该试试来点麻醉剂，你说呢，艾默里？"

艾默里只好作罢，心里平和了许多，慵懒地看着外面的风景，陷入了沉思。斯温伯恩的诗句倒是挺适合此景的。

"啊，冻雨和毁灭终于消逝，
以及延绵不断的积雪和罪蕖，
还有恋人天各一方的日子，
灯光暗淡了，得意的是黑夜，
往昔的记忆是忘却的悲伤，
花儿竞放、早已消灭了严霜，
灌木丛翠绿浓郁上下整齐，

---

1. 新泽西的一处海滨城市。

春天来了，百花争艳未消散，"

"溪水漫溢灯心草——"[1]

"你是什么情况，艾默里？艾默里心中正念叨着诗歌，想着漂亮的鸟儿和花朵。我透过他的眼神可以看出来。"

"不不，我没有想，"他用谎言来掩盖真相。"我是在想《普林斯顿人报》。本来今晚我需要排版，不过我可以打电话告知他们，我想。"

"啊，"凯里心存敬意，说道，"这些重要人物——"

艾默里感觉脸有些发烫，他好像可以体会到作为一个失败的竞争者菲伦比有一点不高兴。当然，凯里也只是在开玩笑罢了，不过他确实不该提起《普林斯顿人报》。

这是一个闲适安静的日子，他们离海边越来越近了，咸咸的海风轻轻地朝他们吹着，一幅大海和绵延数里的大片沙滩以及俯瞰蓝色大海的红色屋顶的美丽画卷浮现在他的脑海中。之后他们匆忙地穿过小城，伴随着四音节的音步，大海恍惚间闯入了他的脑海里……

"啊，天呀！你们看！"他大声喊道。

"是什么？"

"停车，停车，快——八年了，八年没有看到了！啊，先生们，快把车停下！"

"他真是一个奇怪的人！"亚历克说道。

"事实上，我也觉得他有些奇怪。"

汽车缓慢地靠路沿停了下来，艾默里向着海滨木板人行道飞奔而去。起初，他认为大海是蓝色的，大海是茫茫的一片，涛声余音绕梁——确实是人们能联想起来的关于大海的所有老生常谈，可是如果有人真的对他说这些话都是老生常谈，那他一定会瞠目结舌，非常惊讶的。

"好了，我们先去吃点午饭，"凯里建议道，随即与人群一起迈开步伐。"艾默里，走吧，来点实际的。"

"首先我们要找一家最好的饭店，"他继续说着，"之后再慢慢地作进一步的打算。"

---

1. 摘自斯温伯恩诗剧《阿塔兰塔在卡昌顿》（1865），"溪水"句未完。这个是从希腊神话月神和狩猎女神阿尔特弥斯的故事中讲述的悲剧，斯温伯恩也因此声名远扬，更有评论家把该诗剧与雪莱的《被解放了的普罗米修斯》相提并论。

他们在木板人行道上散步，看见了前面最大的旅店，便走了进去，之后进入餐厅，找了张桌子，围在一起坐了下来。

"八杯布朗克斯鸡尾酒，"亚历克叫道，"还有一个总会三明治和切丝蔬菜。吃的给一人，剩下的一人一份。"

艾默里吃得不多，他搬来一把椅子坐了下来，这样他就可以舒服地看大海，并感受着大海的礁石。午饭吃完了，他们几个人坐在那里安静地抽着烟。

"花了多少钱？"

有人拿起账单仔细地看了看。

"八块两角五。"

"坑人呢！拿两块钱给他们，之后再给服务员一块钱。凯里，找的零头你收着。"

服务员走了过来，凯里非常认真地拿出一块钱给了他，之后把两块钱甩在账单上，转身就走。他们不慌不忙地向门口走去，不一会儿，身后那疑惑不解的服务员追了上来。

"不对呀，先生。"

凯里把账单拿过来若有其事地看了一遍。

"没有什么差错呀！"他假装正经地摇摇头，之后把那单子撕成了四块，扔给了服务员，那服务员好像受到了惊吓，一动不动地愣在那里，大概是没有反应过来，脸上没有一丝的表情，而他们则毫无顾忌地嚣张地走出了餐厅。

"他会来找我们吗？"

"不会，"凯里说道，"他的第一反应一定会认为我们是老板的儿子之类的，之后会再仔细地看一遍账单，然后再去叫经理，此时此刻——"

他们把汽车扔在阿斯伯里，坐电车来到艾伦赫斯特镇，在这里停了下来，坐在公园人潮拥挤的亭子里看景，下午四点，在就餐室里吃了点心，这次他们支付的钱相比应当支付的就更少了；他们这些人配合得很好，事情进展得也很顺利，事后没有人追出来。

"艾默里，你看，我们是马克思社会主义者，"凯里解释道。"我们不相信财产，我们让财产经受了巨大的考验。"

"黑夜将要降临了，"艾默里说道。

"小心，你就信任贺拉狄吧。"

到了五点半,他们又开始活跃起来了,他们手拉着手,在木板人行横道上走来走去,摆成了一字型,嘴里还哼唱着忧郁的大海波涛的单调曲子。此刻凯里看到人群中的一张脸,马上引起了他的注意,他离开同伴,回来的时候就带了个姑娘,在艾默里眼里,这是他见过的最难看的人。一张毫无血色的大嘴,还有一排凸出的大牙齿,以及她那双在他大鼻子旁边眯成一条缝的歪斜的眼睛。凯里郑重地向大家介绍了她。

"夏威夷女王,卡路卡家族!请准许我向您介绍康尼奇先生,斯罗恩先生,亨伯德先生,菲伦比先生,以及布莱恩先生。"

姑娘接连不断地向他们行屈膝礼。倒霉的人呀;艾默里在心里琢磨着她在一生中从来没有吸引过他人的眼球——也许她是一个弱智者。她与他们一同用餐(由于凯里邀请她一起共进晚餐)的时候沉默不言,这一点让他们更加不会产生怀疑了。

"她喜欢吃本地的菜,"亚历克念念有词地对服务员说着,"不过也没必要做得太精致。"

从晚餐开始到结束,服务员对她说话的语气都是恭恭敬敬的,而凯里则坐在对面傻里傻气地与她打情骂俏,使她笑得合不拢嘴。艾默里情愿坐在那里看着他们演戏,心里想着凯里这小伙子真是可以,言语轻巧又不失风趣,开始只是单纯的一次意外,却让他玩出了这么多花样,真是精彩生动。他们这些人大概多多少少都有些这方面的技能,与他们在一起可以非常轻松。艾默里一般情况下喜欢一个人待着,可是与别人待在一起的时候,他就对他们有些小恐惧,只有一种情况例外,那就是这群人中他是主角。他心里疑惑着,到底每个人可以为团体奉献多少,毕竟在精神方面每个人都要付出一些的。亚历克与凯里给这一群人带来无限的乐趣,但他们好像并不是主角。从某方面来讲,沉默不语的亨伯德与竭尽全力要展示出一股傲慢心态的斯罗恩,才是他们中的主角。

记得大学一年级刚入学的时候,在艾默里看来,狄克·亨伯德就是一个满身贵族气息的人。他个子很高,并且体型健硕——黑色的卷发,端正的五官,黝黑的皮肤。他每次说话听起来都很稳妥,合乎常理。他有过人的勇气,才能一般,但是非常有荣誉感,并展示出十足的魅力以及贵人理应高尚的思想,所以他的荣誉感和正义感便有些差别。他也会放纵自己,但绝不会出格,重点是他每次放浪不羁的冒险好像从来不会"没事找事"。人们学习他的穿衣风格,模仿他的说话方式……艾默里坚信他能够阻拦别人前进的脚步,但无论如何都改变不了他……

他与健壮的人不相同,那一类人实质上是中产阶级——而他却很少流汗。有些人只有在利益的驱使下才会与一个汽车司机亲近,但亨伯德却能够与一个黑人在餐馆吃饭,虽然人们无论如何也知道这样做并没有什么大碍。他不是一个唯利是图的小人,虽然班里的人他只认识一半。他的朋友遍布各个阶层,不论高低。可是,要真正跟他"交朋友"是不可能发生的事。仆人们很尊敬他,如同神一般的对待他。在高年级学生眼中,要努力成为像他那样的人,他好像永远都是他们的榜样。

"他就好似《插图伦敦新闻》[1]上面登载的英国牺牲的将领的那些画像,"艾默里对亚历克说过。

"哦,"亚历克回答道,"如果你想知道一些匪夷所思的真相,我可以一五一十地告诉你,他的父亲是一名杂货店的店员,在塔科马炒房地产的时候成了暴发户,十年前来到了纽约。"

艾默里心里察觉到一丝无以言表的挫败感。

时至今日,这一帮人之所以会聚在一起,是由于俱乐部选举之后同一个班级的人聚集在一起的缘由——好像是要作最后的殊死一搏,去认识自己,协调内外关系,让俱乐部紧张的气氛消散。这就好似是从他们都严格按遵守的规矩办事的习俗的巅峰猛然下降。

晚餐过后他们把卡路卡送到海滨木板人行道上,之后顺着海滩走,返回阿斯伯里。看着黑夜中的大海仿佛又产生了一种新的感受,由于大海的颜色与白天的自由早已消散,大海好像变成了让斯堪的纳维亚的英雄传奇变得凄惨的一片荒凉;吉卜林的诗句浮现在艾默里的脑海里:

"海豹掠杀者未到时的腊卡农海滩。"[2]

可是它仍然是一种音乐,仅仅是有了无限的悲哀。

到了晚上十点钟,他们的口袋就已经空了。他们用最后的一角一分钱好好地吃了一顿,他们一边走路一边哼歌,从海滨木板的人行道上走过了凉棚,接着走过了灯火辉煌的拱门,忽然驻足,颇有兴趣地听起了管乐队音乐会。在听

---

1. 英国一周刊,一八四二年创,十六页,三十二幅木刻。之后多次改刊,现已停刊。
2. 吉卜林《丛林故事》(1894)第八章"腊卡农"诗第二节第四行。

音乐会的空闲时间，凯里为法国战争孤儿筹集善款，总共得到一块两角钱，他们把这些钱花在了买白兰地上，防止晚上生病。当天最后一个活动是去电影院看电影，他们看的是一个老旧的喜剧，看得他们连连大笑，声音大到惹怒了其他观众。他们的进场明显是早就计划好的，由于他们进场的时候，每个人都把责任推给后边。斯罗恩殿后，直到所有人都进了场开始分散坐下，他就假装一无所知，说和他没有任何关系；之后趁检票怒气冲冲地冲进场的时候，他镇定自若地跟着进了放映室。

之后他们在娱乐场旁边汇集，研究怎么过夜。凯里对值夜的人软磨硬泡，希望能允许他们在台上睡，他们在售货亭收集了许多地毯来作为床垫和褥子，躺在上面谈天说地，直到半夜，之后静悄悄地进入了梦乡，即使艾默里强忍着困意迟迟不肯睡觉，希望能看到唯美的月亮在海上落下的画面。

就这样，他们度过了两天的时光，在海滨游玩，坐电车或者汽车，或者就在海滨木板人行道上散步；偶尔和富人一起用餐，可通常情况下吃得都很节约，让丝毫没有察觉的店老板买单。在快递冲洗店里，他们拍了单人照片。凯里强烈建议要大家一起拍，来一张橄榄球队"校队"的合照，之后又拍了一张纽约东区流氓团伙的合照，大家将衣服反穿，凯里在中间的位置，坐在一个钩子一般的月亮上。摄影师有可能在欺骗他们——毕竟，他们从来都没有对摄影师提出要求。天气十分晴朗，他们继续在一起露宿，艾默里再一次不甘心地进入了梦乡。

星期天来临了，冷淡又得体，就连大海都在嘟囔、埋怨，所以他们也趁机搭上了流动农民的福特车回到普林斯顿，顶着感冒带来的头晕目眩各自分散，值得一提的是，除了感冒以外，这一次的游走没有闹出任何事来。

艾默里在学业上比上一学年更加不思进取了，倒不是因为他故意不想学，只是因为懒，还有就是各式各样的兴趣爱好给他带来的各种诱惑。解析几何学和高乃依和拉辛[1]的忧思六韵步诗行对他来说没有什么兴趣，包括起初他期待已久的心理学，居然也是一门没有吸引力的学科，满堂课都是在讲肌肉反应和生物学术语，丝毫不涉及对性格和感化力的研究。那门课在中午进行，刚踏进教室他就想睡觉。因为他发现"主观与客观，先生"这句话好像是万能的，可以

---

1. 高乃依，法国剧作家、古典主义悲剧奠基人；拉辛（Jean Baptistte Lacine，1639—1699），法国剧作家、古典主义悲剧代表作家之一。

适用于大多数问题，所以当教授向他提问、菲伦比或斯罗恩把他推醒之后，他一鼓作气地说出了这一大段话，这件事也成为了年纪最大的笑话。

一般都有聚会——到奥兰治或是到新泽西海滩，很少去纽约和费城，记得那天晚上，他们从查尔兹酒吧招呼了十四个女招待，与她们一起坐在一辆公交汽车的顶上，奔驰在第五大道上。由于逃课太多，他们已经违背了学校的规章制度，如此一来，下一学期他们必须要多修一门课，但是春天可是一个久违的好时光，任何事情都阻止不了他们跑出校园，进行各式各样的游玩。五月到来了，艾默里成为了二年级的年级舞会筹备委员会的成员，在与亚历克探讨了一个小时之后，他们罗列出了高年级学生会的年级候选人名单，他们都觉得自己是名单上最有可能入选的人之一。高年级学生会大概是由这十八名最具代表性的高年级学生组成，想到亚历克优秀的管理球队的能力以及艾默里在《普林斯顿人报》赢得伯恩·贺拉狄成为主席的可能性，他们的这些想法都是有理有据的。奇怪的是，他们两个人都认为丹维里埃也是候选人之一，如果在一年前同学们听到这个都会浮想联翩，惊讶不已。

在春天这个最美好的时光中，艾默里与伊莎贝尔·伯尔赫一直在持续不断地给对方写信，每次吵架之后都会停一阵儿，之后会再次联系，主要原因是他想找寻传递爱情的方式。他认为伊莎贝尔的信件表达得很小心，所以他非常愤怒，因为她一点都不投入感情，可是他依然心存希望，希望她不是春天花团锦簇的宏大画面上那朵格格不入的花儿，她一定会像在明尼哈哈乡村俱乐部的小房间里一样令他心满意足，十分和睦。五月间，每天晚上他似乎都要挥洒自如地写上三十张信纸，将信封撑得非常鼓，外面还附着"第一部分"与"第二部分"的标注。

"哦，亚历克，就目前而言，我觉得大学生活实在太枯燥无味了，"夕阳西下，他们一起散步的时候，他沮丧地诉说着。

"我也有这样的感受。"

"能让我感到满足的，仅仅是在乡间有一个小小的家，在一个四季如春、天气晴朗的乡间，还有一个老婆，不会每天无所事事，不至于崩溃就好。"

"我也是。"

"我不想上了。"

"你的女朋友是什么看法？"

"啊！"艾默里惊恐地倒吸了一口凉气。"他甚至连结婚都没有想过……意思就是，现在不考虑。但是将来呢，你应该懂的。"

"我的女朋友说想要结婚，我已经和她订婚了。"

"这是真的吗？"

"没错，千万不要告诉其他人我已经订婚的消息。下学期我可能就不来学校了。"

"但是你才二十岁呀！不上大学了吗？"

"哎，艾默里，你忘了刚才你是怎么说的了吗？"

"是的，"艾默里打断了他的话语，"但那只是一个期望罢了，事实上，我绝对不会退学的。只是刚好觉得这几个美好的夜晚心里有些难受，想吐吐苦水罢了。可是我能感觉到这样的夜晚应该一去不复返了，我没有好好地享受这几个夜晚。如果我的女朋友来这里，该是件多么美好的事呀。但是说到结婚——丝毫没有希望。尤其像我父亲说的那样，现在的钱越来越难赚了。"

"这几个夜晚真的很浪费！"亚历克很是赞同。

可是艾默里既痛苦又悔恨，所以开始好好珍惜这几个夜晚。他存着一张伊莎贝尔的快照，完好无损地保存在一块旧怀表里，似乎每晚到了八点钟就把所有灯都灭掉，只留下一盏台灯，痴情地看着照片，坐在打开的窗前，一心一意地给她写着信。

……哦，我特别想念你的时候，根本无法用语言来表达我最真实的感受，对我而言，你早已成了一个梦，那是无以言表的无法书写在纸上的梦。你的上一封信我已经收到了，写得非常好！从头到尾，那一封信我大概读了六遍，特别是最后一部分，可是有的时候，我特别希望，你能再直白一点，让我知道你的真实想法，然而你上一封信把我令得太好了，这让我有些不敢相信，急迫的我，无论如何也等不到六月份了！你一定要做好来我们的年纪舞会的准备。在我看来，舞会一定会非常成功，我打算在一个美好的学年步入尾声的时候带你过来。我时常想起你那天晚上跟我说的话，很想知道那句话的背后究竟是什么？如果这不是和你却是和别人有关——但是你看，我们第　次相见的时候，我还认为你不会是个一心一意的人，出乎意料的是，你的人缘这么好，人见人爱，最没有想到的是你真的最喜欢我。

啊，伊莎贝尔，亲爱的——多么美丽的夜晚。距离校园很远的地方，有人在用曼陀林演奏着"爱月",听着歌声,就仿佛你也一起来到了这里。现在又换成了"再见,小伙子们,我已经结束",这音乐就好似我量身定做的一样。由于我也失去了所有。我已经下定决心不再喝鸡尾酒,并且我还知道我永远也不会恋爱了——因为我不可能再爱了——你在我的脑海里挥之不去,占据了我的大部分光阴,除了你,我根本不会再想着其他姑娘。尽管我在任何时候都可以见到她们,但是我对她们提不起兴趣。我并不是装作厌烦的样子,因为事实的确不是如此。因为我深爱着你。啊,最亲爱的伊莎贝尔(我一直感觉我不能仅仅称呼你伊莎贝尔,今年六月在你们家人面前,我一定要用上"最亲爱的"这个称呼),你一定要来出席我们的舞会,之后再让我去你们家待上一天,如此一来,一切都完美了……

如同这样一般,无止境的简单的话语,可是对他们两个人来说,好像无比地诱人,无比地新鲜。

六月份到了,气温早就开始升高了,一副懒洋洋的样子,哪怕是对考试他们也着实担心不起来,而是整夜整夜地在小楼俱乐部的天井里陶醉着,他们肆意地开着玩笑相互聊天打闹,直到石溪那边的乡村顶部泛着淡蓝的晨雾,网球场周围的丁香花竞相开放,他们不再有所言语,取而代之的是安静地吸着烟……之后漫步在空旷无人的展望大道上,穿过周围传来美丽歌声的麦考什林荫路,径直走向迸发着热烈气氛的纳骚街去。

那几天艾默里与汤姆·丹维里埃很晚才开始出去漫步。一阵赌博的热潮在二年级传播开了,好几个炎热的夜晚,他们都伸着脖子瞪着眼睛专注地看骰子,到三点钟才结束。玩完一把以后,他们走出斯罗恩的房间,看着外面已经有了露水,天空中的星星也逐渐暗淡了。

"我们去找两辆自行车出去转一转吧。"艾默里建议道。

"可以呀,我一点都不疲惫,今天大概是本学期的最后一晚了,确实如此,毕竟年级舞会的事星期一就要着手进行了。"

他们走到了霍尔德楼的院子中,发现了两辆没有上锁的自行车,索性就骑走了,大概到了三点半,他们便已经骑到劳伦斯维尔路了。

"今年暑假有些什么打算,艾默里?"

"没什么变化——和往常一样,我想。在日内瓦湖玩上一两个月——七月份你必须要来啊!你知道——之后我会到明尼阿波利斯去,那里有将近好几百场的夏日舞会，再找几个姑娘们玩耍，之后就什么都不想了——可是，啊，汤姆，"他忽然情不自禁地说了句，"今年真是太美妙了！"

"是啊，"汤姆用力地说道，他已经和原来不一样了，衣着有名的布鲁克斯上衣，脚底下踩的是弗兰克斯名牌皮鞋，"这一次，我胜利了，可是我感觉自己很不喜欢再经历一次。你说得是正确的——你是一个橡皮球，用这句话来形容你，还是有些贴切的，但是我非常不情愿去融入到那个心胸狭小、充满势利风气的世界里。我希望人们不会由于领带的颜色不合时宜或者是衣服老旧的原因就被排挤到其他地方去。"

"这是不可能的，汤姆，"艾默里争论道，他们依然在慢慢退去的夜色中骑着车子，"无论你身在何处，你终究会神不知鬼不觉地用上'有'或'无'如此的标准。无论是对是错，你早已被我们打上标签了；你是一个普林斯顿型的人！"

"哦，那么，"汤姆抱怨道，声音沙哑的他只能用痛苦换来分贝的提高，"到底是什么理由驱使着我回学校来呢？普林斯顿能带给我的东西我全都学到了。仅仅是学一些拘泥守旧的东西，在俱乐部里鬼混，以这种状态在学校再待两年，对自己也不会有太多的好处。经过那番熏陶，我将会被他们彻头彻尾地变成一个做事马虎，从此墨守成规的人。即便我现在已经成为了那种抬不起头的人，再这样下去我就无药可救了。"

"哦，但是你没有发现这个问题的精髓，汤姆，"艾默里打断他说。"你刚才非常敏锐地忽然发现这个世界的势利风气很是不好。这会给一个喜欢思考的人带来一个很好的启迪，普林斯顿一定会给他一个社会意识。"

"你会觉得那是你教给我的，对吗？"他用讽刺的口气说着，悄悄地注视着艾默里。

艾默里内心偷笑着。

"我有教给你吗？"

"有时候，"他大喘气似的说道，"我认为你是我的魔鬼。我原本可以成为一个真正的诗人的。"

"得了吧，这样说就有点不妥了。你选择到一所东部的大学来读书。可能是你瞪大了双眼，清楚地看到人们在利益的驱使下勾心斗角的卑鄙做法，另一种可能是你稀里糊涂的，对此一无所知，但你一定会很不喜欢那种态度的——

就像马蒂·凯那样。"

"是呀,"他很同意那种说法,"你说得没错。那不是我喜欢的模样,但是,要让一个二十来岁的人表现出一副看到社会黑暗愤怒不已的样子也很难。"

"从出生那天,我就是一个看到社会黑暗就愤怒不已的人,"艾默里喃喃说道。"但我脑子里都是一些不切实际的想法。"他顿了顿,没有继续说,也不知道说这样的话代表着什么。

他们骑到了大门紧闭的劳伦斯维尔中学[1],之后往回骑。

"很过瘾,虽然只是一段短暂的骑行,你说呢?"过了一会儿,汤姆说道。

"没错,这是一个很棒的目的地,太棒了,今天晚上的经历都非常好。啊,如果是一个如烤箱一般、疲惫懒散的夏天还有伊莎贝尔,那该多美妙呀!"

"啊,你和你的伊莎贝尔!她一定是一个纯洁的,天真烂漫的女孩子……我们来吟诗吧。"

所以,艾默里向道路两旁的灌木丛朗诵着《夜莺颂》。[2]

"我这辈子都不会成为一个诗人,"艾默里吟诵完了喊道。"事实上我还称不上一个喜欢用心去倾听的人,在我眼里美好的东西不多:女人,春夜,夜间的音乐,大海;我感受不到像'清越吼叫的喇叭声'[3]那种奇妙的东西。或许我最后会成为一个智力很高的人,但却写不出杰出的诗歌。"

当太阳照常升起,在研究生院后面的天空中布满了彩霞的时候,他们骑着自行车进入了普林斯顿,急忙去洗了个澡,一瞬间神清气爽,并借此来填补困意。到了中午时分,校友们组成的乐队以及合唱队穿着华丽的服装把一条条马路堵得水泄不通,一顶顶帐篷外面插上了橙黑相间的旗子,在风中摇曳着,校友们聚在一起,在帐篷里愉快地交谈着。有一顶帐篷上写着"六九级"几个大字,令艾默里在那里停留了很久很久。有几位长者坐在那里安静地聊着天,另一边则是纷繁各异的校友们蜂拥而过,展示了人生的各种画面。

---

1. 与普林斯顿相隔五英里。
2. 英国浪漫主义诗人济慈的《夜莺颂》作于一八一九年,次年发表,诗要表达的是夜莺优美不朽的叫声以及观察者的悲伤,但最终观察者一定认为只有悲伤并没有不朽。诗共十八行,最后两行是:"这是一个幻觉,还是一个醒着的梦?/美妙的歌声消逝了:——我是醒还是睡?"
3. 见济慈叙事诗《圣安格尼斯之夜》(1819)第四章第四行。

第二章 尖顶建筑和怪兽滴水嘴

弧光灯下

之后,六月即将进入尾声,忧伤的绿色的眼睛忽然目不转睛地盯着他。就在他们骑着自行车去劳伦斯维尔骑行了一圈的那一晚过后,一群人集结起来准备去纽约开启骑行经历,到了夜里十二点钟他们才回来,用两辆汽车才装下了他们所有人。这是一群充满乐趣的人,有的人很清醒,有的人却睡意十足,每个人的表现都各不相同。艾默里坐在后面的那辆车里;他们的司机开错了方向迷了路,所以迫不及待地要赶上前一辆车子。

这是一个月朗星稀的夜晚,一路的欢声笑语刺激了他的大脑。隐约中,两节诗在他脑海里浮现出来……

就这样,在一片黑漆漆的夜里,一辆灰色的汽车在向前行进,四周格外寂静,没有丝毫活物在动……沉默无声的大海在鲨鱼面前劈开一条大道,航道亮晶晶的,泛着白光,一轮明月高高地悬在天上,大树被月光照耀得无比美丽,相互衬托着,显得很有意思,黑夜中前行的鸟扇动着翅膀在空中一闪而过……

在一家旅店的光亮与黑暗中驻足了一会儿,那一轮金黄的明月,还有同样金闪闪的客栈——随后便是一阵安宁,最大分贝的笑声不见了……六月的夜晚中汽车再一次迎着风前行,模糊的背影在黑暗中慢慢消失,之后阴影突然被一片蓝色代替……

忽然来了个急刹车,艾默里抬头一望,非常惊讶。路边站着一个女人,在和开车的亚历克谈论着某些事。事后他想起了被她陈旧的和服式的衬衣烘托出的波妇形象,以及她说话时眉头紧锁的嘶哑声音:

"你们认得普林斯顿的同学吗?"

"认得。"

"哎呀,这里有一个人摔死了,另外两个差不多也奄奄一息了。"

"我的天!"

"看!"她的手指着一个方向,我们顺着那个方向看去,全都目瞪口呆了。路边的一盏弧光灯刚好照在那里,正是倒着一个人的地方,那个人脸朝下躺在那里,在那个逐渐扩大的血泊中。

他们跳下车,艾默里忽然想起来那个后脑勺——那头发——那头发……之后那个人被翻了过来。

"是狄克——狄克·亨伯德!"

"啊，天哪！"

"看看还有没有心跳！"

之后，老妇人心急火燎，好像是不容置疑地抱怨道：

"早就断了气了，车都被撞翻了。他们中有两个未受伤的人刚把其他人扶进去，这个人肯定没希望了。"

艾默里急忙向门跑去，其他人跟在他身后，他们筋疲力尽，刚到那间破败不堪又很小的前厅就一股脑儿瘫在了沙发上。斯罗恩的肩膀被穿透了，躺在另外一张床上。他的意识已经开始模糊了，嘴里不知说了什么胡话，好像是在说八点十分有化学课。

"我不清楚到底是怎么发生的，"菲伦比哆哆嗦嗦地说道。"是狄克在开车子，他一直坚持要自己开车，我们说他喝酒喝得太多了——随即而来的就是这个恐怖的弯道——啊，我的上帝！……"他跪到了地板上，瞬间嚎啕大哭起来。

医生来了，艾默里坐到了沙发上，有人把一条被单盖到了他身上。他忽然举起手臂，可手臂又不自觉地垂了下来。他的额头冷得可怕，可是脸上却是一副无以言表的样子。他直勾勾地盯着鞋带——那是早晨狄克帮他系的。鞋带是他系的——然而现在他却成了一具冰冷的尸体，一动不动地躺在那里。他所认识的那个狄克·亨伯德的魅力与人格，如今只剩下——啊，真是太可怕了，言谈举止不再高贵，反而是躺在地上。所有的悲剧都是同样的不堪和龌龊——那又如何？白费力气……如同动物一般的死法……艾默里的思绪回到了他童年时代的小巷的地上躺着的那只不堪入目的已经死去的猫身上。

"找一个人跟菲伦比一起回普林斯顿。"

艾默里在门外踱步，寒冷的夜风吹得他有点打颤——那毫无章法的风吹得残缺的废铁堆里的折断的保险杠发出刺耳、凄惨的声音。

高潮！

第二天，有不幸的人就一定有幸运的人，虽然他们是在混乱中度过的。艾默里独自一人的时候，他竭力阻止自己不去乱想，但是没有办法，绕了多少圈，每次都是那一幕收尾，苍白的脸上那张已经扭曲的充满鲜血的嘴，可是，他依然强忍着，坚强地克服着，让所有的愉快都强行占据了恐怖的记忆，努力让恐惧暂时消退。

四点钟，伊莎贝尔与她母亲驱车进了城，她们路过张灯结彩的展望大道，在充满欢声笑语的人群中驶过，在小楼俱乐部吃着茶点。同一天晚上，所有的俱乐部都举行了宴会，于是晚上七点，他让一个一年级新生带着她，并约定好十一点钟在体操房等她，那一时段高年级同学可以进去参加新生舞会。她的表现和他所想的一样，他非常开心，并且期盼那一夜会变成他所有梦想的中心。九点钟，俱乐部门前站满了高年级同学，为的是观看一年级新生的火炬队愉快地走过去，但艾默里对身着燕尾服的火炬手，在庄严肃穆又漆黑的环境的渲染下，在火炬光辉的指引下，是否可以为全神贯注、兴高采烈的一年级新生把夜空点亮感到很好奇，就像去年他所经历的那样。

　　第二天也是一个混乱的日子。在俱乐部的雅座餐室里，他们六个人在一起欢乐地吃着午饭，而伊莎贝尔和艾默里的面前放着一盆炸鸡，情意绵绵地两眼相视，彼此都能感受到他们会因为爱情永远在一起。年级舞会上的他们一直跳个不停，一直到五点钟，没有女舞伴的男生兴高采烈地前来截舞，争先恐后地和伊莎尔贝跳舞，时间一分一秒的过去，马上就到了黑夜，截舞也随即进入了高潮，他们隐藏在衣帽间外衣口袋里的酒能够让他们变得神清气爽，让他们可以在夜晚继续跳舞。没带舞伴的男生大抵都是如此，他们的脑子好像是由同一个头脑进行支配的。如果有一个黑发美女从前面走了过去，伴随着婀娜舞姿的摇摆，他们就会传出一声轻轻的尖叫。他们当中的一个人便会跳出一个门槛比旁人更精的人，抢着接过她跳起来。之后，当这个六英尺高的女孩子（是你们年级的凯带来的，而且一个晚上都在把你们介绍给她）从前面闪过的时候，这些没带女伴的人全都向后退，并且转讨了头，眼睛向舞厅远端望去，因为凯在焦躁不安地寻找着的正是他们眼前的这位。

　　"喂，老弟，我早已有一个特别喜爱的——"

　　"对不住了，凯，这个是我的了。我必然会争夺和她跳的权利的。"

　　"哦，那么下一个呢？"

　　"什么——啊——呃——任何事都阻止不了我的——她没有舞伴的时候会来找我。"

　　让艾默里欣喜若狂的是，伊莎贝尔建议出去转转，开她的车去转。美妙的一个小时悄然而过，他们从普林斯顿静谧的公路上驶过，婉转又激动地相互展露各自的内心世界。艾默里有一种很奇怪的真诚的感觉，却没有想要吻她的想法。

　　第二天，他们在新泽西的道路上驾车行驶，在纽约吃午饭，下午一起去看了一个问题剧,当第二幕出现的时候,她哽咽了,这让艾默里有些不知所措——虽然看见她哭泣的样子令他不由自主地想要安慰她。他禁不住诱惑,低下身子亲吻她脸颊的眼泪,她趁着周围昏暗的氛围顺势让艾默里温柔地握住了她的手。

到了六点钟,他们来到了伯尔赫家在长岛特别凉爽的别墅中,艾默里急忙上楼去换了餐服。当系上衬衫纽扣的时候,他的心中就在想,一定要珍惜这样美好的时刻,也许以后就没有这个机会了。因为他被自己的青春年少蒙蔽了双眼,所以,现在的他对一切事物都心存敬畏。他汲取了他那一代人中无可比拟的优势并不断发展,来到了普林斯顿。他进入了恋爱的天堂,爱情给了他一个美好的交代。他将所有的灯打开,看着镜子里的自己,努力在自己的脸上找寻着那股致使他与其他人不一样的独有的神秘的气质,然后再指引他当机立断,并再一次显现出他内心的真实想法并跟随着它。生活中他很少有想要改变的事物……牛津或许将会是一番别有洞天的世界。

他暗地里赞美着自己。他有着俊俏的外貌以及恰到好处的餐服。他进了餐厅,忽然听到了脚步声,于是便在楼梯口等候。那是伊莎贝尔,从她光亮的秀发再到她脚下金色的浅口鞋子,在艾默里眼里,今天的她格外耀眼。

"伊莎贝尔!"他带着内心的激动大叫道,与此同时展开了双臂。如同故事中所讲述的那样,她拥入他的怀抱里,当他们的嘴唇第一次触碰在一起的那一刹那,就让他心中的那份被扭曲的自尊心急转直上地到达了巅峰,也是他年少轻狂的巅峰。

第三章　自大的人开始反思

"哎呀！把手松开！"

他将手放下，把两手垂在身体两边。

"出什么事情了？"

"你衬衣的扣子——硌疼我了——你瞧！"他顺着脖子向下瞧去，只见黄豆般大小的一个紫青斑点点缀在了白皙的皮肤上。

"哦，伊莎贝尔，"他很后悔自己的行为，"我实在是荒谬可笑。实在是抱歉——我不应当这么紧地抱着你。"

她抬起头，表现出了一种厌烦。

"哦，艾默里，自然你不是故意的，我也不是特别痛，但是已经到了这一步了，我们接下来应该做什么？"

"做什么？"他重复道，"哦，关于这个斑点，不一会它就会落下去的。"

"它没有消退，"她的眼睛在小斑点上停留了很长的一段时间，"它仍旧在这里——瞧着让人很厌烦——啊，艾默里，我们该做什么！刚刚到你肩膀的位置。"

"在上面揉揉吧，"他提议说，尽量克制自己，几乎要笑出声了。

她将手指放在斑点上慢慢地揉动，之后一颗泪珠从她的眼角偷偷流出来，沿着脸颊滑下。

"啊，艾默里，"她说，一张十分惹人疼爱的脸缓缓抬起，"再揉下去的话我的脖子就要燃烧了。我该怎么做呢？"

他忽然想到了一句台词，忍不住大声背了出来。

"任何一种阿拉伯香料都无法让一只小手变得白皙。"[1]

她昂起头，眼睛中闪烁着泪光，如同圣洁的冰一般。

---

[1] 引自莎士比亚悲剧《麦克白》第五幕第一场，然而菲茨杰拉德用"变得白皙"代替了莎士比亚的"变香"。

085

"你不怎么关心别人。"

艾默里曲解了她话的本意。

"伊莎贝尔，亲爱的，我认为它将——"

"别摸我！"她吼道，"我已经十分烦闷了，而你却站在那儿笑！"

就这样，他再一次讲错了话。

"啊，的确有趣，伊莎贝尔，那天我们所提及的风趣是——"

她的眼睛盯着他，脸上露出的不再是单纯的微笑，却是在她嘴角勉强挤出的模糊、压抑的微笑。

"啊！不要出声了！"忽然她大声嚷道，箭一般的速度冲回她的屋子。独留艾默里站在那里，露出一脸茫然的懊恼。

"坏了！"

再一次见到伊莎贝尔时，她的身上多了一条薄薄的披肩，他们一块下楼，彼此不说话，这种沉默从晚宴开始到结束一直持续着。

"伊莎贝尔，"艾默里言语中带有几分怒气，那时他们刚坐进一辆准备前往格林威治乡村俱乐部舞会的车子，"你动怒了，过不了多久我也会和你一样。我们吻一下，以此作为弥补。"

伊莎贝尔想了想，依旧闷闷不乐。

"我很不喜欢让别人嘲笑。"她终于开口了。

"我不会笑了。现在我就没有笑，你看！"

"你之前笑了。"

"啊，别太女人气了。"

她的嘴唇动了一下，一副嫌弃的表情。

"我喜欢做什么就做什么。"

艾默里努力地压制住脾气，没有冲她发泄。他已经发现，他对伊莎贝尔毫无爱情的感觉，可是她的冷淡已经让他无法忍受了。他想亲吻她，狠狠地吻她，仅仅因为在吻过之后，他隔天早晨离开时才不会再牵挂这件事。但是，如果不吻她，因为这件事造成的苦恼就会让他永远挥之不去……居然吻她一下都不可以，这就会让他怀疑自己是一个征服者的身份。对伊莎贝尔这样一个霸道的勇士请求，让自己甘心认输，这种行径会丢尽颜面。

或许她已经怀疑他的心理。无论她是否怀疑，最终，艾默里眼看着原本能够演变成绝佳的爱情经历的那一晚偷偷过去了,仅仅剩下飞蛾在头顶扑棱,仅仅闻到路边花园浓烈的花香,可是没有熙熙攘攘的说话声,更不存在轻微的叹息声……

之后,他们的晚宴是在备餐室中吃的,饭食有巧克力蛋糕以及干姜水,趁着吃饭的空隙艾默里公布了一个决断。

"明天天一亮我就会离开。"

"为什么?"

"为什么不可以离开?"他反问道。

"不需要。"

"无论怎样,我必须离开。"

"嗯,如果你非得办事如此的滑稽——"

"啊,不可以对我说这样的话。"他斥责道。

"——仅仅是没有让你吻。你认为——"

"你可以,伊莎贝尔,"他插话了,"你明白不是因为这个——就算是因为这个吧。目前我们的关系到了这一步,假如不是亲吻——就会——就会——大家相忘于江湖。似乎事情并非是因为你考虑到道德标准才回绝我的。"

她迟疑了。

"我的确不明白你在我生活中扮演着什么角色,"她不知所措地说道,并且固执地想同他和好,"你看起来太让人捉摸不透了。"

"为什么这么说?"

"额,之前我认为你太踌躇满志了,甚至是自傲自负,你还能想起那天对我说你想做的都能做,想得到的都可以获得吗?"

艾默里脸涨得通红。他的确向她提到过这句话。

"的确。"

"嗯,今晚你好像看起来并没有之前那么自信。或许你的本性就是自傲自负吧!"

"不是这样的,我没有,"他思前想后,憋得说不出话来,"在普林斯顿——"

"啊,你同普林斯顿!从你说话的语气判断,我觉得你将自己想象成世界的全部!或许谈到你亲爱的普林斯顿人时,相较其他人,你可以用更加准确的语言来形容他们,或许一年级的学生会相当崇拜你——"

"你不能明白——"

"不，我明白，"她插话说道，"我太了解了，因为你一直在说你自己，并且之前我也乐意听你说，可是现在——我不想了。"

"今晚我也是这样吗？"

"问题正出在这儿，"伊莎贝尔坚决地说道，"今晚你让所有的事情变得不同。你就是待在那里盯着我的双眼。并且，在我同你交往时必须得谨言慎行——你对别人的要求相当严苛。"

"我让你谨言慎行了吗？"艾默里反问道，言语中带有一些自大。

"你的神经很敏感。"——她刻意强调——"对于你思考每一个细腻的情感以及本能时的行为，我都看不懂。"

"我明白。"艾默里同意她的话，并且无助地晃了晃头。

"咱们该走了。"她站起来。

他站起来，一脸愕然，随后他们便来到楼梯脚处。

"我能够乘坐哪辆车？"

"如果你非走不可的话，九点十一分左右有辆车。"

"的确，我必须走。是的，祝你好梦。"

"好梦。"

"他们现在来到了楼梯顶，艾默里掉头回到他的卧室的时候，好像窥见了她脸上一种模糊不清的不悦的神情。他躺在床上，在黑暗中双眼紧闭，他的心里十分郁闷，很想搞明白自己关心的程度有多少——他忽然体会到的悲惨有几分是因为受伤的自大——是否，仅仅拿脾气秉性来说，他不适合谈恋爱。"

一觉醒来，让人亢奋的感觉遍布他的全身。清晨的微风吹动摩擦轧光印着花的窗帘，他完全没有征兆地苦恼起来，为什么不是在普林斯顿他自己的房间内，五斗橱上方原本是他学校橄榄球队的照片，对面的墙角上是三角形俱乐部。之后，外面传来了落地大钟敲响八点钟的声音，这让他回忆起了昨天晚上的情景。他穿上衣服，走下床，娴熟得如同一道闪电，他要趁着还没有瞧见伊莎贝尔时独自离开别墅。就好像昨天晚上的事情本是让人感到黯然的事情，现在居然转变成了让人厌烦的乏味之事。在八点半，他收拾好了一切，之后他在窗口坐了下来，依稀能体会到他的心还在作痛，相较他预想的估计还要严重。早晨好像变成了让人捧腹大笑的戏谑！——阳光明媚，缕缕清香从花园中飘来，他听到楼下阳光室传来伯尔赫太太说话的声音,心里马上闪过一个念头,伊莎贝尔现在会在哪里呢?

有人敲门了。

"八点五十左右,车子就会抵达,先生。"

他又接着思忖着户外的活动,于是一遍遍地,机械地朗诵着布朗宁的诗句,这是他之前写给伊莎贝尔的一封信中提到的:

"人生追求还未完成,你是否洞悉;

目标仍旧未变,空缺仍要补全:

我们不存在深沉地哀叹,任意地狂笑,

饱、饿、无望绝不会存在——剩下的只是热爱。"[1]

可是他一生追求的不可能做不完。他抑郁寡欢,笃信或许她并不存在太多的意见,仅仅是他对她多虑了;其他的人谁也做不到逼着她动脑,这就是她思想的极端。可是她反对他也正是因为这个;所以艾默里厌烦了思考、不间断的思考!

"让她死去吧!"他喊出了声,带有一腔怒火,"她耽误了我整整一年!"

超人高枕无忧了

九月,正值黄沙漫天的时节,艾默里来到了普林斯顿,同在大街上汗流满面、为了补考的众人们挤在了一起。每天上午就是挤在一个辅导学校的密不透风的教室里,学习着没有结尾的乏味的椎体截面知识,高年级的功课以这样的方式开始好像太枯燥了。鲁尼先生传授的学业,使得原本乏味的内容变得更加枯燥,从上午六点到晚上八点一直是由他传授,画图,解方程同抽蓓尔美尔牌香烟两不误。

"好,朗格达克,如果我之前借助那个公式,那么,我该将我的 A 点设在哪里呢?"

朗格达尔是一个橄榄球球员,他慢悠悠地动了动他那六英尺三的庞大身躯,想要让他的精力集中起来。

"嗯——这个——我如果会的话,太阳就要从西边出来了,鲁尼先生。"

"哈,很对,你肯定不可以使用那个公式。我要你答复的正是这句话。"

---

1. 引自英国诗人布朗宁(Robert Browning, 1812—1889)诗《剧中人》中的一首《青春与艺术》(1864)第十六节。

"嗯，肯定，自然。"

"你明白原因吗？"

"你一定——我认为对吧。"

"如果你还是不能理解，跟我说。我立即就会为你演算。"

"这个，鲁尼先生，如果可以的话，我想请求你再讲一遍这个。"

"我的荣幸。嗯，A 点在这里……"

愚蠢的景象在整个教室随处可见——两个大支架挂着讲课用的纸，脱下外套仅仅披着一件衬衫、矗立在支架跟前的是鲁尼先生，横七竖八地在椅子上坐着的是十几个学生：投球手弗雷德·斯罗恩，他肯定要过关；"瘦子"朗格达克，假如能够有幸获得五十分，今年的秋季赛季便能够打败耶鲁；无忧无虑的麦克道威尔——还在上二年级的小子，他以同这些家喻户晓的运动员在一块温习功课而骄傲。

"那些实在拿不出一点钱来补习功课，所以只能在接下来一个学期奋起直追的人会让我产生怜悯，"有一天他当面告诉艾默里这句话，苍白的嘴唇上咬着一根柔软的香烟，让人感觉非常慵懒但又很亲切，"我觉得那是一件极其乏味的事情，在纽约能够用这个学期做很多事情。无论说什么，我认为他们甚至不明白自己失去了多少东西。"听麦克道威尔先生说话好像有一种"你我之间讲讲，不能传出去"的诡秘的感觉，艾默里听见这话，差一点将他从半开的窗子里扔出去……明年二月他的母亲会有疑问，他为什么不张罗一个储蓄会，借此让他的每月补助变高一些……实在是一个没头没脑的笨蛋……

通过弥漫的烟雾以及充斥在整间教室的庄严浓郁的认真氛围来看，一般情况下会听见不受控制的声音：

"我没有弄明白！再讲一次！鲁尼先生！"他们绝大多数人不是头脑简单，就是太不在意，尽管没弄明白也不会招认，艾默里就是第二类人。他认为他完全没有能力掌握椎体横截面；他们处之泰然、令人憧憬的体面在鲁尼先生发臭的会客室肆意蔓延开来，这种环境让他们的方程式发生了改变，演变成了没有办法解出的猜谜游戏。他拾起任何人都会用的湿毛巾，用了整整一晚上的时间临时复习，之后毫无眷顾地参加补考，可是他内心极其不乐意，不知道春天的朝气与生机为什么会变得无迹可寻。无论如何，在伊莎贝尔抛弃了他之后，他作为本科生的优越感便勾不起他的想象了，他心里思忖着自己或许不能从容不迫地通过补考了，尽管这就代表着他只能任人将他从《普林斯顿人报》的编委中除名，而毫无办法，同时也代表着他无法成功竞选为高年级学生会成员。

他好歹还可以拼一拼运气。

他打了个哈欠，在封面上粗略地写上他的诚信誓言，[1] 淡定地离开了教室。

"如果你没有通过补考，"刚来的亚历克这样说，他们坐在艾默里屋子的窗户上，苦想着怎样布置墙壁，"你就同这世上最愚蠢的笨蛋没什么区别了。无论是在俱乐部还是校园，你的名声就会像电梯一样迅速滑下去。"

"啊，去死吧，我了解。为什么非要说到我的痛处呢！"

"因为你自作自受。任意一位想挑战你最有竞争力位子的人，或许都没有资格坐上普林斯顿人报主席的位子。"

"嗯，不说这个了，"艾默里打断了谈话，"瞧着吧，等着吧，不要再提这件事了。我不想让俱乐部的人都来向我询问这件事，就好像我是打了激素被扔到蔬菜展示厅任人观赏的大土豆一样。"

一周以后的一个夜晚，在前往伦维客咖啡馆的路上，他驻足在自己房间的窗口下，瞧见里面的灯光，喊道：

"嗨，汤姆，有人给我寄信吗？"

窗口处一片漆黑，忽然亚历克的脑袋冒了出来。

"有人，是你的成绩单。"

他的心剧烈地跳动着。

"结果如何，单子是蓝色还是红色？"

"我也不清楚。你最好还是上来一趟吧！"

他走进房间，直接奔向桌子，这才意识到屋子里还有其他客人。

"你好，凯里。"他表现得很谦恭，"啊，全都是普林斯顿的同学。"他们好像大部分是朋友的关系，就这样，他拿起印有"教务处"字样的信封，掂了掂，格外得紧张。

"一张纸的分量还挺重。"

"艾默里，打开吧。"

"考虑到制造效果，我会对你们坦诚，如果我的成绩单是蓝色的，我会从《普

---

1. 普林斯顿大学的"诚信誓言"于一八九三年开始，由一群学生创导，之后经过不断地更新，如今的诚信誓言是："我用我的人格担保，在这次的考试中，我没有违反诚信准则。"

林斯顿人报》编委上除名,我的编者生涯也就至此结束了。"

他犹豫了一会儿,这个空当他头一次瞧见菲伦比的眼睛,目光直勾勾地盯着那个信封,眼神中还带有一丝饥饿与渴望。艾默里也狠狠地瞪了他一眼。

"瞧我的脸庞,先生们,瞧我自然表露出来的情感。"

他慢慢地撕开信封,拿着信对准灯。

"结果如何?"

"是红色还是蓝色?"

"告诉我们吧,结果是什么?"

"我们所有人都很关心这件事呢,艾默里。"

"大笑还是骂街——抑或是一些其他的表现。"

一片沉寂……几秒钟转瞬即逝……之后他瞧了瞧信纸,几秒钟又很快过去了。

"蓝得如同天空一样,各位……"

结果

整整一个学期,从九月的一开始到来年的春天结束,艾默里所做的任何事都是漫无目的的,并且总是想起一出是一出,因此在他身上发现不了任何有价值的东西。自然,那些自己丢失的东西随即让他感到很懊恼。他的成功哲学彻底塌陷了,他在找寻原因。

"完全是因为你自己过于慵懒。"亚历克随后说道。

"不准确——还存在更深层次的原因。我现在认为我从一开始就注定要丢失这个机遇。"

"俱乐部的人都像是在躲着你,你明白;我们的队伍不管少了谁,力量都会变得更加薄弱。"

"我不喜欢这样的看法。"

"自然,稍微努力一些,你仍旧能够卷土重来。"

"不对——我已经没有可能了——就拿在大学中的影响力来说。"

"但是,艾默里,实话实说,最让我觉得愤怒的其实不是你不当普林斯顿人报的编辑主任,不当学生协会成员,而是你对待考试的态度过于敷衍。"

"不是我的原因,"艾默里慢慢地说道,"我追寻的是实实在在的事物,我的慵懒完全是出于我自己的性格,可是,很不幸。"

"你的意思是,问题出在你的性格上。"

"或许是因为这个。"

虽然艾默里的观点是危险的,可是也能说得通。如果将他对周边的环境做出的反应列出一张表,这张图表的起始时间在他的幼年,可以这样描述:

1. 起初的艾默里。
2. 艾默里同贝雅特丽丝。
3. 艾默里同贝雅特丽丝以及明尼阿波利斯。之后圣雷吉士预备学校将他打乱了,使他回到了原点,重新开始。
4. 艾默里同圣雷吉士预备学校。
5. 艾默里同圣雷吉士以及普林斯顿。

这些让他更容易熟悉环境、走向成功。起初的艾默里,性格钟爱想象、慵懒、不合群,好像完全改变了。他熟悉了环境,他获得过成功,可是他的想象,一没有变成现实,二没有被他的成功所理解,所以他万念俱灰,就好像不经意地,将成功赶跑了,所以他再一次成为:

6. 起初的艾默里

经济状况

在感恩节那天,他的父亲毫无征兆地离开了人世。既同日内瓦优美的环境完全不搭调,又与他的母亲庄严并且默不作声的性格不和谐,这一点让他觉得十分有趣,所以他对他父亲的葬礼采取不干预的态度,表现出有趣的宽容。他觉得相较于火葬来说,土葬更好,回想到自己处于童年时候人们的做法——人在去世之后,便会被挂在树顶上逐渐发烂,便觉得十分可笑。葬礼的第二天,他独自躺在空旷的书房中找寻快乐,他躺在长长的沙发上,摆弄着各种优雅俊美的姿势,想要做出选择,等到自己也不得不走出这一步的时候,是应该虔诚地将两只手交叉于胸前(达西大人之前就提倡这样的仪态,觉得较为肃穆),还是应该采用异教徒样式的或是拜伦样式的仪态,两手紧紧地交叉握住,垫在后脑勺下面。

相较于他的父亲最后挣脱繁杂的鸡毛小事离开人世,三方会谈反倒更能引起他的兴趣,就是贝雅特丽丝、巴顿(克罗格曼律师事务所的巴顿先生),还有他本人之间举行的会谈,这件事发生在举行葬礼的几天之后。那是他头一次真正了解到自己家庭的经济情况,意识到他父亲之前继承的财产数额是如此之大。他拿起一本标有"一九零六年"的分类账本，十分认真地从头看到尾。那年的总支出超过十一万元。其中四万是贝雅特丽丝个人所得，对于这笔收入并没有进行详细的说明，全都分到"支票、汇票，并且转交给贝雅特丽丝的信用证"的名下。而其他各种支出则全都详细地一一列举出来：交税以及庄园返修费用将近花费九万元；普普通通的维护保养，包含贝雅特丽丝的电动车以及那年买的一辆法国产的汽车，超过了三万五千元。其他的每条开支都非常详细地记录着，并且总是能看见同分类右栏有出入的项目。

翻到"一九一二年"的分类账目，艾默里瞧见后很是惊慌，他察觉到持有的债券数目降低，导致收入大跌。关于贝雅特丽丝的财富，这一本不怎么明确，但是很明显，他父亲在之前一年内经济上的获利都投资到几笔入不敷出的石油投机生意当中了。石油燃烧得极少，但是斯蒂芬·布莱恩却被烧得十分狼狈。就这样一年接着一年，从第二年到第四年，收入的滑落都表现出相似的情况，导致贝雅特丽丝不得不头一次使用她的私房钱来支撑家庭的正常运行。可是在一九一三年，单单她自己看医生的支出就超过了九千元。

对于收支的真实情况，巴顿先生并非十分了解，并且觉得十分困惑。近期的几笔投资，就目前的收益情况来看，的确存在一些问题，但是他觉得除了这些，还应该有一些投机生意和交易，可是在这方面他并没有向律师咨询过建议。

几个月过后，贝雅特丽丝才想起给他写信，详尽地阐述了整个经济情况。布莱恩以及奥哈拉家剩下的财产除了日内瓦湖旁边的一处农村房产以外，还有五十万左右的现金，这笔财产目前已经投入到较为保守的收益为百分之六的持有财产上。实际上，贝雅特丽丝在信中提到，她在收购铁路以及电车债券等方面投入了很多钱，一旦遇到合适的时机，她会将资金转移到债券上面。

"我敢笃定，"在她写给艾默里的信中提到，"如果存在我们可以百分之百确信的事情，那一定是人们不会在一棵树上吊死。你这位出门就配有福特汽车的人自然能够懂得这个道理。因此，就拿北太平洋公司以及他们称之为电车公司的这些快运公司来说，对于这类工作，我命令巴顿先生一定要花大力气进行钻研。我对没能收购伯利恒钢铁公司的债券而后悔不已，我这辈子都不会宽恕自己这个过失。我听说了让人最为沉醉的消息。你不得不将精力放在金融工作上，艾默里。你肯定会沉醉在这个职业当中的。一开始，你就当一位信差或是一位出纳员，我觉得，之后在那个岗位上再向上升迁——可以说是没有节制的升迁。我笃定，如果我是一名男子汉，我会很乐意同金钱接触；对我来说这种深情已然到了一种无法自拔的地步。我首先得说一件事，之后再转回来接着说。有一位叫比斯帕姆太太的人，她甚至客气得有点过火，她是我在喝茶吃点心的时候碰到的。她告诉我，她那个在耶鲁上学的儿子在写给她的信中提到，那个学校的男生完全不考虑季节而任意搭配衣服，冬天会出现夏天才穿的内衣，甚至在下雪下雨的天气出门都不带雨伞，任凭雨雪打在头上，脚上穿着低帮的鞋子。艾默里，我不了解这种风气在你们普林斯顿那里是否也非常盛行，但是我希望你不要去做这样的蠢事情。如果那样做，即使年轻，肺炎以及骨髓灰质炎也会很容易找上你的，严重的话还会患上肺部疾病，特别是你的肺部极其容易患病。你绝不能将你的身体当成试验品。如今我明白了。我不会闹笑话，有的母亲肯定会那样做，逼着你穿套鞋，虽然我的脑海中总是出现你进进出出穿着套鞋，甚至都不扣一个扣子的画面。我还能想象到，随着你的脚步所发出的哗啦啦的奇怪的声音，你不愿意扣扣子是因为这种做法在外边不流行。第二年的圣诞节，你甚至不去穿浅口胶鞋，无论我说什么，你都不穿。如今你将近二十岁了，亲爱的，我不可能总是陪伴在你的身边，判断你的处事是否合理。"

"这封信所提到的事情都是真实发生的。在上一封信中我提醒过你，因为没钱所以完成不了你想做的事情会让人变得絮絮叨叨、没完没了，可是只要我们懂得节约，无论做任何事情钱还是不成问题的。你要好好照顾自己，孩子，想办法每周最少邮一封信回来，因为如果收不到你的信件，关于你的各种糟糕的情况都可能会出现在我的脑海中。

爱你的
妈妈"

头一次出现"分量大的人物"这一术语

艾默里受到达西大人的邀请——在圣诞节那天，前往哈得逊河畔斯图业特宫廷般的大宅中住上一周，他们在炉火旁边促膝长谈。达西大人身材稍微有些圆润，并且随着体型一天天变大，他的秉性也变得开怀了很多，所以，艾默里坐进矮小、坐垫舒服的椅子，同他一块享受一根雪茄为中年人带来的清醒，他觉得既安适又舒服。

"我不想上学了，大人。"

"出于什么原因呢？"

"我所有的成绩都已经风流云散了；你会觉得这是一件很小的事情，一点都不重要，但是——"

"这很重要。我把这件事看得很重要。你仔仔细细地告诉我。从我们上次分别到现在所发生的全部事情。"

艾默里把能想到的都说了，包括他的自我摧毁也全都说了出来，半小时以后，他声音中的那些厌倦神奇地消失了。

"如果你不上学了，之后的计划是什么？"大人发问说。

"我还没有想好。我非常想有一场旅行。但是很明显这场不惹人喜欢的战争没有为我提供那样的条件。不管怎样，母亲知道我没有念完大学会很生气的。我不知道该怎么做。凯里·贺拉狄想让我同他一块参军，参加法国飞行大队。"

"我清楚你不想去。"

"这也说不准——或许今晚我就会走。"

"啊，假如你那样做，你肯定会更加厌烦生活，你会比我想的还要厌倦。我很清楚你。"

"或许你说得没错，"艾默里表示同意，一脸的不屑，"这个方法好像可以令我很容易地挣脱所有——想到我得再过一年平淡无为、厌倦的生活。"

"很对，我明白；但是实话实说，我并没有太担心你；反而我认为你是在慢慢地进步。"

"不准确，"艾默里辩驳道，"我的个性在一年的时间内被消磨得差不多了。"

"丝毫没有遗失！"达西大人嘲讽着说，"你只是失去了大量的虚荣。"

"我的上帝！我一直有一种感觉，好像我在圣雷吉士预备学校的五年级又上了一年。"

"大错特错，"大人晃了晃头，"之前是一件晦气的事情；但是现在是好事情。无论是什么好事降临，肯定不会经过你去年探寻的渠道了。"

"如今在我身上已经找不到朝气了，我想没有比这个更差劲的事情了！"

"单单就事论事，或许是这样……但是你一直在进步。这种境况下，你就存在思考的空间，你将会丢下很多关于成功或者超人等等这些曾经的负担。我们这类人是不会承认毫不变更的道理的，如同你之前一样。如果我们可以去做下一件事[1]，并且每天可以腾出一个小时来推敲，那么在我们身上就可能会创造奇迹，可是如果任意独断专行，不加思考地支配所有的计划——那么我们肯定会做出傻事的。"

"但是，大人，我对下一件事情毫无想法啊！"

"艾默里，说句掏心窝的话，我自己也只是刚明白如何做。除了从事下一件事情，我能够做很多其他的事，可是只要做那件事我就会遇到瓶颈，就如同今年秋天数学让你受到的磨难一样。"

"为什么我们要从事下一件事情呢？我一直认为那件事同我没有任何关联。"

"我们必须得这样做，因为我们不是个性张扬的人，而是有分量的人。"

"完美——但是你想要表达什么意思呢？"

"个性张扬的人就是你之前认为你所表现的人，你向我提及的凯里以及斯罗恩明显是个性张扬的人。个性好像就是一个物理问题；它会使它影响到的人的身份降低——我瞧见过长时间抱病在床的人个性的泯灭。可是，在一个个性张扬的时刻，它会将'下一件事情'否决。而一个分量大的人物是一点点积累而成的。人们对于一个人的评判，一定会基于他的所作所为。这就如同一根横杆，上面挂着满满当当的东西——有时候看着晃眼睛，正如同我们的东西一样；可是在他使用这些东西的时候，能够凭着冷静的心态来确保事情的成功。"

"可是我身上的几样最为耀眼的东西在我最需要他们的时候却溜走了。"艾默里接着将它比喻成横杆，言语中有些许急促。

"对啊，正是如此；在你觉得将积攒的名声、才能等等值得称赞的东西全都挂出来的时候，你完全不用考虑别人的看法；这些东西你能够极为容易地进行处理。"

"但是，不得不提到，如果在我身上没有发现我所拥有的事物，我就愕然，不明白该怎么办了！"

---

1. 一首具有宗教含义的诗名叫《做下一件事》，作者无名氏，四节，总共二十三行，每一节的最后一句都是"做下一件事"。约翰·沃纳梅克（John Wanamaker,1838—1922），美国宗教领袖、第一家百货商店的创始人、现代广告之父，同时也是"顾客至上"论的主张者，他也说过这样一句常被人引用的话："做下一件事。"他还说："一步一步登山，再高的山也能翻过去。"意思是一样的。

"很对。"

"那当然是个相当不错的观点。"

"这样你就彻彻底底地占了上风——凯里或是斯罗恩完全不会获得的上风。你抛弃三四件对你无用的外衣,头脑一热又摒弃你的其他东西。目前的首要任务就是收集新的东西,目光越远,收集到的东西就会越棒。前提是一定不要忘记,去做你接下来需要做的事情!"

"你能讲道理讲得如此透彻!"

他们就是这样无话不谈,大多数情况下是在说他们自己,有时还会提及哲学、宗教,也会畅谈人生,谈谈游戏般的人生,谈谈谜一般的人生。神父好像在艾默里犹豫的时候,就已经搞明白了他的想法,因为无论是思维还是习惯,这些方面他们都好像是对方的影子。

"为什么我要列个清单?"一天晚上,艾默里提出了这样的疑问,"全部东西都要出现在清单上,为什么?"

"因为你正在努力钻研中世纪问题,"大人回复道。"我们两个人一样。这体现了我们对分类和总结的热爱。"

"这是对得到明确的事物的期望。"

"经济哲学必须围着它转。"

"在来的路上我就察觉到,我变得古怪了。我猜想,这是一种装出来的态度。"

"你不必对这个有所犹豫;对你来说,什么想法都不装才是最虚伪的想法。装模作样——"

"有什么依据?"

"可是得从事下一件事。"

艾默里返回学校后接连收到达西大人寄来的信,信中给了他该如何解决骄傲狂妄的问题的精神食粮。

或许我对于你的安全方面提了过多的建议,可是你一定要铭记,我做这件事是出于对你奋斗的原动力的认同;并不是想当然地认为你没有经过奋斗就能够实现目标。秉性上的那些细微的差异你应该熟悉认可它,但是对其他人掏心窝的时候一定要小心。不能随便动真情,聪明但不奸诈,自大但不狂傲。

不要自己放弃自己,认定自己毫无用处;实际上当你认为自己近乎完美的时候,那才是真正到了没有办法挽救的地步;不要害怕失去你的个性,如同你总是提到的那样；十五岁的你如同清晨的阳光一样生机勃勃，二十岁的你如同月光一般阴郁惆怅。等到你活到我这个年纪，你就会同我一样，散发出下午四点中温柔的金色阳光。

假如你想给我回信，请你一定要发自真情。你的上一封信件，就是那篇有关建筑学的论文，写得很差——如此的"趣味高雅，不切实际"，我将你看成是生活在感情跟知识的真空中。要明确的是，不要将人定义为过于肯定的类型，假如你给碰到的每一个人都贴上鄙视的标签，那同你将玩具用盒子包装起来没什么差别。然而等到你同这个世界格格不入的时候，盒子便会炸开，玩具会对着你翻白眼，鄙视你。视雷奥纳多·达·芬奇这种人为偶像，就现在的情况来看，对你会有极大的帮助。

你的道路一定会曲折，就像我年轻时经历的那样，但是无论那些肯对你提出批评的人怎样，你一定得时刻让自己保持思考，不要太多的谴责自己。

你说让你在"女人的问题"上步步为营完全是因为习俗，可是问题并不是这么简单的，艾默里；那是因为你惧怕一旦涉足就无法收场，你会掌控不住自己，你明白我的意思；那是你以此来觉察邪恶的可以说是能够创造奇迹的第六感，那是你内心深处暂时还没有完全展现的对上帝的敬仰。

无论你未来精通哪一门——建筑、宗教、文学——我笃定你相较于之前更能够领会其中的深意，可是我不会顽固地要你接受我的观点，贸然让你接受我的思想。虽然我个人相信，"天主教裂口里的黑暗"会在你的脚下裂开口子。赶快回信给我。

顺便致以亲切的问候
泰厄．达西

这一阶段艾默里的阅读显得平淡无味；他在朦胧的文学道路上越走越远：于斯曼、瓦尔特·佩特、戈蒂埃，还有拉伯雷、卟迦丘、佩特罗尼乌斯、苏埃托尼乌斯[1]的文章。有一个星期，也是出于好奇，他翻遍了所有同学的藏书，并

---

1. 于斯曼（Joris-Kal Huysmans，1848—1907），法国小说家；瓦尔特·佩特（Walter Pater，1838—1894），英国散文家、文学批评家、小说家，倡导"为艺术而艺术"；戈蒂埃（Theophile Gautier，1811—1872），法国诗人、小说家、评论家，首创"为艺术而艺术"；佩特罗尼乌斯（Gaius Petronius，？—66），古罗马作家；苏埃托尼乌斯（Suetonius，69—104），古罗马传记作家。

且觉察到斯罗恩的书同其他人一样有特色,全部是些集子:吉普林、欧·亨利、古罗马作家小约翰·弗克斯[1],还有理查德·哈丁·戴维斯[2];《中年妇女须知》、诗歌《育空河的魅力》[3];美国诗人詹姆斯·维特科姆·莱雷[4]的一册《附赠本》,许多缺页的加注教科书。最后,出乎他意料的是,他的新发掘之一——美国诗人卢泼特·布鲁克的诗歌摘选。

他同汤姆·丹维里埃在普林斯顿的名人中探寻,想要找到一位有美国诗歌伟大传统[5]的人。

那一年的本科生相较于两年前整个普林斯顿的庸人更加有趣。情况十分活跃,虽然为此付出了新生第一年的天然质朴的魅力。在旧普林斯顿时期,他们无论如何都找寻不到塔纳杜克·怀利。塔纳杜克上二年级,耳朵长得很大,他平时说的,"天地含混涡动穿过久远的预谋预兆灾难的月轮!"他们听见后表情愕然,思忖着怎么会听不明白他的意思,可是绝对不会疑虑这是与众不同的表达方法。起码汤姆以及艾默里是这样想他的。他们义正言辞地告诉他,他的思维仿照雪莱,并且在《纳骚文学杂志》特意登载了他的超自由的自由诗以及散文诗。可是塔纳杜克的天才吸收了时代的很多特点,并且让他们觉得美中不足的是,放荡不羁的生活方式深深地吸引着他。他现在说话一定得说格林威治村,[6]不再去写"午夜涡动的月轮"这种诗句;通过引荐去探访没落的诗人,而且并不是因为学术方面,躲入第四十二大街以及百老汇,不再写那些让他们一饱眼福的雪莱式的梦中的孩子。但是,他们放弃了塔纳杜克,将他送给了未来派,笃定他同他高亢激昂的关系在那一派人中可以发挥得更加完美。汤姆最终提出了一个建议,奉劝他在接下来的两年内不要写作,认真地看四遍亚历山大·蒲柏[7]的诗集,但是艾默里表示反对,他认为让塔纳杜克看蒲柏同放松双脚来治疗

---

1. 小约翰·弗克斯(John Fox, Jr., 1862—1919),美国新闻记者、小说家。
2. 理查德·哈丁·戴维斯(Richard Harding Davis, 1864—1916),美国通俗小说家。
3. 罗伯特·塞尔维斯作,并参见第15页注。
4. 詹姆斯·维特科姆·莱雷(James Whitcomb Riley, 1849—1916),美国诗人。
5. 提到美国诗歌的传统,一般来说,需要收集艾米莉·狄金生、朗费罗、惠特曼等十九世纪诗人的作品。
6. 纽约曼哈顿作家与艺术家聚集的地方,同时也是"垮掉的一代"运动诞生的地方。
7. 蒲柏(Alexander Pope, 1688—1744),英国著名的诗人,擅长讽刺、使用英雄偶体以及翻译荷马史诗。

胃病没什么区别，说完他们热热闹闹地走出了房间，这位天才在他们眼中过于伟大以至于他们消费不起，抑或过于平庸他们嗤之以鼻，这个决定要等到抛完硬币之后才能做出来。

艾默里回避了那位受广大同学欢迎的教授的课，每天晚上他们为尊崇的人写下通俗明了的警句以及几篇如同芳香草白兰地般的文雅诗歌。但凡同死板性格稍微能扯上关系的科目都存在着不能确定的氛围，为此他丧失了信心；他的态度在一首题为《讲堂》的讽刺小说中能够找到依据，他强烈建议汤姆将这首诗歌登在《纳骚文学》的刊物上面。

"早上好，愚蠢的人……
每周三课堂上各种吹嘘
只要你开口说话，我们大眼瞪小眼，完全不知道怎么做，
用你哲学态度的狡诈'嗯啊'
让我们求知若渴的灵魂变得愚昧……
啊，我们如同一百头迷路的羔羊，
鼾声如雷、不闻不问、倾诉衷肠……进入梦乡……
他们都将你看成一位学者；
有一天你费尽心思认真揣摩
一个提纲，我们对它很通晓，
出自一本被世人遗忘的诗集；
你接触了这个时代所有的必读书，
却换来了你的两个鼻孔塞满厚厚的尘土，
所以你从地上爬了起来，
一声震天响的喷嚏将你从故纸堆里拉了回来……
可是有一个人坐在我的右手边，
饥渴的笨驴……大家都说很邪门；
永远有问题要问……他矗立在那里，
表情庄严，双手颤抖着屏住呼吸，
下课后才能告诉你，
他坐了一夜直到隔天的黎明升起；
手捧着你的书……啊，你会矫揉造作而他

也会装出一副精神健硕的姿态，
两个傻蛋，你会张着嘴巴嘿嘿笑出声，
两眼斜视，匆忙地赶回去还要背地里笑出声……

从那时到现在已经整整一星期了，先生，你归还
我的论文，我获益良多
（细读了您写的眉批旁注
每一句、每一条我都没有遗漏）
我鄙视歇后语，简单并且不经大脑，
来一个装模作样的狠批……
'你可以笃定确实是这样说的吗？'
还有
'萧伯纳说的话不能够被当做教条嘛！'
但是饥渴的笨驴，将到手的资料视为真理，
完全与你给他的最高分相背离。

仍旧——我仍旧能够在各个地方遇到你……
甚至你会出现在莎士比亚的演出当中，
一颗过时的、风光不再的星
也会迷倒你这样有问题的学者先生……
一名激进派的成员就会让你大惊小怪，
无神论的正宗面目？——
你所讲的仅仅是平常人都懂的内容，
嘴巴大张着，代表着听众。

有时，甚至拿钟声嗡嗡的教堂来说
也有迷人之处，唤起你有意的谅解与谦恭，
唤起你对真理的率真、欣喜深思；

（甚至康德以及救世军军长布斯[1]也不能独善其身……）
你的生活只能瞧见震惊，
一个缥缈、无力的认同……

到时间了……一个个伸懒腰，打哈欠，
一百位孩子都由幸福的父母所生，
他们在昏暗的走廊里你推我搡，好不热闹；
骗取你一两句话的是脚步的竞走……
忽略了小肚鸡肠的大地，实在惹人怜悯，
突如其来的裂口将你引到了人间。"

四月，凯里·贺拉狄迈出校门，坐船到法国去了，他参加了法国航空大队。一开始艾默里很羡慕他，敬仰凯里能够有勇气迈出这一步，可是等他自己也经历了这件事情以后，他的羡慕以及敬仰瞬间消失了，同时他也没有从中获得太多的益处。可是即使是这样，这件往事在后来三年的时间里总是在他的心中挥之不去。

恶魔

他们离开希利餐厅时已经过了十二点了，之后乘着出租车到了比斯托勒利的咖啡厅。他们里边有艾克西亚·马洛以及菲比·科伦，不久前参加了夏日的花展，还有弗雷德·斯罗恩以及艾默里。夜幕还未完全降临，时间还不晚，他们精力充沛，感觉十分滑稽，所以就仿照酒神节的狂欢者闯进了咖啡厅。

"四位，为我们安排中间位置，"菲比扯着嗓子喊道，"哎，赶紧把酒拿上来，告诉他们一声我们来了！"

"让他们把音乐打开，一定得放'赞美歌'！"斯罗恩也大声嚷道。"要喝什么交给你们两个了；我同菲比得去练练脚劲，为你们献舞。"说完就洒脱地走向昏昏沉沉的人群。仅仅才结识一个小时的艾克西亚以及艾默里挤在一位服务员的身后，他们找了一个好位置，之后坐下来欣赏斯罗恩和菲比的表演。

"那不是纽黑文[2]的芬德尔.马格特生嘛！"瞧见熟人，艾克西亚很激动，

---

1. 布斯（William Booth, 1829—1912），英国基督教循道宗传教士，同时也是救世军第一任军长。
2. 耶鲁大学的所在地。

声音盖过了嘈杂的人群声。"喂,芬德尔!嗨——喂!"

"啊,是艾克西亚!"他向她猛烈地挥手,喊道,"来我们这儿吧!"

"不要离开!"艾默里小声地说。

"不可以,芬德尔,我同其他人在一起呢!明天大概一点给我打电话!"

芬德尔的言行举止经常会引起人们的厌恶,他是酒吧的常客,他的言行完全不着边际,转身面对着光芒四射的金发女郎,带着她到处转。

"他一生下来就是个混蛋,"艾默里说话了。

"嗯,他本性挺好的。"一位男招待走了过来,穿着让人看着很奇怪的衣服,问我是不是要点些什么。

"来两份代基里酒。"

"来四客。"

人们围成一圈不停地旋转着,叫喊声不绝于耳。大部分人都来自大学,还有少数几个男人是百老汇的无所事事的人。女人被划分为两种,高级一些的是歌舞喜剧中的歌舞队合唱女演员。大体上,这些人具有一定的代表性。整个聚会当中有四分之三的活动完全是为了表面效果,所以他们并没有心存不良,到了咖啡厅门口,聚会就宣布告一段落。他们随即赶上五点钟的火车返回耶鲁抑或普林斯顿。大概四分之一的人会继续待在那里喝饮品,直到夜色朦胧才肯罢休,到了不熟悉的地方会被陌生人所忽略。他们聚会的初衷就不是打着什么歪主意。弗雷德·斯罗恩以及菲比·科伦是旧相识,艾克西亚同艾默里是才结交的。可是奇特的事情早在黑夜中酝酿好了,不同寻常的事情是不可能在咖啡厅埋伏的,因为那里是进行普普通通、毫无创意的活动的地方。可是一件不同寻常的事情即将打乱他们就要结束的百老汇的风流之行。不同寻常的事情的发生的确会让人畏惧,让人难以接受,他甚至在这事情发生以后都没有将它当做是经历,可是它又是说不清道不明的悲剧中的一个片段。悲剧在发生的时候你完全察觉不到,可是它想表达的意思又是他所明白的事情。

午夜一点钟左右,他们来到马克希姆酒吧,两点钟他们又换了一家,走进戴维尼埃酒吧。斯罗恩一直在喝酒,已经到了醉醺醺的地步,走起路来歪歪扭扭的;相反艾默里却毫无醉意,仅仅有些厌烦。那些平时帮助他们布置纽约聚会的人,收下别人的行贿来换取香槟的老人,他们一个也没有瞧见。

他们刚刚跳完舞,就要回到座位上时,艾默里好像意识到旁边的一张桌子上的人在看他。他转过身大致晃了一眼……那是一位中年男人，身上披了一件普通的棕色西装，他附近还有一张桌子，一个人坐在那里，全神贯注地盯着他们的聚会。艾默里回过头时，他嘴角上扬，表达出了一丝友善。艾默里回过头，对着要坐下的弗雷德。

"那个一直看我们的笨蛋是谁？"他说道，语气中夹杂着一丝生气的意味。

"在哪？"斯罗恩大喊道。"我们将他赶出去！"说完他站了起来，手提着椅子环顾四周。"他在哪？"

艾克西亚以及菲比忽然俯身凑在一块儿，隔着桌子小声说话，艾默里还没有弄清楚状况，她们就已经走到门口了。

"去哪里？"

"到公寓去，"菲比提议道，"我们有起泡酒以及白兰地——今夜这里的全部看起来都毫无生气。"

艾默里脑子飞转着。他未曾饮下太多的酒，如果他不再喝了，那么他同她们赶紧离开，也是一件经过深思熟虑的事情。实际上，把斯罗恩看得紧一些或许是一件好事，因为他的神智已经模糊、不能听他支配了。所以他抓住艾克西亚的手臂，像一对恋人一样钻进了一辆出租车里，他们在马路上疾驰，停在一幢白石砌的高层公寓面前……他肯定会一辈子都记得那条马路……那条马路十分宽阔，放眼看去，两旁全都是这种高层的白石建筑，一扇扇窗户如同一个个黑洞一般；在洁白的月光的映衬下，建筑变成了银白色。他想着每一幢房子都配有电梯，还有一个开电梯的黑人以及钥匙架；每幢房子高八层，每层都有三户或者四户的套房。他走进菲比家亮堂的客厅，心里很是开心，一头倒进柔软的沙发上，而姑娘们则在到处找寻吃的东西。

"菲比真是太厉害了。"斯罗恩小声地告诉他这个秘密。

"半个小时后我会离开。"艾默里面无表情地说道。他心中有个疑问，不知这是否显得过于拘谨。

"你说什么，"斯罗恩反驳说，"既然到了这儿——我们不要急匆匆的。"

菲比出来了，还端来了三明治、白兰地酒瓶、吸管以及四个酒杯。

"艾默里，由你倒酒，"她说道，"让我们为弗雷德·斯罗恩干一杯，平时他可不会醉成这样。"

"说得很对，"艾克西亚说着走进客厅，"以及艾默里，我喜欢艾默里。"

她在他的身边坐了下来，一头金色的头发倾泻在他的肩上。

"我倒酒，"斯罗恩说，"吸管你来用，菲比。"

他们将酒杯搁在托盘上面。

"好了，酒已经被她端起来了！"

艾默里手中握着酒杯，仍在思忖着。

在接下来一分钟的时间里，诱惑如同暖风一般侵袭进人的身体，蔓延至全身，他的想象溅出了火光，他从菲比手中接过杯子。就是这样；因为在他即将做出抉择的时候，他抬起头，瞧见距离他十码左右的位置上，坐着去过咖啡厅的那个人，他惊了一下，杯子从他的手中掉了下去。那人的身体一半摆出坐着的姿态，另一半却靠在沙发转角的一堆靠垫上面，他的脸色同在咖啡厅中碰见时没什么差别，就好像是使用同一根黄蜡烛制成的，既不像是死人那般无光泽的白——反倒可以说是有活力的白——也不是人们口中那种亚健康的苍白；不如说是一位在矿井下面工作了很长时间的健硕的人，抑或是在潮湿的环境下值过夜班的人。艾默里将这个人从上到下仔细地看了好几遍，假如事后出于需要，他甚至能够将他画在纸上，就连细节也能够反映出来，毫无遗漏。他的嘴巴属于实诚的那种类型，两只眼睛神态自若并且十分庄严，目光慢慢地在他们当中游动，仅仅露出了一丝疑问的神情。艾默里还留意到了他的双手；手指很粗大，但是灵活而又脆弱……双手动作紧张，轻轻地搁在沙发坐垫上面，从未停止过颤抖，一会儿攥紧手，一会儿又张开。之后，艾默里突然瞧见了他的两只脚。一股血窜上他的头顶，他觉察到自己害怕了。他的双脚反方向长着……这种反向是感觉到的，而不是亲眼瞧见的……它如同一位善良女人身上的弱点，也可以看成是缎子上的一点血迹，是一种令人内心忐忑的震惊的不和谐。他没有穿皮鞋，而是穿着一双低帮的莫卡辛那种类型的软鞋。鞋头很尖，从他的鞋子上可以看到十四世纪的影子，鞋尖向上弯起。颜色是深褐色的，瞧起来就像是鞋尖塞着满满的脚趾……那情况实在是让人有种不可名状的畏惧……

他肯定是说了什么话，又或是生病了，因为可以听见从空旷的地方传来的艾克西亚的说话声，一种带着好奇的说话声。

"啊，看艾默里的神情！惹人怜惜的宝贝艾默里是否生病了——脑袋很晕对吗？"

"瞧那个人！"艾默里大声吼道，说着伸出手指指向沙发转角。

"你说的是紫斑马！"艾克西亚风趣地说着。"哈——哈！紫斑马一直看着艾默里！"

斯罗恩在一旁憨笑着。

"斑马认定你了，艾默里？"

鸦雀无声……那个人的目光在他身上看来看去，带有一丝嘲讽……之后，他的耳边传来了说话声：

"我原以为你还清醒着呢，"艾克西亚嘲讽地说道，可是声音听起来却是那么的动听。坐在软沙发上的那个人把沙发变活了，他如同柏油公路上的热浪，又如同一只虫子一样扭动着身体……

"别走！别走！"艾克西亚用手臂勾着他。"艾默里，我的宝贝，你别走，艾默里！"他已经走向门口了。

"别这样，艾默里，同大伙待在一块吧！"

"感觉很难受对吗？"

"坐下待会儿吧！"

"喝些水。"

"品尝一下白兰地……"

电梯门关着，那位黑人一会睡着一会醒来，脸色铁青……艾克西亚央求的声音飘在电梯的上空。两只脚……那两只脚……

就在电梯降到一层的时候，那两只脚再一次出现在了铺满砌砖的门厅的昏暗的灯光下。

小巷中

长长的马路上铺满了月光，艾默里在马路上走着，背对着月亮。距离大约十步、二十步远的地方能听见哒哒哒的脚步声，那声音如同没有关紧的水龙头在往下滴水一样，水滴下来的时候还多少有些迟疑。艾默里的影子停在距离他大概十步远的地方，他的软底鞋差不多停在他身后那么远的距离。出于孩子的本能，艾默里藏身在白色建筑物的灰色影子中，在他迷迷糊糊的片刻间，月光界限分明，他忽然间跟跄慢跑了几步。不过没跑几步，他便立即停住了脚步，思忖着。一定得镇定。他口干舌燥，舌头舔着嘴唇。

假如他碰到一位好人——这个世上还会有好人吗？是否现在所有的好人全都搬进白色的公寓当中了？是否每一个独自走在月光下的人身后都会跟着

一个陌生人？可是纵使他碰到了一位好人，他会理解他的想法，听到这让人头皮发麻的脚步声……就在这个空当，那迅疾的脚步声突然直逼过来，月亮这时又被一片乌云盖住。等到惨淡的月光掠过屋子的檐口，那脚步声似乎移到了他的面前，艾默里认为他听到了喘息的声音。他突然意识到那脚步声并非从他身后传来，从未在他身后，脚步声是从他的前方传来的！他自己并非在躲避脚步声，而是循着脚步声而来！踏声而来！就这样他果断地奔跑起来，没有任何原因，心在剧烈地跳动，双手交叉，紧紧地握在一起。在他正前方很远的一个地方，出现了一个黑点，渐渐地，这个黑点演变成了一个人的模样。好在如今艾默里甩开那脚步声已经有相当长的一段距离了。他从大马路拐进一条小巷当中，那条小巷不但狭窄而且昏暗，甚至还弥漫着一股老旧腐烂的味道。他不停地奔跑着，顺着一条延绵曲折的修长小巷，月光照不进这条巷子，仅仅残存着一点一点、一块一块的亮光……忽然他跌倒了，跌进一排篱笆的角落当中，他大口地呼吸着，筋疲力尽。他前面的脚步声停止了，他能够听到脚步轻轻移动的声音，紧接着是连续不断的哒哒声……如同环绕码头的海浪一般。

　　他将双手盖在脸上，使劲地捂住双眼，勒紧耳朵。就在他一路狂奔的空当，他从来没有考虑过自己是脑子坏掉了还是喝醉酒了。他的脑海中还能够意识到现实的存在，那是物质的东西不能够授予他的意识，并且这种意识同他在这件事以前出现的一切都可以精确地对上号，如同戴手套那样。这种意识没有让他的头脑变得混乱。它如同一道计算题，答案就摆在纸上，可是解的出处他实在弄不明白。他的感受已经超出了惊恐的范畴。他已经看透了那让人惧怕的稀薄的外表，当下是在其他的范围内思考，在这个范围中，他的双脚以及对白色外墙的畏惧都是真实存在的，是活蹦乱跳的生命。在他的内心深处有一团很小的光亮在跳动，在召唤，对他说有人在拽他，想将他拽进门，之后锁上门。门被锁之后，就只剩下脚步声以及月光照耀下的银白色的屋子，甚至他自己也可能会变成脚步声。

　　他居然在篱笆的阴影下停留了五分钟甚至十分钟之久，在这段时间当中，他一直认为存在这样的一团火……相当近，以至于他事后还可以想起来。他记得自己曾大声吼叫：

　　"让那个笨蛋过来，啊，让那个笨蛋过来！"他是对着对面黑压压的篱笆喊的，因为脚步声正是从那处阴影当中冒出来的……拖着脚向前移动的声音。他认为"笨蛋"同"友好"经过之前的结合以后，不清楚什么原因已经结合在一块了。他这样的呼喊，是完全不受意识支配的呐喊——自制力强迫他不再去想马路上的那个人影；完全是出自本能的呐喊，就是很多固有的传统抑或是深夜迫切的恳求。之后一声撞击声传了出来，那声音像极了远处响起的闷锣声，随后一张脸孔猛地就出现在他的眼前，出现在他的两只脚的上方。那张脸面色惨白，有些扭曲，散发着无尽的阴险，脸上的肌肉不住地扭动，如同风中的火焰；但是在闷锣声敲响的那一瞬间，他看清了，这张脸就是狄克·亨伯德的脸。

几分钟过后，他猛地站了起来，好像什么声响都消失了，阴暗的小巷中只剩下他一人。天气格外的冷，他独自稳步地向另一头能看见灯光的马路奔去。

窗口

第二天醒来时，天已经很亮了，酒店床头的电话发疯似的响个不停。他想起来了，是他给酒店留言让他们在十一点把他唤醒。斯罗恩还在沉睡，打鼾的声音震耳欲聋，他的衣服就扔在床边。他们穿好衣服，安静地吃着早饭，吃完饭后外出散步，呼吸着清新的空气。艾默里仔细地梳理着自己的记忆，努力回想着昨晚发生的各种情形，想要从他脑海中充斥着的所有混沌的印象中剥离出几条线索。假如清晨天气阴冷，也许他能够很快就找到往事的脉络，可是那一天的天气却是五月的纽约偶尔才会出现的，第五大道的空气呈现出温柔、浅紫红的颜色。斯罗恩可以回想起多少，是非常多还是极少，艾默里都没有兴趣去了解；很明显，他并不像艾默里那样精神紧张。艾默里心中还萦绕着恐惧的情绪，如同吱吱作响的锯子，前后来回摆动着。

之后百老汇忽然出现在了他们眼前，环境吵闹，一副副盖着胭脂的脸在街上大摇大摆地晃动着，艾默里忽然觉得很厌恶。

"就算是为我好，咱们回去吧！咱们离开——离开此地！"

斯罗恩看着他，表情很诧异。

"为什么啊？"

"这条街，这条街让人畏惧！赶紧！咱们回到第五大道去！"

"你是说，"斯罗恩不念情分地说道，"因为昨晚你肚子塞着满满的，表现如同疯了一般，从此之后不肯踏足百老汇半步，我说的对吗？"

然而就在这时，艾默里已经给斯罗恩贴上了标签，把他归为熙熙攘攘的大众，

109

那个在他眼中诙谐幽默、儒雅、性格外向的斯罗恩已经消失了，他仅仅是混在卑鄙龌龊人群当中一个让人厌烦的人。

"喂！"他大声嚷道，声音洪亮，以至于拐角处的人都转头看了看，一脸愕然的盯着他们，"何其的卑鄙，假如分辨不清，你同卑鄙之人也就没什么差别了！"

"我来这里完全不是出自我的本意，"斯罗恩执拗地说。"你究竟出什么事情了？曾经的悔恨是否再一次激发你了？如果你同我们几个人在一块吃吃喝喝，你的心情就会好过来了！"

"我得离开了，弗雷德，"艾默里支支吾吾地说。他的膝盖剧烈抖动着，他清楚再在这条街上停留一会儿，就会马上晕过去。"我会在范德比特餐厅吃饭。"说完他就大步跑走了，跑向第五大道。回到饭店，他觉得好些了，可是就在他走进理发店，想着做一个头部按摩的时候，迎面而来的扑粉以及洗发露的气味唤起了艾克西亚对他抛媚眼的记忆，所以他慌忙地离开了理发馆。到房间门口时，他的眼前忽然一片黑暗，如同一条分叉的河流。

他醒来后，了解到已经过去了几个小时。他瘫在床上，把脸埋在床单里，内心充满了恐惧，很怕自己突然疯掉。他需要有人陪着他，需要一个清醒的、笨笨的、善良的人。他一动不动地躺在那儿，已经忘了自己在那儿躺了多长时间了。他能感觉到额头上那热乎乎的细细的血管凸了出来，畏惧的感觉像石膏一般烙在了身上。他认为自己再一次穿越了稀薄的令人畏惧的硬壳，并且只有在这时，他才可以分辨出他离开的时候留下的朦朦胧胧的暮色。他肯定又睡着了，因为当他镇定下来之后，他已经支付了饭店账单，在门口叫了一辆出租车。天空中瓢泼大雨倾盆而下。

在开往普林斯顿的车上，他不曾瞧见过任何一个熟人，只是瞧见了一群旅途劳累的费城人。一个涂着厚厚胭脂的女人坐在他的对面，这又让他觉得恶心，所以他换乘了别的车厢，努力将精力放在杂志上的一篇文章上面。可是他一直心不在焉地看着同一段文字，因此他直接放下杂志，身体疲倦地靠在窗户上，发烫的额头顶在湿润的车窗玻璃上面。这节车厢是非禁烟车厢，热气弥漫还夹杂着一丝从国外搬来的居住在这里的侨民的味道。他将窗户打开，雾气迎面吹来，他忍不住打了个哆嗦。两个小时的车程让他觉得像是过了好几天，看着周边慢慢出现的普林斯顿建筑的塔楼以及蓝色的雨中透出的那温馨的灯光，他高兴得几乎要欢呼出来了！

汤姆在房间中间站着，心事重重地吸着一根雪茄。艾默里心想，他的回来让汤姆似乎长长地松了口气。

"昨晚我做了一个恐怖的梦，是关于你的，"雪茄的烟雾夹杂着嘶哑的声音一块传来，"我那时就认为你碰到了困难。"

"不要同我讲这些！"艾默里声音很大，像是在嘶吼。"不要同我讲任何话；我很疲倦，一点儿精力也没有。"

汤姆盯着他，用反常的眼光，之后坐在一把椅子上，翻开他的意大利笔记本。艾默里将外套以及帽子狠狠地摔在地上，解开衣领，随意地从书架上抽出一本小说，作者是威尔斯。"威尔斯的脑子是清醒的，"他在心里嘀咕着，"如果他不能解决矛盾，我就看鲁泼特·布鲁克的著作。"

半个小时过去了。外边刮起了风，瞧见湿漉漉的树枝在风中晃动着，它们的枝桠抓在玻璃窗上，发出啪啪的声响，艾默里感到很惊讶。汤姆低着头，一门心思地做着他的作业，房间中偶尔传来擦亮火柴的声音以及他们在椅子上变换坐姿时皮革摩擦所发出的声响，这些声音让安静的屋子变得活泼了起来。之后发生了一件令人出乎意料的事情。艾默里像弹簧一般从椅子上直挺挺地坐了起来，冻得浑身僵硬。汤姆目不转睛地看着他，嘴角向下弯曲，眼睛瞪得很圆。

"上帝帮帮我们！"艾默里大声吼道。

"啊，上帝！"汤姆也大声说话了，"你瞧瞧后边！"艾默里如同闪电一样转过头。仅仅能看见黑洞洞的玻璃窗，除此之外，什么都没有。

"现在看不见了，"在无声的恐惧中过了一段时间之后，汤姆说了这样的话。"那时有东西在盯着你看。"

艾默里浑身颤抖，再一次坐到了椅子上。

"我一定得跟你说，"他说道，"我碰到了一件令人恐怖的事情。我觉得我——我碰到恶魔了，或是被魔鬼般的东西盯上了。你刚刚瞧见的那张脸是什么样子？——不要说了。"他随即说道。"不要告诉我！"

之后他同汤姆详述了事情的经过。直到深夜才说完，然后他们将屋里能打开的灯全都打开了，两个昏昏欲睡、浑身颤抖的还未成熟的孩子依次读着《新

111

马基雅弗利》[1],直到黎明的阳光照在维瑟斯泼恩大楼上,《普林斯顿人报》被放进门里边,五月的小鸟叽叽喳喳地迎接着昨天暴雨之后升起的朝阳。

---

1. 《新马基雅弗利》(1911),出自英国著名幻想小说作家威尔斯(H.G. Wells, 1866—1946)之手。这部小说是威尔斯从科幻小说创作转向政治和社会问题的分析研究的一个转折点。

第四章　顾影自怜的美少年

　　艾默里在校的最后两年间，也就是普林斯顿的过渡期，他看到了普林斯顿用比夜间游行更好的方式进行改革、开拓，在努力成为能够与她的哥特式建筑相媲美的大学。但是，校园里出现的几个人激发了普林斯顿，同时也触及了他浮夸的内心深处。他们曾经是与艾默里一样的大学一年级的学生，放荡不羁；有些人是艾默里的低年级的同学。他们围坐在纳骚酒店的小桌前，那是在艾默里大学最后一年开始时，他们公开对旧制度开始提出质疑，而在过去，很长时间以来艾默里以及他之前的无数长辈都是在暗地里对这些提出质疑的。开始的时候，而且也是特别偶然的情况，他们联想到几本书，特别清晰，那些书籍属于自传体系列，被艾默里称为"求索"小说。这些"求索"小说中的主人公，在他们人生道路刚刚开始的时候，就用最精良的武器武装自己，公然表露出来要依照一般的方法运用这些武器，来尽可能不假思索地、自私地鼓舞这些武器的拥有者，不过这些"求索"书籍的主人公发现这些武器可能有更为高尚的用途。这一类的书籍有《别无他神》[1]、《凶险街道街道》[2]、《高尚的研究》[3]，其中的第三本小说是最吸引伯恩·贺拉狄的，读完这第三本小说后，他很想知道沉浸在担当年级职务的风光中并且可以展望大道俱乐部里耍手腕的独裁者，最终会有多大的价值，这是他在高年级刚刚开始时心中就有的一个疑团。伯恩的人生道路显然是通过精英分子的渠道找到的。艾默里认识伯恩，是通过凯里的关系，他偶尔会与他有些忽冷忽热的交往，但是他们之间的友谊真正开始是在高年级的元月。

　　一个下着淅淅沥沥的小雨的黄昏，汤姆带着得意的神情走进宿舍，问道："听

---

[1]. 是由英国神甫、作家罗伯特·本森（Robert Hugh Benson,1871—1914）撰写的长篇小说，参看第50页注。
[2]. 是由苏格兰小说家康普顿·麦肯齐(Compton Mackenzie,1883—1972)撰写的长篇小说。
[3]. 是由英国作家威尔斯撰写的长篇小说。

说最新的消息了没？"而往往他们侃侃而谈有了影响之后才会露出那样的表情。

"没啊，难道是有人考试不及格退学了？还是又有一条船沉没了呢？"

"事情的糟糕程度远大于这些，因为大约有三分之一的低年级同学打算退出俱乐部了。"

"啊？"

"这是真的！"

"怎么会这样！"

"比如改革的精神以及类似的东西嘛。策划者是伯恩·贺拉狄。今晚俱乐部的主席都要开会，看这一现象能否被他们联手制止。"

"唉，这样做算怎么回事啊？"

"嗯，说什么普林斯顿的民主空气都被俱乐部损害了；成本特别高；社交界线被划分，浪费时间。有时可以在失望的二年级同学中听到，还是平常的那些说法。例如伍德认为应该解散所有的俱乐部，类似这些等等。"

"但是，真的是这样吗？"

"绝对的，我认为这个现象会扩张开来。"

"哎呦，你把详细情况给我讲一下。"

于是汤姆开始讲道："嗯，这个想法似乎是几个人不约而同地产生的。我与伯恩刚刚就在谈这个问题，他认为这个结论是合乎逻辑的，而且这样的结论必然是一个具有聪明才智的人，在对社交制度进行深入思考之后得出的。他们会召开一个'集体讨论会'，有人在会上提出了解散俱乐部的想法，接着大家听到之后会十分欢跃，这几乎是人人都有的想法，于是导火线出现，事件便爆发了。"

"棒极了！我相信形势会特别有趣的。礼帽和礼服俱乐部有什么样的反应呢？"

"肯定是乱极了。大家全都郑重其事地坐下来，互相争论、吵架、谩骂，变得十分疯狂和情绪化，蛮不讲理。任何一个俱乐部都是如此我全都走了一遍。看到他们不停地提问一名激进分子。"

"那激进分子的表现如何？"

"嗯，还好。伯恩的确是一个能言巧辩的家伙，而且态度十分诚恳，你肯定说不过他。道理我们都明白，我们觉得阻止人们退出俱乐部有着非常重大的意义，可他认为他的意义更加重大，那就是退出俱乐部。我认为同他进行辩论真是吃力不讨好，最终我十分英明地保持中立的立场。而事实上，我觉得伯恩一度认为我已经被他争取过去，说服我变换了立场。"

"你说大约有三分之一的低年级学生打算退出了？"

"说得准确些应该是有四分之一吧。"

"上帝啊，谁会想到变成这个样子！"

伴随着一阵猛烈的敲门声，伯恩走了进来。

"你好，艾默里——你好，汤姆。"

艾默里站了起来

"晚上好，伯恩。你不介意我走得稍微匆忙了些吧，我要去伦威克酒吧。"

伯恩立刻转身和他说道：

"你应该知道我要和汤姆说的话，和私人的事情毫不相关。我希望你留下来。"

"我十分愿意。"艾默里再次坐下来，看到伯恩在一张桌子上坐下来，然后立刻与汤姆辩论了起来。他仔细地注视着这个革命者，比任何时候都要留心。伯恩有着大下巴，浓眉，诚实灰色的眼睛和凯里的一样，眼睛中透露着机灵，他留给人的第一印象是十分大度和有安全感，特别明显的是很倔强，但是不执拗。在听他讨论了五分钟后，艾默里认识到他的强烈热情中没有丝毫的浅薄。

艾默里后来意识到，他对亨伯德的敬佩之情与他从伯恩·贺拉狄身上感觉出来的坚强有力是截然不同的。这次他完全是始丁自己内心的关注，与以往最初他所认为的非常优秀的人相比，情况完全不同，一开始，他是被他们身上的个性特点所吸引，而那种他非常崇拜的即刻产生个性吸引力的，他没有在伯恩的身上发现。但就在那天晚上，他被伯恩严肃认真的态度和诚挚的热情深深打动了，以往的他总会把认真与无药可救的愚蠢联系在一起，而现在这种诚挚的热情却触动了他麻木已久的心弦。伯恩的潜意识中希望自己可以登上陆地——现在差不多是时候出现这片陆地了。汤姆和艾默里以及亚历克已经身处尴尬之中，由于汤姆和亚历克整天在各种委员会里乱忙，艾默里整天得过且过，混日子，从未有过任何新奇的经历，只是分析学校、当代特性及类似这些问题，他们在一起用餐时无数次地讨论这些问题，不计其数。

那天晚上，就俱乐部的问题，他们一直讨论到半夜十二点，伯恩的观点基本上获得了大家的认可。这个问题对于同一宿舍的人来讲，同两年前一样，是极为重要的，而且伯恩提出来的关于社交制度的异议思路，同他们所想的每个方面都十分契合。因此他们不做任何辩论，只是提出问题，同时也羡慕这个有着如此清醒头脑的人，能够站出来，挑战一切传统。

随后艾默里开始提及另一话题，他发现伯恩此时也在想其他事情。对经济学也同样感兴趣的他，正在向一个社会主义者转变。反战主义活跃在他的思想深处，他非常喜欢读《民众》杂志[1]和列夫·托尔斯泰的作品。

"讨论一下关于宗教的问题如何？"

"那个我不了解。很多东西我都很模糊——我开始读书还是因为我刚刚发现自己也是有思想的。"

"读哪类书？"

"任何书都读。当然，也会有目的地阅读，不过那些书都是为了我能更好地思考问题。我目前读的是四福音书[2]和《论形形色色的宗教经验》[3]。"

"你这样做的动力是什么？"

"我认为是威尔斯、托尔斯泰还有爱德华·卡宾特[4]。我阅读他们的著作——其中几个方面，已经有一年多了，通常会去读那些具有实质性意义的内容。"

"诗歌部分呢？"

"哦，说实话，我不读他们眼中的诗歌，也可以这样说，我不读你们读的那种诗歌——当然，你们两个写诗，看待事物的角度是不一样的。吸引我的是惠特曼[5]的诗。"

"惠特曼？"

"对的，他可以作为一种明确意义上的道德影响力。"

---

1. 《民众》杂志是美国一九一一年至一九一七年出版的社会主义进步刊物，撰稿人是报道十月革命《震撼世界十日》（1917）的作者、记者、诗人约翰·里德（John Reed, 1887—1920）等进步人士。
2. 载《圣经·新约》。
3. 即《论形形色色的宗教经验：人性之研究》（1902），是由美国实用主义哲学家、机能心理学家威廉·詹姆斯（Willian James, 1842—1910）所撰写的。
4. 爱德华·卡宾特（Edward Carpenter, 1844—1929），英国十九世纪末二十世纪初著名人士，诗人、作家、哲学家，对威费边社、工党的创建起了很大作用。
5. 惠特曼与爱德华·卡宾特是很好的朋友。

"唉，我非常惭愧，对于惠特曼我一点儿也不了解。汤姆，你了解吗？"

汤姆羞涩地点点头。

伯恩接着说道："当然了，你可以略去不读那些乏味的诗，但我指的是他的整个诗歌。他像托尔斯泰一样非常了不起，他们能够正确地对待问题。从某一方面来说，他们主张的观点多多少少会有一样的，尽管他们不属于一个类型。"

艾默里承认道："伯恩，我被你难倒了，我的确读过他的《安娜·卡列尼娜》和《克鲁采奏鸣曲》[1]，但是我认为他的作品大多都是俄文原文。"

伯恩充满热情地说道："他属于几百年才出现一个的那种最伟大的人，他的画像你们见过吗？是一个一头乱蓬蓬的头发和有着满脸胡子的老人？"

他们无所不谈，话题从生物学谈到有组织的宗教，一直谈到凌晨三点钟。当艾默里哆哆嗦嗦地爬上床的时候，他脑袋中思考了很多，并且感觉非常惊讶，认为他完全有可能走的一条路被另外一个人找到了。伯恩·贺拉狄很明显走在成长的路上——一直以来艾默里认为自己也在成长中，当他面临人生路上所遇到的事物时，也曾深深地陷入愤世嫉俗的思想中去，人的不可完善性他也思考过，萧伯纳和切斯特顿[2]的很多作品他都读了，进而他避免了思想堕落——在过去的一年半里，他自己的全部思想过程突然间好像变得腐败而徒劳了——他的自我实现如此微不足道……今年春天的那件事情如同一个阴郁的背景一般衬托着，使他的每个夜晚都充满了骇人的氛围，以至于他无法进行祈祷。尽管他并不是一名天主教徒，但他唯一模糊不清的道德标准却是天主教那浮华、老一套、似是而非的信仰，而切特斯顿就是

这个信仰的先知，像于斯曼和布尔热[3]这样改邪归正的文学浪荡子是它的捧场者们，崇尚十三世纪大教堂的拉尔夫·亚当斯·克拉姆[4]是它的美国倡导者——是艾默里认为方便并且现有的天主教信仰，没有神甫和圣礼，也没有献祭。

他难以入睡，于是打开台灯，拿下来《克莱采鸣奏曲》，认真寻找令伯恩如此充满热情的真正原因。突然间他发现想要做个像伯恩这样的人比想要做聪

---

1. 《克鲁采奏鸣曲》（1889），是托尔斯泰的所写的一部中篇小说。
2. 二十世纪英国最有影响的作家之一——切斯特顿（G.K Chesterton, 1874—1936），另见第 21 页注。
3. 布尔热（Paul Bourget, 1852—1935）是法国的小说家、批评家。
4. 克拉姆（Ralph Adams Cram,1863—1942），美国小说家、建筑师，推崇哥特式建筑。

明的人的愿望,更加实在和真切了。然而他感慨了……虽然话是这么说,但他也许会有其他缺陷[1]。

他回忆起两年前,那时候的伯恩是一个完全淹没在哥哥的个性下,来去匆匆、神经质的一年级学生。然后他想到一件发生在二年级时候的事情,当时人们猜测是伯恩扮演了一个主要角色。

那时很多人都听到,从枢纽站乘出租车来的系主任贺里斯特和司机吵得特别厉害。"干脆买一辆出租车得了。"在争吵的过程中,系主任说了这样一句话。他在讲完后,付了钱便扬长而去,但第二天,他看到一辆出租车真的就停在他以前放桌子的地方,车上面的牌子上写着"系主任贺里斯特私有财产。账款付清"。两个内行的修理工被系主任叫来拆卸车子,用了半天的时间才把车子拆卸成一个个部件搬走。可见若是领导有方,二年级学生的幽默能够释放出惊人的能量。

依旧是在那年秋天,伯恩再次在校园里引起轰动。有一个校际舞会陪舞者,名字叫做菲莉斯·斯泰尔斯,没有收到观看哈佛—普林斯顿的球赛年度邀请。

在几个星期前她被杰斯·菲伦比带去观看了一场小型比赛,并且把伯恩叫来接待——却因此改变了伯恩讨厌女人的观念。

伯恩不过是搭讪而已,于是想都没想,便问道"你还去看哈佛那场球赛吗"?

菲莉斯迅速地回答道:"你邀请我就来。"

伯恩略显无力地回答说:"当然会邀请你。"他并不了解菲莉斯有怎样的计谋,以为只是随便说说而已。但是一个小时还没到,他就发现自己无法脱身了。菲莉斯盯上了他,并把他的话当真了,还告诉他自己所乘火车的班次,这令他郁闷极了。他其实非常想自己一个人去观看比赛,除了讨厌菲莉斯以外,他还想款待自己几个哈佛的朋友。

他对来他宿舍取笑他的几个人说道:"让她走着瞧吧,这将是她最后一次纠缠天真的年轻人带她看比赛了"。

"不过,伯恩——你怎么想的?不想带她看比赛,为什么还邀请她?"

"伯恩,你自己知道,问题的症结所在是——其实你在暗恋她。"

"伯恩,你有什么打算?你准备如何应对菲莉斯?"

但伯恩只是在那里摇头,好像低声说着这样一句话:"让她走着瞧吧,让

---

1. 原文是"clay feet(泥足)",比喻偶像身上、性格上隐藏的缺点和致命弱点。语出《圣经·旧约·但以理书》第二章第三十一节。另见詹姆斯·乔伊斯:《尤里西斯》第十六章。

她走着瞧吧！"类似这样的具有威胁性的话。

菲莉斯有二十五岁了，她心情愉悦，兴致勃勃地下了火车。却在月台上看到令她非常不开心的一幕。她看到伯恩和斯罗恩全身上下的穿着就像是学校招贴画上的人一般。他们穿着一套耀眼夺目的服装，肩膀被垫得很高，大裤子上宽下窄。潇洒的大学礼帽戴在头上，鲜艳的橘红色与黑色相间的饰带挂在紧扣的胸前，火红的橘红色领带就戴在赛璐珞假领上。橘红的字母"P"被绣在他们的黑色臂章上，普林斯顿的锦旗挂在手杖上，他们同一色调的短袜和露出一角的手帕更是有了好上加好的效果。一只很大的雄猫被涂上颜料，象征着一只老虎，被拴在了一根当啷作响的链条上。

他们已经吸引了月台上拥挤的人群中很大一部分人的目光，有的人很害怕，有的人在喧闹。菲莉斯则是吃惊极了，她惊讶地走近他们，只见两人鞠躬，高喊着学校的口号，声音嘹亮、深沉，特别有新意的是在喊声最后加上了"菲莉斯"的名字。在他们高声呼喊的欢迎和热情中，菲莉斯进入校园，一百多个从村子来的顽童跟在他们身后——几百个校友和参观者，他们中几乎没人知道这是一场闹剧，而在那里闷笑，心里暗自思忖着伯恩和斯罗恩这两个校队的花花公子，竟然带他们的女朋友来大学体验生活了。

在这两个人的陪同下，菲莉斯从哈佛和普林斯顿两个看台走过去，看到坐在看台上十多个她以前的追随者，心情可想而知了。她尝试着走得靠前些，一会儿又靠后些，但都是徒劳的。他们紧跟在她身旁，毫无疑问人家一看便知道她同谁在一起。他们大声呼喊着，讨论着在橄榄队里的朋友，后来她几乎听到身边的朋友在低声说：

"菲莉斯·斯泰尔斯跟在这两个怪人身后，心里该多难受。"

这便是伯恩，有着生机勃勃的幽默，但他的严肃认真是别人无法改变的，他要逐步加以引导的充沛精力在此基础上迸发而出……

就这样，时光一天天流逝，三月转眼间就到来了，艾默里寻找的隐秘的致命缺陷依旧没出现。最后，大概有一百名低年级同学和高年级同学由于满腔的怒愤退出了俱乐部。在极其无奈的情况下，俱乐部把矛头指向了伯恩，使出了最后的杀手锏——嘲弄伯恩。基本上认识伯恩的人都很喜欢他——但他所主张的（尽管他所主张的越来越多）遭遇到很多阻碍。如果是一个性格比他懦弱的人面对这些阻碍，肯定已经垮了。

119

一天艾默里问道:"你难道不怕失去威信吗?"他们已经形成习惯,每个月都要互相走访几次。

"当然了,而且有威信又如何?"

"有人说,你的确是一个政治家,见解如此独到。"

他大声笑起来。

"今天弗雷德·斯罗恩也是这样和我说的。我认为自己对于这个称呼是当之无愧的。"

关于生理属性对于一个人性格的影响问题,一直以来是艾默里最为关注的话题,一天下午他们讨论起来。伯恩就这个问题在生物学上的意义说道:

"身体的健康状况当然很重要——一个身体健康的人行善的机会是身体虚弱的人的两倍。"

"你的说法我不认同——'强身派基督教'是我所不认同的。"

"我坚信——我认为耶稣拥有强壮的体力。"

艾默里反对说:"不对,不对。耶稣活得太辛苦了,我认为他的身体已经不行了,在他要死去的时候——那些圣徒们的身体大都不太好。"

"他们中有一半人身体不好。"

"好,即使如此,我始终不认为健康情况和行善有关系;当然如果一个伟大的圣徒可以承受极度的疲劳,也是非常有意义的。但是那些深得人心的圣徒们,勉强打起精神来忙碌奔走,进行传道,嘴里还宣讲着只有强身健体才可以拯救世界,那样的风尚,我无法认同。"

艾默里迫不及待地问道:"外表?"

"是的。"

艾默里点头说道:"我和汤姆也是这样认为的,我们把过去十年的毕业生刊全部翻阅了一遍,高年级学生会的照片都看过了。我知道你并不看重这个具有威严的机构,但是从一些方面来说,它的确代表了成功。嗯,在这里约有百分之三十五的人是白皮肤金发碧眼的人,的确是真实的浅色——但在每一届高年级学生会中有三分之二是浅色的。请记得,这十年的照片我们都研究过了。可以这样说,有着浅色头发的高年级学生,每十五个人中会有一个人进入高年级学生会;在有着深色头发的高年级学生中,每五十个人中才会有一个人进入高年级学生会。"

伯恩十分认同，说道："的确如此。一般来说，有着浅色头发的人的确高人一等。我曾经就发色的问题研究过美国总统，发现浅色头发的人占一半以上——之后再探讨下人种中数量占优势的深色头发和浅黑色皮肤的人。"

艾默里说道："其实人们会下意识地承认这个观点，因为你常常可以看到，人们大多会认为说话比较多的是浅色头发的人。我们会把一个白皮肤金发碧眼但是不怎么讲话的姑娘，叫作'玩偶'；一个男人如果被看作是傻子，大多是由于他头发是浅色的，并且又沉默寡言。其实'黑皮肤又沉默寡言的人'和没脑子'有着黑色的头发和皮肤又懒惰的人'在这个世界上到处都是，但不知是什么原因，没有人说过他们的话少。"

"毫无疑问，一张优秀的脸就是嘴巴大、下巴宽、鼻子也大。"

艾默里是完全赞同传统的五官特征的，说道："我不能确定。"

这时伯恩从书桌抽屉里拿出来一沓照片，说道："那你看这些。"照片全是托尔斯泰，惠特曼，卡宾特等名人，都有着一脸浓密的胡子和一头浓密的头发。

"好看不？"

艾默里基于礼貌问题，把照片拿来一张张看，之后却把照片扔在一旁，大笑起来。

"伯恩，我认为他们好像是老人院的老人，他们是我见过的人中模样最为丑陋的了。"

伯恩颇为责备地说道："怎么可能，艾默里，你仔细看看爱默生的额头，看看托尔斯泰的眼睛。"

艾默里则摇摇头。

"不对！不对！你想说什么就说什么吧，你可以说他们仪表堂堂——但在我眼中，他们的确是难看的。"

伯恩丝毫不甘示弱，一边轻轻抚摸着那宽大的额头，一边把照片收好放进抽屉里。

他的爱好之一是在夜晚出去散步，于是一天晚上艾默里被他邀请去散步。

艾默里拒绝道："我不喜欢黑暗，而且也没有这样的习惯——除了在我思想沸腾很有想法的时候，但目前我真的十分厌恶去散步——在这件事情上我真是傻到家了。"

"不可能，你了解的。"

"完全可能啊。"

伯恩提出自己的想法："我们向东边走吧，穿过林中的一条条小路。"

艾默里十分勉强地说道："我不认为你说得有多好，不过我们还是走吧。"

他俩从一开始便走得很快，没一会儿就把普林斯顿甩在身后了，只剩下白点的东西。他们十分激烈地讨论着，一个小时的时间里，依旧激情不减。

伯恩特别认真地说："任何一个富有想象力的人都会感到害怕的，我以前害怕的事情就包括夜间出来散步。现在我告诉你，我去哪里都不会害怕的原因是什么。"

艾默里显得有些迫切了，催促他："快接着往下说。"他们向林子的方向大步走去。只要一讲到这个话题，伯恩便越来越有兴致了，语气开始变得紧张而充满热情。

"三个月以前，我常常在夜里独自一人来到这里。嗯，我习惯走到交叉路口时便停下来，就是我们刚刚走过的那个路口。前面的林子就和现在一样影影绰绰，眼睛里看到的都是树的影子，听到的都是狗的叫声，却听不到有人讲话的声音。当然，我认为林子里总会有些恐怖的东西，是不是就和你现在的感受一样呢？"

"嗯，是的。"艾默里并没有否认。

"之后我开始分析自己的这种心理反应——恐怖与黑暗被我顽固地联系到了一起——接着我把想象与黑暗联系起来，代替了恐怖，开始留意着想象——我把自己想象成一只流浪狗、一个逃犯，或者想象成一个鬼走在林中。之后心理似乎就正常了——就是使自己完全换了个角度看待问题，在别人的角度上，似乎一切又恢复正常了。我知道，假如我的确就是流浪狗、是逃犯、是鬼，那么就如同他不会伤害我一样，我也不会去伤害伯恩·贺拉狄。之后，我突然想到我的怀表。我觉得我最好还是把表放回宿舍，然后再回到林子里来。不，我决定了，即使丢失一块怀表，我也不会返回去的。这样可能更加睿智些——于是我便走在林子里了——不仅仅是走在林中，而是穿梭在树木中，最后便不再恐惧了——有一晚我坐在林中休息，竟然在林中睡着了。从那以后，我知道自己再也不害怕黑暗了。"

艾默里小声说道："天哪，如果是我，肯定做不到的。我会在半路便返回去，我可能会在一辆汽车第一次开过去以后，车灯消失了，一切变得更加黑暗时就进去。"

一段时间的沉默之后,伯恩说道:"嗯,我们已经走完林子的一半了,往回走吧。"

在回去的路上,他发起了一场关于意志的讨论。

他下定结论说:"这肯定是问题的全部了,也是善和恶的唯一区分线。既过着堕落的生活又意志薄弱的人,我至今尚未见过。"

"那该怎么解释罪大恶极的罪犯呢?"

"他们大多是精神不正常的人,否则就是意志薄弱的人。所谓的意志坚强又精神正常的罪犯是不存在的。"

"伯恩,你的观点我完全不赞同;那你认为超人是什么样子的呢?"

"嗯?"

"我认为他不仅是邪恶的,同时也是坚强并且精神正常的。"

"虽然我从未见过,但我坚信如果他不是一个傻子,就是一个精神失常的人。"

"我认为你错了,因为我遇见过他无数次,他非但不傻,而且精神也正常。"

"我不认为我错了——除非监禁那些精神失常的人,否则我不相信监禁。"

艾默里不能同意这一观点。他认为意志坚强的罪犯在生活中和历史上是很多见的,他们有着精明的头脑,但往往自欺欺人;无论在政治和商界,还是在老政治家、国王、将军中都是可以被人们找到的。但伯恩不能认同这个观点,于是他们意见出现分歧,开始分道扬镳。

伯恩脱离他周围的世界,开始走得越来越远。他把高年级学生会的副主席职务辞掉了。阅读和散步几乎成了他唯一的爱好。他不会缺席任何一堂研究生的哲学和生物学课程,自愿去学习,似乎在等待老师提出决不会涉及的问题,专注的目光中略显悲伤。偶尔他在座位上扭动身子被艾默里看到了,又会突然喜形于色他内心十分渴望与人交流、争辩。

在路上行走时他开始变得心不在焉,甚至被人说成势力,但是艾默里了解他肯定不是这样的人,一次艾默里看见他在四英尺之外的地方,但他正在思考着千里之外的事情,根本没有看到艾默里,只见他神情愉悦,不着边际的使他都快喘不过气来了。伯恩就好像在攀登山峰,而且那山峰是其他人永远也找不到踏脚点的高峰。

艾默里对汤姆说道:"我跟你说,我遇见的同龄人中,他是第一个智力在我之上的人,这点我承认。"

"你现在说的话太不合时宜了——在人们眼中他从一开始就是一个奇怪的人。"

"人们是不能理解他的——你在同他交流时,自己心里肯定也是这样认为的——哦,天哪,汤姆,过去的你常常会站出来反对'人们'。现在你成功了,便开始因循守旧了。"

汤姆听完特别生气。

"难道他做的事情特别神圣吗?"

"不,他并不是你认为的那种人。他从来没有去过费城社[1],那一套东西他压根不信。他很随性,想喝酒就喝酒;公共游泳池以及一句及时的好话便可以洗刷世间的冤屈,这些他从来不相信。"

"毫无疑问,他得罪某些人了。"

"最近你们谈过没?"

"没。"

"那你根本不了解他。"

虽然争论并没有结果,但是对于伯恩在校园里情绪的巨大变化,艾默里已经更加明白地觉察到了。

一天晚上艾默里开始对汤姆说自己的想法,这时他们两人在这个问题上的态度已经稍微缓解了一些。他说道:"好奇怪,很明显强烈反对伯恩的激烈做法的人都是法利赛人级别的——我是指在学校里最有教养的人——比如你和菲伦比这样的报纸编辑,年轻的教授……无知的运动员像朗格达克那样的认为他变得越来越古怪了,他们会说'伯恩老弟脑子里全是稀奇古怪的念头,'但他们说一次之后便不再提起,——法利赛人级别的人——哎,他始终被他们无情地嘲讽着。"

第二天上午下课后,碰到伯恩在麦克科什小路上匆忙走着。

"头,你要去哪?"

他朝艾默里挥挥手中那份上午出版的《普林斯顿人报》,"去《普林斯顿人报》

---

1. 费城社(the Philadelphian Society),基督教青年会的大学分支,基督教团体是被普林斯顿大学一小群学生于一八二五年创建的。

办公室找菲伦比，他写的社论。"

"要严加批判他吗？"

"并非如此——我被他整糊涂了。如果不是我看错他了，那么就是他在一夜间成为这个世界上最恶劣的激进分子了。"

伯恩匆忙离去，几天过后，艾默里听说了下面他与人的对话。伯恩进入编辑办公室，异常兴奋地铺开报纸。

"嗨，杰西。"

"嗨，萨瓦纳洛拉[1]。"

"你的社论我刚刚拜读了。"

"好家伙——我不知道你竟然还会如此屈尊俯就。"

"杰西，你吓着我了。"

"什么情况？"

"你做的事情如此漠视宗教，你难道就不怕全体教职员都来骂你吗？"

"你说什么？"

"今天上午的事情。"

"究竟是——这是一篇具有指导性的社论。"

"不错，但是那语录——"

杰西直接站起来。

"你指的是什么语录？"

"就是那句'不拥护我的人就是反对我。'"

"嗯，对呀，那怎么了？"

虽然杰西感到十分困惑，但是并不吃惊。

"好，我找下你写的。"于是伯恩把报纸摊开，读道："'正如那位先生所说，不拥护我的人就是反对我。众所周知，他只会作粗枝大叶的区分和幼稚的概述。'"

菲伦比略显忧愁："怎么了？这难道不是奥立弗·克伦威尔说的吗？或者是华盛顿说的？还是哪位圣徒说的？天，我竟然忘记是谁说的了？"

伯恩大笑起来。

"哈哈，杰西你太可爱太善良啦。"

---

1. 萨瓦纳洛拉（Savonarola,1452—1498），意大利政治、宗教改革家，曾领导佛罗伦萨人民起义（1494），后教皇阴谋把他推翻，判火刑处死。

"老天,到底是谁说的呢?"

伯恩停下来,不再大笑,他说:"是耶稣的话被使徒马太引用了[1]。"

杰西大声说道:"天哪!"倒在了身后的废纸篓上。

艾默里作了一首诗

时光流逝,转眼间几个星期过去了。艾默里为了让车子像棒棒糖那样的诱惑力穿透他的性情,要找到一辆崭新的鲜绿色公共汽车,于是偶尔会去纽约闲逛。一天他走进一家剧院,观看一个专业剧团表演的保留剧目,剧名略感熟悉。当表演刚刚开始的时候,一个小姑娘走近视线中,当时他正在漫不经心地观看着。他听到了几句话:何时——?何处——?这几句话开启了他朦胧的记忆之门。

之后,他似乎听到身边有个轻柔而响亮的声音在悄悄诉说:"哦,我的确是个可怜的小傻瓜;如果我做错了什么,一定要告诉我。"

他的心中瞬间有了答案,他立刻想到了伊莎贝尔,心情异常兴奋。

他开始在剧院说明书的空白处奋笔疾书:

"在这隐约的黑暗中,我再次观赏,
在那里,帷幕拉起,岁月也随之流逝;
两年,整整两年——我们有过共鸣,
美好的结局并没有留下烦恼
来打扰我们安宁的心境;我迷恋
你那双充满期望、欢喜、圆睁的眼睛,
嫣然一笑百媚生而台上演的戏
好似岸边的涟漪不易触动我的心弦。

夜晚在哈欠连连、惊叹不已中消失,
我独自观赏……吵吵闹闹必将会
搅乱尚有魅力的仅有场景;
你哭泣了一会儿,我为你心伤未消停,
在此时!只见有男子把头频频摇动,
怀中女子早已倒下不省人事。"

---

[1] 参考《圣经·新约·马太福音》第十二章第三十节以及《路加福音》第十一章第二十三节。

第四章　顾影自怜的美少年

依然平静

亚历克说道："鬼的反应都很慢，它们都是非常愚蠢的。而且鬼的意图总会被我猜透。"

汤姆问道："你是如何猜的？"

"这个嘛，是分场合的。比如在卧室，如果想在卧室不被找到，那你必须要小心翼翼。"

艾默里特别好奇地问道："你快接着讲，如果你感觉鬼在你的卧室中——那你夜晚回家后会做什么？"

亚历克暗自怀着敬畏之心回答说："把一根大约扫帚把那么长的棍子拿在手中，首先要打扫一遍房间——你要闭上眼睛冲进书房把灯全部打开，才可以打扫卫生——之后走进小房间，在门口挥三四下棍子。如果没事，你才能进去看看。记得，一定，一定要拿棍子用力挥几下——一定不要没挥棍子就进去！"

"当然了，这种手法是古代的凯尔特人的。"汤姆说得一本正经。

"对——但他们常常会先祈祷。无论怎样，清理小房间和每扇门的背后用这种方法——"

"还有床，"艾默里提醒道。

亚历克恐惧地说道："不行！艾默里，这样做不对——床应该用不同的手法来对待——先不说床的问题，因为你比较在意说理——如果房间里有鬼，它也只能待三分之一天的时间，而且大部分时间它都会藏在床底下。"

"哎——"艾默里刚刚想说什么。

被亚历克举手制止了。

"当然你不会去看。你在房间中间站着，在鬼反应之前，你就快速扑向床那里——谨记不要离床太近了；对于鬼来说你身上最脆弱的地方就是你的脚踝——只要上了床，你便安全了；即使鬼可能一直待在床底下，你也没必要担忧；但如果你还是害怕，那就把自己蒙在被子里。"

"汤姆，这听起来似乎很有趣。"

亚历克听后十分得意，说道："是么？这些办法都是我——新世界的奥利弗·洛奇爵士[1]——想的。"

---

1. 奥利弗·洛奇爵士（Sir Oliver Joseph Lodge，1851—1940），英国物理学家、作家，无线电报前驱，还热爱灵魂研究。

对于大学生活，艾默里再次燃起热爱之情。再次回来的是那种毅然决然、径直朝前迈进的意识；骚动的青春，有几片新的羽毛在抖动。

甚至他已经把足够的剩余能量储存好了，打算把新的姿态摆出来。

有一天亚历克问道："艾默里，你这是什么意思，怎么总是摆出来一副'正在发呆'的样子？"看到艾默里依旧盯着书看，假装在发呆，亚历克接着说道："哎，你千万不要像伯恩一样在我面前装神秘。"

艾默里满脸无辜地抬起头来。

"什么？"

亚历克学他说道："什么？你准备从这本书读出狂想吗？——把书给我看看。"

他一下子把书拿来，嘲弄地看起来。

艾默里稍显尴尬地问道："怎么了？"

亚历克读出声音来："啊，我的天呀！是《圣特雷萨传》[1]。"

"哎，亚历克。"

"什么？"

"招惹你了吗？"

"你说什么招惹我了？"

"我是否发呆招惹你了么？"

"哦，没——你当然没有惹到我。"

"那就好，不要把别人的好事破坏了。假如我喜欢随处和人家说我自己是个天才，那么就随我说去吧。"

亚历克笑着说道："现在你出名了，因为行为怪异。如果这就是你想要表达的。"

最终艾默里取得了胜利，只有他们两个人留在房间里，亚历克同意了，相信他如果有短暂的时间休息，在其他人面前的表现也肯定只是装下样子；于是对于那些最怪的人、想法极端的研究生、头脑中全是有关上帝和政府的奇怪理论的导师，他全都会设宴款待，并为此付出了很大的代价，这一切都是为了"出风头"。他的行为使那些傲慢的小屋俱乐部的人感到疑惑并且异常惊讶。

---

1. 圣特雷萨（St Terss of Avila,1515—1582），西班牙天主教修女，神秘主义者，作家。她的自传是《圣特雷萨传》。

第四章　顾影自怜的美少年

二月在灿烂的阳光照耀下，也没有那么寒冷了，三月在斗转星移中很快到来了。有几次艾默里都外出同达西大人一起度周末，一次伯恩也被艾默里带去了，效果相当显著，艾默里十分愉悦，十分骄傲，那是因为他们彼此之间都要表现出愉悦和骄傲。有几次他都被达西大人带去见桑顿·汉莫克，还有一两次他被带到一个经常访问罗马的美国人——劳伦斯太太——家中拜访，一见面他便喜欢上了劳伦斯太太。

之后的一天，他收到了一封来自达西大人的加了附言的信，附言写得很有意思：

"你知道吗？克拉拉·佩奇，你的远方表姐，现在在费城过着很辛苦的日子，她的配偶在半年前去世了，你不知道吧？我知道你肯定没见过她，但我盼望你可以去看看她，算是帮我一个忙。她和你年龄相仿，是一个非常出色的女人。"

艾默里叹了一口气，决定帮一次忙，去走一趟。……

克拉拉

她来自遥远的古时候……艾默里和克拉拉根本就不般配，克拉拉的头发是金色的卷发，没有谁是可以和她相般配的。就算把女孩子的有关美德的冗词赘句抛之脑后，她的赞誉也要比那些寻找丈夫的人冗长的道德准则高。

伤心的情愫轻轻地弥漫在她的周围，艾默里来费城看望她的时候，他感觉到她那冷若寒霜的蓝眼睛里表现出来的全是开心的神情，她必须面对的真相在她的内心深处形成了一股潜伏的势力，一个现实主义的姿态。她一个人孤苦无依地在这个世界上，身边跟着年纪还很小的两个孩子，钱不多。最惨的是，好友反而有不少。某一年的冬天他去费城看望她的时候，她正在举办晚会来款待一屋子的男人，但是他非常清楚她家里连一个仆人都没有，她仅仅是叫了一个黑人女孩照顾楼上的小孩。他瞧见城中一个臭名昭著的浪荡子，一个常常喝得大醉、名声狼藉的人，在她的对面坐着，畅谈着女子寄宿学校，神情激动，还装出一副与世无争的模样。克拉拉的心情改变得那么迅速！在客厅那几乎没有什么感情可言的一堆人当中，她说话依旧可以用天花乱坠、乃至谈笑自若来形容。

按照他对情况的猜想，他认为这个女人现在已是身无分文。他觉得人们会对他说方舟街九二一号是一条满目荒凉的街巷，到处都是歪歪斜斜的小房子，他抱着这样的想法来到了费城。等到了这里，才发现情形并不是他所想的那般，这使得他稍微有点消沉。那是一座年代很久远的房子，长期以来这所房子的所有权掌握在她的丈夫手中。因为一个年纪很大的姑妈的阻挠，房子没有被卖出去，她还将十年来的税款都交给了一名律师，接着转身离开，独自一人去了檀香山，留下了房子的供暖系统的问题让克拉拉自己一个人烦恼。所以，开门欢迎他的并不是一个头发乱糟糟的女人，怀里抱着一个由于饥饿而哭泣的小孩，脸上带着仿若阿米莉娅[1]一样伤心的表情。反过来说，从他受到的招待来看，艾默里全然能够将她的生活看作是丰衣足食的。

和她的沉着冷静构成明显对比的，是她那沉稳的活力和轻快的诙谐——有时候她会在这样的精神当中寻求安慰。她能够做最无聊的事情（虽然她非常懂事，从不会去做编织和刺绣这样的"针线活"，让自己变得罗里吧嗦），但是把事情做完之后，她会立马将一本书拿在手上，使得她的思想得以飞翔，就和没有特定形状的云朵一样，随风起伏。她性格当中最深刻的是她释放到周围的金色光芒。就像将浪漫和怜惜释放到一团团坐在火炉边的安适的脸上的黑暗室里的一盆炉火，她也将她的光和影释放到她容身的房间的角角落落，直到她将那个年迈、沉重的叔叔改变成一个稀奇古怪、喜欢思考的魅力四射的人，将那个内向的电报投递员改变成一个蒲克式的促狭鬼[2]，有了别开生面的欢乐心情。刚开始的时候她的这种性格有些让艾默里气恼。他感觉自己拥有特有的性格就已然知足了，但她还要赋予他别的使人兴奋的特点，来适应现场仰慕者的兴趣。他感觉她就像一个文质彬彬却又坚定不移的舞台监督者，尝试着要让他对早已钻研了很长时间的角色，做一个彻底的改观。

克拉拉没休没止地讲着，她将那些微不足道的小事讲得周到细致，说那女帽上的别针，说那喝得神志不清的男人，还说她自己……人们总是在事情结束以后再将她说的故事讲一遍，但是无论怎么做都没有办法还原事情的始末。他们只是单纯地听着，然后不停地微笑，他们已经这样笑了很长时间了。在克拉拉的双眼中几乎看不出泪花，但是听她讲的那些人反而泪眼朦胧，对着她不住

---

1. 这是英国著名作家威廉·M·萨克雷（William Makepeace Thackeray,1811—1863）的小说《名利场》中的一个人物，阿米莉娅因为父亲破产，原来稳定的生活变得动荡起来，和他的浪荡子丈夫谋划，谎称丈夫在滑铁卢战役中牺牲，她独自带着孩子在父母家过着贫穷的生活。
2. 英国神话故事中机智、活泼的精灵，这里使用了梁实秋《莎士比亚全集·仲夏夜之梦》当中的翻译方法。

地笑。

有时候在求婚的人全都离开之后,艾默里还会在这里再留半个小时,他们吃完午饭后会再吃几片抹了酱的面包,喝一会儿茶,抑或是在晚上吃一些他们这里的"槭糖午饭食物"。

"你真的是太棒了,不是吗?"某天晚上六点钟的时候,艾默里在餐桌的中央坐着,显得有一些罗里吧嗦的。

"没什么特别出色的,"克拉拉回答说。她在餐具柜当中翻找着餐巾纸。"我就是一个很平凡,很普通的人。就是一颗心都放在孩子身上、其他的任何事都不在乎的人。"

"这样的话还是给别人讲吧,"艾默里的话语中带有一些讽刺意味。"你知道你十分优秀。"他就是问了她一句他也知道会使她难堪的话。这句话就是第一个招人厌的人告诉亚当的话。

"谈谈你自己吧。"她的回答肯定和亚当说的话一样。

"我自己没什么可说的。"

但是最后,亚当也许会把晚上在沙草地上蝗虫唧唧叫的时候的想法,都告诉那些令人厌恶的人,同时他一定会神采奕奕地说他和夏娃是多么的不同,但是心里却不清楚夏娃到底和他有着什么不一样……无论怎么讲,那天晚上克拉拉讲了许多有关她自己的事情。她从十六岁开始,就经受着苦难的生活,舒适的生活到了终点,她也被迫中途辍学。艾默里翻看着她私藏的书籍,发现了一本年代久远的破破烂烂的书,书被翻开的时候有一张泛黄的纸张从里面掉了出来,他很随意地把这张纸打开了。纸上是一首她在学校里写的诗,大意是阴沉沉的一天,修道院阴沉沉的一道墙,一阵风吹起了一个女孩的斗篷,而那女孩此时正坐在墙头思考着这多姿多彩的世界。通常而言,这样的感情会让他觉得枯燥,但是她把这首诗写得这样朴实无华,氛围描绘得那么沉稳,一幅关于克拉拉的画面在他的脑海当中不经意地出现,那是克拉拉在这样寒冷、阴森的一天,敏感的蓝眼睛注视着前方,想要目睹外面的花园里向她扑来的苦难。她能够写出这样的诗让他很羡慕。他是多么的希望自己也可以在那里亲眼看着她在墙头上坐着,和她叙说着闲话,抑或是对她讲一些肉麻的话,看着她在空中高高地坐着。他开始疯狂地妒忌着和克拉拉有关的一切事物:她的过去,她的小孩,包括那些男男女女,他们结伴而来,欣赏着她冷淡的善意,将他们心里的疲乏驱散，好像在看着使人聚精会神的喜剧演出。

"好像谁都不会引起你的厌恶，"他满不在乎地说着。

"也许这个世界上有一半的人会吧，"她认可道，"我觉得这已经是一个非常好的平均水平了，你认为呢？"说着她转过身去寻找布朗宁在这个方面的诗句。在交谈的间隙，她还停下来去查看章节并引用语录让他看，却也不会使人觉得讨厌，将人的注意力分散开，她是他所遇见的人当中唯一可以这样的一个人，她不停地翻找，抱着很高的热情，态度是那么端庄，这倒对他有着很大的吸引力，看着她的金发披散在书页上，紧皱着眉头，搜寻着她需要的诗句。

每个三月伊始的周末他都在费城度过，这早已成了他的习惯。但是当他在费城的时候，她的家中总是有其他人在，并且她好像并没有迫不及待地想要和他单独在一块，因为他碰到过很多这样的时候，只需要她一句话，他就会开开心心地将他待在那里的时间再加上半个小时。但是他慢慢地喜欢上了她，并且开始胡思乱想，预备娶她。虽然他的这个想法一直在他的心头盘旋，乃至就要一吐为快，但是他以后就会明白他的这个想法并没有在他的心里扎根。有一次他梦到他的梦想成真了，但是他被自己的一身冷汗惊醒了，只是因为在他梦里的克拉拉傻里傻气的，头发是亚麻色的，原来头发上的金色已经消失不见，彻彻底底地成为了另一个人，嘴里嘟囔着老旧的没有什么意义的一番话。不管怎么说她都是他碰到过的第一个出色的女人，是引起他兴趣的少数几个心地善良的人当中的一个。善良成为了她突出的优点。艾默里肯定地认为，对于很多善良的人来讲，善良要不变成了阻碍他们步伐的累赘，要不就是将善良曲解成表面意义上的和善，自然也包含一直存在的自视甚高和虚伪的人——（但艾默里从来没有把他们加入到被拯救了灵魂的人的行列里）。

圣塞西莉娅[1]

"在她灰蒙蒙的丝绒衣服之上，
在她美丽、松软的头发之下，
玫瑰的色彩在假装疼痛伤心，
红晕展开又消失美丽无限；
充斥在她与他之间的空气，

---

1. 圣塞西莉娅（St Cecilia,?—230?），一位罗马基督教女殉教者，是音乐主保圣人。

第四章　顾影自怜的美少年

是灯光和疲倦还有悲叹，
如此模模糊糊他毫无所觉……
闪电的愉快，玫瑰色泽繁杂。"

"你是喜欢我的吗？"

"那是自然。"克拉拉非常严肃地回答道。

"什么原因呢？"

"嗯，我们的性格特点有一些相同的地方。我们身上不经意间流露出的——换句话说就是本来就存在的东西。"

"你的意思是说我对自己不好了？"

克拉拉停顿了一下。

"呃，我说不明白。一个男人理所应当承受更多的苦难，但我生活在别人的保护之下。"

"啊，麻烦你，不要闪烁其词了，克拉拉。"艾默里将她的话打断了，"就只是谈一谈我吧，可以吗？"

"当然可以，我很开心这么做。"她的脸上并没有微笑的样子。

"那就太棒了。首先回答几个提问吧。我是不是自以为是，令人讨厌？"

"呃——不是的，你非常自大，如果留意到这种自大心理影响巨大的人们反而会认为非常有意思。"

"我知道了。"

"其实你内心深处是非常谦恭有礼的。如果你感觉你被人看不起的时候，你就会把自己藏在烦闷尽头。事实上，你的自尊心并没有想象中的强大。"

"你就是两者之间共同的靶心，克拉拉。你究竟是怎么做到的？必须要为我解释一下。"

"自然是这样——如果一个人在讲话，我就没有办法对他做出评价了。但是我要说的还不止这些，我所谓的你缺少真正的自尊，就是说即使你对一个偶然碰到的无能之辈严肃地说，你觉得你是一个天才。我之所以这样讲，是因为你将重要的错误都归咎于自己的同时又言出必行。就像，你常常说你自己是一个酒鬼。"

"但是，从可能发生的概率来讲，事实就是如此。"

"还有你认为自己非常软弱，你觉得你的意志力薄弱。"

133

"我压根就没有意志力——我被情感支配着，被我的喜好支配着，被那些枯燥乏味的心理支配着，被大多数的梦想支配着——"

"这不是你！"她攥紧拳头敲击着另一只手。"你是一发不可收拾地、无药可救地被这世界上的一种东西支配着，那就是你的想象。"

"毫无疑问，你的话引起了我的兴趣。如果你觉得有意思的话，接着讲吧。"

"我留意到，如果你想要迟一天到学校的话，你就会非常自信地准备这样做。你从不会在权衡走还是留的问题上先得出一个结果。你是将你的想法在你的梦想之上攀登几个小时以后，再得出你要的结果。自然而然地，你的思想在搁置了一段时间之后，会找出很多借口来解释留下来的理由，所以当你作出决定的时候，你的决定是不现实的。这样的决定有失公允。"

"不是这样的，"艾默里表示了反对，"但是这难道不是由于我的意志力缺乏，致使我的思想在错误的路上行进吗？"

"我亲爱的弟弟，这就是你的大错误了。这和你的意志力全然不同。无论怎么说，这就是一个无稽之谈；你缺少判断力——是在你清楚你的想象力要玩弄你的时候，只要时机一到就会马上做出决断。"

"天哪，见鬼了！"艾默里惊讶地大声呼叫，"我是无论如何都想不到这一点的。"

克拉拉没有丝毫落井下石的模样。她马上将话题转变到其他地方。但是她的话已然引起了他的深思，他觉得她的话有一部分是对的。他觉得这就像一个工厂老板在批评一个员工作弊以后，发现自己那坐在办公室里的儿子每周都要换一次账本。他一直用来讽刺自己和他的好友的、可悲而又错误看待的意志力，就在他的眼前站着，单纯又无辜。他的判断力离他而去，蹲了牢房，而没有办法监禁的调皮，也就是想象力，反而自得其乐地在他的身旁作陪。克拉拉的话是他自己没有先入为主的结论而求教的唯一忠言——可能，有一种状况除外，那就是他和达西大人在交流的时候。

他是那么的喜欢和克拉拉在一块干活，无论是什么样的活计！和她一块出去买东西是百年难得一见、做梦都想做的事情。在她以前光临的每一家店铺里走着，都可以听到人们的交头接耳声，称呼她为美丽的佩奇夫人。

"我敢这样讲，不需要多长时间她就会嫁人的。"

"喂，不要这么大声。她不是来问你的意见的。"

"她是那么的美丽！"

（一边的巡店专员出现在视野当中——大家都安静下来，要等着他离开。他边走边傻笑。）

"人家是上层社会的人，不是吗？"

"是的呀，但是现在她不是穷了吗，依我看。他们都是这样说的。"

"啊呀！我说，她还有自己的小孩呢！"

而克拉拉不管面对谁都是满脸笑容。艾默里觉得店主们看见她都会给予折扣，有的时候她是清楚的，有的时候她并不知情。他了解她衣着大方，买东西的话总是选择最好的，所以一定能够获得店面巡店员主管的关照，那是不管怎么说都要办到的。

有时候他们会在周末一块去做礼拜，他和她并肩走着，沉醉于她那被清新空气中的水分浸润的脸庞。她特别真诚，真诚的心一直如此，她双膝跪地，她一头金色的头发在彩色玻璃的光线的照射下披散下来，此时她的内心到达什么样的高度，她汲取了怎样的能量，上帝都清楚。

"圣赛西莉娅，"有一天他高声叫道，完全是情不自禁地，人们转过身来看着他，牧师也将布道暂停，克拉拉和艾默里的双颊都变红了。

那是他们一起度过的最后一个周末，因为在那天晚上他将所有的一切都毁了。他难以控制住自己。

他们在夜色里漫步，三月的黄昏温暖得就像是六月一样，他的内心被青春的快乐充斥着，因此他觉得一定要把心里的话讲出来。

"我感觉，"他讲道，声音里带着颤抖，"如果我对你丧失信心了，那么我对上帝的信赖也就消失了。"

她惊慌失措地看着他，所以他问她这是为什么。

"没什么，"她慢吞吞地讲道，"事情就是这样而已；过去的时候也有五个男人跟我讲过相同的话，这句话令我感到害怕。"

"嗯，克拉拉，那就是你注定要承担的吗？！"

她静默着。

"我觉得爱对你而言是——"他刚刚说出口。

她忽然把脸转过来。

"我的世界里根本就没有爱的存在。"

他们继续走着,他慢慢地懂得了她的话里蕴含着怎样的意思……她从来没有爱过……好像她转瞬之间就变成了圣灵光亮之女。他这个人从她的高处跌下来,心里抱着几乎像约瑟[1]对于马利亚的永恒意义的认知,就是希望能抚摸一下她的衣服。但他僵硬地听见自己在讲:

"我是爱你的呀——假如我有哪些伟大的地方的话,那就是……啊,我讲不出来,但是,克拉拉,如果我两年之后再回到这里有迎娶你的条件了——"

她摇摇脑袋。

"不行,"她说,"我是不会再结婚了。我还有两个小孩,我要把我的一切都给了他们。我对你有好感——我对所有的聪慧的男人都有好感,对你的好感超过其他人——然而你非常清楚我,明白我肯定不会嫁给一个机智的男人——"她的话在这个地方戛然而止。

"艾默里。"

"你还要讲什么?"

"你并没有爱上我。你从来没有要和我结婚的想法,是不是?"

"那是模模糊糊的,"他惊讶地讲道。"我没有觉察出我好像是大声讲出来了。但是,我喜欢你——换句话说是倾慕你——又或者说是敬重你——"

"那就是了——你用了五秒钟的时间来查看你的感情记录。"

他笑得很尴尬。

"不要把我当成一个毫无能力的人,克拉拉,有的时候你确实使人感到难过。"

"一个没有能力的人,这样的话是肯定不可以讲的。"她的语气异常坚定,说着就将他的手臂挽住,睁大双眼——茫茫的夜色能够将她眼睛里的友好衬托出来。"没有能力的人,这句话是不可以讲的。"

"空气里弥漫着春天的味道——你的内里被疲倦的可爱装满了。"

她把他的手臂放下来。

"你现在这样就够了,我同样感觉很惬意。给我一支烟吧。你就没有看见过我吸烟,是吧?嗯,我会抽烟,一个月大概抽一次。"

因此,那个很棒的姑娘和艾默里开始向着街角赛跑,宛若两个发了疯的孩童,

---

1. 他是圣母玛利亚的丈夫,详细解说见《圣经·新约·马太福音》第一章第十八节。

136

在那淡蓝色的夜色当中奔跑。

"我明天要去乡下了。"她说,站在那里大口喘着气,避开了街角路灯投射下来的强光。"这段时间天特别灿烂雄伟,那是不容错过的,虽然可能在城里会有更明显的感觉。"

"啊,克拉拉!"艾默里讲,"如果上帝让你的心灵往另一个方向偏一点,你就会是一个特别疯狂的人!"

"可能如此吧,"她回答说,"但是我认为不会这样。我肯定不会真的发疯,之前也从没有出现过。刚才那阵歇斯底里完全是春天造成的。"

"你是特别疯狂的。"他说。

此时他们又走了起来。

"不是这样的——你又讲错了,一个像你一样觉得自己有深谋远虑的人,怎么会总是对我有着错误的观点呢?我是和春天所代表的特点完全相反的人。如果我恰巧有一点和某一个自作多情的古希腊雕塑家所称颂的形象特点相似,那么这是非常不好的,然而我可以明明白白地对你说,如果不是因为我的相貌,只怕我就已经做了女修道院里默默无闻的修女了。"之后她忽然跑起来,他跟在她的身后,听到她大声说道——"我亲爱的孩子,我必须回去看看他们。"

和一个女孩相伴,他可以了解到另外一个男人被相中的原因,她是他所认识的女孩当中唯一一个这样的。艾默里碰到的通常都是人们所说的刚刚进入社交界的妇女,看着这样的女人他心里常常以为她们脸上的表情表达出的意思是这样的:

"呀,如果你可以属于我就好了!"呀,这个男人自负到了什么地步!

但是那个夜晚好像是星光璀璨的一夜,是歌声飞扬的一夜,而克拉拉的高尚的节操仍旧在他们走过的路上发出耀眼的光芒。

"嘹亮的歌声被空气送过来,"面对一个个小水沟,他清唱着……"空气中飘来嘹亮的歌声,声音嘹亮的曼陀林将金色的音符送来,声音嘹亮的小提琴,金色的柱子,漂亮,啊,疲倦的美丽……编织篮里那一团团的线,凡人无法梳理清楚;啊,是哪一位洒脱不羁的神明,想知道也想问问?……谁能将这样嘹亮的……"

艾默里的义愤填膺

逐渐地,无法逃脱地,但是最后忽然翻滚起来,那就是战争,艾默里还在说着话，还在做着很好的梦，战争已经快速入侵海滩，洗刷着普林斯顿玩闹的海滩。每一个晚上健身房里都人声嘈杂，一群一群的人踩踏在地板上，将篮球场上划的线都磨坏了。接下来的那个星期天艾默里抵达华盛顿的时候，他感觉到了一些紧张的氛围，在返程的普尔曼顶级车厢当中，转变为厌恶，只因在过道对面的座位上坐着的散发出臭味的外国人——希腊人，他感觉是，或者是俄国人。他心里思考着，爱国主义的情感在同一种族的人之间很容易就产生了，就像独立前的十三个州那样作战、就像南部邦联那样作战是多么简单呀。那天晚上他没有入睡，而是一直听着那些外国人开怀大笑，打呼，而美国最新的浓郁的味道在车厢里散布着。

在普林斯顿，每一个人都在公共场所说笑，而在心里却告诉自己：如果他们死了，那他们就是英勇就义。文学爱好者怀揣着热情读着鲁泼特·布鲁克的诗，纨绔子弟挂念着政府会不会让军官们身穿英国式样的军装，几个无药可救的懒人给陆军并不太重要的部门写信，申请一些轻松的任务和柔软的车厢。

然后在一周之后，艾默里瞧见了伯恩，他马上就明白了争辩是没有用的——伯恩很明显已经变成了一个和平主义者。看着社会主义的书刊，每句话里都有托尔斯泰，热切希望可以献身于将自己力量充分展现的事业当中，这些原因造就了他最终下定决心把宣传和平当作他的主观梦想。

"德国军队挺进比利时的时候，"他开始说话，"如果市民们能够安静地做着他们自己的事情，德国军队就会土崩瓦解——"

"我明白，"艾默里把他的话打断了，"这些话是我以前就说过的。但是我并不准备和你说有关宣传的事。也许你是对的——但是即使这样，我们与不抵抗主义变成唾手可及的现实的距离还相差甚远。"

"但是，艾默里，你听我——"

"伯恩，我们就讨论——"

"不错。"

"就一点问题——我不强求你将你的家人或者朋友列在考虑范围之内，因为我十分清楚和你的责任心比起来，他们都是无关紧要的——但是，伯恩，你怎么就能够清楚你看的这些书刊，你参加的这些协会，还有你看到的这些理想主义者，就不是显而易见的德国的呢？"

"他们中有一部分是，无可厚非。"

"你怎么辨别他们不都是亲德的——就是那些意志不坚定的人——他们用着德国犹太人的姓名。"

"自然,那也是有可能的,"他语速很慢地讲道。"我之所以站在这样的位置有多少是受到我听见的宣传的影响,这我也不清楚;当然我觉得这是我发自内心的想法——它好像是此刻就在我的面前呈现的一条路。"

艾默里内心纠结万分。

"但是你思考一下这种宣传的荒谬的一面——谁都不会实实在在地用和平主义的罪责将你判处死刑——那只是让你和那些臭名昭著的结交而——"

"我不会信的。"他插话说。

"哦,纽约文化人的气味飘到了我的鼻尖。"

"你想说什么我明白,这也是为何我需不需要煽动还没有把握的理由。"

"你就是独自一人,伯恩——要对那些不愿意听你的人们宣讲——即使你非常擅长这个。"

"很多年以前的圣斯蒂芬[1]肯定也是这样认为的。但是他布道的时候被杀死了。他死的时候也许想过他付出的所有努力都没用了。但你清楚,我时常觉得保罗[2]在去往大马士革的路上想到的也是圣斯蒂芬的去世,就是这件事鼓励着他将整个世界都走遍,去宣讲耶稣的教育。"

"接着说。"

"就这样了——这是我的一个特殊的使命。即便此时的我只是一个微不足道的小人物——就是用作供品罢了。天哪!艾默里,你不要觉得我喜爱德国人!"

"哦,其他的或许我讲不上来——有关不抵抗主义,我已经将它所有逻辑的终点都找到了,我发现这个地方,就仿若一个被排除在外的才能平凡的人,在此时一意孤行、将来坚定不移的人的伟大灵魂上站立着。这个灵魂的身边,托尔斯泰的逻辑必然性在一边站着,尼采的逻辑必然性在另一边站着——"讲到这个地方的时候,艾默里突然停住了。"你什么时候离开?"

"下周离开。"

"那我一定会来送你的。"

他离开的时候,艾默里回忆起两年前在布莱尔拱门下和凯里诀别的场景,

---

1. 这是基督教的第一位殉教者。
2. 详见《圣经·新约·使徒行传》第二十二章第六节。

他们两个脸上的神态非常相像。他的心里郁闷不已,不明白他为什么总是不能将他们最坦诚的一面弄清楚。

"伯恩是一个狂热分子,"他告诉汤姆,"他一定是不对的,我反而觉得,他在毫无察觉的情况下变成了无政府主义出版家和被德国收买的泄密者手里的马前卒——但是他的容颜常常在我的脑海中盘旋——给人以意义非凡的印象——"

一周之后,伯恩在令人感动的氛围中默默地离开了。他将他所有的物品变卖掉,骑着一辆陈旧的自行车,来到住的地方道别。他计划骑着这辆自行车,抵达他的故乡宾夕法尼亚。

"隐士彼得[1]和红衣主教黎塞留[2]告别。"亚历克示意说,伯恩和艾默里握手的时候,他正懒散地在窗台上躺着。

但是艾默里没有接话的心情,他看着伯恩的两条长腿踩在他那辆搞笑的自行车上,在亚历山大楼的后面消失了。他心里非常明白自己在这周将会过得非常伤心。并不是他对战争还抱有怀疑的态度——德国代表着所有令他厌恶的事情,代表着物质至上主义和极大的胡作非为的权势的倾向;而是伯恩的脸颊总在他的记忆当中出现,并且他对已经开始听见的狂躁心情的爆发感到厌恶。

"忽然之间诋毁起歌德来,究竟有什么作用?"他对亚历克和汤姆讲道。"为何要在文章里提到是他发动了战争——抑或是说那个蠢笨、被吹嘘了的席勒[3]是一个虚伪的魔鬼,这又是怎么一回事?"

"你看过他们写的东西没有?"汤姆机智地询问。

"没有看过,"艾默里摇头。

"我也没有看过,"他大笑着说道。

"人们会大声叫出来的,"亚历克小声地回答,"而歌德的作品依然在图书馆同一个书架上,就连摆放的位置都没有变化——谁爱看就让谁看去吧!"

艾默里激昂的心情消失了,这个话题也被丢弃在一边。

---

1. 隐士彼得(Peter the Hermit, 1050?—1115),他是法国的一名僧众,也是第一次十字军入侵东方时的传教士。
2. 参看第22页注解。
3. 席勒(Johann Christoph Friederch von Schiller,1759—1805),他是一名德国诗人、剧作家、评论家、史学家,创作出了《阴谋与爱情》、《三十年战争史》等作品。

"你准备做什么,艾默里?"

"大概是步兵或者是航空兵之类的,我也不好说——我不喜欢机械部队,但是做一名航空兵的话我还是比较适合的——"

"我的看法也是这样,就和艾默里一样。"汤姆说。"不管是步兵还是航空兵——众所周知航空兵听上去好似是战争的比较吸引人的一个方面——就如同以前人们所讲的骑兵一样,你清楚的;但是我同艾默里一样,就连马力和活塞杆是什么都分辨不出来。"

无论怎么讲,艾默里对于自己缺乏热情非常不满,最后演化为尝试着将整个战争归结于他们这一代人的先祖身上……在一八七〇年,所有人都在为德国欢呼[1]……所有的物质至上主义者们都非常疯狂,也包括所有德国科技和效率的推崇者们。他沉醉在自己的内心世界里,在某一天的一节英语课上,他听到教授借用《洛克斯雷大楼》[2],因此他心情压抑地认真钻研起来,一面抱着对丁尼生和他所代表的所有事物的轻视——由于丁尼生被他当作是维多利亚时代人的表率。

"维多利亚时期的人,他们从未学会流泪和悲伤,

他们把种子种下去,获得疼痛的却是你们的后世子孙——"

艾默里将这两行诗在笔记本上写了下来。老师在讲着有关丁尼生诗作的博大精深的一面,所有的学生都在埋头苦记。艾默里翻过笔记本的一页,在另一页上又开始书写起来。

"他们害怕,只因明白达尔文先生著作里的表述,

他们害怕,只因华尔兹流行而纽曼[3]却逝去地匆匆——"

然而华尔兹流行的时间要早上很多,因此他又将这一句划掉。

"题目的话就定为《安定时代之歌》[4]。"那是教授说的话,从远处传来。"安定时代"——我的天呀!所有的一切都被放进箱子里,维多利亚时期的人就坐

---

1. 在这里指的是一八七〇至一八七一年之间的普法战争。
2. 丁尼生在一八三五年写的长诗,全诗共有一百九十四行、九十七个对句,小说下文提到的艾默里说的也是对句。
3. 纽曼(John Henry Newrnan,1801—1890),是英国圣公会内部牛津运动的领导者,后信奉天主教,是天主教神甫、红衣主教,他的作品有《论教会的先知职责》、《大学宣道集》等。
4. 这是斯温伯恩的诗《安定时代之歌》(1852)中第五十六行当中的一句。

在箱盖上心境平和地微笑……布朗宁在他那意大利别墅里英勇地大声叫着:"一切都已圆满结束[1]。"艾默里又拿起笔,继续写起来。

"你在神殿里跪着,他倾身下去来听你的祷告,
你由于'璀璨丰收'对他感恩——替'中国[2]'对他讨伐。"

为何他每一次都只能将一个对子写下来?他写好了一半,此刻他须得想出第二句来押韵:

"你须得用科学来教育他,虽然他曾经犯过错……"

哎,就这样吧……。

"你在家中看见小孩——'我早就把房间收拾好了!'你喊着说,
你在欧洲经历五十个春秋,接着光明正大地——死去。"

"在很大水平上,那就是丁尼生的想法。"这是教授讲的。"完全可以将斯温伯恩的《安定时代之歌》用来作为丁尼生的诗的标题。他不赞成暴乱,不赞成破坏,将和平都理想化了。"

最终艾默里有了想法。他又将笔记本翻过一页,在这节课接下来的二十分钟里笔走龙蛇。写完之后他走到讲台前面,将从他笔记本上撕下来的一页,放置在讲桌上。

"先生,这首诗是献给维多利亚时期的人的。"他态度冷淡地讲道。

教授新奇地将纸片拿起来,而此时艾默里则借机快速地溜出去了。

他的诗是这样写的:

"安定时代之歌

你教我们歌唱,

将愚人的证据销毁,

将生活的答案述写,

狱卒的钥匙塞腰间

铃声哗啦作响,

时间终结了谜语,

我们已将时间用完……

---

1. 引用的是布朗宁《戏剧抒情诗》(1842)中的一首《流亡英国的意大利人》,全诗共一百六十六行。
2. 这里借用的是丁尼生诗句中一个词语。

海洋广阔无边

天空触手可及，

枪炮保护着边疆，

以及防护手套——不是掷球，

千丝万缕涌上心头，

旧调重弹依旧，

安定时代歌声压抑——

语声缭乱，我们歌唱声啾啾。"

万事终结

四月上旬在朦胧的氛围中悄悄逝去——那是弥漫在俱乐部阳台的漫长夜晚的阴霾，房间里的唱机播放的是《可怜的蝴蝶》[1]……由于《可怜的蝴蝶》是在最后一年流行的曲调。战争好像没有给他们带来一点影响，本来这个时候应当如同以前的高年级学生的春天一样，但是现在每隔一天就有军训，但艾默里机敏地注意到这是旧体制下的最后一个春天。

"这是对有理想之人[2]的激烈抵抗。"艾默里讲。

"我有相同的感觉，"亚历克点点头。表示同意。

"他和任何理想国是必定不能相处融洽的。他出现在哪个地方，哪个地方就会遇到困难，隐藏的灾祸就会显现出来，只要他张口讲话，隐藏的灾祸就会让人们晕厥、摇摆。"

"自然，勉强来说他也就是一个有才无德的人。"

"事情就是这样。我认为现在需要思考的最惨的一件事是这个问题——以前都曾经发生过，要多长时间才可以再次发生呢？在爆发滑铁卢战争的五十年以后，对于英国的小学生来讲拿破仑就是与威灵顿公爵比肩的英雄。我们又如何担保我们的子孙就不会对兴登堡[3]尊崇得一塌糊涂呢？"

---

1. 一九一六年美国的流行歌曲正是《可怜的蝴蝶》，雷蒙德·哈贝尔（Reymond Hubbell）作曲，约翰·戈尔顿（John Golden）填词，这首歌的灵感来自于普契尼（Giocomo Puccini,1858—1924）的歌剧《蝴蝶夫人》。
2. 原文应该是"superman（超人）"，尼采哲学中的"完美无缺之人"、"有抱负之人"。
3. 兴登堡（Paul von Hindenburg,1847—1934），他是德国的一个元帅，在第一次世界大战中俄军将俄军打败，在一九一五年担任总参谋长一职。

"是什么造成了现在的局面?"

"时代,妈的,还有那些历史学家。我们只需要学着将灾难看成是灾难就完全不会这样了,不管灾难披着怎样肮脏的外衣,不管这灾难的外表是单一还是瑰丽。"

"天哪!难道这四年的时间里我们还没有将世间的东西都谩骂一通吗?"

然后夜晚降临,这样的夜晚它将会是最后一个。明天一早汤姆和艾默里就要赶往他们各自的训练营,此时他们和平常一样在昏暗的小路上走着,好像依然可以在四周看到熟悉的脸庞。

"今天晚上鬼影会在草地上四散开来。"

"鬼怪会在整个校园肆虐。"

等到了立特尔大楼,他们停下脚步,看着月亮缓缓上升,多德楼石板瓦的屋顶被月光照得满目银白,沙沙作响的树木被照得一片深蓝。

"你清楚,"汤姆低声说,"我们此时的全部感觉都是雄壮的青春的气息,两百年来这里都是声势浩大、自在快乐的青春。"

最终从布莱尔拱门那里传来一阵歌声——恒久的诀别,时断时续的话语。

"我们留在这里的不单是这个年级,还有我们青春的所有的传统。我们仅仅是一代人——这个地方好像把我们跟穿高跟鞋和名声很大的那几代人联系在一起的所有关系,都将要全部斩断。我们与伯尔[1]和'轻骑哈里·李'[2]手拉着手度过了这样深蓝的夜的一半。"

"就是这样的色泽,"汤姆扯开话题,"深蓝色——色彩再添一分都会把氛围破坏掉,就显得不正常了。尖顶的房屋,由代表着黎明的天空做背景,蓝色的光在石板瓦屋顶上驻足——它被破坏了……非常——"

"拜拜,阿伦·伯尔,"艾默里对着纳骚楼高声叫着,"我和你都对人生的陌生角落有了进一步的认识。"

他的声音回响在寂静的夜空当中。

---

1. 伯尔(Aaron Burr,1756—1836),他参加过美国独立战争,是美国第三任总统杰佛逊时期的副总统,于一七七二年在普林斯顿大学毕业。
2. "轻骑哈里·李"也就是亨利·李(Henry Lee,1756—1818),他是独立战争时的骑兵军官,因为战功显赫而得名,他是华盛顿去世时国会决议的起草人,于一七七三年在普林斯顿大学毕业。

第四章　顾影自怜的美少年

"火炬不亮了,"汤姆低声说。"啊,梅萨利纳[1],体育场上狭长的身影将清真寺旁的光塔搭建起来——"

转眼间,一年级时的讲话声在他们四周响起,接着他们互相对视着,眼泪在眼中打着转儿。

"妈的!"

"妈的!"

最后的光芒逐渐隐去,在大地上拂过——低洼、广阔的大地,房屋尖顶下熠熠生辉的大地;夜里的鬼魂又将他们的里拉琴拨动起来,一边游荡在树林间长长的走道上,一边吟唱着悲哀的曲调,惨白的月光照着夜,从塔尖照到塔身。呀,睡了就要做梦,做梦就会没有停歇,睡莲的花瓣被挤压着,得到可以留念的东西,一个小时的精华。

在这与世隔绝的星光和塔尖的幽谷,不要再等待这模糊的月光,因为一个愿望的永久的清晨早已过了时间,来到现实的午后。在这个地方,赫拉克利特斯[2],藏在火和行动的物体中,你是否可以找出他在无精打采的时代言辞激烈地讲出来的预言;今天半夜时分,在余火的黑暗里,在火焰的中心,我的心愿将见证这个世界的雄壮和哀伤。

---

1. 梅萨利纳(Velcria Measalina,22—48),她是罗马皇帝克劳狄一世的第三个妻子,因为祸乱官廷和阴谋夺权而被处死。
2. 赫拉克利特斯(Heraclitus,公元前 535?—前 475),是古希腊的一名哲学家,他的观点是火是万物的根本,变化是永久的。

插曲　一九一七年五月至一九一九年二月

现在，艾默里是一名少尉，隶属长岛弥尔斯营登船港第171步兵团。达西大人于一九一八年一月给艾默里写了一封信。

亲爱的孩子：

关于你自身的情况，我希望你会告诉我，你还像以前一样一切安好；而别的方面，我只需要回忆一下我在你这个年龄时的情况，用一个只表示冷暖的温度计，跟你现在焦灼万分的情绪做一下对照就可以了。

或许，人们会众说纷纭，我和你站在舞台上，互相说着毫无意义的话，最后，啪的一声，那是帷幕掉在了我们那频繁鞠躬致谢的脑袋上所发出的声音。我之所以要给你写信，是因为现在你正在经历着和我相似的事情。人生就像一组放映的幻灯片，而你正在放映的和我放映过的幻灯片是如此的相似，即使只能振臂高呼"愚蠢的人类啊"，那我的这封信也是有价值的。

这代表着一个时期的完结：不论结果如何，或许好，也或许坏。你们这一代正在汲取着时代的营养，奋发向上，尽管我们这一代汲取了九十年代的营养，但是，你们依然比我们要茁壮。你将不再是以前的你，不再是我所认识的艾默里·布莱恩了，而我们再也不会像以前那样见面了。

艾默里，最近我又重新读了一遍《阿伽门农》，这是埃斯库罗斯[1]的作品。这本书通篇采用了高超的讽喻技巧。在这本书中，我找到了答案——关于如今这个悲惨的时期的唯一的答案。答案就是世界已经彻底坍塌，变成了一片废墟，并且与之联系最为密切的相似的年代却回到了那一片无奈的绝望中。外面的人远离堕落的城市，抵御那一盘散沙。正因如此，偶尔我会把他们比作罗马军团。

---

1. 埃斯库罗斯（Aeschylus）公元前525年出生于希腊阿提卡的埃琉西斯，于公元前456年去世。他是古希腊悲剧诗人，与索福克勒斯和欧里庇得斯一起被称为是古希腊最伟大的悲剧作家，有"悲剧之父""有强烈倾向的诗人"的美誉。代表作有《被缚的普罗米修斯》、《阿伽门农》、《善好者》(或称《复仇女神》)等。

显而易见，敌人虽然是一盘散沙，但是却比堕落的城市的居民还要危险。在很多年前的那个维多利亚时代，我们举行庆典，欢庆胜利时传达出来的是对于复仇的狂热之情，面对着敌人的尸体，我们狂欢，我们得意忘形，忘乎所以。

然后，从头至尾的物质主义世界就应运而生，当然还有天主教会。我心里在担忧，你会不会找到适合自己的位置，这位置究竟会是在哪里？不过，你是凯尔特人这件事我是可以确定的。你生下来就是一个凯尔特人，就连死后也依旧是一个凯尔特人。脚踏实地的同时，一定不要忘记仰望星空。

艾默里，我渐渐地发觉我已经步入老年了，我变成了一个老人，和所有的老人一样，我也偶尔做梦，我把我的梦告诉你。在梦里，可能是年轻的时候，我把你当成了我的儿子，我的心情很愉悦，在昏迷状态下，我生下了你。可是等我醒来时，我却忘得一干二净。父亲的本性即是如此。艾默里，我想告诉你，独身主义是与生俱来的，深入骨髓的。

有的时候我觉得我们如此相似的原因或许是因为我们有同一个祖先。我真的发现了这样的一个人，他叫奥唐纳修，他是达西家与奥哈拉家共有的唯一血缘。或许，他叫斯蒂芬，当然，这是我杜撰的。

我们好似连在了一条线上，闪电不管是击中了你还是我，都等同于击中了我们两个人。在你还没有到达登船港的时候，我就已经拿到了我的证件，准备去罗马了。我时时刻刻都在等待着去罗马的通知，我需要知道我该如何上船。估计等你收到这封信的时候，我就已经在海上了，然后就该你了。走上战场是你应该做的事情，就像你读中学，考大学一样，都是理所应当的。你像一个壮志凌云的战士一样走向战场。那些吵吵嚷嚷和高呼英雄主义的事情还是让中产阶级去做比较好，毕竟，他们是内行。

那是在去年，三月份的一个周末，你曾带着伯恩·赫拉狄来拜访我。你还记得吗？你们是从普利斯顿过来的。他真是一个好孩子！后来，你来信说，他认为我是一个杰出的人，这可真的吓到我了。他怎么会这么认为呢？一定是受到了蒙蔽。杰出这个词不能用来形容你，也不能用来形容我。杰出这个词不能用在我们身上。形容我们两个的词语有很多——可以说我们非比寻常，我们聪慧。或许也可以说我们才华盖世。我们能吸引别人的目光，我们也可以营造氛围，或许我们在细枝末节中还会失去我们作为凯尔特人特有的灵魂。我们甚至可以一直独树一帜，但是说我们杰出——这是坚决不可以的！

我带着令人吃惊的文件去罗马，当然，还有很多介绍信——能让我很顺利地前往欧洲的每一个首都。如果我到了那里，肯定会引起很大的"轰动"。我是多么希望你能与我一起同行啊！这句话似乎有点炫耀的意味，绝不是我作为一个中年的神职人员对你这样一个将要奔赴前线的年轻人应该说的话，我唯一可以用来解释的就是这句话是我对自己说的。你知道，我们都把秘密隐藏在内心深处，你像我一样清楚那秘密是什么。我们都有高尚的品格，所有狡猾的辩解都不能影响我们。特别是我们拥有像孩子一样纯真的心灵，这能阻止我们展示出实实在在的恶意。

下面是我为你写的一首挽歌，虽然你的脸颊还不如我在诗中描绘得那样美丽，但是我相信你会在漫漫长夜边抽烟边读诗——

闲言免叙，诗抄录如下：

为养子将要出发征战外国国王而作挽歌。

"哎呀呀[1]

你已离我远去我心爱的儿子，

如风华正茂的少年安格斯，[2]

卓越的安格斯，

思维敏锐如穆伊尔蒂姆的古楚林[3]。

Awirra sthrue

洁白的额头如梅弗[4]的奶牛，

绯红的面颊如树上的红樱桃，

圣母正在哺育圣子而樱桃树正向她弯腰。

Aveelia Vrone

---

1. 原文为爱尔兰感叹词 ochone，挽歌的结尾也是 och ochone，代表伤心、吃惊，挽歌每一节每一句都是表示同样感情的不同表达方式，因此仍保留原文的拼写。
2. 安格斯爱尔兰神话中头上飞着象征吻的四只鸟的爱神。
3. 古楚林是爱尔兰民间传说中的英雄，爱尔兰戏剧家和民间文学家奥古斯塔·葛里高利夫人著有《穆尔蒂姆的古楚林》一书，获得了爱尔兰传奇文学学者的一致好评。
4. 梅弗，爱尔兰神话中的康诺特女王。

插曲　一九一七年五月至一九一九年二月

他金色的头发好似塔拉山[1]国王的护领，
深邃的双眼像极了爱尔兰的那个灰色的大海，
氤氲在绵绵的雨丝里。

Mavrone go Gudyo
他会毅然出战、在头领中奋勇杀敌，
他们尽显英雄本色，
或许他们将英勇就义，
我紧绷的心弦也会松弛。

A Vich Deelish
我将与我的儿同在，
我的生命与他的生命融为一体，
一个人可以在他儿子的生命里
再年轻一次。

Jia du Vaha Alanav
希望圣子一直在他的周围守护他，
希望上帝能将敌人的眼睛蒙蔽，
希望博爱的女王能牵着他的手使他在敌人的阵地上来去自如，
希望所有的神圣的人都能保佑他，
让他去往前线。
哎呀，哎呀呀！"

我深切地呼唤你，艾默里，艾默里……我觉得很害怕，我不知所措，感觉一切都要结束了，或你或我，会丧命于这场残酷的战役。一直以来，我都想说，在这几年中，你就是我的转世化身，意义那样重大。我们两个人那么相像，又是那么的不同。

再见了，上帝会保佑你，我亲爱的孩子。

秦厄·达西

---

1. 爱尔兰东北一村庄，在都柏林西南，古代爱尔兰国王之乡。

暗夜登船

空荡荡的甲板上，艾默里一直在向前走，电灯把他的影子拉得很长。终于，他在一盏灯下停了下来，坐在旁边的凳子上。他从军装的口袋里摸索出铅笔和信纸，开始认真地，费劲地写道：

"我们的部队今晚开拔，
悄无声息地，我们走向空无一人的马路，
黑漆漆的队伍缓缓前进，
百鬼震惶，或许他们听到了我们低沉的脚步声。
在这个黑夜，我们背好行囊，出发；
低沉却又整齐的脚步声传到了远处的船坞上，
我们夜以继日地训练，不知疲倦。

甲板上，只剩下我们徘徊的脚步，
遥远的海岸，看过去，只有一个朦胧的影子，
漫长的岁月，灰暗得像是尸骨残骸。
啊，是否悲伤总是这样如影随形
反抗也枉然！
眼前的大海，白茫茫一片，
云层已经散去，月光清冷，
空洞的通道两旁泛着青光，
海浪拍打着船尾，波涛汹涌，
长夜漫漫，唯有夜曲，伴我们远航，
……今夜，我们出发。在船上。"

艾默里写了一封信，给T·P·丹维里埃。他是佐治亚州高顿营的少尉。这封信的发信地址是布列斯特，发信日期是一九一九年三月三十一日。

亲爱的博德莱尔：——

我们将在这个月的三十号，在哈曼顿见面；之后，我们就去租赁公寓，公寓一定要漂亮和舒适。我和你，当然还有亚历克。我在给你写信，而他现在就在我的旁边看着。对于未来，我很迷茫，但是我有一个念头，想要从政。在美国，我们的从政人员大多粗鄙，而英国的从政人员大多毕业于剑桥或者牛津大

学。我们的从政人员是被党派的基层机构培养的，在党派集会上进行训练，然后挑选适合的人送往国会。他们大都是一些中饱私囊，浑水摸鱼的人，他们被评论员说成是没有独立"灵魂"，也没有独立"思想"的人。尽管在四十年以前，我们的政界都有卓越的人、称职的人。但是，我们的培养目标却是不适宜的。我们的目标是，要让人们了解自己，要让人知道"我们是由什么材质组成的"。美国人的生活太愚昧，太糟糕了，有时候，我多么希望自己出生在英国，是一个英国人。

贝雅特丽斯去世了，她真是可怜。我会得到一部分遗产，但是仅仅是一小部分。我的母亲，在行将就木的时候，突然开始信奉宗教，所以，将会拿出一半的遗产捐给教堂和神学院。这是唯一一点我不能谅解我的母亲的地方。巴顿先生是我的律师，他写信给我。信中说道，我的财富正在急速缩水。因为我的千万财富投资的是亏损的公交公司。该公司的车费只需要五分钱，这或许就是他们亏损的原因。很难想象我每个月要给一个不认识字的人付三百五十元的工资。然而，面对这一切，我还是心存希望的。尽管我的千万财富就这样渐渐地消失了，消失的原因是失败的投资，是铺张浪费的奢靡生活，是不合理的民主管理，还有荒谬的所得税。这一切是如此的人性化，现代化，民主化，这就是我的人生，亲爱的。

闲话少叙，我们将来会有一间漂亮而舒适的房间，如果你愿意的话，可以在附近的时尚杂志社找一份工作。亚历克可以去锌矿公司工作，或者去任意一家他们家开的公司工作。亚历克在看我写信，他说他要去铜矿公司而不是锌矿公司，管他什么公司呢，我觉得都没有什么关系。你觉得呢？不管在哪里赚钱，不管是锌矿公司还是铜矿公司，或许都有一样的偷税漏税，或许都是一样的泥沙俱下。不过要说起我，我可是赫赫有名的艾默里啊，可是要写出流传千古的经典之作的，前提是得有一定的分寸并敢于大胆地写出来。如若要给后代子孙留下一份特别的礼物，最好的就是老生常谈了，不过还是要说得巧妙一点。

汤姆，你为什么不信奉天主教？为什么不做一名虔诚的天主教徒？很显然，这样的话，你得抛弃你曾经告诉我的那些狠毒的鬼蜮伎俩了。你可以写出更棒的诗歌以及那些长长的歌颂和平的颂诗，不过这需要一个前提，就是你得与金光闪闪的高大的烛台联系在一起。如我母亲所说，美国的神父都是相当无聊的，很是低趣味。你最好还是要找一个美丽一点高雅一点的教堂，我会给你介绍一个很卓越的人,他是一位神父,叫秦厄·达西。

凯里的死亡对我和杰西来说都是一个沉重的打击。我有强烈的好奇心,我很想知道伯恩到底是去哪了,会不会躲在世界的某一个神奇的角落里呢?又或者是不是被化了名顶替别人进了监狱?战争,正常情况下,会把人变得更有血性、更正统。但是相反,战争没有把我变得正统,却激发了我内心深处的强烈好奇心,我变成了一个探索者。近来,罗马天主教会频频遭遇挫折,它的羽翼已经不再丰满,作用也不值一提,更不用说会出现什么优秀的作家了。切斯特顿[1]的著作我已经读了好几遍了,读得厌倦了。

我发现,只有一个叫唐纳德·汉基[2]的军人经受住了被宣扬的满城风雨的精神危机的考验。我所认识的他已经成熟,正在攻读牧师的职位,可以担任这个角色。我的确认为,这都是无稽之谈,虽然对于那些在国内的人来说是精神上的安慰,也会让家长们为自己养育大的孩子而骄傲。但是这种由于危机而引发的宗教一点价值也没有,有的话也只会是昙花一现。或许会有四个人能找到帕里斯[3],而能找到上帝的人只有一个。

可是我和你还有亚历克——我们,啊,我们一定要请一个来自日本的男管家,我们穿着华丽的衣服出席晚宴,优雅地品尝着佐餐葡萄酒。我们过着奢华、毫无感情的生活,直到我们厌倦了,我们突然觉醒,我们决定拿起机关枪与那些财产拥有者站在同一战线,或者与布尔什维克们站在一起,一起投炸弹。哦,上帝!汤姆,我希望我们大干一场,我心神不宁,坐立难安,像魔鬼一样,不愿意变胖,不愿意因为恋爱而变得啰里啰嗦。

我把日内瓦湖的房子出租出去了,并且上岸之后我不会回去,我会先去找巴顿先生,了解一下他的近况。如果你给我写信,可以寄到芝加哥,然后请莱克斯帮忙转交。

愿一切安好,亲爱的鲍士威尔。

撒缪尔·约翰逊

---

1. 参考第 32 页注,切斯特顿(G. K. Chesterton,1874—1936 年)以写布朗神甫的侦探小说而著称。
2. 唐纳德·汉基,英国军人,代表作《弃学从戎》。
3. 希腊神话中特洛伊王子,因为诱走斯巴达王的妻子而引发特洛伊战争。

第二卷

一个重要人物所受的教育

第一章　刚入社交圈的少女

那时是二月，地点在纽约第六十八大街康尼奇家住宅的一间大而精致的卧房。那是一个小女生的屋子：墙面是粉红色的、窗帘也是粉红色的，粉红色的床单铺在奶黄色的床上。这个房间的主色调是粉红色和奶黄色，房间里那个奢侈的梳妆台是仅有的全景家具。梳妆台上面有玻璃台面，还有三个面的镜子。一幅价格高昂的彩色石印画《成熟的樱桃》[1]，几幅兰德西尔的柔顺的小狗[2]，和一张麦克斯菲尔·帕里什的装点画作《年幼的黑岛国王》[3]在墙上面挂着。

房间里杂乱无章地摆放着如下物品：（1）七八个空了的纸盒子，有一截薄棉纸裸露着挂在盒子口；（2）各式各样上街穿的衣服，和晚礼服一起全都被放在桌子上，很明显是刚买的；（3）一卷已经丧失了尊严，胡乱地纠缠着眼前的所有的物件的纱网；（4）还有两把小椅子上摆着一批难以描述的内衣裤。人们非常想要瞧一瞧购买面前这些奢侈衣物的凭据，而且也非常想要看一眼公主的美貌，由于这些都是为了她——看！有人过来了！真没意思！她就是一个仆人，来搜寻一些东西的——她从椅子上抓起来一把物件——不在这个地方；她又在梳妆台上、五斗橱的抽屉中，抓了一下。她找到了几件美丽的无袖宽内衣和一件使人震惊的睡衣，然而这些都不是她要寻找的——她走了出去。

旁边的房间有难以辨别的嘀咕声传出来。

太好了，我们开始高兴起来。这是亚历克的妈妈康尼奇夫人，她体格健壮，庄重，胭脂擦得和她遗孀的身份很匹配，她特别疲惫。她一边搜寻那东西，一边在嘴里振振有词。她搜寻得不像女仆那么仔细，但她搜寻的时候却夹杂着怒火，这填补了她搜寻东西时的粗心大意。她被一卷纱网绊了一下，嘴里吐出清楚的"该

---

1. 这是由英国画家约翰·艾弗列特·米莱斯（John Everett Milais,1829—1896）所作。
2. 英国画家艾德温·亨利·兰德西尔（Sir Edwin Henry Landseer,1802—1873），以画动物画闻名于世，就像马、狗、鹿。
3. 这是美国画家麦克斯菲尔·帕里什（Maxfield Parrish,1870—1966）以《天方夜谭》作为创作题材画的一幅装饰画。

死"一词。之后她空着手离开了。

外面滔滔不绝的声音愈加多了起来,还有一个娇惯的女孩用软绵绵的声音说:"那些全部蠢笨的人都——"

暂停了一下,第三个要搜寻东西的人进来了,不是讲话软绵绵的那个她,而是年纪较小的那个。这是赛西丽娅·康尼奇,十六岁,长得很好看,聪慧活泼,生来风趣。她的晚装,一件晚礼服,也许是样式的朴素使得她烦躁。她走到距离她最近的一堆衣物前面,看中了一条粉红色的裙子,拿起来观察了一下。

赛西丽娅:粉红色的吗?

罗莎琳:(舞台之外)嗯!

赛西丽娅:非常流行的吗?

罗莎琳:是的!

赛西丽娅:嗯,就是它了!

(她在梳妆台镜子当中瞧见了自己,心里暖烘烘的,开始摇摆起身体来。)

罗莎琳:(舞台之外)你在干什么——在试衣服吗?

(赛西丽娅停下照镜子的动作,将裙子搭在右肩上走了出去。亚历克·康尼奇在另一边的门那边,向周围快速地扫了一眼,用非常嘹亮的声音叫道:母亲!旁边的门里传来一阵埋怨声,他听见声音后向着门那边走过去,然而又传出一阵声音使得他停了下来。)

亚历克:你们原来都在这儿呀!艾默里·布莱恩来了。

赛西丽娅:(快速麻利地)把他带到楼下去。

亚历克:嗯,他早就在楼下了。

康尼奇夫人:那就带他去他的房间瞧瞧吧。告诉他我非常抱歉现在还不可以见他。

亚历克:你们所有人的情况他早就很了解了。你们就快一些吧。爸爸在和他谈论战争的问题,他早就有些坐不住了。他这个人有些容易兴奋。

(这最后的一句话使得赛西丽娅进入了房间。)

赛西丽娅:(她在堆放得很高的内衣裤上坐了下来。)你这句话是什么意思——容易兴奋?以前在信上你也经常这样讲。

亚历克:嗯,他就是写一些东西。

赛西丽娅:他知道怎么弹钢琴吗?

155

亚历克：应该不知道。

赛西丽娅：（新奇地）饮酒吗？

亚历克：嗯——他饮酒并不稀奇。

赛西丽娅：钱很多吗？

亚历克：天哪——你去问问他吧，他以前非常富有，此时也有一些收入。

（康尼奇夫人出场。）

康尼奇夫人：亚历克，你的任何一个好友我们都非常愿意见——

亚历克：你理所应当地应该和艾默里见上一面。

康尼奇夫人：自然，我想要和他见一面。但是你也太任性了一点，条件这样好的家放着不住，就要跟两个男生搬到什么乱七八糟的公寓里去。我希望这不是由于你们几个人想要尽情地喝酒的原因。（她的话停了一下。）今天晚上对他有些招待不周了。这个星期是属于罗莎琳的，你清楚。一个刚刚进入社交场合的女孩子，应该拿出足够重视的态度来对待她。

罗莎琳：（舞台之外）那行啊，你应该有所表示，过来将我的扣子扣一下。

（康尼奇夫人下台。）

亚历克：罗莎琳依旧是这样，丝毫都没有改变。

赛西丽娅：（压低声音）她是被惯坏了。

亚历克：今天晚上她碰到对手了。

赛西丽娅：谁呀？艾默里·布莱恩先生吗？

（亚历克点点头表示赞同。）

赛西丽娅：呃，罗莎琳非要去见她没有追上的那个人。说句实在的，亚历克，她在男人面前的表现实在是太糟糕了。她会羞辱别人，讽刺别人，经常爽约，还在别人面前打哈欠——但是他们仍旧会回头遭罪。

亚历克：那是他们自己乐意。

赛西丽娅：他们是不喜欢。她仿佛一个——她和荒唐的荡妇有一些相似，我感觉——她会让女孩子做她经常想做的那些事——只是她对女孩子非常厌恶。

亚历克：我们家遗传下来的性格吧。

赛西丽娅：（无可奈何地）我觉得还没有轮到我就已经遗传完了。

亚历克：罗莎琳表现得如何？

赛西丽娅：不是太好。呀，她也是表现得很普通——有时候吸烟，饮潘趣酒，常常会叫别人亲她——就是这样，就是这样——任何一个人都清楚——这也是战争所造成的影响吧，你清楚。

（康尼奇夫人上台。）

康尼奇夫人：罗莎琳就要准备好了，就能够下楼和你的好友见一面了。

（亚历克和他的妈妈下台。）

罗莎琳：（舞台之外）呀，母亲——

赛西丽娅：母亲到楼下去了。

（此时罗莎琳上台。罗莎琳就是——彻彻底底的罗莎琳。一些女孩子不需要做任何努力就可以让男人们为她们倾倒，罗莎琳就是这样的一个女孩子。两种男人肯定做不到：蠢笨的男人对于她的聪慧很是惧怕，而聪慧的男人又恐惧她的美丽。这两种类型除外，剩下的依靠与生俱来的优越性都是属于她的。）

假如要惯就可以惯坏，到了此刻惯的过程也早就结束了，但真相是，她的脾气秉性绝对不应当是这般的；她想要的任何东西她都想要拥有，一旦她没有如愿以偿，也许她就会让她四周的人一个个都特别难过——但是认真讲起来，她也并不是被惯坏的。她那充足的激情，她那成长和学习的力量，她对于那些充满生机的梦幻事情的无限信心，她的英勇和骨子里的诚实——这些好的地方都没有被抹杀。

很长的一段时间里她从心底里对这个家庭感到很是厌恶。她的生活当中缺乏准则，她的理念是自己要醉生梦死，对别人则使用互不干扰的态度。她喜欢听一些耸人听闻的故事，她有和生性华而不实的人相一致的粗心大意的毛病。她希望别人都喜欢她，然而如果别人不喜欢她，她也不会感觉不开心，也不会因为这个对自己进行改变。

她一定不会是一个典范人物。

所有美丽的女人获得的教育就是认识男人。罗莎琳对那些作为个人的一个个男人都非常绝望，但是她非常信任那些作为一个性别的男人。提到女人她就非常厌恶。她们代表着她自己感觉得到而且特别看不起的性格特点——平凡、自傲、胆小、小家子气的诓骗。以前她告诉一房间的母亲的好友，女人存在的唯一的理由是男人们需要一个弄得他们心神不安的人。她跳舞跳得非常好；精于画画，然而画得特别草率；文字特别流畅，但是只是针对情书。

然而指责她的所有人最后还是会说她很美丽。她有一头非常夺人眼球的金发,如果要学会装扮这样的头发会给染料业提供很大的帮助。那张让人永远也吻不够的嘴巴,小巧,有些许肉感,让人完全抵挡不住它的魅力。灰色的眼睛,白皙无暇的皮肤,即便那上面有两个难以察觉的色块。她的身材健康纤细,不存在发育不好的地方,看着她在房间里走来走去,看着她在马路上来回行走,或是做一个"侧手翻",会使得人心花怒放。

最后一个要求——她的伶俐、瞬时展现的性格与艾默里在伊莎贝尔身上瞧见的故意表现、做作的性格分隔开。达西大人见到她也会感觉困扰,究竟说她是一个特别的人呢,还是说她是一个重要的人呢。也许她是一个将优雅、难以言说、百年难得一见的特色集于一身的人。

在她刚刚步入社交场合的第一晚,她表现得特别像一个小女孩,她虽然有奇怪并且不经意间表露的聪慧。她妈妈的仆人刚刚为她弄好头发,但她烦躁地感觉她自己弄会弄得更好。现在的她特别紧张,心烦气躁,不愿意在同一个地方待着。我们觉得这是由于她是在一间杂乱的卧房中呆着的原因。她要准备讲话了。伊莎贝尔的女低音仿佛是小提琴的声响,但假如你可以听见罗莎琳讲话,你会感觉她的声音仿佛瀑布一样好听。

罗莎琳:说实在的,我只爱穿世界上的这两种衣服——(在梳妆台前坐着梳头。)

一种是有窄裤的圈环裙;另一种是连体的泳衣。我穿这两种衣服都很好看。

赛西丽娅:要进入社交圈了开心吗?

罗莎琳:开心。你不开心吗?

赛西丽娅:(嘲讽地)你开心的原因是因为这样你就能够结婚了,能够和一群轻佻、年幼的已婚之人到长岛上去居住。你想要你的生活是一环接一环的调情,每一个男人都在一个环上。

罗莎琳:想过这样的日子!你是想说我早已发现生活是这般的。

赛西丽娅:呵呵!

罗莎琳:赛西丽娅,亲爱的,你不清楚这是多么大的磨练,对于——如我这般。我走在马路上要提防男人对我眨眼睛,我必须使我的脸保持坚定,仿若一块铁板。如果我坐在剧院的第一排不住地笑着,一整晚喜剧演员就会朝着我演戏了。如果我在舞会上小声地讲话,低着脑袋跳舞,抑或是手帕掉了,我的舞伴就会一整个礼拜天天给我打电话。

赛西丽娅：那样的话实在是太耗费精力了。

罗莎琳：最令人头疼的是，我唯一感兴趣的几个男人一点都配不上。假如——假如我非常贫穷，我就去做演员了。

赛西丽娅：嗯，你还是根据表演的多少挣钱吧。

罗莎琳：有的时候我觉得自己非常高兴，我心想，为什么要在一个人的身上花费全部心思呢？

赛西丽娅：通常在你觉得非常糟心的时候，我就搞不懂了为何把心思都耗在一家人身上。（站起身来。）我觉得我要下楼去和艾默里·布莱恩先生见一面。我对容易兴奋的男人感兴趣。

罗莎莉：世界上是不存在这样的人的。男人不清楚怎么真正发火，不清楚怎么实实在在地开心——假如真明白，就有问题了。

赛西丽娅：嗯哼，我很开心自己没有你的那些忧愁。我很忙。

罗莎琳：（讥讽地笑）订婚了[1]？哼，你这小疯子！如果母亲听见你这么讲，她一定会将你送到住宿学校，那里对于你来讲最适合。

赛西丽娅：但是你是不会对她说的，只因我清楚我有能够对你讲的事情——你真的太自私了！

罗莎琳：（有些气恼）赶紧走，小丫头！和谁订婚了，那个送冰的还是那个开杂货店的？

赛西丽娅：真蠢——再见，亲爱的，再见。

罗莎琳：呀，千万要记住——你可以起到大作用。

（赛西丽娅走下舞台。罗莎琳把头发梳完，站起身，嘴上哼唱着曲调。她对着镜子走过去，站在镜子前在软软的地毯上舞动起来。她的眼睛没有看向脚，而是直视着眼睛——不是随意瞧一眼，而是聚精会神地瞧，即便是她在微笑的时候。门忽然被打开了，艾默里走了进来，和平时无二，冷静、洒脱。他马上就变得紧张起来。）

男的：呀，真抱歉。我还以为——

女的：（高兴地笑着）嗯，你就是艾默里·布莱恩，对吗？

男的：（细细地打量着她）你是罗莎琳？

---

1. "忙着"与"订婚"可以用作同一个字。

女的：我称呼你艾默里吧——呀，进来吧——没事的——母亲马上要过来的——（把声音压低）太不好了。

男的：（四下看了看）我倒感觉很新奇。

女的：这是一个没有人收拾的地方。

男的：这是你——你——（停顿）

女的：嗯——这些物件都是。（她走到梳妆台跟前。）看，我使用的唇膏——眼线笔。

男的：之前我不了解你是这样的。

女的：你认为是怎样的？

男的：之前我感觉你有些——有些——男孩子气，你明白，游泳，打高尔夫球。

女的：嗯，就是这样——但是我工作的时候不去。

男的：工作的时候？

女的：六点到两点——严格来讲。

男的：我觉得你拥有有限责任公司的一部分股份。

女的：嗯，不是什么有限责任公司——就是"罗莎琳无限公司"罢了。百分之五十一的股份，声望，信誉，每一样都加在一块，每年两万五千元。

男的：（不认可地）好像是一单使人不感兴趣的生意。

女的：哎，艾默里，你没有不同的意见——是吗？当我和一个两周之后还不会让我极度厌恶的男人遇上以后，情况可能就不一样了。

男的：奇怪，你对于男人的观点和我对于女人的观点不谋而合。

女的：我不是真正的女人，你清楚——在我的头脑里。

男的：（产生了兴致）讲下去。

女的：不行，你讲——你讲下去——是你让我讲我自己的。否则就违反规则了。

男的：违反规则？

女的：我自己制定的规则——但是你——呀，艾默里，我听别人说你满腹经纶。父母对你的期望很高。

男的：多么振奋人心哪！

女的：亚历克说是你教会他怎样思考，是不是？我觉得谁都不可能做到。

男的：是的。我的确很蠢。

（明显他不想让人对这句话太较真。）

女的：骗人。

男的：我——崇尚宗教——我喜欢文学。我——我甚至还作诗。

女的：自由诗——太厉害了！（她开始诵读。）

"绿色大树

小鸟在树上鸣叫，

女孩饮了毒药

小鸟飞了女孩死了。"

男的：（哈哈大笑）不是，不是这样的诗。

女的：（忽然地）我喜欢你。

男的：不要。

女的：还会客气——

男的：我害怕你。我常常对女孩子很恐惧——在我亲她之前。

女的：（加重语调）啊呀呀，已经没有战争了。

男的：因此我会对你一直很恐惧。

女的：（有些小难过）我觉得你会的。

（两个人都有些踌躇。）

男的：（稍加思考）听着。这是一个非常令人害怕的问题。

女的：（清楚要问的是什么）五分钟之后。

男的：我是想问你会——亲我吗？还是你害怕了？

女的：我就不知道害怕是什么——但是你提出的缘由太卑劣了。

男的：罗沙琳，我的确想亲你。

女的：我也是这样想的。

（他们接吻——清清楚楚地、深深地。）

男的：（无法呼吸的时候）哎，满足你的好奇心了吗？

女的：你呢？

男的：没有满足，恰恰相反引起了我的好奇心。

（瞧得出是真的。）

女的：（隐约中）十几个男人都被我亲过。我觉得我还会和十几个男人接吻。

161

男的：（愣神中）对，我觉得你会——像这般。

女的：我这样的亲吻大多数人都喜欢。

男的：（猛然惊醒）啊呀，对的。再亲我一下，罗莎琳。

女的：不行——通常情况下我的好奇心一次就能够满足了。

男的：（心灰意冷地）这也是一条规定吗？

女的：我是看状况制定规定。

男的：我们两个有些相似——就是我的经验要比你多一些。

女的：你年龄多大了？

男的：将近二十三了。你的年龄呢？

女的：十九岁——刚刚好。

男的：我觉得你是流行学校教出来的学生。

女的：不对——我还未被雕琢过。我是斯潘思学校开除的——但是至于什么原因我忘了。

男的：讲讲你一般的性格，都有什么？

女的：嗯，我聪颖，特别自私，只要受到激发就会感情繁多，喜欢让别人赞美——

男的：（忽然地）我并不想和你谈恋爱——

女的：（紧锁眉头）我又没有求你这么做。

男的：（依然面无表情）但是也许我会。我喜欢你的嘴唇。

女的：住口！请不要喜欢我的嘴唇——头发、眼睛、肩膀、鞋子都可以——但是不要喜欢我的嘴唇。每一个人都喜欢我的嘴唇。

男的：你的嘴唇很好看。

女的：我的嘴巴有些小。

男的：不，不小——让我瞧一下。

（他如同先前一样含情脉脉地吻她。）

女的：（有些激动）讲点动听的。

男的：（被吓了一跳）天呀。

女的：（退后）好了，不要说了——假如没有办法讲的话。

男的：我们要做做样子吗？这么快？

女的：就快和慢来说的话，我们和其他人的衡量标准并不一样。

男的：你已经说——其他人了。

女的：我们做做样子嘛。

男的：不可以——我不会装——这是感情的问题。

女的：你没有感情吗？

男的：没有，我是浪漫——多情的人觉得事情会持续很长时间——浪漫的人对待事情的时间不会很长，心里怀有一丝希冀。多情是情绪化了的。

女的：你不是吗？（半闭着眼睛。）也许你认为那是高人一等的姿态。

男的：呃——罗莎琳，罗莎琳，不要争辩了——再亲我一下吧。

女的：（此时很平静）不可以——我不想亲你。

男的：（丝毫掩饰不住他的震惊）刚才你还想要亲我呢。

女的：我指的是现在。

男的：那我还是离开吧。

女的：我觉得也是。

（他向门边走去。）

女的：呀！

　　　（男的调转身体。）

女的：（哈哈大笑）比分——主队：一百分——客队：零分。

　　　（他回过头走出去。）

女的：（猛地）天下雨——暂停比赛。

（男的走下舞台。）

（女的偷偷地走到五斗橱前，把一盒香烟拿出来，藏到一张桌子旁边的抽屉里。她的妈妈走上舞台，手里拿着一个本子。）

康尼奇夫人：好——下楼之前我一直想要和你单独聊聊。

罗莎琳：啊呀！你要把我卟死了！

康尼奇夫人：罗莎琳，你花钱太不计后果了。

罗莎琳：（局促地）对的。

康尼奇夫人：你清楚你父亲的收入不能和以前相比了。

罗莎琳：（做了个鬼脸）呀，请不要讲什么钱不钱的了。

康尼奇夫人：没有钱你不能做成任何事。今年是我们在这座房子中住的最后一年了——除非局势有所转变，否则赛西丽娅就不会有你这么优异的条件了。

163

罗莎琳：（烦躁地）呀——有什么问题？

康尼奇夫人：因此我让你留意写在我本子上的这几件事。第一条：不要和男人一块失去踪迹。这样重要的时刻可能会来的，但是目前我要你就待在舞池里，让我可以找到你。有几个人你得见一见，你躲在玻璃暖房的哪个犄角旮旯里和什么人聊天这一点我非常不喜欢——你也不能去听别人聊天。

罗莎琳：（讽刺地）是，只是听的话还好一些。

康尼奇夫人：不可以和一群大学生去浪费时间——十九、二十岁的学生娃娃。我不反对你参加班级舞会或是观看橄榄球赛，但是不可以参加那些乘人之危的晚会，和杂七杂八的人到熙熙攘攘的地区的小咖啡馆吃吃喝喝——

罗莎琳：（说出她的行为规范，而且也讲得有理有据，和她妈妈讲得一样都很偏激）母亲，全都结束了——现在你不可以把什么事情都依照你们九十年代那样的做法来安排。

康尼奇夫人：（丝毫不在意）今天晚上我要和你爸爸的几个单身汉朋友见一面——年龄还小的男人。

罗莎琳：（聪敏地点点头）大概四十五岁？

康尼奇夫人：（严肃道）有什么不行的？

罗莎琳：呀，特别行——他们懂得生活，满脸憔悴，使人仰望（摇头）——然而他们乐意跳舞。

康尼奇夫人：布莱恩先生我还没有见过——但是我觉得你不会倾心于他的。他看起来不是一个擅长挣钱的人。

罗莎琳：母亲，钱不钱的从来不在我的考虑范围内。

康尼奇夫人：你和别人的关系从没坚持到要思考钱的时候。

罗莎琳：（叹了一口气）是的，我觉将来有一天我就嫁给钞票好了——等到我对什么事情都没有兴趣了。

康尼奇夫人：（打开本子）从哈特福那边发来了一个电报。是道生·莱恩要到这里来。这个年轻人可是我特别喜欢的一个，他就是一个在钱堆上躺着的人。我总感觉既然你对霍华德·吉雷斯皮有些不喜欢，那就鼓励一下莱德先生吧。这是他在一个月的时间里第三次来我们家做客。

罗莎琳：你是如何得知我对霍华德·吉雷斯皮不喜欢的？

康尼奇夫人：这个年轻人每一次过来都表现得惹人怜惜。

第一章　刚入社交圈的少女

罗莎琳：那些都是他真情流露前的一种浪漫方法。有些不对劲。

康尼奇夫人：（她的观点都讲完了）无论怎么讲，你今晚都要使我们觉得自豪。

罗莎琳：你认为我不美丽吗？

康尼奇夫人：你非常清楚你的美丽。

（这时一把小提琴调弦的呜呜声从楼下传来，还伴随着鼓发出的隆隆声。康尼奇夫人迅速地把脸转过来对着她的女儿。）

康尼奇夫人：咱们走吧！

罗莎琳：等一下！

（她妈妈离开了。罗莎琳走到镜子前面，心满意足地看着镜子里的自己。她亲吻着自己的手，接着又用手去抚摸镜子中的她的嘴唇。之后她把灯关上，从房间离开了。忽然有片刻的安静。钢琴弹奏出的几声乐调，模模糊糊鼓的轻柔的嘭嘭的声音，刚刚穿在身上的丝绸裙子的细碎的声响，在楼梯口汇集然后纠缠在一起，传到了那打开了一半的门里。一大群人走在灯光照耀着的楼道里。楼下传过来的笑声越来越大。接着有人走到房间里，把门关上，将灯打开了。那个人是赛西丽娅。她走近五斗橱，翻看着抽屉里的东西，犹豫了一下——接着她走到桌子前，将抽屉里的烟盒拿起来，从里面抽出了一支香烟。然后她把烟点燃，抽了一口，接着又吐出来，一边向着镜子走过去。）

赛西丽娅：（用很老成的语气讲）呀，对了，"第一次接触社交界"此时早就变成这么搞笑的一幕闹剧，你清楚。在你十七岁之前的确能够尽情地四处游玩，与此对比这的确是让人不高兴的事。（与那些只出现在梦里的中年贵族握手。）嗯，大人——我觉得您已经被我姐姐提起了。吸一支吧——特别好吸的烟。名字叫做——叫做花冠[1]香烟。难道，你不吸烟？多么令人惋惜呀！国王不允许，照我的观点的话。嗯，我跳一支舞吧。

（因此她随着楼下曲子的节奏在房间里跳起舞来，两只手臂向着她想象中的舞伴伸出去，她手中的香烟随着手在舞动着。）

几个时辰过去

在楼下那个小房间的一个角落里，一个特别舒服的皮卧榻在那里摆放着。

---

[1] 古巴的一种雪茄。

皮卧榻两边的上方各自有一盏灯,在卧榻的中间位置的上边挂着一幅画,是一个衣服特别老旧、特别庄重的绅士,时间是在一八六零年。狐步舞曲的乐声在外面洋溢着。

罗莎琳在卧榻上坐着,霍华德·吉雷斯皮在她的左边,那是一个大概二十四岁的死气沉沉的青年。很明显可以看出来他特别不开心,而罗莎琳则感觉特别无聊。

吉雷斯皮:(没有办法地)你说我不一样了是什么意思。我对你的感觉还是一样啊。

罗莎琳:但是就我看来你的模样是不一样了。

吉雷斯皮:三周以前,你经常说你喜欢我的原因是我从容不迫,麻木不仁——我依旧如此。

罗莎琳:但是我不是原来的样子了啊。以前我对你很喜欢的原因是你有一双棕色的眼睛,有一双又长又细的腿。

吉雷斯皮:(迷茫不知所以)腿还是一样的细长呀,双眼还是棕色的呀。你就是会勾引男人的人,情况就是这样。

罗莎琳:要是说到吸引男人的话,我就是按照钢琴总谱来做。对于如何使得男人心情烦躁,我是十分自然。以前我以为你肯定不会吃醋的。但是此时我觉得你的眼睛一直在跟着我的身影走。

吉雷斯皮:那是我爱你呀。

罗莎琳:(冷漠地)对于这一点我很了解。

吉雷斯皮:你都两周没有和我接吻了。我还想着,女孩子让别人亲过以后,她的心——就属于——那个人了。

罗莎琳:那早就成为过去式了。你每一次见我都是一个全新的开始。

吉雷斯皮:你确定?

罗莎琳:和平时没有多少变化。以前接吻的话要分成两种类型:一种是女孩被亲了,接着又被丢弃了;另一种是,他们订婚了。现在这个时代又有第三种类型出现了,就是男人被女孩亲了,接着被丢弃了。如果琼斯先生在九十年代炫耀说他亲了一个女孩子,大家听到后的第一反应就是他和这个女孩子好事将近了。如果琼斯先生在一九一九年也这样炫耀,大家的第一反应就是他不可能再和她接吻了。如果有了一个好的开始,此时哪一个女孩儿都要比男人强很多。

第一章　刚入社交圈的少女

吉雷斯皮：那你为什么要把男人玩弄于股掌之间呢？

罗莎琳：（弯腰向前好像不能让别人听到）就是在开始的一瞬间，在他正兴致勃勃的时候。曾经有那么一瞬间——嗯，就是在亲吻以前，一句悄悄话——值得一讲的那些话。

吉雷斯皮：还有什么？

罗莎琳：接下来是接过吻以后，你就让他说说自己的事情。过不了多长时间，他就只想着一件事了，那就是和你在一块——他气得闷不做声，他不会再争，他也不想再玩了——胜利了！

（道森·莱恩走上台，他今年二十六岁，美丽，有钱，对自己的信仰很忠诚，他可能是一个使人厌恶的人，但是他很坚持，有成功的信心。）

莱德：我觉得现在是我跳舞的时间了，罗莎琳。

罗莎琳：嗯，道森，这么说来你认得我了。呃，我清楚地知道我妆化得有些淡。莱德先生，这位先生是吉雷斯皮。

（他们握手问好，接着吉雷斯皮转身离去，一副无精打采的模样。）

莱德：毫无疑问你的晚会非常成功。

罗莎琳：是这样吗——近期我也没有参加过什么晚会。我感觉非常累——你介意到外面去坐一会儿吗？

莱德：介意——我有点太兴奋了。你非常了解我就是对做事情"匆匆忙忙"的很讨厌。昨天和一个女孩见面，今天和一个女孩见面，明天又和另一个女孩见面。

罗莎琳：道森·莱恩！

莱德：嗯？

罗莎琳：我心里在想着你是不是对于你喜欢我这一点清楚。

莱德：（大吃一惊）你说什么——呀——你对于你的优秀非常清楚！

罗莎琳：由于你非常清楚我是一个非常可怕的人，谁要是娶了我谁就会遇上麻烦了。我非常小心眼儿——小心眼儿。

莱德：呃，我是不会讲这样的话的。

罗莎琳：啊，对，我特别小心眼——对最亲密的人尤其是这样。（她站起身子。）哎，我们回去吧。也许母亲要生气了。

（俩人一起走下台。亚历克和赛西丽娅走上舞台。）

赛西丽娅：能和自己的哥哥一块休息，真是太幸运了。

亚历克：（难过地）如果你不想让我待在这里，那我就离开。

赛西丽娅：天呀，不要离开——我下一个舞伴找谁呢？（叹息一声。）自从法国军官回国以后，情调这个东西在舞台上就再也不存在了。

亚历克：（做沉思状）我不想要艾默里喜欢上罗莎琳。

赛西丽娅：哎，怎么我感觉你就是盼望他们相爱呢。

亚历克：是呀，但是在见到这些女孩之后——我就不清楚了。我很欣赏艾默里。他这个人非常敏感，我不希望看到他因为哪一个讨厌他的人而难过。

赛西丽娅：他长得很好看。

亚历克：（依然思考）她是不会嫁给他的，但是一个女孩如果要让一个男孩难过的话，也没有必要和他结婚。

赛西丽娅：那我们应该做些什么呢？希望我能够了解这其中的精髓。

亚历克：哎，你就是个没有感情的家伙。这对一些人来讲真的很幸运，上帝把一个狮子鼻赠送给了你。

（康尼奇夫人走上舞台。）

康尼奇夫人：罗莎琳究竟跑到什么地方去了？

亚历克：（拐弯抹角地）要找她的话你自然是找对人了。她一定会来我们这个地方的。

康尼奇夫人：你父亲让她见他找的那八个百万富翁单身汉。

亚历克：你都能够凑成一个班来到大厅里了。

康尼奇夫人：我是很认真的——她可能会在刚刚进入社交之夜就和哪个橄榄球运动员去椰林夜总会了呢。你去左边找找看，我就——

亚历克：（草率地）你让男管家去地下室找一下，不是更好吗？

康尼奇夫人：（极其严肃地）嗯，你认为她会在那个地方吗？

赛西丽娅：他跟你开玩笑的，母亲。

亚历克：母亲一定认为她和一个跨栏运动员在旋桶塞摆啤酒呢。

康尼奇夫人：我们立即去找找看。

（他们一起离开。罗莎琳和吉雷斯皮一块走进来。）

吉雷斯皮：罗莎琳——我再问你一次。你就丝毫没有把我放在心上吗？

（艾默里迈着轻快的脚步走上舞台。）

第一章 刚入社交圈的少女

艾默里：我跳舞的时间到了。

罗莎琳：吉雷斯皮先生，这位是布莱恩先生。

吉雷斯皮：你来自日内瓦湖，对吗？

艾默里：是的。

吉雷斯皮：（使人生气地）那个地方我以前去过。那里地处——中西部，是吗？

艾默里：（讽刺地）好像是吧。但是我一直都认为我宁可是乡下气味浓厚的辣味玉米粉蒸肉，也不想要没有一点调料的汤。

吉雷斯皮：你说什么！

艾默里：嗯，见笑了。

（吉雷斯皮俯了俯身，离开了。）

罗莎琳：他这个人就是太自命不凡了。

艾默里：以前我就喜欢上一个自命不凡的人。

罗莎琳：那你们的结局呢？

艾默里：嗯，对——她叫伊莎贝尔——她对什么都是一问三不知的样子，都是在我说了以后才清楚。

罗莎琳：然后呢？

艾默里：结局就是我让她坚信她比我还要聪明——因此她就离开我了。她还说我挑肥拣瘦，不切实际，你清楚。

罗莎琳：你说的不切实际怎么讲？

艾默里：嗯——就是会开车，但不会更换轮胎。

罗莎琳：你有什么计划没有？

艾默里：不太确定——竞选总统，写作——

罗莎琳：格林威治村是吗？

艾默里：天呀，当然不是——我说的是写作——并没有说喝酒。

罗莎琳：我对那些经商人都很喜欢。智商很高的人经常是容貌一般的。

艾默里：我对你有一点相见恨晚的感觉。

罗莎琳：呃，你是不是打算从"金字塔"的故事开始写？

艾默里：不是——我将故事的发生地定在了法国。我是路易十四，那你呢，你就是我的一个——一个——（改变语气）假设——我们坠入爱河。

罗莎琳：我说过我们装模作样一下。

169

艾默里：我们如果真这么做的话，事情就闹大了。

罗莎莉：为什么这么说？

艾默里：从某种意义上来讲，那是由于自私的人极其有可能对于演这样的爱情故事很不擅长。

罗莎琳：（将她的两片嘴唇送上去）装模作样。

（他们不慌不忙地接吻。）

艾默里：我不会讲一些好听的话。但是你的确非常美丽。

罗莎琳：我想要的不是这个。

艾默里：那你想要什么？

罗莎琳：（伤心地）嗯，也没有什么——只是我想要的是感情，真实的感情——但是我从来就没有拥有过。

艾默里：在这个世界上，我也从没有得到过其他的什么东西——我恨这个世界。

罗莎琳：要找到一个符合你艺术兴趣的男人实在是太难了。

（有人把一扇门给打开了，因此华尔兹舞曲的音乐声飘进了房间。罗莎琳站起身。）

罗莎琳：你听！他们弹奏的是《再吻我》[1]。

（他目不转睛地盯着她）

艾默里：嗯？

罗莎琳：嗯？

艾默里：（慢慢地——退缩了）我喜欢你。

罗莎琳：我喜欢你——此时此刻。

（他们拥吻。）

艾默里：呀，天哪，我在做什么？

罗莎琳：你什么也没有做。呀，别讲话了，再亲我一下。

艾默里：我不知道是什么原因，也不知道发生了什么，就是喜欢你——第一眼看见你就喜欢你。

罗莎琳：我也是这样——我——我——哦，今天就是不一样。

---

[1] 一九〇五年在百老汇首演的两幕轻歌剧《莫提斯小姐》（Mlle Modiste）中的歌曲，二十世纪初在美国流行起来。

（她哥哥走进房间，大吃一惊，接着高声说道："呀，抱歉，"讲完就离开了。）

罗莎琳：（她的两片嘴唇保持着原来的姿势）不要把我放开——我才不理会都是谁发现我干了什么。

艾默里：讲出来吧。

罗莎琳：我喜欢你——在此时此刻。（他们彼此拉开距离。）啊——谢谢上帝我还很年轻——谢谢上帝，赐予我美貌——我非常幸福，谢谢上帝，谢谢上帝——（她停了一下，接着忽然觉察到了一些什么，就又加上了一句）可怜的艾默里！

（他又一次向她吻去。）

缘分

还没有到两个星期，艾默里和罗莎琳的感情就已经特别深厚，处于热恋中了。那些损害了他们两个人各自十几次浪漫遭遇的重要特点，在他们热烈巨浪的映衬下显得毫无光泽了。

"这可能是一个刺激的恋爱事件，"她告诉她那心情焦躁的妈妈，"但着肯定不会是愚昧的恋爱。"

三月伊始，热烈的浪头将艾默里卷进了一家广告公司，因此他一边用充沛的精力优秀地完成了工作；一边怀揣着梦想，梦想自己瞬间变成了有钱人，带着罗莎琳在意大利旅游。

他们两个人一直在一块待着，不管是午饭还是晚饭，并且几乎每天晚上也都待在 起——一直在一片静谧中相处，好像他们担心魔法随时会解除，他们也随时会被赶出这玫瑰与激情的海洋。然而着魔状况上升到迷恋，而且他们好像一天要比一天迷恋；他们开始交谈有关七月的事——六月就结婚。所有的生活都跟随着他们的爱情发生了改变，所有的经验，所有的心愿，所有的壮志凌云，都失去了意义——他们的诙谐都藏到角落里休息了。他们原来的恋爱好像是有些可笑、完全不用觉得抱歉的幼稚行为。

艾默里人生当中第二次彻底陷入了混乱的状况，正急急忙忙地要奋起超过他这一代人。

一个小插曲

艾默里在林荫大道上犹豫不决，内心里感觉这夜晚最终是属于他的——厚重的夜色和模糊的街道上一片华丽和快乐……好像他终于把和谐意味逐渐淡薄

171

的书本合上了,走上了心旷神怡、满是活力的康庄大道。那里到处都是数不清的灯火,夜晚的街道和欢唱带来的希冀——他带着如梦似幻的情绪在人群当中走过,好像在盼望着罗莎琳从每一个角落踩着匆忙的步伐向他走来……夜色中一张张难以忘怀的脸都融进了她的脸庞之中,数不清的脚步接踵而来,仿佛无尽的序曲,融到她的脚步声中。她目不转睛看着他时的柔和的目光要比酒更使人沉醉。乃至他此时的梦是飘扬的小提琴声,和夏天的声音一样飘荡在夏日的空气当中。

房间到处都是黑黢黢的,只有汤姆的烟发出一点微弱的红光,他倚靠在打开的窗台上。身后的门被关上了,艾默里保持着背靠门的姿势站了一会儿。

"哎,本维奴托·布莱恩[1]。今天的广告生意做得怎么样?"

艾默里在长沙发上将四肢伸展开。

"我还是一如既往地厌恶做生意!"转眼之间在脑海里消失的生意兴旺的广告公司立刻被另一幅画面所代替。

"天啊,她真的让人惊叹!"

汤姆叹了一口气。

"我不可以对你说,"艾默里再次说道,"她究竟多么令人惊叹。我并不想你知道这些。我也不想其他的任何一个人知道。"

窗台上又有一阵叹息声传来——特别无可奈何的叹气。

"她就是我的生活,是我的希望,是我此时的一切。"

他觉察到有眼泪在眼睛中打转儿。

"呀,我的天,汤姆!"

苦中作乐

"如同我们这样坐。"她悄悄地说。

他在大椅子上坐下来,把双臂张开,如此一来她就能够靠在他的怀抱当中了。

"我就知道你今天晚上会过来的,"她温柔地说,"就好像夏天一样,就在我特别需要你的时候……亲爱的……亲爱的……"

---

1. 本维奴托·切里尼(Benvenuto Cellini,1500—1571),是意大利文艺复兴时期佛罗伦萨的一位金匠、画家、雕刻家、音乐家,他还创作过一部著名的自传,语言诙谐幽默,有多种英译本,其中就有英国诗人、文学批评家塞蒙兹(John Addington Symonds,1840—1893)在一八八八年所作的,在文学界有很大的影响力。

第一章　刚入社交圈的少女

他的嘴唇在她的脸上慵懒地蹭着。

"你的滋味真不错，"他叹息着。

"你是怎么想的，亲爱的？"

"嗯，真美味，真美味……"他抱得她更紧了。

"艾默里，"她小声说着，"等你准备好和我在一起的时候，就是我要嫁给你的时候。"

"刚开始我们所拥有的的东西不会太多。"

"不要这样说！"她大叫着。"如果你由于不能够给我太多东西而责怪自己的话，这让我听到会很难过的。我已经得到了最宝贵的你了——我认为这样已经很好了。"

"告诉我……"

"你不是早就已经清楚了吗？呃，你了解的。"

"是的，但是我要听你亲口说出来。"

"我喜欢你，艾默里，我全心全意地喜欢你。"

"永永远远，可以吗？"

"长长久久——呀，艾默里——"

"你说什么？"

"我要变成你的人。我要将你的家人也都变成我的家人。我要和你生孩子。"

"但是我的家人都已经不在了。"

"不要嘲笑我，艾默里。你还是亲吻我吧。"

"你要我怎么做我都照办，"他回答说。

"不对，是你要我怎么做我就怎么做。如果说的是我们的话就是说你——不是说的我。啊，你是我最宝贵的一部分，几乎要成为我的一切了……"

他将眼睛闭上。

"我真是太兴奋了，几乎都要变成惊恐了。如果这就是——这就是我最享受的时刻的话……难道这不是令人非常害怕的事情吗？"

她精神恍惚地盯着他看。

"美貌和爱情已经成为过去式了，我都明白……然而，嗯，伤心还是剩下了。我觉得所有的一切都是那么幸福，除了有些伤感。美貌是玫瑰散发的香气，但玫瑰的死亡——"

173

"对我们来说,艾默里,是最美好的,我明白。我始终坚信上帝是爱我们的——"

"上帝爱你。你就是他所拥有的最珍贵的财富。"

"我不属于他,我是属于你的。艾默里,我是你的。我是第一次后悔以前的那些亲吻,现在我才明白一个亲吻代表的含义有多大。"

然后他们吸烟,他把一天之内在办公室完成的事情讲给她听——包括他们能够住在哪个地方。有的时候,他讲话尤其多的时候,她也会在他的怀抱当中熟睡,然而他就是喜欢这样的一个罗莎琳——罗莎琳的一切,因为他在这个世界上从来没有把爱给予过任何人。很难捉摸、转瞬即逝的时刻,无法缅怀的时刻。

水上事件

某一天,艾默里和吉雷斯皮非常碰巧地在闹市中心遇见,他们俩就一块去吃了午饭,吃饭的时候艾默里听说了一件使他觉得非常开心的事情。吉雷斯皮在喝了几杯鸡尾酒之后,话就变得多了起来。这要从罗莎琳讲起,他告诉艾默里,非常确定地说罗莎琳的脾气有一些奇怪。

以前他曾和她在韦斯切斯特县参加过一个游泳运动,那时有人提到安内特·凯勒曼[1]有一天曾在那里做采访,并站在高达三十英尺的摇晃不定的避暑别墅的房顶跳水。罗莎琳听说以后马上强迫霍华德和她一块到屋顶上去感受感受。

过了一段时间之后,他刚刚在房檐边上坐下来,两条腿都悬在高空,一个身影嗖的一下从他身边飞出;罗莎琳将双臂展开,在空中摆了一个华丽的直体向前跳水的动作,跳进了清亮的水中。

"自然,我也就只能和她一起往下跳——我几乎要把自己的生命葬送在这里。当时我的心里就想着,我可以跳一下就已经非常好了。那些参加过游泳活动的人都没有进行过这样的尝试。哼,结束以后罗莎琳竟然还问我,为什么我跳的时候背没有挺直。'这样的姿势并没有使跳水变得简单。'她说,'这样的动作只是会使你的信心全部失去。'我问一下你,对于这样的一个女孩儿,一个男人究竟应当如何?没有进行下去的可能了,在我看来。"

吉雷斯皮不知道艾默里为什么在吃饭的时候一直都笑容不断。他心里暗暗思忖,也许他就是那些狡诈的乐观主义者当中的一个。

---

1. 安内特·凯勒曼(Annette Kellerman,1887—1975),是澳大利亚职业旅游运动员,也是女子泳装改良的先驱,同时又是一位影星,还是一位作家。

五周之后

还是在康尼奇家的书房里。罗莎琳自己一个人在睡榻上坐着,有点郁郁寡欢,双眼都直愣愣的,双目无神。她的改变已经可以明显地看出来了——先是人有一些消瘦,原来炯炯有神的双眼已经看不出神采,非常容易就能看出她的年龄又增加了一岁。

她妈妈走进房间,身上披着晚礼服斗篷。她惶惶不安地看了一下罗莎琳。

康尼奇夫人:今天晚上有谁要来?

(罗莎琳没有听进去她的讲话,最起码是没有留意到。)

康尼奇夫人:亚历克要过来接我去看一场巴里的喜剧《原来有你,布鲁特斯》[1]。(她看出自己是在自说自话,根本没有人在听。)罗莎琳!我是在问你今天晚上有谁要来?

罗莎琳:(吓了一跳)哦——你说什么——哦——艾默里——

康尼奇夫人:(讽刺地)近来你有那么多的告白者,我怎么清楚究竟是哪一位。(罗莎琳没有接她的话)道森·莱德比我想象中有毅力多了。这周你一个晚上都没有和他在一起。

罗莎琳:(脸上出现刚刚才有的特别厌恶的神情。)母亲——请你——

康尼奇夫人:嗯,我不干预你。你早就在一个想象中的天才身上折腾了两个多月的时间,但他的账户上一分钱都没有,你就这样和他谈下去吧,把你的一辈子都耗费在他的身上。我不干预你的决定。

罗莎琳:(就像是在背诵令人生厌的课业一样)你清楚他有一些收入——你也清楚他在广告公司一周可以获得三十五块钱的酬劳——

康尼奇夫人:就这点钱还不够你买衣服的。(她停了一下,但是罗莎琳依旧没有接她的话。)

---

[1] 巴里(Sir Jame Mathew Barrie,1860—1937),是英国剧作家、小说家。在这里康尼奇夫人说的剧名是不正确的,应该是巴里的三幕剧《亲爱的布鲁特斯》,剧名来自于莎士比亚悲剧《尤利厄斯·凯撒》第一幕第二场卡希厄斯教唆布鲁特斯时讲的话:"有时候人可以主宰自己的生命:/亲爱的布鲁特斯,我们变成了一个听从命令的人/这并不是我们的命运的错误,重点在于我们本身。"巴里这个戏也是创作的"仲夏夜之梦"的故事,假如人们有一次机会重新作出选择,情形又会是怎样的呢?而"原来有你,布鲁特斯?"则是《尤利厄斯·凯撒》第三幕第一场凯撒被刺杀时所讲的话。

我警告你万万不可迈出你将来会后悔的那一步，我是站在你的角度为你思考的。这件事可不是你爸爸能够做得到的事情。最近他的日子也特别不好过，他的年龄大了。你嫁给他的话就是嫁给了一个空想家，容貌出众，家世优渥，令人遗憾的是就是一个空想家——他就有点小聪明。（她的话外音就是，以她的角度来看，这一性格特点本身就是特别不好的。）

罗莎琳：就看在上帝的面子上，母亲——

（这时一个女仆走进房间，禀报布莱恩先生来了，女仆的话还没有说完，他就跟着一起进了房间。艾默里的好友们这十天以来都觉得他"仿佛遭了天谴"，他也的确是这样。事实上在过去的三十六个小时里，他都没有吃过一点儿食物。）

艾默里：晚上好，康尼奇夫人。

康尼奇夫人：（并没有把不友善的一面表现出来）晚上好，艾默里。

（艾默里和罗莎琳互相看了一下，交换了一下眼神——然后亚历克走近房间。亚历克的态度一直不偏不倚。他私下以为他们的结合会使得艾默里感觉很平淡，而罗莎琳会感觉特别难过，但他特别怜悯这两个人。）

亚历克：你好，艾默里！

艾默里：你好，亚历克！汤姆告诉我说他在剧院等着你。

亚历克：嗯，我刚刚就是和他见的面。今天的广告怎么样了？写出来什么精彩的文字了吗？

艾默里：嗯，都还可以。我的薪酬涨了——（每一个人都用热切的眼光注视着他）——一个星期两块钱。（大家都觉得很扫兴。）

康尼奇夫人：我们走吧，亚历克，我听到车子的响声了。

（非常美好的一个夜晚，但也存在使人失望的时候。康尼奇夫人和亚历克离开以后，一阵沉默接踵而至。罗莎琳仍旧是神情木讷地盯着壁炉看。艾默里向她走过来，伸出手来将她抱住。）

艾默里：亲爱的。

（他们互相亲吻。接下来又是一阵静默，然后她紧紧地抓住他的手，不住地亲吻着，接着将他的手放在了她的胸口上。）

罗莎琳：（伤心地）我喜欢你的手，我最喜欢的就是你的手。你从我这里离开以后——特别没有精神的模样，我经常可以看见你的手，我清楚地知道你手上的每一条掌纹。多么可爱的手呀！

（他们互相盯着看了一会儿，然后她大声啼哭起来——没有眼泪流出来的哭泣。）

艾默里：罗莎琳！

罗莎琳：哎，我们是那么的可怜！

艾默里：罗莎琳！

罗莎琳：呀，我真想现在就去死！

艾默里：罗莎琳！如果我再经历这样一个晚上的话，我的精神就要完全支撑不住了。你这个模样已经过去四天了。你一定要带给人更多的激励，不然的话我就没有办法静心工作，吃不下也睡不好。（他茫然无措地四下看了看，好像要找到一个没有用过的词语，用来将那些不流行的、腐朽的表达方法包装起来。）我们的生活必须有一个非常好的开始。我喜欢我们一起来创造一个美好的开始。（忽然他站起身，在房间里走来走去。）这都怪道森·莱德，就是因为他才这样的。是他把你纠缠得心情烦躁的。已经一周了，他每天下午都和你在一起。有人跑过来告诉我，说看到他和你在一起了，但我就只能够装作不在意地微笑着点点头，装作这些对我没有产生一点影响。但是随着事情一天天进展下去，你什么都不愿意对我吐露。

罗莎琳：艾默里，你如果再站着的话我就要疯了。

艾默里：（突然在她的旁边坐了下来）啊，我的天啊。

罗莎琳：（将他的手轻轻地抓起来）我爱你你很清楚的，对不对？

艾默里：是的。

罗莎琳：你也明白我的爱会永远属于你的——

艾默里：不要这样说；你这样令我觉得非常害怕。你说的话听上去就好像我们两个要分开了。

（她哭了一会儿，起身离开睡榻，坐在椅了上。）

一整个下午我都觉得事情越来越不好了。我在办公室当中几乎要发疯了——就连一行字也无法写出来。你将事情都给我说说吧。

罗莎琳：这没有什么好讲的，你明白吗？我就是心情不好。

艾默里：罗莎琳，你是在苦恼要不要和道森·莱德结婚的问题吗？

罗莎琳：（停顿了一下）他每天都在恳求我。

艾默里：哼，他真有本事！

177

罗莎琳：（又停顿了一下）我对他也很喜欢。

艾默里：你不要这样讲。我听到之后会非常难过的。

罗莎琳：不要犯傻了。你很清楚你是唯一的一个我以前爱、未来还爱的人。

艾默里：（快速地）罗莎琳，我们结婚吧——就下周。

罗莎琳：我们不可能办到的。

艾默里：怎么就做不到了？

罗莎琳：嗯，做不到的。我就当你的媳妇——在一个穷苦的地方过日子。

艾默里：我们的月收入有两百七十五块钱呀。

罗莎琳：亲爱的，我平时就连自己的头发都没有机会做了。

艾默里：我为你做。

罗莎琳：（似哭非笑地）谢谢你了。

艾默里：罗莎琳，你不可以将要同别人结婚的事情放到脑袋里。你告诉我！你一直瞒着我。如果你对我说的话，我就能够帮助你抵抗到底了。

罗莎琳：我就是在想——我们。我们多么可怜呀，就这么一件小事。使我爱上你的那些所谓的优点，都是会让你永远不会出人头地的缺点。

艾默里：（气愤地）讲下去。

罗莎琳：嗯——就是道森·莱德。他让人特别有安全感，我好像能够感觉出来他会是一个——一个起映衬作用的人。

艾默里：但是你并不喜欢他呀。

罗莎琳：我非常清楚这一点，但是我尊敬他，而且他是一个非常和善的人，坚毅的人。

艾默里：（委屈地）嗯——他就是这样一个人。

罗莎琳：呃——我可以给你讲一件很小的事情。周二的下午我们在麦城[1]遇见了一个惹人怜惜的小孩子——呀，道森将他抱起来让小孩坐在他的膝头，和他交流，还允诺送给他一件印第安人的衣服——第二天的时候他还记得并且买了一件——呀，特别漂亮的衣服，我心里忍不住想到他肯定会好好地对——对我们的孩子的——将他们照顾得很好——这样一来我就没有担心的必要了。

艾默里：（失望地）罗莎琳！罗莎琳！

---

1. 麦城（Rye），是位于纽约州威斯切斯特县的一座城镇。

罗莎琳：（有些许调皮地）不要故意作出一副难受的模样。

艾默里：我们彼此伤害，多么狠呀！

罗莎琳：（又开始抽泣）我们真是天造地设的一对——你和我。我一直希望，但是从来没有想过有一天我们会拥有的梦想是如此地相似。第一次真实的毫无保留的体验，我倾其一生都无法体会到的一切。我不可以什么都不做地任其在丝毫没有情调的氛围当中消逝。

艾默里：不会这样的——一定不会的。

罗莎琳：我反而非常希望可以将它当作是一个美好的回忆——将它埋藏在我的心底深处。

艾默里：嗯，女人可以做到——然而男人是无法做到的。我将会永远记得它，我要记住的不是那毫无保留的体验带给我的美好感受，而是牢牢地将痛苦记下来，很长一段时间的痛苦。

罗莎琳：你不要这样！

艾默里：我不会再见到你，失去了亲吻你的资格，仿佛那道大门被紧紧地关上了——你害怕做我的新娘。

罗莎琳：不是这样的——不是这样的——我走的是一条最难走的路，但也是最牢不可破的路。我嫁给你的话带来的只是霉运，但是我从来没有做过——你的脚步再不停下来的话，依旧这样来来回回地走着，我就要发狂了！

（他再一次失望地在睡榻上瘫坐着。）

艾默里：你到这边来，亲我一下。

罗莎琳：我不要。

艾默里：你难道不想要亲我吗？

罗莎琳：今天晚上我要你心平气和、态度冷静地爱我。

艾默里：揭示最后结局的端倪。

罗莎琳：（忽然嘴巴里吐露出令人深思的观点）艾默里，你还很年轻。我也很年轻。现在人们会对我们的自以为是选择包容，包容我们的不知深浅，包容我们将他们看作桑丘[1]的行为，即便他们没有发现我们的做法。他们此时包容我们。但是你会连续不断地碰到难题——

---

1. 他是游侠骑士堂·吉诃德的仆从。

179

艾默里：你就是担心会和我一块面对。

罗莎琳：不是的，事情不是这样的。我曾经看过一首诗——你肯定觉得这是爱拉·维拉·威尔科克斯[1]创作的，感到好笑——但是你最好还是听一下：

"由于这就是聪慧——敢爱、敢生活，

服从命运的指派和神的处置，

不要过多地询问，也不要再祈祷，

接吻抚摸头发不应缠绕不止，

感情喷涌时勿忘把持情感，

拥有了享受了就不要再——妄想。"

艾默里：但是我们还没有彼此属于对方呀。

罗莎琳：艾默里，我已经是你的人了——你明白的。光上个月就有好多次，如果你讲出来的话，我就彻底属于你了。但是不可以和你结婚，这会把我们两个人的一辈子都毁了的。

艾默里：我们可以抓住幸福的时机。

罗莎琳：道森告诉我说，我会学着去爱他的。

（艾默里双手捧着头，一动也不动。生命的迹象好像忽然从他的身上消失不见了。）

罗莎琳：亲爱的！亲爱的！我不知道究竟该怎么和你说，没有你的生活我实在是想象不出来。

艾默里：罗莎琳，我们两个人都在给彼此制造麻烦，我们的神经好像都被绷直了一般，这一周——

（他的声音听上去有些奇怪。她走上前去，双手将他的脸捧起来，亲吻他。）

罗莎琳：我不可以的，艾默里。我不能在没有绿树和花草的空间，将自己封闭在一间窄小的公寓当中，等着你回家。你会对等候在窄小房间里的我感到厌恶的，我也会逼得你对我厌恶的。

（她又没有控制住眼泪，任它模糊了双眼。）

艾默里：罗莎琳——

罗莎琳：啊，亲爱的，离开吧——不要让事情变得越来越复杂！我不能接

---

1. 爱拉·维拉·威尔科克斯（Ella Wheeler Wilcox,1850—1919），是美国女作家、诗人，同时也是通俗诗歌的创作者。这儿引用的并不是她的诗句。

受这样的——

艾默里：（他的脸紧紧地绷着，语调有些别扭）你明白你讲的是什么吗？你是说我们以后都这样了吗？

（他们的苦痛有着本质上的区别。）

罗莎琳：难道你不清楚——

艾默里：只怕我是搞不懂你是否爱我。你是担心和我在一起会经历两年的困难时光吧。

罗莎琳：我不是那个你爱着的罗莎琳。

艾默里：（情绪如此冲动地）我是不会放弃你的！我不会的，就是不会的！我必须要得到你！

罗莎琳：（她用尖酸的语气讲道）现在的你和一个小孩子一般无二。

艾默里：（狂躁地）我什么都不管了！你将我们的整个人生都摧毁了！

罗莎琳：我在做一件非常理智的事情，这是我目前唯一可以做的事情。

艾默里：你是要嫁给道森·莱德，对吗？

罗莎琳：呃，这件事你不要问我。你非常清楚，在某些方面我是一个成年人——但在一些方面——嗯，我还是未成年而已。我需要太阳的光芒，我需要和煦的阳光，我需要快乐——我害怕对一些事情负责。我不想去操心杯碟、锅碗瓢盆、扫帚簸箕的事情。我想要关心的是我在夏天游泳的时候，我的腿能否变得光滑，皮肤的颜色是否会加重。

艾默里：你依然爱我。

罗莎琳：这也是我们为什么要结束的原因。随遇而安实在是太破坏感情了。这样的情况在我们之间不要再出现了。

（她把手上的戒指摘下来还给他。泪水又把他们的双眼打湿了。）

艾默里：（他的嘴唇在她湿漉漉的脸颊上贴着）不要还给我！请你将它留下来吧——嗯，不要再让我难过了！

（她把戒指轻轻地放在他的手中。）

罗莎琳：（悲伤地）你还是离开这里吧。

艾默里：再见——

（她再次看向他，眼中含着深切的希冀，无尽的悲伤。）

罗莎琳：你一定要记得我，艾默里——

艾默里：再见——

（他走向门口，伸手去找门把手，接着抓住——她亲眼看到他把头抬起来——他离开了。离开了——她几乎要从睡榻上跳起来，然后扑倒在睡榻上，将脸埋藏在枕头里。）

罗莎琳：天哪，上帝呀，我都想要死了！（一段时间以后她站起身，双眼闭合，试探地走到了门口。接着她把身子转过来，又看了一眼房间的摆设。他们曾经在这里坐过，有过他们的小梦想；她以前常常为他在那个烟灰缸里放满火柴，他们曾经在星期天小心翼翼地把那个遮阳的窗帘拉低了整整一个下午。她双眼模糊地站立着，将这些都记住吧：她大声地告诉自己。）哎，艾默里，我哪里对不住你呢？

（随着时间的消逝，苦痛也会随之消失，不过在这难过心痛之下，罗莎琳觉得她已经失去了一些什么，但她又不清楚是什么失去了，也不清楚她究竟为什么会失去它们。）

第二章　康复实验

　　分享喜悦的麦克斯菲尔·帕里什[1]、色彩丰富的壁画《老国王科尔》令纽约州人酒吧增光添彩、高朋满座、热闹非凡。艾默里驻足在门口，瞧了瞧手表。他特别想知道精确的时间，因为他已经把心里的某件事进行了归类编码，愿意将事情办得认真细致、不拖泥带水。以后想起"完成那件事情的精确时间是一九一九年六月十日八点二十分"，他朦朦胧胧地也会觉得非常满意。如此计算时间是将他走出家门后所走的路程所用的时间也计算在内了——事后他对这段路丝毫没有印象了。

　　他的精神状态有些奇怪：他因为两天的烦忧和不安而寝食难安，最终决定以感情危机和罗莎琳的意外作为事情的结束——他的精神状态因为这件事紧张到了麻木不仁的境地。当他坐在免费午餐的桌子上，拙笨地用手去拿青果时，有一个人走来同他谈话，青果从他哆嗦的手中掉在了地上。

　　"额，艾默里……"

　　这个人是他以前在普林斯顿结识的；可他的名字他不晓得了。

　　"嗨！兄弟——"他听见自己如此打招呼。

　　"我的名字叫做吉姆·威尔逊——你不记得了？"

　　"那是，当然，吉姆。我没有忘记。"

　　"去参加同学聚会吗？"

　　"你知道！"他话刚一讲出口立刻回过味来，此行并不是去参加同学聚会。

　　"去海外？"

　　艾默里点头，双眼怪诞地瞅着。他想给人让路后退一步，可是却将桌子上的青果连带着碟子一同打翻到了地上。

　　"真倒霉，"他嘀咕道。"喝酒吗？"

　　威尔逊大方地伸出笨拙的手拍了一下他的肩膀。

---

1. 帕里什的壁画作于一八九四年，取材于童谣《老国王科尔》。

"你酒喝多了,兄弟。"

艾默里一声不响地瞧着威尔逊,盯得他十分尴尬。

"喝多了?不可能的事!"艾默里最后说出一句话。"我今天滴酒未沾。"

威尔逊半信半疑。

"到底喝不喝?"艾默里粗鲁地说道。

他们一同向吧台走去。

"高杯黑麦威士忌。"

"给我来一杯布朗斯鸡尾酒。"

威尔逊又点了一杯酒,艾默里又喝了几杯。他们打算入座。到了十点钟,卡林代替了威尔逊,他是一五级的。艾默里此时已经喝得天旋地转了,可是他精神的淤血依然得到了那层层的温柔的满足和宽慰,他对战争高谈阔论,没有停止的意思。

"那是精神的荒芜,"他以大智者的口吻接连说道,"在知识的空虚中度过了两年多的时间,遗弃了理想主义,成为了一头畜生。"他表情丰富地向着《老国王科尔》这幅壁画舞动拳头,"变成普鲁士式的人,对于所有事情都是这个模样,特别是对女人。以前是非常直接地对女子学院讲话,现在丝毫不放在心上了。"他伸手一挥,将一个德国赛尔脱兹矿泉水打到了地上,哗啦一声碎了,以此来表示他本人没有原则,可是这一行为并未将他的话打断。"如果可以寻找到快乐,那就去寻找,因为明天就要去死。从此时此刻开始,这便是我的哲学。"

卡林打哈欠了,而艾默里,愈发健谈,他继续说道:

"以前对所有事情都感到好奇—— 人们退让了,生活态度采用了一半对一半的方式。现在不觉得奇怪了,不奇怪了。"他为了让卡林确信他丝毫都不觉得奇怪,逐渐加重了语气,结果他不记得自己之前讲了什么,最后朝着酒吧里的所有人宣称他是一头"畜牲",敷衍地结束了这件事。

"艾默里,你在讲什么呢?"

艾默里真心实意地弯着身子向前。

"宣布我人生的消亡。紧急的关头将我的人生毁灭了。这个不能和你说——"

卡林对酒吧侍者说的一句话传进了他的耳朵:

"给他镇静剂。"

艾默里愤怒地摇着头。

"别给我这个东西!"

"但是你听我讲,艾默里,你喝了太多的酒。脸色苍白得如同幽灵一样。"

艾默里在思索这句话。他打算看一下镜子中的自己。但是他即便眯着一只眼,也仅仅能看见吧台后面那一排瓶子这么远的距离。

"人要活得体面些。我们去整来一些色拉。"

他收拾了一下外套,摆出一副冷酷的模样,可是离开吧台对于他来讲是非常困难的,结果他还是摔倒在了椅背上。

"我们去香利餐馆去。"卡林建议道,一面伸出胳膊,以便让他抓住。

有了这帮助,艾默里终于可以迈动两条腿了,死扛着走过了第四十二大街。

香利餐厅灯光昏暗。他觉得自己是在高声讲话,他感觉自己在讲打算将人们都踩在脚下,说得非常直接,十分有说服力。他食用了三个总会三明治,一个接一个,仿佛是在吃巧克力颗粒糖。随后罗莎琳又浮现在他脑海里,从他的嘴型上,可以判断出是在呼喊她的名字。之后他便沉沉欲睡,迷迷糊糊、昏昏沉沉的,觉得人们身穿燕尾服,或许是侍者,绕着桌子……

……他来到一间卧室,卡林在讲他的鞋带被系成了死结。

"没事,"他迷迷糊糊讲出一句话。"穿着睡觉……"

还没有醒酒

他大声笑着苏醒过来,慵懒地看着四周的环境,很明显这是一家高档饭店里的客房,里面有浴室。他的头还在嗡嗡地响着,一幅幅画面出现在眼前,之后又变得模糊,最终逐渐消失,可是除了想乐以外,他没有做出任何有意识的反应。他伸手拿起床边的电话机。

"喂——这个饭店叫什么名字?"

"尼克勃克[1]?那好,我要两杯黑麦威士忌,请送上来——"

他躺了一会儿,无聊地思索着,不清楚他们会端来一瓶还是端来两个小玻璃杯子。然后他费劲地,从床上挣扎着起身,慢慢地向浴室走去。

他走出浴室,慵懒地拿着一块毛巾在身上擦着,这个时候酒吧的侍者来送酒,于是他忽然有了一个要作弄他的想法。又考虑到这么一来有失尊严,于是便叫他离开了。

---

1. 即纽约人州人饭店

他喝了新酒,感到全身发热,前一天所发生的事像电影胶片又渐渐地开始由一个个独立的画面拼凑而成。他又瞧见了罗莎琳的身体蜷缩着,趴在床头哭泣,他又感觉到自己的脸被她的泪水打湿。他又听见她所讲的话:"一定不要忘记我,艾默里——一定不要忘记我——"

"见鬼!"他大喊了一声,之后便哽咽了,伤心地颤抖起来,瘫在了床上。过了一会儿,他睁开双眼,注视着天花板。

"大笨蛋!"他生气地喊了一声,发出长长的叹气声,起身走下床,走到那瓶酒跟前。他又喝了一杯酒之后,流下了眼泪。他脑海中浮现起一件件小事——这些事发生在已经逝去的春天,他喃喃自语地讲出心里的激动,结果他更加伤心了。

"我们那时候多么幸福啊,"他讲话就好像表演一样,"特别特别幸福。"然后他放声痛哭,跪在床边,一半的脑袋埋在枕头上。

"我自己的女人——我自己的——啊——"

他用力地咬着牙齿,于是哗哗地流下了眼泪。

"啊……亲爱的女人,属于我的一切,我想得到的一切!……啊,我的女人,回到我身边,赶紧回来吧!……我需要你……需要你……我们太可怜了……我们留给彼此的只有痛哭……她从我身边消失了……我看不见她。我能成为她朋友了。肯定是这样的——肯定是——"

之后他又讲:

"我们那么幸福,特别特别幸福……"

他从地板上站起来,激动地扑在床上,然后他疲惫不堪地翻身躺着,同时他渐渐地清楚了,他前一晚喝得烂醉如泥,现在仍然昏昏沉沉的。他高声笑着,起身走下床,又忘记了所有事情……

中午,在比尔特莫酒吧偶然碰上一群人,放纵再一次开始。他过后还隐隐约约地记得,那时候与一个自称是"皇家步兵康恩上尉"的英国军官谈论过法国诗歌,他还记得在午餐桌上试着朗读诗歌《月光》[1],然后昏睡在一个又大又软的椅子上,一直睡到快要五点钟的时候,又来了一群人,他才被叫起。之后又是喝酒,凭借这个来调节几种心态,准备忍受正餐的折磨。他们决定使用泰

---

1. 法国象征主义诗歌代表人物之一魏尔兰(Paul Verlaine,1844—1896)的诗作,并参阅第6页注。

森酒店的剧院入场券去看戏,因为在这个戏里有四次喝酒的演出——这个戏有两个丝毫没有变化的语调,烟雾缭绕并且昏暗的场景,灯光效果很不容易习惯,即便他的反应这么棒。他事后猜测这个戏演得肯定是《玩笑盛宴》[1]……

……之后又去了椰树林夜总会,在那里,艾默里在外面的小露台上又睡着了。到达杨克色的香利酒吧时,他几乎已经头脑清楚了,他小心翼翼地掌控了自己喝高杯酒的杯数,变得清醒,而且滔滔不绝地讲话。他发现参加聚会的有五个人,其中的两个人他有些印象。他支付自己的费用,给人一种正直的感觉,而且高声坚持,他马上安排所有的事情,以此来让他身边几桌的人高兴……

有人讲了一句话,旁边桌子的座位上有一位歌舞明星——名字叫做卡巴莱,于是艾默里起身,大胆地走上前去介绍自己……他因为这一行为陷入了一场争吵,开始是与她的同伴争吵,然后又同酒吧的领班争论——艾默里摆出一副高傲、过分热情的姿态……在面临着没有什么可以反驳的理论后,他同意在别人的陪同下返回自己的座位上。

"我决定自杀了,"他忽然宣称。

"什么时间?明年?"

"现在。明天早上。我打算在海军准将饭店包房里的一个房间,将热水装满浴缸,之后切断血管。"

"他是有病了!"

"你应当再喝一杯黑麦,老弟!"

"我们明天再说这些。"

但是不管身边的人如何劝解,艾默里都选择不听了,最起码在言语上。

"你之前也是如此吗?"他偷偷问道。

"是啊!"

"常常吗?"

"我总是如此。"

这一句话惹起了争论。有个人说他在一些时候情绪非常低落,是会如此认真思考的。另一个人表示同意,说人活在世界上是一件没有什么意义的事。"康恩[2]上尉"不晓得什么时间参与进来,他说根据他自己的想法,这种感觉最容易

---

1. 意大利剧作家贝尼利(Sem Benelli,1877—1949)的四幕喜剧(1909)。
2. "康恩"(com)在美国英语里意思为"玉米"。

在一个人身体情况很差的时候产生。艾默里提议所有人都点一杯布朗克斯鸡尾酒,将碎玻璃倒进里面,然后全喝了。让他安心的是无人同意他的看法,于是他饮用了高杯黑麦威士忌后,将自己的胳膊肘放在桌子上,手托着下巴——一个十分儒雅、丝毫不会被人发觉的睡觉姿势,他安心下来——没有了知觉,陷入了沉睡……

一个女人叫醒了他,将他抱在怀里。那是一个美丽的女人,长着褐色、凌乱的头发,有一双深蓝色的眼睛。

"送我回家!"她说道。

"喂!"艾默里眨动着眼睛说。

"我喜欢你。"她轻声说道。

"我也喜欢你。"

他留意到她身后有一个人,那人一脸凶相,正在与他的同伴在吵架。

"跟我在一起的那个人非常没用,"长着蓝眼睛的女人偷偷说道,"我厌烦他。我希望和你一块回家。"

"你喝醉了?"艾默里聪明地问道。

她腼腆地点点头。

"跟他一块回家,"他严肃地对她讲,"你是跟着他来的。"

这时候,她身后那个一脸凶相的人推开抓着他争吵的人,向他们走来。

"喂!"他凶巴巴地说道,"这个女孩是跟着我来的,你这是要半道抢走吗?"

艾默里冷冷地瞧着他,而姑娘反倒是将他抱得更紧了。

"你松开那个女孩!"凶恶的人说道。

艾默里将眼睛睁大。

"你去死吧!"他最后命令道,然后转身朝向那个女孩。

"一见钟情。"他说。

"我爱你。"她一面娇羞地说着,一面依靠在他身上。她的眼睛真的很好看。

有人凑近他的耳朵讲话。

"她的名字叫做格利特·戴蒙。她喝醉了,她是跟着那个人来的。你最好松开她。"

"那好,让他照看好这个姑娘!"艾默里生气地大喊道,"我不在基督教女青年会工作,对吧?——对不对?"

"松开她！"

桌子四周的人越发多了，眼看着就要打起来了，可是一个狡诈的侍者拽住了马格利特·戴蒙的手指，强迫她放开艾默里。这时她打了侍者一记耳光，发出响亮的声音，又举起双手愤怒地打在之前那位同伴的身上。

"啊，上帝！"艾默里叫道。

"我们走！"

"快一些，一会就叫不到出租车了！"

"喂，服务员。"

"走，艾默里。你的风流停止吧。"

艾默里大声地笑着。

"你不晓得你讲得太对了。不晓得，这就是问题的所在。"

艾默里的劳资关系

两天后的一个早上，艾默里来到巴斯科姆——巴罗广告公司，抬手敲着主管的门。

"进来！"

艾默里踉跄地走进办公室。

"早上好，巴罗先生。"

巴罗先生戴上眼镜观察着客人，嘴巴稍微张开，如此一来他就能仔细听了。

"哦，布莱恩先生。好些天没见到你了。"

"是啊，"艾默里说道，"我要辞职。"

"呃——呃——这是——"

"我不喜欢在这里上班。"

"很可惜。我认为我们关系一直——呃——很愉快。我认为你干活很卖力——或许你也稍微倾向于写新奇的文字说明——"

"没有别的原因，我只是有些厌烦了，"艾默里非常粗鲁地打断了他的话，"我根本不在乎海尔贝尔的面粉是否比其他家的好。实际上，我向来不食用他们的面粉。所以说我已经厌倦了这些面粉的好与坏——啊，我清楚我一直在喝酒——"

巴罗先生的面部表情已经僵硬了。

"你想要被提拔——"

艾默里挥手打断了他的讲话。

"而且我觉得我的工资太低了，一个礼拜三十五块钱——都没一个娴熟的木工工资高。"

"你刚刚入职，以前你一直没有干过这个工作。"巴罗先生冷漠地说道。

"但是我花了一万元在我的教育上，难道只是了给你写这种东西？无论如何，只看工作年限，在你这儿工作的速记员，工作五年了，一个礼拜才有十五元的工资。"

"我不愿意跟你争论，先生。"巴罗先生说着站起身来。

"我也不想跟你争论。我仅仅是想跟你说我不想干了。"

他们站在那里，冷冷地看着对方，随后艾默里转身走出了办公室。

稍稍平静

事情发生四天之后，他终于返回了公寓。汤姆在低头为《新民主》杂志写书评，他是这个杂志的编辑。他们见面后彼此安静地看着对方。

"哦？"

"哦？"

"上帝啊，艾默里，谁把你的眼睛打得乌青——还有下巴，发生了什么事情？"

艾默里哈哈一笑。

"没有什么事。"

他脱掉外套，将两个肩膀显露出来。

"你看这里！"

汤姆轻声地吹了一声口哨。

"谁打的？"

艾默里再一次哈哈大笑。

"啊，许多人。他们把我狠狠地揍了一顿。确实是这样。"他缓慢地将衬衣穿好，"被打也是早晚的事，我肯定是无法躲避的。"

"谁打的？"

"哦，打我的有几个酒吧服务员，两个海员，还有几个路人，我觉得。那种感觉很奇怪。你要是希望能感受下这种感觉，就得被人狠狠地打一顿。过不了多长时间，你就倒下了，每个人好像都在劈头盖脸地使劲揍你，最终你倒在地上——随后他们用力踢向你的身体。"

第二章　康复实验

汤姆点着一支烟。

"我花了一天的时间四处找你，艾默里。但是你总比我技高一筹。我可以说你是跟一帮人在一起。"

艾默里迅速地坐到一把椅子上，向汤姆要了一支香烟。

"你现在没有喝多吧？"汤姆探问道。

"丝毫没有。为何这么问呢？"

"哦，亚历克搬出去了。他的父母一直在看着他，要求他搬回家里，因此他——"

他心里涌出一阵悲痛，令他心乱如麻。

"太糟糕了。"

"是啊，太糟糕了。我们打算在这里住下去就必须去找其他人。房租又贵了。"

"是啊。找谁都可以。你来决定吧，汤姆。"

艾默里返回自己的屋子。他第一眼就看到了罗莎琳的照片——靠在梳妆台上的一面镜子上，他之前打算把照片用镜框裱起来的。他看着照片一点反应都没有。此时的他只能够在脑海里回忆关于她的一幕幕鲜活的画面，相比之下，她的相片显得十分怪异而又不真实。他又返回书房。

"你有没有纸盒子？"

"没有，"汤姆回答道，不清楚他是何意，"我要纸盒子有什么用？哦，对啦——没准儿亚历克的屋子里有。"

艾默里终于找见了他期望已久的纸盒子，于是他走到梳妆台前，将装有信件、一截项链、两块小手帕以及几张照片的抽屉打开。当他非常小心地将这些东西移动到纸盒里时，他的目光已经被一本书吸引了过去，这本书讲述了主人公将失去的恋人的一块肥皂保存了一年之久，最后使用这块肥皂洗手，洗清了一切的东西。他发出哈哈的笑声，哼唱起《自你走了以后》[1]这首歌……瞬间停止……

绳子断了两回，又重新接好，他将这包东西丢到了箱子的最底下，合上箱子的盖子后，他又返回了书房。

"外出吗？"汤姆担忧地问道。

"呜呜。"

1.《自你走了以后》，一九一八年创作的美国流行歌曲，特纳◇雷顿（Tumer Layton）作曲，亨利◇克里默（Henry Creamer）作词，火来很多爵士歌曲依此创作。

"去什么地方?"

"不能告诉你,小伙子。"

"一块吃顿饭吧。"

"对不起,我已经和苏凯·布列特约好了要一块儿吃。"

"哦。"

"再见。"

艾默里走到马路对面,饮用了一杯高杯威士忌;随后他来到华盛顿广场,跳到一辆公共汽车上,找到了一个车顶上的座位。公共汽车到达四十三大街后,他下车径直向比尔特莫酒吧走去。

"嗨!艾默里!"

"你想喝点什么?"

"喂!服务员!"

心理正常

当禁止"解渴先行"的法令下达后,艾默里马上就不再借酒消愁了,有一天早上他一觉醒来后发觉先前的"往返于酒吧"的时光已经彻底结束了,他不后悔过去三个礼拜的所作所为,同时也不遗憾这样的日子不会再出现。他使用了最强烈、虽然是最无力的方法自保,抵抗回忆带来的痛苦,而且虽然他不会用这样的方法去劝慰别人,可是他最后觉得这是个很奏效的方法:他已经熬过了一开始的痛苦。

千万不要误解!罗莎琳得到了艾默里无与伦比的爱,不会再有活着的人得到艾默里这样的爱了。罗莎琳已经带走了艾默里的青春活力,从他从来没有探索过的心灵深处挖掘出让他惊讶的温存,除了罗莎琳,没有任何一个人得到过他的温柔与无私。艾默里后来又谈过几场恋爱,可那些都是不一样的爱情;他在那些恋爱中恢复了许更典型的心理状态,在这种情况下,女孩变成了一面镜子,来反映着他的情绪。罗莎琳在他身上挖掘的不仅是富有激情的爱恋;他对于罗莎琳的感情是深厚的、永不消退的。

但是,在快要结束的时刻,他的状况像极了舞台上所演的悲剧,而且最后出现了三个礼拜放纵狂饮的令人难以理解的情形,他目前在感情上已经疲惫不堪了。冷漠和虚伪的人和环境浮现在他的脑海里,现在仿佛非常能够成为他的抚慰。他用父亲的去世为背景写了一个故事,十分愤世嫉俗,邮递到一家杂志,获得了一张六十元的支票，并获得邀请——希望他可以再给他们杂志编写同种类型的故事。这一下满足了他的虚荣心，可是他并没有因此受到激励而继续写作。

他阅读了大量的书籍。《一个青年艺术家的肖像》[1]令他迷惑和沮丧；《琼和彼得》和《永不熄灭的火》[2]令他兴趣十足；他在一个名字叫做门肯[3]的批评家的文章中找到的几部十分优秀的美国小说，令他非常惊叹；《凡多佛与兽性》[4]，《特伦·威尔的毁灭》[5]，还有《珍妮姑娘》[6]。麦肯奇、切斯特顿、高尔撕华绥、贝尼特在他心里，现在已经从看透所有、富有生活气质的天才，沦为只为娱乐的同时代的人，萧伯纳出众的清晰与才华，还有 H·G 威尔斯非常沉醉地把浪漫主义的均匀相称的钥匙插进捉摸不透的真理之锁，仅凭这一点就已经吸引了他的目光，令他十分痴迷。

他打算去拜访达西大人，因为他刚回国就给他写信了，可是到目前为止他还没有收到回信；并且他也清楚去看达西大人就代表着要说罗莎琳的事，而一想到要将他们的事重新讲述一遍，就令他胆战心惊。

在挑选从容镇静的人的时候他想起了劳伦斯夫人，一个极为聪慧、很有尊严的夫人，教会的一名皈依者，非常虔诚地崇拜着达西大人。

一天，他给劳伦斯夫人打了个电话。对，她还清晰地记得他；没有，达西大人不在城里，她觉得达西大人身处波士顿；他答应过只要回来就来参加晚宴。艾默里是否能来一同享用午餐呢？

"我觉得我还是能到吧，劳伦斯夫人，"他到达之后意思模糊地说道。

---

1. 爱尔兰著名作家詹姆斯·乔伊斯（James Joyce, 1882—1941）出版于一九一六年的中篇小说。
2. 英国作家 H·G·威尔斯著，《琼和彼得》出版于一九一八年，《永不熄灭的火》出版于一九一九年。
3. 门肯（H.L Mencken,1880—1956），美国记者、散文家、美国生活和文化的辛辣批评家、二十世纪前五十年间美国最有影响的作家和散文家之一。
4. 美国自然主义小说家佛兰克·艾里斯（Frank Norris, 1870—1902）的小说，一九一四年根据他生前未完成的手稿出版。
5. 美国《纽约时报》驻伦敦记者、小说家哈罗德·佛雷德里克（Harold Frederic, 1856—1898）的小说，发表于一八九六年，批评界认为是美国的一部经典小说，尽管一般读者并不熟悉。
6. 美国小说家西奥多·德莱赛（Theodore Dreiser, 1871—1945）的第二部长篇小说，出版于一九一一年。

"大人上个礼拜还在这儿呢，"劳伦斯夫人后悔地说。"他非常想见到你，可是你的地址被他落在家里了。"

"他是否觉得我已经信奉布尔什维克主义了？"艾默里饶有兴趣地问道。

"他目前心情很差。"

"什么原因呢？"

"由于爱尔兰共和国。他认为缺少尊严。"

"怎么回事？"

"爱尔兰总统抵达的时候，他已经去了波士顿。可是他内心很难受，因为借贷委员在坐车时，会用胳膊搀扶总统。"

"我不怪罪他的。"

"哎，你在部队的时候什么给你留下了最深刻的印象？你瞧上去成长了不少。"

"那是因为另外一场，并且更具毁灭性的战役，"他回答道，并且还情不自禁地大笑起来，"但是要谈论部队——我考虑一下——哦，我觉得一个人身体状况很大程度上决定了身体的勇敢程度，我觉得我跟身边的人一样有胆量——以前这点总让我担忧。"

"还有其他的吗？"

"呃，就是觉得只要习惯了，任何事情都能够忍受，我还有一个条件便是心理学考试时取得了不错的成绩。"

劳伦斯夫人哈哈大笑起来。艾默里感觉来到这座位于滨河大道凉爽的宅子里，内心是十分惬意的，这里距离人口密集的纽约很远，不会产生一种人们向一个狭窄的空间吐出许多气的感觉。恍惚间，劳伦斯夫人让他回忆起贝雅特丽斯，并不是在气质上，而是在柔媚的风度和得体的举止间。这座宅子，室内的摆设，还有席间上菜的方法与他在长岛有名望的人家见到的情况有着非常大的不同，那里的仆人太鲁莽，一定应当赶走他们，甚至和更为保守的"联谊俱乐部"[1]会员的宅子中所见的也不能相提并论。他有些困惑，这种匀称约束的气氛，这种魅力，虽然他认为富有欧洲大陆的格调，可是不晓得是否是依靠劳伦斯夫人家族的新英格兰渊源汇集而成的，或者是由于她长时间生活在意大利和西班牙。

---

1. 纽约市"联谊俱乐部"（Union Club）是美国最老的私人俱乐部，创办于一八六三年，会员中有包括美国总统、工业巨头在内的很多大人物。

他在午饭时喝了两杯法国苏特恩白葡萄酒，随之话也逐渐增多了，他自认为很有旧时魅力的气派，畅谈宗教和文学，还有步步紧逼的社会等级现象。很明显他很受劳伦斯夫人喜爱，他的见解尤其受她关注；艾默里也希望人们能够再次欣赏他的见解——用不了多长时间这里也许就会变成非常美好的居住地。

"达西大人依旧觉得你是他的化身，觉得你的信仰终究会渐渐变得明朗。"

"或许吧，"他认同道，"现在我还不信奉宗教。那只是由于宗教与我这个岁数的生活好像没有一点联系。"

从她家离开的时候，他在河滨大道上走着，有些得意洋洋。现在再来探讨斯蒂芬·文森特·贝尼特[1]这个年轻的诗人，或是谈论爱尔兰共和国，真的令人充满兴趣。无论是律师爱德华·卡森[2]或者是科哈兰法官[3]的惹人厌恶的控诉，他对爱尔兰问题已经完全厌烦了；但是，有一段时间，他自身的凯尔特人的性格特征成为了他个人哲学的支撑。

他仿佛忽然之间感觉到生活具有充裕的遗产，只要这种先前的兴致再次出现并不代表着他重新逃离生活——逃离生活本身。

忐忑不安

"我的岁数已经很大了，很倦怠了，汤姆。"一天艾默里如此说道，一面坐在舒服的窗台上伸着懒腰。他常常很自然地采用斜靠的姿势。

"你在没写作之前是一个很有趣的人，"他接着说道，"现在你隐藏起你觉得能够付印的内心的想法。"

生活又归于平静，又回到了没有志向的状态。他们觉得如果俭朴一些，依旧可以负担得起这套公寓的费用，汤姆具有老猫的习性——总待在家里不外出，他越来越喜欢这套公寓了。汤姆拥有一副挂在墙上的英国狩猎图版画的印制品，还有借来的大挂毯，大学姜靡时期的一件纪念品，非常多的没有人认领的蜡扦，雕花的路易十四椅子，可是无论什么人坐在这把椅子上不到一分钟就会感到脊椎酸痛——汤姆觉得这是因为人们坐在了蒙特斯庞[4]阴魂的膝头上——不管怎

---

1. 斯蒂芬·文森特·贝尼特（Stephen Vincent Benet，1898—1943），美国作家、诗人，因一部写美国内战的长诗《约翰⊠布朗的遗体》，于一九二九年获普利策奖。
2. 爱德华⊠卡森（Edward Carson，1854—1935），北爱尔兰统一党领袖、律师。
3. 科哈兰法官（Daniel Florence Cohalan，1867—1946？），美国爱尔兰人法官。
4. 路易十四的情妇。

说，出于对汤姆这些家具的考虑，他们决定继续居住下去。

  他们不怎么外出：有时候会去看一场戏，或者去豪华餐馆或普林斯顿俱乐部吃顿饭。因为禁止喝酒，这个有名的见面地也遭遇了他们的要命的伤害；你以后不会在午夜十二点或者早上五点钟漫步到比尔特莫酒吧，而心情仍然非常高兴，无论是汤姆还是艾默里都已经没有心情去二十夜总会（别称"老家伙夜总会"）或者广场饭店的玫瑰厅，挑寻中西部或是新泽西刚刚加入社交场合的女孩子跳舞了——另外，就如艾默里之前对一位胆战心惊的夫人所讲的，纵然如此，也得饮用几杯鸡尾酒"方可将智力降低到在场女人的水平"。

  艾默里最近收到了几封来自巴顿先生的信，这些信令人非常担忧。信里讲日内瓦湖的房子太大，租出去非常困难；现在可以收到的租金只够交付今年的税款和必要的修缮，除去这些费用就没剩多少钱了；事实上，律师的意见是虽然艾默里拥有整个房产权在名义上听起来不错，但是实际上却是个负担。但即便未来三年里他不能从整个房产中得到一分钱，艾默里出于模糊的情感上的思索决定，现在，无论怎么讲，他不会卖掉房产。

  他对汤姆讲出了自己内心厌恶的那个具体的日子是非常典型的。他睡到中午才起床，起床以后和劳伦斯夫人共同享用了午餐。之后坐在他最喜爱的公共汽车顶部，满心空落地返回家中。

  "为什么你不应该感到倦怠，"汤姆打着哈欠说道，"像你这个岁数和条件的人，这应该是惯有的心态啊。"

  "不错，"艾默里一边深思一边讲道，"但是不光是倦怠；我是内心忐忑。"

  "那是由于战争和恋爱。"

  "哦，"艾默里考虑着，"我不清楚战争本身无论是对你还是对我能不能造成很大的影响——但是毋庸置疑，战争毁掉了我们之前的背景，仿佛剔除了我们这代人身上的个人主义。"

  汤姆惊异地将头抬起。

  "的确是这样，"艾默里坚定地认为。"我不清楚战争能不能铲除整个世界的个人主义。啊，上帝，之前多么高兴，能够做梦，幻想自己能够变成一个真正的大独裁者，或是一个作家，或是一个宗教的领袖或是政治领袖——而现在，纵然是再出现一个雷奥纳多·达·芬奇，或是再出现一个洛伦佐·德·梅迪奇[1]，也一定不会是世界上真正老式的水火不容的人物。生活覆盖得太广，太复杂了。一片荒芜掩埋了整个世界，甚至伸出一个手指头都不可以，而我就是想成为这样一个伟大的手指头——"

"我不赞同你的说法，"汤姆制止了他的话，"自打——哦，自打开始法国大革命，在这个唯我独尊的位置上还一直没有出现过这样的人。"

艾默里极其不赞成。

"你对这个时代的理解是错误的，在这个时代所有愚蠢的人都是个人主义已经表现了一个时期的个人主义者。威尔逊[2]仅仅在他反抗的时候才是强悍的；他只能一再地退让。只要托洛茨基和列宁站在明确、相同的立场，他们就变成和只有两分钟的克伦斯基[3]同样的名人。即便是福熙[4]，也没有"石壁"杰克逊[5]的一半重要。人类最富有个人主义色彩的事便是战争，可是战争中的人民英雄不但没有威望，也不承担责任；基纳麦和中士约克[6]就是个例子。一个小学生不可能将潘兴[7]当作一个英雄。一个大人物压根就没有时间真的去做每一件事，他就是坐着成为伟大的人物的。"

"那么你觉得未来就不会出现永远的世界英雄了吗？"

"没错——从历史上来看——不通过生活中来看。卡莱尔[8]估计很难寻找到

---

1. 梅迪奇（Lorenzo de Medici，1449—1492），佛罗伦萨统治者（1469—1492）。
2. 威尔逊（Thomas Woodrow Wilson，1856—1924），普林斯顿大学校长（1902—1910），美国第二十八任总统（1913—1921），在第一次世界大战期间于一九一七年四月向国会提出对德宣战。
3. 克伦斯基（Alexandr Fyodorovich Kerensky，1881—1970），俄国社会革命党人，临时政府（1917）最高司令，十月革命后逃亡国外。
4. 福熙（Ferdinand Foch，1851—1929），法国元帅，第一次世界大战法军总参谋长。
5. "石壁"杰克逊（Thomas Jonathan Jackson，1824—1863），美国内战时期南部联军将领，因一八六一年内战第一仗地面战役的胜利而得名。
6. 基纳麦（George Guynemer，1894—1917）第一次世界大战法国民族英雄，在空战中失踪。约克中士（Alvin York，1887—1964），第一次世界大战美国战斗英雄。一九四一年美国把他的事迹拍成影片《陆军中士约克》。
7. 潘兴（John Joseph Pershing，1860—1948），美国将军，第一次世界大战美国远征军将领。
8. 卡莱尔（Thomas Caryle，1795—1881），苏格兰讽刺作家、散文家、历史学家，著作有《法国大革命》《论英雄、英雄崇拜及历史上的英雄事迹》等，对英国维多利亚时期文化有很大影响。

材料来写新的章节讲述'大人物英雄'。"

"继续讲。我今天要认真听。"

"现在人们全力信任领袖人物,可怜地用光所有力气。但是我们刚发现一个受人拥戴的改革家或者政治家或者军人或者作家或者哲学家——发现了一个像罗斯福、像托尔斯泰、像伍德[1]、像萧伯纳、像尼采这类的人物,一旦出现这类的人物,他便会被批评的逆流冲走。天啊,如今的世界,不会有永远存在的人。这是一条通往默默无闻最靠得住的道路。当人们反复听见同一个人的名字就会觉得厌倦。"

"于是你便归罪于新闻舆论?"

"完全正确。拿你来说吧,你在《新民主》杂志做编辑,这个杂志是全国最棒的,是会被一个志向远大的人阅读的。你有什么任务?啊,对分配给你去评价的每一个人,每一个理论,每一本书,每一个政策,都要竭尽全力描写得精妙,富有趣味,尽可能地表现出愤世嫉俗的态度。你能在所争论的问题上投入更多的关注,激起更多精神上的愤怒,你就会赚到他们更多的钱,就会有更多的人购买这期刊物。你,汤姆·丹维里埃,一个历经煎熬的雪莱式的诗人,擅长变革,擅长应对,聪慧,为了达到目的能够用尽一切手段,是人类批评意识的代表——哦,你别反对,我清楚这类东西。我在读大学时就时常写书评;诚实、仔细地书写,说出一个理论或者一个解决方法,当作'又一种作为我们夏天放松阅读的深受欢迎的补充'我觉得引用最新出版的这一类图书,真是一种不错的消遣。好了,你就认同吧。"

汤姆哈哈大笑,而艾默里则洋洋自得,接着说道:

"我们打算相信。青年学生打算信任老一代的作者,选民们打算信任他们在国会里的代表,民众们打算信任他们的政治家,但是他们不可以。有太多的声音,有太多不集中、不合理、不成熟的批评。报刊的情况更差。所有富裕却不进步的旧党,只要具备那种能够称之为金融天赋的非常贪心、紧紧抓住不放手的心态,就能够拥有一家报纸,而报纸便是数以万计精疲力竭、行色匆匆的人的精神食量和饮品,他们为现代生活的事务投入太多精力,只能整个吃下已经事先消化的食物。投票人花两分钱买下了他的政治见解,买下了成见,买下

---

1. 伍德(Leonard Wood,1860—1927),美国将领,曾任志愿兵骑兵团司令。参加过美西战争(1898)。

了哲学观点。一年以后，形成了一个新的政治集团，或者报纸的所有权发生了改变，结果是：更大的动乱，更多的冲突，新思想的猛然出现，新思想的糅合，新思想的净化，对新思想的抵抗——"

他停下来，稍微歇息一下。

"这就是我为何立下誓言不再写作的理由，除非我拥有清晰的看法，要么任何看法也没有了；即便不将危险、粗浅的警句灌输到人们的脑袋里，我的心灵也已经拥有太多的罪恶了；也许我会导致一个可怜、不侵犯人的资本家和炸弹产生卑劣的联系，或者叫一个天真烂漫的小布尔什维克和一颗机枪子弹发生纠葛——"

对于借他与《新民主》杂志的关系加以嘲讽的那种态度，汤姆愈发觉得担忧了。

"这一切跟你的心情倦怠有什么关联呢？"

艾默里则觉得有非常大的关联。

"哪里是我的位置？"他问道。"什么是我所拥护的？宣传人类？参照美国小说里的说法，我们要被他们引导相信，年龄在十九岁至二十五岁的'健康的美国男子'是彻彻底底的无性的动物。实际上，他越是健壮这句话越是错误的。拥有强烈的兴趣是令你兴奋起来的唯一解决方法。行了，战争已经结束了；我目前太注重作者的职责，因此还无法成为作家。至于做生意，即使不讲也清楚。只跟经济学有一丝丝实用主义的联系，除此之外，它和这世界上我有兴致的所有事情都没有关联。平平庸庸地当一个小职员，我可以瞧见的是我一生中即将到来的最珍贵的十年就会包含一部工业电影脑力劳动的内容。"

"试着写小说。"汤姆提出建议。

"主要是我只要写故事就会感到烦躁——担心我是在写小说而不是生活——会考虑或许生活会在奢华饭店的日式花园里，或是在大西洋域，或是在曼哈顿东区的南面等候我。"

"无论怎么讲，"他接着说道，"必需的冲动在我身上是不存在的。之前我打算做一个正常的人，但是女孩子肯定不会和我想的一样。"

"你还会找到的。"

"上帝！别再这么想了。你为什么不跟我讲'一个值得爱的女孩是会等着你的'？不对，先生，确实值得爱的女孩是不会等任何一个人的。假如我当时认为还会有别的女孩子，那我便会丧失对人性仅有的信心。或许我能这么干——可是普天之下，我心动的女孩只有罗莎琳。"

"唉，"汤姆打着哈欠说道，"作为倾听者，我已经听你说了整整一个小时。但是，话又说回来，对事物你又开始拥有激烈的看法了，这令我很高兴。"

"我也很高兴，"艾默里勉强表示认同。"可是在我见到生活甜蜜的一家人的时候，我心里就觉得不舒服——"

"生活甜蜜的家庭就需要人们有这种感受。"汤姆粗暴地说道。

吹毛求疵的汤姆

艾默里也有听别人说个不停的时候——汤姆在烟雾缭绕中洋洋自得地批判美国文学。他却无言以对。

"一年五万块，"他大声叫道，"上帝！看看他们，看看他们——爱德娜·费尔伯[1]、格弗娜·莫里斯[2]、芬妮·赫斯特[3]、玛丽·罗伯茨·莱恩哈特[4]——他们所写的作品——不管是长篇还是短篇，没有一个能够活十年的。这个名字叫做科伯的人——我觉得他不但愚蠢而且无趣——并且更重要的是，我认为除了编辑们以外，不会有很多人认为他既聪明又有趣。他是被广告欺骗了。还有——哦，哈罗德·贝尔·赖特[5]，哦，萨恩·格雷[6]——"

"他们付出了努力。"

"不对，他们甚至不努力。他们有的可以写，可是他们不愿意坐下来稳稳当当地写一部小说。他们大部分人不会写，我觉得。我觉得鲁泼特·修斯[7]想要描写真实、完整的美国生活，可是他的特色和视角粗鄙并且毫不规范。厄内斯特·蒲尔[8]和多萝西·凯菲尔[9]希望写好，可是他们一点也不幽默，因此他们希望

---

1. 爱德娜·费尔伯（Edna Ferber，1885—1968），美国小说家、剧作家。
2. 格弗娜·莫里斯（Gouverneur Morris，1752—1816），美国政治家，宪法起草人之一。
3. 芬妮·赫斯特（Fanny Hurst，1889—1968），美国小说家。
4. 见第16页注。
5. 哈罗德·贝尔·赖特（Harold Bell Wright，1872—1944），美国二十世纪初畅销小说家。
6. 萨恩·格雷（Zane Grey，1872—1939），美国小说家，以描写西部冒险经历著称。
7. 鲁泼特·修斯（Rupert Hughes，1872—1956），美国历史学家、小说家、好莱坞电影导演。
8. 厄内斯特·蒲尔（Ernest Poole，1880—1950），美国小说家，一九〇二年毕业于普林斯顿大学。
9. 多萝西·凯菲尔（Dorothy Canfield，1879—1958），教育改革家，社会活动家，畅销小说家。

写好的想法受到了很大的阻碍；但是最起码他们的文章都写得很饱满，而不是写得很单薄。任何一个作家在写任何一篇文章前都应该想象着完成作品的时候自己就即将被处死了。"

"这里有两层意思吗？"

"别打断！还有少数几个人，他们好像有一些文化背景，还有一些灵性，还富有文学才气，可是他们就是不想稳稳当当地写文章；他们每一个人都会讲好的作品没有读者。那么，威尔斯，康拉德，高尔斯华绥，萧伯纳，贝尼特，还有别的人，究竟为什么要在美国投入他们作品的一半以上的销量呢？"

"对于诗人来讲，可爱的托米有什么高明的见解吗？"

汤姆犯难了。他将两个手臂放下，之后任由手臂在椅子边垂下，与此同时，嘴里还在小声地嘟囔着。

"我在创作一首具有讽刺意味的诗，名字叫做《波士顿诗人与赫斯特[1] 书评人》。[2]"

"愿闻其详。"艾默里急不可耐地说道。

"我只是将结尾的几行诗写完了。"

"那倒是很新奇。听起来很有意思，那就念一下吧。"

汤姆从口袋中拿出一份折叠好的稿件，开始朗诵，时不时地停顿下来，想让艾默里明白这是一首自由体的诗歌：

"于是

瓦尔特·艾伦斯伯格[3]，

阿尔弗莱德·克雷姆伯格，

卡尔·桑德伯格，

路易斯·恩特梅厄，

尤尼斯·泰琼斯，

克拉拉·莎娜费尔特，

詹姆斯·欧本海姆，

---

1. 纽约美国私人报业集团。
2. 仿拜伦的《英格兰诗人与苏格兰书评人》（1809）。
3. 此处所列的都是后来在美国文学史上有一定地位的人，不过在菲茨杰拉德写作本书时，他们仍是年轻的作家和诗人。

麦克斯维尔·伯顿海姆，

理查德·格雷恩泽，

莎穆尔·伊利斯，

康拉德·艾肯，

我将你们的名字写在这里，

如此一来你们的生命可以延续，

即便只是虚名，

弯弯曲曲、深紫色的名字，

活在我的小时候

作品全集中[1]。"

艾默里不停地大笑。

"你赢得了铁三色堇花。由于你结尾的两行诗写得很有傲气，我决定请你吃饭。"

艾默里并不十分赞同汤姆将美国作家和诗人，全盘否定的观点。他喜欢瓦彻尔·林赛[2]和布思·塔金顿[3]的作品，也敬佩埃德加·李·马斯特斯[4]的仔细严肃的艺术手法，尽管稍显羸弱。

"我厌恶这种愚笨的无聊话，什么'我是上帝——我是人——我乘风而来——我看清云雾——我就是生活的意义。'"

"太差劲了！"

"我反倒希望美国的小说可以不再尝试将正经事变为浪漫而有意思的事。没有人愿意读这类的小说，除非写的故事是虚假的。如果写的是很有趣的题材，他们便会去买来詹姆斯·J·希尔[5]传记阅读，而不会选择总是谈到烟雾的重要性的啰嗦的办公室悲剧——"

---

1. 仿拜伦针对勃鲁厄姆爵士（Henry Peter Brougham, 1778—1868）在《爱丁堡评论》上贬低他的第一部作品《闲暇时刻》(Hours Of Idleness) 为"一潭死水"而写的讽刺诗《英格兰诗人与苏格兰书评人》。
2. 瓦彻尔·林赛（Vachel Lindsay, 1879—1931），美国诗人，被认为是吟唱诗歌之父。
3. 布思·塔金顿（Booth Tarkington, 1869—1946），美国小说家、戏剧家，两部小说获普利策奖。
4. 埃德加·李·马斯特斯（Edgar Lee Masters, 1868—1950），美国诗人、传记作家、戏剧家。
5. 詹姆斯·J·希尔（James J Hill, 1838—1916），美国铁路大王。

"除了烟雾还有阴暗,"汤姆说道,"那是另一个受作家欢迎的题材,可是我觉得俄国人独占了这个题材。我们擅长写小女孩的故事,写她们折断了脊柱骨,被脾气粗暴的老人收养,因为她们经常喜欢笑。你会感到我们这个国度是愉快的瘸子的国度,而俄国农民有着同样的结局——便是自杀。"

"六点钟了,"艾默里瞅了一眼手表说道,"就凭着小时候的作品全集这句话,我决定晚上请你吃顿大餐。"

回顾

热得叫人难以呼吸的七月,在度过最后一个炎热的礼拜以后,终于告一段落,艾默里在又一阵内心的躁动中觉察到,从他与罗莎琳第一次约会到现在恰好是五个月。但是,他已经无法想象那时候一个小伙子怀着一颗完好的心刚从车上下来时,急切地期望着生活的冒险。一天晚上,令人无法呼吸、身心俱疲的热浪,向他的卧室涌来,而他坐在房间里挖空心思地想了好几个小时,恍惚中尽力要把之前的艰辛往事写下来,永远留给未来。

二月的大街上,晚上寒风凛冽,夹杂着怪异而又断断续续的雨滴,打湿了荒凉的街道,在连续一个小时的积雪的融化和星光里,在路灯照耀下迸溅的雪花闪动着点点光亮,犹如天上的一台机器在向外喷洒着黄灿灿的油。

怪异的雨水——那是很多人的眼睛,在风雪的间歇,熙来攘往,富有活力……啊,我还非常年轻,因为我还能再来找寻你,非常平凡而又非常美丽,再来欣赏历历在目的梦境,在你的嘴唇上,美妙而又清新。

……午夜的空气中弥漫着浓郁的味道——安静已经死去,喧哗还未醒来——生命如同冰层一般发出声响——耳旁飘荡着悦耳的乐声,只看见你在那里站着,明亮却又苍白……春天已经到来。(一截截冰柱子在屋檐上悬挂着,变幻中的城令人神魂颠倒。)

我们的思维便是檐口冷意刺骨的雾气;我们两个幽灵在接吻,在高高的天空中,在长长的复杂的丝网上——令人恐惧的笑声在这里飘荡,留下了一声传递天真期望的叹息;后悔追逐着她的热爱,留下了悠长的沙哑一声。

另一个结局

一封达西大人的信在八月中旬被寄来,很明显在不久之前,达西大人碰巧知道了艾默里的地址。

亲爱的孩子:

看过你的上一封来信，令我为你担忧起来。这与你的性格一点也不一样。我能够在你信中的言语间感觉到你和这位姑娘的婚约让你难过不已，我感觉到你已经丧失了战前对爱情的所有感觉。假如你觉得没有宗教信仰也可以浪漫，那你真的犯下了天大的错误。有时候我在思考，对于我们两个人来讲，我们一旦发现了成功，它的诀窍就成了我们身体上的秘密成分：我们的身体里被注入了能放大我们个性的某样东西，而当这东西褪去之后，我们的个性便缩小了；我觉得你的上两次来信非常干枯。你要留心防范在另一个人的个性里迷失自己，不管是男人还是女人。

现在我正与红衣主教奥尼尔大人还有波士顿大主教在一块，所以此时的我甚至连写信的时间都没有，可是希望你将来能够来到我身边，哪怕只是呆一个星期。这个礼拜我要前往华盛顿。

我还未决定以后要做些什么。假如在八个月之内红衣主教由没有才能的人担当，我不会觉得惊讶，这话也只是咱们两人之间闲聊，不能和别人说。无论怎么讲，我希望在纽约或者华盛顿拥有一座房子，这样你也就能在周末过来玩了。

艾默里，我们两个人依然在世，这令我十分高兴；一个幸福的家庭很有可能会被这场战争毁灭；不过谈到婚姻这个话题，现在是你人生最危险的时候。你也许能够仓促地结婚，之后再平静地悔恨，但是我觉得你是不会这样做的。根据你信上所讲，你现在正处在灾难性的经济危机中，从这一点来看，你无法获得你想要的东西。但是，假如依照我一般采用的方法来对你做一个评判，我想说，在一年之内，在你身上会发生例如感情危机的事情。

记得经常给我写信。很难受，我一点都不不清楚你现在的情况。

非常爱你
泰厄·达西

收到这封信后还不到一个礼拜，他们这个小小的家就解体了。直接的原因是汤姆的母亲身患重病，或许已经很多年了。于是他们储藏好家具，准备将这个公寓转租给别人，心情低落的他们在宾夕法尼亚车站握手分别。艾默里和汤姆好像经常要告别。

汤姆离开后，艾默里异常孤独，于是就一时冲动，前往南方，想要去华盛顿寻找达西大人。可是他们错过了两个钟头，没能见上一面。他便决定拜访他依然记得的岁数很大的舅舅，在他那住上几天，他一路奔波，穿越了马里兰州物茂盛的田野，到达了拉密利县。可是，原本想要住上两天就走，没想到他竟然住了一个多月，从八月中旬一直住到九月快要结束，因为他在马里兰碰到了艾里诺。

第三章　狂妄的嘲讽

　　在之后的很多年中，艾默里每次想起艾里诺的时候，好像依旧能听到风呼啸着吹过他的耳边，随之传来一阵阵刺骨的冰冷，不仅仅直接侵入了他的内心，就连除了心以外的地方都能感受到那种寒气。在那个夜晚，他们爬到山顶上去，看着空中漂浮着的云，苍白的月亮悬挂其中，他仿佛又丢失了部分的自我，而这部分的自我是无论如何都没有办法重新恢复的；并且每次丧失它的时候连同想要再反悔的力气也一起失去了。艾里诺可能是被美丽的面孔所遮掩着的邪恶对艾默里最后一次的偷袭，是让他丧失自我、把他的内心击成碎片的最后一个离奇又怪异的东西。

　　每次她在旁边的时候，他就会不自觉地生出他无穷无尽的幻想，也正是因为这个原因，他们爬上了最高的山峰，欣赏邪恶的月亮慢慢升起，因为在那个时候他们就晓得自己能够发现自己身上的罪恶。然而艾里诺——艾默里在梦中有没有见到她？在之后的日子里他们的灵魂居无定所、飘来飘去，但是他们彼此都从心底里期盼着不要再看到对方了。是她瞳孔里那深深的哀伤让他沉迷，还是他从她心底的那片像镜子一般的纯洁中看到了自己的影子？她可能永远都不会再有像艾默里一般的奇遇了，但是如果她看到这儿所写的句子，她可能就会这样说：

　　"他也可能永远都不会再有我这样的奇遇。"

　　他不会因此而叹气，同样的她也不会。

　　之前，她在纸上写过这些话来表达她内心的情感：

　　"仅仅知道一件淡漠的事情

　　我们依旧会将它忘记……

　　抛弃在一边……

　　盼着能够跟着冰雪一块消融，

　　但是梦里的情境让我欲罢不能，

第三章 狂妄的嘲讽

一直到现在都念念不忘:
黎明忽然到来,我们开心地迎接,
每个人都能够看到,却没有人能够享受,
这也仅仅是黎明……如果能够再一次看见他
就当从来没有遇到过。

我爱的人……不会流眼泪哪怕只是一滴……
不用再说别的
我心甘情愿
尽管经常回忆到我们之前的亲密接触——
我也不再缄默不言
即便是我们之间的对视,
旧的灵魂也有宽广的地界去遨游,
遨游的地方还有一望无际的海面……
深色的东西在海面撞击产生的泡沫下飘来飘去
我们却从来不能看到它的表面。"

他们不顾一切无休止地吵闹,因为艾默里觉得"面"和"面"这两个字即便是一样,也不算是押韵[1]。随后艾里诺朗读了另外一段诗句,然而她并没有整理好这段诗句的开头那句应该怎么说:

"……然而聪慧逐渐消逝……但时间依旧如此
赐给我们聪慧……岁月将持续不断
再次回到古稀——眼泪早已流尽
我们对此毫不知情。"

艾里诺对马里兰恨得咬牙切齿。她在拉密利县历史最悠久的家族中长大,跟她的爷爷一起住在那个又大又昏暗的屋子里。她从小在法国生长,长大之后……我觉得我的开头出错了。我重新讲吧。

艾默里觉得这是件很枯燥的事情,他每次下乡的时候这种感觉就出现。他经常自己一个人走路,一直走到离刚开始特别远的地方去——没有任何目的地

---

1. 文章里是说"sea"(大海)与"see"(看到)不算是押韵。

行走，走的过程中还对着玉米地朗诵《乌拉鲁姆》，对在那种沾沾自喜的氛围当中，因喝酒喝得太多而死掉的坡[1]表示喝彩。

在一天下午，他顺着一条他不常走的小道，一直走了大概有几英里远，误信了一个黑人女士的指路，进到了一片树林里……完全找不到东南西北。眼看着暴雨马上要到来了，并且现在的天空已经被乌云遮住了，面前黑压压的一片，这让他更加焦虑了。没一会儿，倾盆大雨就撞击在了旁边的树木上，突然这倾盆大雨好像又变得藏头露尾，蹑手蹑脚的。雷声轰隆隆地充斥着整个山谷，声音越来越大，一波接着一波在整个树林里来回滚动。他步履蹒跚，小心翼翼地向前试探着，也分辨不出到底应该往哪个方向前进，只是单纯地想要找到一个出口。最终他穿过了树林里错综复杂的枝枝杈杈，隐约望见这个树林里有一个像是出口的地方，就在这个时候闪电突然而至，照亮了这片宽广又突兀的地方。他朝那个林子的缺口方向奔跑起来，可随之他又踌躇不前，不晓得到底是应该横穿这片田地，还是应该想办法找一个小茅屋暂时避雨，因为他已经看到了在半山腰上有一处灯光从一个小屋子里透了出来。那个时候时辰还早，大概是刚过五点半的样子，然而，现在的能见度大概只有十步左右，超过十步的地方就是一片漆黑，也只是在闪电袭来的那一瞬间，才能看到这片田地附近的一切，非常奇异。

忽然间，一个奇怪的声音传进他的耳朵里。好像是一首歌，声音是从一个女孩儿的嘴里发出来的，低沉又沙哑，无论唱歌的是谁，听起来就在他身边。如果这种情况发生在一年之前，他在这个时候可能会大笑，也可能会颤栗；然而现在出现在他心里的情绪只有焦虑不安，也正因为这样，他仅仅站在那个地方，仔细地倾听，从这首歌里他听见了一些歌词：

"哽咽哀声

乐声嘤嘤

秋景瑟瑟

我心悲伤

---

1. 埃德加·爱伦·坡（Edgar Allen Poe,1809—1849），美国作家、诗人、文学评论家、现代侦探小说的始祖，浪漫主义学派的代表人物。坡去世的原因常常被说成是饮酒太多，然而至今他去世的真正原因仍然很神秘。《乌拉鲁姆》（Ulalume,1847）诗共计一百零四句，主要是描述作者已去世的爱人。

只有苍茫

忧郁零落。"

闪电将天空划开，然而歌声依旧悠扬，没有悄然而止，也没有颤栗。很明显那女孩儿就在那片空旷的田地上，这歌声听起来好像就是从距离他面前大约二十英尺远的草丛里传出来的。

之后歌声就消失了，歌声就这么消失了，紧接着又从那位姑娘的嘴里传出歌声，那声音奇特、高低起伏、蜿蜒曲折，跟暴雨的哗哗声混合在一起：

"气息奄奄

惨白难消

钟声阵阵

旧事蜿蜒

争先恐后

哭泣难忍……"[1]

"究竟是拉密利县的什么人在那里唱歌，"艾默里大声地喊叫着，"对着已经被雨浇透的草丛用随性自编的歌词来唱魏尔兰诗句的是谁？"

"有人走过来了！"传来一个声音，那声音听起来一点惊慌失措的感觉也没有，"你是哪位？——是曼弗雷德[2]，是圣克里斯托弗[3]，还是维多利亚女王？"

"我是唐璜[4]！"艾默里一时紧张，脱口而出，因为雨声和风声较大，他不得不用力大声喊叫。

一阵愉悦的尖叫声从草垛里传了出来。

"我晓得你是哪位——你就是热爱《乌拉鲁姆》的那个长有一头金发的男生——我能够认出你的声音。"

---

1. 原文引用的是法国诗人魏尔兰《秋声》诗（1866）的前两章（共三章）。
2. 曼弗雷德（Manfred），英国著名诗人拜伦于一八一六年到一八一七年期间创作的与主人公名字相同的鬼戏，浮士德式的权贵。
3. 圣克里斯托弗（St. Christopher），被罗马天主教所崇拜的殉难教徒，于罗马皇帝黛西乌斯在位（249—251）的时候逝世。
4. 拜伦是英国的著名诗人，他创作的十六章又十四节、总计一万六千行与在世的时候还没有完成的诗歌著作《唐璜》中的男主角、欧洲传闻当中的唐璜，在拜伦的著作里从奢侈的贵族，演变成好心的愤青。西班牙语"Don,"翻译成"唐"，一译作"唐"，常位于姓氏的前面表示尊敬，也就是"先生"的意思。

"我要怎么做才可以上去？"他站在草垛脚下大声喊叫道，因为他已经来到草垛这边，被暴雨淋得浑身湿透了。草垛的一边冒出来一个人影——然而天空被乌云遮住，艾默里也仅仅能看到那一头湿漉漉的头发，还有那双像猫眼一样明亮的眼睛。

"往后走几步！"一个声音从上面传了出来，"之后就往这边使劲跳，我能够握住你的手——错了，不是在那里——往另外一边走走。"

他按照那个声音说的做，张开双手双脚在草垛的边缘处趴着，就这样让自己陷进草垛当中，就在这个时刻，在草垛的最里面出现了一双小且白嫩的手，握住他的双手，将他拽到草垛的上方。

"可以了，璜，"她的头发也被淋得湿漉漉的，"你不会因为我不叫你唐而介意吧？"

"咱俩的大拇指竟然一模一样！"他惊奇地叫道。

"你还不把我的手放开，别人长什么样你还没有亲眼看到就抓着别人的手不放开，这样多危险啊。"他马上把她的手松开了。

上天好像是为了对他的要求做出回答，让一道闪电划破了漆黑的夜，她就站在那个已经被暴雨浇透的草垛中，大概离地面十英尺，离他非常近，他那期盼的目光注视着她。然而她的脸被遮挡住了，在他的视线里只呈现出了她那婀娜多姿的身材，一头乌黑、被暴雨打湿了的短发，白白嫩嫩的小手，大拇指跟他的一模一样，都向后弯曲着。

"坐这儿吧，"她表现得非常懂事，这个时候的天色看起来比之前更加黑暗了，"如果你坐到我对面这个有些陷下去的地方，我的雨衣可以分给你一半用来遮风挡雨，我之前本来打算是把这件雨衣当成帐篷来防水的，这下可好，你完全把我的安排给打乱了，真是计划赶不上变化。"

"是有人邀请我来的，"艾默里语气欢快地说着，"不是你邀请我上来的吗——你要晓得我是被你邀请上来的。"

"唐璜总是用这个方法，"她说着，一边放声大笑，"但是我以后不叫你这个名字了，因为你的头发上呈现出一些红色。而且你也会朗诵《乌拉鲁姆》，我决定当普塞克[1]，当你的灵魂。"

---

1. 普赛克（Psyche）是希腊神话中代表人类灵魂的少女，与爱神厄洛斯（Eros）相爱；《乌拉鲁姆》的叙述者把他的灵魂人格化为古希腊的普赛克。

第三章 狂妄的嘲讽

艾默里觉得有点不好意思,也幸亏这个时候风吹得更厉害了,雨下得更大了,把他的面部表情都遮住了,什么也看不出来。他们就这样坐在草丛陷下去的地方,面对面注视着对方,头上依旧披着雨衣,几乎将两个人一大半的身体都遮住了,剩下的那一小部分没有遮住的地方就这么在外面露着,任凭风吹雨打。艾默里看着普塞克,心里非常想看清她的样子,然而上天好像听不见他的恳求,闪电再也没有划破天空照耀这片田地,他也只能心急地干等着。我的天啊!要是她不是个美丽的女子——要是她是一个年过四十而且做事又循规蹈矩的死板女人——哦,我的上帝!要是,我只是假想一下,要是她是个疯癫的女子。其实他心底里也明白他最后的那个假想是不可能成立的。就好比是上帝让人来找本维奴托·塞利尼去暗杀谁似的,这个时候上帝让一个这样的女子来使他心情愉悦,他现在的内心活动就是:她不会因为是恰好完成了自己的使命——使我的情绪变好而疯癫了吧?

"我怎么可能会疯癫。"她觉得有些可笑。

"嗯?什么意思?"

"我怎么会变成疯子呢?更何况我刚开始看到你的那一刻并没有认为你是个疯子,所以你要是认为我是个疯子的话,你不觉得这很不公平吗?"

"那这种情况究竟是怎样——"

现在的情境是艾里诺和艾默里彼此都认识,那他们"对同一个话题感兴趣"的可能性就太大了,然而他们彼此又不好意思说,即便内心就是在思考这个问题。但是大概过了十分钟后大声说出来的时候,又发现他们彼此的思维活动一直想的是同一件事情的同一个情境,不谋而合,两个人的想法十分一致,他人可能会认为跟最开始的那个话题一点关系也没有的想法。

"你可以告诉我,"他对她说,而且身体向前倾斜着,有些等不及的感觉,"你怎么会读过《乌拉鲁姆》的——你又是从哪里了解到我头发上的颜色的?对了,你的名字是什么?现在你待在这个地方做什么呢?赶紧都跟我说说!"

霎那间,闪电划破了天空,那明亮的光芒照耀着田地上的一切,所以他看见了艾里诺的脸,之前的时候从来没有看到过她眼睛的他,这次也看到了。天啊,她长得真漂亮,简直让我心动——白白嫩嫩的皮肤,就好比是大理石在满天星光的照耀下闪闪发光,弯弯的柳叶眉,翠绿色的瞳孔就好像是那绿宝石似的闪闪发亮。她看起来是个温婉贤淑的女孩儿,他看着她的脸庞,她大概像是十九岁的样子,灵敏,让人着迷,她的嘴唇的上方露出一些空白,让人忍不住想靠近,也令人觉得愉悦。他尖叫了一声,倚在旁边的草丛壁上。

"这下你终于看见我的脸了,"她一脸平静地说着,"我还觉得你可能即将脱口而出的就是我那绿色的瞳孔简直都能透视你的大脑了。"

"你头发的颜色是什么?"他有些心急地想知道,"你的头发并不长,剪的短发是吗?"

"是啊,是短发。我也不太清楚这颜色是什么。"她一边想着该怎么回答一边说着,"好多人都问过这个问题。可能是中间的颜色吧,我觉得——从来没人长时间地盯着我的头发看。但是他们都说我的眼睛很好看,对吧。其实你的看法对我来说也不是很重要,反正我的眼睛就是很好看。"

"你还没答复我刚才问的问题呢,梅德琳。"

"我好像忘记你刚才的问题问的是什么了——我现在要说的是我并不是叫梅德琳这个名字,我的名字是艾里诺。"

"我刚才其实就已经猜到了。你长得跟艾里诺一样——你的神态看起来就是艾里诺。你应该能懂我说话的含义吧[1]?"

之后他们就这样一直沉默着,静静地听着下雨的声音。

"雨都顺着我的脖子流到衣服里了,这位疯子哥哥。"过了好半天她才说出这么一句话。

"你还没回答我刚才的问题。"

"额——我姓萨威奇,名字是艾里诺;我的家是一座看起来历史悠久的大宅子,距离我们现在待的地方大概有一英里远;在世上跟我关系最为亲密的,是我的爷爷——拉密利·萨威奇;他大概有五英尺四英寸高;3077W 是他的表壳号;他长有一个看起来非常精致的鹰钩鼻;性格嘛,有些奇怪——"

"我,"艾默里将她的话打断了,"你是从哪儿发现我的存在的?"

"这个啊,这个世上总有那么一些男人,"她的态度突然变得很高傲,"总是对我唧唧歪歪得没完没了,你就属于这类人当中的一个。对了,兄弟,上周一个天气挺好的日子,我在篱笆的一边躺着沐浴阳光,就在这个时候,一个人走了过来,嘴里唠叨个没完没了,语调抑扬顿挫,很有带动性,而且很容易使

---

1. 英文名"艾里诺(Eleanor)"是"海伦(Helen)"的异体字,"海伦"在希腊神话当中被认为是斯巴达王的妻子,之后被帕里斯强行掳走,继而造成了特洛伊大战。

第三章 狂妄的嘲讽

人有身临其境的感觉":

"这个时刻黑夜已经呈现出风烛残年"

(他念叨着)

"斗转星移黎明将近

路的末端看着朦胧一片"

(他继续念叨着)

"即将冉冉升起的就是朝霞。"[1]

"我听见有人念叨的时候就抬头看着篱笆旁边的那个人,然而那个时候你就开始狂奔了,也不知道是什么原因,所以我看到的也仅有你那好看的背影,'天啊!'我情不自禁地说出口,'这应该可能是一个被很多人思念的人吧。'之后我就接着跟我的脾气争斗——"

"够了,"艾默里把她想要继续说的话打断了,"继续说说关于你自己的事情吧。"

"当然,我原本就想告诉你的。我本身是和普通的人没什么区别,我生存在这个世界上的意义就是故意去给别人制造出一些惊恐或者是危机感,但是对我自己来说基本上没有碰到过,也仅仅是像现在这种时刻,我看到男人后才会自恋地以为别人对我有好感。我的勇气是足够支撑我去登上舞台表演节目的,但是我并没有那么多的空闲时间;我其实是不能够静下心来去出一本书的;而且在之前这么久以来我还没有碰到任何一个人——我一看到他就想嫁给他。但是,我还年轻,毕竟我才十八岁,还有的是时间。"

大雨已经逐渐变小了,仅剩下暴风仍然在叫嚣着,草垛被大风吹得弯了腰,来回摆动。艾默里有些走神。他认为现在这种时候是应该好好珍惜的。他在之前的那么长时间里都没有碰到过一个这样的女生——她永远也不会有跟之前一样的表现。他竟然从来没有产生自己是一个生活在剧中的人的感觉,也就是跟不同寻常的情景非常符合的那种感觉——相反的,他现在有一种在家里的感觉。

"就在刚才,我已经做出一个很重要的决定,"大概过了有一秒钟的时间,艾里诺继续说道,"那就是我会来到这里的具体原因,这也可以说是我回答了你剩下的那个问题吧。因为我刚才做的决定就是,我根本不会认为有永生

---

1. 引用于埃德加·艾伦·坡《乌拉鲁姆》诗中的第四章(共九章)。

213

的存在。"

"什么！那么庸俗！"

"简直俗不可耐，"她说道，"然而，即便是很庸俗，其中却包含有压抑、一点生机都没有的郁闷的感觉，让人喘不过气来。我是从家里跑出来的，到这里被暴雨淋了个底儿朝天——简直就是一只落汤鸡；但是落汤鸡的脑子却没有坏掉，时刻保持清醒。"她最后补充了一句。

"继续说。"艾默里非常有礼貌地说道。

"啊——我是个不害怕黑的人，所以我从家里出来的时候也只是披上油布雨衣，脚上穿上雨鞋，仅此而已。你要明白，在之前的时候，我总是感到恐怖，我害怕说不相信有上帝——因为我特别害怕被雷劈——但是我这个时候还好好地站在这里，并没有被雷劈，的确是没有。然而现在最重要的问题是，这一次我不再感到恐怖，不跟去年的时候一样，那是我还是基督教科学派的一份子。然而这个时候我已经明白我事实上是个唯物论者，当你从家里出来，在这片树林边缘徘徊，害怕得简直要没命的时候，我就已经在草丛上面待着了。"

"切，你这个小玩意儿——"艾默里非常生气地说着"对什么感到恐怖？"

"就是你！"她大叫着，他吓得跳了起来。她捧腹大笑，"你看看——看见了！良知——就跟我似的将它杀死在摇篮里！艾里诺·萨威奇，唯物论者——不会被吓得跳起来，更不会大喊大叫，很早的时候就来——"

"然而在我身体里存在一个灵魂是非常有必要的，"他不认为那个观点正确，"我从来不会生活得那么理智——我的生活不会那么精细。"

她的身子朝他倾斜，用赤裸裸的眼神一直注视着他的脸，用她那不容置喙的语气，小声又性感地在他耳边说道：

"我就知道最终会是这样的情况，璜，就是这个才让我一直很焦虑——你的理智不强，经常用感情来判断是非。我们两个在这点上一点也不同。我认为我是一个浪漫的唯物论者。"

"我不是所有的事情都用感情来判断是非——在浪漫这一方面我认为我们两个人是相同的。现在最根本的问题是，你明白，用感情来判断是非的人总会觉得事情的发展会一直持续很久——而浪漫的人对于事情的发展根本不会持续很久这一方面的立场非常坚决。"（这就是艾默里经历过很多事情之后总结出来的看法。）

"非常正确。现在我该往家里走了，"她心里非常郁闷地说着，"我们从草垛上跳下去，一起往那个路口走吧。"

之后他们就慢吞吞地从草垛的上面爬下来。下草垛的时候她坚持不让他扶，一面说着让他站到一边去，一面弯曲着自己的身子动作华丽地蹦到了旁边那松松软软的泥土地上，然后继续在那儿坐了一小段时间，她觉得自己很好笑。之后她一下子跳了起来，把自己的手放到了他的手里，然后他们踮着脚跟从这片田地穿了过去，脚下面踩着干燥的土地，跳过眼前这个水坑的时候用力地甩着胳膊，好像这里的任何一个水坑里都承载着超乎寻常的快乐，这个时候月亮已经逐渐地升上了天空，狂风暴雨瞬间转走，跑到了马里兰的西方。当艾里诺的胳膊触碰到他的那一刻，他觉得他的手冰凉，对他手里拿着的抽象的画笔可能会不属于自己这件事情感到恐怖极了，因为在他的脑海里就是用这只抽象的画笔在画着她那充满魅力的一面。再跟她肩并肩走路的时候，他和往常一样用眼睛的余光看着她——她那张美丽的脸让人看到后就会心情愉悦，她又给人一种呆萌的感觉，现在他最大的梦想就是能一直坐在草垛上，用她那像猫一样的绿色瞳孔去观察生活。就在那个晚上他的异教徒信仰突然膨胀了很多倍，她的身影最终消失在了路上，黑漆漆的一片，简直就像一个幽灵，那片田地上又传来了歌声，听起来比之前深沉了很多，歌声一直延续到他回到家中。整个晚上，艾默里的窗户都敞开着，夏天的飞蛾顺着窗口一会儿飞进来，一会儿又飞出去；整个晚上，他的耳旁响着在安静中显得更为清楚的声音。银白色的光芒穿了进来，一会儿高昂，一会儿低沉，好像是在那神秘莫测的梦里一样——他躺在床上，浸没在一片寂静里，没有闭上眼睛。

九月

艾默里从很多的草叶里挑出来一片，很熟悉地放到了嘴里咀嚼起来。

"我之前没有在八九月份的时候谈过恋爱。"他说着。

"那你会在什么时候谈恋爱？"

"大概是在圣诞节，也有可能是复活节。在礼拜仪式这方面我会很严格地遵守。"

"复活节！"她皱了下她的鼻子。"额！那个时候我们就会穿上紧身衣了吧，因为那个季节是春季！"

"春天这个季节会因为有复活节而使人感到很无聊，你觉得呢？因为复活节的时候人们都会把头发扎成辫子,然后穿上之前定做好的紧身衣。"

"系紧你的鞋带,哦,你的手脚利索。

你两只脚的色彩和速度都被遮掩了——"

艾里诺不自觉地就朗诵出了这句诗[1],紧接着她又说了一句:"我觉得比感恩节更加适合在秋天度过的节日就数诸圣日的前夕了。"

"对啊,我也感觉更加适合——在冬天这个季节度过圣诞夜的前夕简直妙极了,但是夏天这个季节……"

"这些有代表性的节日不会在夏天出现,"她说着,"夏天的恋爱是绝对不会在我们之间发生的。这世上有多少人在之前的时候都尝试过夏天的恋爱,也正因为这个原因已经没有人不知道这名称了。夏天也仅仅是春天还没有实现的承诺而已,是假冒我四月时候在梦里都想得到的微风习习的晚上的骗子。它简直就是一个没有生命力的充满苦难和悲伤的季节……在夏日里不存在节日。"

"有七月四日[2],"艾默里调戏地说着。

"别不正经!"她说着,还用非常严肃的目光注视着他。

"嗯,那么如何能够让春天里的承诺实现呢?"

她沉思了一段时间。

"嗯,我觉得上帝能够做到这些,要是真的存在上帝的话。"她最后又补充道。"一个异教徒的上帝——我认为你可能是一个唯物论者。"她语无伦次地念叨着。

"你从哪里看出来的?"

"因为你的脸长得很像那张相片上的鲁泼特·布鲁克。"

在艾默里跟艾里诺相识的这段时间里,他都在竭尽全力地假扮鲁泼特·布鲁克,好使他们看起来更加相似。

从他的嘴里说出来的话,他本身的生活姿态,他在面对她的时候所表现出来的样式,他对自己生活的态度,基本上跟这位已经去世了的英国人的文学基调的写照。大多时候都是她在草地上坐着,一阵阵微风袭来,将她那不太长的头发吹得飞舞,那些诗句都被她用沙哑的声音一点点地朗诵了出来,从《葛朗

---

1. 这两句诗引用于斯温伯恩的《阿塔兰塔在卡吕顿》的第七十七句和七十八句。另注于第71页。
2. 美国独立纪念日。

第三章 狂妄的嘲讽

切斯特老教区牧师住所》，到《威基基》，不管是多长或者是多短[1]。艾里诺每次朗诵这些诗句的时候，都带着特别炽热的情感。他们每次朗诵诗句的时候，好像两人之间的距离就缩短了，不仅仅是精神上，而且肉体上也是，比她跌倒在他的怀抱里的那个时刻的距离更短，这种事情也是时不时就会发生的，因为他们俩好像从刚开始见面就已经彼此有好感了。但是艾默里这个时候可以相爱吗？他从头到尾都可以在半个小时之内将所有的感情都展露无疑，但是即便是在他们都遨游在幻想当中的时候他也非常明白，他们俩人都不会跟之前的时候一样对感情那么认真——这就是他们，向后加布鲁克、斯温伯恩、向雪莱寻求帮助的原因。跟这些诗人结缘是由于他们很可能会让所有的事情都变得更好与完美无瑕，华丽并且能够引人幻想；他们一定得让那金色的小触须从他的幻想里延伸到她的幻想里，这样以后就能够代替那种爱，那种不会让人感到非常亲密，也不会像梦境一样那么宏伟、深厚的爱。

他们反反复复朗诵的有一首诗，就是那首《时光的胜利》[2]，是斯温伯恩写的。一直沉寂在他的回忆当中的是其中的四句诗，那是一个晚上，温度适中，他的眼睛里呈现的是昏暗的树干之间，飞来飞去的萤火虫；耳朵里听到的是一群青蛙在叫，那声音听起来很低沉。再之后艾里诺好像又从又远又黑的地方走了过来，就停在他的旁边，他的耳朵里传来她那低沉的声音，那种声调好像是绒毛鼓锤在敲响的感觉，重复了一遍又一遍：

"值得淌着眼泪，用掉一个钟点的时间，
对那一去不复返的煎熬与痛苦进行追溯？
果子失去了外壳而花朵呈现出空茫茫的状态，
难道曾经的梦境、之前的所作所为还要用嘴来述说？"

过了两天的时间，他们彼此才开始全面地认识，他的舅妈将她家的情况告诉了他。拉密利的家这个时候也仅剩两个人了：拉密利这位老人以及他的孙女艾里诺。她现在在法国定居，跟她母亲一起，她母亲现在有些浮躁，艾默里认为她的性格和她母亲有些相似。在母亲过世之后，她返回美国，在马里兰定居。

---

1. 鲁泼特·布鲁克作，《葛朗切斯特老教区牧师住所》，一百四十二句，一九一二年在柏林所写；《威基基》，十四句，一九一三年在檀香山郊区附近的威基基所写。
2. 写于一八八六年，整部诗一共四十九节，共计三百九十二句，描述的是由时光与爱情（爱情的拒绝）的消逝给人们所带来的悲伤和忧虑。

217

她最开始的时候是去巴尔的摩，与那个大叔一起居住，那个大叔还是个单身，在那个地方时她非得在十七岁的时候就踏入社交圈。她一整个冬天都在吵吵闹闹，下乡的时候已经是大概三月份了，由于她跟巴尔的摩那个地方的全部亲朋好友都吵了个遍，所以他们中的任何一个人都对她感到害怕，不情愿接受她。那个时候没多久就有一大群人聚在了一起，他们在看起来高端又很奢侈的小型客车里品尝鸡尾酒，他们用随便的态度，对待年长的人，肆无忌惮，毫不知礼，而且艾里诺这个时候已经被街头上的浓厚习气所污染，把很多仍然会让人联想到圣提摩西女子学校和法明顿女子学校[1]的无辜的人，引上了歧途，使她们的行为出现了那种流浪者身上调皮的气息。她的叔叔是生活在一个比这还要虚假的时代里，对待生活的态度懒懒散散、目中无人的人，他在听别人说了这些情况以后发了很大一通脾气，艾里诺在外表上看起来很顺服的样子，内心里仍旧感到愤怒并且一点也不服气，所以这个情境出现之后她就开始跑到她爷爷的家中进行躲避，然而她爷爷一直在乡下生活，这个时候也已经是行将就木了。当然，这些情况都是道听途说，其他一些细微方面的事情也有她亲自告诉我的，但是那都是后来发生的事情了。

　　他们时不时就会去游泳，艾默里经常漂浮在水面上呈现出一副懒洋洋的姿态，他的脑子里一片空白，什么都没有，只剩下一个模糊的充满肥皂泡沫的天地，在风中摇摇晃晃的大树被阳光照耀着。每当百花绽放的月份过了的时候，在这个季节更替的时刻，不包括玩水、跳水、安静地坐着发呆，根本不会有人还在继续沉思、继续忧虑、继续做其他的事情。就这样纵容时间流逝吧——哀痛、回忆、悲伤在外面反反复复地呈现，然而，在这个地方，在他要去处理这些哀痛的事情以前，他的愿望就是再放纵自己一次，沉溺在这种年轻有活力的感觉当中。

　　在个别的情况下，艾默里的内心也会感到非常不公平，之前走的是一条有着美好前景，并且十分宽广的道路，风景五颜六色，而这个时候竟然是一系列瞬息万变、毫无关系的场景——两年的辛苦奋斗，被罗莎琳刺激而产生的那种忽然的、荒谬的成为一个父亲的本能。和艾里诺在一起的这个秋天一半是感官的、一半是神经质的表现特点。他认为，要是能够将这么多处理起来非常困难、

---

1. 圣提摩西女子学校系马里兰州的一个著名的私立学校；这个地方所写的法明顿女子学校可能是指康涅狄格州明顿城"波特小姐女子学校"（Miss Poter's School）。

第三章　狂妄的嘲讽

令人感到很怪异的相片都粘到他人生所设置的剪贴本子上面，必须得让自己身心全部放到里面去，这个事情要想做到，单凭他自己的能力还远远不够。这就好比是要参加一场晚会，他在这个晚会期间要单纯地只是坐着花费他青年时期的半个小时，又必须得将人世间所有的美味佳肴全都品尝过。

朦朦胧胧中他觉得自己应该用些时间将这一切都结合起来。一连几个月，他认为自己有时候要被那爱与沉迷的洪水所淹没，有时候又要被浪直接冲到最底部，然而每当真的被冲到最底部的时候，他并未生出思考的欲望，而只是等待着再一次被冲上浪尖，然后继续被淹没。

"让人感到失望、垂死挣扎的秋季和我们之间产生的感情——两者相处得是那么的和谐！"有这么一天，他们都弄得浑身湿透，就这样安静地躺在河边，艾里诺有些悲伤地说着。

"我们两人心里的那个小阳春——"他说了半截突然停了下来。

"继续说下去，"她最终还是开口问了，"她皮肤的颜色是浅色还是深色？"

"浅色吧。"

"她长得比我更好看是吗？"

"这个我确实不太清楚。"艾默里的回复简单明了。

有一天晚上的时候他们一起出去溜达，这个时候月亮已经开始往上升了，将这个小院子映照得一片金灿灿。艾默里和艾里诺好像身处在仙境中，他们两个人就如幻影一般，浅浅淡淡，内心含着特殊的精灵的恋爱感情，展现出了永远的魅力。再之后他们走出了月亮照耀的地方来到一个黑漆漆的地方，那个地方有一个塔形的架子，上面挂满了葡萄藤的枝蔓，这个塔形架子下散发出阵阵的香味，让人产生悲伤的情绪，几乎到了能发出乐音的境界了。

"把这根火柴点上，"她小声地说着，"我现在想看见你的脸。"

嗤的一声！火柴点着了！

晚上的星空与已经起皮的大树看起来就像是一个大型舞台上的背景，艾默里和艾里诺一块儿走到了这个地方，模模糊糊，扑朔迷离，眼下这个场景看起来有些怪异而且似曾相识。他心想只有过去才显得有些奇怪而难以相信。火柴燃烧完了。

"黑乎乎的一片。"

"这个时候我们也只能听到声音了，"艾里诺小声念叨着，"也只剩下孤独的声音了。再点亮一根火柴。"

"刚才点就是最后一根了。"

突然间他将她抱住，圈在了自己的怀里。

"你是属于我的——你要明白你是属于我的！"他大声地说着，几乎要发疯……月光穿透了那纵横交错的葡萄枝子照射在地上，好像在听什么声音……萤火虫也在侧着耳朵听他们小声地讲话，就好像是希望他们那亮晶晶的瞳孔能够停落在自己身上，哪怕只是一秒钟的时间。

夏的终结

"草地上连一点点微风也没有，现在也没有要起风的意思……水在湖泊里隐藏着，清澈得像一面镜子，面对着天空上的月亮，把那金灿灿的象征镶嵌在这苍白的湖泊上，"艾里诺看着这些枝子指着天空的林子说着，"你觉得这个地方是否给人一种奇怪的感觉，并且让人感到很恐怖？要是你可以让马前面的蹄子稳住了，我们就能够走过这片树林去找寻那被隐藏起来的湖泊。"

"我们这是要进行探险，你可能会遇见妖魔鬼怪的，"他不赞同地说着，"我平时并没有骑过马，对马很陌生，在这黑乎乎的大晚上就更不敢骑马了。"

"行了，我知道了，你这个大笨蛋，"她小声地嘀咕着跟这些并没有什么联系的话语，而且倾斜着身子用赶马的鞭子有一下没一下地打在他的身上，"你可以将这匹上了年纪的马绑在我们家马厩的旁边，等明天的时候我再给你牵过来。"

"但是我的舅舅在明天清晨七点的时候可能需要用这匹上了年纪的马将我送到车站去。"

"能不能别扫兴——你要知道，你的性格经常会让你做出的决定反反复复定不下来，要是定不下来你就不可能成为我人生道路上指路的灯塔。"

艾默里将马掉了头儿，牵到了她的旁边，他俯下身来，握住她的手。

"我就是你人生道路上指路的灯塔——赶紧的，否则我就要将你拽过来，让你坐在我后面。"

她抬起头看着他，脸上挂满了笑容，高兴地来回摆头。

"啊，走呀！——要不然我们就不走了！到底是什么原因让这一切愉快的事情都让人感到悲伤，就好比是打仗，也像是去冒险，还像是在加拿大滑雪？而且，我们现在要做的事情是爬哈帕尔山。我之前做的规划是要在大概五点钟

第二章 狂妄的嘲讽

的时候开始爬山。"

"你这个调皮的孩子，"艾默里有些生气地嘀咕着，"你的意思是让我一整晚都不睡觉，明日白天的时候像那些从外乡过来的移民那样一上火车就开始蒙头大睡，一觉醒来就到纽约吗？"

"不要再说话了！有人从路那边过来了——我们赶紧离开这里！呜——呜！"一声喊叫令这些在半夜里赶路的行人浑身打颤，她将马头掉转过来，走到林子里去，后面慢吞吞地跟着艾默里，就如同他三周以来没日没夜地跟着她一样。

夏天已经悄悄地走了，但是在这么多天内他一直都很留意艾里诺的行为举止，她就好比是一个优雅、灵敏的曼弗莱德，一边沉迷于不能很好控制自己情绪的十几岁女孩的装模作样，一边还在为她自己修建理性和幻想的金字塔，他们有时候在吃饭的时候会作几首诗。

一百个开心的六月以前，每次虚荣亲吻了虚荣，他盯着她的脸像是喘不过气来的样子，也好比是所有的人或许都明白的，他将她那双漂亮的眸子跟生命结合在一块：

"我会用时间来挽救我的爱情！"他说着……但是那个漂亮的人儿跟着他的呼吸不见了，她也跟着她的爱人们一块死掉了……

——永恒的是他的聪明智慧而不是她那漂亮的眼睛，永恒的是他的技艺而不是她那亮丽的秀发：

"到底是谁能够运用诗句当中那些技巧，在他的十四行诗句前明智地终止"……所以我说的一切语言，即便是非常合理的，也只是把你歌唱到第一千个六月而已，然而谁都不清楚你之前还做过一个下午的漂亮女子。

某天他写了这样一部作品，他在思考我们对于《十四行诗的黑肤女子》[1]的态度是那么的高冷，也没有像大诗人所期盼的那样将她铭记，我们脑海里关于她的回忆是那么的少。

原因是，那个美人现在本应该还在世的，这肯定是莎士比亚所期盼的，他居然可以非凡的绝望来描述……如今我们对她不再关注了……而令人感到非常具有嘲讽意味的是如果他在意更多的是关于这首诗，而不是这首诗当中所描绘

---

1. 萧伯纳在一九一〇年作的短剧，描述的是莎士比亚跟他的十四行诗第一二七首到第一五二首（共计一五四首）里的人物、诗人所喜爱的"黑肤女子"。

221

的美人的话，十四行诗也仅仅只是个毫无色彩、具有抄袭性的句子，再过二十年也就没有人再提起了……

这天是艾默里跟艾里诺在一起的最后一个晚上。他在明天的清晨就要跟她告别了，他们都对在还有苍白的月光的时候，进行一次骑马远游的分别仪式十分赞同。她本来想说些什么，她说道——这可能是她的生命中最后一回看起来非常理智了（她的意思是摆成一个更为舒服的姿势）。之后他们就一起骑着马进到了林子里去，一晃就过了半个小时，两个人谁都没有开口说话，唯一例外的是在一根非常多余的枝子挡在她眼前的时候，她小声嘀咕了一句"他妈的！"——那是其他任何一个漂亮女子都不会说出口的一句话。之后他们牵着那匹看起来已经快要跑不动的马，开始爬哈帕尔山。

"我的上帝！这里怎么会这么安静！"艾里诺小声说着，"跟那片树林比起来显得更荒凉了。"

"我对树林并不是很感兴趣，"艾默里一边说着一边打了个冷颤，"在晚上不管是什么叶子，什么样的草丛，我都不感兴趣。到了这个宽广的地方，让人感觉精神上很放松。"

"连续不断的山脉，连续不断的山坡。"

"苍白的月光照射在这无数个大大小小的山坡上。"

"你和我两个人，就成了最重要的角色。"

那一天晚上非常安静——他们在山上的一条非常顺直的小路上走着，一直走到了悬崖的边缘处，无论在什么时候都不可能留下很多的印迹。也只剩下偶然间能看到的黑人住的那个木头做的小屋子，在那照射着无数座山脉的月光底下呈现出一片银灰的颜色，将那条长长的而且什么都没有的小路拦截住了；小木屋的后方是那片林子的边缘，黑漆漆的一片，好像是在白色的奶油蛋糕上涂了一层巧克力酱一般，前面的是显而易见的、比那片树林高出很多的地平线。空气好像要凝结了——让人觉得寒气扑面而来，将他们心里的一个个温暖的晚上全都驱赶走了。

"夏季已经悄悄地走了，"艾里诺小声地说着，"你听见马蹄的响声了吗？'踏——踏——踏——踏。'你的头脑现在开始发热了没有，把全部响声都进行详细分类，变成踏——踏——踏的响声，一直到你能够起誓永远都能够详细地划分成各种各样的踏踏声？我现在已经有这样的感觉了——上了年纪的马匹

第三章 狂妄的嘲讽

走路就会发出这样的响声……我认为这可能就是马和钟表与人类的差距所在。人类走路时要是发出踏踏踏的声音就要发狂了。"

风在呼啸着,好像声音更响了,艾里诺把披风紧了紧,忍不住打了一个寒颤。

"你感觉冷得受不了吗?"艾默里关心地问道。

"不是很冷,我是在对我自己进行反思——我的内心是阴暗的,而我真实的自己,生下来就具备的诚实会让我察觉到自己的罪过,反而让我从那些心怀不轨的罪过当中挣脱出来了。"

他们骑上马一直走到了悬崖边缘处的地方,艾默里低头向下看,看见了那距这里大概有一百英尺的山沟,下面的小山坡好像跟地面连在了一起,一条黑漆漆的小山路形成了一条显而易见的线,中间的是很急的水流,远远看起来上面星星点点地发着亮光。

"沉沦,沉沦的旧时代,"艾里诺忽然说出了这么一句话,"然而最令人感到怜悯的人就是我——哦,我怎么就是一个女孩子呢?我怎么就不能是一个笨——?我感觉你,你比我笨太多了,不是特别笨,就是有那么一点儿笨,但是你就能够四处跑跑跳跳,讨厌这个城市了就能够换另一个城市继续跑跑跳跳,你能够随便将女孩子玩弄于股掌之中也不必担心被卷到情感纠纷中而出不来,无论你要做什么事情都没有错——但是我自己,我还能够做什么,空有聪明智慧,但是又要被未来婚姻所束缚着最终沉到海底。如果我能早出生一百多年,那其实也还好,但是我眼前还剩下什么呢——我也只能找个人嫁了,这就是不容置喙的事情。嫁给谁呢?对于这个时代的很多男人来讲,我比别人聪明太多了,然而我也只能够将就着他们的智商,为了能够让他们更加关心我,我自己的聪明智慧要受到他们的管制和约束。就这样一年又一年的时间过去了,要是我自己嫁不出去,再想找一个优质男结婚的几率就变得更加渺茫了。最多我也只能在附近的这一两个地方进行筛选,很明显的是我肯定是要跟一个家境富裕的人结婚的。"

"你听好了,"她又倾斜着身子离他近了一些,"我对有智慧的男人有好感,当然长相好的男人我也喜欢,很明显估计没有人能跟我一样如此在乎一个人的品质。啊,能从五十个人里面能挑出一个稍微明白什么是性的人就很好了。我看过一点儿费洛伊德等人的理论,但是,很不巧,这个时代里哪怕只有极少的真正的爱情,其中百分之九十九的就是那控制不住的肉体欲望,还有一点儿

223

就是妒忌。"她忽然说了很长一段文字，之后又戛然而止。

"的确是，我非常赞同你说的，"艾默里觉得这很正确，"让人觉得非常厌恶的强大力量，才是能够推动世界上所有运转的不可缺少的一部分。这简直就是一个故意让你了解到他的表演技巧的演员！稍等一会儿，我想一个更好的表述方式……"

他静止不动，想要找出一个更合适的说法。他们刚才走过的路已经将悬崖绕了过去，现在是沿着距离边缘处大概有五十英尺的小路行走。

"你瞧瞧，这里的任何一个人都得有一件自己的披风将自己包裹在里面。颇有才华的人里面的那些庸俗的人，也就是柏拉图所说的属于二流的人，使用的就是被守旧情感稀释的浪漫主义的英雄品质的残渣——而将自己看作是有学问的我们，装作这就是我们的另一面，跟我们的才华一点关系也没有，而是将它掩藏住；我们都假装懂得这一点，这样才可以从根本上免于被伤害。然而，问题在于性就在我们简单的幻想当中，离我们非常近，我们的视线都变得朦胧了……这个时候我想要亲吻你而且也想要……"他在马背上朝她俯身而去，然而她却躲开了。

"我觉得我不应该——我现在不应该跟你亲吻——我对这些非常敏感。"

"你的意思是你更笨，"他的耐心基本上已经被用尽了，"日常习惯不能够帮助你抵挡性的诱惑，聪明智慧也帮不了你什么大忙……"

"那你觉得什么能够帮助我？"她情绪有些不稳定地说着，"你觉得是罗马天主教会，还是孔夫子的箴言？"

艾默里听完这句话之后猛地把头抬了起来，吓了一大跳。

"那些都是你的锦囊妙计，是不是？"她大声喊道，"啊，看来你也仅仅是个装腔作势的小人而已。数以千计沉沦的神甫教意大利人和没有文化的爱尔兰人都感觉非常后悔，由于他们的嘴里说出很多第六戒和第九戒[1]的愚蠢的话语。这些都是遮住事实的外套，情感、精神色彩、锦囊妙计，全都算是。我跟你说，这个世界上根本没有上帝，就连绝对抽象的善都没有。也正是这个原因，这些不得不由自己去为自己处理，如同我这般额头长得比较高而且白白嫩嫩的人，但是像你呢，你身上书呆子的气息有些浓重，肯定不愿意坦白这个问题。"她

---

1. 根据《圣经·旧约·出埃及记》，摩西所吩咐的十戒当中的第六戒就是"不可杀人"，第九戒是"不可做假见证"。

把手里拿着的缰绳放了下来,对着满天星空摆动着她那小巧的拳头。

"要是这个世界上真有上帝,那么就请他对我施行惩戒吧——惩戒我吧!"

"你又在模仿那些所谓的无神论者的理论来对上帝进行谈论了。"艾默里的声音有些尖锐。他那所谓的唯物论充其量也不过是一件薄薄的外套而已,但是这个时候已经被艾里诺这几句尖锐的话语粉粹成渣了……对于这一方面她其实是明白的,正因为如此,他才被惹得怒火朝天。

"就好比是那些发现不了跟自己的信念相配套的文化的人似的,"他用非常冷淡的口吻说着,"就好比拿破仑和王尔德还有你们这群人似的,你们到临死的时候才大声地喊叫要把神甫招来。"

艾里诺忽然就勒紧了马的缰绳,他在她的身边也勒住了马。

"你认为我会这样吗?"她的口吻有些怪异,让他感觉到了害怕,"你觉得我会这样吗?看清楚了!我能够从悬崖上飞过去!"他都还来不及阻止她的行为,她就已经让马调头,冲向了高原尽头,过程看起来非常惊悚。

他也让马调头,在她的身后紧追不舍,他浑身上下像冰一样没有温度,他的神经系统一直在噼里啪啦地响。现在这种情况已经制止不了了。乌云飘了过来,将月亮遮住了,她骑的那匹马总是毫无目的地乱闯,最终跑到了距离悬崖边大概十英尺的地方,她忽然高分贝地喊叫了一声,那匹马将她摔到了旁边——从马背上掉在了地上,顺势在地面上打了两个滚儿,然后跌在了距离悬崖处五英尺远的草堆里。马也开始嘶叫起来,随后从悬崖上摔了下去。他马上向艾里诺的身旁奔跑过去,映入视线里的是她那两只眼睛。

"艾里诺!"他紧张地大叫道。

她没有回复他的话,但是嘴唇轻轻地动了一下,顿时泪流满面。

"艾里诺,你伤到了哪里吗?"

"没有受伤,我感觉应该没有。"她一点力气也没有了,随后就开始大哭。

"我的马是不是掉到悬崖下面摔死了?"

"我的天啊——是掉下去了!"

"哇!"她抱头大,"我本来以为可以跨越过去的。我真的不晓得——"

他抱住她的胳膊,慢慢地把她拉起来,而且把她扶上了他的那匹马。然后,他们就开始往家的方向走去。艾默里在前面拉着缰绳,她在马背上趴着,哭得非常痛苦。

"我可能是头脑不清醒了，"她语无伦次地说着，"我在之前的时候也发生过两次这样的事情。在我十二岁的时候我妈妈开——开始疯了——嘴里一直胡说八道颠三倒四。我们那个时候居住在维也纳——"

回家的这一路，她结结巴巴地叙述着自己的身世，艾默里的爱情也随着月亮逐渐地不见了。到她家大门口的时候，他们习惯性地亲吻对方，算是告别，然而她没有被圈进他的怀抱里，他们也不会像之前要看见她的时候那样用心。他们在她家的大门口逗留了一段时间，彼此之间也只剩下仇恨，只剩下悲伤和痛苦。然而，就像是艾默里在艾里诺身上喜爱的是他自己的影子一样，他现在仇恨的也只剩下那面镜子了。他们的装模作样在已经开始露白的黎明时刻就像玻璃渣子一样散落了一地。天上早就没有了星星的影子，剩下的只有那一阵阵袭来的微风，还有当这阵微风停止时的安静时刻……但是那赤裸裸的灵魂总是被看不起，没过多长时间他就扭头往家走去了，去迎接太阳带来的新的光明。

过了几年之后艾里诺写给艾默里的一首诗

"这时，田地的女儿，听着水流的哗哗声，
好像水的美妙，承载着那轻快的阳光，
玩耍的小女孩快乐又潇洒，尽情地拥抱白天……
这时我们之间的悄悄话没有外人偷听，不用害怕晚上来临。
我们蹒跚而行……我们是成功还是意犹未尽，
在这长发飘飘的美妙的夏季里？
地面上呈现出的一片奇形怪状的图案是我们所喜爱的树影投射而成，
好像是壁画，奥妙，幽暗，让人惊叹不已。

那是一个白天……夜晚展现出的是另一番美景，
朦朦胧胧的一个个树影苍白的颜色像是在梦里一般——
正在寻找那之前已经没落的辉煌的是那络绎不绝的星星鬼影
在悲风的吹动下低声耳语诉说着这一片安宁，
诉说白昼将旧时光流失的信念彻底摧毁掉，
廉价的青春换来的是月光的惊喜；
那就是我们之前历经的全部期盼和至关重要的言辞
那就是我们需要赔偿给债务者六月的恩惠。

这时，梦境使我产生了困惑，在幽幽的小河边，
水流并没有使人记起我们那没必要晓得的曾经，
假如只剩下阳光却听不到小河的低声耳语，
好像我们依旧在一起……我在之前的时候也把情感告诉……
夏天这个季节已经跟我们告别，最终的那个晚上又有什么吸引人的地方，
竟然指引着我们再次来到了那变幻莫测的林中空地的家？
究竟是什么在偷窥夜晚中成片的红花草
我的上帝啊！……等到你从梦中醒来……受了很大的惊吓……

哎……我们已经度过了……我们早就看过那令人恐怖的幽暗。
让人觉得好奇的铁块是从划破天空掉下来的陨石上落下的；
田地的女儿不知道什么是疲乏，依旧躺在那幽幽的小溪旁边，十分困顿，
我这个人精就是凭借着那个猜不准心思而且又丑又笨的孩子……
恐怖是因为我们追忆到了安全之女的回声；
这时我们也开始有脸也有声……过不了多久可能就要老化
在那哗哗的水流声中小声诉说着我们彼此的爱心……
廉价的青春换来的是月光的潇洒。"

艾默里写给艾里诺的一首诗，这首诗被他称作"夏天风暴"
"虚弱的风，歌声逐渐消失，落叶萧瑟，
虚弱的风，笑声在远方也逐渐消失……
雨声哗哗的，喊叫声充斥着田野……

头顶上方被风吹散的乌云慌里慌张地消失了，
向太阳飘去，连带着几片黑云，
一起被吹走。那个影子是一只白鸽的
停在鸽子棚上，大树仿佛长出了翅膀似的；
风雨在暴走中，黑漆漆的一片；眼里满是疯狂
大海的凄凉苦楚被清新的空气捎带了来
还有那纤细又持续的雷声……

然而我的耐心仍旧……
等到薄雾将天空充满，天色变黑，哗哗地下着大雨——
呼啸着的风好像要将这即将降临的命运帷幕彻底颠覆，
习习微风要将她的头发捋顺；
然而他们不断地
使我受伤、训斥我、空气都变得更沉闷了
压榨我，狂风我忍受了，还有那暴风雨。
有一个夏天降水量少而且使人燥热；
有一个季节吹的都是干燥的热风使我的心烦躁不已……

然而这个时候你在朦朦胧胧的雾气中从我的身边路过……头发凌乱
像是被雨水淋湿过了，双唇湿润着向上翘起，
那简直是狂妄的嘲笑，那简直是绝望在算计你，
这就是之前看见你的时候你显得成熟的原因；
在暴雨倾盆而下之前你像个孤魂一般漂浮着，
手里捏着没有柄的花儿，在田野间游荡，
依旧承载着你早期的盼望、枯萎的叶子还有惆怅——
像梦境一样幽暗，到嘴边又停止的话是在描述旧日的时光
（低声耳语会融入到浓郁的夜晚当中……
吵闹声也停止在树木的枝头）
夜晚来临
撕扯着她湿漉漉的胸口已经脏掉的衣裙，
从雨水蒙蒙的山脉处悄悄溜走，眼里含着泪水，看起来晶莹剔透，
她用头发遮住了那奇特的绿眸……
喜爱夜晚的肃穆……喜爱事后的晶莹剔透；
树木安静无声一直到树顶部的枝梢上……寂静幽暗……

虚弱的风，来自远方的笑声逐渐消失……"

第四章　鄙视一切的牺牲

艾默里再次来到大西洋城。夕阳西下，汹涌澎湃的海浪像猛兽一样不断地拍打着海岸，发出嘶吼。艾默里落寞地走在海滨木板人行道上。眼前的景色，使他的心情变得很宁静。海风夹杂着海水特有的咸涩，以及那令人悲伤的气味扑面而来。此刻，他想，比起背叛了自己的陆地，大海显然更加珍惜自己的记忆。大海好像依旧喁喁细语地诉说着那个画着渡鸦图形的旗子在海洋世界撑起时的样子，古代斯堪的纳维亚的囚犯们的战舰在广袤无边的大海上乘风破浪的景象，还有灰色城堡里的文明，以及大不列颠战舰的英勇无畏——它在一个充斥着阴霾的七月，发动马达，冲破一切阻隔，势不可挡地驶入北海。

"嘿——艾默里·布莱恩！"

一辆低底盘的赛车在艾默里脚下的马路上停了下来，驾驶位的车窗处探出一张熟悉的洋溢着欢乐的笑容的脸。

亚历克朝他大喊道："傻瓜，快下来！"

艾默里向他打了个招呼，顺着一排木头的台阶，走到车前。他和亚历克经常见面，但是，罗莎琳一直是横在两人之间的难以跨越的障碍。为此，他十分悲伤，他不想失去亚历克这个朋友。

"这位是沃特逊小姐，这位是威恩小姐，这位是塔利先生。"

"大家好！"

"艾默里，你上车吧，我们去一个幽静的好地方喝一点波旁威士忌。"亚历克兴奋地说。

艾默里心里有些纠结。

"真是一个不错的主意！"

"快上来吧！吉尔，你往里坐一点，艾默里会十分感激你的。"

艾默里坐到后排的一个衣着华丽，浓妆艳抹的金发女郎的旁边的座位上。

"嘿，我叫达格·费尔邦克斯，"她轻浮地问道，"你在海边散步是为了锻炼吗？还是在找人呢？"

艾默里不苟言笑地说："我在统计有多少海浪，我热爱统计学。"

"达格，你又在开玩笑。"

亚历克将车子停到了路旁浓重的阴影里，这是一条很僻静的街道。

亚历克一边将一大瓶波旁威士忌从地毯下拿出来，一边说："艾默里，这么冷的天儿，你跑到这儿来干什么？"

到这儿来好像并没有特别清晰的目的。艾默里心里这么想着，但是没有说出来。

他问："你是否还能回忆起大二时我们的那个聚会？"

"你是在问我吗？当然，我记得当时我们睡在了阿士伯花园的亭子里——"

"哦！亚历克！我真的很难想象杰西，迪克和凯里，他们三个人都已经去世了。"

亚历克感到一阵寒意。

"你们不要再说了，直到现在，当我回忆起那些布满阴霾的秋日，我都觉得萎靡不振。"

吉尔似乎也很认同。

"不知为什么，达格现在好像有点抑郁，"她说道，"现如今很少有波旁威士忌的，让他多喝一点。"

"艾默里，其实，我想问你，你在哪里？"

"噢，我在纽约，我看——"

"我是说，今夜，之所以我这样问是想请你帮个忙，如果你还没有下榻的地方的话。"

"我的荣幸。"

"情况是这样的，我和塔利各自在莱尼埃饭店订了一间房，其中有一个是浴室。但是，他要回纽约。我呢，不想再换一个地方了。所以，你愿意来那个房间住吗？"

当然愿意，艾默里心想，如果他现在就能进房间的话。

"房间登记的是我的名字，钥匙在办公室里。"

艾默里下车了，因为他实在是不想再附和，不想再麻烦了。他又来到了木板人行道上踱步，慢慢地走回了饭店。

第四章 鄙视一切的牺牲

艾默里不想工作，也没有激情来写作，他不想恋爱，也不想放浪形骸，好似被卷进了深深的旋涡中，可他却不想挣扎。第一次，他如此热切地期盼着死神的来临，希望死神浇灭他们这一代人的猥琐的狂欢之火，夺取他们萎靡的斗志和奢靡迂腐的生活。这次他来到海滨，所感受到的，是从未感觉到过的落寞，这不同于四年前的融洽、愉悦的朋友出游。他从没像现在这样萎靡不振，好像失去了所有的活力。当时，倒头酣睡是他人生中最平常不过的事。萎靡不振填满了他与生俱来的对于美的意识和一切欲望逝去所带来的缺口。

"女人只有抓住男人最大的弱点，才能留住男人。[1]"大概在每个情绪糟糕的夜晚，他都会思考这个问题。他觉得今夜也不会有所不同。他的思绪已经飘到了这个问题的各个方面。他对罗莎琳所有的疯狂的爱恋现在只剩下了无处安放的激情，疯狂的妒忌，还有他强烈的征服欲和占有欲。这些感觉，都是对他萎靡不振的惩罚——爱情是糖衣包裹的苦涩，欢愉只是短暂的。

到了房间，艾默里脱掉了衣服。窗子是打开的，他坐到了窗子旁边的扶手椅上。十月的天气十分寒冷，艾默里在身上裹了条毛毯来保暖，他睡意沉沉。

他脑海里回忆起前几个月读过的一首诗：

"啊，赤胆忠心的人呐，你为我奔波受累，

可我却四处流浪荒废青春——"

可是，他认定是生活抛弃了他。他意识不到荒废的时光，意识不到现在的愿望隐藏着荒废时光的意思。

"罗莎琳！罗莎琳！"他把这个名字慢声细语地吐露出来，吐露到夜幕降临的黑暗中，直到'罗莎琳'充盈了整间房间。苦涩且又潮湿的海风渐渐打湿了他的头发。圆月高悬在空中，把帘幕照得扑朔迷离。他，进入了梦乡。

等到他醒来，天色已晚，四周很静。身上裹着的毯子早已滑落，手臂又湿又冷。

忽然，他听到一阵焦急的低声密谈，声源距离他最多十英尺远。

他也渐渐地紧张了起来。

"嘘，别发出声音！"那是亚历克在说话，"你有没有听到，吉尔？"

"嗯——"他们在浴室，把说话的声音压得很低。

忽然，艾默里听到一阵响亮的声音从外面走廊的某个地方传来了。是男人

---

[1] 引自王尔德的剧作《少奶奶的扇子》第三幕："如果女人打算留住一个男人，她只要抓住他的最大弱点就可以了。"

的说话声，模模糊糊的，接着就是接连不断的咚咚的敲门的声音。他拿掉身上的毯子，走到了浴室门的附近。

"啊！你不能弄到外边去呀！"里边传来女孩子的声音。

"嘘！"

突然，响起一阵急躁且连续的敲门声，这次，声音是从艾默里客厅的门上传来的。同时，穿着睡衣的亚历克和同样穿着睡衣且嘴唇鲜红的吉尔从浴室走了出来。

亚历克着急地低声说："艾默里！"

"发生了什么事？"

"饭店的私家侦探。哦，上帝，艾默里——他们只是想找个案子，可以供他们演习——"

"原来是这样，那我来开门吧！"

"你不懂，根据曼恩法案[1]，他们是可以把我抓起来的。"

吉尔小心翼翼地跟在他的身后，她的样子在黑暗中显得愈发的可怜，很难不让人泛起恻隐之心。

很快，艾默里想出了一个解决办法。

"亚历克你尽量地大声吵闹，把注意力吸引到你房间去，然后我带着吉尔从这儿溜出去。"艾默里紧张地建议道。

"他们肯定会留一些人在这儿守着的。"

"那你能不能用假名字呢？"

"不能的，艾默里，我的房间登记的是自己的名字，况且，他们会查汽车牌照的。"

"那么，就说你们是夫妻。"

"行不通的，吉尔说这儿有一个私家侦探认识她。"

吉尔已经轻轻地走向床，并爬上去；她蜷缩在床上，显得更加可怜，听着门外的敲门声越来越急促，越来越响。然后，一个男人怒气冲冲地喊道：

"快点开门，不然我们就硬闯了！"

喊声突然停下来，一片寂静，安静得让艾默里觉得这个房间里除了他们三

---

1. 美国国会于一九一〇年通过的禁止州与州之间贩运妇女的法案。

第四章　鄙视一切的牺牲

个外还弥漫着其他的东西——它笼罩着蜷缩在床上的吉尔的头顶和房间的四周，造成一种神秘的氛围，像月光似的阴冷，它的颜色更是像极了走了味的淡葡萄酒，然而这种恐怖的氛围已经笼罩了他们，在房间里四处游荡……还有别的东西在随风摆动的窗帘之间隐藏着，没有一定的形状，也没有特别的气味，很难辨别，熟悉又神秘……同时，艾默里眼前出现了两个并排的大盒子，这些念头冲击着艾默里的脑海，然而事实上，这才用了不足十秒钟的时间。

他心里闪过的第一个意识是牺牲是具有客观性的——他意识到我们所认为的爱恨情仇，是非对错，这些与牺牲一点关系都没有。正如和今天是什么日子一样没有丝毫的关系。此刻，他的脑海里回想起一则有关牺牲的故事，那是他在上大学的时候听到的。大学里的一次考试中，有一位同学作弊被抓了，作弊者的一位舍友一时义气承担了全部责任。作弊毕竟是可耻的行为，懊悔与失败笼罩着这个无辜者的未来，压得他喘不过气。让人愤恨的是，当时的作弊的人一点都不知道感激。结局是无辜者最终因为羞耻而选择自杀，几年后真相浮出了水面。那件事深深地震撼了当时的艾默里，他既疑惑又悲伤。其中蕴含的道理，他现在才慢慢地明白，便是牺牲不能换来自由。就像是一个选举大会，就像权力的继承——在特定的时刻对于特定的人来说，牺牲是必不可少的奢侈，附带的不是保证而是要肩负责任。并且还要冒着巨大的风险。仅仅是它的动力就能摧毁一切——随着维系着这一切的感情纽带被切断，掀起这波浪的人将永远被留在寂寞的孤岛上，孤独终老。

……艾默里知道如果他这么做，亚历克肯定会偷偷怀恨在心，恨他为什么要揽下这一摊事。

……这所有的事情，就像滚落在他脚下的一副被打开了的画卷。而那两股与他没有丝毫联系的、却又密切窥探他的力量，正屏息凝神，仔细倾听着；弥漫到姑娘头顶以及满房间的恐怖的氛围再加上窗口那熟悉又神秘的东西。

牺牲，是孤高的，是客观的；牺牲者总是睥睨群雄的。

不要为我悲伤，为你们自己悲伤吧，为你们的子孙而悲伤吧。[1]

不论如何，上帝会这样说的。艾默里心想。

做出了决定以后，艾默里不由得感到一阵轻松，一阵喜悦之情跃上心头。

1.《圣经·新约·路加福音》第二十三章第二十六节，耶稣钉死在十字架上时，对赶来现场的女人说的。

此时，笼罩在房间里的恐怖的氛围，就像电影里的逐渐暗下去的人脸一样，消失不见了；窗口神秘的影子变得越来越熟悉，他几乎都能叫出影子的名字了，影子在此停留了一瞬，然后，倏地被风吹走了。艾默里握紧拳头，瞬间感到一阵无与伦比的喜悦，并且越来越强烈……十秒钟转眼就到了……

"你俩按照我说的办，明白吗？亚历克，你明白吗？"

亚历克脸上露出十分为难的神情，他久久地盯着艾默里，不知道该说什么。

艾默里缓缓地说道："你有家人，有父母，你绝对不能卷入这件事情，这很重要，你明白了吗？"他又清清楚楚地一字一顿地重复了一遍他的话，"你明白了吗，亚历克？"

"嗯，明白了。"亚历克说话的声音很轻，而他的眼睛则一直全神贯注地盯着艾默里的双眸。

"你就躺在这里，亚历克。倘若有人进来，你就装作喝醉了。你就这么做——否则，我或许会杀了你。"艾默里郑重地说道。

他们互相对视了一眼。然后艾默里拿起了他放在梳妆台上的简装版的书，向吉尔招手。模糊中，他好像听到亚历克嘟囔了一个词，发音像"监狱"。然后，艾默里和吉尔一起走进了浴室。关好门并且上了保险。

艾默里用严厉的口吻对吉尔说："你今晚与我在一起，一整晚都是。"

吉尔点头，压低嗓子应了一声。

然后，他打开了另一扇门。门一开就立刻进来三个人，伴随着电灯发出的强烈的光，艾默里站在门口，光刺得他睁不开眼睛。

"年轻人，你这么玩有点危险呀！"

"哈哈哈——"艾默里大笑。

"如何？"

三个男人中地位最高的人点了点头，同时用命令的神态看向其中一个身材健硕，穿着带格子的衣服的男人。

"就这样吧，奥尔逊。"

"奥梅先生，我知道该怎么做。"奥尔逊边点头边说道。其余两个人用好奇的目光上下打量着他们的对象，然后气愤地走出了房间，"砰"地一声关上了门。

身材健硕的男人用鄙视的目光打量着艾默里。

"你知道曼恩法案吗？你带着她一起南下到这儿，这真的不是一个明智的

第四章　鄙视一切的牺牲

决定。"说着他用手指了指我身旁的吉尔，"你的车挂的可是纽约的牌照，可是你却到大西洋城的这种酒店来。"他很无奈地摇摇头，意思是他曾尽力帮助艾默里，不过现在帮不了了。

"嗯，那你想怎么办？"艾默里很是紧张地说。

"快点穿上衣服！叫那个姑娘别吵了！"在床上蜷缩着轻声呜咽的吉尔听到这句话的时候立马停止了呜咽，然后绷着脸，抓起自己的衣服快步地走向浴室。艾默里在穿亚历克的内衣的时候，他发现亚历克对眼前这一幕的态度让人忍俊不禁，尤其是那个身材健硕的男人流露出虚假的好意的时候，让他真想笑出声来。

奥尔逊目光谨慎地打量着四周，问："这儿除了你们俩以外，还有其他人吗？"

"有，不过他喝已经得不省人事了，从六点一直睡到现在。哦，是他订的这个房间。"

"一会儿我过去看看。"

艾默里不解地问道："你们是如何发现的？"

"夜里，你们带着她上楼的时候被前台值班的人发现了。"

艾默里点点头。吉尔穿戴整齐之后，从浴室里走了出来，即使不算是整整齐齐，也算是穿得很规矩得体了。

奥尔逊掏出本子，说："现在，我要记录下你们的名字，不要说你叫约翰·史密斯或是玛丽·布朗米，我要的是你们的真实姓名。"

"请等一下，"艾默里低声说道，"那个倒霉的醉鬼就算了吧，我们被抓到了，就那么回事儿。"

奥尔逊严厉地问："叫什么？"他瞪圆眼睛，看起来更严厉了。

艾默里说了姓名和他在纽约的住址。

"那你呢？"

"我叫吉尔。"

奥尔逊气愤地说："呵！你省省吧，我又不是小孩子，别用小把戏糊弄我！到底叫什么？萨拉·默菲？米妮·杰克逊？"

吉尔小姐双手捂脸，泪水从脸上滑落，说道："哦，上帝！我不想让我妈妈知道这件事，我真的不想！"

"别啰嗦了，快说！"

艾默里看不过去，朝奥尔逊喊道："不要嚷了！"

235

周围一阵安静。

之后，姑娘断断续续地说："我叫斯黛拉·罗宾逊，住在新罕布什尔州腊格威，存局候领。"

"啪"地一声，奥尔逊合上本子，深表同情地看着他们两人。

"按照常理来说，只要饭店把我们掌握的这些证据交给警方，你们就会进监狱的，就要坐牢。你心怀不轨地把这个姑娘从纽约带到了大西洋城，是违反了曼恩法案的。"他停顿了一会，好让他们能明白他说的话的重要性，"但是，饭店呢，不打算追究了。"

吉尔惊喜地喊道："那是打算放了我们了，啊，不用登报了！"

虚惊一场，艾默里现在才意识到，原来他会惹来那么大的麻烦。好在现在已经没事了。

"但是，"奥尔逊接着说，"这种事数不胜数，所以饭店之间组成了一个保护性的组织。饭店跟报社有一个交易，他们不提饭店的名字，只是有一行字说你们在这里违反了条例，你们登一次报。可以吧？"

"可以可以，当然可以！"

"你真是宽宏大量，这真是从轻处罚了，但是——"

"啊，快走吧，我们不用来一个告别仪式了吧？"艾默里用轻松欢快的语气说道。

奥尔逊穿过浴室，顺便朝一动不动躺着的亚历克看了一眼。他关了灯，挥手让他们跟着他。进电梯的时候，艾默里还在考虑他要不要做一个虚张声势的动作——最终他打消了这个念头。他抬手碰了一下奥尔逊的小臂。

"电梯里有女士，方便摘下帽子吗？"

奥尔逊缓缓拿下了帽子。他们在饭店大堂明亮的灯光下经历了漫长而尴尬的两分钟。用好奇的目光打量他们的不只是在大堂里前台值夜班的接待员还有几位刚刚到的客人。姑娘衣着鲜艳，却低着头。帅气的少年倔强地抬着下巴。结论是不言而喻的。然后，他们走出了饭店，寒气扑面而来——户外清晨的第一缕曙光中的海风夹杂着的咸味变得更加清新浓烈。

"你们现在可以逃之夭夭了，或许可以叫一辆路边的出租车。"奥尔逊用手指着路边停着的出租车，而司机可能正在酣睡。

奥尔逊把手伸进口袋，做了一个提示性动作，说："再见了。"艾默里不动声色地用鼻音"嗯"了一声，拉起吉尔，转身叫了一辆出租车。

月朗星稀，他们在空旷的马路上疾驰的时候，吉尔小姐问道："我们要去哪里？"

"去火车站。"

吉尔紧张地说："那个人会不会写信给我妈妈——"

"不会的，除非是我们的朋友和敌人，不会有别的人知道这件事的。"

太阳逐渐升起，朝霞映红了海面。

"天亮了！"她说。

"嗯，还很蓝。"艾默里抬头看了一眼，表示赞同。然后他想起他们还没有吃早饭，"现在到了吃早餐的时间了吧，你想吃点什么？"

吉尔轻松欢快地说："吃东西？就是因为这个才闹出了这么多事呢。凌晨两点左右，我们有点饿，订了一份大餐，要服务员送到房间里，亚历克没有给小费，我猜，正是因为这样，那个贱人就去告发我们了。"

随着黑夜的消失，吉尔糟糕的情绪好像也消失不见了，甚至比黑夜消失得还要迅速。她义正言辞地说："倘若你要组织这种聚会，一定记着不能喝酒，倘若想保持和谐的氛围，就一定要走出房间。"

"好的，我会记住的。"

突然，他用手指敲了敲车窗，车子停在一家二十四小时营业的餐馆前。

"亚历克和你是好朋友吗？"吉尔问道。他们走进餐馆，坐在高凳子上。吉尔把胳膊撑在已经褪色泛黄的柜台上。

"以前是的。只是现在他可能不再想要我这个好朋友了——但是我一直不知道原因。"

"你可真傻，替他背黑锅，他对你来说就那么重要吗，比你自己还要重要？"艾默里哈哈大笑起来。

"以后再看吧，问题就是这个。"艾默里答道。

精神支柱的坍塌

在回到纽约的两天后，艾默里看到了他最近一直在关心的消息，在一页报纸上，有十几行字，向某些可能会关心这些消息的人宣布：艾默里·布莱恩先生，后边跟着的是他当时说的在纽约居住的地址。因为带一位并非他妻子的女士到大西洋城的一家饭店且与之共处一室而被赶出了饭店。

接着他看到了一则消息——让他大为吃惊,甚至他的手都不由自主地颤抖起来。在这几行字的上方,还有这样一段话,导语大意是:

"兹有里兰·R·康尼奇夫妇在这里隆重宣布,小女罗莎琳与康涅狄格州首府哈特福的J·道森·莱德先生订婚了——"

艾默里放下手中的报纸,瘫倒在床上,他感觉心痛如绞。他彻彻底底地失去她了,这,就是最终的结局。就算到现在,艾默里的内心仍旧抱有一丝希望,他相信,罗莎琳会来找他的,跟他哭诉,告诉他,这只是一场误会。她的心只会为他而痛苦煎熬。想要得到她,即使是奢望,他也再不可能了——肯定不会是这个罗莎琳,这么无情,这么衰老——而不是等到他四十岁的中年时期想象的年老色衰的丑陋女人——艾默里想要的,是她年轻的岁月,是她散发的活力与朝气,是她现在已经没有的东西。对他来说,年轻光鲜的罗莎琳已经去世了,不存在了。

一天之后,他收到一封信,来自芝加哥的巴顿先生。他的来信言简意赅。就是告诉他因为有三家电车公司已经宣布破产,所以,他目前不会再收到这三家公司的汇款了。最后,在一个迷茫的周末的深夜,传来了一个噩耗——一份电报将达西大人五天前死于费城的消息带给了他。

此时,他才意识到,在大西洋城,出现在他客房窗帘之间的影子是什么。

第五章　自傲的人变得重要起来

"朦胧中我浑然入睡
旧时渴盼，曾受抑制，
大吼一声起死回生，
模糊中暗夜破门消散；
只为寻找共同信念
我来寻觅那自信的白天……
但是陈旧曲调仍在：
雨中之路望不到边。
啊，祈愿我能再次站起！祈愿
褪去旧日的酒的躁动
欢迎崭新的清晨崭新的天，
醉人高塔，星罗棋布；
每一个美景在空中展现
是代表，梦幻不见了……
但是陈旧曲调仍在：
雨中末路一眼难见。"

艾默里在一家剧院的玻璃吊门下站着，盯着那最开始颗粒非常大的雨点噼里啪啦地落下来，随后在人行道上铺散开来，最终变成了黢黑的污渍。天空变得昏暗起来，还来杂着污浊的气息；忽然街上的一盏孤零零的灯亮了起来，将马路对面一扇窗子的模样照得十分清晰；然后又有一盏灯被点亮；接着数以百计的灯间隔着亮了起来，映入人们的眼帘。在他的脚底，好像钉了严严实实的铁钉的天光变黄了；马路上出租车车灯的强光在早已变黑的路面上照着。令人不满意的十一月的雨像和谁对着干一样将一天中的最后时刻都偷走了，将它卖给了古老的收赃人，夜晚。

他身后安静的剧院，传来了一声非常古怪的"啪"的响声，接下来便是人们站起来时的吵闹声和很多人同时讲话的喧哗声。日场电影结束了。

他后退到边上，几乎将自己暴露在雨中，为熙熙攘攘的人群让开路。从门口冲出来一个小男孩，他呼吸着湿润、清新的空气，然后竖起毛衣领子来；有三四个人急速地向外走，他们在走出剧院的时候全都是瞪大眼睛先看一下被雨浸润的土地，接着是盯着空中下着的雨，最后就是看一下阴森森的天空；最后离开剧院的是闲适地迈着步、携朋带友的那些人，鼻尖的气味使他觉得莫名的烦躁，那是从男人身上散发的烟草味和女人身上陈腐的扑粉的恶臭混杂在一起的味道。在这一群成群结队的人的身后，又有几个结伴走出门口的人，是五六个人，还有一个靠丁字形拐杖行走的男人。最后从剧院里传出乒乒乓乓的翻动座椅时的声音，这恰恰表示了剧院的引座员正在工作。

纽约好像还在沉睡之中，刚才就是在床上的一个翻身而已。脸上毫无血色的男人步履匆匆，都将身上的大衣的领子夹紧；成群结队的疲乏却又吵吵闹闹的姑娘们从百货公司冲出来，一边不停地尖叫着，一边三个人一块儿挤在同一把雨伞下面；一个齐步迈进的警察小分队从她们的身边经过，使人震惊的是，他们身上披着油布雨衣的披风。

下雨带给艾默里一种冷冰冰的感觉，口袋里没有钱的城市生活使得无数令人讨厌的场面一个接着一个地让他碰到。那拥挤的使人难以忍受的、臭气熏天的地铁——车厢里的广告映入眼帘，向你瞥了一眼，仿佛是那些令人讨厌的人硬拽着你将陈年旧事重新讲一遍；使人心情烦躁，又有些担忧，谁知道那些人有没有靠在你的身上；一个男人不会心甘情愿地将他的座位让给一个女人，因此为了不让座位而对她感到厌烦；女人也因为这个男人没有把座位让给她而讨厌他；从最糟糕的一面来看，那就是呼气、穿在人身上的旧衣服和人们食用的餐食那不好的味道时不时地散发出来——从好的一面来看，就仅仅是人而已——太狂躁抑或是漠不关心，太疲惫，太忧心。

那些人的住所的画面在他的脑海里慢慢铺展开来——他们的房间里早已皱巴的墙纸上的图案是以绿和黄作为背景画的深沉、不断重复的向日葵，马口铁制成的浴盆在房间里摆着，门厅内阴森森的，房间的后面是没有绿意点缀的、又脏又乱的空地；在他们居住的那个地方就连爱都被看做是赤裸裸的勾引——在那周围有骇人听闻的命案发生过，楼上公寓里的未婚生子的母亲还在那里住着。因为考虑到节约,每到冬天屋里都被封得很严实,等到了更难熬的潮湿闷热的夏天就会出现在墙壁的包围下被汗流浃背的可怖场景……餐馆里脏乱不堪,在里面用餐的粗俗顽劣却又疲惫不已的人们用自己用过的咖啡匙舀糖,以至于碗底都沉淀下了褐色的硬块。

假如只是男人在这里生活,或者就只是女人的话,这一切也许就不会变得那么糟糕了;但是当在非常糟糕的环境里男人和女人碰到一块的时候,所有的事情便都脱离了轨道。每当男人看到女人辛苦劳作的时候,女人的心里都会感到难堪——而对于那些男人来说,看到辛苦劳作的女人,会没由来地觉得讨厌。甚至比他所看到的任何战场上的场景更甚,比淤泥、汗水、危险交织在一起的所有的现实苦恼更令人无法直面,就是在这样的氛围中,出生、嫁娶、去世都变成了使人厌恶的、秘密的事情。

他的印象里有这么一件事,某一天在地铁里,一个送货的人将一个由鲜花制成的大花圈带进了车厢,污浊的空气霎时被花香清洗了,车厢里的人也感到了短暂的愉悦。

"我不喜欢没有钱的人,"艾默里忽然冒出了这样一个想法,"我不喜欢他们的穷。或许以前贫穷是美好的,然而此时此刻贫穷早已变得粗鄙不堪。它就是世界上最让人看不起的。粗鄙而富裕比清白而贫穷在本质上更清白。"他好像又看见了一个人的身影,以前他的重要性给他留下了不可磨灭的印象——一个穿着时尚的年轻人从夜总会的窗口看着底下的第五大道,正和他的好友们说着话,脸上带着一种明显是极其讨厌的表情。"也许,"艾默里在心里想,"他讲的话是:'我的天哪!人真是让人喜欢不起来!'"

艾默里从出生到现在压根就没有将贫困的人放在心里过。他非常难过地以为他缺乏对人的同情心。欧·亨利在那些穷人中寻觅到了浪漫、悲伤、真爱、悔恨——但是映入艾默里的眼帘的就只有粗俗、身体的肮脏和愚昧无知。他也没有对自己有任何的不满:他没有因为他那些自然而坦诚的情感而谴责自己。他始终相信他所有的反应都属于他自身的组成部分,无可更改,不存在道德观念。贫穷这一问题,假如性质不一样了,范围更广了,变成了某一个更加伟大、更加庄严的想法的一部分,也许在将来的某一天这个问题会变成他的;目前看来这个问题只是将他那深深的厌恶勾起而已。

他迈步走向第五大道,在路上一直躲避着没长眼睛的雨伞的可恶威胁,最后他站在德尔莫尼可餐厅的门前向一辆公共汽车示意。他将大衣的纽扣牢牢地扣上,上了汽车的顶端,孤单地坐在车上,头上还下着毛毛细雨,脸上又湿又冷的感觉刺激着他的神经。在他的脑海中一直有一段对话,讲得更准确一些,是因为他的聚精会神而再次将对话接了上去。这段对话并不是两个人在交谈,而是一个人,一个人在自问自答:

问:——嗯——事情怎么样了?

答:——此时的问题是我名下大概有二十四块钱。

问:——日内瓦湖的产业也是属于你的呀。

答:——但是我并不想动用这份产业呀。

问:——你可以自在地活着吗?

答:——这是我无法想象的情景。人们凭借书挣钱,我觉得我也可以用这个方法来挣钱。事实上这也是我可以做的唯一一件事情。

问:——再讲清楚一些。

答:——我也不清楚我究竟要做什么——我也没觉得自己有多大的猎奇心。明天我就要和纽约说再见了。这就是一个糟糕的城市,除非你处于这个城市的上层。

问:——你很希望有很多的钱吗?

答:——不是这样。我只是不想没有钱而已。

问:——你会害怕吗?

答:——也就是被动地害怕罢了。

问:——你要去哪个地方流浪?

答:——我也不清楚!

问:——你不要考虑一下吗?

答:——是要考虑的。我不想在精神上杀死自己。

问:——你就没有留下什么吸引你的东西?

答:——我早已把所有的美好的品质都抛弃了。就像一个正在冷却过程中的咖啡壶一直有热量向外散发一样,我们在自己的青少年时期同样在将美德的卡路里散发出去。那就是我们通常所说的年少无知。

问:——你讲得很吸引人。

答:——这也是为什么"好人倒霉"很引人注意的原因。人们在好人的身旁站着，他所散发的卡路里会让他们切实地感觉到和煦。萨拉曾经讲过一句很朴实的话，人们听到之后的第一反应就是在脸上露出傻笑的表情——"可怜的孩子多么单纯呀！"她的美德让他们感到温馨。然而萨拉也瞧见了人们的傻笑，没有再讲这句话。就是自那以后她觉得有一些失望。

问：——你所有的卡路里都不见了吗？

答：——对呀。我开始凭借着别人的美好的品质来使自己觉得温暖。

问：——你已经沉沦了吗？

答：——在我看来是这样。我也无法确定。我现在再也无法掌控那些善与恶了。

问：——这本身就是不好的预兆吗？

答：——也不能这么说。

问：——那我们可以用什么来检测是否已经沉沦了呢？

答：——真正地使自己变得虚伪——觉得自己"不是这么不好的人"，感觉我因为失去青春而懊恼，但事实上我仅仅只是羡慕失去青春反而带给我愉悦的心情。青春好像是拥有一大盘糖果，感情用事的人觉得他们想让自己保持吃糖果之前的朴实的快乐。其实他们也不想这样，他们想做的就是再享受一次吃糖果的快乐。已婚妇女并不想回到出嫁之前的女孩的模样——她就是想要再有一次度蜜月。我也不想要使我的无知再现，我只想获得再次将天真失去的快乐。

问：——你想要到哪个地方去流浪？

这段交谈极其怪异地进入了他心中的熟悉状态里——期望、担心、表面印象和身体反应古怪地混在一起。

第一二七大街——也许是第一三七大街……二和三瞧上去非常相似——不是的，也不是那么的相像。座位被淋湿了……是衣服将座位上的雨水吸收了，还是座位将衣服上的干燥都吸收了？……在潮湿的位置上坐着容易得阑尾炎，蛙喉帕克的母亲就是这样讲的。哎，他已经得了阑尾炎了——我要和轮船公司打官司，贝雅特丽丝讲，我舅舅在这里拥有四分之一的股份——贝雅特丽丝上天了吗？……也许事实并非如此——他代表着贝雅特丽丝的永垂不朽，还有那些从来没有想起过他的很多已经去世的男人的恋爱……假如没有得阑尾炎的话，他也许会感冒。什么意思？第一二〇大街？原先的地方肯定是第一一二。一〇二，而不是所说的一二七。罗莎琳和贝雅特丽丝有些不一样，而艾里诺和贝雅特丽丝则很相像，就是她更加疯狂一些，也更加聪敏一些。这一带公寓的租金价格都很高——一个月的租金可能有一百五十——也许是两百。姨夫在明尼阿波利斯的大房子一个月的租金只需要一百而已。还有一个问题——你进来的时候楼梯是在你的左边还是在你的右边？无论怎么讲，大学十二号的楼梯直达里面，是在左边。这是多么脏乱差的一条河呀——想要到那个地方瞧一眼，是不是真像说的那般脏乱差——法国的河流有的是褐色的，有的是黑色的，美国南方的河流也是这样。二十四块钱等于四百八十个炸面圈。有了这二十四块钱他就可以很好地度过接下来的三个月，休息可以到公园去。不清楚吉尔如今在哪里——吉尔·培恩斯，或者是费恩斯、赛恩斯？——谁又知道她的姓氏呢——脖子有些胀痛，座位让他非常不舒服。一点都不情愿和吉尔一块睡，亚历克究竟看上了她哪一点？亚历克看女人的眼光太庸俗了。就他自己的审美观最好，伊莎贝尔、克拉拉、罗莎琳、艾里诺，她们都是具有美国地域风情的女人。艾里诺也许擅长左手投球。罗莎琳可以作为外场手，或者是优异的击球手，克拉拉也可以作为一垒。也不清楚亨伯德的尸体究竟如何了。假如他没有担任刺刀教练一职的话，只怕在三个月以前他就到前线作战去了，或许早就殒命了。那他的尸体又会在何方呢……

雾气和滴水的树木将河滨大道的门牌号掩盖住了，艾默里根本没有时间去仔细观察，但是最终还是有一个门牌号映入了他的眼帘——第一二七大街。他跳下车来，心里也没有想出到底要做什么，因此就沿着一条曲曲折折、越来越低的人行道朝前方走去，到了路口，再往前走就是江边了，尤其是前面还有一个长码头和毫无次序隔开分布的船坞，那里被各种小船挤得水泄不通，有小游艇、独木舟、划艇、单桅帆船。他转过头来顺着江边向北走去，中途跳过一个小铁丝制成的围栏墙，来到了一个和码头相连的混杂的大船坞。首先进入眼帘的是四周许许多多的修理到不同进度的船架，有木屑和汽油的味道飘进了他的鼻子，一块儿飘进来的还有那几乎闻不到的哈得逊河的淡淡的腥臭味。一个人伴着浓厚的夜幕向他走过来。

"你好。"艾默里讲道。

"你有这里的通行证吗？"

"我没有。这里不对外开放吗？"

"这里是哈得逊河运动游艇俱乐部。"

244

"啊！对不起，我不清楚。我就是随便散步，走到哪儿就在哪儿停一下。"

"呃——"这个人带着疑问的语气说。

"这里不能停留的话我马上就离开。"

这个人模棱两可地咳嗽了一声，就离开了。艾默里在一条翻过来的船上，心神恍惚地低下头去，他的一只手支撑着下巴。

"只要遭遇不好的事情，就很容易让别人讨厌。"他慢慢地说道。

意志低迷之时

毛毛细雨一直下着，丝毫没有停歇的打算，艾默里沮丧地回顾着他人生的溪流，回想溪流所有值得表扬的地方，回想它那令人厌恶的海滩。首先，他的心里仍然充满着恐惧——不是害怕那些有形的东西，他是害怕人，害怕偏见，害怕疼痛，害怕枯燥。但是，在他那悲伤的内心深处，他也有所怀疑，不明白他是不是比所有人都要厄运缠身。他非常清楚他最终也许会变得圆滑，喜欢装糊涂，告诉别人他的懦弱无能都是拜周围的环境所赐。通常像他这样一个自傲的人在自己生闷气的时候，总会有一个声音谄媚地对他说："不是这样的。你就是天才！"发出这样的声音，就是自身害怕的一个表现，也是这个声音在告诉他伟大和聪明不可兼得，告诉他说天才正是他脑袋里那些使人很难理解的习惯与新玩法的交汇，还告诉他说一切的戒律都会起到相反的作用，让天才变得庸俗。也许和其他的一切短板和不足比起来，艾默里更看不起他自己的性格——他讨厌相信明天并且在这之后的三年时间里，他也许会像一个三流的音乐家或者是一个一级演员一样，听到别人的讨好就会心花怒放，听到别人的批评就会满心怒意。他感觉非常惭愧，那些特别朴素单纯的人常常都对他持怀疑态度。他对那些一跟他在一起就丢失了自己的性格的人通常都非常冷淡——那是几个小女孩，还有偶尔遇到的大学同学，那些都是被他的不好的习惯所影响的人。有时候也会有人和他一起参加心灵冒险，然而往往就只有他一个人可以原模原样地逃离那冒险。

像今天这样的夜晚最近常常出现，在这样的晚上，他通常都可以从这样的令人沉醉的反省中脱离出来，因为他的心里记挂着那些孩子们和孩子们的不可估量的前程——他低下身子来仔细听着，果然听到了马路对过的一间房间里一个小孩被惊醒了，嘤嘤抽泣的声音将夜晚的安静打破了。他如同闪电一般快速地转身离开，心里泛起不知名的慌乱，他也不清楚他那毫无希望的思考的情绪是不是会在小孩的内心深处留下阴影。他觉得胆战心惊。假如将来有一天他的镇定也失去了，他变成一个专门恐吓小孩子的妖怪，趁着天黑潜入房间，神志不清地和那些幽灵狼狈为奸，而恰恰就是这些幽灵将那些无法见人的隐秘告诉在那一片黑暗的月球上生活的疯子的，假如那一天确实来到了他又该怎么办……

艾默里的脸上显现出一丝微笑。

"你将你自己紧紧地封闭在了一个地方。"他的耳朵里传来这样的声音。

接着又听到——

"离开那个地方吧，让自己做一些脚踏实地的工作——"

"不要沮丧了——"

他的脑海里不停地闪现着他以后也许会说的话。

"就是这样——以前的我可能就是一个处在初级阶段的自傲的人，但是我没过多长时间就发现了过多地思考自己会使我处于忧郁的境地。"

就在这时他忽然有一种马上就走的冲动——但也并不是像一个君子那样满腔热血、行为冲动地行走，而是平安顺遂、满心快乐地消失。他想象着自己在墨西哥的一座土砖堆砌成的房间里，在一张垫着垫子的睡榻上躺着，他那细小、颇具魅力的手指上夹着一支香烟，他还听着吉他伴随着卡斯蒂里亚挽歌的节拍将那悲伤的低音弹奏出来，在他的身边有一个橄榄色皮肤、深红色嘴唇的女孩在抚摸着他的头发。在这个地方他能够进行一些平时并不常见的祈祷，能够身处净世，摆脱天狗，和每一个神明（那神秘莫测的墨西哥神除外，由于他自身慵懒，而且沉迷于东方香料）——将成功、希冀和贫穷摆脱，进入那条秘密的长滑坡里，因为毕竟这条滑坡会通往死亡的人工湖。

可以使得一个人舒舒服服地堕落的地方有很多：塞得港、上海、土耳其斯坦[1]的部分领土、君士坦丁堡[2]、南太平洋——那些都是令人伤心的、盘旋在耳际的乐声和很多香料的故乡，在这些地方欲望可以是生活的方式和呈现，在那些地方夜空和夕阳的明暗交替好像就仅仅是激昂情绪的变幻莫测的体现：嘴唇和鸦片的颜色。

依然消除

以前他可以使人特别惊讶地闻出罪恶的味道，就仿佛马可以在夜里找出断

---

1. 一些外国人通常这样称呼里海以东的广大中亚地区。
2. 旧时土耳其最大城市伊斯坦布尔的名称。

桥的踪迹一样,但是菲比家里的那个双脚很怪异的人变小了,幻化成了吉尔脑袋上的那种气氛。出于本能他发现了贫穷的臭气熏天,然而他再也没有办法发现傲慢和肉欲的更深层次的邪恶。

那些满腹学识的人都消失了;英雄也从人间消失了;伯恩·贺拉狄也彻底消失了,就好像他从来就没有在这个世界出现过;达西大人离开人间了。艾默里早已经长大了,他的成长超越读上千部图书,胜过听上千句谎话。以前的他常常仔细倾听假装明白一切、事实上一点儿都不明白的人的讲话。以前在万籁俱寂时那些使得他肃然起敬的圣徒那神秘的虚幻的想象,此刻使得他的内心升起一阵阵厌恶的感觉。那些在山顶上站着的傲视人间的拜伦和布鲁克的模仿者们,终究也不过是些花花公子和虚张声势的人而已,从好的一面来看,他们是将勇敢的幻影当成是智慧的化身了。他的恍然大悟,场面看上去特别雄伟,那是一群年代相差很远的人,他们一个接一个地在他的面前涌现,他们当中有先知、雅典人、殉教者、圣徒、科学家、唐璜们、耶稣会会士、清教徒、浮士德们、诗人、反战主义者;他们就仿佛是大学校友会上盛装打扮的校友,从他的面前走过去,因为他们的丰富多彩的梦想、性格和信仰都在他的内心深处交替出现。他们每一人都尽力地展现着他们生活的壮阔和人的巨大的重要性;他们每一个人都自恋地说他们早已将过去所发生的一切都融进了自己那并不可信的理论中;他们都还需要依靠固定的舞台和戏剧的习惯,这就是,人们盼望在找到信仰的时候,能将距离自己最近、最便捷的精神食粮加以利用来养护自己的心灵。

女人——他对她们曾经抱着很大的希望;以前的他渴盼将她们的美好转化为艺术的形式;她们那无法预料的能力,虽然非常使人震惊并且无法述说,但是他也想过要按照经验来保存那些东西——她们现在做的就只是在为她们自己的后代做贡献而已。伊莎贝尔、克拉拉、罗莎琳、艾里诺,就是由于男人们被她们漂亮的外表迷得团团转的原因,使得此时的她们就只剩下了一颗后悔的心和一页疑惑的话要写,除此之外,要做任何贡献都是不可能的了。

艾默里已经对别人的帮助完全没有了信心的论断是在几个总结性的推论的基础上建立的。假设他这一代人,无论这场维多利亚时期的冲突究竟带给了他们多么大的伤害和损伤,都是那个时代进步的传承人。如果得到的结果有些不同意见可以置之不理,即使这些不一样的观点有时会带走几百万年轻人的生命,但是这些不一样的观点也可以经由双方的互相解释来抹去——假如最终伯纳·萧[1]和伯恩哈狄，伯纳尔·劳和特曼·霍尔威格都是进步的传承者，即便他们的观点也就在反对躲避妖娆女人的方面相同——如果不将他们当做是对立的两个方面，而是特殊对待这些好像是担任领导角色的人，那么，关于这些人自身存在的不同和分歧他也早就觉得厌烦了。

就拿桑顿·汉科克[2]来说吧，知识界有一半的人觉得他在阐述人生方面有很大的威信，一个能够证明并且坚信他所遵守的道德准则的人，一个表现优异的教育家，担当总统顾问的人——但是艾默里了解这个人，在他的心里，依然要依靠另一种宗教的神明。

而达西大人，虽然红衣教主的位置已经为期不远了，他还是有觉得古怪和恐怖的危险的时候——这对于一种就连有疑问都可以凭借它自身的信仰来解答的宗教来讲，是很难理解的：如果你对于魔鬼持有怀疑的态度，那么这个让你怀疑的东西就是魔鬼本身。以前他就看到过达西大人在那些愚昧无知又缺乏文化教育的人的家里进出，看很多通俗小说，忙于日常事务，借着这个逃离那些害怕的心理。

但是就是这样的一个牧师，有着一个聪敏的脑袋，但是又有着略显单纯的内心，艾默里心里明白，年纪也不见得就会比他大。

艾默里的内心很寂寞——他走出那个窄小的围场，来到一个特别大的迷宫里。此时他处境就像是歌德准备写《浮士德》时的场景一般；此时他的境况就像是康拉德写《阿尔梅耶的愚蠢》[3]时的境况一般。

艾默里告诉自己，因为自然的清晰或者因为猛然间的清醒，而离开那窄小的围场去寻找一个大迷宫的人基本上就只有两种。一种就是以威尔斯和柏拉图为代表的人，他们潜意识里拥有一个奇奇怪怪、神神秘秘的正统思想，他们自己都只相信大家都认可的事情——无药可救的浪漫主义者，他们拼尽全力却仍旧没有办法让自己孤零零的灵魂找到迷宫；另一种就是仿佛剑一般的激进的人，

---

1. 通常翻译为"萧伯纳"，由于要和以B开头的人名保持一致，所以这样翻译。伯恩哈狄(Friedrich Adolf Julius von Bernhardi,1849—1930)，普鲁士将军、军事历史学家；伯纳尔·劳(Andrew Bonar Law,1858—1923)，英国保守党领袖、首相（1922—1923）；贝特曼·霍尔威格(Bethmann Hollweg,1856—1921)，德国总理（1909—1917）。
2. 这个人在第24页出现过。
3. 闻名于世的英国小说家约瑟夫·康拉德（Joseph Conrad,1857—1924）依照他在马来地区的所见所闻写的第一部小说，在一八九五年出版。

像撒缪尔·波特勒[1]、勒南[2]、伏尔泰，他们的进步要落后一大截儿，然而他们的思想却也更深刻，并不是仅仅在理论哲学的直接悲观路线方面，而是放在关注不断尝试将积极的意义投放在生活上的方面……

艾默里没有再进行下去。这是他第一次开始对一切总结性的话语和精辟语言抱着怀疑的心态。这些话对于大众的心理来说太简单了，但也存在着危险。但是所有的思想在三十年以后常常是以某一个形式深入人心的：本森和切斯特顿普席卷了于斯曼和纽曼；萧伯纳将尼采、易卜生、叔本华都美化了。普通的人经由另一个人的似是而非的妙语连珠和起说教作用的耐人寻味的言辞听到了已经去世的天才的结论。

生活就是一团乱麻……是一场人人处于越位的位置、并且没有裁判的橄榄球赛——每一个都觉得只要裁判在的话那自己肯定是可以得到他的支持的。

进步就好像是一座迷宫……人们毫无理由地向前冲，接着又一哄而散，大声叫嚷着自己早就找到了……隐形的王者——生命力——进化的道理……写书，挑起战争，创立学校。

艾默里，即便他是一个非常无私的人，他也会从自己的角度来对这一切进行探索。他就是他自己最好的老师——在雨中坐着，一个有着鲜明的性格特征、有着超强自尊的人，他败给了巧合和他自己享受着爱的慰藉的性格和保护起来帮助树立人类富有生命力的思想的孩子们。

在内心深处的自责、孤单和理想消亡的状态下，他来到了迷宫的入口处。

又一个黎明笼罩着江面；一辆隐身在黑暗中的出租车在马路上匆忙开过，车灯仍旧闪着亮光，仿佛是喝了一整晚的酒以后发白的脸上那双猩红的眼睛。忧伤的汽笛声从很远处的江面上传了过来。

达西大人

艾默里一直在思考着达西大人究竟有多么喜欢他自己的葬礼。葬礼的流程完全就是按照天主教的要求和礼拜仪式进行的，场面十分庄严。奥尼尔主教歌唱赞颂庄严肃穆的大弥撒，红衣教主宣布那最终的赦免。桑顿·汉科克、劳伦

---

1. 撒缪尔·波特勒（Samuel Butler,1835—1902），英国作家，反对基督教教义，对正统教达尔文主义表示敌视。他的作品有长篇小说《众生之路》、乌托邦游记小说《埃瑞洪》等。
2. 勒南（Ernest Renan,1823—1892），法国哲学家、历史学家，他用历史视角研读宗教，主要作品有《基督教起源史》。

斯夫人、英国和意大利大使、罗马教皇的发言人，很多的朋友和牧师在葬礼上现身——但是那无法阻挡的剪子还是将达西大人双手一直在收集的网线给剪断了。他平静地在棺材里躺着，法衣上放着他那一直握紧的双手，艾默里看着这样的景象，心里不禁泛起悲哀之情。达西大人的脸没有发生丝毫的变化，因为他也不清楚他何时会死去，所以他的脸上没有痛苦，也没有害怕。他是艾默里最亲密的好朋友，同时也是别人的好朋友——从教堂里那挤满的人群就可以看出来，那些人都表现出了震惊的样子，地位最高的好像也是对他的死亡最悲痛的。

红衣教主就像是一个身穿斗篷式法衣、头戴主教帽子的天使长，他将圣水洒了出去；风琴的声音传出来；合唱队开始唱 Requien Eternam[1]。

他们这些人都很伤心，因为他们在某种程度上都是听从达西大人的。他们的伤心远远不是对于（用威尔斯的话来讲）"他讲话时总是发出的沙哑声和他走路时从不循规蹈矩的样子"的情感。这些人对达西大人都有一种盲目的崇拜，依赖着他寻找到快乐的真谛，将宗教转化成光和影之类的东西，将所有的光和影都只变成上帝的相貌。只要他在人们身边，他们就会感到安心。

从艾默里想要作出的牺牲中涅槃而生的仅仅是他恍然大悟的充分实现，而在达西大人的葬礼中涅槃而生的是那具有童话色彩的小精灵，而且将追随着他的脚步一块进入到迷宫里。他寻找到了以前他特别想要的东西、他至今还在憧憬的东西、在不远的将来他想要的东西——并不是他所担心的那般，是值得人们赞颂夸耀的东西；也并不是他一直要相信的那般，是让人爱的东西；而是人们都必须有的东西，不可缺少的东西。他的脑海中闪现出了他在伯恩的身上找到的安全感。

生活在忽然爆发的耀眼光芒中柳暗花明，以前有一句名言总是在他的心里千回百转，然而此时艾默里忽然想要将它永远抛弃了："重要的事情不常出现，没有什么事情是很重要的。"

相反，想要带给别人安全感的强烈念头在艾默里的内心深处孕育而生。

戴着防护镜的大个子

艾默里开始向普利斯顿出发的那一天，天空看起来就像是一个没有着色的穹隆，冷淡，目中无人，然而没有一点要下雨的征兆。那天的天空灰蒙蒙的，

---

[1] 这是莫扎特创作的《安魂曲》（1791）。

第五章 自傲的人变得重要起来

那是挑不起人的征服欲望的天气。这一天是属于梦想的，是距离希望还有一大截的一天，是有明确想法的一天。在这一天里你很容易就会把抽象的真理和单纯关联在一起，而那些抽象的真理和纯洁将会在阳光的照射下融化消失，而你可以借着月亮的光辉看见它们在人们嘲讽的笑声中逐渐失去了踪迹。树木和云层是依照朴实无华的风格雕成的；乡间的声音就像是和谐的单音调，仿佛喇叭一样的金属声，如同希腊瓮一般压抑。

这一天，艾默里一边走一边聚精会神地思考着，将四周的世界都抛之脑后了，这样造成的后果就是给几个开车的人造成了很大的困扰，他们没有办法，只能尽量让车子慢一点，再慢一点，不然的话车子就会将他撞翻。他陷入自己的想法中无法挣脱，满脑子装的都是自己的事，对于这种不可理解的现象完全不觉得震惊——在距离曼哈顿五十英里的地方展现出的热情友善——就在这个时候，一辆经过的汽车在他的身边缓缓地停了下来，有一个声音在向他打招呼。他抬起头，就看见一辆牵引车，有两个中年男人在车里坐着，其中一个个子很矮，神情很是烦躁，样子看上去就好像是用人工手段从另外一个身材高大、戴着防护眼镜、器宇不凡的人培育成的。

"你需要坐车吗？"像是人工培育出来的人问道，他一边说一边看了身旁那个器宇不凡的人一眼，就好像是习惯性地、暗示般地征得他的同意。

"如果可以的话自然是想的。非常感谢。"

司机将车门打开，艾默里爬进车里，在后排座位的中间位置坐了下来。他细细地观察着那两个人，觉得非常新奇。个子很高的那个人的主要的特点是特别自信，他的那种自信将他身边的那些烦躁无味都给消除掉了。暗藏在防护眼镜下面的那一部分脸可以用平常所说的"豪放"来形容，并没有显得搞笑的赘肉在下巴旁边层层堆积着，下巴的上方是一个又大义薄的嘴巴和一个并不精致的高鼻梁鹰钩鼻，脸下面的肩膀塌陷下来，直接和那庞大有力的胸部和腹部相连。他的穿着打扮很是简单大方，衣服的颜色并不是很艳丽的那种。艾默里觉察到他喜欢一直盯着司机的后脑勺，好像在不停地思考着那没有办法解决的硬头发多的问题。

小个子的特点是他完完全全沉醉在另一个人的个性当中。他就是属于级别很低的秘书之类的人，已经是四十岁的年纪了，在他的名片上有这样的一行字："总裁助理"，心甘情愿地将自己的一生都投入到模仿别人的世界里。

251

"还有很远吗？"小个子问道，他说话的口吻冷淡却又平和。

"是很远。"

"你是在散步锻炼身体吗？"

"哦，不是这样的，"艾默里简明扼要地回答说，"我之所以走路是因为我没有坐车的钱。"

"啊，是这样呀。"

他接着又说：

"你是在找工作吗？工作的种类多种多样。"他讲话的语气有些急，"大家都说找不到工作。但是西部的劳动力就很匮乏呀。"他在说到西部的时候摆了一个横扫千军的手势。艾默里颇有礼貌地点了点头表示认可。

"你有什么特别擅长的吗？"

没有——艾默里并没有学到什么东西。

"你是文职人员，呃？"

也不是——艾默里并不是文职人员。

"无论你是做什么的吧，"小个子说道，好像对艾默里刚才所讲的话非常认可，"此时恰恰就是寻找机遇和商业缺口的好时光。"他又看了一眼那个个子很高的人，就仿若一个正在询问证人的律师不由自主地向陪审团看了一眼一样。

艾默里下定决心，他觉得自己此时应该讲些什么，但是如果让他讲话的话，他也只能想到一件可以讲出来的事情。

"我当然是渴望挣很多很多钱的——"

个子矮小的那个人嘻嘻哈哈地笑着，但是他的神情却表明他是非常认真的。

"钱是每一个人都非常想要拥有的东西，但是每一个人又都不想要为此付出努力。"

"这是很正常、也很合理的愿望。几乎所有人都不想付出努力就能拥有很多金钱——除了那些问题剧中的金融家以外，他们就想'无所顾忌'。你难道不是抱着这样的想法吗？"

"当然是的，"做秘书的人愤愤不平地说道。

"但是，"艾默里并没有对他的回答作出评说，他接着讲道，"现在我没有钱，因此我在思考是不是应该把社会主义当做我的特长。"

两个人都表情古怪地看了他一眼。

"那些投掷炸弹的人——"刚一听到高个子要把自己的心里话说出来的时候,小个子就不再说下去了。

"假如我认为你是哪个抛炸弹的人,我就会把你送到纽瓦克[1]监狱去。这也是我对社会主义的看法。"

艾默里破口大笑。

"你究竟是什么人?"高个子说道,"你是不是和那些空手套白狼的布尔什维克人一样,也是那种空想家?我没觉得我能够察觉到这两种人有什么不一样。那些空想家四处流浪,老是写一些东西来激发那些贫困的移民的思想。"

"哎,"艾默里讲,"如果空想家能够保得自身的平安又可以得到一些好处,那么我恐怕迟早会变成他们的一员。"

"你是遇到什么麻烦了吗?工作丢了?"

"说丢工作的话也不至于,但是——哎,还是不要说了吧。"

"你是做什么的?"

"为一家广告公司写广告词。"

"在广告公司可以挣很多钱呀。"

艾默里拘谨地笑了一下。

"啊,我也认为如果一直留在那里的话能够挣很多钱。人才不会再被饥饿困扰着。现在就连一个搞艺术的都能挣钱养家。画家为杂志画封面,画广告画,做音乐的都可以动用脑子给剧院写散拍乐。印刷业更是大规模商业化了,这就为每一个天才创造出了一个安全而又高尚的职业,他们可以在当中获得一个自己能够胜任的职位。然而那些将艺术家和空谈家两者合二为一的人就必须要小心戒备了。那些早已和社会脱节的人——现在的卢梭啊、托尔斯泰啊、撒缪尔·波特勒啊、艾默里·布莱恩啊——"

"最后一个人是谁?"矮个子的人怀疑地问道。

"嗯,"艾默里讲,"他就是一个——他就是一个知识分子,现在人们很少能够听到他的名字。"

小个子禁不住笑起来,笑得非常认真,但是在艾默里的眼光瞥向他的时候

---

[1]这是位于美国新泽西州东北部的一个港市。

253

又突然严肃起来。

"你在笑什么？"

"那些知识分子——"

"你了解什么是知识吗？"

小个子的双眼忽然有些紧张地不停地眨着。

"好吧，这个的意思就是——"

"它的意思是说一直有一个聪明的大脑，接受过良好的教育。"艾默里将他的话打断了接着讲道，"它代表着掌控人类经验的能够促进人类进步的知识。"艾默里决心要粗暴一回。他转过身对那个高个子的人说道："这个年轻人，"他用大拇指指向那个做秘书的人，他口中的年轻人这三个字让人听上去就好像是在说饭店的伙计似的，在他的口中听不出一点"年轻"的意思，"他口中的通俗易懂的词句说出来都是含糊其辞的意思。"

"你讨厌资方控制印刷业吗？"个子高大的那人问道，他那戴着防护罩的眼睛一转不转地看着他。

"是的——我不喜欢替他们工作。我好像觉得在我周围所能看到的所有企业里，归根结底最根本的问题就是，招进来一些愿意听从命令的新人，干活的时候要加班加点，但是挣的钱却是少之又少。"

"说到这儿，"个子很高的那个人又接话了，"你必须承认工人的薪金的确是非常高的——每天上五六个小时的班——让人觉得很好笑。你在工会会员那里还要不来这样老老实实的活儿呢。"

"那都是你们自己找的，"艾默里仍然坚持他的观点，"你们的人不到万不得已的情况是根本不会作出让步的。"

"那是什么样的人？"

"属于你们的阶层。我直到最近都还是这个阶层的一份子。有的人是通过继承，有的人是通过勤劳，有的人则是凭借自己聪明的大脑，有的则是通过欺骗，变成了有产阶级的一员。"

"你觉得假如那边的修路工人有了钱，他还愿意放弃不要吗？"

"当然不会这样，但是那又怎样呢？"

年纪大的人低头沉思着。

"是不怎么样，我也承认这没有任何的关联，但是听上去又像是有些联系的。"

"事实上，"艾默里接着说，"那样的话他会更加糟糕的。劳工阶层的人心胸会更加狭隘，更不会得到别人的喜欢，人也只是想着自己——这明显是更愚昧的想法。但是这所有的一切和我们说的问题没有一点儿关系。"

"那你说得再明确一点，什么才是我们所说的问题呢？"

讲到这里，艾默里也必须想一下明确的问题究竟是什么。

艾默里凭空创造词语

"只要生活将一个得到过非常好的教育的聪明人给抓住了，"艾默里慢慢地说，"这也就是说，只要他成了家，就以现在的社会条件来说，十有八九，他会变成一个保守的人。他或许会非常无私，心地也很好，即便是就他个人来说是这样，然而他的首要工作就是要养家糊口，就是要牢牢地抓住生活的尾巴。他的妻子老是催着他，从一年的一万年薪到一年的两万，再接着不停地挣钱，在一间窄小的、就连窗户都不存在的地方，做着极度耗费体力的活。他的精力早就被损耗殆尽！生活已经彻彻底底地将他抓在手里了！他已经无药可救了！他就是那个在精神上已经成家的人。"

艾默里歇了一下，感觉他说的这个词非常好。

"有一些人，"他接着说，"因此逃跑了，他们并没有被生活抓住。这可能是由于他们的妻子并没有社会野心；也可能是他们找到了一本他们喜欢看的'危险的书'，看到了一两句话；他们也如同我一般，刚刚开始做这样繁杂的工作就被踢出局了。但是不管怎么样，他们是你无法收买的国会议员，不是政治家出身的总统，也不是那些只被五六个女人孩子倾心的摸彩袋的作家、演说家、科学家、政治家。"

"他出生就是激进人士吗？"

"嗯，"艾默里答道，"他们也许会是各种各样的人，他们的身份从将那些虚幻都抛弃的批评家老桑顿·汉科克，一直到托洛茨基，都是有可能的。并且那些在精神上未成家的人并不会带来直接的影响，因为那些在精神上成家的人，作为他们金钱追求的衍生品，早已经搜集了大报、通俗杂志、有影响力的周刊——因此报纸夫人、杂志夫人、周刊夫人用着比马路对面石油老板家属和周围水泥老板家属们更加高档的汽车。"

"为什么不能？"

"如此一来,有钱人就会变成世界知识良心的保护者了。自然,一个被一整套社会习俗影响着的有钱人,理所当然不会同意要求另外一整套社会习俗的叫喊声在报纸上刊登出来,从而陷入毁灭他们自己幸福的漩涡中。"

"但是这些还是被报道出来了呀。"高个子的人讲道。

"被报道在什么地方?——刊登在早就坏了名声的媒介上。质量极其低劣,纸张价格低廉的周刊上。"

"那好——接着说下去吧。"

"嗯,我首先要讲的问题就是借由以家庭为主的社会条件的混合,有两种极其聪明的人诞生了。其中一种人依照实际的情况对待人生,他们利用人性的怯懦、人性的弱点和优点来达到自己的目的。和这种人相对而生的就是另外一类人了,他们因为是精神上的未婚人士,所以不停地寻找掌控人性或者能够和人性对抗的新制度。他们的问题要难上很多。复杂的不是生活本身,而是指引和掌控生活的战斗。这也是他们的争斗。他们自己本身就是进步的一份子——但那些在精神上已婚的人就不是如此。"

高个子的人拿出来三支大雪茄放在他那肥大的手掌上递给他们。矮个子的那个人拿起一支,艾默里摇头表示不需要,转而伸手摸出一支香烟。

"你再接着讲,"高个子的那个人说道,"我一直盼着可以和你们这样的人交流交流。"

极速前进

"现代化的生活方式,"艾默里接着说,"生活方式的改变早就不需要一百年一个变动了,它就是一年一个变化,速度是原来的十倍都不止——人口的数量也在原来的基础上增加了近一倍,一个文明国家愈加紧密地和其他的文明国家融合在一起,他们在经济上互相依赖着对方,其中的种族问题,还有——我们是在逛街。我想说的是我们的速度必须要提上去,再快一些。"他着重强调了最后几个词,而司机也在不知不觉中将车子的速度加快了。艾默里和那个个子很高的人捧腹大笑;小个子的人停顿了一下,也跟着大笑起来。

"每一个小孩,"艾默里说,"都应该有一个共同的起点。如果他的爸爸能够将他那魁梧的身材传承给他,他的妈妈可以在他的早期教育中赐予他判断是非的能力,那这就是他双亲的遗传。如果他的爸爸不能将他那魁梧的身材传承给他,如果他的妈妈在她应该专心致志地教育孩子的时候却只是跟随在男人的身后，那么他们的小孩的命运就会更糟糕。他不应该是花费金钱揠苗助长的产物，也不应当被送到那些耸人听闻的辅导学校去承受折磨，也不应该勉强地将大学读完……每一个孩子都拥有享有同等起点的权利。"

"接着说吧，"高个子的那个人说，他的防护镜对此没有作出丝毫的表示。

"第二步我就要尝试运行所有产业的政府所有权制度。"

"但是事实已经说明那是行不通的。"

"不是——它只是没有成功罢了。如果我们推行政府所有制，这样的结果就是我们在政府里有了一个为目标工作，而不是仅仅为了他们自己工作的最优异的分析型经营头脑。我们就会重用麦凯式的人才，也用不着害怕伯尔逊那样的人；而我们的财政部要重用摩根那样的人；如果说管理州际商务的话自然要重用希尔型的人；参议员的工作只能由最优异的律师来担任。"

"他们的兢兢业业可不是白白得来的。麦卡杜[1]——"

"也不都是这样的，"艾默里反对说，"金钱并不是调动一个人积极性的唯一激励方法，即便是在美国也是这样。"

"你之前还说是的。"

"现在也是。然而如果金钱超过一定的数目的话就会变成不合法的，这样优秀的人才就会朝着诱惑人的另外一种酬劳——荣耀靠拢。"

高个子的人嘴里发出类似 boo[2] 的音调。

"讲到现在你这句话最不可理喻。"

"不是这样的，这话并没有让人觉得不可理喻。这话说得是非常对的。如果你上过大学那你肯定会被大学里为各种小小的荣耀努力学习的精神所折服，他们就如同那些艰苦奋斗养家糊口的人一样刻苦。"

"小孩子——那只是开玩笑而已！"他的对手嘲讽地说道。

"根本就不是在开玩笑——除非你承认我们都是小孩儿。你有没有见到过一个成年人要申请加入一个秘密机构——或是一个新兴的家族自己的姓名在一个俱乐部出现的场景？他们会因为听到自己家族的名字而兴奋地跳起来。如果

---

1. 好像是指麦卡杜（William Cibbs McAdoo,1863—1941），曾经担任美国财务部长（1913—1918），他制订了联邦储备法案，将联邦储备系统创立起来。艾默里这里提到的人是虚指，指的是优秀人才。
2. 表示轻视、看不起的语气助词。

只是让一个人尽心工作就把钱财放到他的面前的话，这只是在表面上治愈而已，根本没有办法根治。这个方法我们早就用了很长时间了，谁都没有再想出其他更好的办法。我们早就把那个要使用另一个方法的天地创造出来了。让我给你普及一下"——艾默里加重了说话的口气——"如果有十个人在这里，无论这些人是贫穷还是富有，我们都有一个提前的防护措施，接着如果这些人每天工作五个小时我们就发给他一条绿绶带，如果一天工作十个小时的话就送给他们一条蓝绶带，那么他们当中的九个人必然会为蓝绶带而努力奋斗。这种竞争的本能就只是想要为他们自己赢得一个标志罢了。他们居住的房间的大小就是他们努力要获得蓝绶带的标志。如果就只有一条蓝绶带的话，我觉得他们也会付出一样的辛劳。他们在有些时候就是这样做的。"

"我对你的这个观点持反对意见。"

"我就知道是这样，"艾默里悲伤地点点头，"但是现在说这些已经没有意义了。我觉得这些人很快就会过来取走他们势必要夺取的东西了。"

个子很小的那个人对此发出刺耳的嘲笑声。

"是机关枪！"

"啊，但是你早就教会他们如何使用了。"

个子很高的那个人摇头表示反对。

"这个国家有自己的财富的人并不在少数，他们是不准许发生这样的事情的。"

艾默里现在无比希望他熟知财产所有者和非财产所有者的信息，他打算换一个话题来说。

然而个子很高的那个人此时的兴致正浓。

"你说'带走东西'，这样讲话非常危险。"

"不带走的话他们怎么能够得到这些东西？很长时间人们都被承诺蒙蔽了双眼。对我们来说社会主义也许并不是社会的进步，但是不得不说红旗的威胁确确实实就是所有的改革振奋人心的力量。如果你要引起人们关注的话就必须制造轰动。"

"俄国就可以当做你行善暴力的榜样，这话正不正确？"

"非常有可能，"艾默里表示认可，"但是，它也确实和法国大革命一般做得有些过头了，但我可以很肯定地告诉你那是一个非常了不起的实验，它值得我们冒险一试。"

"难道你就没有想过用一些比较温和的方式吗?"

"你是不会认可温和派的观点的,并且现在也已经来不及了。实际情况就是,大家已经做了一件一百多年以来他们从未接触过的惊险刺激、耸人听闻的大事件。他们对这个思想已经了解得很深了。"

"他们了解的是什么思想?"

"这个思想就是无论人们拥有多少知识和能力,他们的肚子从根本上来说都是一样的。"

小个子讲话了

"如果你的手里掌握了世界上的全部金钱,"个子矮小的那个人话里有话地说道,"你要和所有人平分——"

"呃,你不要说了!"艾默里直接地说道,他对于个子矮小的那个人的生气的眼光视而不见,接着论述自己的看法。

"所有人的肚子——"他开始讲,然而个子很高的那个人很烦躁地把他的话打断了。

"我能够允许你说一下自己的观点,你很明白这一点,"他说,"但是请你不要再讲什么肚子之类的。这一整天我都感觉自己有一个肚子。无论怎么讲,你讲的话我有一半不认同。不管你怎么解释最后总是在说政府所有制。政府所有制永远逃不开腐朽的命运。人们并不会将自己所有的精力都投入到争夺蓝绶带中去,那简直就是在胡说八道。"

在他的讲话中止的间隙,那个个子很小的人非常坚决地表示了赞同,好像这一次他要非常勇敢地将自己的看法公之于众。

"这个世界上还有一种叫做人性的东西存在着,"他讲道,双眼露出仿若猫头鹰一般的神色,"在以前的时候一直存在着,将来也还会存在,那是我们穷尽一生都无法改变的东西。"

艾默里神色茫然地看看那个个子矮小的人,再扭头看看那个个子高大的人。

"你听听他说的是什么话!这就是导致我对进步丧失信心的原因。你听听!一白多种可以被人的意志左右的自然现象我张口就来——人的身上有一百种被文明消除抑或是被抑制的本能。这个人刚刚说的话几千年以来一直就是世界上那一伙蠢笨的人的最后的避难场所。全部的科学家、政治家、道德家、改革家、医生、哲学家尽心尽力地为人类贡献了他们的一生，但是他们所做的一切都被这句话给否定了。他的那句话，就是对人性中所有的闪光点的公然侮辱。对于每一个如此冷漠地将这种观点发表出来的二十五岁以上的人，我们都应当将他的公民权利取消。"

那个个子很小的人在车子的座椅背上靠着，脸都被气得发紫了。艾默里接着讲他的看法，但是他明显是说给大个子听的。

"就像你这个朋友一样只是接受过那些水平比较低的、思想陈旧的教育的人，他们觉得他们明白提出的每一个问题，仔细看的话你会发现他们这样的人脑里都被浆糊填满了。一会儿说'那些普鲁士人蛮横不讲道理'——一会儿又说'我们应该让德国人在我们的领土上永远消失'。他们一直认为'此时的情势十分危机'，然而'他们又对那些空想家缺乏信任'。一会儿他们又觉得威尔逊'仅仅是一个幻想家，一点都不实际'——一年之后他们又批判他，认为他把幻想转变成了实实在在的东西。他们能做的就只有用尽全力地去和一切变化作斗争，而对任何一个问题都没有给出一个明明白白的合乎常规的看法。在他们看来那些没有接受过教育的人，就没有获得高昂薪水的资格，但是他们并没有搞清楚如果没有接受过教育的人就没有资格获得高昂的薪水的话，那么这些人的孩子就没有钱接受教育，如此这般我们就会不停地循环下去。这就是你口中意义非凡的中产阶级！"

个子很高的那个人的脸上的笑容就一直没有中断过，他低下头对个子矮小的那个人说：

"你被臭骂了一顿，加文。你现在是什么感觉呢？"

小个子想在脸上伪装出笑容来，他表现出一副整件事好像特别搞笑的模样，他简直不屑看一下。但是艾默里要说的还没有完。

"人们是否能够管好自己的理论就要看这个人了。如果他能够给予他们良好的教育，清楚、简单、合理地去思考问题，将那专门找一些老生常谈、偏见和感情用事的话来当掩护的坏毛病摆脱掉，那么我就可以做一个好斗的社会主义者了。如果他教育得不好的话，那么人类或者是人类的制度出现什么问题，无论是在现在还是在不久的将来，我都觉得不重要了。"

"我感觉这样的话不但有趣而且非常好玩，"高个子的那个人说，"你的年龄还很小。"

"这句话的意思就是,现代的经验既没有将我腐蚀掉,也没有使我变得谨小慎微。我拥有的是最宝贵的经验,人类的经验,原因是虽然我上过大学,但是我还是再次接受了良好的教育。"

"你很会讲话。"

"这些话都说得非常有道理,"艾默里感情充沛地讲道,"这是我第一次谈论社会主义。社会主义也是我了解的解决问题的唯一有效方法。我的心绪始终不安。我们这一代也将永远心绪难安。那些有钱人想要得到美丽的女人就可以得到,而那些没有收入的美术家就只能在纽扣工厂里将自己的才能出卖掉,我对这样的一个制度始终喜欢不起来。即便我并没有才干,我也不会毫不勉强地在这里干十年活,被迫独自一人,亦或是偷偷摸摸地放纵自己,让别人家的公子哥儿可以有钱来买车。"

"但是,如果你说不允许的话——"

"那样也没有关系,"艾默里人声说。"我的情况已经是最糟糕的了。一场社会大变革也许会将我推上社会的顶端。当然我也是非常自私的。我觉得我就仿佛是那太多的陈旧体制下的一条离开了水的鱼儿。我的大学同班同学当中接受过良好教育的就有二十几个,也许我还可以算得上是其中的一个。但是他们只允许受过专门辅导的笨蛋去踢橄榄球,我是没有那个资格的,因为那几个愚昧的老家伙觉得我们大家都应该从别处获得利益。我不喜欢军队。我也不喜欢经商。我特别喜欢改革,所以我已经将我的善良给扼杀了——"

"因此向前进的时候我们还要大叫着再快一些。"

"这一点,无论怎么说,都是非常正确的。"艾默里坚持着自己的看法,"改革永远也追不上文明的脚步,除非我们强力施压。自由放任的政策就和说孩子到时候就会变得更好,结果却宠坏了他一样。他终究会变好的   如果强迫他的话。"

"你所说的这些社会主义的废话你也没有全都相信呀。"

"我也不清楚。在我和你讲这些话之前我从没有仔细地想过这个问题。我跟你讲的这些话我也没有多大的自信坚信它就是正确的。"

"你让我有点晕晕乎乎的,"高个子的那个人说,"但是你们都是一样的。他们说,萧伯纳,他的理论我们暂且置之不理,在他的稿费上是所有的戏剧家中最计较的人,就连半个便士都不能少。"

261

"啊，"艾默里讲，"我就直接说吧，我属于始终暴躁的那一代人的反复无常头脑的产物——有充足的理由使我的思想和秃笔与激进分子作伴。即便我在心里认为，在这个庞大的世界上我们都是盲目的微粒，就好像是钟摆的摆动一样只带来微弱的力量，我和我的同道中人也会团结起来抵抗传统。最起码，我们要想办法使新的语言代替那落后的词不达意的词语。我这样想过，对于人生的各个时期我的观点是很正确的，但是信仰非常困难。有一点我是非常清楚的。如果活着不是在追求渴望实现的目标，那么生活对于我们来讲就是特别无聊的游戏。"

突然间两人都不再说话，接着个子高大的那个人问：

"你是在哪所大学上的学？"

"普林斯顿。"

个子高大的那个人忽然有了兴趣，他的眼睛防护罩的表情也出现了一点细微的改变。

"我的儿子也在普林斯顿上大学。"

"是吗？"

"没准你还认识他呢。他叫做杰斯·菲伦比。去年的时候他死在了法国战场上。"

"我非常了解他。事实上，他还是我非常特别的一个朋友。"

"他是——一个——非常不错的孩子。我们之间的关系很亲近。"

艾默里现在才发现这位父亲和他那早逝的儿子之间相似的地方，他在心里默默地告诉自己，他一直感觉他非常熟悉。他一直以来期盼的荣誉让杰斯·菲伦比获得了。这件事已经过去了很久了。当时他们都还是很小的孩子，都为了蓝绶带而努力着——

汽车在一个大庄园的门口慢了下来，大庄园周围是巨大的围栏和高大的铁丝网。

"一起进去用午饭方便吗？"

艾默里摇了摇头。

"非常感谢您，菲伦比先生，但是我不得不接着赶路了。"

那个个子很高的人把手伸了出来。艾默里发觉，因为他对于杰斯实在太了解了，所以他的看法所造成的不好的影响也就一带而过了。人啊，真是一起相处的奇怪东西呀！就连那个个子很小的人都把手伸过来硬要和他握手告别。

"拜拜！"菲比轮先生大声说道，就在这个时候他的汽车转弯了，进入了车道，"你的好运陪伴你，坏运陪伴你的观点。"

"同样祝您幸运，先生。"艾默里大声喊出来，微笑着挥了挥手。

"离开火炉，走出小屋"[1]

在距离普林斯顿大概八个小时路程的地方，艾默里在新泽西州的路边坐了下来，放眼眺望经历了霜冻的田野。大自然作为一个非常粗略的现象，大体上，假如凑过去看，就会发现是由被蛾子咬食的花儿，和在草叶上漫无止境地旅行的蚂蚁所构成的，它一直让人感觉应当将幻想都丢掉。蔚蓝的天空和清澈见底的河水和那遥远的地平线所代表的大自然更加惹人喜爱。霜冻和夏天的来临使得此时此刻的他觉得特别开心，令他回想起了圣雷吉士中学和格罗顿中学之间的一场刺激的球赛，那都是很多年以前的事情了，好像是在七年前——令他想起了一年前还在法国时的那个秋天，当时他匍匐在长得很茂盛的草地上，他那一边的人没精打采地在他的身旁坐着，等着拍打刘易斯轻机枪手的肩膀。他一瞧见这两幅画面，就感觉心里涌现出了原始的激动——他玩过的两个游戏，虽然困难的程度各有不同，但是它们之间有关联，所以和罗莎琳是不一样的，和迷宫的问题也是不尽相同的，因为那毕竟是人生的大事。

"我非常自私"他在心里想着。

"这也不是会在我'瞧见人在受难'抑或是'失去父母'或者是'援助别人'的时候就会更改的品质。"

"这种自私不单单是我自身不可分割的一部分，它还是最为活跃的一部分。"

"唯有想办法跨越自私，而不是设法避开自私，我才能为我的生活带来安宁与祥和。"

"我可以采用任何无私的美德，我可以作出任何牺牲，我也可以有慈悲的心，我还可以救助一个朋友，我还可以因为一个朋友而忍受苦难，我也可以为一个朋友舍去自己的性命——这都是因为我这样的做法或许是最能表达我自己的方法，但是这里面我并没有掺杂进去一滴人情的乳汁[2]。"

---

1. 这句话出自鲁泼特·布鲁克的诗《夜行》（1913）的第五节。
2. "人情的乳汁"一词出自莎士比亚悲剧《麦克白》第一幕当中的第五场。

对于艾默里来讲，邪恶的问题早就变成了性的问题。他已经开始将邪恶和布鲁克的诗歌与威尔斯早期作品中坚定的阴茎崇拜等同起来。和邪恶紧密地结合在一起的是美——美，仍旧是那不断加重的喧哗；艾里诺温柔的声音，在黑夜哼唱一首老歌的时候，穿越生命随意宣泄，就如同那叠印的瀑布，有一半处在和谐里，有一半被黑暗浸没。艾默里心里清楚每一次他希望倾听这声音的时候，它总是带着邪恶的古怪的面具斜着眼瞪他。伟大崇高的艺术之美，欢愉享乐之美，特别显眼的就是女性的美。

究其根本，美与尽情享受和沉醉其中有太多的关联。脆弱的东西通常都是美丽的，但是脆弱的东西并不是美好的。无论他可以获得多么大的成功，他最终的选择都是孤独。在他这样的新的孤单的情绪里，美一定是相对的，亦或是，因为它自己就是和谐，所以它只能创造不和谐。

从某种意义上来讲，美的这种渐渐的抛弃就是他彻底抛弃幻想之后迈出的第二步。他觉得他将他也许会成为某种艺术家的机遇抛在身后了。成为一个某种类型的人的重要性好像远远超过做一个艺术家。

他的想法忽然之间改变了，他自己开始主动思考起罗马天主教。在依仗正统宗教的人的身上总是有某种内在的需求，这个想法在他的心中已经根深蒂固了，而宗教对于艾默里来讲就是罗马天主教。完全能够想象出来，这是一个空洞乏味的流程，但是他好像是抵制道德沦丧的唯一促进同化的传统的堡垒。除非很多乌合之众能够教育好，形成了道德上的认知，不然的话就必须要有一个人高声叫着："你万万不能！"但是，对于现在来说，那是难以置信的。他非常需要时间，他不需要更大的压力。他也不想把树装扮起来，他要充分认识这一新开始的方向和势头。

午后的时光早就从三点钟的清新变成了四点钟的金色美景。随后他在一轮西斜的残阳连续的疼痛中行进着，这时就连那云彩都好像在滴血，黄昏的时候他走到了一处墓地。空气中弥漫着一股晦涩的、温柔的花的气息，天上出现了一轮模模糊糊的新月，到处都能看见影子。他油然生出一种冲动，想要把那建在半山腰上的锈迹斑斑的墓穴的门打开。墓穴被打扫得非常干净，上面被晚开的花完全覆盖了，那是湿漉漉的蔚蓝色的花，也许它们是从死人的眼睛上长出来的，接触以后粘在手上，有着刺鼻的气味，闻之令人作呕。

艾默里的手想要抚摸"威廉·黛菲尔，一八六四"。

他觉得惊讶，坟墓会使人感到生无可恋。不明白怎么一回事，活着他也并没有觉得没有希望。全部的残垣断壁、交握的双手、鸽子、天使都代表着浪漫。他想象着在一百年之后他也想要叫年轻人猜测他的眼睛是褐色的还是蓝色的，他还满含热情地想着，在他的墓地上会笼罩着很多年以前的氛围。他好像感觉很新奇，在那一排联邦政府军士兵的坟墓当中，有两三个人使得他记起了早已消失的爱情和早就死亡的恋人，但是实际上他们的坟墓和其他人的完全相同，就连那坟墓前发黄的苔藓也是如此。

　　早就已经过了午夜了，普林斯顿的大楼和建筑的屋顶还可以看到，还有孤单的要度过漫漫黑夜的灯在亮着——钟声在一片黑暗当中敲响。钟声不停地响着，像是无休止的梦一般。往日的精神在新的一代人的心头缠绕，他们是从那杂乱无章、随波逐流的世界当中选出来的，依然浪漫地从早就去世的政治家和诗人的错误和将要被遗忘的梦想中吸收养分。他们就是全新的一代人，在那漫漫黑夜和白天的思考当中，叫喊着昨日的口号，学习着昨日的条例；他们最终的结局都是迈出去，投身到那肮脏不堪的混乱当中，去追寻那爱和自尊。那是对于贫穷的担忧和对成功的推崇比上一代人更加念念不忘的一代人；等到他们长大的时候，他们却发现那所有的神都已经不见了踪迹，所有的战争早就已经结束，他们对于人类的全部信仰早就崩塌了……

　　虽然艾默里也为他们感到难过，但是他仍旧没有为他自己伤心——艺术、政治、宗教，无论采取什么样的方法。但是他非常清楚现在的他是安全的，一定不会撕心裂肺地发作——他能够接受所有的可以接受的行为方式,漂泊、成熟、叛逆、在很多个夜晚蒙头大睡……

　　上帝早就在他的心中消失了，他很明白这一点。他的思想仍然躁动不安，记忆的苦恼一直伴随着他。对于他那早就流逝的青春的忏悔——然而后悔的河水也还是在他的心灵深处留下了积淀，那是责任和对生活的喜爱，原来的野心勃勃和来不及实现的梦想在轻轻地跳动。但是——啊，罗莎琳！罗莎琳！……

　　"也就勉强可以算作是笨拙的替代品而已。"他悲伤地说道。

　　他也讲不明白为什么努力是值得的，为什么他坚定地想努力利用他自己和他早就超越的重要人物遗留下来的传统……

　　他向着晶莹剔透的天空展开双臂。

　　"我对我自己非常了解，"他大叫道，"但是也仅仅是这样罢了。"

THIS SIDE OF PARADISE

F.Scott Fitzgerald [work]

Contents

BOOK ONE—The Romantic Egotist

CHAPTER 1 Amory, Son of Beatrice / 002

CHAPTER 2 Spires and Gargoyles / 024

CHAPTER 3 The Egotist Considers / 059

CHAPTER 4 Narcissus Off Duty / 080

BOOK TWO—The Education of a Personage

CHAPTER 1 The Debutante / 110

CHAPTER 2 Experiments in Convalescence / 131

CHAPTER 3 Young Irony / 147

CHAPTER 4 The Supercilious Sacrifice / 162

CHAPTER 5 The Egotist Becomes a Personage / 170

BOOK ONE

The Romantic Egotist

CHAPTER 1 Amory, Son of Beatrice

Amory Blaine inherited from his mother every trait, except the stray inexpressible few, that made him worth while. His father, an ineffectual, inarticulate man with a taste for Byron and a habit of drowsing over the Encyclopedia Britannica, grew wealthy at thirty through the death of two elder brothers, successful Chicago brokers, and in the first flush of feeling that the world was his, went to Bar Harbor and met Beatrice O'Hara. In consequence, Stephen Blaine handed down to posterity his height of just under six feet and his tendency to waver at crucial moments, these two abstractions appearing in his son Amory. For many years he hovered in the background of his family's life, an unassertive figure with a face half-obliterated by lifeless, silky hair, continually occupied in "taking care" of his wife, continually harassed by the idea that he didn't and couldn't understand her.

But Beatrice Blaine! There was a woman! Early pictures taken on her father's estate at Lake Geneva, Wisconsin, or in Rome at the Sacred Heart Convent—an educational extravagance that in her youth was only for the daughters of the exceptionally wealthy—showed the exquisite delicacy of her features, the consummate art and simplicity of her clothes. A brilliant education she had—her youth passed in renaissance glory, she was versed in the latest gossip of the Older Roman Families; known by name as a fabulously wealthy American girl to Cardinal Vitori and Queen Margherita and more subtle celebrities that one must have had some culture even to have heard of. She learned in England to prefer whiskey and soda to wine, and her small talk was broadened in two senses during a winter in Vienna. All in all Beatrice O'Hara absorbed the sort of education that will be quite impossible ever again; a tutelage measured by the number of things and people one could be contemptuous of and charming about; a culture rich in all arts and traditions, barren of all ideas, in the last of those days when the great gardener clipped the inferior roses to produce one perfect bud.

In her less important moments she returned to America, met Stephen Blaine and married him—this almost entirely because she was a little bit weary, a little bit sad. Her only child was carried through a tiresome season and brought into the world on a spring day in ninety-six.

When Amory was five he was already a delightful companion for her. He was an auburn-haired boy, with great, handsome eyes which he would grow up to in time, a facile imaginative mind and a taste for fancy dress. From his fourth to his tenth year he did the country with his mother in her father's private car, from Coronado, where his mother

CHAPTER 1 Amory, Son of Beatrice

became so bored that she had a nervous breakdown in a fashionable hotel, down to Mexico City, where she took a mild, almost epidemic consumption. This trouble pleased her, and later she made use of it as an intrinsic part of her atmosphere—especially after several astounding bracers.

So, while more or less fortunate little rich boys were defying governesses on the beach at Newport, or being spanked or tutored or read to from "Do and Dare," or "Frank on the Mississippi," Amory was biting acquiescent bell-boys in the Waldorf, outgrowing a natural repugnance to chamber music and symphonies, and deriving a highly specialized education from his mother.

"Amory."

"Yes, Beatrice." (Such a quaint name for his mother; she encouraged it.)

"Dear, don't think of getting out of bed yet. I've always suspected that early rising in early life makes one nervous. Clothilde is having your breakfast brought up."

"All right."

"I am feeling very old to-day, Amory," she would sigh, her face a rare cameo of pathos, her voice exquisitely modulated, her hands as facile as Bernhardt's. "My nerves are on edge—on edge. We must leave this terrifying place to-morrow and go searching for sunshine."

Amory's penetrating green eyes would look out through tangled hair at his mother. Even at this age he had no illusions about her.

"Amory."

"Oh, yes."

"I want you to take a red-hot bath as hot as you can bear it, and just relax your nerves. You can read in the tub if you wish."

She fed him sections of the "Fetes Galantes" before he was ten; at eleven he could talk glibly, if rather reminiscently, of Brahms and Mozart and Beethoven. One afternoon, when left alone in the hotel at Hot Springs, he sampled his mother's apricot cordial, and as the taste pleased him, he became quite tipsy. This was fun for a while, but he essayed a cigarette in his exaltation, and succumbed to a vulgar, plebeian reaction. Though this incident horrified Beatrice, it also secretly amused her and became part of what in a later generation would have been termed her "line."

"This son of mine," he heard her tell a room full of awestruck, admiring women one day, "is entirely sophisticated and quite charming—but delicate—we're all delicate; here, you know." Her hand was radiantly outlined against her beautiful bosom; then sinking her voice to a whisper, she told them of the apricot cordial. They rejoiced, for she was a brave raconteuse, but many were the keys turned in sideboard locks that night against the possible defection of little Bobby or Barbara....

These domestic pilgrimages were invariably in state; two maids, the private car, or Mr. Blaine when available, and very often a physician. When Amory had the whooping-cough four disgusted specialists glared at each other hunched around his bed; when he took scarlet fever the number of attendants, including physicians and nurses, totalled fourteen. However, blood being thicker than broth, he was pulled through.

The Blaines were attached to no city. They were the Blaines of Lake Geneva; they had quite enough relatives to serve in place of friends, and an enviable standing from Pasadena to Cape Cod. But Beatrice grew more and more prone to like only new acquaintances, as there were certain stories, such as the history of her constitution and its many amendments, memories of her years abroad, that it was necessary for her to repeat at regular intervals. Like Freudian dreams, they must be thrown off, else they would sweep in and lay siege to her nerves. But Beatrice was critical about American women, especially the floating population of ex-Westerners.

"They have accents, my dear," she told Amory, "not Southern accents or Boston accents, not an accent attached to any locality, just an accent"—she became dreamy. "They pick up old, moth-eaten London accents that are down on their luck and have to be used by some one. They talk as an English butler might after several years in a Chicago grand-opera company." She became almost incoherent—"Suppose—time in every Western woman's life—she feels her husband is prosperous enough for her to have—accent—they try to impress me, my dear—"

Though she thought of her body as a mass of frailties, she considered her soul quite as ill, and therefore important in her life. She had once been a Catholic, but discovering that priests were infinitely more attentive when she was in process of losing or regaining faith in Mother Church, she maintained an enchantingly wavering attitude. Often she deplored the bourgeois quality of the American Catholic clergy, and was quite sure that had she lived in the shadow of the great Continental cathedrals her soul would still be a thin flame on the mighty altar of Rome. Still, next to doctors, priests were her favorite sport.

"Ah, Bishop Wiston," she would declare, "I do not want to talk of myself. I can imagine the stream of hysterical women fluttering at your doors, beseeching you to be simpatico"—then after an interlude filled by the clergyman—"but my mood—is—oddly dissimilar."

Only to bishops and above did she divulge her clerical romance. When she had first returned to her country there had been a pagan, Swinburnian young man in Asheville, for whose passionate kisses and unsentimental conversations she had taken a decided penchant—they had discussed the matter pro and con with an intellectual romancing quite devoid of sappiness. Eventually she had decided to marry for background, and the young pagan from Asheville had gone through a spiritual crisis, joined the Catholic Church, and was now—Monsignor Darcy.

"Indeed, Mrs. Blaine, he is still delightful company—quite the cardinal's right-hand man."

"Amory will go to him one day, I know," breathed the beautiful lady, "and Monsignor Darcy will understand him as he understood me."

CHAPTER 1 Amory, Son of Beatrice

Amory became thirteen, rather tall and slender, and more than ever on to his Celtic mother. He had tutored occasionally—the idea being that he was to "keep up," at each place "taking up the work where he left off," yet as no tutor ever found the place he left off, his mind was still in very good shape. What a few more years of this life would have made of him is problematical. However, four hours out from land, Italy bound, with Beatrice, his appendix burst, probably from too many meals in bed, and after a series of frantic telegrams to Europe and America, to the amazement of the passengers the great ship slowly wheeled around and returned to New York to deposit Amory at the pier. You will admit that if it was not life it was magnificent.

After the operation Beatrice had a nervous breakdown that bore a suspicious resemblance to delirium tremens, and Amory was left in Minneapolis, destined to spend the ensuing two years with his aunt and uncle. There the crude, vulgar air of Western civilization first catches him—in his underwear, so to speak.

A KISS FOR AMORY

His lip curled when he read it.

"I am going to have a bobbing party," it said, *"on Thursday, December the seventeenth, at five o'clock, and I would like it very much if you could come.*

Yours truly,

R.S.V.P.   Myra St. Claire.

He had been two months in Minneapolis, and his chief struggle had been the concealing from "the other guys at school" how particularly superior he felt himself to be, yet this conviction was built upon shifting sands. He had shown off one day in French class (he was in senior French class) to the utter confusion of Mr. Reardon, whose accent Amory damned contemptuously, and to the delight of the class. Mr. Reardon, who had spent several weeks in Paris ten years before, took his revenge on the verbs, whenever he had his book open. But another time Amory showed off in history class, with quite disastrous results, for the boys there were his own age, and they shrilled innuendoes at each other all the following week:

"Aw—I b'lieve, doncherknow, the Umuricun revolution was lawgely an affair of the middul clawses," or

"Washington came of very good blood—aw, quite good—I b'lieve."

Amory ingeniously tried to retrieve himself by blundering on purpose. Two years before he had commenced a history of the United States which, though it only got as far as the Colonial Wars, had been pronounced by his mother completely enchanting.

His chief disadvantage lay in athletics, but as soon as he discovered that it was the touchstone of power and popularity at school, he began to make furious, persistent efforts to excel in the winter sports, and with his ankles aching and bending in spite of his efforts, he skated valiantly around the Lorelie rink every afternoon, wondering how soon he would be able to carry a hockey-stick without getting it inexplicably tangled in his skates.

The invitation to Miss Myra St. Claire's bobbing party spent the morning in his coat pocket, where it had an intense physical affair with a dusty piece of peanut brittle. During the afternoon he brought it to light with a sigh, and after some consideration and a preliminary draft in the back of Collar and Daniel's "First-Year Latin," composed an answer:

My dear Miss St. Claire:

Your truly charming envitation for the evening of next Thursday evening was truly delightful to receive this morning. I will be charm and inchanted indeed to present my compliments on next Thursday evening.

Faithfully,
Amory Blaine.

On Thursday, therefore, he walked pensively along the slippery, shovel-scraped sidewalks, and came in sight of Myra's house, on the half-hour after five, a lateness which he fancied his mother would have favored. He waited on the door-step with his eyes nonchalantly half-closed, and planned his entrance with precision. He would cross the floor, not too hastily, to Mrs. St. Claire, and say with exactly the correct modulation:

"My dear Mrs. St. Claire, I'm frightfully sorry to be late, but my maid"—he paused there and realized he would be quoting—"but my uncle and I had to see a fella—Yes, I've met your enchanting daughter at dancing-school."

Then he would shake hands, using that slight, half-foreign bow, with all the starchy little females, and nod to the fellas who would be standing 'round, paralyzed into rigid groups for mutual protection.

A butler (one of the three in Minneapolis) swung open the door. Amory stepped inside and divested himself of cap and coat. He was mildly surprised not to hear the shrill squawk of conversation from the next room, and he decided it must be quite formal. He approved of that—as he approved of the butler.

"Miss Myra," he said.

To his surprise the butler grinned horribly.

"Oh, yeah," he declared, "she's here." He was unaware that his failure to be cockney was ruining his standing. Amory considered him coldly.

"But," continued the butler, his voice rising unnecessarily, "she's the only one what is here. The party's gone."

Amory gasped in sudden horror.

"What?"

"She's been waitin' for Amory Blaine. That's you, ain't it? Her mother says that if you showed up by five-thirty you two was to go after 'em in the Packard."

Amory's despair was crystallized by the appearance of Myra herself, bundled to the ears in a polo coat, her face plainly sulky, her voice pleasant only with difficulty.

"'Lo, Amory."

CHAPTER 1 Amory, Son of Beatrice

"'Lo, Myra." He had described the state of his vitality.

"Well—you got here, anyways."

"Well—I'll tell you. I guess you don't know about the auto accident," he romanced. Myra's eyes opened wide.

"Who was it to?"

"Well," he continued desperately, "uncle 'n aunt 'n I."

"Was any one killed?"

Amory paused and then nodded.

"Your uncle?"—alarm.

"Oh, no just a horse—a sorta gray horse."

At this point the Erse butler snickered.

"Probably killed the engine," he suggested. Amory would have put him on the rack without a scruple.

"We'll go now," said Myra coolly. "You see, Amory, the bobs were ordered for five and everybody was here, so we couldn't wait—"

"Well, I couldn't help it, could I?"

"So mama said for me to wait till ha'past five. We'll catch the bobs before it gets to the Minnehaha Club, Amory."

Amory's shredded poise dropped from him. He pictured the happy party jingling along snowy streets, the appearance of the limousine, the horrible public descent of him and Myra before sixty reproachful eyes, his apology—a real one this time. He sighed aloud.

"What?" inquired Myra.

"Nothing. I was just yawning. Are we going to surely catch up with 'em before they get there?" He was encouraging a faint hope that they might slip into the Minnehaha Club and meet the others there, be found in blasé seclusion before the fire and quite regain his lost attitude.

"Oh, sure Mike, we'll catch 'em all right—let's hurry."

He became conscious of his stomach. As they stepped into the machine he hurriedly slapped the paint of diplomacy over a rather box-like plan he had conceived. It was based upon some "trade-lasts" gleaned at dancing-school, to the effect that he was "awful good-looking and English, sort of,"

"Myra," he said, lowering his voice and choosing his words carefully, "I beg a thousand pardons. Can you ever forgive me?" She regarded him gravely, his intent green eyes, his mouth, that to her thirteen-year-old, arrow-collar taste was the quintessence of romance. Yes, Myra could forgive him very easily.

"Why—yes—sure."

He looked at her again, and then dropped his eyes. He had lashes.

"I'm awful," he said sadly. "I'm diff'runt. I don't know why I make faux pas. 'Cause I don't care, I s'pose." Then, recklessly: "I been smoking too much. I've got t'bacca heart."

007

Myra pictured an all-night tobacco debauch, with Amory pale and reeling from the effect of nicotined lungs. She gave a little gasp.

"Oh, Amory, don't smoke. You'll stunt your growth!"

"I don't care," he persisted gloomily. "I gotta. I got the habit. I've done a lot of things that if my fambly knew"—he hesitated, giving her imagination time to picture dark horrors—"I went to the burlesque show last week."

Myra was quite overcome. He turned the green eyes on her again. "You're the only girl in town I like much," he exclaimed in a rush of sentiment. "You're simpatico."

Myra was not sure that she was, but it sounded stylish though vaguely improper.

Thick dusk had descended outside, and as the limousine made a sudden turn she was jolted against him; their hands touched.

"You shouldn't smoke, Amory," she whispered. "Don't you know that?"

He shook his head.

"Nobody cares."

Myra hesitated.

"I care."

Something stirred within Amory.

"Oh, yes, you do! You got a crush on Froggy Parker. I guess everybody knows that."

"No, I haven't," very slowly.

A silence, while Amory thrilled. There was something fascinating about Myra, shut away here cosily from the dim, chill air. Myra, a little bundle of clothes, with strands of yellow hair curling out from under her skating cap.

"Because I've got a crush, too—" He paused, for he heard in the distance the sound of young laughter, and, peering through the frosted glass along the lamp-lit street, he made out the dark outline of the bobbing party. He must act quickly. He reached over with a violent, jerky effort, and clutched Myra's hand—her thumb, to be exact.

"Tell him to go to the Minnehaha straight," he whispered. "I wanta talk to you—I got to talk to you."

Myra made out the party ahead, had an instant vision of her mother, and then—alas for convention—glanced into the eyes beside. "Turn down this side street, Richard, and drive straight to the Minnehaha Club!" she cried through the speaking tube. Amory sank back against the cushions with a sigh of relief.

"I can kiss her," he thought. "I'll bet I can. I'll bet I can!"

Overhead the sky was half crystalline, half misty, and the night around was chill and vibrant with rich tension. From the Country Club steps the roads stretched away, dark creases on the white blanket; huge heaps of snow lining the sides like the tracks of giant moles. They lingered for a moment on the steps, and watched the white holiday moon.

"Pale moons like that one"—Amory made a vague gesture—"make people mysterieuse. You look like a young witch with her cap off and her hair sorta mussed"—her hands clutched at her hair—"Oh, leave it, it looks good."

They drifted up the stairs and Myra led the way into the little den of his dreams, where a cosy fire was burning before a big sink-down couch. A few years later this was to be a great stage for Amory, a cradle for many an emotional crisis. Now they talked for a moment about bobbing parties.

"There's always a bunch of shy fellas," he commented, "sitting at the tail of the bob, sorta lurkin' an' whisperin' an' pushin' each other off. Then there's always some crazy cross-eyed girl"—he gave a terrifying imitation—"she's always talkin' hard, sorta, to the chaperon."

"You're such a funny boy," puzzled Myra.

"How d'y' mean?" Amory gave immediate attention, on his own ground at last.

"Oh—always talking about crazy things. Why don't you come ski-ing with Marylyn and I to-morrow?"

"I don't like girls in the daytime," he said shortly, and then, thinking this a bit abrupt, he added: "But I like you." He cleared his throat. "I like you first and second and third."

Myra's eyes became dreamy. What a story this would make to tell Marylyn! Here on the couch with this wonderful-looking boy—the little fire—the sense that they were alone in the great building—

Myra capitulated. The atmosphere was too appropriate.

"I like you the first twenty-five," she confessed, her voice trembling, "and Froggy Parker twenty-sixth."

Froggy had fallen twenty-five places in one hour. As yet he had not even noticed it.

But Amory, being on the spot, leaned over quickly and kissed Myra's cheek. He had never kissed a girl before, and he tasted his lips curiously, as if he had munched some new fruit. Then their lips brushed like young wild flowers in the wind.

"We're awful," rejoiced Myra gently. She slipped her hand into his, her head drooped against his shoulder. Sudden revulsion seized Amory, disgust, loathing for the whole incident. He desired frantically to be away, never to see Myra again, never to kiss any one; he became conscious of his face and hers, of their clinging hands, and he wanted to creep out of his body and hide somewhere safe out of sight, up in the corner of his mind.

"Kiss me again." Her voice came out of a great void.

"I don't want to," he heard himself saying. There was another pause.

"I don't want to!" he repeated passionately.

Myra sprang up, her cheeks pink with bruised vanity, the great bow on the back of her head trembling sympathetically.

"I hate you!" she cried. "Don't you ever dare to speak to me again!"

"What?" stammered Amory.

"I'll tell mama you kissed me! I will too! I will too! I'll tell mama, and she won't let me play with you!"

009

Amory rose and stared at her helplessly, as though she were a new animal of whose presence on the earth he had not heretofore been aware.

The door opened suddenly, and Myra's mother appeared on the threshold, fumbling with her lorgnette.

"Well," she began, adjusting it benignantly, "the man at the desk told me you two children were up here—How do you do, Amory."

Amory watched Myra and waited for the crash—but none came. The pout faded, the high pink subsided, and Myra's voice was placid as a summer lake when she answered her mother.

"Oh, we started so late, mama, that I thought we might as well—"

He heard from below the shrieks of laughter, and smelled the vapid odor of hot chocolate and tea-cakes as he silently followed mother and daughter down-stairs. The sound of the graphophone mingled with the voices of many girls humming the air, and a faint glow was born and spread over him:

"Casey-Jones—mounted to the cab-un

Casey-Jones—'th his orders in his hand.

Casey-Jones—mounted to the cab-un

Took his farewell journey to the prom-ised land."

SNAPSHOTS OF THE YOUNG EGOTIST

Amory spent nearly two years in Minneapolis. The first winter he wore moccasins that were born yellow, but after many applications of oil and dirt assumed their mature color, a dirty, greenish brown; he wore a gray plaid mackinaw coat, and a red toboggan cap. His dog, Count Del Monte, ate the red cap, so his uncle gave him a gray one that pulled down over his face. The trouble with this one was that you breathed into it and your breath froze; one day the darn thing froze his cheek. He rubbed snow on his cheek, but it turned bluish-black just the same.

The Count Del Monte ate a box of bluing once, but it didn't hurt him. Later, however, he lost his mind and ran madly up the street, bumping into fences, rolling in gutters, and pursuing his eccentric course out of Amory's life. Amory cried on his bed.

"Poor little Count," he cried. "Oh, poor little Count!"

After several months he suspected Count of a fine piece of emotional acting.

Amory and Frog Parker considered that the greatest line in literature occurred in Act III of "Arsene Lupin."

They sat in the first row at the Wednesday and Saturday matinees. The line was:

"If one can't be a great artist or a great soldier, the next best thing is to be a great criminal."

Amory fell in love again, and wrote a poem. This was it:

"Marylyn and Sallee,

Those are the girls for me.

CHAPTER 1 Amory, Son of Beatrice

Marylyn stands above
Sallee in that sweet, deep love."

He was interested in whether McGovern of Minnesota would make the first or second All-American, how to do the card-pass, how to do the coin-pass, chameleon ties, how babies were born, and whether Three-fingered Brown was really a better pitcher than Christie Mathewson.

Among other things he read: "For the Honor of the School," "Little Women" (twice), "The Common Law," "Sapho," "Dangerous Dan McGrew," "The Broad Highway" (three times), "The Fall of the House of Usher," "Three Weeks," "Mary Ware, the Little Colonel's Chum," "Gunga Din," The Police Gazette, and Jim-Jam Jems.

He had all the Henty biasses in history, and was particularly fond of the cheerful murder stories of Mary Roberts Rinehart.

School ruined his French and gave him a distaste for standard authors. His masters considered him idle, unreliable and superficially clever.

He collected locks of hair from many girls. He wore the rings of several. Finally he could borrow no more rings, owing to his nervous habit of chewing them out of shape. This, it seemed, usually aroused the jealous suspicions of the next borrower.

All through the summer months Amory and Frog Parker went each week to the Stock Company. Afterward they would stroll home in the balmy air of August night, dreaming along Hennepin and Nicollet Avenues, through the gay crowd. Amory wondered how people could fail to notice that he was a boy marked for glory, and when faces of the throng turned toward him and ambiguous eyes stared into his, he assumed the most romantic of expressions and walked on the air cushions that lie on the asphalts of fourteen.

Always, after he was in bed, there were voices—indefinite, fading, enchanting—just outside his window, and before he fell asleep he would dream one of his favorite waking dreams, the one about becoming a great half-back, or the one about the Japanese invasion, when he was rewarded by being made the youngest general in the world. It was always the becoming he dreamed of, never the being. This, too, was quite characteristic of Amory.

CODE OF THE YOUNG EGOTIST

Before he was summoned back to Lake Geneva, he had appeared, shy but inwardly glowing, in his first long trousers, set off by a purple accordion tie and a "Belmont" collar with the edges unassailably meeting, purple socks, and handkerchief with a purple border peeping from his breast pocket. But more than that, he had formulated his first philosophy, a code to live by, which, as near as it can be named, was a sort of aristocratic egotism.

He had realized that his best interests were bound up with those of a certain variant, changing person, whose label, in order that his past might always be identified with him, was Amory Blaine. Amory marked himself a fortunate youth, capable of infinite expansion for good or evil. He did not consider himself a "strong char'c'ter," but relied on his facility (learn things sorta quick) and his superior mentality (read a lotta deep books). He was proud of the fact that he could never become a mechanical or scientific genius. From no other heights was he debarred.

Physically.—Amory thought that he was exceedingly handsome. He was. He fancied himself an athlete of possibilities and a supple dancer.

Socially.—Here his condition was, perhaps, most dangerous. He granted himself personality, charm, magnetism, poise, the power of dominating all contemporary males, the gift of fascinating all women.

Mentally.—Complete, unquestioned superiority.

Now a confession will have to be made. Amory had rather a Puritan conscience. Not that he yielded to it—later in life he almost completely slew it—but at fifteen it made him consider himself a great deal worse than other boys... unscrupulousness... the desire to influence people in almost every way, even for evil... a certain coldness and lack of affection, amounting sometimes to cruelty... a shifting sense of honor... an unholy selfishness... a puzzled, furtive interest in everything concerning sex.

There was, also, a curious strain of weakness running crosswise through his make-up... a harsh phrase from the lips of an older boy (older boys usually detested him) was liable to sweep him off his poise into surly sensitiveness, or timid stupidity... he was a slave to his own moods and he felt that though he was capable of recklessness and audacity, he possessed neither courage, perseverance, nor self-respect.

Vanity, tempered with self-suspicion if not self-knowledge, a sense of people as automatons to his will, a desire to "pass" as many boys as possible and get to a vague top of the world... with this background did Amory drift into adolescence.

PREPARATORY TO THE GREAT ADVENTURE

The train slowed up with midsummer languor at Lake Geneva, and Amory caught sight of his mother waiting in her electric on the gravelled station drive. It was an ancient electric, one of the early types, and painted gray. The sight of her sitting there, slenderly erect, and of her face, where beauty and dignity combined, melting to a dreamy recollected smile, filled him with a sudden great pride of her. As they kissed coolly and he stepped into the electric, he felt a quick fear lest he had lost the requisite charm to measure up to her.

"Dear boy—you're so tall... look behind and see if there's anything coming..."

She looked left and right, she slipped cautiously into a speed of two miles an hour, beseeching Amory to act as sentinel; and at one busy crossing she made him get out and run ahead to signal her forward like a traffic policeman. Beatrice was what might be termed a careful driver.

"You are tall—but you're still very handsome—you've skipped the awkward age, or is that sixteen; perhaps it's fourteen or fifteen; I can never remember; but you've skipped it."

"Don't embarrass me," murmured Amory.

"But, my dear boy, what odd clothes! They look as if they were a set—don't they? Is your underwear purple, too?"

CHAPTER 1 Amory, Son of Beatrice

Amory grunted impolitely.

"You must go to Brooks' and get some really nice suits. Oh, we'll have a talk to-night or perhaps to-morrow night. I want to tell you about your heart—you've probably been neglecting your heart—and you don't know."

Amory thought how superficial was the recent overlay of his own generation. Aside from a minute shyness, he felt that the old cynical kinship with his mother had not been one bit broken. Yet for the first few days he wandered about the gardens and along the shore in a state of superloneliness, finding a lethargic content in smoking "Bull" at the garage with one of the chauffeurs.

The sixty acres of the estate were dotted with old and new summer houses and many fountains and white benches that came suddenly into sight from foliage-hung hiding-places; there was a great and constantly increasing family of white cats that prowled the many flower-beds and were silhouetted suddenly at night against the darkening trees. It was on one of the shadowy paths that Beatrice at last captured Amory, after Mr. Blaine had, as usual, retired for the evening to his private library. After reproving him for avoiding her, she took him for a long tete-a-tete in the moonlight. He could not reconcile himself to her beauty, that was mother to his own, the exquisite neck and shoulders, the grace of a fortunate woman of thirty.

"Amory, dear," she crooned softly, "I had such a strange, weird time after I left you."

"Did you, Beatrice?"

"When I had my last breakdown"—she spoke of it as a sturdy, gallant feat.

"The doctors told me"—her voice sang on a confidential note—"that if any man alive had done the consistent drinking that I have, he would have been physically shattered, my dear, and in his grave—long in his grave."

Amory winced, and wondered how this would have sounded to Froggy Parker.

"Yes," continued Beatrice tragically, "I had dreams—wonderful visions." She pressed the palms of her hands into her eyes. "I saw bronze rivers lapping marble shores, and great birds that soared through the air, parti-colored birds with iridescent plumage. I heard strange music and the flare of barbaric trumpets—what?"

Amory had snickered.

"What, Amory?"

"I said go on, Beatrice."

"That was all—it merely recurred and recurred—gardens that flaunted coloring against which this would be quite dull, moons that whirled and swayed, paler than winter moons, more golden than harvest moons—"

"Are you quite well now, Beatrice?"

"Quite well—as well as I will ever be. I am not understood, Amory. I know that can't express it to you, Amory, but—I am not understood."

Amory was quite moved. He put his arm around his mother, rubbing his head gently

013

against her shoulder.

"Poor Beatrice—poor Beatrice."

"Tell me about you, Amory. Did you have two horrible years?"

Amory considered lying, and then decided against it.

"No, Beatrice. I enjoyed them. I adapted myself to the bourgeoisie. I became conventional." He surprised himself by saying that, and he pictured how Froggy would have gaped.

"Beatrice," he said suddenly, "I want to go away to school. Everybody in Minneapolis is going to go away to school."

Beatrice showed some alarm.

"But you're only fifteen."

"Yes, but everybody goes away to school at fifteen, and I want to, Beatrice."

On Beatrice's suggestion the subject was dropped for the rest of the walk, but a week later she delighted him by saying:

"Amory, I have decided to let you have your way. If you still want to, you can go to school."

"Yes?"

"To St. Regis's in Connecticut."

Amory felt a quick excitement.

"It's being arranged," continued Beatrice. "It's better that you should go away. I'd have preferred you to have gone to Eton, and then to Christ Church, Oxford, but it seems impracticable now—and for the present we'll let the university question take care of itself."

"What are you going to do, Beatrice?"

"Heaven knows. It seems my fate to fret away my years in this country. Not for a second do I regret being American—indeed, I think that a regret typical of very vulgar people, and I feel sure we are the great coming nation—yet"—and she sighed—"I feel my life should have drowsed away close to an older, mellower civilization, a land of greens and autumnal browns—"

Amory did not answer, so his mother continued:

"My regret is that you haven't been abroad, but still, as you are a man, it's better that you should grow up here under the snarling eagle—is that the right term?"

Amory agreed that it was. She would not have appreciated the Japanese invasion.

"When do I go to school?"

"Next month. You'll have to start East a little early to take your examinations. After that you'll have a free week, so I want you to go up the Hudson and pay a visit."

"To who?"

"To Monsignor Darcy, Amory. He wants to see you. He went to Harrow and then to Yale—became a Catholic. I want him to talk to you—I feel he can be such a help—" She stroked his auburn hair gently. "Dear Amory, dear Amory—"

CHAPTER 1 Amory, Son of Beatrice

"Dear Beatrice—"

So early in September Amory, provided with "six suits summer underwear, six suits winter underwear, one sweater or T shirt, one jersey, one overcoat, winter, etc.," set out for New England, the land of schools.

There were Andover and Exeter with their memories of New England dead—large, college-like democracies; St. Mark's, Groton, St. Regis'—recruited from Boston and the Knickerbocker families of New York; St. Paul's, with its great rinks; Pomfret and St. George's, prosperous and well-dressed; Taft and Hotchkiss, which prepared the wealth of the Middle West for social success at Yale; Pawling, Westminster, Choate, Kent, and a hundred others; all milling out their well-set-up, conventional, impressive type, year after year; their mental stimulus the college entrance exams; their vague purpose set forth in a hundred circulars as "To impart a Thorough Mental, Moral, and Physical Training as a Christian Gentleman, to fit the boy for meeting the problems of his day and generation, and to give a solid foundation in the Arts and Sciences."

At St. Regis' Amory stayed three days and took his exams with a scoffing confidence, then doubling back to New York to pay his tutelary visit. The metropolis, barely glimpsed, made little impression on him, except for the sense of cleanliness he drew from the tall white buildings seen from a Hudson River steamboat in the early morning. Indeed, his mind was so crowded with dreams of athletic prowess at school that he considered this visit only as a rather tiresome prelude to the great adventure. This, however, it did not prove to be.

Monsignor Darcy's house was an ancient, rambling structure set on a hill overlooking the river, and there lived its owner, between his trips to all parts of the Roman-Catholic world, rather like an exiled Stuart king waiting to be called to the rule of his land. Monsignor was forty-four then, and bustling—a trifle too stout for symmetry, with hair the color of spun gold, and a brilliant, enveloping personality. When he came into a room clad in his full purple regalia from thatch to toe, he resembled a Turner sunset, and attracted both admiration and attention. He had written two novels: one of them violently anti-Catholic, just before his conversion, and five years later another, in which he had attempted to turn all his clever jibes against Catholics into even cleverer innuendoes against Episcopalians. He was intensely ritualistic, startlingly dramatic, loved the idea of God enough to be a celibate, and rather liked his neighbor.

Children adored him because he was like a child; youth revelled in his company because he was still a youth, and couldn't be shocked. In the proper land and century he might have been a Richelieu—at present he was a very moral, very religious (if not particularly pious) clergyman, making a great mystery about pulling rusty wires, and appreciating life to the fullest, if not entirely enjoying it.

He and Amory took to each other at first sight—the jovial, impressive prelate who could dazzle an embassy ball, and the green-eyed, intent youth, in his first long trousers, accepted in their own minds a relation of father and son within a half-hour's conversation.

"My dear boy, I've been waiting to see you for years. Take a big chair and we'll have a chat."

"I've just come from school—St. Regis's, you know."

"So your mother says—a remarkable woman; have a cigarette—I'm sure you smoke. Well, if you're like me, you loathe all science and mathematics—"

Amory nodded vehemently.

"Hate 'em all. Like English and history."

"Of course. You'll hate school for a while, too, but I'm glad you're going to St. Regis's."

"Why?"

"Because it's a gentleman's school, and democracy won't hit you so early. You'll find plenty of that in college."

"I want to go to Princeton," said Amory. "I don't know why, but I think of all Harvard men as sissies, like I used to be, and all Yale men as wearing big blue sweaters and smoking pipes."

Monsignor chuckled.

"I'm one, you know."

"Oh, you're different—I think of Princeton as being lazy and good-looking and aristocratic—you know, like a spring day. Harvard seems sort of indoors—"

"And Yale is November, crisp and energetic," finished Monsignor.

"That's it."

They slipped briskly into an intimacy from which they never recovered.

"I was for Bonnie Prince Charlie," announced Amory.

"Of course you were—and for Hannibal—"

"Yes, and for the Southern Confederacy." He was rather sceptical about being an Irish patriot—he suspected that being Irish was being somewhat common—but Monsignor assured him that Ireland was a romantic lost cause and Irish people quite charming, and that it should, by all means, be one of his principal biasses.

After a crowded hour which included several more cigarettes, and during which Monsignor learned, to his surprise but not to his horror, that Amory had not been brought up a Catholic, he announced that he had another guest. This turned out to be the Honorable Thornton Hancock, of Boston, ex-minister to The Hague, author of an erudite history of the Middle Ages and the last of a distinguished, patriotic, and brilliant family.

"He comes here for a rest," said Monsignor confidentially, treating Amory as a contemporary. "I act as an escape from the weariness of agnosticism, and I think I'm the only man who knows how his staid old mind is really at sea and longs for a sturdy spar like the Church to cling to."

Their first luncheon was one of the memorable events of Amory's early life. He was quite radiant and gave off a peculiar brightness and charm. Monsignor called out the best

CHAPTER 1 Amory, Son of Beatrice

that he had thought by question and suggestion, and Amory talked with an ingenious brilliance of a thousand impulses and desires and repulsions and faiths and fears. He and Monsignor held the floor, and the older man, with his less receptive, less accepting, yet certainly not colder mentality, seemed content to listen and bask in the mellow sunshine that played between these two. Monsignor gave the effect of sunlight to many people; Amory gave it in his youth and, to some extent, when he was very much older, but never again was it quite so mutually spontaneous.

"He's a radiant boy," thought Thornton Hancock, who had seen the splendor of two continents and talked with Parnell and Gladstone and Bismarck—and afterward he added to Monsignor: "But his education ought not to be intrusted to a school or college."

But for the next four years the best of Amory's intellect was concentrated on matters of popularity, the intricacies of a university social system and American Society as represented by Biltmore Teas and Hot Springs golf-links.

... In all, a wonderful week, that saw Amory's mind turned inside out, a hundred of his theories confirmed, and his joy of life crystallized to a thousand ambitions. Not that the conversation was scholastic—heaven forbid! Amory had only the vaguest idea as to what Bernard Shaw was—but Monsignor made quite as much out of "The Beloved Vagabond" and "Sir Nigel," taking good care that Amory never once felt out of his depth.

But the trumpets were sounding for Amory's preliminary skirmish with his own generation.

"You're not sorry to go, of course. With people like us our home is where we are not," said Monsignor.

"I am sorry—"

"No, you're not. No one person in the world is necessary to you or to me."

"Well—"

"Good-by."

THE EGOTIST DOWN

Amory's two years at St. Regis', though in turn painful and triumphant, had as little real significance in his own life as the American "prep" school, crushed as it is under the heel of the universities, has to American life in general. We have no Eton to create the self-consciousness of a governing class; we have, instead, clean, flaccid and innocuous preparatory schools.

He went all wrong at the start, was generally considered both conceited and arrogant, and universally detested. He played football intensely, alternating a reckless brilliancy with a tendency to keep himself as safe from hazard as decency would permit. In a wild panic he backed out of a fight with a boy his own size, to a chorus of scorn, and a week later, in desperation, picked a battle with another boy very much bigger, from which he emerged badly beaten, but rather proud of himself.

He was resentful against all those in authority over him, and this, combined with a lazy indifference toward his work, exasperated every master in school. He grew discouraged and imagined himself a pariah; took to sulking in corners and reading after lights. With a dread of being alone he attached a few friends, but since they were not among the elite of the school, he used them simply as mirrors of himself, audiences before which he might do that posing absolutely essential to him. He was unbearably lonely, desperately unhappy.

There were some few grains of comfort. Whenever Amory was submerged, his vanity was the last part to go below the surface, so he could still enjoy a comfortable glow when "Wookey-wookey," the deaf old housekeeper, told him that he was the best-looking boy she had ever seen. It had pleased him to be the lightest and youngest man on the first football squad; it pleased him when Doctor Dougall told him at the end of a heated conference that he could, if he wished, get the best marks in school. But Doctor Dougall was wrong. It was temperamentally impossible for Amory to get the best marks in school.

Miserable, confined to bounds, unpopular with both faculty and students—that was Amory's first term. But at Christmas he had returned to Minneapolis, tight-lipped and strangely jubilant.

"Oh, I was sort of fresh at first," he told Frog Parker patronizingly, "but I got along fine—lightest man on the squad. You ought to go away to school, Froggy. It's great stuff."

INCIDENT OF THE WELL-MEANING PROFESSOR

On the last night of his first term, Mr. Margotson, the senior master, sent word to study hall that Amory was to come to his room at nine. Amory suspected that advice was forthcoming, but he determined to be courteous, because this Mr. Margotson had been kindly disposed toward him.

His summoner received him gravely, and motioned him to a chair. He hemmed several times and looked consciously kind, as a man will when he knows he's on delicate ground.

"Amory," he began. "I've sent for you on a personal matter."

"Yes, sir."

"I've noticed you this year and I—I like you. I think you have in you the makings of a—a very good man."

"Yes, sir," Amory managed to articulate. He hated having people talk as if he were an admitted failure.

"But I've noticed," continued the older man blindly, "that you're not very popular with the boys."

"No, sir." Amory licked his lips.

"Ah—I thought you might not understand exactly what it was they—ah—objected to. I'm going to tell you, because I believe—ah—that when a boy knows his difficulties he's better able to cope with them—to conform to what others expect of him." He a-hemmed again with delicate reticence, and continued: "They seem to think that you're—ah—rather too fresh—"

Amory could stand no more. He rose from his chair, scarcely controlling his voice when he spoke.

"I know—oh, don't you s'pose I know." His voice rose. "I know what they think; do you s'pose you have to tell me!" He paused. "I'm—I've got to go back now—hope I'm not rude—"

He left the room hurriedly. In the cool air outside, as he walked to his house, he exulted in his refusal to be helped.

"That damn old fool!" he cried wildly. "As if I didn't know!"

He decided, however, that this was a good excuse not to go back to study hall that night, so, comfortably couched up in his room, he munched Nabiscos and finished "The White Company."

INCIDENT OF THE WONDERFUL GIRL

There was a bright star in February. New York burst upon him on Washington's Birthday with the brilliance of a long-anticipated event. His glimpse of it as a vivid whiteness against a deep-blue sky had left a picture of splendor that rivalled the dream cities in the Arabian Nights; but this time he saw it by electric light, and romance gleamed from the chariot-race sign on Broadway and from the women's eyes at the Astor, where he and young Paskert from St. Regis' had dinner. When they walked down the aisle of the theatre, greeted by the nervous twanging and discord of untuned violins and the sensuous, heavy fragrance of paint and powder, he moved in a sphere of epicurean delight. Everything enchanted him. The play was "The Little Millionaire," with George M. Cohan, and there was one stunning young brunette who made him sit with brimming eyes in the ecstasy of watching her dance.

"Oh—you—wonderful girl,
What a wonderful girl you are—"

sang the tenor, and Amory agreed silently, but passionately.

"All—your—wonderful words
Thrill me through—"

The violins swelled and quavered on the last notes, the girl sank to a crumpled butterfly on the stage, a great burst of clapping filled the house. Oh, to fall in love like that, to the languorous magic melody of such a tune!

The last scene was laid on a roof-garden, and the 'cellos sighed to the musical moon, while light adventure and facile froth-like comedy flitted back and forth in the calcium. Amory was on fire to be an habitui of roof-gardens, to meet a girl who should look like that—better, that very girl; whose hair would be drenched with golden moonlight, while at his elbow sparkling wine was poured by an unintelligible waiter. When the curtain fell for the last time he gave such a long sigh that the people in front of him twisted around and stared and said loud enough for him to hear:

"What a remarkable-looking boy!"

This took his mind off the play, and he wondered if he really did seem handsome to the population of New York.

Paskert and he walked in silence toward their hotel. The former was the first to speak. His uncertain fifteen-year-old voice broke in in a melancholy strain on Amory's musings:

"I'd marry that girl to-night."

There was no need to ask what girl he referred to.

"I'd be proud to take her home and introduce her to my people," continued Paskert.

Amory was distinctly impressed. He wished he had said it instead of Paskert. It sounded so mature.

"I wonder about actresses; are they all pretty bad?"

"No, sir, not by a darn sight," said the worldly youth with emphasis, "and I know that girl's as good as gold. I can tell."

They wandered on, mixing in the Broadway crowd, dreaming on the music that eddied out of the cafes. New faces flashed on and off like myriad lights, pale or rouged faces, tired, yet sustained by a weary excitement. Amory watched them in fascination. He was planning his life. He was going to live in New York, and be known at every restaurant and cafe, wearing a dress-suit from early evening to early morning, sleeping away the dull hours of the forenoon.

"Yes, sir, I'd marry that girl to-night!"

HEROIC IN GENERAL TONE

October of his second and last year at St. Regis' was a high point in Amory's memory. The game with Groton was played from three of a snappy, exhilarating afternoon far into the crisp autumnal twilight, and Amory at quarter-back, exhorting in wild despair, making impossible tackles, calling signals in a voice that had diminished to a hoarse, furious whisper, yet found time to revel in the blood-stained bandage around his head, and the straining, glorious heroism of plunging, crashing bodies and aching limbs. For those minutes courage flowed like wine out of the November dusk, and he was the eternal hero, one with the sea-rover on the prow of a Norse galley, one with Roland and Horatius, Sir Nigel and Ted Coy, scraped and stripped into trim and then flung by his own will into the breach, beating back the tide, hearing from afar the thunder of cheers... finally bruised and weary, but still elusive, circling an end, twisting, changing pace, straight-arming... falling behind the Groton goal with two men on his legs, in the only touchdown of the game.

THE PHILOSOPHY OF THE SLICKER

From the scoffing superiority of sixth-form year and success Amory looked back with cynical wonder on his status of the year before. He was changed as completely as Amory Blaine could ever be changed. Amory plus Beatrice plus two years in Minneapolis—these had been his ingredients when he entered St. Regis'. But the Minneapolis years were not a thick enough overlay to conceal the "Amory plus Beatrice" from the ferreting eyes of a boarding-school, so St. Regis' had very painfully drilled Beatrice out of him, and begun to lay down new and more conventional planking on the fundamental Amory. But both St. Regis' and Amory were unconscious of the fact that this fundamental Amory had not in

CHAPTER 1 Amory, Son of Beatrice

himself changed. Those qualities for which he had suffered, his moodiness, his tendency to pose, his laziness, and his love of playing the fool, were now taken as a matter of course, recognized eccentricities in a star quarter-back, a clever actor, and the editor of the St. Regis Tattler: it puzzled him to see impressionable small boys imitating the very vanities that had not long ago been contemptible weaknesses.

After the football season he slumped into dreamy content. The night of the pre-holiday dance he slipped away and went early to bed for the pleasure of hearing the violin music cross the grass and come surging in at his window. Many nights he lay there dreaming awake of secret cafes in Mont Martre, where ivory women delved in romantic mysteries with diplomats and soldiers of fortune, while orchestras played Hungarian waltzes and the air was thick and exotic with intrigue and moonlight and adventure. In the spring he read "L'Allegro," by request, and was inspired to lyrical outpourings on the subject of Arcady and the pipes of Pan. He moved his bed so that the sun would wake him at dawn that he might dress and go out to the archaic swing that hung from an apple-tree near the sixth-form house. Seating himself in this he would pump higher and higher until he got the effect of swinging into the wide air, into a fairyland of piping satyrs and nymphs with the faces of fair-haired girls he passed in the streets of Eastchester. As the swing reached its highest point, Arcady really lay just over the brow of a certain hill, where the brown road dwindled out of sight in a golden dot.

He read voluminously all spring, the beginning of his eighteenth year: "The Gentleman from Indiana," "The New Arabian Nights," "The Morals of Marcus Ordeyne," "The Man Who Was Thursday," which he liked without understanding; "Stover at Yale," that became somewhat of a text-book; "Dombey and Son," because he thought he really should read better stuff; Robert Chambers, David Graham Phillips, and E. Phillips Oppenheim complete, and a scattering of Tennyson and Kipling. Of all his class work only "L'Allegro" and some quality of rigid clarity in solid geometry stirred his languid interest.

As June drew near, he felt the need of conversation to formulate his own ideas, and, to his surprise, found a co-philosopher in Rahill, the president of the sixth form. In many a talk, on the highroad or lying belly-down along the edge of the baseball diamond, or late at night with their cigarettes glowing in the dark, they threshed out the questions of school, and there was developed the term "slicker."

"Got tobacco?" whispered Rahill one night, putting his head inside the door five minutes after lights.

"Sure."

"I'm coming in."

"Take a couple of pillows and lie in the window-seat, why don't you."

Amory sat up in bed and lit a cigarette while Rahill settled for a conversation. Rahill's favorite subject was the respective futures of the sixth form, and Amory never tired of outlining them for his benefit.

"Ted Converse? 'At's easy. He'll fail his exams, tutor all summer at Harstrum's, get into Sheff with about four conditions, and flunk out in the middle of the freshman year. Then he'll go back West and raise hell for a year or so; finally his father will make him go into the paint business. He'll marry and have four sons, all bone heads. He'll always think St. Regis's spoiled him, so he'll send his sons to day school in Portland. He'll die of locomotor ataxia when he's forty-one, and his wife will give a baptizing stand or whatever you call it to the Presbyterian Church, with his name on it—"

"Hold up, Amory. That's too darned gloomy. How about yourself?"

"I'm in a superior class. You are, too. We're philosophers."

"I'm not."

"Sure you are. You've got a darn good head on you." But Amory knew that nothing in the abstract, no theory or generality, ever moved Rahill until he stubbed his toe upon the concrete minutiae of it.

"Haven't," insisted Rahill. "I let people impose on me here and don't get anything out of it. I'm the prey of my friends, damn it—do their lessons, get 'em out of trouble, pay 'em stupid summer visits, and always entertain their kid sisters; keep my temper when they get selfish and then they think they pay me back by voting for me and telling me I'm the 'big man' of St. Regis's. I want to get where everybody does their own work and I can tell people where to go. I'm tired of being nice to every poor fish in school."

"You're not a slicker," said Amory suddenly.

"A what?"

"A slicker."

"What the devil's that?"

"Well, it's something that—that—there's a lot of them. You're not one, and neither am I, though I am more than you are."

"Who is one? What makes you one?"

Amory considered.

"Why—why, I suppose that the sign of it is when a fellow slicks his hair back with water."

"Like Carstairs?"

"Yes—sure. He's a slicker."

They spent two evenings getting an exact definition. The slicker was good-looking or clean-looking; he had brains, social brains, that is, and he used all means on the broad path of honesty to get ahead, be popular, admired, and never in trouble. He dressed well, was particularly neat in appearance, and derived his name from the fact that his hair was inevitably worn short, soaked in water or tonic, parted in the middle, and slicked back as the current of fashion dictated. The slickers of that year had adopted tortoise-shell spectacles as badges of their slickerhood, and this made them so easy to recognize that Amory and Rahill never missed one. The slicker seemed distributed through school, always a little

CHAPTER 1 Amory, Son of Beatrice

wiser and shrewder than his contemporaries, managing some team or other, and keeping his cleverness carefully concealed.

Amory found the slicker a most valuable classification until his junior year in college, when the outline became so blurred and indeterminate that it had to be subdivided many times, and became only a quality. Amory's secret ideal had all the slicker qualifications, but, in addition, courage and tremendous brains and talents—also Amory conceded him a bizarre streak that was quite irreconcilable to the slicker proper.

This was a first real break from the hypocrisy of school tradition. The slicker was a definite element of success, differing intrinsically from the prep school "big man."

"THE SLICKER"

1. Clever sense of social values.
2. Dresses well. Pretends that dress is superficial—but knows that it isn't.
3. Goes into such activities as he can shine in.
4. Gets to college and is, in a worldly way, successful.
5. Hair slicked.

"THE BIG MAN"

1. Inclined to stupidity and unconscious of social values.
2. Thinks dress is superficial, and is inclined to be careless about it.
3. Goes out for everything from a sense of duty.
4. Gets to college and has a problematical future. Feels lost without his circle, and always says that school days were happiest, after all. Goes back to school and makes speeches about what St. Regis's boys are doing.
5. Hair not slicked.

Amory had decided definitely on Princeton, even though he would be the only boy entering that year from St. Regis'. Yale had a romance and glamour from the tales of Minneapolis, and St. Regis' men who had been "tapped for Skull and Bones," but Princeton drew him most, with its atmosphere of bright colors and its alluring reputation as the pleasantest country club in America. Dwarfed by the menacing college exams, Amory's school days drifted into the past. Years afterward, when he went back to St. Regis', he seemed to have forgotten the successes of sixth-form year, and to be able to picture himself only as the unadjustable boy who had hurried down corridors, jeered at by his rabid contemporaries mad with common sense.

CHAPTER 2　Spires and Gargoyles

At first Amory noticed only the wealth of sunshine creeping across the long, green swards, dancing on the leaded window-panes, and swimming around the tops of spires and towers and battlemented walls. Gradually he realized that he was really walking up University Place, self-conscious about his suitcase, developing a new tendency to glare straight ahead when he passed any one. Several times he could have sworn that men turned to look at him critically. He wondered vaguely if there was something the matter with his clothes, and wished he had shaved that morning on the train. He felt unnecessarily stiff and awkward among these white-flannelled, bareheaded youths, who must be juniors and seniors, judging from the savoir faire with which they strolled.

He found that 12 University Place was a large, dilapidated mansion, at present apparently uninhabited, though he knew it housed usually a dozen freshmen. After a hurried skirmish with his landlady he sallied out on a tour of exploration, but he had gone scarcely a block when he became horribly conscious that he must be the only man in town who was wearing a hat. He returned hurriedly to 12 University, left his derby, and, emerging bareheaded, loitered down Nassau Street, stopping to investigate a display of athletic photographs in a store window, including a large one of Allenby, the football captain, and next attracted by the sign "Jigger Shop" over a confectionary window. This sounded familiar, so he sauntered in and took a seat on a high stool.

"Chocolate sundae," he told a colored person.

"Double chocolate jiggah? Anything else?"

"Why—yes."

"Bacon bun?"

"Why—yes."

He munched four of these, finding them of pleasing savor, and then consumed another double-chocolate jigger before ease descended upon him. After a cursory inspection of the pillow-cases, leather pennants, and Gibson Girls that lined the walls, he left, and continued along Nassau Street with his hands in his pockets. Gradually he was learning to distinguish between upper classmen and entering men, even though the freshman cap would not appear until the following Monday. Those who were too obviously, too nervously at home were freshmen, for as each train brought a new contingent it was immediately absorbed into the hatless, white-shod, book-laden throng, whose function seemed to be to drift endlessly up and down the street, emitting great clouds of smoke from brand-new pipes. By afternoon Amory realized that now the newest arrivals were taking him for an upper classman, and he

CHAPTER 2 Spires and Gargoyles

tried conscientiously to look both pleasantly blasé and casually critical, which was as near as he could analyze the prevalent facial expression.

At five o'clock he felt the need of hearing his own voice, so he retreated to his house to see if any one else had arrived. Having climbed the rickety stairs he scrutinized his room resignedly, concluding that it was hopeless to attempt any more inspired decoration than class banners and tiger pictures. There was a tap at the door.

"Come in!"

A slim face with gray eyes and a humorous smile appeared in the doorway.

"Got a hammer?"

"No—sorry. Maybe Mrs. Twelve, or whatever she goes by, has one."

The stranger advanced into the room.

"You an inmate of this asylum?"

Amory nodded.

"Awful barn for the rent we pay."

Amory had to agree that it was.

"I thought of the campus," he said, "but they say there's so few freshmen that they're lost. Have to sit around and study for something to do."

The gray-eyed man decided to introduce himself.

"My name's Holiday."

"Blaine's my name."

They shook hands with the fashionable low swoop. Amory grinned.

"Where'd you prep?"

"Andover—where did you?"

"St. Regis's."

"Oh, did you? I had a cousin there."

They discussed the cousin thoroughly, and then Holiday announced that he was to meet his brother for dinner at six.

"Come along and have a bite with us."

"All right."

At the Kenilworth Amory met Burne Holiday—he of the gray eyes was Kerry—and during a limpid meal of thin soup and anaemic vegetables they stared at the other freshmen, who sat either in small groups looking very ill at ease, or in large groups seeming very much at home.

"I hear Commons is pretty bad," said Amory.

"That's the rumor. But you've got to eat there—or pay anyways."

"Crime!"

"Imposition!"

"Oh, at Princeton you've got to swallow everything the first year. It's like a damned prep school."

Amory agreed.

"Lot of pep, though," he insisted. "I wouldn't have gone to Yale for a million."

"Me either."

"You going out for anything?" inquired Amory of the elder brother.

"Not me—Burne here is going out for the Prince—the Daily Princetonian, you know."

"Yes, I know."

"You going out for anything?"

"Why—yes. I'm going to take a whack at freshman football."

"Play at St. Regis's?"

"Some," admitted Amory depreciatingly, "but I'm getting so damned thin."

"You're not thin."

"Well, I used to be stocky last fall."

"Oh!"

After supper they attended the movies, where Amory was fascinated by the glib comments of a man in front of him, as well as by the wild yelling and shouting.

"Yoho!"

"Oh, honey-baby—you're so big and strong, but oh, so gentle!"

"Clinch!"

"Oh, Clinch!"

"Kiss her, kiss 'at lady, quick!"

"Oh-h-h—!"

A group began whistling "By the Sea," and the audience took it up noisily. This was followed by an indistinguishable song that included much stamping and then by an endless, incoherent dirge.

"Oh-h-h-h-h

She works in a Jam Factoree

And—that-may-be-all-right

But you can't-fool-me

For I know—DAMN—WELL

That she DON'T-make-jam-all-night!

Oh-h-h-h!"

As they pushed out, giving and receiving curious impersonal glances, Amory decided that he liked the movies, wanted to enjoy them as the row of upper classmen in front had enjoyed them, with their arms along the backs of the seats, their comments Gaelic and caustic, their attitude a mixture of critical wit and tolerant amusement.

"Want a sundae—I mean a jigger?" asked Kerry.

"Sure."

They suppered heavily and then, still sauntering, eased back to 12.

CHAPTER 2 Spires and Gargoyles

"Wonderful night."

"It's a whiz."

"You men going to unpack?"

"Guess so. Come on, Burne."

Amory decided to sit for a while on the front steps, so he bade them good night.

The great tapestries of trees had darkened to ghosts back at the last edge of twilight. The early moon had drenched the arches with pale blue, and, weaving over the night, in and out of the gossamer rifts of moon, swept a song, a song with more than a hint of sadness, infinitely transient, infinitely regretful.

He remembered that an alumnus of the nineties had told him of one of Booth Tarkington's amusements: standing in mid-campus in the small hours and singing tenor songs to the stars, arousing mingled emotions in the couched undergraduates according to the sentiment of their moods.

Now, far down the shadowy line of University Place a white-clad phalanx broke the gloom, and marching figures, white-shirted, white-trousered, swung rhythmically up the street, with linked arms and heads thrown back:

"Going back—going back,

Going—back—to—Nas-sau—Hall,

Going back—going back—

To the—Best—Old—Place—of—All.

Going back—going back,

From all—this—earth-ly—ball,

We'll—clear—the—track—as—we—go—back—

Going—back—to—Nas-sau—Hall!"

Amory closed his eyes as the ghostly procession drew near. The song soared so high that all dropped out except the tenors, who bore the melody triumphantly past the danger-point and relinquished it to the fantastic chorus. Then Amory opened his eyes, half afraid that sight would spoil the rich illusion of harmony.

He sighed eagerly. There at the head of the white platoon marched Allenby, the football captain, slim and defiant, as if aware that this year the hopes of the college rested on him, that his hundred-and-sixty pounds were expected to dodge to victory through the heavy blue and crimson lines.

Fascinated, Amory watched each rank of linked arms as it came abreast, the faces indistinct above the polo shirts, the voices blent in a paean of triumph—and then the procession passed through shadowy Campbell Arch, and the voices grew fainter as it wound eastward over the campus.

The minutes passed and Amory sat there very quietly. He regretted the rule that would forbid freshmen to be outdoors after curfew, for he wanted to ramble through the shadowy

027

scented lanes, where Witherspoon brooded like a dark mother over Whig and Clio, her Attic children, where the black Gothic snake of Little curled down to Cuyler and Patton, these in turn flinging the mystery out over the placid slope rolling to the lake.

Princeton of the daytime filtered slowly into his consciousness—West and Reunion, redolent of the sixties, Seventy-nine Hall, brick-red and arrogant, Upper and Lower Pyne, aristocratic Elizabethan ladies not quite content to live among shopkeepers, and, topping all, climbing with clear blue aspiration, the great dreaming spires of Holder and Cleveland towers.

From the first he loved Princeton—its lazy beauty, its half-grasped significance, the wild moonlight revel of the rushes, the handsome, prosperous big-game crowds, and under it all the air of struggle that pervaded his class. From the day when, wild-eyed and exhausted, the jerseyed freshmen sat in the gymnasium and elected some one from Hill School class president, a Lawrenceville celebrity vice-president, a hockey star from St. Paul's secretary, up until the end of sophomore year it never ceased, that breathless social system, that worship, seldom named, never really admitted, of the bogey "Big Man."

First it was schools, and Amory, alone from St. Regis', watched the crowds form and widen and form again; St. Paul's, Hill, Pomfret, eating at certain tacitly reserved tables in Commons, dressing in their own corners of the gymnasium, and drawing unconsciously about them a barrier of the slightly less important but socially ambitious to protect them from the friendly, rather puzzled high-school element. From the moment he realized this Amory resented social barriers as artificial distinctions made by the strong to bolster up their weak retainers and keep out the almost strong.

Having decided to be one of the gods of the class, he reported for freshman football practice, but in the second week, playing quarter-back, already paragraphed in corners of the Princetonian, he wrenched his knee seriously enough to put him out for the rest of the season. This forced him to retire and consider the situation.

"12 Univee" housed a dozen miscellaneous question-marks. There were three or four inconspicuous and quite startled boys from Lawrenceville, two amateur wild men from a New York private school (Kerry Holiday christened them the "plebeian drunks"), a Jewish youth, also from New York, and, as compensation for Amory, the two Holidays, to whom he took an instant fancy.

The Holidays were rumored twins, but really the dark-haired one, Kerry, was a year older than his blond brother, Burne. Kerry was tall, with humorous gray eyes, and a sudden, attractive smile; he became at once the mentor of the house, reaper of ears that grew too high, censor of conceit, vendor of rare, satirical humor. Amory spread the table of their future friendship with all his ideas of what college should and did mean. Kerry, not inclined as yet to take things seriously, chided him gently for being curious at this inopportune time about the intricacies of the social system, but liked him and was both interested and amused.

Burne, fair-haired, silent, and intent, appeared in the house only as a busy apparition,

CHAPTER 2 Spires and Gargoyles

gliding in quietly at night and off again in the early morning to get up his work in the library—he was out for the Princetonian, competing furiously against forty others for the coveted first place. In December he came down with diphtheria, and some one else won the competition, but, returning to college in February, he dauntlessly went after the prize again. Necessarily, Amory's acquaintance with him was in the way of three-minute chats, walking to and from lectures, so he failed to penetrate Burne's one absorbing interest and find what lay beneath it.

Amory was far from contented. He missed the place he had won at St. Regis', the being known and admired, yet Princeton stimulated him, and there were many things ahead calculated to arouse the Machiavelli latent in him, could he but insert a wedge. The upper-class clubs, concerning which he had pumped a reluctant graduate during the previous summer, excited his curiosity: Ivy, detached and breathlessly aristocratic; Cottage, an impressive mélange of brilliant adventurers and well-dressed philanderers; Tiger Inn, broad-shouldered and athletic, vitalized by an honest elaboration of prep-school standards; Cap and Gown, anti-alcoholic, faintly religious and politically powerful; flamboyant Colonial; literary Quadrangle; and the dozen others, varying in age and position.

Anything which brought an under classman into too glaring a light was labelled with the damning brand of "running it out." The movies thrived on caustic comments, but the men who made them were generally running it out; talking of clubs was running it out; standing for anything very strongly, as, for instance, drinking parties or teetotalling, was running it out; in short, being personally conspicuous was not tolerated, and the influential man was the non-committal man, until at club elections in sophomore year every one should be sewed up in some bag for the rest of his college career.

Amory found that writing for the Nassau Literary Magazine would get him nothing, but that being on the board of the Daily Princetonian would get any one a good deal. His vague desire to do immortal acting with the English Dramatic Association faded out when he found that the most ingenious brains and talents were concentrated upon the Triangle Club, a musical comedy organization that every year took a great Christmas trip. In the meanwhile, feeling strangely alone and restless in Commons, with new desires and ambitions stirring in his mind, he let the first term go by between an envy of the embryo successes and a puzzled fretting with Kerry as to why they were not accepted immediately among the elite of the class.

Many afternoons they lounged in the windows of 12 Univee and watched the class pass to and from Commons, noting satellites already attaching themselves to the more prominent, watching the lonely grind with his hurried step and downcast eye, envying the happy security of the big school groups.

"We're the damned middle class, that's what!" he complained to Kerry one day as he lay stretched out on the sofa, consuming a family of Fatimas with contemplative precision.

"Well, why not? We came to Princeton so we could feel that way toward the small colleges—have it on 'em, more self-confidence, dress better, cut a swathe—"

"Oh, it isn't that I mind the glittering caste system," admitted Amory. "I like having a bunch of hot cats on top, but gosh, Kerry, I've got to be one of them."

"But just now, Amory, you're only a sweaty bourgeois."

Amory lay for a moment without speaking.

"I won't be—long," he said finally. "But I hate to get anywhere by working for it. I'll show the marks, don't you know."

"Honorable scars." Kerry craned his neck suddenly at the street. "There's Langueduc, if you want to see what he looks like—and Humbird just behind."

Amory rose dynamically and sought the windows.

"Oh," he said, scrutinizing these worthies, "Humbird looks like a knock-out, but this Langueduc—he's the rugged type, isn't he? I distrust that sort. All diamonds look big in the rough."

"Well," said Kerry, as the excitement subsided, "you're a literary genius. It's up to you."

"I wonder"—Amory paused—"if I could be. I honestly think so sometimes. That sounds like the devil, and I wouldn't say it to anybody except you."

"Well—go ahead. Let your hair grow and write poems like this guy D'Invilliers in the Lit."

Amory reached lazily at a pile of magazines on the table.

"Read his latest effort?"

"Never miss 'em. They're rare."

Amory glanced through the issue.

"Hello!" he said in surprise, "he's a freshman, isn't he?"

"Yeah."

"Listen to this! My God!

"'A serving lady speaks:
Black velvet trails its folds over the day,
White tapers, prisoned in their silver frames,
Wave their thin flames like shadows in the wind,
Pia, Pompia, come—come away—'

"Now, what the devil does that mean?"

"It's a pantry scene."

"'*Her toes are stiffened like a stork's in flight;*
She's laid upon her bed, on the white sheets,
Her hands pressed on her smooth bust like a saint,
Bella Cunizza, come into the light!'

"My gosh, Kerry, what in hell is it all about? I swear I don't get him at all, and I'm a literary bird myself."

"It's pretty tricky," said Kerry, "only you've got to think of hearses and stale milk when

CHAPTER 2 Spires and Gargoyles

you read it. That isn't as pash as some of them."

Amory tossed the magazine on the table.

"Well," he sighed, "I sure am up in the air. I know I'm not a regular fellow, yet I loathe anybody else that isn't. I can't decide whether to cultivate my mind and be a great dramatist, or to thumb my nose at the Golden Treasury and be a Princeton slicker."

"Why decide?" suggested Kerry. "Better drift, like me. I'm going to sail into prominence on Burne's coat-tails."

"I can't drift—I want to be interested. I want to pull strings, even for somebody else, or be Princetonian chairman or Triangle president. I want to be admired, Kerry."

"You're thinking too much about yourself."

Amory sat up at this.

"No. I'm thinking about you, too. We've got to get out and mix around the class right now, when it's fun to be a snob. I'd like to bring a sardine to the prom in June, for instance, but I wouldn't do it unless I could be damn debonaire about it—introduce her to all the prize parlor-snakes, and the football captain, and all that simple stuff."

"Amory," said Kerry impatiently, "you're just going around in a circle. If you want to be prominent, get out and try for something; if you don't, just take it easy." He yawned. "Come on, let's let the smoke drift off. We'll go down and watch football practice."

Amory gradually accepted this point of view, decided that next fall would inaugurate his career, and relinquished himself to watching Kerry extract joy from 12 Univee.

They filled the Jewish youth's bed with lemon pie; they put out the gas all over the house every night by blowing into the jet in Amory's room, to the bewilderment of Mrs. Twelve and the local plumber; they set up the effects of the plebeian drunks—pictures, books, and furniture—in the bathroom, to the confusion of the pair, who hazily discovered the transposition on their return from a Trenton spree; they were disappointed beyond measure when the plebeian drunks decided to take it as a joke; they played red-dog and twenty-one and jackpot from dinner to dawn, and on the occasion of one man's birthday persuaded him to buy sufficient champagne for a hilarious celebration. The donor of the party having remained sober, Kerry and Amory accidentally dropped him down two flights of stairs and called, shame-faced and penitent, at the infirmary all the following week.

"Say, who are all these women?" demanded Kerry one day, protesting at the size of Amory's mail. "I've been looking at the postmarks lately—Farmington and Dobbs and Westover and Dana Hall—what's the idea?"

Amory grinned.

"All from the Twin Cities." He named them off. "There's Marylyn De Witt—she's pretty, got a car of her own and that's damn convenient; there's Sally Weatherby—she's getting too fat; there's Myra St. Claire, she's an old flame, easy to kiss if you like it—"

"What line do you throw 'em?" demanded Kerry. "I've tried everything, and the mad wags aren't even afraid of me."

031

"You're the 'nice boy' type," suggested Amory.

"That's just it. Mother always feels the girl is safe if she's with me. Honestly, it's annoying. If I start to hold somebody's hand, they laugh at me, and let me, just as if it wasn't part of them. As soon as I get hold of a hand they sort of disconnect it from the rest of them."

"Sulk," suggested Amory. "Tell 'em you're wild and have 'em reform you—go home furious—come back in half an hour—startle 'em."

Kerry shook his head.

"No chance. I wrote a St. Timothy girl a really loving letter last year. In one place I got rattled and said: 'My God, how I love you!' She took a nail scissors, clipped out the 'My God' and showed the rest of the letter all over school. Doesn't work at all. I'm just 'good old Kerry' and all that rot."

Amory smiled and tried to picture himself as "good old Amory." He failed completely.

February dripped snow and rain, the cyclonic freshman mid-years passed, and life in 12 Univee continued interesting if not purposeful. Once a day Amory indulged in a club sandwich, cornflakes, and Julienne potatoes at "Joe's," accompanied usually by Kerry or Alec Connage. The latter was a quiet, rather aloof slicker from Hotchkiss, who lived next door and shared the same enforced singleness as Amory, due to the fact that his entire class had gone to Yale. "Joe's" was unaesthetic and faintly unsanitary, but a limitless charge account could be opened there, a convenience that Amory appreciated. His father had been experimenting with mining stocks and, in consequence, his allowance, while liberal, was not at all what he had expected.

"Joe's" had the additional advantage of seclusion from curious upper-class eyes, so at four each afternoon Amory, accompanied by friend or book, went up to experiment with his digestion. One day in March, finding that all the tables were occupied, he slipped into a chair opposite a freshman who bent intently over a book at the last table. They nodded briefly. For twenty minutes Amory sat consuming bacon buns and reading "Mrs. Warren's Profession" (he had discovered Shaw quite by accident while browsing in the library during mid-years); the other freshman, also intent on his volume, meanwhile did away with a trio of chocolate malted milks.

By and by Amory's eyes wandered curiously to his fellow-luncher's book. He spelled out the name and title upside down—"Marpessa," by Stephen Phillips. This meant nothing to him, his metrical education having been confined to such Sunday classics as "Come into the Garden, Maude," and what morsels of Shakespeare and Milton had been recently forced upon him.

Moved to address his vis-a-vis, he simulated interest in his book for a moment, and then exclaimed aloud as if involuntarily:

"Ha! Great stuff!"

The other freshman looked up and Amory registered artificial embarrassment.

CHAPTER 2 Spires and Gargoyles

"Are you referring to your bacon buns?" His cracked, kindly voice went well with the large spectacles and the impression of a voluminous keenness that he gave.

"No," Amory answered. "I was referring to Bernard Shaw." He turned the book around in explanation.

"I've never read any Shaw. I've always meant to." The boy paused and then continued: "Did you ever read Stephen Phillips, or do you like poetry?"

"Yes, indeed," Amory affirmed eagerly. "I've never read much of Phillips, though." (He had never heard of any Phillips except the late David Graham.)

"It's pretty fair, I think. Of course he's a Victorian." They sallied into a discussion of poetry, in the course of which they introduced themselves, and Amory's companion proved to be none other than "that awful highbrow, Thomas Parke D'Invilliers," who signed the passionate love-poems in the Lit. He was, perhaps, nineteen, with stooped shoulders, pale blue eyes, and, as Amory could tell from his general appearance, without much conception of social competition and such phenomena of absorbing interest. Still, he liked books, and it seemed forever since Amory had met any one who did; if only that St. Paul's crowd at the next table would not mistake him for a bird, too, he would enjoy the encounter tremendously. They didn't seem to be noticing, so he let himself go, discussed books by the dozens—books he had read, read about, books he had never heard of, rattling off lists of titles with the facility of a Brentano's clerk. D'Invilliers was partially taken in and wholly delighted. In a good-natured way he had almost decided that Princeton was one part deadly Philistines and one part deadly grinds, and to find a person who could mention Keats without stammering, yet evidently washed his hands, was rather a treat.

"Ever read any Oscar Wilde?" he asked.

"No. Who wrote it?"

"It's a man—don't you know?"

"Oh, surely." A faint chord was struck in Amory's memory. "Wasn't the comic opera, 'Patience,' written about him?"

"Yes, that's the fella. I've just finished a book of his, 'The Picture of Dorian Gray,' and I certainly wish you'd read it. You'd like it. You can borrow it if you want to."

"Why, I'd like it a lot thanks."

"Don't you want to come up to the room? I've got a few other books."

Amory hesitated, glanced at the St. Paul's group—one of them was the magnificent, exquisite Humbird—and he considered how determinate the addition of this friend would be. He never got to the stage of making them and getting rid of them—he was not hard enough for that—so he measured Thomas Parke D'Invilliers' undoubted attractions and value against the menace of cold eyes behind tortoise-rimmed spectacles that he fancied glared from the next table.

"Yes, I'll go."

So he found "Dorian Gray" and the "Mystic and Somber Dolores" and the "Belle Dame

033

sans Merci"; for a month was keen on naught else. The world became pale and interesting, and he tried hard to look at Princeton through the satiated eyes of Oscar Wilde and Swinburne—or "Fingal O'Flaherty" and "Algernon Charles," as he called them in precieuse jest. He read enormously every night—Shaw, Chesterton, Barrie, Pinero, Yeats, Synge, Ernest Dowson, Arthur Symons, Keats, Sudermann, Robert Hugh Benson, the Savoy Operas—just a heterogeneous mixture, for he suddenly discovered that he had read nothing for years.

Tom D'Invilliers became at first an occasion rather than a friend. Amory saw him about once a week, and together they gilded the ceiling of Tom's room and decorated the walls with imitation tapestry, bought at an auction, tall candlesticks and figured curtains. Amory liked him for being clever and literary without effeminacy or affectation. In fact, Amory did most of the strutting and tried painfully to make every remark an epigram, than which, if one is content with ostensible epigrams, there are many feats harder. 12 Univee was amused. Kerry read "Dorian Gray" and simulated Lord Henry, following Amory about, addressing him as "Dorian" and pretending to encourage in him wicked fancies and attenuated tendencies to ennui. When he carried it into Commons, to the amazement of the others at table, Amory became furiously embarrassed, and after that made epigrams only before D'Invilliers or a convenient mirror.

One day Tom and Amory tried reciting their own and Lord Dunsany's poems to the music of Kerry's graphophone.

"Chant!" cried Tom. "Don't recite! Chant!"

Amory, who was performing, looked annoyed, and claimed that he needed a record with less piano in it. Kerry thereupon rolled on the floor in stifled laughter.

"Put on 'Hearts and Flowers'!" he howled. "Oh, my Lord, I'm going to cast a kitten."

"Shut off the damn graphophone," Amory cried, rather red in the face. "I'm not giving an exhibition."

In the meanwhile Amory delicately kept trying to awaken a sense of the social system in D'Invilliers, for he knew that this poet was really more conventional than he, and needed merely watered hair, a smaller range of conversation, and a darker brown hat to become quite regular. But the liturgy of Livingstone collars and dark ties fell on heedless ears; in fact D'Invilliers faintly resented his efforts; so Amory confined himself to calls once a week, and brought him occasionally to 12 Univee. This caused mild titters among the other freshmen, who called them "Doctor Johnson and Boswell."

Alec Connage, another frequent visitor, liked him in a vague way, but was afraid of him as a highbrow. Kerry, who saw through his poetic patter to the solid, almost respectable depths within, was immensely amused and would have him recite poetry by the hour, while he lay with closed eyes on Amory's sofa and listened:

"*Asleep or waking is it? for her neck*
Kissed over close, wears yet a purple speck

CHAPTER 2 Spires and Gargoyles

*Wherein the pained blood falters and goes out;
Soft and stung softly—fairer for a fleck..."*

"That's good," Kerry would say softly. "It pleases the elder Holiday. That's a great poet, I guess." Tom, delighted at an audience, would ramble through the "Poems and Ballades" until Kerry and Amory knew them almost as well as he.

Amory took to writing poetry on spring afternoons, in the gardens of the big estates near Princeton, while swans made effective atmosphere in the artificial pools, and slow clouds sailed harmoniously above the willows. May came too soon, and suddenly unable to bear walls, he wandered the campus at all hours through starlight and rain.

A DAMP SYMBOLIC INTERLUDE

The night mist fell. From the moon it rolled, clustered about the spires and towers, and then settled below them, so that the dreaming peaks were still in lofty aspiration toward the sky. Figures that dotted the day like ants now brushed along as shadowy ghosts, in and out of the foreground. The Gothic halls and cloisters were infinitely more mysterious as they loomed suddenly out of the darkness, outlined each by myriad faint squares of yellow light. Indefinitely from somewhere a bell boomed the quarter-hour, and Amory, pausing by the sun-dial, stretched himself out full length on the damp grass. The cool bathed his eyes and slowed the flight of time—time that had crept so insidiously through the lazy April afternoons, seemed so intangible in the long spring twilights. Evening after evening the senior singing had drifted over the campus in melancholy beauty, and through the shell of his undergraduate consciousness had broken a deep and reverent devotion to the gray walls and Gothic peaks and all they symbolized as warehouses of dead ages.

The tower that in view of his window sprang upward, grew into a spire, yearning higher until its uppermost tip was half invisible against the morning skies, gave him the first sense of the transiency and unimportance of the campus figures except as holders of the apostolic succession. He liked knowing that Gothic architecture, with its upward trend, was peculiarly appropriate to universities, and the idea became personal to him. The silent stretches of green, the quiet halls with an occasional late-burning scholastic light held his imagination in a strong grasp, and the chastity of the spire became a symbol of this perception.

"Damn it all," he whispered aloud, wetting his hands in the damp and running them through his hair. "Next year I work!" Yet he knew that where now the spirit of spires and towers made him dreamily acquiescent, it would then overawe him. Where now he realized only his own inconsequence, effort would make him aware of his own impotency and insufficiency.

The college dreamed on—awake. He felt a nervous excitement that might have been the very throb of its slow heart. It was a stream where he was to throw a stone whose faint ripple would be vanishing almost as it left his hand. As yet he had given nothing, he had taken nothing.

A belated freshman, his oilskin slicker rasping loudly, slushed along the soft path. A voice from somewhere called the inevitable formula, "Stick out your head!" below an unseen window. A hundred little sounds of the current drifting on under the fog pressed in finally on his consciousness.

"Oh, God!" he cried suddenly, and started at the sound of his voice in the stillness. The rain dripped on. A minute longer he lay without moving, his hands clinched. Then he sprang to his feet and gave his clothes a tentative pat.

"I'm very damn wet!" he said aloud to the sun-dial.

HISTORICAL

The war began in the summer following his freshman year. Beyond a sporting interest in the German dash for Paris the whole affair failed either to thrill or interest him. With the attitude he might have held toward an amusing melodrama he hoped it would be long and bloody. If it had not continued he would have felt like an irate ticket-holder at a prize-fight where the principals refused to mix it up.

That was his total reaction.

"HA-HA HORTENSE!"

"All right, ponies!"

"Shake it up!"

"Hey, ponies—how about easing up on that crap game and shaking a mean hip?"

"Hey, ponies!"

The coach fumed helplessly, the Triangle Club president, glowering with anxiety, varied between furious bursts of authority and fits of temperamental lassitude, when he sat spiritless and wondered how the devil the show was ever going on tour by Christmas.

"All right. We'll take the pirate song."

The ponies took last drags at their cigarettes and slumped into place; the leading lady rushed into the foreground, setting his hands and feet in an atmospheric mince; and as the coach clapped and stamped and tumped and da-da'd, they hashed out a dance.

A great, seething ant-hill was the Triangle Club. It gave a musical comedy every year, travelling with cast, chorus, orchestra, and scenery all through Christmas vacation. The play and music were the work of undergraduates, and the club itself was the most influential of institutions, over three hundred men competing for it every year.

Amory, after an easy victory in the first sophomore Princetonian competition, stepped into a vacancy of the cast as Boiling Oil, a Pirate Lieutenant. Every night for the last week they had rehearsed "Ha-Ha Hortense!" in the Casino, from two in the afternoon until eight in the morning, sustained by dark and powerful coffee, and sleeping in lectures through the interim. A rare scene, the Casino. A big, barnlike auditorium, dotted with boys as girls, boys as pirates, boys as babies; the scenery in course of being violently set up; the spotlight man rehearsing by throwing weird shafts into angry eyes; over all the constant tuning of the orchestra or the cheerful tumpty-tump of a Triangle tune. The boy who writes the lyrics

CHAPTER 2 Spires and Gargoyles

stands in the corner, biting a pencil, with twenty minutes to think of an encore; the business manager argues with the secretary as to how much money can be spent on "those damn milkmaid costumes"; the old graduate, president in ninety-eight, perches on a box and thinks how much simpler it was in his day.

How a Triangle show ever got off was a mystery, but it was a riotous mystery, anyway, whether or not one did enough service to wear a little gold Triangle on his watch-chain. "Ha-Ha Hortense!" was written over six times and had the names of nine collaborators on the programme. All Triangle shows started by being "something different—not just a regular musical comedy," but when the several authors, the president, the coach and the faculty committee finished with it, there remained just the old reliable Triangle show with the old reliable jokes and the star comedian who got expelled or sick or something just before the trip, and the dark-whiskered man in the pony-ballet, who "absolutely won't shave twice a day, doggone it!"

There was one brilliant place in "Ha-Ha Hortense!" It is a Princeton tradition that whenever a Yale man who is a member of the widely advertised "Skull and Bones" hears the sacred name mentioned, he must leave the room. It is also a tradition that the members are invariably successful in later life, amassing fortunes or votes or coupons or whatever they choose to amass. Therefore, at each performance of "Ha-Ha Hortense!" half-a-dozen seats were kept from sale and occupied by six of the worst-looking vagabonds that could be hired from the streets, further touched up by the Triangle make-up man. At the moment in the show where Firebrand, the Pirate Chief, pointed at his black flag and said, "I am a Yale graduate—note my Skull and Bones!"—at this very moment the six vagabonds were instructed to rise conspicuously and leave the theatre with looks of deep melancholy and an injured dignity. It was claimed though never proved that on one occasion the hired Elis were swelled by one of the real thing.

They played through vacation to the fashionable of eight cities. Amory liked Louisville and Memphis best: these knew how to meet strangers, furnished extraordinary punch, and flaunted an astonishing array of feminine beauty. Chicago he approved for a certain verve that transcended its loud accent—however, it was a Yale town, and as the Yale Glee Club was expected in a week the Triangle received only divided homage. In Baltimore, Princeton was at home, and every one fell in love. There was a proper consumption of strong waters all along the line; one man invariably went on the stage highly stimulated, claiming that his particular interpretation of the part required it. There were three private cars; however, no one slept except in the third car, which was called the "animal car," and where were herded the spectacled wind-jammers of the orchestra. Everything was so hurried that there was no time to be bored, but when they arrived in Philadelphia, with vacation nearly over, there was rest in getting out of the heavy atmosphere of flowers and grease-paint, and the ponies took off their corsets with abdominal pains and sighs of relief.

When the disbanding came, Amory set out post haste for Minneapolis, for Sally

Weatherby's cousin, Isabelle Borge, was coming to spend the winter in Minneapolis while her parents went abroad. He remembered Isabelle only as a little girl with whom he had played sometimes when he first went to Minneapolis. She had gone to Baltimore to live—but since then she had developed a past.

Amory was in full stride, confident, nervous, and jubilant. Scurrying back to Minneapolis to see a girl he had known as a child seemed the interesting and romantic thing to do, so without compunction he wired his mother not to expect him... sat in the train, and thought about himself for thirty-six hours.

"PETTING"

On the Triangle trip Amory had come into constant contact with that great current American phenomenon, the "petting party."

None of the Victorian mothers—and most of the mothers were Victorian—had any idea how casually their daughters were accustomed to be kissed. "Servant-girls are that way," says Mrs. Huston-Carmelite to her popular daughter. "They are kissed first and proposed to afterward."

But the Popular Daughter becomes engaged every six months between sixteen and twenty-two, when she arranges a match with young Hambell, of Cambell & Hambell, who fatuously considers himself her first love, and between engagements the P. D. (she is selected by the cut-in system at dances, which favors the survival of the fittest) has other sentimental last kisses in the moonlight, or the firelight, or the outer darkness.

Amory saw girls doing things that even in his memory would have been impossible: eating three-o'clock, after-dance suppers in impossible cafes, talking of every side of life with an air half of earnestness, half of mockery, yet with a furtive excitement that Amory considered stood for a real moral let-down. But he never realized how wide-spread it was until he saw the cities between New York and Chicago as one vast juvenile intrigue.

Afternoon at the Plaza, with winter twilight hovering outside and faint drums downstairs... they strut and fret in the lobby, taking another cocktail, scrupulously attired and waiting. Then the swinging doors revolve and three bundles of fur mince in. The theatre comes afterward; then a table at the Midnight Frolic—of course, mother will be along there, but she will serve only to make things more secretive and brilliant as she sits in solitary state at the deserted table and thinks such entertainments as this are not half so bad as they are painted, only rather wearying. But the P. D. is in love again... it was odd, wasn't it?—that though there was so much room left in the taxi the P. D. and the boy from Williams were somehow crowded out and had to go in a separate car. Odd! Didn't you notice how flushed the P. D. was when she arrived just seven minutes late? But the P. D. "gets away with it."

The "belle" had become the "flirt," the "flirt" had become the "baby vamp." The "belle" had five or six callers every afternoon. If the P. D., by some strange accident, has two, it is made pretty uncomfortable for the one who hasn't a date with her. The "belle"

CHAPTER 2 Spires and Gargoyles

was surrounded by a dozen men in the intermissions between dances. Try to find the P. D. between dances, just try to find her.

The same girl... deep in an atmosphere of jungle music and the questioning of moral codes. Amory found it rather fascinating to feel that any popular girl he met before eight he might quite possibly kiss before twelve.

"Why on earth are we here?" he asked the girl with the green combs one night as they sat in some one's limousine, outside the Country Club in Louisville.

"I don't know. I'm just full of the devil."

"Let's be frank—we'll never see each other again. I wanted to come out here with you because I thought you were the best-looking girl in sight. You really don't care whether you ever see me again, do you?"

"No—but is this your line for every girl? What have I done to deserve it?"

"And you didn't feel tired dancing or want a cigarette or any of the things you said? You just wanted to be—"

"Oh, let's go in," she interrupted, "if you want to analyze. Let's not talk about it."

When the hand-knit, sleeveless jerseys were stylish, Amory, in a burst of inspiration, named them "petting shirts." The name travelled from coast to coast on the lips of parlor-snakes and P. D.'s.

DESCRIPTIVE

Amory was now eighteen years old, just under six feet tall and exceptionally, but not conventionally, handsome. He had rather a young face, the ingenuousness of which was marred by the penetrating green eyes, fringed with long dark eyelashes. He lacked somehow that intense animal magnetism that so often accompanies beauty in men or women; his personality seemed rather a mental thing, and it was not in his power to turn it on and off like a water-faucet. But people never forgot his face.

ISABELLE

She paused at the top of the staircase. The sensations attributed to divers on spring-boards, leading ladies on opening nights, and lumpy, husky young men on the day of the Big Game, crowded through her. She should have descended to a burst of drums or a discordant blend of themes from "Thais" and "Carmen." She had never been so curious about her appearance, she had never been so satisfied with it. She had been sixteen years old for six months.

"Isabelle!" called her cousin Sally from the doorway of the dressing-room.

"I'm ready." She caught a slight lump of nervousness in her throat.

"I had to send back to the house for another pair of slippers. It'll be just a minute."

Isabelle started toward the dressing-room for a last peek in the mirror, but something decided her to stand there and gaze down the broad stairs of the Minnehaha Club. They curved tantalizingly, and she could catch just a glimpse of two pairs of masculine feet in the hall below. Pump-shod in uniform black, they gave no hint of identity, but she wondered eagerly if one pair were attached to Amory Blaine. This young man, not as yet encountered, had nevertheless taken up a considerable part of her day—the first day of her arrival. Coming up in the machine from the station, Sally had volunteered, amid a rain of question, comment, revelation, and exaggeration:

"You remember Amory Blaine, of course. Well, he's simply mad to see you again. He's stayed over a day from college, and he's coming to-night. He's heard so much about you—says he remembers your eyes."

This had pleased Isabelle. It put them on equal terms, although she was quite capable of staging her own romances, with or without advance advertising. But following her happy tremble of anticipation, came a sinking sensation that made her ask:

"How do you mean he's heard about me? What sort of things?"

Sally smiled. She felt rather in the capacity of a showman with her more exotic cousin.

"He knows you're—you're considered beautiful and all that"—she paused—"and I guess he knows you've been kissed."

At this Isabelle's little fist had clinched suddenly under the fur robe. She was accustomed to be thus followed by her desperate past, and it never failed to rouse in her the same feeling of resentment; yet—in a strange town it was an advantageous reputation. She was a "Speed," was she? Well—let them find out.

Out of the window Isabelle watched the snow glide by in the frosty morning. It was ever so much colder here than in Baltimore; she had not remembered; the glass of the side door was iced, the windows were shirred with snow in the corners. Her mind played still with one subject. Did he dress like that boy there, who walked calmly down a bustling business street, in moccasins and winter-carnival costume? How very Western! Of course he wasn't that way: he went to Princeton, was a sophomore or something. Really she had no distinct idea of him. An ancient snap-shot she had preserved in an old kodak book had impressed her by the big eyes (which he had probably grown up to by now). However, in the last month, when her winter visit to Sally had been decided on, he had assumed the proportions of a worthy adversary. Children, most astute of match-makers, plot their campaigns quickly, and Sally had played a clever correspondence sonata to Isabelle's excitable temperament. Isabelle had been for some time capable of very strong, if very transient emotions....

They drew up at a spreading, white-stone building, set back from the snowy street. Mrs. Weatherby greeted her warmly and her various younger cousins were produced from the corners where they skulked politely. Isabelle met them tactfully. At her best she allied all with whom she came in contact—except older girls and some women. All the impressions she made were conscious. The half-dozen girls she renewed acquaintance with that morning were all rather impressed and as much by her direct personality as by her reputation. Amory Blaine was an open subject. Evidently a bit light of love, neither popular nor unpopular—every girl there seemed to have had an affair with him at some time or other, but no one volunteered any really useful information. He was going to fall for her.... Sally had

CHAPTER 2 Spires and Gargoyles

published that information to her young set and they were retailing it back to Sally as fast as they set eyes on Isabelle. Isabelle resolved secretly that she would, if necessary, force herself to like him—she owed it to Sally. Suppose she were terribly disappointed. Sally had painted him in such glowing colors—he was good-looking, "sort of distinguished, when he wants to be," had a line, and was properly inconstant. In fact, he summed up all the romance that her age and environment led her to desire. She wondered if those were his dancing-shoes that fox-trotted tentatively around the soft rug below.

All impressions and, in fact, all ideas were extremely kaleidoscopic to Isabelle. She had that curious mixture of the social and the artistic temperaments found often in two classes, society women and actresses. Her education or, rather, her sophistication, had been absorbed from the boys who had dangled on her favor; her tact was instinctive, and her capacity for love-affairs was limited only by the number of the susceptible within telephone distance. Flirt smiled from her large black-brown eyes and shone through her intense physical magnetism.

So she waited at the head of the stairs that evening while slippers were fetched. Just as she was growing impatient, Sally came out of the dressing-room, beaming with her accustomed good nature and high spirits, and together they descended to the floor below, while the shifting search-light of Isabelle's mind flashed on two ideas: she was glad she had high color to-night, and she wondered if he danced well.

Down-stairs, in the club's great room, she was surrounded for a moment by the girls she had met in the afternoon, then she heard Sally's voice repeating a cycle of names, and found herself bowing to a sextet of black and white, terribly stiff, vaguely familiar figures. The name Blaine figured somewhere, but at first she could not place him. A very confused, very juvenile moment of awkward backings and bumpings followed, and every one found himself talking to the person he least desired to. Isabelle manoeuvred herself and Froggy Parker, freshman at Harvard, with whom she had once played hop-scotch, to a seat on the stairs. A humorous reference to the past was all she needed. The things Isabelle could do socially with one idea were remarkable. First, she repeated it rapturously in an enthusiastic contralto with a soupcon of Southern accent; then she held it off at a distance and smiled at it—her wonderful smile; then she delivered it in variations and played a sort of mental catch with it, all this in the nominal form of dialogue. Froggy was fascinated and quite unconscious that this was being done, not for him, but for the green eyes that glistened under the shining carefully watered hair, a little to her left, for Isabelle had discovered Amory. As an actress even in the fullest flush of her own conscious magnetism gets a deep impression of most of the people in the front row, so Isabelle sized up her antagonist. First, he had auburn hair, and from her feeling of disappointment she knew that she had expected him to be dark and of garter-advertisement slenderness.... For the rest, a faint flush and a straight, romantic profile; the effect set off by a close-fitting dress suit and a silk ruffled shirt of the kind that women still delight to see men wear, but men were just beginning to

041

get tired of.

During this inspection Amory was quietly watching.

"Don't you think so?" she said suddenly, turning to him, innocent-eyed.

There was a stir, and Sally led the way over to their table. Amory struggled to Isabelle's side, and whispered:

"You're my dinner partner, you know. We're all coached for each other."

Isabelle gasped—this was rather right in line. But really she felt as if a good speech had been taken from the star and given to a minor character.... She mustn't lose the leadership a bit. The dinner-table glittered with laughter at the confusion of getting places and then curious eyes were turned on her, sitting near the head. She was enjoying this immensely, and Froggy Parker was so engrossed with the added sparkle of her rising color that he forgot to pull out Sally's chair, and fell into a dim confusion. Amory was on the other side, full of confidence and vanity, gazing at her in open admiration. He began directly, and so did Froggy:

"I've heard a lot about you since you wore braids—"

"Wasn't it funny this afternoon—"

Both stopped. Isabelle turned to Amory shyly. Her face was always enough answer for any one, but she decided to speak.

"How—from whom?"

"From everybody—for all the years since you've been away." She blushed appropriately. On her right Froggy was hors de combat already, although he hadn't quite realized it.

"I'll tell you what I remembered about you all these years," Amory continued. She leaned slightly toward him and looked modestly at the celery before her. Froggy sighed—he knew Amory, and the situations that Amory seemed born to handle. He turned to Sally and asked her if she was going away to school next year. Amory opened with grape-shot.

"I've got an adjective that just fits you." This was one of his favorite starts—he seldom had a word in mind, but it was a curiosity provoker, and he could always produce something complimentary if he got in a tight corner.

"Oh—what?" Isabelle's face was a study in enraptured curiosity.

Amory shook his head.

"I don't know you very well yet."

"Will you tell me—afterward?" she half whispered.

He nodded.

"We'll sit out."

Isabelle nodded.

"Did any one ever tell you, you have keen eyes?" she said.

Amory attempted to make them look even keener. He fancied, but he was not sure, that her foot had just touched his under the table. But it might possibly have been only the table leg. It was so hard to tell. Still it thrilled him. He wondered quickly if there would be any difficulty in securing the little den up-stairs.

BABES IN THE WOODS

Isabelle and Amory were distinctly not innocent, nor were they particularly brazen. Moreover, amateur standing had very little value in the game they were playing, a game that would presumably be her principal study for years to come. She had begun as he had, with good looks and an excitable temperament, and the rest was the result of accessible popular novels and dressing-room conversation culled from a slightly older set. Isabelle had walked with an artificial gait at nine and a half, and when her eyes, wide and starry, proclaimed the ingenue most. Amory was proportionately less deceived. He waited for the mask to drop off, but at the same time he did not question her right to wear it. She, on her part, was not impressed by his studied air of blasé sophistication. She had lived in a larger city and had slightly an advantage in range. But she accepted his pose—it was one of the dozen little conventions of this kind of affair. He was aware that he was getting this particular favor now because she had been coached; he knew that he stood for merely the best game in sight, and that he would have to improve his opportunity before he lost his advantage. So they proceeded with an infinite guile that would have horrified her parents.

After the dinner the dance began... smoothly. Smoothly?—boys cut in on Isabelle every few feet and then squabbled in the corners with: "You might let me get more than an inch!" and "She didn't like it either—she told me so next time I cut in." It was true—she told every one so, and gave every hand a parting pressure that said: "You know that your dances are making my evening."

But time passed, two hours of it, and the less subtle beaux had better learned to focus their pseudo-passionate glances elsewhere, for eleven o'clock found Isabelle and Amory sitting on the couch in the little den off the reading-room up-stairs. She was conscious that they were a handsome pair, and seemed to belong distinctively in this seclusion, while lesser lights fluttered and chattered down-stairs.

Boys who passed the door looked in enviously—girls who passed only laughed and frowned and grew wise within themselves.

They had now reached a very definite stage. They had traded accounts of their progress since they had met last, and she had listened to much she had heard before. He was a sophomore, was on the Princetonian board, hoped to be chairman in senior year. He learned that some of the boys she went with in Baltimore were "terrible speeds" and came to dances in states of artificial stimulation; most of them were twenty or so, and drove alluring red Stutzes. A good half seemed to have already flunked out of various schools and colleges, but some of them bore athletic names that made him look at her admiringly. As a matter of fact, Isabelle's closer acquaintance with the universities was just commencing. She had bowing acquaintance with a lot of young men who thought she was a "pretty kid—worth keeping an eye on." But Isabelle strung the names into a fabrication of gayety that would have dazzled a Viennese nobleman. Such is the power of young contralto voices on sink-down sofas.

He asked her if she thought he was conceited. She said there was a difference between conceit and self-confidence. She adored self-confidence in men.

"Is Froggy a good friend of yours?" she asked.

"Rather—why?"

"He's a bum dancer."

Amory laughed.

"He dances as if the girl were on his back instead of in his arms."

She appreciated this.

"You're awfully good at sizing people up."

Amory denied this painfully. However, he sized up several people for her. Then they talked about hands.

"You've got awfully nice hands," she said. "They look as if you played the piano. Do you?"

I have said they had reached a very definite stage—nay, more, a very critical stage. Amory had stayed over a day to see her, and his train left at twelve-eighteen that night. His trunk and suitcase awaited him at the station; his watch was beginning to hang heavy in his pocket.

"Isabelle," he said suddenly, "I want to tell you something." They had been talking lightly about "that funny look in her eyes," and Isabelle knew from the change in his manner what was coming—indeed, she had been wondering how soon it would come. Amory reached above their heads and turned out the electric light, so that they were in the dark, except for the red glow that fell through the door from the reading-room lamps. Then he began:

"I don't know whether or not you know what you—what I'm going to say. Lordy, Isabelle—this sounds like a line, but it isn't."

"I know," said Isabelle softly.

"Maybe we'll never meet again like this—I have darned hard luck sometimes." He was leaning away from her on the other arm of the lounge, but she could see his eyes plainly in the dark.

"You'll meet me again—silly." There was just the slightest emphasis on the last word—so that it became almost a term of endearment. He continued a bit huskily:

"I've fallen for a lot of people—girls—and I guess you have, too—boys, I mean, but, honestly, you—" he broke off suddenly and leaned forward, chin on his hands: "Oh, what's the use—you'll go your way and I suppose I'll go mine."

Silence for a moment. Isabelle was quite stirred; she wound her handkerchief into a tight ball, and by the faint light that streamed over her, dropped it deliberately on the floor. Their hands touched for an instant, but neither spoke. Silences were becoming more frequent and more delicious. Outside another stray couple had come up and were experimenting on the

CHAPTER 2 Spires and Gargoyles

piano in the next room. After the usual preliminary of "chopsticks," one of them started "Babes in the Woods" and a light tenor carried the words into the den:

"Give me your hand
I'll understand
We're off to slumberland."

Isabelle hummed it softly and trembled as she felt Amory's hand close over hers.

"Isabelle," he whispered. "You know I'm mad about you. You do give a darn about me."

"Yes."

"How much do you care—do you like any one better?"

"No." He could scarcely hear her, although he bent so near that he felt her breath against his cheek.

"Isabelle, I'm going back to college for six long months, and why shouldn't we—if I could only just have one thing to remember you by—"

"Close the door...." Her voice had just stirred so that he half wondered whether she had spoken at all. As he swung the door softly shut, the music seemed quivering just outside.

"Moonlight is bright,
Kiss me good night."

What a wonderful song, she thought—everything was wonderful to-night, most of all this romantic scene in the den, with their hands clinging and the inevitable looming charmingly close. The future vista of her life seemed an unending succession of scenes like this: under moonlight and pale starlight, and in the backs of warm limousines and in low, cosy roadsters stopped under sheltering trees—only the boy might change, and this one was so nice. He took her hand softly. With a sudden movement he turned it and, holding it to his lips, kissed the palm.

"Isabelle!" His whisper blended in the music, and they seemed to float nearer together. Her breath came faster. "Can't I kiss you, Isabelle—Isabelle?" Lips half parted, she turned her head to him in the dark. Suddenly the ring of voices, the sound of running footsteps surged toward them. Quick as a flash Amory reached up and turned on the light, and when the door opened and three boys, the wrathy and dance-craving Froggy among them, rushed in, he was turning over the magazines on the table, while she sat without moving, serene and unembarrassed, and even greeted them with a welcoming smile. But her heart was beating wildly, and she felt somehow as if she had been deprived.

It was evidently over. There was a clamor for a dance, there was a glance that passed between them—on his side despair, on hers regret, and then the evening went on, with the reassured beaux and the eternal cutting in.

At quarter to twelve Amory shook hands with her gravely, in the midst of a small crowd assembled to wish him good-speed. For an instant he lost his poise, and she felt a bit rattled when a satirical voice from a concealed wit cried:

"Take her outside, Amory!" As he took her hand he pressed it a little, and she returned the pressure as she had done to twenty hands that evening—that was all.

At two o'clock back at the Weatherbys' Sally asked her if she and Amory had had a "time" in the den. Isabelle turned to her quietly. In her eyes was the light of the idealist, the inviolate dreamer of Joan-like dreams.

"No," she answered. "I don't do that sort of thing any more; he asked me to, but I said no."

As she crept in bed she wondered what he'd say in his special delivery to-morrow. He had such a good-looking mouth—would she ever—?

"Fourteen angels were watching o'er them," sang Sally sleepily from the next room.

"Damn!" muttered Isabelle, punching the pillow into a luxurious lump and exploring the cold sheets cautiously. "Damn!"

CARNIVAL

Amory, by way of the Princetonian, had arrived. The minor snobs, finely balanced thermometers of success, warmed to him as the club elections grew nigh, and he and Tom were visited by groups of upper classmen who arrived awkwardly, balanced on the edge of the furniture and talked of all subjects except the one of absorbing interest. Amory was amused at the intent eyes upon him, and, in case the visitors represented some club in which he was not interested, took great pleasure in shocking them with unorthodox remarks.

"Oh, let me see—" he said one night to a flabbergasted delegation, "what club do you represent?"

With visitors from Ivy and Cottage and Tiger Inn he played the "nice, unspoilt, ingenuous boy" very much at ease and quite unaware of the object of the call.

When the fatal morning arrived, early in March, and the campus became a document in hysteria, he slid smoothly into Cottage with Alec Connage and watched his suddenly neurotic class with much wonder.

There were fickle groups that jumped from club to club; there were friends of two or three days who announced tearfully and wildly that they must join the same club, nothing should separate them; there were snarling disclosures of long-hidden grudges as the Suddenly Prominent remembered snubs of freshman year. Unknown men were elevated into importance when they received certain coveted bids; others who were considered "all set" found that they had made unexpected enemies, felt themselves stranded and deserted, talked wildly of leaving college.

In his own crowd Amory saw men kept out for wearing green hats, for being "a damn tailor's dummy," for having "too much pull in heaven," for getting drunk one night "not like a gentleman, by God," or for unfathomable secret reasons known to no one but the wielders of the black balls.

CHAPTER 2 Spires and Gargoyles

This orgy of sociability culminated in a gigantic party at the Nassau Inn, where punch was dispensed from immense bowls, and the whole down-stairs became a delirious, circulating, shouting pattern of faces and voices.

"Hi, Dibby—'gratulations!"

"Goo' boy, Tom, you got a good bunch in Cap."

"Say, Kerry—"

"Oh, Kerry—I hear you went Tiger with all the weight-lifters!" "Well, I didn't go Cottage—the parlor-snakes' delight."

"They say Overton fainted when he got his Ivy bid—Did he sign up the first day?—oh, no. Tore over to Murray-Dodge on a bicycle—afraid it was a mistake."

"How'd you get into Cap—you old roue?"

"'Gratulations!'"

"'Gratulations yourself. Hear you got a good crowd."

When the bar closed, the party broke up into groups and streamed, singing, over the snow-clad campus, in a weird delusion that snobbishness and strain were over at last, and that they could do what they pleased for the next two years.

Long afterward Amory thought of sophomore spring as the happiest time of his life. His ideas were in tune with life as he found it; he wanted no more than to drift and dream and enjoy a dozen new-found friendships through the April afternoons.

Alec Connage came into his room one morning and woke him up into the sunshine and peculiar glory of Campbell Hall shining in the window.

"Wake up, Original Sin, and scrape yourself together. Be in front of Renwick's in half an hour. Somebody's got a car." He took the bureau cover and carefully deposited it, with its load of small articles, upon the bed.

"Where'd you get the car?" demanded Amory cynically.

"Sacred trust, but don't be a critical goopher or you can't go!"

"I think I'll sleep," Amory said calmly, resettling himself and reaching beside the bed for a cigarette.

"Sleep!"

"Why not? I've got a class at eleven-thirty."

"You damned gloom! Of course, if you don't want to go to the coast—"

With a bound Amory was out of bed, scattering the bureau cover's burden on the floor. The coast... he hadn't seen it for years, since he and his mother were on their pilgrimage.

"Who's going?" he demanded as he wriggled into his B. V. D.'s.

"Oh, Dick Humbird and Kerry Holiday and Jesse Ferrenby and—oh about five or six. Speed it up, kid!"

In ten minutes Amory was devouring cornflakes in Renwick's, and at nine-thirty they bowled happily out of town, headed for the sands of Deal Beach.

"You see," said Kerry, "the car belongs down there. In fact, it was stolen from Asbury

047

Park by persons unknown, who deserted it in Princeton and left for the West. Heartless Humbird here got permission from the city council to deliver it."

"Anybody got any money?" suggested Ferrenby, turning around from the front seat.

There was an emphatic negative chorus.

"That makes it interesting."

"Money—what's money? We can sell the car."

"Charge him salvage or something."

"How're we going to get food?" asked Amory.

"Honestly," answered Kerry, eying him reprovingly, "do you doubt Kerry's ability for three short days? Some people have lived on nothing for years at a time. Read the Boy Scout Monthly."

"Three days," Amory mused, "and I've got classes."

"One of the days is the Sabbath."

"Just the same, I can only cut six more classes, with over a month and a half to go."

"Throw him out!"

"It's a long walk back."

"Amory, you're running it out, if I may coin a new phrase."

"Hadn't you better get some dope on yourself, Amory?"

Amory subsided resignedly and drooped into a contemplation of the scenery. Swinburne seemed to fit in somehow.

"Oh, winter's rains and ruins are over,
And all the seasons of snows and sins;
The days dividing lover and lover,
The light that loses, the night that wins;
And time remembered is grief forgotten,
And frosts are slain and flowers begotten,
And in green underwood and cover,
Blossom by blossom the spring begins.

"The full streams feed on flower of—"

"What's the matter, Amory? Amory's thinking about poetry, about the pretty birds and flowers. I can see it in his eye."

"No, I'm not," he lied. "I'm thinking about the Princetonian. I ought to make up tonight; but I can telephone back, I suppose."

"Oh," said Kerry respectfully, "these important men—"

Amory flushed and it seemed to him that Ferrenby, a defeated competitor, winced a little. Of course, Kerry was only kidding, but he really mustn't mention the Princetonian.

It was a halcyon day, and as they neared the shore and the salt breezes scurried by, he began to picture the ocean and long, level stretches of sand and red roofs over blue sea. Then they hurried through the little town and it all flashed upon his consciousness to a mighty paean of emotion....

"Oh, good Lord! Look at it!" he cried.

"What?"

"Let me out, quick—I haven't seen it for eight years! Oh, gentlefolk, stop the car!"

"What an odd child!" remarked Alec.

"I do believe he's a bit eccentric."

The car was obligingly drawn up at a curb, and Amory ran for the boardwalk. First, he realized that the sea was blue and that there was an enormous quantity of it, and that it roared and roared—really all the banalities about the ocean that one could realize, but if any one had told him then that these things were banalities, he would have gaped in wonder.

"Now we'll get lunch," ordered Kerry, wandering up with the crowd. "Come on, Amory, tear yourself away and get practical."

"We'll try the best hotel first," he went on, "and thence and so forth."

They strolled along the boardwalk to the most imposing hostelry in sight, and, entering the dining-room, scattered about a table.

"Eight Bronxes," commanded Alec, "and a club sandwich and Juliennes. The food for one. Hand the rest around."

Amory ate little, having seized a chair where he could watch the sea and feel the rock of it. When luncheon was over they sat and smoked quietly.

"What's the bill?"

Some one scanned it.

"Eight twenty-five."

"Rotten overcharge. We'll give them two dollars and one for the waiter. Kerry, collect the small change."

The waiter approached, and Kerry gravely handed him a dollar, tossed two dollars on the check, and turned away. They sauntered leisurely toward the door, pursued in a moment by the suspicious Ganymede.

"Some mistake, sir."

Kerry took the bill and examined it critically.

"No mistake!" he said, shaking his head gravely, and, tearing it into four pieces, he handed the scraps to the waiter, who was so dumfounded that he stood motionless and expressionless while they walked out.

"Won't he send after us?"

"No," said Kerry; "for a minute he'll think we're the proprietor's sons or something; then he'll look at the check again and call the manager, and in the meantime—"

They left the car at Asbury and street-car'd to Allenhurst, where they investigated the crowded pavilions for beauty. At four there were refreshments in a lunch-room, and this time they paid an even smaller per cent on the total cost; something about the appearance and savoir-faire of the crowd made the thing go, and they were not pursued.

"You see, Amory, we're Marxian Socialists," explained Kerry. "We don't believe in property and we're putting it to the great test."

"Night will descend," Amory suggested.

"Watch, and put your trust in Holiday."

They became jovial about five-thirty and, linking arms, strolled up and down the boardwalk in a row, chanting a monotonous ditty about the sad sea waves. Then Kerry saw a face in the crowd that attracted him and, rushing off, reappeared in a moment with one of the homeliest girls Amory had ever set eyes on. Her pale mouth extended from ear to ear, her teeth projected in a solid wedge, and she had little, squinty eyes that peeped ingratiatingly over the side sweep of her nose. Kerry presented them formally.

"Name of Kaluka, Hawaiian queen! Let me present Messrs. Connage, Sloane, Humbird, Ferrenby, and Blaine."

The girl bobbed courtesies all around. Poor creature; Amory supposed she had never before been noticed in her life—possibly she was half-witted. While she accompanied them (Kerry had invited her to supper) she said nothing which could discountenance such a belief.

"She prefers her native dishes," said Alec gravely to the waiter, "but any coarse food will do."

All through supper he addressed her in the most respectful language, while Kerry made idiotic love to her on the other side, and she giggled and grinned. Amory was content to sit and watch the by-play, thinking what a light touch Kerry had, and how he could transform the barest incident into a thing of curve and contour. They all seemed to have the spirit of it more or less, and it was a relaxation to be with them. Amory usually liked men individually, yet feared them in crowds unless the crowd was around him. He wondered how much each one contributed to the party, for there was somewhat of a spiritual tax levied. Alec and Kerry were the life of it, but not quite the centre. Somehow the quiet Humbird, and Sloane, with his impatient superciliousness, were the centre.

Dick Humbird had, ever since freshman year, seemed to Amory a perfect type of aristocrat. He was slender but well-built—black curly hair, straight features, and rather a dark skin. Everything he said sounded intangibly appropriate. He possessed infinite courage, an averagely good mind, and a sense of honor with a clear charm and noblesse oblige that varied it from righteousness. He could dissipate without going to pieces, and even his most bohemian adventures never seemed "running it out." People dressed like him, tried to talk as he did.... Amory decided that he probably held the world back, but he wouldn't have changed him. ...

He differed from the healthy type that was essentially middle class—he never seemed to perspire. Some people couldn't be familiar with a chauffeur without having it returned;

Humbird could have lunched at Sherry's with a colored man, yet people would have somehow known that it was all right. He was not a snob, though he knew only half his class. His friends ranged from the highest to the lowest, but it was impossible to "cultivate" him. Servants worshipped him, and treated him like a god. He seemed the eternal example of what the upper class tries to be.

"He's like those pictures in the Illustrated London News of the English officers who have been killed," Amory had said to Alec. "Well," Alec had answered, "if you want to know the shocking truth, his father was a grocery clerk who made a fortune in Tacoma real estate and came to New York ten years ago."

Amory had felt a curious sinking sensation.

This present type of party was made possible by the surging together of the class after club elections—as if to make a last desperate attempt to know itself, to keep together, to fight off the tightening spirit of the clubs. It was a let-down from the conventional heights they had all walked so rigidly.

After supper they saw Kaluka to the boardwalk, and then strolled back along the beach to Asbury. The evening sea was a new sensation, for all its color and mellow age was gone, and it seemed the bleak waste that made the Norse sagas sad; Amory thought of Kipling's

"Beaches of Lukanon before the sealers came."

It was still a music, though, infinitely sorrowful.

Ten o'clock found them penniless. They had suppered greatly on their last eleven cents and, singing, strolled up through the casinos and lighted arches on the boardwalk, stopping to listen approvingly to all band concerts. In one place Kerry took up a collection for the French War Orphans which netted a dollar and twenty cents, and with this they bought some brandy in case they caught cold in the night. They finished the day in a moving-picture show and went into solemn systematic roars of laughter at an ancient comedy, to the startled annoyance of the rest of the audience. Their entrance was distinctly strategic, for each man as he entered pointed reproachfully at the one just behind him. Sloane, bringing up the rear, disclaimed all knowledge and responsibility as soon as the others were scattered inside; then as the irate ticket-taker rushed in he followed nonchalantly.

They reassembled later by the Casino and made arrangements for the night. Kerry wormed permission from the watchman to sleep on the platform and, having collected a huge pile of rugs from the booths to serve as mattresses and blankets, they talked until midnight, and then fell into a dreamless sleep, though Amory tried hard to stay awake and watch that marvellous moon settle on the sea.

So they progressed for two happy days, up and down the shore by street-car or machine, or by shoe-leather on the crowded boardwalk; sometimes eating with the wealthy, more frequently dining frugally at the expense of an unsuspecting restaurateur. They had their photos taken, eight poses, in a quick-development store. Kerry insisted on grouping them as a "varsity" football team, and then as a tough gang from the East Side, with their coats inside out, and himself sitting in the middle on a cardboard moon. The photographer probably has them yet—at least, they never called for them. The weather was perfect, and again they slept outside, and again Amory fell unwillingly asleep.

Sunday broke stolid and respectable, and even the sea seemed to mumble and complain, so they returned to Princeton via the Fords of transient farmers, and broke up with colds in their heads, but otherwise none the worse for wandering.

Even more than in the year before, Amory neglected his work, not deliberately but lazily and through a multitude of other interests. Co-ordinate geometry and the melancholy hexameters of Corneille and Racine held forth small allurements, and even psychology, which he had eagerly awaited, proved to be a dull subject full of muscular reactions and biological phrases rather than the study of personality and influence. That was a noon class, and it always sent him dozing. Having found that "subjective and objective, sir," answered most of the questions, he used the phrase on all occasions, and it became the class joke when, on a query being levelled at him, he was nudged awake by Ferrenby or Sloane to gasp it out.

Mostly there were parties—to Orange or the Shore, more rarely to New York and Philadelphia, though one night they marshalled fourteen waitresses out of Childs' and took them to ride down Fifth Avenue on top of an auto bus. They all cut more classes than were allowed, which meant an additional course the following year, but spring was too rare to let anything interfere with their colorful ramblings. In May Amory was elected to the Sophomore Prom Committee, and when after a long evening's discussion with Alec they made out a tentative list of class probabilities for the senior council, they placed themselves among the surest. The senior council was composed presumably of the eighteen most representative seniors, and in view of Alec's football managership and Amory's chance of nosing out Burne Holiday as Princetonian chairman, they seemed fairly justified in this presumption. Oddly enough, they both placed D'Invilliers as among the possibilities, a guess that a year before the class would have gaped at.

All through the spring Amory had kept up an intermittent correspondence with Isabelle Borge, punctuated by violent squabbles and chiefly enlivened by his attempts to find new words for love. He discovered Isabelle to be discreetly and aggravatingly unsentimental in letters, but he hoped against hope that she would prove not too exotic a bloom to fit the large spaces of spring as she had fitted the den in the Minnehaha Club. During May he wrote thirty-page documents almost nightly, and sent them to her in bulky envelopes exteriorly labelled "Part I" and "Part II."

"Oh, Alec, I believe I'm tired of college," he said sadly, as they walked the dusk together.

"I think I am, too, in a way."

"All I'd like would be a little home in the country, some warm country, and a wife, and

CHAPTER 2 Spires and Gargoyles

just enough to do to keep from rotting."

"Me, too."

"I'd like to quit."

"What does your girl say?"

"Oh!" Amory gasped in horror. "She wouldn't think of marrying... that is, not now. I mean the future, you know."

"My girl would. I'm engaged."

"Are you really?"

"Yes. Don't say a word to anybody, please, but I am. I may not come back next year."

"But you're only twenty! Give up college?"

"Why, Amory, you were saying a minute ago—"

"Yes," Amory interrupted, "but I was just wishing. I wouldn't think of leaving college. It's just that I feel so sad these wonderful nights. I sort of feel they're never coming again, and I'm not really getting all I could out of them. I wish my girl lived here. But marry—not a chance. Especially as father says the money isn't forthcoming as it used to be."

"What a waste these nights are!" agreed Alec.

But Amory sighed and made use of the nights. He had a snap-shot of Isabelle, enshrined in an old watch, and at eight almost every night he would turn off all the lights except the desk lamp and, sitting by the open windows with the picture before him, write her rapturous letters.

> ... Oh it's so hard to write you what I really feel when I think about you so much; you've gotten to mean to me a dream that I can't put on paper any more. Your last letter came and it was wonderful! I read it over about six times, especially the last part, but I do wish, sometimes, you'd be more frank and tell me what you really do think of me, yet your last letter was too good to be true, and I can hardly wait until June! Be sure and be able to come to the prom. It'll be fine, I think, and I want to bring you just at the end of a wonderful year. I often think over what you said on that night and wonder how much you meant. If it were anyone but you but you see I thought you were fickle the first time I saw you and you are so popular and everthing that I can't imagine you really liking me best.
>
> Oh, Isabelle, dear it's a wonderful night. Somebody is playing "Love Moon" on a mandolin far across the campus, and the music seems to bring you into the window. Now he's playing "Good-by, Boys, I'm Through," and how well it suits me. For I am through with everything. I have decided never to take a cocktail again,

053

and I know I'll never again fall in love—I couldn't—you've been
too much a part of my days and nights to ever let me think of
another girl. I meet them all the time and they don't interest me.
I'm not pretending to be blasé, because it's not that. It's just
that I'm in love. Oh, dearest Isabelle (somehow I can't call you
just Isabelle, and I'm afraid I'll come out with the "dearest"
 before your family this June), you've got to come to the prom,
and then I'll come up to your house for a day and everything'll be
perfect....

And so on in an eternal monotone that seemed to both of them infinitely charming, infinitely new.

June came and the days grew so hot and lazy that they could not worry even about exams, but spent dreamy evenings on the court of Cottage, talking of long subjects until the sweep of country toward Stony Brook became a blue haze and the lilacs were white around tennis-courts, and words gave way to silent cigarettes.... Then down deserted Prospect and along McCosh with song everywhere around them, up to the hot joviality of Nassau Street.

Tom D'Invilliers and Amory walked late in those days. A gambling fever swept through the sophomore class and they bent over the bones till three o'clock many a sultry night. After one session they came out of Sloane's room to find the dew fallen and the stars old in the sky.

"Let's borrow bicycles and take a ride," Amory suggested.

"All right. I'm not a bit tired and this is almost the last night of the year, really, because the prom stuff starts Monday."

They found two unlocked bicycles in Holder Court and rode out about half-past three along the Lawrenceville Road.

"What are you going to do this summer, Amory?"

"Don't ask me—same old things, I suppose. A month or two in Lake Geneva—I'm counting on you to be there in July, you know—then there'll be Minneapolis, and that means hundreds of summer hops, parlor-snaking, getting bored—But oh, Tom," he added suddenly, "hasn't this year been slick!"

"No," declared Tom emphatically, a new Tom, clothed by Brooks, shod by Franks, "I've won this game, but I feel as if I never want to play another. You're all right—you're a rubber ball, and somehow it suits you, but I'm sick of adapting myself to the local snobbishness of this corner of the world. I want to go where people aren't barred because of the color of their neckties and the roll of their coats."

"You can't, Tom," argued Amory, as they rolled along through the scattering night; "wherever you go now you'll always unconsciously apply these standards of 'having it' or 'lacking it.' For better or worse we've stamped you; you're a Princeton type!"

"Well, then," complained Tom, his cracked voice rising plaintively, "why do I have to come back at all? I've learned all that Princeton has to offer. Two years more of mere pedantry and lying around a club aren't going to help. They're just going to disorganize me, conventionalize me completely. Even now I'm so spineless that I wonder how I get away with it."

"Oh, but you're missing the real point, Tom," Amory interrupted. "You've just had your eyes opened to the snobbishness of the world in a rather abrupt manner. Princeton invariably gives the thoughtful man a social sense."

"You consider you taught me that, don't you?" he asked quizzically, eying Amory in the half dark.

Amory laughed quietly.

"Didn't I?"

"Sometimes," he said slowly, "I think you're my bad angel. I might have been a pretty fair poet."

"Come on, that's rather hard. You chose to come to an Eastern college. Either your eyes were opened to the mean scrambling quality of people, or you'd have gone through blind, and you'd hate to have done that—been like Marty Kaye."

"Yes," he agreed, "you're right. I wouldn't have liked it. Still, it's hard to be made a cynic at twenty."

"I was born one," Amory murmured. "I'm a cynical idealist." He paused and wondered if that meant anything.

They reached the sleeping school of Lawrenceville, and turned to ride back.

"It's good, this ride, isn't it?" Tom said presently.

"Yes; it's a good finish, it's knock-out; everything's good to-night. Oh, for a hot, languorous summer and Isabelle!"

"Oh, you and your Isabelle! I'll bet she's a simple one... let's say some poetry."

So Amory declaimed "The Ode to a Nightingale" to the bushes they passed.

"I'll never be a poet," said Amory as he finished. "I'm not enough of a sensualist really; there are only a few obvious things that I notice as primarily beautiful: women, spring evenings, music at night, the sea; I don't catch the subtle things like 'silver-snarling trumpets.' I may turn out an intellectual, but I'll never write anything but mediocre poetry."

They rode into Princeton as the sun was making colored maps of the sky behind the graduate school, and hurried to the refreshment of a shower that would have to serve in place of sleep. By noon the bright-costumed alumni crowded the streets with their bands and choruses, and in the tents there was great reunion under the orange-and-black banners that curled and strained in the wind. Amory looked long at one house which bore the legend "Sixty-nine." There a few gray-haired men sat and talked quietly while the classes swept by in panorama of life.

UNDER THE ARC-LIGHT

Then tragedy's emerald eyes glared suddenly at Amory over the edge of June. On the night after his ride to Lawrenceville a crowd sallied to New York in quest of adventure, and started back to Princeton about twelve o'clock in two machines. It had been a gay party and different stages of sobriety were represented. Amory was in the car behind; they had taken the wrong road and lost the way, and so were hurrying to catch up.

It was a clear night and the exhilaration of the road went to Amory's head. He had the ghost of two stanzas of a poem forming in his mind. ...

> So the gray car crept nightward in the dark and there was no life
> stirred as it went by.... As the still ocean paths before the
> shark in starred and glittering waterways, beauty-high, the
> moon-swathed trees divided, pair on pair, while flapping
> nightbirds cried across the air....
>
> A moment by an inn of lamps and shades, a yellow inn under a
> yellow moon—then silence, where crescendo laughter fades... the
> car swung out again to the winds of June, mellowed the shadows
> where the distance grew, then crushed the yellow shadows into
> blue....

They jolted to a stop, and Amory peered up, startled. A woman was standing beside the road, talking to Alec at the wheel. Afterward he remembered the harpy effect that her old kimono gave her, and the cracked hollowness of her voice as she spoke:

"You Princeton boys?"

"Yes."

"Well, there's one of you killed here, and two others about dead."

"My God!"

"Look!" She pointed and they gazed in horror. Under the full light of a roadside arc-light lay a form, face downward in a widening circle of blood.

They sprang from the car. Amory thought of the back of that head—that hair—that hair... and then they turned the form over.

"It's Dick—Dick Humbird!"

"Oh, Christ!"

"Feel his heart!"

Then the insistent voice of the old crone in a sort of croaking triumph:

"He's quite dead, all right. The car turned over. Two of the men that weren't hurt just carried the others in, but this one's no use."

Amory rushed into the house and the rest followed with a limp mass that they laid on the sofa in the shoddy little front parlor. Sloane, with his shoulder punctured, was on another lounge. He was half delirious, and kept calling something about a chemistry lecture at 8:10.

"I don't know what happened," said Ferrenby in a strained voice. "Dick was driving and

CHAPTER 2 Spires and Gargoyles

he wouldn't give up the wheel; we told him he'd been drinking too much—then there was this damn curve—oh, my God!..." He threw himself face downward on the floor and broke into dry sobs.

The doctor had arrived, and Amory went over to the couch, where some one handed him a sheet to put over the body. With a sudden hardness, he raised one of the hands and let it fall back inertly. The brow was cold but the face not expressionless. He looked at the shoe-laces—Dick had tied them that morning. He had tied them—and now he was this heavy white mass. All that remained of the charm and personality of the Dick Humbird he had known—oh, it was all so horrible and unaristocratic and close to the earth. All tragedy has that strain of the grotesque and squalid—so useless, futile... the way animals die.... Amory was reminded of a cat that had lain horribly mangled in some alley of his childhood.

"Some one go to Princeton with Ferrenby."

Amory stepped outside the door and shivered slightly at the late night wind—a wind that stirred a broken fender on the mass of bent metal to a plaintive, tinny sound.

CRESCENDO!

Next day, by a merciful chance, passed in a whirl. When Amory was by himself his thoughts zigzagged inevitably to the picture of that red mouth yawning incongruously in the white face, but with a determined effort he piled present excitement upon the memory of it and shut it coldly away from his mind.

Isabelle and her mother drove into town at four, and they rode up smiling Prospect Avenue, through the gay crowd, to have tea at Cottage. The clubs had their annual dinners that night, so at seven he loaned her to a freshman and arranged to meet her in the gymnasium at eleven, when the upper classmen were admitted to the freshman dance. She was all he had expected, and he was happy and eager to make that night the centre of every dream. At nine the upper classes stood in front of the clubs as the freshman torchlight parade rioted past, and Amory wondered if the dress-suited groups against the dark, stately backgrounds and under the flare of the torches made the night as brilliant to the staring, cheering freshmen as it had been to him the year before.

The next day was another whirl. They lunched in a gay party of six in a private dining-room at the club, while Isabelle and Amory looked at each other tenderly over the fried chicken and knew that their love was to be eternal. They danced away the prom until five, and the stags cut in on Isabelle with joyous abandon, which grew more and more enthusiastic as the hour grew late, and their wines, stored in overcoat pockets in the coat room, made old weariness wait until another day. The stag line is a most homogeneous mass of men. It fairly sways with a single soul. A dark-haired beauty dances by and there is a half-gasping sound as the ripple surges forward and some one sleeker than the rest darts out and cuts in. Then when the six-foot girl (brought by Kaye in your class, and to whom he has been trying to introduce you all evening) gallops by, the line surges back and the groups face about and become intent on far corners of the hall, for Kaye, anxious and perspiring,

057

appears elbowing through the crowd in search of familiar faces.

"I say, old man, I've got an awfully nice—"

"Sorry, Kaye, but I'm set for this one. I've got to cut in on a fella."

"Well, the next one?"

"What—ah—er—I swear I've got to go cut in—look me up when she's got a dance free."

It delighted Amory when Isabelle suggested that they leave for a while and drive around in her car. For a delicious hour that passed too soon they glided the silent roads about Princeton and talked from the surface of their hearts in shy excitement. Amory felt strangely ingenuous and made no attempt to kiss her.

Next day they rode up through the Jersey country, had luncheon in New York, and in the afternoon went to see a problem play at which Isabelle wept all through the second act, rather to Amory's embarrassment—though it filled him with tenderness to watch her. He was tempted to lean over and kiss away her tears, and she slipped her hand into his under cover of darkness to be pressed softly.

Then at six they arrived at the Borges' summer place on Long Island, and Amory rushed up-stairs to change into a dinner coat. As he put in his studs he realized that he was enjoying life as he would probably never enjoy it again. Everything was hallowed by the haze of his own youth. He had arrived, abreast of the best in his generation at Princeton. He was in love and his love was returned. Turning on all the lights, he looked at himself in the mirror, trying to find in his own face the qualities that made him see clearer than the great crowd of people, that made him decide firmly, and able to influence and follow his own will. There was little in his life now that he would have changed. ... Oxford might have been a bigger field.

Silently he admired himself. How conveniently well he looked, and how well a dinner coat became him. He stepped into the hall and then waited at the top of the stairs, for he heard footsteps coming. It was Isabelle, and from the top of her shining hair to her little golden slippers she had never seemed so beautiful.

"Isabelle!" he cried, half involuntarily, and held out his arms. As in the story-books, she ran into them, and on that half-minute, as their lips first touched, rested the high point of vanity, the crest of his young egotism.

CHAPTER 3 The Egotist Considers

"Ouch! Let me go!"

He dropped his arms to his sides.

"What's the matter?"

"Your shirt stud—it hurt me—look!" She was looking down at her neck, where a little blue spot about the size of a pea marred its pallor.

"Oh, Isabelle," he reproached himself, "I'm a goopher. Really, I'm sorry—I shouldn't have held you so close."

She looked up impatiently.

"Oh, Amory, of course you couldn't help it, and it didn't hurt much; but what are we going to do about it?"

"Do about it?" he asked. "Oh—that spot; it'll disappear in a second."

"It isn't," she said, after a moment of concentrated gazing, "it's still there—and it looks like Old Nick—oh, Amory, what'll we do! It's just the height of your shoulder."

"Massage it," he suggested, repressing the faintest inclination to laugh.

She rubbed it delicately with the tips of her fingers, and then a tear gathered in the corner of her eye, and slid down her cheek.

"Oh, Amory," she said despairingly, lifting up a most pathetic face, "I'll just make my whole neck flame if I rub it. What'll I do?"

A quotation sailed into his head and he couldn't resist repeating it aloud.

"All the perfumes of Arabia will not whiten this little hand."

She looked up and the sparkle of the tear in her eye was like ice.

"You're not very sympathetic."

Amory mistook her meaning.

"Isabelle, darling, I think it'll—"

"Don't touch me!" she cried. "Haven't I enough on my mind and you stand there and laugh!"

Then he slipped again.

"Well, it is funny, Isabelle, and we were talking the other day about a sense of humor being—"

She was looking at him with something that was not a smile, rather the faint, mirthless echo of a smile, in the corners of her mouth.

"Oh, shut up!" she cried suddenly, and fled down the hallway toward her room. Amory stood there, covered with remorseful confusion.

"Damn!"

When Isabelle reappeared she had thrown a light wrap about her shoulders, and they descended the stairs in a silence that endured through dinner.

"Isabelle," he began rather testily, as they arranged themselves in the car, bound for a dance at the Greenwich Country Club, "you're angry, and I'll be, too, in a minute. Let's kiss and make up."

Isabelle considered glumly.

"I hate to be laughed at," she said finally.

"I won't laugh any more. I'm not laughing now, am I?"

"You did."

"Oh, don't be so darned feminine."

Her lips curled slightly.

"I'll be anything I want."

Amory kept his temper with difficulty. He became aware that he had not an ounce of real affection for Isabelle, but her coldness piqued him. He wanted to kiss her, kiss her a lot, because then he knew he could leave in the morning and not care. On the contrary, if he didn't kiss her, it would worry him.... It would interfere vaguely with his idea of himself as a conqueror. It wasn't dignified to come off second best, pleading, with a doughty warrior like Isabelle.

Perhaps she suspected this. At any rate, Amory watched the night that should have been the consummation of romance glide by with great moths overhead and the heavy fragrance of roadside gardens, but without those broken words, those little sighs....

Afterward they supped on ginger ale and devil's food in the pantry, and Amory announced a decision.

"I'm leaving early in the morning."

"Why?"

"Why not?" he countered.

"There's no need."

"However, I'm going."

"Well, if you insist on being ridiculous—"

"Oh, don't put it that way," he objected.

"—just because I won't let you kiss me. Do you think—"

"Now, Isabelle," he interrupted, "you know it's not that—even suppose it is. We've reached the stage where we either ought to kiss—or—or—nothing. It isn't as if you were refusing on moral grounds."

She hesitated.

"I really don't know what to think about you," she began, in a feeble, perverse attempt at conciliation. "You're so funny."

CHAPTER 3 The Egotist Considers

"How?"

"Well, I thought you had a lot of self-confidence and all that; remember you told me the other day that you could do anything you wanted, or get anything you wanted?"

Amory flushed. He had told her a lot of things.

"Yes."

"Well, you didn't seem to feel so self-confident to-night. Maybe you're just plain conceited."

"No, I'm not," he hesitated. "At Princeton—"

"Oh, you and Princeton! You'd think that was the world, the way you talk! Perhaps you can write better than anybody else on your old Princetonian; maybe the freshmen do think you're important—"

"You don't understand—"

"Yes, I do," she interrupted. "I do, because you're always talking about yourself and I used to like it; now I don't."

"Have I to-night?"

"That's just the point," insisted Isabelle. "You got all upset to-night. You just sat and watched my eyes. Besides, I have to think all the time I'm talking to you—you're so critical."

"I make you think, do I?" Amory repeated with a touch of vanity.

"You're a nervous strain"—this emphatically—"and when you analyze every little emotion and instinct I just don't have 'em."

"I know." Amory admitted her point and shook his head helplessly.

"Let's go." She stood up.

He rose abstractedly and they walked to the foot of the stairs.

"What train can I get?"

"There's one about 9:11 if you really must go."

"Yes, I've got to go, really. Good night."

"Good night."

They were at the head of the stairs, and as Amory turned into his room he thought he caught just the faintest cloud of discontent in her face. He lay awake in the darkness and wondered how much he cared—how much of his sudden unhappiness was hurt vanity— whether he was, after all, temperamentally unfitted for romance.

When he awoke, it was with a glad flood of consciousness. The early wind stirred the chintz curtains at the windows and he was idly puzzled not to be in his room at Princeton with his school football picture over the bureau and the Triangle Club on the wall opposite. Then the grandfather's clock in the hall outside struck eight, and the memory of the night before came to him. He was out of bed, dressing, like the wind; he must get out of the house before he saw Isabelle. What had seemed a melancholy happening, now seemed a tiresome anticlimax. He was dressed at half past, so he sat down by the window; felt that the sinews

061

of his heart were twisted somewhat more than he had thought. What an ironic mockery the morning seemed!—bright and sunny, and full of the smell of the garden; hearing Mrs. Borge's voice in the sun-parlor below, he wondered where was Isabelle.

There was a knock at the door.

"The car will be around at ten minutes of nine, sir."

He returned to his contemplation of the outdoors, and began repeating over and over, mechanically, a verse from Browning, which he had once quoted to Isabelle in a letter:

"Each life unfulfilled, you see,
 It hangs still, patchy and scrappy;
 We have not sighed deep, laughed free,
  Starved, feasted, despaired—been happy."

But his life would not be unfulfilled. He took a sombre satisfaction in thinking that perhaps all along she had been nothing except what he had read into her; that this was her high point, that no one else would ever make her think. Yet that was what she had objected to in him; and Amory was suddenly tired of thinking, thinking!

"Damn her!" he said bitterly, "she's spoiled my year!"

THE SUPERMAN GROWS CARELESS

On a dusty day in September Amory arrived in Princeton and joined the sweltering crowd of conditioned men who thronged the streets. It seemed a stupid way to commence his upper-class years, to spend four hours a morning in the stuffy room of a tutoring school, imbibing the infinite boredom of conic sections. Mr. Rooney, pander to the dull, conducted the class and smoked innumerable Pall Malls as he drew diagrams and worked equations from six in the morning until midnight.

"Now, Langueduc, if I used that formula, where would my A point be?"

Langueduc lazily shifts his six-foot-three of football material and tries to concentrate.

"Oh—ah—I'm damned if I know, Mr. Rooney."

"Oh, why of course, of course you can't use that formula. That's what I wanted you to say."

"Why, sure, of course."

"Do you see why?"

"You bet—I suppose so."

"If you don't see, tell me. I'm here to show you."

"Well, Mr. Rooney, if you don't mind, I wish you'd go over that again."

"Gladly. Now here's 'A'..."

The room was a study in stupidity—two huge stands for paper, Mr. Rooney in his shirt-sleeves in front of them, and slouched around on chairs, a dozen men: Fred Sloane, the pitcher, who absolutely had to get eligible; "Slim" Langueduc, who would beat Yale this fall, if only he could master a poor fifty per cent; McDowell, gay young sophomore, who

CHAPTER 3   The Egotist Considers

thought it was quite a sporting thing to be tutoring here with all these prominent athletes.

"Those poor birds who haven't a cent to tutor, and have to study during the term are the ones I pity," he announced to Amory one day, with a flaccid camaraderie in the droop of the cigarette from his pale lips. "I should think it would be such a bore, there's so much else to do in New York during the term. I suppose they don't know what they miss, anyhow." There was such an air of "you and I" about Mr. McDowell that Amory very nearly pushed him out of the open window when he said this. ... Next February his mother would wonder why he didn't make a club and increase his allowance... simple little nut....

Through the smoke and the air of solemn, dense earnestness that filled the room would come the inevitable helpless cry:

"I don't get it! Repeat that, Mr. Rooney!" Most of them were so stupid or careless that they wouldn't admit when they didn't understand, and Amory was of the latter. He found it impossible to study conic sections; something in their calm and tantalizing respectability breathing defiantly through Mr. Rooney's fetid parlors distorted their equations into insoluble anagrams. He made a last night's effort with the proverbial wet towel, and then blissfully took the exam, wondering unhappily why all the color and ambition of the spring before had faded out. Somehow, with the defection of Isabelle the idea of undergraduate success had loosed its grasp on his imagination, and he contemplated a possible failure to pass off his condition with equanimity, even though it would arbitrarily mean his removal from the Princetonian board and the slaughter of his chances for the Senior Council.

There was always his luck.

He yawned, scribbled his honor pledge on the cover, and sauntered from the room.

"If you don't pass it," said the newly arrived Alec as they sat on the window-seat of Amory's room and mused upon a scheme of wall decoration, "you're the world's worst goopher. Your stock will go down like an elevator at the club and on the campus."

"Oh, hell, I know it. Why rub it in?"

"'Cause you deserve it. Anybody that'd risk what you were in line for ought to be ineligible for Princetonian chairman."

"Oh, drop the subject," Amory protested. "Watch and wait and shut up. I don't want every one at the club asking me about it, as if I were a prize potato being fattened for a vegetable show." One evening a week later Amory stopped below his own window on the way to Renwick's, and, seeing a light, called up:

"Oh, Tom, any mail?"

Alec's head appeared against the yellow square of light.

"Yes, your result's here."

His heart clamored violently.

"What is it, blue or pink?"

"Don't know. Better come up."

He walked into the room and straight over to the table, and then suddenly noticed that there were other people in the room.

"'Lo, Kerry." He was most polite. "Ah, men of Princeton." They seemed to be mostly friends, so he picked up the envelope marked "Registrar's Office," and weighed it nervously.

"We have here quite a slip of paper."

"Open it, Amory."

"Just to be dramatic, I'll let you know that if it's blue, my name is withdrawn from the editorial board of the Prince, and my short career is over."

He paused, and then saw for the first time Ferrenby's eyes, wearing a hungry look and watching him eagerly. Amory returned the gaze pointedly.

"Watch my face, gentlemen, for the primitive emotions."

He tore it open and held the slip up to the light.

"Well?"

"Pink or blue?"

"Say what it is."

"We're all ears, Amory."

"Smile or swear—or something."

There was a pause... a small crowd of seconds swept by... then he looked again and another crowd went on into time.

"Blue as the sky, gentlemen...."

AFTERMATH

What Amory did that year from early September to late in the spring was so purposeless and inconsecutive that it seems scarcely worth recording. He was, of course, immediately sorry for what he had lost. His philosophy of success had tumbled down upon him, and he looked for the reasons.

"Your own laziness," said Alec later.

"No—something deeper than that. I've begun to feel that I was meant to lose this chance."

"They're rather off you at the club, you know; every man that doesn't come through makes our crowd just so much weaker."

"I hate that point of view."

"Of course, with a little effort you could still stage a comeback."

"No—I'm through—as far as ever being a power in college is concerned."

"But, Amory, honestly, what makes me the angriest isn't the fact that you won't be chairman of the Prince and on the Senior Council, but just that you didn't get down and pass that exam."

"Not me," said Amory slowly; "I'm mad at the concrete thing. My own idleness was quite in accord with my system, but the luck broke."

"Your system broke, you mean."

CHAPTER 3 The Egotist Considers

"Maybe."

"Well, what are you going to do? Get a better one quick, or just bum around for two more years as a has-been?"

"I don't know yet..."

"Oh, Amory, buck up!"

"Maybe."

Amory's point of view, though dangerous, was not far from the true one. If his reactions to his environment could be tabulated, the chart would have appeared like this, beginning with his earliest years:

1. *The fundamental Amory.*
2. *Amory plus Beatrice.*
3. *Amory plus Beatrice plus Minneapolis.*

Then St. Regis' had pulled him to pieces and started him over again:

4. *Amory plus St. Regis'.*
5. *Amory plus St. Regis' plus Princeton.*

That had been his nearest approach to success through conformity. The fundamental Amory, idle, imaginative, rebellious, had been nearly snowed under. He had conformed, he had succeeded, but as his imagination was neither satisfied nor grasped by his own success, he had listlessly, half-accidentally chucked the whole thing and become again:

6. *The fundamental Amory.*

FINANCIAL

His father died quietly and inconspicuously at Thanksgiving. The incongruity of death with either the beauties of Lake Geneva or with his mother's dignified, reticent attitude diverted him, and he looked at the funeral with an amused tolerance. He decided that burial was after all preferable to cremation, and he smiled at his old boyhood choice, slow oxidation in the top of a tree. The day after the ceremony he was amusing himself in the great library by sinking back on a couch in graceful mortuary attitudes, trying to determine whether he would, when his day came, be found with his arms crossed piously over his chest (Monsignor Darcy had once advocated this posture as being the most distinguished), or with his hands clasped behind his head, a more pagan and Byronic attitude.

What interested him much more than the final departure of his father from things mundane was a tri-cornered conversation between Beatrice, Mr. Barton, of Barton and Krogman, their lawyers, and himself, that took place several days after the funeral. For the first time he came into actual cognizance of the family finances, and realized what a tidy fortune had once been under his father's management. He took a ledger labelled "1906" and ran through it rather carefully. The total expenditure that year had come to something over one hundred and ten thousand dollars. Forty thousand of this had been Beatrice's own income, and there had been no attempt to account for it: it was all under the heading, "Drafts,

065

checks, and letters of credit forwarded to Beatrice Blaine." The dispersal of the rest was rather minutely itemized: the taxes and improvements on the Lake Geneva estate had come to almost nine thousand dollars; the general up-keep, including Beatrice's electric and a French car, bought that year, was over thirty-five thousand dollars. The rest was fully taken care of, and there were invariably items which failed to balance on the right side of the ledger.

In the volume for 1912 Amory was shocked to discover the decrease in the number of bond holdings and the great drop in the income. In the case of Beatrice's money this was not so pronounced, but it was obvious that his father had devoted the previous year to several unfortunate gambles in oil. Very little of the oil had been burned, but Stephen Blaine had been rather badly singed. The next year and the next and the next showed similar decreases, and Beatrice had for the first time begun using her own money for keeping up the house. Yet her doctor's bill for 1913 had been over nine thousand dollars.

About the exact state of things Mr. Barton was quite vague and confused. There had been recent investments, the outcome of which was for the present problematical, and he had an idea there were further speculations and exchanges concerning which he had not been consulted.

It was not for several months that Beatrice wrote Amory the full situation. The entire residue of the Blaine and O'Hara fortunes consisted of the place at Lake Geneva and approximately a half million dollars, invested now in fairly conservative six-per-cent holdings. In fact, Beatrice wrote that she was putting the money into railroad and street-car bonds as fast as she could conveniently transfer it.

"I am quite sure," she wrote to Amory, "that if there is one thing we can be positive of, it is that people will not stay in one place. This Ford person has certainly made the most of that idea. So I am instructing Mr. Barton to specialize on such things as Northern Pacific and these Rapid Transit Companies, as they call the street-cars. I shall never forgive myself for not buying Bethlehem Steel. I've heard the most fascinating stories. You must go into finance, Amory. I'm sure you would revel in it. You start as a messenger or a teller, I believe, and from that you go up—almost indefinitely. I'm sure if I were a man I'd love the handling of money; it has become quite a senile passion with me. Before I get any farther I want to discuss something. A Mrs. Bispam, an overcordial little lady whom I met at a tea the other day, told me that her son, he is at Yale, wrote her that all the boys there wore their summer underwear all during the winter, and also went about with their heads wet and in low shoes on the coldest days. Now, Amory, I don't know whether that is a fad at

Princeton too, but I don't want you to be so foolish. It not only inclines a young man to pneumonia and infantile paralysis, but to all forms of lung trouble, to which you are particularly inclined. You cannot experiment with your health. I have found that out. I will not make myself ridiculous as some mothers no doubt do, by insisting that you wear overshoes, though I remember one Christmas you wore them around constantly without a single buckle latched, making such a curious swishing sound, and you refused to buckle them because it was not the thing to do. The very next Christmas you would not wear even rubbers, though I begged you. You are nearly twenty years old now, dear, and I can't be with you constantly to find whether you are doing the sensible thing.

"This has been a very practical letter. *I warned you in my last that the lack of money to do the things one wants to makes one quite prosy and domestic, but there is still plenty for everything if we are not too extravagant. Take care of yourself, my dear boy, and do try to write at least once a week, because I imagine all sorts of horrible things if I don't hear from you. Affectionately,*

MOTHER."

FIRST APPEARANCE OF THE TERM "PERSONAGE"

Monsignor Darcy invited Amory up to the Stuart palace on the Hudson for a week at Christmas, and they had enormous conversations around the open fire. Monsignor was growing a trifle stouter and his personality had expanded even with that, and Amory felt both rest and security in sinking into a squat, cushioned chair and joining him in the middle-aged sanity of a cigar.

"I've felt like leaving college, Monsignor."

"Why?"

"All my career's gone up in smoke; you think it's petty and all that, but—"

"Not at all petty. I think it's most important. I want to hear the whole thing. Everything you've been doing since I saw you last."

Amory talked; he went thoroughly into the destruction of his egotistic highways, and in a half-hour the listless quality had left his voice.

"What would you do if you left college?" asked Monsignor.

"Don't know. I'd like to travel, but of course this tiresome war prevents that. Anyways, mother would hate not having me graduate. I'm just at sea. Kerry Holiday wants me to go over with him and join the Lafayette Esquadrille."

"You know you wouldn't like to go."

"Sometimes I would—to-night I'd go in a second."

"Well, you'd have to be very much more tired of life than I think you are. I know you."

"I'm afraid you do," agreed Amory reluctantly. "It just seemed an easy way out of everything—when I think of another useless, draggy year."

"Yes, I know; but to tell you the truth, I'm not worried about you; you seem to me to be progressing perfectly naturally."

"No," Amory objected. "I've lost half my personality in a year."

"Not a bit of it!" scoffed Monsignor. "You've lost a great amount of vanity and that's all."

"Lordy! I feel, anyway, as if I'd gone through another fifth form at St. Regis's."

"No." Monsignor shook his head. "That was a misfortune; this has been a good thing. Whatever worth while comes to you, won't be through the channels you were searching last year."

"What could be more unprofitable than my present lack of pep?"

"Perhaps in itself... but you're developing. This has given you time to think and you're casting off a lot of your old luggage about success and the superman and all. People like us can't adopt whole theories, as you did. If we can do the next thing, and have an hour a day to think in, we can accomplish marvels, but as far as any high-handed scheme of blind dominance is concerned—we'd just make asses of ourselves."

"But, Monsignor, I can't do the next thing."

"Amory, between you and me, I have only just learned to do it myself. I can do the one hundred things beyond the next thing, but I stub my toe on that, just as you stubbed your toe on mathematics this fall."

"Why do we have to do the next thing? It never seems the sort of thing I should do."

"We have to do it because we're not personalities, but personages."

"That's a good line—what do you mean?"

"A personality is what you thought you were, what this Kerry and Sloane you tell me of evidently are. Personality is a physical matter almost entirely; it lowers the people it acts on—I've seen it vanish in a long sickness. But while a personality is active, it overrides 'the next thing.' Now a personage, on the other hand, gathers. He is never thought of apart from what he's done. He's a bar on which a thousand things have been hung—glittering things sometimes, as ours are; but he uses those things with a cold mentality back of them."

"And several of my most glittering possessions had fallen off when I needed them." Amory continued the simile eagerly.

"Yes, that's it; when you feel that your garnered prestige and talents and all that are hung out, you need never bother about anybody; you can cope with them without difficulty."

"But, on the other hand, if I haven't my possessions, I'm helpless!"

"Absolutely."

CHAPTER 3 The Egotist Considers

"That's certainly an idea."

"Now you've a clean start—a start Kerry or Sloane can constitutionally never have. You brushed three or four ornaments down, and, in a fit of pique, knocked off the rest of them. The thing now is to collect some new ones, and the farther you look ahead in the collecting the better. But remember, do the next thing!"

"How clear you can make things!"

So they talked, often about themselves, sometimes of philosophy and religion, and life as respectively a game or a mystery. The priest seemed to guess Amory's thoughts before they were clear in his own head, so closely related were their minds in form and groove.

"Why do I make lists?" Amory asked him one night. "Lists of all sorts of things?"

"Because you're a mediaevalist," Monsignor answered. "We both are. It's the passion for classifying and finding a type."

"It's a desire to get something definite."

"It's the nucleus of scholastic philosophy."

"I was beginning to think I was growing eccentric till I came up here. It was a pose, I guess."

"Don't worry about that; for you not posing may be the biggest pose of all. Pose—"

"Yes?"

"But do the next thing."

After Amory returned to college he received several letters from Monsignor which gave him more egotistic food for consumption.

> I am afraid that I gave you too much assurance of your inevitable safety, and you must remember that I did that through faith in your springs of effort; not in the silly conviction that you will arrive without struggle. Some nuances of character you will have to take for granted in yourself, though you must be careful in confessing them to others. You are unsentimental, almost incapable of affection, astute without being cunning and vain without being proud.
>
> Don't let yourself feel worthless; often through life you will really be at your worst when you seem to think best of yourself; and don't worry about losing your "personality," as you persist in calling it; at fifteen you had the radiance of early morning, at twenty you will begin to have the melancholy brilliance of the moon, and when you are my age you will give out, as I do, the genial golden warmth of 4 P.M.
>
> If you write me letters, please let them be natural ones. Your

last, that dissertation on architecture, was perfectly awful—
so "highbrow" that I picture you living in an intellectual and
emotional vacuum; and beware of trying to classify people too
definitely into types; you will find that all through their youth
they will persist annoyingly in jumping from class to class, and
by pasting a supercilious label on every one you meet you are
merely packing a Jack-in-the-box that will spring up and leer at
you when you begin to come into really antagonistic contact with
the world. An idealization of some such a man as Leonardo da
Vinci would be a more valuable beacon to you at present.

You are bound to go up and down, just as I did in my youth, but
do keep your clarity of mind, and if fools or sages dare to
criticise don't blame yourself too much.

You say that convention is all that really keeps you straight in
this "woman proposition"; but it's more than that, Amory; it's
the fear that what you begin you can't stop; you would run amuck,
and I know whereof I speak; it's that half-miraculous sixth sense
by which you detect evil, it's the half-realized fear of God in
your heart.

Whatever your metier proves to be—religion, architecture,
literature—I'm sure you would be much safer anchored to the
Church, but I won't risk my influence by arguing with you even
though I am secretly sure that the "black chasm of Romanism"
yawns beneath you. Do write me soon.

    With affectionate regards,   THAYER DARCY.

Even Amory's reading paled during this period; he delved further into the misty side streets of literature: Huysmans, Walter Pater, Theophile Gautier, and the racier sections of Rabelais, Boccaccio, Petronius, and Suetonius. One week, through general curiosity, he inspected the private libraries of his classmates and found Sloane's as typical as any: sets of Kipling, O. Henry, John Fox, Jr., and Richard Harding Davis; "What Every Middle-Aged Woman Ought to Know," "The Spell of the Yukon"; a "gift" copy of James Whitcomb Riley, an assortment of battered, annotated schoolbooks, and, finally, to his surprise, one of his own late discoveries, the collected poems of Rupert Brooke.

    Together with Tom D'Invilliers, he sought among the lights of Princeton for some one who might found the Great American Poetic Tradition.

CHAPTER 3 The Egotist Considers

The undergraduate body itself was rather more interesting that year than had been the entirely Philistine Princeton of two years before. Things had livened surprisingly, though at the sacrifice of much of the spontaneous charm of freshman year. In the old Princeton they would never have discovered Tanaduke Wylie. Tanaduke was a sophomore, with tremendous ears and a way of saying, "The earth swirls down through the ominous moons of preconsidered generations!" that made them vaguely wonder why it did not sound quite clear, but never question that it was the utterance of a supersoul. At least so Tom and Amory took him. They told him in all earnestness that he had a mind like Shelley's, and featured his ultrafree free verse and prose poetry in the Nassau Literary Magazine. But Tanaduke's genius absorbed the many colors of the age, and he took to the Bohemian life, to their great disappointment. He talked of Greenwich Village now instead of "noon-swirled moons," and met winter muses, unacademic, and cloistered by Forty-second Street and Broadway, instead of the Shelleyan dream-children with whom he had regaled their expectant appreciation. So they surrendered Tanaduke to the futurists, deciding that he and his flaming ties would do better there. Tom gave him the final advice that he should stop writing for two years and read the complete works of Alexander Pope four times, but on Amory's suggestion that Pope for Tanaduke was like foot-ease for stomach trouble, they withdrew in laughter, and called it a coin's toss whether this genius was too big or too petty for them.

Amory rather scornfully avoided the popular professors who dispensed easy epigrams and thimblefuls of Chartreuse to groups of admirers every night. He was disappointed, too, at the air of general uncertainty on every subject that seemed linked with the pedantic temperament; his opinions took shape in a miniature satire called "In a Lecture-Room," which he persuaded Tom to print in the Nassau Lit.

"Good-morning, Fool...
> Three times a week
You hold us helpless while you speak,
Teasing our thirsty souls with the
Sleek 'yeas' of your philosophy...
Well, here we are, your hundred sheep,
Tune up, play on, pour forth... we sleep...
You are a student, so they say;
You hammered out the other day
A syllabus, from what we know
Of some forgotten folio;
You'd sniffled through an era's must,
Filling your nostrils up with dust,
And then, arising from your knees,
Published, in one gigantic sneeze...
But here's a neighbor on my right,

An Eager Ass, considered bright;
Asker of questions.... How he'll stand,
With earnest air and fidgy hand,
After this hour, telling you
He sat all night and burrowed through
Your book.... Oh, you'll be coy and he
Will simulate precosity,
And pedants both, you'll smile and smirk,
And leer, and hasten back to work....

Twas this day week, sir, you returned
A theme of mine, from which I learned
(Through various comment on the side
Which you had scrawled) that I defied
The highest rules of criticism
For cheap and careless witticism....
'Are you quite sure that this could be?'
And
'Shaw is no authority!'
But Eager Ass, with what he's sent,
Plays havoc with your best per cent.

Still—still I meet you here and there...
When Shakespeare's played you hold a chair,
And some defunct, moth-eaten star
Enchants the mental prig you are...
A radical comes down and shocks
The atheistic orthodox?
You're representing Common Sense,
Mouth open, in the audience.
And, sometimes, even chapel lures
That conscious tolerance of yours,
That broad and beaming view of truth
(Including Kant and General Booth...)
And so from shock to shock you live,
A hollow, pale affirmative...

The hour's up... and roused from rest
One hundred children of the blest

CHAPTER 3   The Egotist Considers

Cheat you a word or two with feet
That down the noisy aisle-ways beat...
Forget on narrow-minded earth
The Mighty Yawn that gave you birth."

In April, Kerry Holiday left college and sailed for France to enroll in the Lafayette Esquadrille. Amory's envy and admiration of this step was drowned in an experience of his own to which he never succeeded in giving an appropriate value, but which, nevertheless, haunted him for three years afterward.

THE DEVIL

Healy's they left at twelve and taxied to Bistolary's. There were Axia Marlowe and Phoebe Column, from the Summer Garden show, Fred Sloane and Amory. The evening was so very young that they felt ridiculous with surplus energy, and burst into the cafe like Dionysian revellers.

"Table for four in the middle of the floor," yelled Phoebe. "Hurry, old dear, tell 'em we're here!"

"Tell 'em to play 'Admiration'!" shouted Sloane. "You two order; Phoebe and I are going to shake a wicked calf," and they sailed off in the muddled crowd. Axia and Amory, acquaintances of an hour, jostled behind a waiter to a table at a point of vantage; there they took seats and watched.

"There's Findle Margotson, from New Haven!" she cried above the uproar. "'Lo, Findle! Whoo-ee!"

"Oh, Axia!" he shouted in salutation. "C'mon over to our table." "No!" Amory whispered.

"Can't do it, Findle; I'm with somebody else! Call me up to-morrow about one o'clock!"

Findle, a nondescript man-about-Bisty's, answered incoherently and turned back to the brilliant blonde whom he was endeavoring to steer around the room.

"There's a natural damn fool," commented Amory.

"Oh, he's all right. Here's the old jitney waiter. If you ask me, I want a double Daiquiri."

"Make it four."

The crowd whirled and changed and shifted. They were mostly from the colleges, with a scattering of the male refuse of Broadway, and women of two types, the higher of which was the chorus girl. On the whole it was a typical crowd, and their party as typical as any. About three-fourths of the whole business was for effect and therefore harmless, ended at the door of the cafe, soon enough for the five-o'clock train back to Yale or Princeton; about one-fourth continued on into the dimmer hours and gathered strange dust from strange places. Their party was scheduled to be one of the harmless kind. Fred Sloane and Phoebe Column were old friends; Axia and Amory new ones. But strange things are prepared even in the dead of night, and the unusual, which lurks least in the cafe, home of the prosaic and inevitable, was preparing to spoil for him the waning romance of Broadway. The way it took was so inexpressibly terrible, so unbelievable, that afterward he never thought of it as experience; but it was a scene from a misty tragedy, played far behind the veil, and that it meant something definite he knew.

About one o'clock they moved to Maxim's, and two found them in Deviniere's. Sloane had been drinking consecutively and was in a state of unsteady exhilaration, but Amory was quite tiresomely sober; they had run across none of those ancient, corrupt buyers of champagne who usually assisted their New York parties. They were just through dancing and were making their way back to their chairs when Amory became aware that some one at a near-by table was looking at him. He turned and glanced casually... a middle-aged man dressed in a brown sack suit, it was, sitting a little apart at a table by himself and watching their party intently. At Amory's glance he smiled faintly. Amory turned to Fred, who was just sitting down.

"Who's that pale fool watching us?" he complained indignantly.

"Where?" cried Sloane. "We'll have him thrown out!" He rose to his feet and swayed back and forth, clinging to his chair. "Where is he?"

Axia and Phoebe suddenly leaned and whispered to each other across the table, and before Amory realized it they found themselves on their way to the door.

"Where now?"

"Up to the flat," suggested Phoebe. "We've got brandy and fizz—and everything's slow down here to-night."

Amory considered quickly. He hadn't been drinking, and decided that if he took no more, it would be reasonably discreet for him to trot along in the party. In fact, it would be, perhaps, the thing to do in order to keep an eye on Sloane, who was not in a state to do his own thinking. So he took Axia's arm and, piling intimately into a taxicab, they drove out over the hundreds and drew up at a tall, white-stone apartment-house. ... Never would he forget that street.... It was a broad street, lined on both sides with just such tall, white-stone buildings, dotted with dark windows; they stretched along as far as the eye could see, flooded with a bright moonlight that gave them a calcium pallor. He imagined each one to have an elevator and a colored hall-boy and a key-rack; each one to be eight stories high and full of three and four room suites. He was rather glad to walk into the cheeriness of Phoebe's living-room and sink onto a sofa, while the girls went rummaging for food.

"Phoebe's great stuff," confided Sloane, sotto voce.

"I'm only going to stay half an hour," Amory said sternly. He wondered if it sounded priggish.

"Hell y' say," protested Sloane. "We're here now—don't le's rush."

"I don't like this place," Amory said sulkily, "and I don't want any food."

Phoebe reappeared with sandwiches, brandy bottle, siphon, and four glasses.

"Amory, pour 'em out," she said, "and we'll drink to Fred Sloane, who has a rare, distinguished edge."

"Yes," said Axia, coming in, "and Amory. I like Amory." She sat down beside him and laid her yellow head on his shoulder.

"I'll pour," said Sloane; "you use siphon, Phoebe."

They filled the tray with glasses.

"Ready, here she goes!"

Amory hesitated, glass in hand.

There was a minute while temptation crept over him like a warm wind, and his imagination turned to fire, and he took the glass from Phoebe's hand. That was all; for at the second that his decision came, he looked up and saw, ten yards from him, the man who had been in the cafe, and with his jump of astonishment the glass fell from his uplifted hand. There the man half sat, half leaned against a pile of pillows on the corner divan. His face was cast in the same yellow wax as in the cafe, neither the dull, pasty color of a dead man—rather a sort of virile pallor—nor unhealthy, you'd have called it; but like a strong man who'd worked in a mine or done night shifts in a damp climate. Amory looked him over carefully and later he could have drawn him after a fashion, down to the merest details. His mouth was the kind that is called frank, and he had steady gray eyes that moved slowly from one to the other of their group, with just the shade of a questioning expression. Amory noticed his hands; they weren't fine at all, but they had versatility and a tenuous strength... they were nervous hands that sat lightly along the cushions and moved constantly with little jerky openings and closings. Then, suddenly, Amory perceived the feet, and with a rush of blood to the head he realized he was afraid. The feet were all wrong ... with a sort of wrongness that he felt rather than knew.... It was like weakness in a good woman, or blood on satin; one of those terrible incongruities that shake little things in the back of the brain. He wore no shoes, but, instead, a sort of half moccasin, pointed, though, like the shoes they wore in the fourteenth century, and with the little ends curling up. They were a darkish brown and his toes seemed to fill them to the end.... They were unutterably terrible....

He must have said something, or looked something, for Axia's voice came out of the void with a strange goodness.

"Well, look at Amory! Poor old Amory's sick—old head going 'round?"

"Look at that man!" cried Amory, pointing toward the corner divan.

"You mean that purple zebra!" shrieked Axia facetiously. "Ooo-ee! Amory's got a purple zebra watching him!"

Sloane laughed vacantly.

"Ole zebra gotcha, Amory?"

There was a silence.... The man regarded Amory quizzically.... Then the human voices fell faintly on his ear:

"Thought you weren't drinking," remarked Axia sardonically, but her voice was good to hear; the whole divan that held the man was alive; alive like heat waves over asphalt, like wriggling worms....

"Come back! Come back!" Axia's arm fell on his. "Amory, dear, you aren't going, Amory!" He was half-way to the door.

"Come on, Amory, stick 'th us!"

"Sick, are you?"

"Sit down a second!"

"Take some water."

"Take a little brandy...." ·

The elevator was close, and the colored boy was half asleep, paled to a livid bronze... Axia's beseeching voice floated down the shaft. Those feet... those feet...

As they settled to the lower floor the feet came into view in the sickly electric light of the paved hall.

IN THE ALLEY

Down the long street came the moon, and Amory turned his back on it and walked. Ten, fifteen steps away sounded the footsteps. They were like a slow dripping, with just the slightest insistence in their fall. Amory's shadow lay, perhaps, ten feet ahead of him, and soft shoes was presumably that far behind. With the instinct of a child Amory edged in under the blue darkness of the white buildings, cleaving the moonlight for haggard seconds, once bursting into a slow run with clumsy stumblings. After that he stopped suddenly; he must keep hold, he thought. His lips were dry and he licked them.

If he met any one good—were there any good people left in the world or did they all live in white apartment-houses now? Was every one followed in the moonlight? But if he met some one good who'd know what he meant and hear this damned scuffle... then the scuffling grew suddenly nearer, and a black cloud settled over the moon. When again the pale sheen skimmed the cornices, it was almost beside him, and Amory thought he heard a quiet breathing. Suddenly he realized that the footsteps were not behind, had never been behind, they were ahead and he was not eluding but following... following. He began to run, blindly, his heart knocking heavily, his hands clinched. Far ahead a black dot showed itself, resolved slowly into a human shape. But Amory was beyond that now; he turned off the street and darted into an alley, narrow and dark and smelling of old rottenness. He twisted down a long, sinuous blackness, where the moonlight was shut away except for tiny glints and patches... then suddenly sank panting into a corner by a fence, exhausted. The steps ahead stopped, and he could hear them shift slightly with a continuous motion, like waves around a dock.

He put his face in his hands and covered eyes and ears as well as he could. During all this time it never occurred to him that he was delirious or drunk. He had a sense of reality such as material things could never give him. His intellectual content seemed to submit passively to it, and it fitted like a glove everything that had ever preceded it in his life. It did not muddle him. It was like a problem whose answer he knew on paper, yet whose

CHAPTER 3 The Egotist Considers

solution he was unable to grasp. He was far beyond horror. He had sunk through the thin surface of that, now moved in a region where the feet and the fear of white walls were real, living things, things he must accept. Only far inside his soul a little fire leaped and cried that something was pulling him down, trying to get him inside a door and slam it behind him. After that door was slammed there would be only footfalls and white buildings in the moonlight, and perhaps he would be one of the footfalls.

During the five or ten minutes he waited in the shadow of the fence, there was somehow this fire... that was as near as he could name it afterward. He remembered calling aloud:

"I want some one stupid. Oh, send some one stupid!" This to the black fence opposite him, in whose shadows the footsteps shuffled ... shuffled. He supposed "stupid" and "good" had become somehow intermingled through previous association. When he called thus it was not an act of will at all—will had turned him away from the moving figure in the street; it was almost instinct that called, just the pile on pile of inherent tradition or some wild prayer from way over the night. Then something clanged like a low gong struck at a distance, and before his eyes a face flashed over the two feet, a face pale and distorted with a sort of infinite evil that twisted it like flame in the wind; but he knew, for the half instant that the gong tanged and hummed, that it was the face of Dick Humbird.

Minutes later he sprang to his feet, realizing dimly that there was no more sound, and that he was alone in the graying alley. It was cold, and he started on a steady run for the light that showed the street at the other end.

AT THE WINDOW

It was late morning when he woke and found the telephone beside his bed in the hotel tolling frantically, and remembered that he had left word to be called at eleven. Sloane was snoring heavily, his clothes in a pile by his bed. They dressed and ate breakfast in silence, and then sauntered out to get some air. Amory's mind was working slowly, trying to assimilate what had happened and separate from the chaotic imagery that stacked his memory the bare shreds of truth. If the morning had been cold and gray he could have grasped the reins of the past in an instant, but it was one of those days that New York gets sometimes in May, when the air on Fifth Avenue is a soft, light wine. How much or how little Sloane remembered Amory did not care to know; he apparently had none of the nervous tension that was gripping Amory and forcing his mind back and forth like a shrieking saw.

Then Broadway broke upon them, and with the babel of noise and the painted faces a sudden sickness rushed over Amory.

"For God's sake, let's go back! Let's get off of this—this place!"

Sloane looked at him in amazement.

"What do you mean?"

"This street, it's ghastly! Come on! let's get back to the Avenue!"

"Do you mean to say," said Sloane stolidly, "that 'cause you had some sort of indigestion that made you act like a maniac last night, you're never coming on Broadway again?"

Simultaneously Amory classed him with the crowd, and he seemed no longer Sloane of the debonair humor and the happy personality, but only one of the evil faces that whirled along the turbid stream.

"Man!" he shouted so loud that the people on the corner turned and followed them with their eyes, "it's filthy, and if you can't see it, you're filthy, too!"

"I can't help it," said Sloane doggedly. "What's the matter with you? Old remorse getting you? You'd be in a fine state if you'd gone through with our little party."

"I'm going, Fred," said Amory slowly. His knees were shaking under him, and he knew that if he stayed another minute on this street he would keel over where he stood. "I'll be at the Vanderbilt for lunch." And he strode rapidly off and turned over to Fifth Avenue. Back at the hotel he felt better, but as he walked into the barber-shop, intending to get a head massage, the smell of the powders and tonics brought back Axia's sidelong, suggestive smile, and he left hurriedly. In the doorway of his room a sudden blackness flowed around him like a divided river.

When he came to himself he knew that several hours had passed. He pitched onto the bed and rolled over on his face with a deadly fear that he was going mad. He wanted people, people, some one sane and stupid and good. He lay for he knew not how long without moving. He could feel the little hot veins on his forehead standing out, and his terror had hardened on him like plaster. He felt he was passing up again through the thin crust of horror, and now only could he distinguish the shadowy twilight he was leaving. He must have fallen asleep again, for when he next recollected himself he had paid the hotel bill and was stepping into a taxi at the door. It was raining torrents.

On the train for Princeton he saw no one he knew, only a crowd of fagged-looking Philadelphians. The presence of a painted woman across the aisle filled him with a fresh burst of sickness and he changed to another car, tried to concentrate on an article in a popular magazine. He found himself reading the same paragraphs over and over, so he abandoned this attempt and leaning over wearily pressed his hot forehead against the damp window-pane. The car, a smoker, was hot and stuffy with most of the smells of the state's alien population; he opened a window and shivered against the cloud of fog that drifted in over him. The two hours' ride were like days, and he nearly cried aloud with joy when the towers of Princeton loomed up beside him and the yellow squares of light filtered through the blue rain.

Tom was standing in the centre of the room, pensively relighting a cigar-stub. Amory fancied he looked rather relieved on seeing him.

"Had a hell of a dream about you last night," came in the cracked voice through the cigar smoke. "I had an idea you were in some trouble."

"Don't tell me about it!" Amory almost shrieked. "Don't say a word; I'm tired and pepped out."

Tom looked at him queerly and then sank into a chair and opened his Italian note-book. Amory threw his coat and hat on the floor, loosened his collar, and took a Wells novel at random from the shelf. "Wells is sane," he thought, "and if he won't do I'll read Rupert Brooke."

Half an hour passed. Outside the wind came up, and Amory started as the wet branches moved and clawed with their finger-nails at the window-pane. Tom was deep in his work, and inside the room only the occasional scratch of a match or the rustle of leather as they shifted in their chairs broke the stillness. Then like a zigzag of lightning came the change. Amory sat bolt upright, frozen cold in his chair. Tom was looking at him with his mouth drooping, eyes fixed.

"God help us!" Amory cried.

"Oh, my heavens!" shouted Tom, "look behind!" Quick as a flash Amory whirled around. He saw nothing but the dark window-pane. "It's gone now," came Tom's voice after a second in a still terror. "Something was looking at you."

Trembling violently, Amory dropped into his chair again.

"I've got to tell you," he said. "I've had one hell of an experience. I think I've—I've seen the devil or—something like him. What face did you just see?—or no," he added quickly, "don't tell me!"

And he gave Tom the story. It was midnight when he finished, and after that, with all lights burning, two sleepy, shivering boys read to each other from "The New Machiavelli," until dawn came up out of Witherspoon Hall, and the Princetonian fell against the door, and the May birds hailed the sun on last night's rain.

CHAPTER 4　　Narcissus Off Duty

During Princeton's transition period, that is, during Amory's last two years there, while he saw it change and broaden and live up to its Gothic beauty by better means than night parades, certain individuals arrived who stirred it to its plethoric depths. Some of them had been freshmen, and wild freshmen, with Amory; some were in the class below; and it was in the beginning of his last year and around small tables at the Nassau Inn that they began questioning aloud the institutions that Amory and countless others before him had questioned so long in secret. First, and partly by accident, they struck on certain books, a definite type of biographical novel that Amory christened "quest" books. In the "quest" book the hero set off in life armed with the best weapons and avowedly intending to use them as such weapons are usually used, to push their possessors ahead as selfishly and blindly as possible, but the heroes of the "quest" books discovered that there might be a more magnificent use for them. "None Other Gods," "Sinister Street," and "The Research Magnificent" were examples of such books; it was the latter of these three that gripped Burne Holiday and made him wonder in the beginning of senior year how much it was worth while being a diplomatic autocrat around his club on Prospect Avenue and basking in the high lights of class office. It was distinctly through the channels of aristocracy that Burne found his way. Amory, through Kerry, had had a vague drifting acquaintance with him, but not until January of senior year did their friendship commence.

"Heard the latest?" said Tom, coming in late one drizzly evening with that triumphant air he always wore after a successful conversational bout.

"No. Somebody flunked out? Or another ship sunk?"

"Worse than that. About one-third of the junior class are going to resign from their clubs."

"What!"

"Actual fact!"

"Why!"

"Spirit of reform and all that. Burne Holiday is behind it. The club presidents are holding a meeting to-night to see if they can find a joint means of combating it."

"Well, what's the idea of the thing?"

"Oh, clubs injurious to Princeton democracy; cost a lot; draw social lines, take time; the regular line you get sometimes from disappointed sophomores. Woodrow thought they should be abolished and all that."

"But this is the real thing?"

CHAPTER 4 Narcissus Off Duty

"Absolutely. I think it'll go through."

"For Pete's sake, tell me more about it."

"Well," began Tom, "it seems that the idea developed simultaneously in several heads. I was talking to Burne awhile ago, and he claims that it's a logical result if an intelligent person thinks long enough about the social system. They had a 'discussion crowd' and the point of abolishing the clubs was brought up by some one—everybody there leaped at it—it had been in each one's mind, more or less, and it just needed a spark to bring it out."

"Fine! I swear I think it'll be most entertaining. How do they feel up at Cap and Gown?"

"Wild, of course. Every one's been sitting and arguing and swearing and getting mad and getting sentimental and getting brutal. It's the same at all the clubs; I've been the rounds. They get one of the radicals in the corner and fire questions at him."

"How do the radicals stand up?"

"Oh, moderately well. Burne's a damn good talker, and so obviously sincere that you can't get anywhere with him. It's so evident that resigning from his club means so much more to him than preventing it does to us that I felt futile when I argued; finally took a position that was brilliantly neutral. In fact, I believe Burne thought for a while that he'd converted me."

"And you say almost a third of the junior class are going to resign?"

"Call it a fourth and be safe."

"Lord—who'd have thought it possible!"

There was a brisk knock at the door, and Burne himself came in. "Hello, Amory—hello, Tom."

Amory rose.

"'Evening, Burne. Don't mind if I seem to rush; I'm going to Renwick's."

Burne turned to him quickly.

"You probably know what I want to talk to Tom about, and it isn't a bit private. I wish you'd stay."

"I'd be glad to." Amory sat down again, and as Burne perched on a table and launched into argument with Tom, he looked at this revolutionary more carefully than he ever had before. Broad-browed and strong-chinned, with a fineness in the honest gray eyes that were like Kerry's, Burne was a man who gave an immediate impression of bigness and security—stubborn, that was evident, but his stubbornness wore no stolidity, and when he had talked for five minutes Amory knew that this keen enthusiasm had in it no quality of dilettantism.

The intense power Amory felt later in Burne Holiday differed from the admiration he had had for Humbird. This time it began as purely a mental interest. With other men of whom he had thought as primarily first-class, he had been attracted first by their personalities, and in Burne he missed that immediate magnetism to which he usually swore allegiance. But that night Amory was struck by Burne's intense earnestness, a quality he was accustomed to associate only with the dread stupidity, and by the great enthusiasm that struck dead chords in his heart. Burne stood vaguely for a land Amory hoped he was drifting toward—and it was almost time that land was in sight. Tom and Amory and Alec had reached an impasse; never did they seem to have new experiences in common, for Tom and Alec had been as blindly busy with their committees and boards as Amory had been blindly idling, and the things they had for dissection—college, contemporary personality and the like—they had hashed and rehashed for many a frugal conversational meal.

That night they discussed the clubs until twelve, and, in the main, they agreed with Burne. To the roommates it did not seem such a vital subject as it had in the two years before, but the logic of Burne's objections to the social system dovetailed so completely with everything they had thought, that they questioned rather than argued, and envied the sanity that enabled this man to stand out so against all traditions.

Then Amory branched off and found that Burne was deep in other things as well. Economics had interested him and he was turning socialist. Pacifism played in the back of his mind, and he read The Masses and Lyoff Tolstoi faithfully.

"How about religion?" Amory asked him.

"Don't know. I'm in a muddle about a lot of things—I've just discovered that I've a mind, and I'm starting to read."

"Read what?"

"Everything. I have to pick and choose, of course, but mostly things to make me think. I'm reading the four gospels now, and the 'Varieties of Religious Experience.'"

"What chiefly started you?"

"Wells, I guess, and Tolstoi, and a man named Edward Carpenter. I've been reading for over a year now—on a few lines, on what I consider the essential lines."

"Poetry?"

"Well, frankly, not what you call poetry, or for your reasons—you two write, of course, and look at things differently. Whitman is the man that attracts me."

"Whitman?"

"Yes; he's a definite ethical force."

"Well, I'm ashamed to say that I'm a blank on the subject of Whitman. How about you, Tom?"

Tom nodded sheepishly.

"Well," continued Burne, "you may strike a few poems that are tiresome, but I mean the mass of his work. He's tremendous—like Tolstoi. They both look things in the face, and, somehow, different as they are, stand for somewhat the same things."

"You have me stumped, Burne," Amory admitted. "I've read 'Anna Karenina' and the 'Kreutzer Sonata' of course, but Tolstoi is mostly in the original Russian as far as I'm concerned."

"He's the greatest man in hundreds of years," cried Burne enthusiastically. "Did you

CHAPTER 4 Narcissus Off Duty

ever see a picture of that shaggy old head of his?"

They talked until three, from biology to organized religion, and when Amory crept shivering into bed it was with his mind aglow with ideas and a sense of shock that some one else had discovered the path he might have followed. Burne Holiday was so evidently developing—and Amory had considered that he was doing the same. He had fallen into a deep cynicism over what had crossed his path, plotted the imperfectability of man and read Shaw and Chesterton enough to keep his mind from the edges of decadence—now suddenly all his mental processes of the last year and a half seemed stale and futile—a petty consummation of himself... and like a sombre background lay that incident of the spring before, that filled half his nights with a dreary terror and made him unable to pray. He was not even a Catholic, yet that was the only ghost of a code that he had, the gaudy, ritualistic, paradoxical Catholicism whose prophet was Chesterton, whose claqueurs were such reformed rakes of literature as Huysmans and Bourget, whose American sponsor was Ralph Adams Cram, with his adulation of thirteenth-century cathedrals—a Catholicism which Amory found convenient and ready-made, without priest or sacraments or sacrifice.

He could not sleep, so he turned on his reading-lamp and, taking down the "Kreutzer Sonata," searched it carefully for the germs of Burne's enthusiasm. Being Burne was suddenly so much realler than being clever. Yet he sighed... here were other possible clay feet.

He thought back through two years, of Burne as a hurried, nervous freshman, quite submerged in his brother's personality. Then he remembered an incident of sophomore year, in which Burne had been suspected of the leading role.

Dean Hollister had been heard by a large group arguing with a taxi-driver, who had driven him from the junction. In the course of the altercation the dean remarked that he "might as well buy the taxicab." He paid and walked off, but next morning he entered his private office to find the taxicab itself in the space usually occupied by his desk, bearing a sign which read "Property of Dean Hollister. Bought and Paid for."... It took two expert mechanics half a day to dissemble it into its minutest parts and remove it, which only goes to prove the rare energy of sophomore humor under efficient leadership.

Then again, that very fall, Burne had caused a sensation. A certain Phyllis Styles, an intercollegiate prom-trotter, had failed to get her yearly invitation to the Harvard-Princeton game.

Jesse Ferrenby had brought her to a smaller game a few weeks before, and had pressed Burne into service—to the ruination of the latter's misogyny.

"Are you coming to the Harvard game?" Burne had asked indiscreetly, merely to make conversation.

"If you ask me," cried Phyllis quickly.

"Of course I do," said Burne feebly. He was unversed in the arts of Phyllis, and was sure that this was merely a vapid form of kidding. Before an hour had passed he knew that he was indeed involved. Phyllis had pinned him down and served him up, informed him the train she was arriving by, and depressed him thoroughly. Aside from loathing Phyllis, he had particularly wanted to stag that game and entertain some Harvard friends.

"She'll see," he informed a delegation who arrived in his room to josh him. "This will be the last game she ever persuades any young innocent to take her to!"

"But, Burne—why did you invite her if you didn't want her?"

"Burne, you know you're secretly mad about her—that's the real trouble."

"What can you do, Burne? What can you do against Phyllis?"

But Burne only shook his head and muttered threats which consisted largely of the phrase: "She'll see, she'll see!"

The blithesome Phyllis bore her twenty-five summers gayly from the train, but on the platform a ghastly sight met her eyes. There were Burne and Fred Sloane arrayed to the last dot like the lurid figures on college posters. They had bought flaring suits with huge peg-top trousers and gigantic padded shoulders. On their heads were rakish college hats, pinned up in front and sporting bright orange-and-black bands, while from their celluloid collars blossomed flaming orange ties. They wore black arm-bands with orange "P's," and carried canes flying Princeton pennants, the effect completed by socks and peeping handkerchiefs in the same color motifs. On a clanking chain they led a large, angry tom-cat, painted to represent a tiger.

A good half of the station crowd was already staring at them, torn between horrified pity and riotous mirth, and as Phyllis, with her svelte jaw dropping, approached, the pair bent over and emitted a college cheer in loud, far-carrying voices, thoughtfully adding the name "Phyllis" to the end. She was vociferously greeted and escorted enthusiastically across the campus, followed by half a hundred village urchins—to the stifled laughter of hundreds of alumni and visitors, half of whom had no idea that this was a practical joke, but thought that Burne and Fred were two varsity sports showing their girl a collegiate time.

Phyllis's feelings as she was paraded by the Harvard and Princeton stands, where sat dozens of her former devotees, can be imagined. She tried to walk a little ahead, she tried to walk a little behind—but they stayed close, that there should be no doubt whom she was with, talking in loud voices of their friends on the football team, until she could almost hear her acquaintances whispering:

"Phyllis Styles must be awfully hard up to have to come with those two."

That had been Burne, dynamically humorous, fundamentally serious. From that root had blossomed the energy that he was now trying to orient with progress....

So the weeks passed and March came and the clay feet that Amory looked for failed to appear. About a hundred juniors and seniors resigned from their clubs in a final fury of righteousness, and the clubs in helplessness turned upon Burne their finest weapon: ridicule. Every one who knew him liked him—but what he stood for (and he began to stand for more all the time) came under the lash of many tongues, until a frailer man than he would have

CHAPTER 4 Narcissus Off Duty

been snowed under.

"Don't you mind losing prestige?" asked Amory one night. They had taken to exchanging calls several times a week.

"Of course I don't. What's prestige, at best?"

"Some people say that you're just a rather original politician."

He roared with laughter.

"That's what Fred Sloane told me to-day. I suppose I have it coming."

One afternoon they dipped into a subject that had interested Amory for a long time—the matter of the bearing of physical attributes on a man's make-up. Burne had gone into the biology of this, and then:

"Of course health counts—a healthy man has twice the chance of being good," he said.

"I don't agree with you—I don't believe in 'muscular Christianity.'"

"I do—I believe Christ had great physical vigor."

"Oh, no," Amory protested. "He worked too hard for that. I imagine that when he died he was a broken-down man—and the great saints haven't been strong."

"Half of them have."

"Well, even granting that, I don't think health has anything to do with goodness; of course, it's valuable to a great saint to be able to stand enormous strains, but this fad of popular preachers rising on their toes in simulated virility, bellowing that calisthenics will save the world—no, Burne, I can't go that."

"Well, let's waive it—we won't get anywhere, and besides I haven't quite made up my mind about it myself. Now, here's something I do know—personal appearance has a lot to do with it."

"Coloring?" Amory asked eagerly.

"Yes."

"That's what Tom and I figured," Amory agreed. "We took the year-books for the last ten years and looked at the pictures of the senior council. I know you don't think much of that august body, but it does represent success here in a general way. Well, I suppose only about thirty-five per cent of every class here are blonds, are really light—yet two-thirds of every senior council are light. We looked at pictures of ten years of them, mind you; that means that out of every fifteen light-haired men in the senior class one is on the senior council, and of the dark-haired men it's only one in fifty."

"It's true," Burne agreed. "The light-haired man is a higher type, generally speaking. I worked the thing out with the Presidents of the United States once, and found that way over half of them were light-haired yet think of the preponderant number of brunettes in the race."

"People unconsciously admit it," said Amory. "You'll notice a blond person is expected to talk. If a blond girl doesn't talk we call her a 'doll'; if a light-haired man is silent he's considered stupid. Yet the world is full of 'dark silent men' and 'languorous brunettes' who haven't a brain in their heads, but somehow are never accused of the dearth."

"And the large mouth and broad chin and rather big nose undoubtedly make the superior face."

"I'm not so sure." Amory was all for classical features.

"Oh, yes—I'll show you," and Burne pulled out of his desk a photographic collection of heavily bearded, shaggy celebrities—Tolstoi, Whitman, Carpenter, and others.

"Aren't they wonderful?"

Amory tried politely to appreciate them, and gave up laughingly.

"Burne, I think they're the ugliest-looking crowd I ever came across. They look like an old man's home."

"Oh, Amory, look at that forehead on Emerson; look at Tolstoi's eyes." His tone was reproachful.

Amory shook his head.

"No! Call them remarkable-looking or anything you want—but ugly they certainly are."

Unabashed, Burne ran his hand lovingly across the spacious foreheads, and piling up the pictures put them back in his desk.

Walking at night was one of his favorite pursuits, and one night he persuaded Amory to accompany him.

"I hate the dark," Amory objected. "I didn't use to—except when I was particularly imaginative, but now, I really do—I'm a regular fool about it."

"That's useless, you know."

"Quite possibly."

"We'll go east," Burne suggested, "and down that string of roads through the woods."

"Doesn't sound very appealing to me," admitted Amory reluctantly, "but let's go."

They set off at a good gait, and for an hour swung along in a brisk argument until the lights of Princeton were luminous white blots behind them.

"Any person with any imagination is bound to be afraid," said Burne earnestly. "And this very walking at night is one of the things I was afraid about. I'm going to tell you why I can walk anywhere now and not be afraid."

"Go on," Amory urged eagerly. They were striding toward the woods, Burne's nervous, enthusiastic voice warming to his subject.

"I used to come out here alone at night, oh, three months ago, and I always stopped at that cross-road we just passed. There were the woods looming up ahead, just as they do now, there were dogs howling and the shadows and no human sound. Of course, I peopled the woods with everything ghastly, just like you do; don't you?"

"I do," Amory admitted.

"Well, I began analyzing it—my imagination persisted in sticking horrors into the dark—so I stuck my imagination into the dark instead, and let it look out at me—I let it play stray dog or escaped convict or ghost, and then saw myself coming along the road. That

CHAPTER 4 Narcissus Off Duty

made it all right—as it always makes everything all right to project yourself completely into another's place. I knew that if I were the dog or the convict or the ghost I wouldn't be a menace to Burne Holiday any more than he was a menace to me. Then I thought of my watch. I'd better go back and leave it and then essay the woods. No; I decided, it's better on the whole that I should lose a watch than that I should turn back—and I did go into them—not only followed the road through them, but walked into them until I wasn't frightened any more—did it until one night I sat down and dozed off in there; then I knew I was through being afraid of the dark."

"Lordy," Amory breathed. "I couldn't have done that. I'd have come out half-way, and the first time an automobile passed and made the dark thicker when its lamps disappeared, I'd have come in."

"Well," Burne said suddenly, after a few moments' silence, "we're half-way through, let's turn back."

On the return he launched into a discussion of will.

"It's the whole thing," he asserted. "It's the one dividing line between good and evil. I've never met a man who led a rotten life and didn't have a weak will."

"How about great criminals?"

"They're usually insane. If not, they're weak. There is no such thing as a strong, sane criminal."

"Burne, I disagree with you altogether; how about the superman?"

"Well?"

"He's evil, I think, yet he's strong and sane."

"I've never met him. I'll bet, though, that he's stupid or insane."

"I've met him over and over and he's neither. That's why I think you're wrong."

"I'm sure I'm not—and so I don't believe in imprisonment except for the insane."

On this point Amory could not agree. It seemed to him that life and history were rife with the strong criminal, keen, but often self-deluding; in politics and business one found him and among the old statesmen and kings and generals; but Burne never agreed and their courses began to split on that point.

Burne was drawing farther and farther away from the world about him. He resigned the vice-presidency of the senior class and took to reading and walking as almost his only pursuits. He voluntarily attended graduate lectures in philosophy and biology, and sat in all of them with a rather pathetically intent look in his eyes, as if waiting for something the lecturer would never quite come to. Sometimes Amory would see him squirm in his seat; and his face would light up; he was on fire to debate a point.

He grew more abstracted on the street and was even accused of becoming a snob, but Amory knew it was nothing of the sort, and once when Burne passed him four feet off, absolutely unseeingly, his mind a thousand miles away, Amory almost choked with the romantic joy of watching him. Burne seemed to be climbing heights where others would be

087

forever unable to get a foothold.

"I tell you," Amory declared to Tom, "he's the first contemporary I've ever met whom I'll admit is my superior in mental capacity."

"It's a bad time to admit it—people are beginning to think he's odd."

"He's way over their heads—you know you think so yourself when you talk to him—Good Lord, Tom, you used to stand out against 'people.' Success has completely conventionalized you."

Tom grew rather annoyed.

"What's he trying to do—be excessively holy?"

"No! not like anybody you've ever seen. Never enters the Philadelphian Society. He has no faith in that rot. He doesn't believe that public swimming-pools and a kind word in time will right the wrongs of the world; moreover, he takes a drink whenever he feels like it."

"He certainly is getting in wrong."

"Have you talked to him lately?"

"No."

"Then you haven't any conception of him."

The argument ended nowhere, but Amory noticed more than ever how the sentiment toward Burne had changed on the campus.

"It's odd," Amory said to Tom one night when they had grown more amicable on the subject, "that the people who violently disapprove of Burne's radicalism are distinctly the Pharisee class—I mean they're the best-educated men in college—the editors of the papers, like yourself and Ferrenby, the younger professors.... The illiterate athletes like Langueduc think he's getting eccentric, but they just say, 'Good old Burne has got some queer ideas in his head,' and pass on—the Pharisee class—Gee! they ridicule him unmercifully."

The next morning he met Burne hurrying along McCosh walk after a recitation.

"Whither bound, Tsar?"

"Over to the Prince office to see Ferrenby," he waved a copy of the morning's Princetonian at Amory. "He wrote this editorial."

"Going to flay him alive?"

"No—but he's got me all balled up. Either I've misjudged him or he's suddenly become the world's worst radical."

Burne hurried on, and it was several days before Amory heard an account of the ensuing conversation. Burne had come into the editor's sanctum displaying the paper cheerfully.

"Hello, Jesse."

"Hello there, Savonarola."

"I just read your editorial."

"Good boy—didn't know you stooped that low."

"Jesse, you startled me."

"How so?"

CHAPTER 4 Narcissus Off Duty

"Aren't you afraid the faculty'll get after you if you pull this irreligious stuff?"

"What?"

"Like this morning."

"What the devil—that editorial was on the coaching system."

"Yes, but that quotation—"

Jesse sat up.

"What quotation?"

"You know: 'He who is not with me is against me.'"

"Well—what about it?"

Jesse was puzzled but not alarmed.

"Well, you say here—let me see." Burne opened the paper and read: "'He who is not with me is against me, as that gentleman said who was notoriously capable of only coarse distinctions and puerile generalities.'"

"What of it?" Ferrenby began to look alarmed. "Oliver Cromwell said it, didn't he? or was it Washington, or one of the saints? Good Lord, I've forgotten."

Burne roared with laughter.

"Oh, Jesse, oh, good, kind Jesse."

"Who said it, for Pete's sake?"

"Well," said Burne, recovering his voice, "St. Matthew attributes it to Christ."

"My God!" cried Jesse, and collapsed backward into the waste-basket.

AMORY WRITES A POEM

The weeks tore by. Amory wandered occasionally to New York on the chance of finding a new shining green auto-bus, that its stick-of-candy glamour might penetrate his disposition. One day he ventured into a stock-company revival of a play whose name was faintly familiar. The curtain rose—he watched casually as a girl entered. A few phrases rang in his ear and touched a faint chord of memory. Where—? When—?

Then he seemed to hear a voice whispering beside him, a very soft, vibrant voice: "Oh, I'm such a poor little fool; do tell me when I do wrong."

The solution came in a flash and he had a quick, glad memory of Isabelle.

He found a blank space on his programme, and began to scribble rapidly:

"Here in the figured dark I watch once more,
 There, with the curtain, roll the years away;
 Two years of years—there was an idle day
 Of ours, when happy endings didn't bore
 Our unfermented souls; I could adore
  Your eager face beside me, wide-eyed, gay,
  Smiling a repertoire while the poor play
 Reached me as a faint ripple reaches shore.

089

"Yawning and wondering an evening through,
  I watch alone... and chatterings, of course,
  Spoil the one scene which, somehow, did have charms;
You wept a bit, and I grew sad for you
  Right here! Where Mr. X defends divorce
  And What's-Her-Name falls fainting in his arms."

STILL CALM

"Ghosts are such dumb things," said Alec, "they're slow-witted. I can always outguess a ghost."

"How?" asked Tom.

"Well, it depends where. Take a bedroom, for example. If you use any discretion a ghost can never get you in a bedroom."

"Go on, s'pose you think there's maybe a ghost in your bedroom—what measures do you take on getting home at night?" demanded Amory, interested.

"Take a stick" answered Alec, with ponderous reverence, "one about the length of a broom-handle. Now, the first thing to do is to get the room cleared—to do this you rush with your eyes closed into your study and turn on the lights—next, approaching the closet, carefully run the stick in the door three or four times. Then, if nothing happens, you can look in. Always, always run the stick in viciously first—never look first!"

"Of course, that's the ancient Celtic school," said Tom gravely.

"Yes—but they usually pray first. Anyway, you use this method to clear the closets and also for behind all doors—"

"And the bed," Amory suggested.

"Oh, Amory, no!" cried Alec in horror. "That isn't the way—the bed requires different tactics—let the bed alone, as you value your reason—if there is a ghost in the room and that's only about a third of the time, it is almost always under the bed."

"Well" Amory began.

Alec waved him into silence.

"Of course you never look. You stand in the middle of the floor and before he knows what you're going to do make a sudden leap for the bed—never walk near the bed; to a ghost your ankle is your most vulnerable part—once in bed, you're safe; he may lie around under the bed all night, but you're safe as daylight. If you still have doubts pull the blanket over your head."

"All that's very interesting, Tom."

"Isn't it?" Alec beamed proudly. "All my own, too—the Sir Oliver Lodge of the new world."

Amory was enjoying college immensely again. The sense of going forward in a direct, determined line had come back; youth was stirring and shaking out a few new feathers. He

CHAPTER 4   Narcissus Off Duty

had even stored enough surplus energy to sally into a new pose.

"What's the idea of all this 'distracted' stuff, Amory?" asked Alec one day, and then as Amory pretended to be cramped over his book in a daze: "Oh, don't try to act Burne, the mystic, to me."

Amory looked up innocently.

"What?"

"What?" mimicked Alec. "Are you trying to read yourself into a rhapsody with—let's see the book."

He snatched it; regarded it derisively.

"Well?" said Amory a little stiffly.

"'The Life of St. Teresa,'" read Alec aloud. "Oh, my gosh!"

"Say, Alec."

"What?"

"Does it bother you?"

"Does what bother me?"

"My acting dazed and all that?"

"Why, no—of course it doesn't bother me."

"Well, then, don't spoil it. If I enjoy going around telling people guilelessly that I think I'm a genius, let me do it."

"You're getting a reputation for being eccentric," said Alec, laughing, "if that's what you mean."

Amory finally prevailed, and Alec agreed to accept his face value in the presence of others if he was allowed rest periods when they were alone; so Amory "ran it out" at a great rate, bringing the most eccentric characters to dinner, wild-eyed grad students, preceptors with strange theories of God and government, to the cynical amazement of the supercilious Cottage Club.

As February became slashed by sun and moved cheerfully into March, Amory went several times to spend week-ends with Monsignor; once he took Burne, with great success, for he took equal pride and delight in displaying them to each other. Monsignor took him several times to see Thornton Hancock, and once or twice to the house of a Mrs. Lawrence, a type of Rome-haunting American whom Amory liked immediately.

Then one day came a letter from Monsignor, which appended an interesting P. S.:

"Do you know," it ran, "that your third cousin, Clara Page,
widowed six months and very poor, is living in Philadelphia?
I don't think you've ever met her, but I wish, as a favor to me,
you'd go to see her. To my mind, she's rather a remarkable woman,
and just about your age."

Amory sighed and decided to go, as a favor....

091

CLARA

She was immemorial.... Amory wasn't good enough for Clara, Clara of ripply golden hair, but then no man was. Her goodness was above the prosy morals of the husband-seeker, apart from the dull literature of female virtue.

Sorrow lay lightly around her, and when Amory found her in Philadelphia he thought her steely blue eyes held only happiness; a latent strength, a realism, was brought to its fullest development by the facts that she was compelled to face. She was alone in the world, with two small children, little money, and, worst of all, a host of friends. He saw her that winter in Philadelphia entertaining a houseful of men for an evening, when he knew she had not a servant in the house except the little colored girl guarding the babies overhead. He saw one of the greatest libertines in that city, a man who was habitually drunk and notorious at home and abroad, sitting opposite her for an evening, discussing girls' boarding-schools with a sort of innocent excitement. What a twist Clara had to her mind! She could make fascinating and almost brilliant conversation out of the thinnest air that ever floated through a drawing-room.

The idea that the girl was poverty-stricken had appealed to Amory's sense of situation. He arrived in Philadelphia expecting to be told that 921 Ark Street was in a miserable lane of hovels. He was even disappointed when it proved to be nothing of the sort. It was an old house that had been in her husband's family for years. An elderly aunt, who objected to having it sold, had put ten years' taxes with a lawyer and pranced off to Honolulu, leaving Clara to struggle with the heating-problem as best she could. So no wild-haired woman with a hungry baby at her breast and a sad Amelia-like look greeted him. Instead, Amory would have thought from his reception that she had not a care in the world.

A calm virility and a dreamy humor, marked contrasts to her level-headedness—into these moods she slipped sometimes as a refuge. She could do the most prosy things (though she was wise enough never to stultify herself with such "household arts" as knitting and embroidery), yet immediately afterward pick up a book and let her imagination rove as a formless cloud with the wind. Deepest of all in her personality was the golden radiance that she diffused around her. As an open fire in a dark room throws romance and pathos into the quiet faces at its edge, so she cast her lights and shadows around the rooms that held her, until she made of her prosy old uncle a man of quaint and meditative charm, metamorphosed the stray telegraph boy into a Puck-like creature of delightful originality. At first this quality of hers somehow irritated Amory. He considered his own uniqueness sufficient, and it rather embarrassed him when she tried to read new interests into him for the benefit of what other adorers were present. He felt as if a polite but insistent stage-manager were attempting to make him give a new interpretation of a part he had conned for years.

But Clara talking, Clara telling a slender tale of a hatpin and an inebriated man and herself.... People tried afterward to repeat her anecdotes but for the life of them they could

CHAPTER 4 Narcissus Off Duty

make them sound like nothing whatever. They gave her a sort of innocent attention and the best smiles many of them had smiled for long; there were few tears in Clara, but people smiled misty-eyed at her.

Very occasionally Amory stayed for little half-hours after the rest of the court had gone, and they would have bread and jam and tea late in the afternoon or "maple-sugar lunches," as she called them, at night.

"You are remarkable, aren't you!" Amory was becoming trite from where he perched in the centre of the dining-room table one six o'clock.

"Not a bit," she answered. She was searching out napkins in the sideboard. "I'm really most humdrum and commonplace. One of those people who have no interest in anything but their children."

"Tell that to somebody else," scoffed Amory. "You know you're perfectly effulgent." He asked her the one thing that he knew might embarrass her. It was the remark that the first bore made to Adam.

"Tell me about yourself." And she gave the answer that Adam must have given.

"There's nothing to tell."

But eventually Adam probably told the bore all the things he thought about at night when the locusts sang in the sandy grass, and he must have remarked patronizingly how different he was from Eve, forgetting how different she was from him... at any rate, Clara told Amory much about herself that evening. She had had a harried life from sixteen on, and her education had stopped sharply with her leisure. Browsing in her library, Amory found a tattered gray book out of which fell a yellow sheet that he impudently opened. It was a poem that she had written at school about a gray convent wall on a gray day, and a girl with her cloak blown by the wind sitting atop of it and thinking about the many-colored world. As a rule such sentiment bored him, but this was done with so much simplicity and atmosphere, that it brought a picture of Clara to his mind, of Clara on such a cool, gray day with her keen blue eyes staring out, trying to see her tragedies come marching over the gardens outside. He envied that poem. How he would have loved to have come along and seen her on the wall and talked nonsense or romance to her, perched above him in the air. He began to be frightfully jealous of everything about Clara: of her past, of her babies, of the men and women who flocked to drink deep of her cool kindness and rest their tired minds as at an absorbing play.

"Nobody seems to bore you," he objected.

"About half the world do," she admitted, "but I think that's a pretty good average, don't you?" and she turned to find something in Browning that bore on the subject. She was the only person he ever met who could look up passages and quotations to show him in the middle of the conversation, and yet not be irritating to distraction. She did it constantly, with such a serious enthusiasm that he grew fond of watching her golden hair bent over a book, brow wrinkled ever so little at hunting her sentence.

Through early March he took to going to Philadelphia for week-ends. Almost always there was some one else there and she seemed not anxious to see him alone, for many occasions presented themselves when a word from her would have given him another delicious half-hour of adoration. But he fell gradually in love and began to speculate wildly on marriage. Though this design flowed through his brain even to his lips, still he knew afterward that the desire had not been deeply rooted. Once he dreamt that it had come true and woke up in a cold panic, for in his dream she had been a silly, flaxen Clara, with the gold gone out of her hair and platitudes falling insipidly from her changeling tongue. But she was the first fine woman he ever knew and one of the few good people who ever interested him. She made her goodness such an asset. Amory had decided that most good people either dragged theirs after them as a liability, or else distorted it to artificial geniality, and of course there were the ever-present prig and Pharisee—(but Amory never included them as being among the saved).

ST. CECILIA

"Over her gray and velvet dress,
Under her molten, beaten hair,
Color of rose in mock distress
Flushes and fades and makes her fair;
Fills the air from her to him
With light and languor and little sighs,
Just so subtly he scarcely knows...
Laughing lightning, color of rose."

"Do you like me?"

"Of course I do," said Clara seriously.

"Why?"

"Well, we have some qualities in common. Things that are spontaneous in each of us—or were originally."

"You're implying that I haven't used myself very well?"

Clara hesitated.

"Well, I can't judge. A man, of course, has to go through a lot more, and I've been sheltered."

"Oh, don't stall, please, Clara," Amory interrupted; "but do talk about me a little, won't you?"

"Surely, I'd adore to." She didn't smile.

"That's sweet of you. First answer some questions. Am I painfully conceited?"

"Well—no, you have tremendous vanity, but it'll amuse the people who notice its preponderance."

"I see."

CHAPTER 4 Narcissus Off Duty

"You're really humble at heart. You sink to the third hell of depression when you think you've been slighted. In fact, you haven't much self-respect."

"Centre of target twice, Clara. How do you do it? You never let me say a word."

"Of course not—I can never judge a man while he's talking. But I'm not through; the reason you have so little real self-confidence, even though you gravely announce to the occasional philistine that you think you're a genius, is that you've attributed all sorts of atrocious faults to yourself and are trying to live up to them. For instance, you're always saying that you are a slave to high-balls."

"But I am, potentially."

"And you say you're a weak character, that you've no will."

"Not a bit of will—I'm a slave to my emotions, to my likes, to my hatred of boredom, to most of my desires—"

"You are not!" She brought one little fist down onto the other. "You're a slave, a bound helpless slave to one thing in the world, your imagination."

"You certainly interest me. If this isn't boring you, go on."

"I notice that when you want to stay over an extra day from college you go about it in a sure way. You never decide at first while the merits of going or staying are fairly clear in your mind. You let your imagination shinny on the side of your desires for a few hours, and then you decide. Naturally your imagination, after a little freedom, thinks up a million reasons why you should stay, so your decision when it comes isn't true. It's biassed."

"Yes," objected Amory, "but isn't it lack of will-power to let my imagination shinny on the wrong side?"

"My dear boy, there's your big mistake. This has nothing to do with will-power; that's a crazy, useless word, anyway; you lack judgment—the judgment to decide at once when you know your imagination will play you false, given half a chance."

"Well, I'll be darned!" exclaimed Amory in surprise, "that's the last thing I expected."

Clara didn't gloat. She changed the subject immediately. But she had started him thinking and he believed she was partly right. He felt like a factory-owner who after accusing a clerk of dishonesty finds that his own son, in the office, is changing the books once a week. His poor, mistreated will that he had been holding up to the scorn of himself and his friends, stood before him innocent, and his judgment walked off to prison with the unconfinable imp, imagination, dancing in mocking glee beside him. Clara's was the only advice he ever asked without dictating the answer himself—except, perhaps, in his talks with Monsignor Darcy.

How he loved to do any sort of thing with Clara! Shopping with her was a rare, epicurean dream. In every store where she had ever traded she was whispered about as the beautiful Mrs. Page.

"I'll bet she won't stay single long."

"Well, don't scream it out. She ain't lookin' for no advice."

"Ain't she beautiful!"

(Enter a floor-walker—silence till he moves forward, smirking.)

"Society person, ain't she?"

"Yeah, but poor now, I guess; so they say."

"Gee! girls, ain't she some kid!"

And Clara beamed on all alike. Amory believed that tradespeople gave her discounts, sometimes to her knowledge and sometimes without it. He knew she dressed very well, had always the best of everything in the house, and was inevitably waited upon by the head floor-walker at the very least.

Sometimes they would go to church together on Sunday and he would walk beside her and revel in her cheeks moist from the soft water in the new air. She was very devout, always had been, and God knows what heights she attained and what strength she drew down to herself when she knelt and bent her golden hair into the stained-glass light.

"St. Cecelia," he cried aloud one day, quite involuntarily, and the people turned and peered, and the priest paused in his sermon and Clara and Amory turned to fiery red.

That was the last Sunday they had, for he spoiled it all that night. He couldn't help it.

They were walking through the March twilight where it was as warm as June, and the joy of youth filled his soul so that he felt he must speak.

"I think," he said and his voice trembled, "that if I lost faith in you I'd lose faith in God."

She looked at him with such a startled face that he asked her the matter.

"Nothing," she said slowly, "only this: five men have said that to me before, and it frightens me."

"Oh, Clara, is that your fate!"

She did not answer.

"I suppose love to you is—" he began.

She turned like a flash.

"I have never been in love."

They walked along, and he realized slowly how much she had told him... never in love.... She seemed suddenly a daughter of light alone. His entity dropped out of her plane and he longed only to touch her dress with almost the realization that Joseph must have had of Mary's eternal significance. But quite mechanically he heard himself saying:

"And I love you—any latent greatness that I've got is... oh, I can't talk, but Clara, if I come back in two years in a position to marry you—"

She shook her head.

"No," she said; "I'd never marry again. I've got my two children and I want myself for them. I like you—I like all clever men, you more than any—but you know me well enough to know that I'd never marry a clever man—" She broke off suddenly.

"Amory."

"What?"

"You're not in love with me. You never wanted to marry me, did you?"

"It was the twilight," he said wonderingly. "I didn't feel as though I were speaking aloud. But I love you—or adore you—or worship you—"

"There you go—running through your catalogue of emotions in five seconds."

He smiled unwillingly.

"Don't make me out such a light-weight, Clara; you are depressing sometimes."

"You're not a light-weight, of all things," she said intently, taking his arm and opening wide her eyes—he could see their kindliness in the fading dusk. "A light-weight is an eternal nay."

"There's so much spring in the air—there's so much lazy sweetness in your heart."

She dropped his arm.

"You're all fine now, and I feel glorious. Give me a cigarette. You've never seen me smoke, have you? Well, I do, about once a month."

And then that wonderful girl and Amory raced to the corner like two mad children gone wild with pale-blue twilight.

"I'm going to the country for to-morrow," she announced, as she stood panting, safe beyond the flare of the corner lamp-post. "These days are too magnificent to miss, though perhaps I feel them more in the city."

"Oh, Clara!" Amory said; "what a devil you could have been if the Lord had just bent your soul a little the other way!"

"Maybe," she answered; "but I think not. I'm never really wild and never have been. That little outburst was pure spring."

"And you are, too," said he.

They were walking along now.

"No—you're wrong again, how can a person of your own self-reputed brains be so constantly wrong about me? I'm the opposite of everything spring ever stood for. It's unfortunate, if I happen to look like what pleased some soppy old Greek sculptor, but I assure you that if it weren't for my face I'd be a quiet nun in the convent without"—then she broke into a run and her raised voice floated back to him as he followed—"my precious babies, which I must go back and see."

She was the only girl he ever knew with whom he could understand how another man might be preferred. Often Amory met wives whom he had known as debutantes, and looking intently at them imagined that he found something in their faces which said:

"Oh, if I could only have gotten you!" Oh, the enormous conccit of the man!

But that night seemed a night of stars and singing and Clara's bright soul still gleamed on the ways they had trod.

"Golden, golden is the air—" he chanted to the little pools of water. ... "Golden is the air, golden notes from golden mandolins, golden frets of golden violins, fair, oh, wearily

097

fair.... Skeins from braided basket, mortals may not hold; oh, what young extravagant God, who would know or ask it?... who could give such gold..."

AMORY IS RESENTFUL

Slowly and inevitably, yet with a sudden surge at the last, while Amory talked and dreamed, war rolled swiftly up the beach and washed the sands where Princeton played. Every night the gymnasium echoed as platoon after platoon swept over the floor and shuffled out the basket-ball markings. When Amory went to Washington the next week-end he caught some of the spirit of crisis which changed to repulsion in the Pullman car coming back, for the berths across from him were occupied by stinking aliens—Greeks, he guessed, or Russians. He thought how much easier patriotism had been to a homogeneous race, how much easier it would have been to fight as the Colonies fought, or as the Confederacy fought. And he did no sleeping that night, but listened to the aliens guffaw and snore while they filled the car with the heavy scent of latest America.

In Princeton every one bantered in public and told themselves privately that their deaths at least would be heroic. The literary students read Rupert Brooke passionately; the lounge-lizards worried over whether the government would permit the English-cut uniform for officers; a few of the hopelessly lazy wrote to the obscure branches of the War Department, seeking an easy commission and a soft berth.

Then, after a week, Amory saw Burne and knew at once that argument would be futile—Burne had come out as a pacifist. The socialist magazines, a great smattering of Tolstoi, and his own intense longing for a cause that would bring out whatever strength lay in him, had finally decided him to preach peace as a subjective ideal.

"When the German army entered Belgium," he began, "if the inhabitants had gone peaceably about their business, the German army would have been disorganized in—"

"I know," Amory interrupted, "I've heard it all. But I'm not going to talk propaganda with you. There's a chance that you're right—but even so we're hundreds of years before the time when non-resistance can touch us as a reality."

"But, Amory, listen—"

"Burne, we'd just argue—"

"Very well."

"Just one thing—I don't ask you to think of your family or friends, because I know they don't count a picayune with you beside your sense of duty—but, Burne, how do you know that the magazines you read and the societies you join and these idealists you meet aren't just plain German?"

"Some of them are, of course."

"How do you know they aren't all pro-German—just a lot of weak ones—with German-Jewish names."

"That's the chance, of course," he said slowly. "How much or how little I'm taking this stand because of propaganda I've heard, I don't know; naturally I think that it's my most

CHAPTER 4 Narcissus Off Duty

innermost conviction—it seems a path spread before me just now."

Amory's heart sank.

"But think of the cheapness of it—no one's really going to martyr you for being a pacifist—it's just going to throw you in with the worst—"

"I doubt it," he interrupted.

"Well, it all smells of Bohemian New York to me."

"I know what you mean, and that's why I'm not sure I'll agitate."

"You're one man, Burne—going to talk to people who won't listen—with all God's given you."

"That's what Stephen must have thought many years ago. But he preached his sermon and they killed him. He probably thought as he was dying what a waste it all was. But you see, I've always felt that Stephen's death was the thing that occurred to Paul on the road to Damascus, and sent him to preach the word of Christ all over the world."

"Go on."

"That's all—this is my particular duty. Even if right now I'm just a pawn—just sacrificed. God! Amory—you don't think I like the Germans!"

"Well, I can't say anything else—I get to the end of all the logic about non-resistance, and there, like an excluded middle, stands the huge spectre of man as he is and always will be. And this spectre stands right beside the one logical necessity of Tolstoi's, and the other logical necessity of Nietzsche's—" Amory broke off suddenly. "When are you going?"

"I'm going next week."

"I'll see you, of course."

As he walked away it seemed to Amory that the look in his face bore a great resemblance to that in Kerry's when he had said good-by under Blair Arch two years before. Amory wondered unhappily why he could never go into anything with the primal honesty of those two.

"Burne's a fanatic," he said to Tom, "and he's dead wrong and, I'm inclined to think, just an unconscious pawn in the hands of anarchistic publishers and German-paid rag wavers—but he haunts me—just leaving everything worth while—"

Burne left in a quietly dramatic manner a week later. He sold all his possessions and came down to the room to say good-by, with a battered old bicycle, on which he intended to ride to his home in Pennsylvania.

"Peter the Hermit bidding farewell to Cardinal Richelieu," suggested Alec, who was lounging in the window-seat as Burne and Amory shook hands.

But Amory was not in a mood for that, and as he saw Burne's long legs propel his ridiculous bicycle out of sight beyond Alexander Hall, he knew he was going to have a bad week. Not that he doubted the war—Germany stood for everything repugnant to him; for materialism and the direction of tremendous licentious force; it was just that Burne's face stayed in his memory and he was sick of the hysteria he was beginning to hear.

"What on earth is the use of suddenly running down Goethe," he declared to Alec and Tom. "Why write books to prove he started the war—or that that stupid, overestimated Schiller is a demon in disguise?"

"Have you ever read anything of theirs?" asked Tom shrewdly.

"No," Amory admitted.

"Neither have I," he said laughing.

"People will shout," said Alec quietly, "but Goethe's on his same old shelf in the library—to bore any one that wants to read him!"

Amory subsided, and the subject dropped.

"What are you going to do, Amory?"

"Infantry or aviation, I can't make up my mind—I hate mechanics, but then of course aviation's the thing for me—"

"I feel as Amory does," said Tom. "Infantry or aviation—aviation sounds like the romantic side of the war, of course—like cavalry used to be, you know; but like Amory I don't know a horse-power from a piston-rod."

Somehow Amory's dissatisfaction with his lack of enthusiasm culminated in an attempt to put the blame for the whole war on the ancestors of his generation... all the people who cheered for Germany in 1870.... All the materialists rampant, all the idolizers of German science and efficiency. So he sat one day in an English lecture and heard "Locksley Hall" quoted and fell into a brown study with contempt for Tennyson and all he stood for—for he took him as a representative of the Victorians.

Victorians, Victorians, who never learned to weep

Who sowed the bitter harvest that your children go to reap—

scribbled Amory in his note-book. The lecturer was saying something about Tennyson's solidity and fifty heads were bent to take notes. Amory turned over to a fresh page and began scrawling again.

"They shuddered when they found what Mr. Darwin was about,

They shuddered when the waltz came in and Newman hurried out—"

But the waltz came in much earlier; he crossed that out.

"And entitled A Song in the Time of Order," came the professor's voice, droning far away. "Time of Order"—Good Lord! Everything crammed in the box and the Victorians sitting on the lid smiling serenely.... With Browning in his Italian villa crying bravely: "All's for the best." Amory scribbled again.

"You knelt up in the temple and he bent to hear you pray,

You thanked him for your 'glorious gains'—reproached him for

'Cathay.'"

Why could he never get more than a couplet at a time? Now he needed something to rhyme with:

> "You would keep Him straight with science, tho He had gone wrong before..."

Well, anyway....

> "You met your children in your home—'I've fixed it up!' you cried,
> Took your fifty years of Europe, and then virtuously—died."

"That was to a great extent Tennyson's idea," came the lecturer's voice. "Swinburne's Song in the Time of Order might well have been Tennyson's title. He idealized order against chaos, against waste."

At last Amory had it. He turned over another page and scrawled vigorously for the twenty minutes that was left of the hour. Then he walked up to the desk and deposited a page torn out of his note-book.

"Here's a poem to the Victorians, sir," he said coldly.

The professor picked it up curiously while Amory backed rapidly through the door.

Here is what he had written:
"Songs in the time of order
You left for us to sing,
Proofs with excluded middles,
Answers to life in rhyme,
Keys of the prison warder
And ancient bells to ring,
Time was the end of riddles,
We were the end of time...

Here were domestic oceans
And a sky that we might reach,
Guns and a guarded border,
Gauntlets—but not to fling,
Thousands of old emotions
And a platitude for each,
Songs in the time of order—
And tongues, that we might sing."

THE END OF MANY THINGS

Early April slipped by in a haze—a haze of long evenings on the club veranda with the graphophone playing "Poor Butterfly" inside... for "Poor Butterfly" had been the song of that last year. The war seemed scarcely to touch them and it might have been one of the senior springs of the past, except for the drilling every other afternoon, yet Amory realized poignantly that this was the last spring under the old regime.

"This is the great protest against the superman," said Amory.

"I suppose so," Alec agreed.

"He's absolutely irreconcilable with any Utopia. As long as he occurs, there's trouble and all the latent evil that makes a crowd list and sway when he talks."

"And of course all that he is is a gifted man without a moral sense."

"That's all. I think the worst thing to contemplate is this—it's all happened before, how soon will it happen again? Fifty years after Waterloo Napoleon was as much a hero to English school children as Wellington. How do we know our grandchildren won't idolize Von Hindenburg the same way?"

"What brings it about?"

"Time, damn it, and the historian. If we could only learn to look on evil as evil, whether it's clothed in filth or monotony or magnificence."

"God! Haven't we raked the universe over the coals for four years?"

Then the night came that was to be the last. Tom and Amory, bound in the morning for different training-camps, paced the shadowy walks as usual and seemed still to see around them the faces of the men they knew.

"The grass is full of ghosts to-night."

"The whole campus is alive with them."

They paused by Little and watched the moon rise, to make silver of the slate roof of Dodd and blue the rustling trees.

"You know," whispered Tom, "what we feel now is the sense of all the gorgeous youth that has rioted through here in two hundred years."

A last burst of singing flooded up from Blair Arch—broken voices for some long parting.

"And what we leave here is more than this class; it's the whole heritage of youth. We're just one generation—we're breaking all the links that seemed to bind us here to top-booted and high-stocked generations. We've walked arm and arm with Burr and Light-Horse Harry Lee through half these deep-blue nights."

"That's what they are," Tom tangented off, "deep blue—a bit of color would spoil them, make them exotic. Spires, against a sky that's a promise of dawn, and blue light on the slate roofs—it hurts... rather—"

"Good-by, Aaron Burr," Amory called toward deserted Nassau Hall, "you and I knew strange corners of life."

His voice echoed in the stillness.

"The torches are out," whispered Tom. "Ah, Messalina, the long shadows are building minarets on the stadium—"

For an instant the voices of freshman year surged around them and then they looked at

102

each other with faint tears in their eyes.

"Damn!"

"Damn!"

The last light fades and drifts across the land—the low, long land, the sunny land of spires; the ghosts of evening tune again their lyres and wander singing in a plaintive band down the long corridors of trees; pale fires echo the night from tower top to tower: Oh, sleep that dreams, and dream that never tires, press from the petals of the lotus flower something of this to keep, the essence of an hour.

No more to wait the twilight of the moon in this sequestered vale of star and spire, for one eternal morning of desire passes to time and earthy afternoon. Here, Heraclitus, did you find in fire and shifting things the prophecy you hurled down the dead years; this midnight my desire will see, shadowed among the embers, furled in flame, the splendor and the sadness of the world.

INTERLUDE

May, 1917-February, 1919

A letter dated January, 1918, written by Monsignor Darcy to Amory, who is a second lieutenant in the 171st Infantry, Port of Embarkation, Camp Mills, Long Island.

MY DEAR BOY:

All you need tell me of yourself is that you still are; for the rest I merely search back in a restive memory, a thermometer that records only fevers, and match you with what I was at your age. But men will chatter and you and I will still shout our futilities to each other across the stage until the last silly curtain falls plump! upon our bobbing heads. But you are starting the spluttering magic-lantern show of life with much the same array of slides as I had, so I need to write you if only to shriek the colossal stupidity of people....

This is the end of one thing: for better or worse you will never again be quite the Amory Blaine that I knew, never again will we meet as we have met, because your generation is growing hard, much harder than mine ever grew, nourished as they were on the stuff of the nineties.

Amory, lately I reread Aeschylus and there in the divine irony of the "Agamemnon" I find the only answer to this bitter age—all the world tumbled about our ears, and the closest parallel ages back in that hopeless resignation. There are times when I think of the men out there as Roman legionaries, miles from their corrupt city, stemming back the hordes... hordes a little more menacing, after all, than the corrupt city... another blind blow at the race, furies that we passed with ovations years ago, over whose corpses we bleated triumphantly all through the Victorian era....

And afterward an out-and-out materialistic world—and the Catholic Church. I wonder where you'll fit in. Of one thing I'm sure—Celtic you'll live and Celtic you'll die; so if you don't use heaven as a continual referendum for your ideas you'll find earth a continual recall to your ambitions.

Amory, I've discovered suddenly that I'm an old man. Like all old men, I've had dreams sometimes and I'm going to tell you of them. I've enjoyed imagining that you were my son, that perhaps when I was young I went into a state of coma and begat you, and when I came to, had no recollection of it... it's the paternal instinct, Amory—celibacy goes deeper than the flesh....

Sometimes I think that the explanation of our deep resemblance is some common ancestor, and I find that the only blood that the Darcys and the O'Haras have in common is that of the O'Donahues... Stephen was his name, I think....

When the lightning strikes one of us it strikes both: you had hardly arrived at the port of embarkation when I got my papers to start for Rome, and I am waiting every moment to be told where to take ship. Even before you get this letter I shall be on the ocean; then will come your turn. You went to war as a gentleman should, just as you went to school and college, because it was the thing to do. It's better to leave the blustering and tremulo-heroism to the middle classes; they do it so much better.

Do you remember that week-end last March when you brought Burne Holiday from Princeton to see me? What a magnificent boy he is! It gave me a frightful shock afterward when you wrote that he thought me splendid; how could he be so deceived? Splendid is the one thing that neither you nor I are. We are many other things—we're extraordinary, we're clever, we could be said, I suppose, to be brilliant. We can attract people, we can make atmosphere, we can almost lose our Celtic souls in Celtic subtleties, we can almost always have our own way; but splendid—rather not!

I am going to Rome with a wonderful dossier and letters of introduction that cover every capital in Europe, and there will be "no small stir" when I get there. How I wish you were with me! This sounds like a rather cynical paragraph, not at all the sort of thing that a middle-aged clergyman should write to a youth about to depart for the war; the only excuse is that the middle-aged clergyman is talking to himself. There are deep things in us and you know what they are as well as I do. We have great faith, though yours at present is uncrystallized; we have a terrible honesty that all our sophistry cannot destroy and, above all, a childlike simplicity that keeps us from ever being really malicious.

I have written a keen for you which follows. I am sorry your cheeks are not up to the description I have written of them, but you will smoke and read all night—

At any rate here it is:

A Lament for a Foster Son, and He going to the War Against the King of Foreign.

"Ochone

He is gone from me the son of my mind

And he in his golden youth like Angus Oge
Angus of the bright birds
And his mind strong and subtle like the mind of Cuchulin on Muirtheme.

Awirra sthrue
His brow is as white as the milk of the cows of Maeve
And his cheeks like the cherries of the tree
And it bending down to Mary and she feeding the Son of God.

Aveelia Vrone
His hair is like the golden collar of the Kings at Tara
And his eyes like the four gray seas of Erin.
And they swept with the mists of rain.

Mavrone go Gudyo
He to be in the joyful and red battle
Amongst the chieftains and they doing great deeds of valor
His life to go from him
It is the chords of my own soul would be loosed.

A Vich Deelish
My heart is in the heart of my son
And my life is in his life surely
A man can be twice young
In the life of his sons only.

Jia du Vaha Alanav
May the Son of God be above him and beneath him, before him and behind him
May the King of the elements cast a mist over the eyes of the King of Foreign,
May the Queen of the Graces lead him by the hand the way he can go through the midst of his enemies and they not seeing him

May Patrick of the Gael and Collumb of the Churches and the five thousand Saints of Erin be better than a shield to him
And he got into the fight.
Och Ochone."

Amory—Amory—I feel, somehow, that this is all; one or both of us is not going to last out this war.... I've been trying to tell you how much this reincarnation of myself in you has meant in the last few years... curiously alike we are... curiously unlike. Good-by, dear boy, and God be with you. THAYER DARCY.

EMBARKING AT NIGHT

Amory moved forward on the deck until he found a stool under an electric light. He searched in his pocket for note-book and pencil and then began to write, slowly, laboriously:

"We leave to-night...
Silent, we filled the still, deserted street,
A column of dim gray,
And ghosts rose startled at the muffled beat
Along the moonless way;
The shadowy shipyards echoed to the feet
That turned from night and day.

And so we linger on the windless decks,
See on the spectre shore
Shades of a thousand days, poor gray-ribbed wrecks...
Oh, shall we then deplore
Those futile years!
See how the sea is white!
The clouds have broken and the heavens burn
To hollow highways, paved with gravelled light
The churning of the waves about the stern
Rises to one voluminous nocturne,
... We leave to-night."

A letter from Amory, headed "Brest, March 11th, 1919," to Lieutenant T. P. D'Invilliers, Camp Gordon, Ga.

DEAR BAUDELAIRE:—

We meet in Manhattan on the 30th of this very mo.; we then proceed to take a very sporty apartment, you and I and Alec, who is at me elbow as I write. I don't know what I'm going to do but I have a vague dream of going into politics. Why is it that the pick of the young Englishmen from Oxford and Cambridge go into politics and in the U. S. A. we leave it to the muckers?—raised in the ward, educated in the assembly and sent to Congress, fat-paunched bundles of corruption, devoid of "both ideas and ideals" as the debaters used to say. Even forty years ago we had good men in politics, but we, we are brought up to pile up a million and "show what we are made of." Sometimes I wish I'd been an Englishman;

American life is so damned dumb and stupid and healthy.

Since poor Beatrice died I'll probably have a little money, but very darn little. I can forgive mother almost everything except the fact that in a sudden burst of religiosity toward the end, she left half of what remained to be spent in stained-glass windows and seminary endowments. Mr. Barton, my lawyer, writes me that my thousands are mostly in street railways and that the said Street R.R. s are losing money because of the five-cent fares. Imagine a salary list that gives $350 a month to a man that can't read and write!—yet I believe in it, even though I've seen what was once a sizable fortune melt away between speculation, extravagance, the democratic administration, and the income tax—modern, that's me all over, Mabel.

At any rate we'll have really knock-out rooms—you can get a job on some fashion magazine, and Alec can go into the Zinc Company or whatever it is that his people own— he's looking over my shoulder and he says it's a brass company, but I don't think it matters much, do you? There's probably as much corruption in zinc-made money as brass-made money. As for the well-known Amory, he would write immortal literature if he were sure enough about anything to risk telling any one else about it. There is no more dangerous gift to posterity than a few cleverly turned platitudes.

Tom, why don't you become a Catholic? Of course to be a good one you'd have to give up those violent intrigues you used to tell me about, but you'd write better poetry if you were linked up to tall golden candlesticks and long, even chants, and even if the American priests are rather burgeois, as Beatrice used to say, still you need only go to the sporty churches, and I'll introduce you to Monsignor Darcy who really is a wonder.

Kerry's death was a blow, so was Jesse's to a certain extent. And I have a great curiosity to know what queer corner of the world has swallowed Burne. Do you suppose he's in prison under some false name? I confess that the war instead of making me orthodox, which is the correct reaction, has made me a passionate agnostic. The Catholic Church has had its wings clipped so often lately that its part was timidly negligible, and they haven't any good writers any more. I'm sick of Chesterton.

I've only discovered one soldier who passed through the much-advertised spiritual crisis, like this fellow, Donald Hankey, and the one I knew was already studying for the ministry, so he was ripe for it. I honestly think that's all pretty much rot, though it seemed to give sentimental comfort to those at home; and may make fathers and mothers appreciate their children. This crisis-inspired religion is rather valueless and fleeting at best. I think four men have discovered Paris to one that discovered God.

But us—you and me and Alec—oh, we'll get a Jap butler and dress for dinner and have wine on the table and lead a contemplative, emotionless life until we decide to use machine-guns with the property owners—or throw bombs with the Bolshevik God! Tom, I hope something happens. I'm restless as the devil and have a horror of getting fat or falling in love and growing domestic.

The place at Lake Geneva is now for rent but when I land I'm going West to see Mr. Barton and get some details. Write me care of the Blackstone, Chicago.

S'ever, dear Boswell,

SAMUEL JOHNSON.

BOOK TWO

The Education of a Personage

CHAPTER 1 | The Debutante

The time is February. The place is a large, dainty bedroom in the Connage house on Sixty-eighth Street, New York. A girl's room: pink walls and curtains and a pink bedspread on a cream-colored bed. Pink and cream are the motifs of the room, but the only article of furniture in full view is a luxurious dressing-table with a glass top and a three-sided mirror. On the walls there is an expensive print of "Cherry Ripe," a few polite dogs by Landseer, and the "King of the Black Isles," by Maxfield Parrish.

Great disorder consisting of the following items: (1) seven or eight empty cardboard boxes, with tissue-paper tongues hanging panting from their mouths; (2) an assortment of street dresses mingled with their sisters of the evening, all upon the table, all evidently new; (3) a roll of tulle, which has lost its dignity and wound itself tortuously around everything in sight, and (4) upon the two small chairs, a collection of lingerie that beggars description. One would enjoy seeing the bill called forth by the finery displayed and one is possessed by a desire to see the princess for whose benefit—Look! There's some one! Disappointment! This is only a maid hunting for something—she lifts a heap from a chair—Not there; another heap, the dressing-table, the chiffonier drawers. She brings to light several beautiful chemises and an amazing pajama but this does not satisfy her—she goes out.

An indistinguishable mumble from the next room.

Now, we are getting warm. This is Alec's mother, Mrs. Connage, ample, dignified, rouged to the dowager point and quite worn out. Her lips move significantly as she looks for IT. Her search is less thorough than the maid's but there is a touch of fury in it, that quite makes up for its sketchiness. She stumbles on the tulle and her "damn" is quite audible. She retires, empty-handed.

More chatter outside and a girl's voice, a very spoiled voice, says: "Of all the stupid people—"

After a pause a third seeker enters, not she of the spoiled voice, but a younger edition. This is Cecelia Connage, sixteen, pretty, shrewd, and constitutionally good-humored. She is dressed for the evening in a gown the obvious simplicity of which probably bores her. She goes to the nearest pile, selects a small pink garment and holds it up appraisingly.

CECELIA: Pink?
ROSALIND: (Outside) Yes!
CECELIA: Very snappy?
ROSALIND: Yes!
CECELIA: I've got it!

CHAPTER 1 The Debutante

(She sees herself in the mirror of the dressing-table and commences to shimmy enthusiastically.)

ROSALIND: (Outside) What are you doing—trying it on?

(CECELIA ceases and goes out carrying the garment at the right shoulder.

From the other door, enters ALEC CONNAGE. He looks around quickly and in a huge voice shouts: Mama! There is a chorus of protest from next door and encouraged he starts toward it, but is repelled by another chorus.)

ALEC: So that's where you all are! Amory Blaine is here.

CECELIA: (Quickly) Take him down-stairs.

ALEC: Oh, he is down-stairs.

MRS. CONNAGE: Well, you can show him where his room is. Tell him I'm sorry that I can't meet him now.

ALEC: He's heard a lot about you all. I wish you'd hurry. Father's telling him all about the war and he's restless. He's sort of temperamental.

(This last suffices to draw CECELIA into the room.)

CECELIA: (Seating herself high upon lingerie) How do you mean—temperamental? You used to say that about him in letters.

ALEC: Oh, he writes stuff.

CECELIA: Does he play the piano?

ALEC: Don't think so.

CECELIA: (Speculatively) Drink?

ALEC: Yes—nothing queer about him.

CECELIA: Money?

ALEC: Good Lord—ask him, he used to have a lot, and he's got some income now.

(MRS. CONNAGE appears.)

MRS. CONNAGE: Alec, of course we're glad to have any friend of yours—

ALEC: You certainly ought to meet Amory.

MRS. CONNAGE: Of course, I want to. But I think it's so childish of you to leave a perfectly good home to go and live with two other boys in some impossible apartment. I hope it isn't in order that you can all drink as much as you want. (She pauses.) He'll be a little neglected to-night. This is Rosalind's week, you see. When a girl comes out, she needs all the attention.

ROSALIND: (Outside) Well, then, prove it by coming here and hooking me.

(MRS. CONNAGE goes.)

ALEC: Rosalind hasn't changed a bit.

CECELIA: (In a lower tone) She's awfully spoiled.

ALEC: She'll meet her match to-night.

CECELIA: Who—Mr. Amory Blaine?

(ALEC nods.)

111

CECELIA: Well, Rosalind has still to meet the man she can't outdistance. Honestly, Alec, she treats men terribly. She abuses them and cuts them and breaks dates with them and yawns in their faces—and they come back for more.

ALEC: They love it.

CECELIA: They hate it. She's a—she's a sort of vampire, I think—and she can make girls do what she wants usually—only she hates girls.

ALEC: Personality runs in our family.

CECELIA: (Resignedly) I guess it ran out before it got to me.

ALEC: Does Rosalind behave herself?

CECELIA: Not particularly well. Oh, she's average—smokes sometimes, drinks punch, frequently kissed—Oh, yes—common knowledge—one of the effects of the war, you know.

(Emerges MRS. CONNAGE.)

MRS. CONNAGE: Rosalind's almost finished so I can go down and meet your friend.

(ALEC and his mother go out.)

ROSALIND: (Outside) Oh, mother—

CECELIA: Mother's gone down.

(And now ROSALIND enters. ROSALIND is—utterly ROSALIND. She is one of those girls who need never make the slightest effort to have men fall in love with them. Two types of men seldom do: dull men are usually afraid of her cleverness and intellectual men are usually afraid of her beauty. All others are hers by natural prerogative.

If ROSALIND could be spoiled the process would have been complete by this time, and as a matter of fact, her disposition is not all it should be; she wants what she wants when she wants it and she is prone to make every one around her pretty miserable when she doesn't get it—but in the true sense she is not spoiled. Her fresh enthusiasm, her will to grow and learn, her endless faith in the inexhaustibility of romance, her courage and fundamental honesty—these things are not spoiled.

There are long periods when she cordially loathes her whole family. She is quite unprincipled; her philosophy is carpe diem for herself and laissez faire for others. She loves shocking stories: she has that coarse streak that usually goes with natures that are both fine and big. She wants people to like her, but if they do not it never worries her or changes her. She is by no means a model character.

The education of all beautiful women is the knowledge of men. ROSALIND had been disappointed in man after man as individuals, but she had great faith in man as a sex. Women she detested. They represented qualities that she felt and despised in herself— incipient meanness, conceit, cowardice, and petty dishonesty. She once told a roomful of her mother's friends that the only excuse for women was the necessity for a disturbing element among men. She danced exceptionally well, drew cleverly but hastily, and had a startling facility with words, which she used only in love-letters.

But all criticism of ROSALIND ends in her beauty. There was that shade of glorious

CHAPTER 1   The Debutante

yellow hair, the desire to imitate which supports the dye industry. There was the eternal kissable mouth, small, slightly sensual, and utterly disturbing. There were gray eyes and an unimpeachable skin with two spots of vanishing color. She was slender and athletic, without underdevelopment, and it was a delight to watch her move about a room, walk along a street, swing a golf club, or turn a "cartwheel."

A last qualification—her vivid, instant personality escaped that conscious, theatrical quality that AMORY had found in ISABELLE. MONSIGNOR DARCY would have been quite up a tree whether to call her a personality or a personage. She was perhaps the delicious, inexpressible, once-in-a-century blend.

On the night of her debut she is, for all her strange, stray wisdom, quite like a happy little girl. Her mother's maid has just done her hair, but she has decided impatiently that she can do a better job herself. She is too nervous just now to stay in one place. To that we owe her presence in this littered room. She is going to speak. ISABELLE'S alto tones had been like a violin, but if you could hear ROSALIND, you would say her voice was musical as a waterfall.)

ROSALIND: Honestly, there are only two costumes in the world that I really enjoy being in—(Combing her hair at the dressing-table.) One's a hoop skirt with pantaloons; the other's a one-piece bathing-suit. I'm quite charming in both of them.

CECELIA: Glad you're coming out?

ROSALIND: Yes; aren't you?

CECELIA: (Cynically) You're glad so you can get married and live on Long Island with the fast younger married set. You want life to be a chain of flirtation with a man for every link.

ROSALIND: Want it to be one! You mean I've found it one.

CECELIA: Ha!

ROSALIND: Cecelia, darling, you don't know what a trial it is to be—like me. I've got to keep my face like steel in the street to keep men from winking at me. If I laugh hard from a front row in the theatre, the comedian plays to me for the rest of the evening. If I drop my voice, my eyes, my handkerchief at a dance, my partner calls me up on the 'phone every day for a week.

CECELIA: It must be an awful strain.

ROSALIND: The unfortunate part is that the only men who interest me at all are the totally ineligible ones. Now—if I were poor I'd go on the stage.

CECELIA: Yes, you might as well get paid for the amount of acting you do.

ROSALIND: Sometimes when I've felt particularly radiant I've thought, why should this be wasted on one man?

CECELIA: Often when you're particularly sulky, I've wondered why it should all be wasted on just one family. (Getting up.) I think I'll go down and meet Mr. Amory Blaine. I like temperamental men.

113

ROSALIND: There aren't any. Men don't know how to be really angry or really happy—and the ones that do, go to pieces.

CECELIA: Well, I'm glad I don't have all your worries. I'm engaged.

ROSALIND: (With a scornful smile) Engaged? Why, you little lunatic! If mother heard you talking like that she'd send you off to boarding-school, where you belong.

CECELIA: You won't tell her, though, because I know things I could tell—and you're too selfish!

ROSALIND: (A little annoyed) Run along, little girl! Who are you engaged to, the iceman? the man that keeps the candy-store?

CECELIA: Cheap wit—good-by, darling, I'll see you later.

ROSALIND: Oh, be sure and do that—you're such a help.

(Exit CECELIA. ROSALIND finished her hair and rises, humming. She goes up to the mirror and starts to dance in front of it on the soft carpet. She watches not her feet, but her eyes—never casually but always intently, even when she smiles. The door suddenly opens and then slams behind AMORY, very cool and handsome as usual. He melts into instant confusion.)

HE: Oh, I'm sorry. I thought—

SHE: (Smiling radiantly) Oh, you're Amory Blaine, aren't you?

HE: (Regarding her closely) And you're Rosalind?

SHE: I'm going to call you Amory—oh, come in—it's all right—mother'll be right in—(under her breath) unfortunately.

HE: (Gazing around) This is sort of a new wrinkle for me.

SHE: This is No Man's Land.

HE: This is where you—you—(pause)

SHE: Yes—all those things. (She crosses to the bureau.) See, here's my rouge—eye pencils.

HE: I didn't know you were that way.

SHE: What did you expect?

HE: I thought you'd be sort of—sort of—sexless, you know, swim and play golf.

SHE: Oh, I do—but not in business hours.

HE: Business?

SHE: Six to two—strictly.

HE: I'd like to have some stock in the corporation.

SHE: Oh, it's not a corporation—it's just "Rosalind, Unlimited." Fifty-one shares, name, good-will, and everything goes at $25,000 a year.

HE: (Disapprovingly) Sort of a chilly proposition.

SHE: Well, Amory, you don't mind—do you? When I meet a man that doesn't bore me to death after two weeks, perhaps it'll be different.

HE: Odd, you have the same point of view on men that I have on women.

CHAPTER 1 The Debutante

SHE: I'm not really feminine, you know—in my mind.

HE: (Interested) Go on.

SHE: No, you—you go on—you've made me talk about myself. That's against the rules.

HE: Rules?

SHE: My own rules—but you—Oh, Amory, I hear you're brilliant. The family expects so much of you.

HE: How encouraging!

SHE: Alec said you'd taught him to think. Did you? I didn't believe any one could.

HE: No. I'm really quite dull.

(He evidently doesn't intend this to be taken seriously.)

SHE: Liar.

HE: I'm—I'm religious—I'm literary. I've—I've even written poems.

SHE: Vers libre—splendid! (She declaims.)

"The trees are green,

The birds are singing in the trees,

The girl sips her poison

The bird flies away the girl dies."

HE: (Laughing) No, not that kind.

SHE: (Suddenly) I like you.

HE: Don't.

SHE: Modest too—

HE: I'm afraid of you. I'm always afraid of a girl—until I've kissed her.

SHE: (Emphatically) My dear boy, the war is over.

HE: So I'll always be afraid of you.

SHE: (Rather sadly) I suppose you will.

(A slight hesitation on both their parts.)

HE: (After due consideration) Listen. This is a frightful thing to ask.

SHE: (Knowing what's coming) After five minutes.

HE: But will you—kiss me? Or are you afraid?

SHE: I'm never afraid—but your reasons are so poor.

HE: Rosalind, I really want to kiss you.

SHE: So do I.

(They kiss—definitely and thoroughly.)

HE: (After a breathless second) Well, is your curiosity satisfied?

SHE: Is yours?

HE: No, it's only aroused.

(He looks it.)

115

SHE: (Dreamily) I've kissed dozens of men. I suppose I'll kiss dozens more.

HE: (Abstractedly) Yes, I suppose you could—like that.

SHE: Most people like the way I kiss.

HE: (Remembering himself) Good Lord, yes. Kiss me once more, Rosalind.

SHE: No—my curiosity is generally satisfied at one.

HE: (Discouraged) Is that a rule?

SHE: I make rules to fit the cases.

HE: You and I are somewhat alike—except that I'm years older in experience.

SHE: How old are you?

HE: Almost twenty-three. You?

SHE: Nineteen—just.

HE: I suppose you're the product of a fashionable school.

SHE: No—I'm fairly raw material. I was expelled from Spence—I've forgotten why.

HE: What's your general trend?

SHE: Oh, I'm bright, quite selfish, emotional when aroused, fond of admiration—

HE: (Suddenly) I don't want to fall in love with you—

SHE: (Raising her eyebrows) Nobody asked you to.

HE: (Continuing coldly) But I probably will. I love your mouth.

SHE: Hush! Please don't fall in love with my mouth—hair, eyes, shoulders, slippers—but not my mouth. Everybody falls in love with my mouth.

HE: It's quite beautiful.

SHE: It's too small.

HE: No it isn't—let's see.

(He kisses her again with the same thoroughness.)

SHE: (Rather moved) Say something sweet.

HE: (Frightened) Lord help me.

SHE: (Drawing away) Well, don't—if it's so hard.

HE: Shall we pretend? So soon?

SHE: We haven't the same standards of time as other people.

HE: Already it's—other people.

SHE: Let's pretend.

HE: No—I can't—it's sentiment.

SHE: You're not sentimental?

HE: No, I'm romantic—a sentimental person thinks things will last—a romantic person hopes against hope that they won't. Sentiment is emotional.

SHE: And you're not? (With her eyes half-closed.) You probably flatter yourself that that's a superior attitude.

HE: Well—Rosalind, Rosalind, don't argue—kiss me again.

SHE: (Quite chilly now) No—I have no desire to kiss you.

116

CHAPTER 1 The Debutante

HE: (Openly taken aback) You wanted to kiss me a minute ago.

SHE: This is now.

HE: I'd better go.

SHE: I suppose so.

(He goes toward the door.)

SHE: Oh!

(He turns.)

SHE: (Laughing) Score—Home Team: One hundred—Opponents: Zero.

(He starts back.)

SHE: (Quickly) Rain—no game.

(He goes out.)

(She goes quietly to the chiffonier, takes out a cigarette-case and hides it in the side drawer of a desk. Her mother enters, note-book in hand.)

MRS. CONNAGE: Good—I've been wanting to speak to you alone before we go down-stairs.

ROSALIND: Heavens! you frighten me!

MRS. CONNAGE: Rosalind, you've been a very expensive proposition.

ROSALIND: (Resignedly) Yes.

MRS. CONNAGE: And you know your father hasn't what he once had.

ROSALIND: (Making a wry face) Oh, please don't talk about money.

MRS. CONNAGE: You can't do anything without it. This is our last year in this house—and unless things change Cecelia won't have the advantages you've had.

ROSALIND: (Impatiently) Well—what is it?

MRS. CONNAGE: So I ask you to please mind me in several things I've put down in my note-book. The first one is: don't disappear with young men. There may be a time when it's valuable, but at present I want you on the dance-floor where I can find you. There are certain men I want to have you meet and I don't like finding you in some corner of the conservatory exchanging silliness with any one—or listening to it.

ROSALIND: (Sarcastically) Yes, listening to it is better.

MRS. CONNAGE: And don't waste a lot of time with the college set—little boys nineteen and twenty years old. I don't mind a prom or a football game, but staying away from advantageous parties to eat in little cafes down-town with Tom, Dick, and Harry—

ROSALIND: (Offering her code, which is, in its way, quite as high as her mother's) Mother, it's done—you can't run everything now the way you did in the early nineties.

MRS. CONNAGE: (Paying no attention) There are several bachelor friends of your father's that I want you to meet to-night—youngish men.

ROSALIND: (Nodding wisely) About forty-five?

MRS. CONNAGE: (Sharply) Why not?

ROSALIND: Oh, quite all right—they know life and are so adorably tired looking

117

(shakes her head)—but they will dance.

MRS. CONNAGE: I haven't met Mr. Blaine—but I don't think you'll care for him. He doesn't sound like a money-maker.

ROSALIND: Mother, I never think about money.

MRS. CONNAGE: You never keep it long enough to think about it.

ROSALIND: (Sighs) Yes, I suppose some day I'll marry a ton of it—out of sheer boredom.

MRS. CONNAGE: (Referring to note-book) I had a wire from Hartford. Dawson Ryder is coming up. Now there's a young man I like, and he's floating in money. It seems to me that since you seem tired of Howard Gillespie you might give Mr. Ryder some encouragement. This is the third time he's been up in a month.

ROSALIND: How did you know I was tired of Howard Gillespie?

MRS. CONNAGE: The poor boy looks so miserable every time he comes.

ROSALIND: That was one of those romantic, pre-battle affairs. They're all wrong.

MRS. CONNAGE: (Her say said) At any rate, make us proud of you to-night.

ROSALIND: Don't you think I'm beautiful?

MRS. CONNAGE: You know you are.

(From down-stairs is heard the moan of a violin being tuned, the roll of a drum. MRS. CONNAGE turns quickly to her daughter.)

MRS. CONNAGE: Come!

ROSALIND: One minute!

(Her mother leaves. ROSALIND goes to the glass where she gazes at herself with great satisfaction. She kisses her hand and touches her mirrored mouth with it. Then she turns out the lights and leaves the room. Silence for a moment. A few chords from the piano, the discreet patter of faint drums, the rustle of new silk, all blend on the staircase outside and drift in through the partly opened door. Bundled figures pass in the lighted hall. The laughter heard below becomes doubled and multiplied. Then some one comes in, closes the door, and switches on the lights. It is CECELIA. She goes to the chiffonier, looks in the drawers, hesitates—then to the desk whence she takes the cigarette-case and extracts one. She lights it and then, puffing and blowing, walks toward the mirror.)

CECELIA: (In tremendously sophisticated accents) Oh, yes, coming out is such a farce nowadays, you know. One really plays around so much before one is seventeen, that it's positively anticlimax. (Shaking hands with a visionary middle-aged nobleman.) Yes, your grace—I b'lieve I've heard my sister speak of you. Have a puff—they're very good. They're—they're Coronas. You don't smoke? What a pity! The king doesn't allow it, I suppose. Yes, I'll dance.

(So she dances around the room to a tune from down-stairs, her arms outstretched to an imaginary partner, the cigarette waving in her hand.)

SEVERAL HOURS LATER

CHAPTER 1 The Debutante

The corner of a den down-stairs, filled by a very comfortable leather lounge. A small light is on each side above, and in the middle, over the couch hangs a painting of a very old, very dignified gentleman, period 1860. Outside the music is heard in a fox-trot.

ROSALIND is seated on the lounge and on her left is HOWARD GILLESPIE, a vapid youth of about twenty-four. He is obviously very unhappy, and she is quite bored.

GILLESPIE: (Feebly) What do you mean I've changed. I feel the same toward you.

ROSALIND: But you don't look the same to me.

GILLESPIE: Three weeks ago you used to say that you liked me because I was so blasé, so indifferent—I still am.

ROSALIND: But not about me. I used to like you because you had brown eyes and thin legs.

GILLESPIE: (Helplessly) They're still thin and brown. You're a vampire, that's all.

ROSALIND: The only thing I know about vamping is what's on the piano score. What confuses men is that I'm perfectly natural. I used to think you were never jealous. Now you follow me with your eyes wherever I go.

GILLESPIE: I love you.

ROSALIND: (Coldly) I know it.

GILLESPIE: And you haven't kissed me for two weeks. I had an idea that after a girl was kissed she was—was—won.

ROSALIND: Those days are over. I have to be won all over again every time you see me.

GILLESPIE: Are you serious?

ROSALIND: About as usual. There used to be two kinds of kisses: First when girls were kissed and deserted; second, when they were engaged. Now there's a third kind, where the man is kissed and deserted. If Mr. Jones of the nineties bragged he'd kissed a girl, every one knew he was through with her. If Mr. Jones of 1919 brags the same every one knows it's because he can't kiss her any more. Given a decent start any girl can beat a man nowadays.

GILLESPIE: Then why do you play with men?

ROSALIND: (Leaning forward confidentially) For that first moment, when he's interested. There is a moment—Oh, just before the first kiss, a whispered word—something that makes it worth while.

GILLESPIE: And then?

ROSALIND: Then after that you make him talk about himself. Pretty soon he thinks of nothing but being alone with you—he sulks, he won't fight, he doesn't want to play—Victory!

(Enter DAWSON RYDER, twenty-six, handsome, wealthy, faithful to his own, a bore perhaps, but steady and sure of success.)

RYDER: I believe this is my dance, Rosalind.

119

ROSALIND: Well, Dawson, so you recognize me. Now I know I haven't got too much paint on. Mr. Ryder, this is Mr. Gillespie.

(They shake hands and GILLESPIE leaves, tremendously downcast.)

RYDER: Your party is certainly a success.

ROSALIND: Is it—I haven't seen it lately. I'm weary—Do you mind sitting out a minute?

RYDER: Mind—I'm delighted. You know I loathe this "rushing" idea. See a girl yesterday, to-day, to-morrow.

ROSALIND: Dawson!

RYDER: What?

ROSALIND: I wonder if you know you love me.

RYDER: (Startled) What—Oh—you know you're remarkable!

ROSALIND: Because you know I'm an awful proposition. Any one who marries me will have his hands full. I'm mean—mighty mean.

RYDER: Oh, I wouldn't say that.

ROSALIND: Oh, yes, I am—especially to the people nearest to me. (She rises.) Come, let's go. I've changed my mind and I want to dance. Mother is probably having a fit.

(Exeunt. Enter ALEC and CECELIA.)

CECELIA: Just my luck to get my own brother for an intermission.

ALEC: (Gloomily) I'll go if you want me to.

CECELIA: Good heavens, no—with whom would I begin the next dance? (Sighs.) There's no color in a dance since the French officers went back.

ALEC: (Thoughtfully) I don't want Amory to fall in love with Rosalind.

CECELIA: Why, I had an idea that that was just what you did want.

ALEC: I did, but since seeing these girls—I don't know. I'm awfully attached to Amory. He's sensitive and I don't want him to break his heart over somebody who doesn't care about him.

CECELIA: He's very good looking.

ALEC: (Still thoughtfully) She won't marry him, but a girl doesn't have to marry a man to break his heart.

CECELIA: What does it? I wish I knew the secret.

ALEC: Why, you cold-blooded little kitty. It's lucky for some that the Lord gave you a pug nose.

(Enter MRS. CONNAGE.)

MRS. CONNAGE: Where on earth is Rosalind?

ALEC: (Brilliantly) Of course you've come to the best people to find out. She'd naturally be with us.

MRS. CONNAGE: Her father has marshalled eight bachelor millionaires to meet her.

ALEC: You might form a squad and march through the halls.

CHAPTER 1 The Debutante

MRS. CONNAGE: I'm perfectly serious—for all I know she may be at the Cocoanut Grove with some football player on the night of her debut. You look left and I'll—

ALEC: (Flippantly) Hadn't you better send the butler through the cellar?

MRS. CONNAGE: (Perfectly serious) Oh, you don't think she'd be there?

CECELIA: He's only joking, mother.

ALEC: Mother had a picture of her tapping a keg of beer with some high hurdler.

MRS. CONNAGE: Let's look right away.

(They go out. ROSALIND comes in with GILLESPIE.)

GILLESPIE: Rosalind—Once more I ask you. Don't you care a blessed thing about me?

(AMORY walks in briskly.)

AMORY: My dance.

ROSALIND: Mr. Gillespie, this is Mr. Blaine.

GILLESPIE: I've met Mr. Blaine. From Lake Geneva, aren't you?

AMORY: Yes.

GILLESPIE: (Desperately) I've been there. It's in the—the Middle West, isn't it?

AMORY: (Spicily) Approximately. But I always felt that I'd rather be provincial hot-tamale than soup without seasoning.

GILLESPIE: What!

AMORY: Oh, no offense.

(GILLESPIE bows and leaves.)

ROSALIND: He's too much people.

AMORY: I was in love with a people once.

ROSALIND: So?

AMORY: Oh, yes—her name was Isabelle—nothing at all to her except what I read into her.

ROSALIND: What happened?

AMORY: Finally I convinced her that she was smarter than I was—then she threw me over. Said I was critical and impractical, you know.

ROSALIND: What do you mean impractical?

AMORY: Oh—drive a car, but can't change a tire.

ROSALIND: What are you going to do?

AMORY: Can't say—run for President, write—

ROSALIND: Greenwich Village?

AMORY: Good heavens, no—I said write—not drink.

ROSALIND: I like business men. Clever men are usually so homely.

AMORY: I feel as if I'd known you for ages.

ROSALIND: Oh, are you going to commence the "pyramid" story?

AMORY: No—I was going to make it French. I was Louis XIV and you were one of

121

my—my—(Changing his tone.) Suppose—we fell in love.

ROSALIND: I've suggested pretending.

AMORY: If we did it would be very big.

ROSALIND: Why?

AMORY: Because selfish people are in a way terribly capable of great loves.

ROSALIND: (Turning her lips up) Pretend.

(Very deliberately they kiss.)

AMORY: I can't say sweet things. But you are beautiful.

ROSALIND: Not that.

AMORY: What then?

ROSALIND: (Sadly) Oh, nothing—only I want sentiment, real sentiment—and I never find it.

AMORY: I never find anything else in the world—and I loathe it.

ROSALIND: It's so hard to find a male to gratify one's artistic taste.

(Some one has opened a door and the music of a waltz surges into the room. ROSALIND rises.)

ROSALIND: Listen! they're playing "Kiss Me Again."

(He looks at her.)

AMORY: Well?

ROSALIND: Well?

AMORY: (Softly—the battle lost) I love you.

ROSALIND: I love you—now.

(They kiss.)

AMORY: Oh, God, what have I done?

ROSALIND: Nothing. Oh, don't talk. Kiss me again.

AMORY: I don't know why or how, but I love you—from the moment I saw you.

ROSALIND: Me too—I—I—oh, to-night's to-night.

(Her brother strolls in, starts and then in a loud voice says: "Oh, excuse me," and goes.)

ROSALIND: (Her lips scarcely stirring) Don't let me go—I don't care who knows what I do.

AMORY: Say it!

ROSALIND: I love you—now. (They part.) Oh—I am very youthful, thank God—and rather beautiful, thank God—and happy, thank God, thank God—(She pauses and then, in an odd burst of prophecy, adds) Poor Amory!

(He kisses her again.)

KISMET

Within two weeks Amory and Rosalind were deeply and passionately in love. The critical qualities which had spoiled for each of them a dozen romances were dulled by the great wave of emotion that washed over them.

CHAPTER 1   The Debutante

"It may be an insane love-affair," she told her anxious mother, "but it's not inane."

The wave swept Amory into an advertising agency early in March, where he alternated between astonishing bursts of rather exceptional work and wild dreams of becoming suddenly rich and touring Italy with Rosalind.

They were together constantly, for lunch, for dinner, and nearly every evening—always in a sort of breathless hush, as if they feared that any minute the spell would break and drop them out of this paradise of rose and flame. But the spell became a trance, seemed to increase from day to day; they began to talk of marrying in July—in June. All life was transmitted into terms of their love, all experience, all desires, all ambitions, were nullified—their senses of humor crawled into corners to sleep; their former love-affairs seemed faintly laughable and scarcely regretted juvenalia.

For the second time in his life Amory had had a complete bouleversement and was hurrying into line with his generation.

A LITTLE INTERLUDE

Amory wandered slowly up the avenue and thought of the night as inevitably his—the pageantry and carnival of rich dusk and dim streets ... it seemed that he had closed the book of fading harmonies at last and stepped into the sensuous vibrant walks of life. Everywhere these countless lights, this promise of a night of streets and singing—he moved in a half-dream through the crowd as if expecting to meet Rosalind hurrying toward him with eager feet from every corner.... How the unforgettable faces of dusk would blend to her, the myriad footsteps, a thousand overtures, would blend to her footsteps; and there would be more drunkenness than wine in the softness of her eyes on his. Even his dreams now were faint violins drifting like summer sounds upon the summer air.

The room was in darkness except for the faint glow of Tom's cigarette where he lounged by the open window. As the door shut behind him, Amory stood a moment with his back against it.

"Hello, Benvenuto Blaine. How went the advertising business to-day?"

Amory sprawled on a couch.

"I loathed it as usual!" The momentary vision of the bustling agency was displaced quickly by another picture.

"My God! She's wonderful!"

Tom sighed.

"I can't tell you," repeated Amory, "just how wonderful she is. I don't want you to know. I don't want any one to know."

Another sigh came from the window—quite a resigned sigh.

"She's life and hope and happiness, my whole world now."

He felt the quiver of a tear on his eyelid.

"Oh, Golly, Tom!"

BITTER SWEET

123

"Sit like we do," she whispered.

He sat in the big chair and held out his arms so that she could nestle inside them.

"I knew you'd come to-night," she said softly, "like summer, just when I needed you most... darling... darling..."

His lips moved lazily over her face.

"You taste so good," he sighed.

"How do you mean, lover?"

"Oh, just sweet, just sweet..." he held her closer.

"Amory," she whispered, "when you're ready for me I'll marry you."

"We won't have much at first."

"Don't!" she cried. "It hurts when you reproach yourself for what you can't give me. I've got your precious self—and that's enough for me."

"Tell me..."

"You know, don't you? Oh, you know."

"Yes, but I want to hear you say it."

"I love you, Amory, with all my heart."

"Always, will you?"

"All my life—Oh, Amory—"

"What?"

"I want to belong to you. I want your people to be my people. I want to have your babies."

"But I haven't any people."

"Don't laugh at me, Amory. Just kiss me."

"I'll do what you want," he said.

"No, I'll do what you want. We're you—not me. Oh, you're so much a part, so much all of me..."

He closed his eyes.

"I'm so happy that I'm frightened. Wouldn't it be awful if this was—was the high point?..."

She looked at him dreamily.

"Beauty and love pass, I know.... Oh, there's sadness, too. I suppose all great happiness is a little sad. Beauty means the scent of roses and then the death of roses—"

"Beauty means the agony of sacrifice and the end of agony...."

"And, Amory, we're beautiful, I know. I'm sure God loves us—"

"He loves you. You're his most precious possession."

"I'm not his, I'm yours. Amory, I belong to you. For the first time I regret all the other kisses; now I know how much a kiss can mean."

Then they would smoke and he would tell her about his day at the office—and where they might live. Sometimes, when he was particularly loquacious, she went to sleep in his arms, but he loved that Rosalind—all Rosalinds—as he had never in the world loved any one else. Intangibly fleeting, unrememberable hours.

AQUATIC INCIDENT

One day Amory and Howard Gillespie meeting by accident down-town took lunch together, and Amory heard a story that delighted him. Gillespie after several cocktails was in a talkative mood; he began by telling Amory that he was sure Rosalind was slightly eccentric.

He had gone with her on a swimming party up in Westchester County, and some one mentioned that Annette Kellerman had been there one day on a visit and had dived from the top of a rickety, thirty-foot summer-house. Immediately Rosalind insisted that Howard should climb up with her to see what it looked like.

A minute later, as he sat and dangled his feet on the edge, a form shot by him; Rosalind, her arms spread in a beautiful swan dive, had sailed through the air into the clear water.

"Of course I had to go, after that—and I nearly killed myself. I thought I was pretty good to even try it. Nobody else in the party tried it. Well, afterward Rosalind had the nerve to ask me why I stooped over when I dove. 'It didn't make it any easier,' she said, 'it just took all the courage out of it.' I ask you, what can a man do with a girl like that? Unnecessary, I call it."

Gillespie failed to understand why Amory was smiling delightedly all through lunch. He thought perhaps he was one of these hollow optimists.

FIVE WEEKS LATER

Again the library of the Connage house. ROSALIND is alone, sitting on the lounge staring very moodily and unhappily at nothing. She has changed perceptibly—she is a trifle thinner for one thing; the light in her eyes is not so bright; she looks easily a year older.

Her mother comes in, muffled in an opera-cloak. She takes in ROSALIND with a nervous glance.

MRS. CONNAGE: Who is coming to-night?

(ROSALIND fails to hear her, at least takes no notice.)

MRS. CONNAGE: Alec is coming up to take me to this Barrie play, "Et tu, Brutus." (She perceives that she is talking to herself.) Rosalind! I asked you who is coming to-night?

ROSALIND: (Starting) Oh—what—oh—Amory—

MRS. CONNAGE: (Sarcastically) You have so many admirers lately that I couldn't imagine which one. (ROSALIND doesn't answer.) Dawson Ryder is more patient than I thought he'd be. You haven't given him an evening this week.

ROSALIND: (With a very weary expression that is quite new to her face.) Mother—please—

MRS. CONNAGE: Oh, I won't interfere. You've already wasted over two months on a theoretical genius who hasn't a penny to his name, but go ahead, waste your life on him. I won't interfere.

ROSALIND: (As if repeating a tiresome lesson) You know he has a little income—and you know he's earning thirty-five dollars a week in advertising—

MRS. CONNAGE: And it wouldn't buy your clothes. (She pauses but ROSALIND makes no reply.) I have your best interests at heart when I tell you not to take a step you'll spend your days regretting. It's not as if your father could help you. Things have been hard for him lately and he's an old man. You'd be dependent absolutely on a dreamer, a nice, well-born boy, but a dreamer—merely clever. (She implies that this quality in itself is rather vicious.)

ROSALIND: For heaven's sake, mother—

(A maid appears, announces Mr. Blaine who follows immediately. AMORY'S friends have been telling him for ten days that he "looks like the wrath of God," and he does. As a matter of fact he has not been able to eat a mouthful in the last thirty-six hours.)

AMORY: Good evening, Mrs. Connage.

MRS. CONNAGE: (Not unkindly) Good evening, Amory.

(AMORY and ROSALIND exchange glances—and ALEC comes in. ALEC'S attitude throughout has been neutral. He believes in his heart that the marriage would make AMORY mediocre and ROSALIND miserable, but he feels a great sympathy for both of them.)

ALEC: Hi, Amory!

AMORY: Hi, Alec! Tom said he'd meet you at the theatre.

ALEC: Yeah, just saw him. How's the advertising to-day? Write some brilliant copy?

AMORY: Oh, it's about the same. I got a raise—(Every one looks at him rather eagerly)—of two dollars a week. (General collapse.)

MRS. CONNAGE: Come, Alec, I hear the car.

(A good night, rather chilly in sections. After MRS. CONNAGE and ALEC go out there is a pause. ROSALIND still stares moodily at the fireplace. AMORY goes to her and puts his arm around her.)

AMORY: Darling girl.

(They kiss. Another pause and then she seizes his hand, covers it with kisses and holds it to her breast.)

ROSALIND: (Sadly) I love your hands, more than anything. I see them often when you're away from me—so tired; I know every line of them. Dear hands!

(Their eyes meet for a second and then she begins to cry—a tearless sobbing.)

AMORY: Rosalind!

ROSALIND: Oh, we're so darned pitiful!

AMORY: Rosalind!

ROSALIND: Oh, I want to die!

AMORY: Rosalind, another night of this and I'll go to pieces. You've been this way four days now. You've got to be more encouraging or I can't work or eat or sleep. (He looks around helplessly as if searching for new words to clothe an old, shopworn phrase.) We'll

CHAPTER 1 The Debutante

have to make a start. I like having to make a start together. (His forced hopefulness fades as he sees her unresponsive.) What's the matter? (He gets up suddenly and starts to pace the floor.) It's Dawson Ryder, that's what it is. He's been working on your nerves. You've been with him every afternoon for a week. People come and tell me they've seen you together, and I have to smile and nod and pretend it hasn't the slightest significance for me. And you won't tell me anything as it develops.

ROSALIND: Amory, if you don't sit down I'll scream.

AMORY: (Sitting down suddenly beside her) Oh, Lord.

ROSALIND: (Taking his hand gently) You know I love you, don't you?

AMORY: Yes.

ROSALIND: You know I'll always love you—

AMORY: Don't talk that way; you frighten me. It sounds as if we weren't going to have each other. (She cries a little and rising from the couch goes to the armchair.) I've felt all afternoon that things were worse. I nearly went wild down at the office—couldn't write a line. Tell me everything.

ROSALIND: There's nothing to tell, I say. I'm just nervous.

AMORY: Rosalind, you're playing with the idea of marrying Dawson Ryder.

ROSALIND: (After a pause) He's been asking me to all day.

AMORY: Well, he's got his nerve!

ROSALIND: (After another pause) I like him.

AMORY: Don't say that. It hurts me.

ROSALIND: Don't be a silly idiot. You know you're the only man I've ever loved, ever will love.

AMORY: (Quickly) Rosalind, let's get married—next week.

ROSALIND: We can't.

AMORY: Why not?

ROSALIND: Oh, we can't. I'd be your squaw—in some horrible place.

AMORY: We'll have two hundred and seventy-five dollars a month all told.

ROSALIND: Darling, I don't even do my own hair, usually.

AMORY: I'll do it for you.

ROSALIND: (Between a laugh and a sob) Thanks.

AMORY: Rosalind, you can't be thinking of marrying some one else. Tell me! You leave me in the dark. I can help you fight it out if you'll only tell me.

ROSALIND: It's just—us. We're pitiful, that's all. The very qualities I love you for are the ones that will always make you a failure.

AMORY: (Grimly) Go on.

ROSALIND: Oh—it is Dawson Ryder. He's so reliable, I almost feel that he'd be a—a background.

AMORY: You don't love him.

127

ROSALIND: I know, but I respect him, and he's a good man and a strong one.

AMORY: (Grudgingly) Yes—he's that.

ROSALIND: Well—here's one little thing. There was a little poor boy we met in Rye Tuesday afternoon—and, oh, Dawson took him on his lap and talked to him and promised him an Indian suit—and next day he remembered and bought it—and, oh, it was so sweet and I couldn't help thinking he'd be so nice to—to our children—take care of them—and I wouldn't have to worry.

AMORY: (In despair) Rosalind! Rosalind!

ROSALIND: (With a faint roguishness) Don't look so consciously suffering.

AMORY: What power we have of hurting each other!

ROSALIND: (Commencing to sob again) It's been so perfect—you and I. So like a dream that I'd longed for and never thought I'd find. The first real unselfishness I've ever felt in my life. And I can't see it fade out in a colorless atmosphere!

AMORY: It won't—it won't!

ROSALIND: I'd rather keep it as a beautiful memory—tucked away in my heart.

AMORY: Yes, women can do that—but not men. I'd remember always, not the beauty of it while it lasted, but just the bitterness, the long bitterness.

ROSALIND: Don't!

AMORY: All the years never to see you, never to kiss you, just a gate shut and barred—you don't dare be my wife.

ROSALIND: No—no—I'm taking the hardest course, the strongest course. Marrying you would be a failure and I never fail—if you don't stop walking up and down I'll scream!

(Again he sinks despairingly onto the lounge.)

AMORY: Come over here and kiss me.

ROSALIND: No.

AMORY: Don't you want to kiss me?

ROSALIND: To-night I want you to love me calmly and coolly.

AMORY: The beginning of the end.

ROSALIND: (With a burst of insight) Amory, you're young. I'm young. People excuse us now for our poses and vanities, for treating people like Sancho and yet getting away with it. They excuse us now. But you've got a lot of knocks coming to you—

AMORY: And you're afraid to take them with me.

ROSALIND: No, not that. There was a poem I read somewhere—you'll say Ella Wheeler Wilcox and laugh—but listen:

"For this is wisdom—to love and live,
　To take what fate or the gods may give,
　To ask no question, to make no prayer,
　To kiss the lips and caress the hair,
　Speed passion's ebb as we greet its flow,

To have and to hold, and, in time—let go."

AMORY: But we haven't had.

ROSALIND: Amory, I'm yours—you know it. There have been times in the last month I'd have been completely yours if you'd said so. But I can't marry you and ruin both our lives.

AMORY: We've got to take our chance for happiness.

ROSALIND: Dawson says I'd learn to love him.

(AMORY with his head sunk in his hands does not move. The life seems suddenly gone out of him.)

ROSALIND: Lover! Lover! I can't do with you, and I can't imagine life without you.

AMORY: Rosalind, we're on each other's nerves. It's just that we're both high-strung, and this week—

(His voice is curiously old. She crosses to him and taking his face in her hands, kisses him.)

ROSALIND: I can't, Amory. I can't be shut away from the trees and flowers, cooped up in a little flat, waiting for you. You'd hate me in a narrow atmosphere. I'd make you hate me.

(Again she is blinded by sudden uncontrolled tears.)

AMORY: Rosalind—

ROSALIND: Oh, darling, go—Don't make it harder! I can't stand it—

AMORY: (His face drawn, his voice strained) Do you know what you're saying? Do you mean forever?

(There is a difference somehow in the quality of their suffering.)

ROSALIND: Can't you see—

AMORY: I'm afraid I can't if you love me. You're afraid of taking two years' knocks with me.

ROSALIND: I wouldn't be the Rosalind you love.

AMORY: (A little hysterically) I can't give you up! I can't, that's all! I've got to have you!

ROSALIND: (A hard note in her voice) You're being a baby now

AMORY: (Wildly) I don't care! You're spoiling our lives!

ROSALIND: I'm doing the wise thing, the only thing.

AMORY: Are you going to marry Dawson Ryder?

ROSALIND: Oh, don't ask me. You know I'm old in some ways—in others well, I'm just a little girl. I like sunshine and pretty things and cheerfulness—and I dread responsibility. I don't want to think about pots and kitchens and brooms. I want to worry whether my legs will get slick and brown when I swim in the summer.

AMORY: And you love me.

129

ROSALIND: That's just why it has to end. Drifting hurts too much. We can't have any more scenes like this.

(She draws his ring from her finger and hands it to him. Their eyes blind again with tears.)

AMORY: (His lips against her wet cheek) Don't! Keep it, please—oh, don't break my heart!

(She presses the ring softly into his hand.)

ROSALIND: (Brokenly) You'd better go.

AMORY: Good-by—

(She looks at him once more, with infinite longing, infinite sadness.)

ROSALIND: Don't ever forget me, Amory—

AMORY: Good-by—

(He goes to the door, fumbles for the knob, finds it—she sees him throw back his head—and he is gone. Gone—she half starts from the lounge and then sinks forward on her face into the pillows.)

ROSALIND: Oh, God, I want to die! (After a moment she rises and with her eyes closed feels her way to the door. Then she turns and looks once more at the room. Here they had sat and dreamed: that tray she had so often filled with matches for him; that shade that they had discreetly lowered one long Sunday afternoon. Misty-eyed she stands and remembers; she speaks aloud.) Oh, Amory, what have I done to you?

(And deep under the aching sadness that will pass in time, Rosalind feels that she has lost something, she knows not what, she knows not why.)

CHAPTER 2　Experiments in Convalescence

The Knickerbocker Bar, beamed upon by Maxfield Parrish's jovial, colorful "Old King Cole," was well crowded. Amory stopped in the entrance and looked at his wrist-watch; he wanted particularly to know the time, for something in his mind that catalogued and classified liked to chip things off cleanly. Later it would satisfy him in a vague way to be able to think "that thing ended at exactly twenty minutes after eight on Thursday, June 10, 1919." This was allowing for the walk from her house—a walk concerning which he had afterward not the faintest recollection.

He was in rather grotesque condition: two days of worry and nervousness, of sleepless nights, of untouched meals, culminating in the emotional crisis and Rosalind's abrupt decision—the strain of it had drugged the foreground of his mind into a merciful coma. As he fumbled clumsily with the olives at the free-lunch table, a man approached and spoke to him, and the olives dropped from his nervous hands.

"Well, Amory..."

It was some one he had known at Princeton; he had no idea of the name.

"Hello, old boy—" he heard himself saying.

"Name's Jim Wilson—you've forgotten."

"Sure, you bet, Jim. I remember."

"Going to reunion?"

"You know!" Simultaneously he realized that he was not going to reunion.

"Get overseas?"

Amory nodded, his eyes staring oddly. Stepping back to let some one pass, he knocked the dish of olives to a crash on the floor.

"Too bad," he muttered. "Have a drink?"

Wilson, ponderously diplomatic, reached over and slapped him on the back.

"You've had plenty, old boy."

Amory eyed him dumbly until Wilson grew embarrassed under the scrutiny.

"Plenty, hell!" said Amory finally. "I haven't had a drink to-day."

Wilson looked incredulous.

"Have a drink or not?" cried Amory rudely.

Together they sought the bar.

"Rye high."

"I'll just take a Bronx."

Wilson had another; Amory had several more. They decided to sit down. At ten o'clock

Wilson was displaced by Carling, class of '15. Amory, his head spinning gorgeously, layer upon layer of soft satisfaction setting over the bruised spots of his spirit, was discoursing volubly on the war.

"'S a mental was'e," he insisted with owl-like wisdom. "Two years my life spent inalleshual vacuity. Los' idealism, got be physcal anmal," he shook his fist expressively at Old King Cole, "got be Prussian 'bout ev'thing, women 'specially. Use' be straight 'bout women college. Now don'givadam." He expressed his lack of principle by sweeping a seltzer bottle with a broad gesture to noisy extinction on the floor, but this did not interrupt his speech. "Seek pleasure where find it for to-morrow die. 'At's philos'phy for me now on."

Carling yawned, but Amory, waxing brilliant, continued:

"Use' wonder 'bout things—people satisfied compromise, fif'y-fif'y att'tude on life. Now don' wonder, don' wonder—" He became so emphatic in impressing on Carling the fact that he didn't wonder that he lost the thread of his discourse and concluded by announcing to the bar at large that he was a "physcal anmal."

"What are you celebrating, Amory?"

Amory leaned forward confidentially.

"Cel'brating blowmylife. Great moment blow my life. Can't tell you 'bout it—"

He heard Carling addressing a remark to the bartender:

"Give him a bromo-seltzer."

Amory shook his head indignantly.

"None that stuff!"

"But listen, Amory, you're making yourself sick. You're white as a ghost."

Amory considered the question. He tried to look at himself in the mirror but even by squinting up one eye could only see as far as the row of bottles behind the bar.

"Like som'n solid. We go get some—some salad."

He settled his coat with an attempt at nonchalance, but letting go of the bar was too much for him, and he slumped against a chair.

"We'll go over to Shanley's," suggested Carling, offering an elbow.

With this assistance Amory managed to get his legs in motion enough to propel him across Forty-second Street.

Shanley's was very dim. He was conscious that he was talking in a loud voice, very succinctly and convincingly, he thought, about a desire to crush people under his heel. He consumed three club sandwiches, devouring each as though it were no larger than a chocolate-drop. Then Rosalind began popping into his mind again, and he found his lips forming her name over and over. Next he was sleepy, and he had a hazy, listless sense of people in dress suits, probably waiters, gathering around the table....

... He was in a room and Carling was saying something about a knot in his shoe-lace.

"Nemmine," he managed to articulate drowsily. "Sleep in 'em...."

CHAPTER 2   Experiments in Convalescence

STILL ALCOHOLIC

He awoke laughing and his eyes lazily roamed his surroundings, evidently a bedroom and bath in a good hotel. His head was whirring and picture after picture was forming and blurring and melting before his eyes, but beyond the desire to laugh he had no entirely conscious reaction. He reached for the 'phone beside his bed.

"Hello—what hotel is this—?

"Knickerbocker? All right, send up two rye high-balls—"

He lay for a moment and wondered idly whether they'd send up a bottle or just two of those little glass containers. Then, with an effort, he struggled out of bed and ambled into the bathroom.

When he emerged, rubbing himself lazily with a towel, he found the bar boy with the drinks and had a sudden desire to kid him. On reflection he decided that this would be undignified, so he waved him away.

As the new alcohol tumbled into his stomach and warmed him, the isolated pictures began slowly to form a cinema reel of the day before. Again he saw Rosalind curled weeping among the pillows, again he felt her tears against his cheek. Her words began ringing in his ears: "Don't ever forget me, Amory—don't ever forget me—"

"Hell!" he faltered aloud, and then he choked and collapsed on the bed in a shaken spasm of grief. After a minute he opened his eyes and regarded the ceiling.

"Damned fool!" he exclaimed in disgust, and with a voluminous sigh rose and approached the bottle. After another glass he gave way loosely to the luxury of tears. Purposely he called up into his mind little incidents of the vanished spring, phrased to himself emotions that would make him react even more strongly to sorrow.

"We were so happy," he intoned dramatically, "so very happy." Then he gave way again and knelt beside the bed, his head half-buried in the pillow.

"My own girl—my own—Oh—"

He clinched his teeth so that the tears streamed in a flood from his eyes.

"Oh... my baby girl, all I had, all I wanted!... Oh, my girl, come back, come back! I need you... need you... we're so pitiful ... just misery we brought each other.... She'll be shut away from me.... I can't see her; I can't be her friend. It's got to be that way—it's got to be—"

And then again:

"We've been so happy, so very happy...."

He rose to his feet and threw himself on the bed in an ecstasy of sentiment, and then lay exhausted while he realized slowly that he had been very drunk the night before, and that his head was spinning again wildly. He laughed, rose, and crossed again to Lethe....

At noon he ran into a crowd in the Biltmore bar, and the riot began again. He had a vague recollection afterward of discussing French poetry with a British officer who was introduced to him as "Captain Corn, of his Majesty's Foot," and he remembered attempting

133

to recite "Clair de Lune" at luncheon; then he slept in a big, soft chair until almost five o'clock when another crowd found and woke him; there followed an alcoholic dressing of several temperaments for the ordeal of dinner. They selected theatre tickets at Tyson's for a play that had a four-drink programme—a play with two monotonous voices, with turbid, gloomy scenes, and lighting effects that were hard to follow when his eyes behaved so amazingly. He imagined afterward that it must have been "The Jest."...

... Then the Cocoanut Grove, where Amory slept again on a little balcony outside. Out in Shanley's, Yonkers, he became almost logical, and by a careful control of the number of high-balls he drank, grew quite lucid and garrulous. He found that the party consisted of five men, two of whom he knew slightly; he became righteous about paying his share of the expense and insisted in a loud voice on arranging everything then and there to the amusement of the tables around him....

Some one mentioned that a famous cabaret star was at the next table, so Amory rose and, approaching gallantly, introduced himself... this involved him in an argument, first with her escort and then with the headwaiter—Amory's attitude being a lofty and exaggerated courtesy... he consented, after being confronted with irrefutable logic, to being led back to his own table.

"Decided to commit suicide," he announced suddenly.

"When? Next year?"

"Now. To-morrow morning. Going to take a room at the Commodore, get into a hot bath and open a vein."

"He's getting morbid!"

"You need another rye, old boy!"

"We'll all talk it over to-morrow."

But Amory was not to be dissuaded, from argument at least.

"Did you ever get that way?" he demanded confidentially fortaccio.

"Sure!"

"Often?"

"My chronic state."

This provoked discussion. One man said that he got so depressed sometimes that he seriously considered it. Another agreed that there was nothing to live for. "Captain Corn," who had somehow rejoined the party, said that in his opinion it was when one's health was bad that one felt that way most. Amory's suggestion was that they should each order a Bronx, mix broken glass in it, and drink it off. To his relief no one applauded the idea, so having finished his high-ball, he balanced his chin in his hand and his elbow on the table—a most delicate, scarcely noticeable sleeping position, he assured himself—and went into a deep stupor....

He was awakened by a woman clinging to him, a pretty woman, with brown, disarranged hair and dark blue eyes.

CHAPTER 2 Experiments in Convalescence

"Take me home!" she cried.

"Hello!" said Amory, blinking.

"I like you," she announced tenderly.

"I like you too."

He noticed that there was a noisy man in the background and that one of his party was arguing with him.

"Fella I was with's a damn fool," confided the blue-eyed woman. "I hate him. I want to go home with you."

"You drunk?" queried Amory with intense wisdom.

She nodded coyly.

"Go home with him," he advised gravely. "He brought you."

At this point the noisy man in the background broke away from his detainers and approached.

"Say!" he said fiercely. "I brought this girl out here and you're butting in!"

Amory regarded him coldly, while the girl clung to him closer.

"You let go that girl!" cried the noisy man.

Amory tried to make his eyes threatening.

"You go to hell!" he directed finally, and turned his attention to the girl.

"Love first sight," he suggested.

"I love you," she breathed and nestled close to him. She did have beautiful eyes.

Some one leaned over and spoke in Amory's ear.

"That's just Margaret Diamond. She's drunk and this fellow here brought her. Better let her go."

"Let him take care of her, then!" shouted Amory furiously. "I'm no W. Y. C. A. worker, am I?—am I?"

"Let her go!"

"It's her hanging on, damn it! Let her hang!"

The crowd around the table thickened. For an instant a brawl threatened, but a sleek waiter bent back Margaret Diamond's fingers until she released her hold on Amory, whereupon she slapped the waiter furiously in the face and flung her arms about her raging original escort.

"Oh, Lord!" cried Amory.

"Let's go!"

"Come on, the taxis are getting scarce!"

"Check, waiter."

"C'mon, Amory. Your romance is over."

Amory laughed.

"You don't know how true you spoke. No idea. 'At's the whole trouble."

AMORY ON THE LABOR QUESTION

135

Two mornings later he knocked at the president's door at Bascome and Barlow's advertising agency.

"Come in!"

Amory entered unsteadily.

"'Morning, Mr. Barlow."

Mr. Barlow brought his glasses to the inspection and set his mouth slightly ajar that he might better listen.

"Well, Mr. Blaine. We haven't seen you for several days."

"No," said Amory. "I'm quitting."

"Well—well—this is—"

"I don't like it here."

"I'm sorry. I thought our relations had been quite—ah—pleasant. You seemed to be a hard worker—a little inclined perhaps to write fancy copy—"

"I just got tired of it," interrupted Amory rudely. "It didn't matter a damn to me whether Harebell's flour was any better than any one else's. In fact, I never ate any of it. So I got tired of telling people about it—oh, I know I've been drinking—"

Mr. Barlow's face steeled by several ingots of expression.

"You asked for a position—"

Amory waved him to silence.

"And I think I was rottenly underpaid. Thirty-five dollars a week—less than a good carpenter."

"You had just started. You'd never worked before," said Mr. Barlow coolly.

"But it took about ten thousand dollars to educate me where I could write your darned stuff for you. Anyway, as far as length of service goes, you've got stenographers here you've paid fifteen a week for five years."

"I'm not going to argue with you, sir," said Mr. Barlow rising.

"Neither am I. I just wanted to tell you I'm quitting."

They stood for a moment looking at each other impassively and then Amory turned and left the office.

A LITTLE LULL

Four days after that he returned at last to the apartment. Tom was engaged on a book review for The New Democracy on the staff of which he was employed. They regarded each other for a moment in silence.

"Well?"

"Well?"

"Good Lord, Amory, where'd you get the black eye—and the jaw?"

Amory laughed.

"That's a mere nothing."

He peeled off his coat and bared his shoulders.

CHAPTER 2 Experiments in Convalescence

"Look here!"

Tom emitted a low whistle.

"What hit you?"

Amory laughed again.

"Oh, a lot of people. I got beaten up. Fact." He slowly replaced his shirt. "It was bound to come sooner or later and I wouldn't have missed it for anything."

"Who was it?"

"Well, there were some waiters and a couple of sailors and a few stray pedestrians, I guess. It's the strangest feeling. You ought to get beaten up just for the experience of it. You fall down after a while and everybody sort of slashes in at you before you hit the ground—then they kick you."

Tom lighted a cigarette.

"I spent a day chasing you all over town, Amory. But you always kept a little ahead of me. I'd say you've been on some party."

Amory tumbled into a chair and asked for a cigarette.

"You sober now?" asked Tom quizzically.

"Pretty sober. Why?"

"Well, Alec has left. His family had been after him to go home and live, so he—"

A spasm of pain shook Amory.

"Too bad."

"Yes, it is too bad. We'll have to get some one else if we're going to stay here. The rent's going up."

"Sure. Get anybody. I'll leave it to you, Tom."

Amory walked into his bedroom. The first thing that met his glance was a photograph of Rosalind that he had intended to have framed, propped up against a mirror on his dresser. He looked at it unmoved. After the vivid mental pictures of her that were his portion at present, the portrait was curiously unreal. He went back into the study.

"Got a cardboard box?"

"No," answered Tom, puzzled. "Why should I have? Oh, yes—there may be one in Alec's room."

Eventually Amory found what he was looking for and, returning to his dresser, opened a drawer full of letters, notes, part of a chain, two little handkerchiefs, and some snap-shots. As he transferred them carefully to the box his mind wandered to some place in a book where the hero, after preserving for a year a cake of his lost love's soap, finally washed his hands with it. He laughed and began to hum "After you've gone" ... ceased abruptly...

The string broke twice, and then he managed to secure it, dropped the package into the bottom of his trunk, and having slammed the lid returned to the study.

"Going out?" Tom's voice held an undertone of anxiety.

"Uh-huh."

137

"Where?"

"Couldn't say, old keed."

"Let's have dinner together."

"Sorry. I told Sukey Brett I'd eat with him."

"Oh."

"By-by."

Amory crossed the street and had a high-ball; then he walked to Washington Square and found a top seat on a bus. He disembarked at Forty-third Street and strolled to the Biltmore bar.

"Hi, Amory!"

"What'll you have?"

"Yo-ho! Waiter!"

TEMPERATURE NORMAL

The advent of prohibition with the "thirsty-first" put a sudden stop to the submerging of Amory's sorrows, and when he awoke one morning to find that the old bar-to-bar days were over, he had neither remorse for the past three weeks nor regret that their repetition was impossible. He had taken the most violent, if the weakest, method to shield himself from the stabs of memory, and while it was not a course he would have prescribed for others, he found in the end that it had done its business: he was over the first flush of pain.

Don't misunderstand! Amory had loved Rosalind as he would never love another living person. She had taken the first flush of his youth and brought from his unplumbed depths tenderness that had surprised him, gentleness and unselfishness that he had never given to another creature. He had later love-affairs, but of a different sort: in those he went back to that, perhaps, more typical frame of mind, in which the girl became the mirror of a mood in him. Rosalind had drawn out what was more than passionate admiration; he had a deep, undying affection for Rosalind.

But there had been, near the end, so much dramatic tragedy, culminating in the arabesque nightmare of his three weeks' spree, that he was emotionally worn out. The people and surroundings that he remembered as being cool or delicately artificial, seemed to promise him a refuge. He wrote a cynical story which featured his father's funeral and despatched it to a magazine, receiving in return a check for sixty dollars and a request for more of the same tone. This tickled his vanity, but inspired him to no further effort.

He read enormously. He was puzzled and depressed by "A Portrait of the Artist as a Young Man"; intensely interested by "Joan and Peter" and "The Undying Fire," and rather surprised by his discovery through a critic named Mencken of several excellent American novels: "Vandover and the Brute," "The Damnation of Theron Ware," and "Jennie Gerhardt." Mackenzie, Chesterton, Galsworthy, Bennett, had sunk in his appreciation from sagacious, life-saturated geniuses to merely diverting contemporaries. Shaw's aloof clarity and brilliant consistency and the gloriously intoxicated efforts of H. G. Wells to fit the key

CHAPTER 2 Experiments in Convalescence

of romantic symmetry into the elusive lock of truth, alone won his rapt attention.

He wanted to see Monsignor Darcy, to whom he had written when he landed, but he had not heard from him; besides he knew that a visit to Monsignor would entail the story of Rosalind, and the thought of repeating it turned him cold with horror.

In his search for cool people he remembered Mrs. Lawrence, a very intelligent, very dignified lady, a convert to the church, and a great devotee of Monsignor's.

He called her on the 'phone one day. Yes, she remembered him perfectly; no, Monsignor wasn't in town, was in Boston she thought; he'd promised to come to dinner when he returned. Couldn't Amory take luncheon with her?

"I thought I'd better catch up, Mrs. Lawrence," he said rather ambiguously when he arrived.

"Monsignor was here just last week," said Mrs. Lawrence regretfully. "He was very anxious to see you, but he'd left your address at home."

"Did he think I'd plunged into Bolshevism?" asked Amory, interested.

"Oh, he's having a frightful time."

"Why?"

"About the Irish Republic. He thinks it lacks dignity."

"So?"

"He went to Boston when the Irish President arrived and he was greatly distressed because the receiving committee, when they rode in an automobile, would put their arms around the President."

"I don't blame him."

"Well, what impressed you more than anything while you were in the army? You look a great deal older."

"That's from another, more disastrous battle," he answered, smiling in spite of himself. "But the army—let me see—well, I discovered that physical courage depends to a great extent on the physical shape a man is in. I found that I was as brave as the next man—it used to worry me before."

"What else?"

"Well, the idea that men can stand anything if they get used to it, and the fact that I got a high mark in the psychological examination."

Mrs. Lawrence laughed. Amory was finding it a great relief to be in this cool house on Riverside Drive, away from more condensed New York and the sense of people expelling great quantities of breath into a little space. Mrs. Lawrence reminded him vaguely of Beatrice, not in temperament, but in her perfect grace and dignity. The house, its furnishings, the manner in which dinner was served, were in immense contrast to what he had met in the great places on Long Island, where the servants were so obtrusive that they had positively to be bumped out of the way, or even in the houses of more conservative "Union Club" families. He wondered if this air of symmetrical restraint, this grace, which

139

he felt was continental, was distilled through Mrs. Lawrence's New England ancestry or acquired in long residence in Italy and Spain.

Two glasses of sauterne at luncheon loosened his tongue, and he talked, with what he felt was something of his old charm, of religion and literature and the menacing phenomena of the social order. Mrs. Lawrence was ostensibly pleased with him, and her interest was especially in his mind; he wanted people to like his mind again—after a while it might be such a nice place in which to live.

"Monsignor Darcy still thinks that you're his reincarnation, that your faith will eventually clarify."

"Perhaps," he assented. "I'm rather pagan at present. It's just that religion doesn't seem to have the slightest bearing on life at my age."

When he left her house he walked down Riverside Drive with a feeling of satisfaction. It was amusing to discuss again such subjects as this young poet, Stephen Vincent Benet, or the Irish Republic. Between the rancid accusations of Edward Carson and Justice Cohalan he had completely tired of the Irish question; yet there had been a time when his own Celtic traits were pillars of his personal philosophy.

There seemed suddenly to be much left in life, if only this revival of old interests did not mean that he was backing away from it again—backing away from life itself.

RESTLESSNESS

"I'm tres old and tres bored, Tom," said Amory one day, stretching himself at ease in the comfortable window-seat. He always felt most natural in a recumbent position.

"You used to be entertaining before you started to write," he continued. "Now you save any idea that you think would do to print."

Existence had settled back to an ambitionless normality. They had decided that with economy they could still afford the apartment, which Tom, with the domesticity of an elderly cat, had grown fond of. The old English hunting prints on the wall were Tom's, and the large tapestry by courtesy, a relic of decadent days in college, and the great profusion of orphaned candlesticks and the carved Louis XV chair in which no one could sit more than a minute without acute spinal disorders—Tom claimed that this was because one was sitting in the lap of Montespan's wraith—at any rate, it was Tom's furniture that decided them to stay.

They went out very little: to an occasional play, or to dinner at the Ritz or the Princeton Club. With prohibition the great rendezvous had received their death wounds; no longer could one wander to the Biltmore bar at twelve or five and find congenial spirits, and both Tom and Amory had outgrown the passion for dancing with mid-Western or New Jersey debbies at the Club-de-Vingt (surnamed the "Club de Gink") or the Plaza Rose Room—besides even that required several cocktails "to come down to the intellectual level of the women present," as Amory had once put it to a horrified matron.

Amory had lately received several alarming letters from Mr. Barton—the Lake Geneva

CHAPTER 2 Experiments in Convalescence

house was too large to be easily rented; the best rent obtainable at present would serve this year to little more than pay for the taxes and necessary improvements; in fact, the lawyer suggested that the whole property was simply a white elephant on Amory's hands. Nevertheless, even though it might not yield a cent for the next three years, Amory decided with a vague sentimentality that for the present, at any rate, he would not sell the house.

This particular day on which he announced his ennui to Tom had been quite typical. He had risen at noon, lunched with Mrs. Lawrence, and then ridden abstractedly homeward atop one of his beloved buses.

"Why shouldn't you be bored," yawned Tom. "Isn't that the conventional frame of mind for the young man of your age and condition?"

"Yes," said Amory speculatively, "but I'm more than bored; I am restless."

"Love and war did for you."

"Well," Amory considered, "I'm not sure that the war itself had any great effect on either you or me—but it certainly ruined the old backgrounds, sort of killed individualism out of our generation."

Tom looked up in surprise.

"Yes it did," insisted Amory. "I'm not sure it didn't kill it out of the whole world. Oh, Lord, what a pleasure it used to be to dream I might be a really great dictator or writer or religious or political leader—and now even a Leonardo da Vinci or Lorenzo de Medici couldn't be a real old-fashioned bolt in the world. Life is too huge and complex. The world is so overgrown that it can't lift its own fingers, and I was planning to be such an important finger—"

"I don't agree with you," Tom interrupted. "There never were men placed in such egotistic positions since—oh, since the French Revolution."

Amory disagreed violently.

"You're mistaking this period when every nut is an individualist for a period of individualism. Wilson has only been powerful when he has represented; he's had to compromise over and over again. Just as soon as Trotsky and Lenin take a definite, consistent stand they'll become merely two-minute figures like Kerensky. Even Foch hasn't half the significance of Stonewall Jackson. War used to be the most individualistic pursuit of man, and yet the popular heroes of the war had neither authority nor responsibility: Guynemer and Sergeant York. How could a schoolboy make a hero of Pershing? A big man has no time really to do anything but just sit and be big."

"Then you don't think there will be any more permanent world heroes?"

"Yes—in history—not in life. Carlyle would have difficulty getting material for a new chapter on 'The Hero as a Big Man.'"

"Go on. I'm a good listener to-day."

"People try so hard to believe in leaders now, pitifully hard. But we no sooner get a popular reformer or politician or soldier or writer or philosopher—a Roosevelt, a Tolstoi, a

Wood, a Shaw, a Nietzsche, than the cross-currents of criticism wash him away. My Lord, no man can stand prominence these days. It's the surest path to obscurity. People get sick of hearing the same name over and over."

"Then you blame it on the press?"

"Absolutely. Look at you; you're on The New Democracy, considered the most brilliant weekly in the country, read by the men who do things and all that. What's your business? Why, to be as clever, as interesting, and as brilliantly cynical as possible about every man, doctrine, book, or policy that is assigned you to deal with. The more strong lights, the more spiritual scandal you can throw on the matter, the more money they pay you, the more the people buy the issue. You, Tom d'Invilliers, a blighted Shelley, changing, shifting, clever, unscrupulous, represent the critical consciousness of the race—Oh, don't protest, I know the stuff. I used to write book reviews in college; I considered it rare sport to refer to the latest honest, conscientious effort to propound a theory or a remedy as a 'welcome addition to our light summer reading.' Come on now, admit it."

Tom laughed, and Amory continued triumphantly.

"We want to believe. Young students try to believe in older authors, constituents try to believe in their Congressmen, countries try to believe in their statesmen, but they can't. Too many voices, too much scattered, illogical, ill-considered criticism. It's worse in the case of newspapers. Any rich, unprogressive old party with that particularly grasping, acquisitive form of mentality known as financial genius can own a paper that is the intellectual meat and drink of thousands of tired, hurried men, men too involved in the business of modern living to swallow anything but predigested food. For two cents the voter buys his politics, prejudices, and philosophy. A year later there is a new political ring or a change in the paper's ownership, consequence: more confusion, more contradiction, a sudden inrush of new ideas, their tempering, their distillation, the reaction against them—"

He paused only to get his breath.

"And that is why I have sworn not to put pen to paper until my ideas either clarify or depart entirely; I have quite enough sins on my soul without putting dangerous, shallow epigrams into people's heads; I might cause a poor, inoffensive capitalist to have a vulgar liaison with a bomb, or get some innocent little Bolshevik tangled up with a machine-gun bullet—"

Tom was growing restless under this lampooning of his connection with The New Democracy.

"What's all this got to do with your being bored?"

Amory considered that it had much to do with it.

"How'll I fit in?" he demanded. "What am I for? To propagate the race? According to the American novels we are led to believe that the 'healthy American boy' from nineteen to twenty-five is an entirely sexless animal. As a matter of fact, the healthier he is the less that's true. The only alternative to letting it get you is some violent interest. Well, the war

CHAPTER 2 Experiments in Convalescence

is over; I believe too much in the responsibilities of authorship to write just now; and business, well, business speaks for itself. It has no connection with anything in the world that I've ever been interested in, except a slim, utilitarian connection with economics. What I'd see of it, lost in a clerkship, for the next and best ten years of my life would have the intellectual content of an industrial movie."

"Try fiction," suggested Tom.

"Trouble is I get distracted when I start to write stories—get afraid I'm doing it instead of living—get thinking maybe life is waiting for me in the Japanese gardens at the Ritz or at Atlantic City or on the lower East Side.

"Anyway," he continued, "I haven't the vital urge. I wanted to be a regular human being but the girl couldn't see it that way."

"You'll find another."

"God! Banish the thought. Why don't you tell me that 'if the girl had been worth having she'd have waited for you'? No, sir, the girl really worth having won't wait for anybody. If I thought there'd be another I'd lose my remaining faith in human nature. Maybe I'll play—but Rosalind was the only girl in the wide world that could have held me."

"Well," yawned Tom, "I've played confidant a good hour by the clock. Still, I'm glad to see you're beginning to have violent views again on something."

"I am," agreed Amory reluctantly. "Yet when I see a happy family it makes me sick at my stomach—"

"Happy families try to make people feel that way," said Tom cynically.

TOM THE CENSOR

There were days when Amory listened. These were when Tom, wreathed in smoke, indulged in the slaughter of American literature. Words failed him.

"Fifty thousand dollars a year," he would cry. "My God! Look at them, look at them—Edna Ferber, Gouverneur Morris, Fanny Hurst, Mary Roberts Rinehart—not producing among 'em one story or novel that will last ten years. This man Cobb—I don't tink he's either clever or amusing—and what's more, I don't think very many people do, except the editors. He's just groggy with advertising. And—oh Harold Bell Wright oh Zane Grey—"

"They try."

"No, they don't even try. Some of them can write, but they won't sit down and do one honest novel. Most of them can't write, I'll admit. I believe Rupert Hughes tries to give a real, comprehensive picture of American life, but his style and perspective are barbarous. Ernest Poole and Dorothy Canfield try but they're hindered by their absolute lack of any sense of humor; but at least they crowd their work instead of spreading it thin. Every author ought to write every book as if he were going to be beheaded the day he finished it."

"Is that double entente?"

"Don't slow me up! Now there's a few of 'em that seem to have some cultural background, some intelligence and a good deal of literary felicity but they just simply won't

143

write honestly; they'd all claim there was no public for good stuff. Then why the devil is it that Wells, Conrad, Galsworthy, Shaw, Bennett, and the rest depend on America for over half their sales?"

"How does little Tommy like the poets?"

Tom was overcome. He dropped his arms until they swung loosely beside the chair and emitted faint grunts.

"I'm writing a satire on 'em now, calling it 'Boston Bards and Hearst Reviewers.'"

"Let's hear it," said Amory eagerly.

"I've only got the last few lines done."

"That's very modern. Let's hear 'em, if they're funny."

Tom produced a folded paper from his pocket and read aloud, pausing at intervals so that Amory could see that it was free verse:

"So
Walter Arensberg,
Alfred Kreymborg,
Carl Sandburg,
Louis Untermeyer,
Eunice Tietjens,
Clara Shanafelt,
James Oppenheim,
Maxwell Bodenheim,
Richard Glaenzer,
Scharmel Iris,
Conrad Aiken,
I place your names here
So that you may live
If only as names,
Sinuous, mauve-colored names,
In the Juvenalia
Of my collected editions."

Amory roared.

"You win the iron pansy. I'll buy you a meal on the arrogance of the last two lines."

Amory did not entirely agree with Tom's sweeping damnation of American novelists and poets. He enjoyed both Vachel Lindsay and Booth Tarkington, and admired the conscientious, if slender, artistry of Edgar Lee Masters.

"What I hate is this idiotic drivel about 'I am God—I am man—I ride the winds—I look through the smoke—I am the life sense.'"

"It's ghastly!"

144

CHAPTER 2 Experiments in Convalescence

"And I wish American novelists would give up trying to make business romantically interesting. Nobody wants to read about it, unless it's crooked business. If it was an entertaining subject they'd buy the life of James J. Hill and not one of these long office tragedies that harp along on the significance of smoke—"

"And gloom," said Tom. "That's another favorite, though I'll admit the Russians have the monopoly. Our specialty is stories about little girls who break their spines and get adopted by grouchy old men because they smile so much. You'd think we were a race of cheerful cripples and that the common end of the Russian peasant was suicide—"

"Six o'clock," said Amory, glancing at his wrist-watch. "I'll buy you a grea' big dinner on the strength of the Juvenalia of your collected editions."

LOOKING BACKWARD

July sweltered out with a last hot week, and Amory in another surge of unrest realized that it was just five months since he and Rosalind had met. Yet it was already hard for him to visualize the heart-whole boy who had stepped off the transport, passionately desiring the adventure of life. One night while the heat, overpowering and enervating, poured into the windows of his room he struggled for several hours in a vague effort to immortalize the poignancy of that time.

> The February streets, wind-washed by night, blow full of strange
> half-intermittent damps, bearing on wasted walks in shining sight
> wet snow plashed into gleams under the lamps, like golden oil
> from some divine machine, in an hour of thaw and stars.
>
> Strange damps—full of the eyes of many men, crowded with life
> borne in upon a lull.... Oh, I was young, for I could turn
> again to you, most finite and most beautiful, and taste the stuff
> of half-remembered dreams, sweet and new on your mouth.
>
> ... There was a tanging in the midnight air—silence was dead and
> sound not yet awoken—Life cracked like ice!—one brilliant note
> and there, radiant and pale, you stood... and spring had broken.
> (The icicles were short upon the roofs and the changeling city
> swooned.)
>
> Our thoughts were frosty mist along the eaves; our two ghosts
> kissed, high on the long, mazed wires—eerie half-laughter echoes
> here and leaves only a fatuous sigh for young desires; regret has
> followed after things she loved, leaving the great husk.

ANOTHER ENDING

145

In mid-August came a letter from Monsignor Darcy, who had evidently just stumbled on his address:

MY DEAR BOY:—

Your last letter was quite enough to make me worry about you. It was not a bit like yourself. Reading between the lines I should imagine that your engagement to this girl is making you rather unhappy, and I see you have lost all the feeling of romance that you had before the war. You make a great mistake if you think you can be romantic without religion. Sometimes I think that with both of us the secret of success, when we find it, is the mystical element in us: something flows into us that enlarges our personalities, and when it ebbs out our personalities shrink; I should call your last two letters rather shrivelled. Beware of losing yourself in the personality of another being, man or woman.

His Eminence Cardinal O'Neill and the Bishop of Boston are staying with me at present, so it is hard for me to get a moment to write, but I wish you would come up here later if only for a week-end. I go to Washington this week.

What I shall do in the future is hanging in the balance. Absolutely between ourselves I should not be surprised to see the red hat of a cardinal descend upon my unworthy head within the next eight months. In any event, I should like to have a house in New York or Washington where you could drop in for week-ends.

Amory, I'm very glad we're both alive; this war could easily have been the end of a brilliant family. But in regard to matrimony, you are now at the most dangerous period of your life. You might marry in haste and repent at leisure, but I think you won't. From what you write me about the present calamitous state of your finances, what you want is naturally impossible. However, if I judge you by the means I usually choose, I should say that there will be something of an emotional crisis within the next year.

Do write me. I feel annoyingly out of date on you.

With greatest affection,

THAYER DARCY.

Within a week after the receipt of this letter their little household fell precipitously to pieces. The immediate cause was the serious and probably chronic illness of Tom's mother. So they stored the furniture, gave instructions to sublet and shook hands gloomily in the Pennsylvania Station. Amory and Tom seemed always to be saying good-by.

Feeling very much alone, Amory yielded to an impulse and set off southward, intending to join Monsignor in Washington. They missed connections by two hours, and, deciding to spend a few days with an ancient, remembered uncle, Amory journeyed up through the luxuriant fields of Maryland into Ramilly County. But instead of two days his stay lasted from mid-August nearly through September, for in Maryland he met Eleanor.

CHAPTER 3 | Young Irony

For years afterward when Amory thought of Eleanor he seemed still to hear the wind sobbing around him and sending little chills into the places beside his heart. The night when they rode up the slope and watched the cold moon float through the clouds, he lost a further part of him that nothing could restore; and when he lost it he lost also the power of regretting it. Eleanor was, say, the last time that evil crept close to Amory under the mask of beauty, the last weird mystery that held him with wild fascination and pounded his soul to flakes.

With her his imagination ran riot and that is why they rode to the highest hill and watched an evil moon ride high, for they knew then that they could see the devil in each other. But Eleanor—did Amory dream her? Afterward their ghosts played, yet both of them hoped from their souls never to meet. Was it the infinite sadness of her eyes that drew him or the mirror of himself that he found in the gorgeous clarity of her mind? She will have no other adventure like Amory, and if she reads this she will say:

"And Amory will have no other adventure like me."

Nor will she sigh, any more than he would sigh.

Eleanor tried to put it on paper once:

"The fading things we only know
   We'll have forgotten...
     Put away...
Desires that melted with the snow,
   And dreams begotten
     This to-day:
The sudden dawns we laughed to greet,
   That all could see, that none could share,
Will be but dawns... and if we meet
   We shall not care.

Dear... not one tear will rise for this...
   A little while hence
     No regret
Will stir for a remembered kiss—
   Not even silence,
     When we've met,

Will give old ghosts a waste to roam,
　　　Or stir the surface of the sea...
　　If gray shapes drift beneath the foam
　　　We shall not see."

　　They quarrelled dangerously because Amory maintained that sea and see couldn't possibly be used as a rhyme. And then Eleanor had part of another verse that she couldn't find a beginning for:
　　"... But wisdom passes... still the years
　　　Will feed us wisdom.... Age will go
　　　Back to the old—
　　　　For all our tears
　　　　　We shall not know."

　　Eleanor hated Maryland passionately. She belonged to the oldest of the old families of Ramilly County and lived in a big, gloomy house with her grandfather. She had been born and brought up in France.... I see I am starting wrong. Let me begin again.
　　Amory was bored, as he usually was in the country. He used to go for far walks by himself—and wander along reciting "Ulalume" to the corn-fields, and congratulating Poe for drinking himself to death in that atmosphere of smiling complacency. One afternoon he had strolled for several miles along a road that was new to him, and then through a wood on bad advice from a colored woman... losing himself entirely. A passing storm decided to break out, and to his great impatience the sky grew black as pitch and the rain began to splatter down through the trees, become suddenly furtive and ghostly. Thunder rolled with menacing crashes up the valley and scattered through the woods in intermittent batteries. He stumbled blindly on, hunting for a way out, and finally, through webs of twisted branches, caught sight of a rift in the trees where the unbroken lightning showed open country. He rushed to the edge of the woods and then hesitated whether or not to cross the fields and try to reach the shelter of the little house marked by a light far down the valley. It was only half past five, but he could see scarcely ten steps before him, except when the lightning made everything vivid and grotesque for great sweeps around.
　　Suddenly a strange sound fell on his ears. It was a song, in a low, husky voice, a girl's voice, and whoever was singing was very close to him. A year before he might have laughed, or trembled; but in his restless mood he only stood and listened while the words sank into his consciousness:
　　"Les sanglots longs
　　　Des violons
　　　　De l'automne
　　　Blessent mon coeur

CHAPTER 3 Young Irony

D'une langueur
Monotone."

The lightning split the sky, but the song went on without a quaver. The girl was evidently in the field and the voice seemed to come vaguely from a haystack about twenty feet in front of him.

Then it ceased: ceased and began again in a weird chant that soared and hung and fell and blended with the rain:

"Tout suffocant
Et bleme quand
Sonne l'heure
Je me souviens
Des jours anciens
Et je pleure...."

"Who the devil is there in Ramilly County," muttered Amory aloud, "who would deliver Verlaine in an extemporaneous tune to a soaking haystack?"

"Somebody's there!" cried the voice unalarmed. "Who are you?—Manfred, St. Christopher, or Queen Victoria?"

"I'm Don Juan!" Amory shouted on impulse, raising his voice above the noise of the rain and the wind.

A delighted shriek came from the haystack.

"I know who you are—you're the blond boy that likes 'Ulalume'—I recognize your voice."

"How do I get up?" he cried from the foot of the haystack, whither he had arrived, dripping wet. A head appeared over the edge—it was so dark that Amory could just make out a patch of damp hair and two eyes that gleamed like a cat's.

"Run back!" came the voice, "and jump and I'll catch your hand—no, not there—on the other side."

He followed directions and as he sprawled up the side, knee-deep in hay, a small, white hand reached out, gripped his, and helped him onto the top.

"Here you are, Juan," cried she of the damp hair. "Do you mind if I drop the Don?"

"You've got a thumb like mine!" he exclaimed.

"And you're holding my hand, which is dangerous without seeing my face." He dropped it quickly.

As if in answer to his prayers came a flash of lightning and he looked eagerly at her who stood beside him on the soggy haystack, ten feet above the ground. But she had covered her face and he saw nothing but a slender figure, dark, damp, bobbed hair, and the small white hands with the thumbs that bent back like his.

149

"Sit down," she suggested politely, as the dark closed in on them. "If you'll sit opposite me in this hollow you can have half of the raincoat, which I was using as a water-proof tent until you so rudely interrupted me."

"I was asked," Amory said joyfully; "you asked me—you know you did."

"Don Juan always manages that," she said, laughing, "but I shan't call you that any more, because you've got reddish hair. Instead you can recite 'Ulalume' and I'll be Psyche, your soul."

Amory flushed, happily invisible under the curtain of wind and rain. They were sitting opposite each other in a slight hollow in the hay with the raincoat spread over most of them, and the rain doing for the rest. Amory was trying desperately to see Psyche, but the lightning refused to flash again, and he waited impatiently. Good Lord! supposing she wasn't beautiful—supposing she was forty and pedantic—heavens! Suppose, only suppose, she was mad. But he knew the last was unworthy. Here had Providence sent a girl to amuse him just as it sent Benvenuto Cellini men to murder, and he was wondering if she was mad, just because she exactly filled his mood.

"I'm not," she said.

"Not what?"

"Not mad. I didn't think you were mad when I first saw you, so it isn't fair that you should think so of me."

"How on earth—"

As long as they knew each other Eleanor and Amory could be "on a subject" and stop talking with the definite thought of it in their heads, yet ten minutes later speak aloud and find that their minds had followed the same channels and led them each to a parallel idea, an idea that others would have found absolutely unconnected with the first.

"Tell me," he demanded, leaning forward eagerly, "how do you know about 'Ulalume'—how did you know the color of my hair? What's your name? What were you doing here? Tell me all at once!"

Suddenly the lightning flashed in with a leap of overreaching light and he saw Eleanor, and looked for the first time into those eyes of hers. Oh, she was magnificent—pale skin, the color of marble in starlight, slender brows, and eyes that glittered green as emeralds in the blinding glare. She was a witch, of perhaps nineteen, he judged, alert and dreamy and with the tell-tale white line over her upper lip that was a weakness and a delight. He sank back with a gasp against the wall of hay.

"Now you've seen me," she said calmly, "and I suppose you're about to say that my green eyes are burning into your brain."

"What color is your hair?" he asked intently. "It's bobbed, isn't it?"

"Yes, it's bobbed. I don't know what color it is," she answered, musing, "so many men have asked me. It's medium, I suppose—No one ever looks long at my hair. I've got beautiful eyes, though, haven't I. I don't care what you say, I have beautiful eyes."

CHAPTER 3 Young Irony

"Answer my question, Madeline."

"Don't remember them all—besides my name isn't Madeline, it's Eleanor."

"I might have guessed it. You look like Eleanor—you have that Eleanor look. You know what I mean."

There was a silence as they listened to the rain.

"It's going down my neck, fellow lunatic," she offered finally.

"Answer my questions."

"Well—name of Savage, Eleanor; live in big old house mile down road; nearest living relation to be notified, grandfather—Ramilly Savage; height, five feet four inches; number on watch-case, 3077 W; nose, delicate aquiline; temperament, uncanny—"

"And me," Amory interrupted, "where did you see me?"

"Oh, you're one of those men," she answered haughtily, "must lug old self into conversation. Well, my boy, I was behind a hedge sunning myself one day last week, and along comes a man saying in a pleasant, conceited way of talking:

"'And now when the night was senescent'
    (says he)
'And the star dials pointed to morn
At the end of the path a liquescent'
    (says he)
'And nebulous lustre was born.'

"So I poked my eyes up over the hedge, but you had started to run, for some unknown reason, and so I saw but the back of your beautiful head. 'Oh!' says I, 'there's a man for whom many of us might sigh,' and I continued in my best Irish—"

"All right," Amory interrupted. "Now go back to yourself."

"Well, I will. I'm one of those people who go through the world giving other people thrills, but getting few myself except those I read into men on such nights as these. I have the social courage to go on the stage, but not the energy; I haven't the patience to write books; and I never met a man I'd marry. However, I'm only eighteen."

The storm was dying down softly and only the wind kept up its ghostly surge and made the stack lean and gravely settle from side to side. Amory was in a trance. He felt that every moment was precious. He had never met a girl like this before—she would never seem quite the same again. He didn't at all feel like a character in a play, the appropriate feeling in an unconventional situation—instead, he had a sense of coming home.

"I have just made a great decision," said Eleanor after another pause, "and that is why I'm here, to answer another of your questions. I have just decided that I don't believe in immortality."

"Really! how banal!"

"Frightfully so," she answered, "but depressing with a stale, sickly depression, nevertheless. I came out here to get wet—like a wet hen; wet hens always have great clarity

151

of mind," she concluded.

"Go on," Amory said politely.

"Well—I'm not afraid of the dark, so I put on my slicker and rubber boots and came out. You see I was always afraid, before, to say I didn't believe in God—because the lightning might strike me—but here I am and it hasn't, of course, but the main point is that this time I wasn't any more afraid of it than I had been when I was a Christian Scientist, like I was last year. So now I know I'm a materialist and I was fraternizing with the hay when you came out and stood by the woods, scared to death."

"Why, you little wretch—" cried Amory indignantly. "Scared of what?"

"Yourself!" she shouted, and he jumped. She clapped her hands and laughed. "See—see! Conscience—kill it like me! Eleanor Savage, materiologist—no jumping, no starting, come early—"

"But I have to have a soul," he objected. "I can't be rational—and I won't be molecular."

She leaned toward him, her burning eyes never leaving his own and whispered with a sort of romantic finality:

"I thought so, Juan, I feared so—you're sentimental. You're not like me. I'm a romantic little materialist."

"I'm not sentimental—I'm as romantic as you are. The idea, you know, is that the sentimental person thinks things will last—the romantic person has a desperate confidence that they won't." (This was an ancient distinction of Amory's.)

"Epigrams. I'm going home," she said sadly. "Let's get off the haystack and walk to the cross-roads."

They slowly descended from their perch. She would not let him help her down and motioning him away arrived in a graceful lump in the soft mud where she sat for an instant, laughing at herself. Then she jumped to her feet and slipped her hand into his, and they tiptoed across the fields, jumping and swinging from dry spot to dry spot. A transcendent delight seemed to sparkle in every pool of water, for the moon had risen and the storm had scurried away into western Maryland. When Eleanor's arm touched his he felt his hands grow cold with deadly fear lest he should lose the shadow brush with which his imagination was painting wonders of her. He watched her from the corners of his eyes as ever he did when he walked with her—she was a feast and a folly and he wished it had been his destiny to sit forever on a haystack and see life through her green eyes. His paganism soared that night and when she faded out like a gray ghost down the road, a deep singing came out of the fields and filled his way homeward. All night the summer moths flitted in and out of Amory's window; all night large looming sounds swayed in mystic revery through the silver grain—and he lay awake in the clear darkness.

SEPTEMBER

Amory selected a blade of grass and nibbled at it scientifically.

"I never fall in love in August or September," he proffered.

"When then?"

"Christmas or Easter. I'm a liturgist."

"Easter!" She turned up her nose. "Huh! Spring in corsets!"

"Easter would bore spring, wouldn't she? Easter has her hair braided, wears a tailored suit."

"Bind on thy sandals, oh, thou most fleet.

Over the splendor and speed of thy feet—"

quoted Eleanor softly, and then added: "I suppose Hallowe'en is a better day for autumn than Thanksgiving."

"Much better—and Christmas eve does very well for winter, but summer..."

"Summer has no day," she said. "We can't possibly have a summer love. So many people have tried that the name's become proverbial. Summer is only the unfulfilled promise of spring, a charlatan in place of the warm balmy nights I dream of in April. It's a sad season of life without growth.... It has no day."

"Fourth of July," Amory suggested facetiously.

"Don't be funny!" she said, raking him with her eyes.

"Well, what could fulfil the promise of spring?"

She thought a moment.

"Oh, I suppose heaven would, if there was one," she said finally, "a sort of pagan heaven—you ought to be a materialist," she continued irrelevantly.

"Why?"

"Because you look a good deal like the pictures of Rupert Brooke."

To some extent Amory tried to play Rupert Brooke as long as he knew Eleanor. What he said, his attitude toward life, toward her, toward himself, were all reflexes of the dead Englishman's literary moods. Often she sat in the grass, a lazy wind playing with her short hair, her voice husky as she ran up and down the scale from Grantchester to Waikiki. There was something most passionate in Eleanor's reading aloud. They seemed nearer, not only mentally, but physically, when they read, than when she was in his arms, and this was often, for they fell half into love almost from the first. Yet was Amory capable of love now? He could, as always, run through the emotions in a half hour, but even while they revelled in their imaginations, he knew that neither of them could care as he had cared once before—I suppose that was why they turned to Brooke, and Swinburne, and Shelley. Their chance was to make everything fine and finished and rich and imaginative; they must bend tiny golden tentacles from his imagination to hers, that would take the place of the great, deep love that was never so near, yet never so much of a dream.

One poem they read over and over; Swinburne's "Triumph of Time," and four lines of it rang in his memory afterward on warm nights when he saw the fireflies among dusky tree trunks and heard the low drone of many frogs. Then Eleanor seemed to come out of the night and stand by him, and he heard her throaty voice, with its tone of a fleecy-headed drum, repeating:

"Is it worth a tear, is it worth an hour,
  To think of things that are well outworn;
 Of fruitless husk and fugitive flower,
  The dream foregone and the deed foreborne?"

They were formally introduced two days later, and his aunt told him her history. The Ramillys were two: old Mr. Ramilly and his granddaughter, Eleanor. She had lived in France with a restless mother whom Amory imagined to have been very like his own, on whose death she had come to America, to live in Maryland. She had gone to Baltimore first to stay with a bachelor uncle, and there she insisted on being a debutante at the age of seventeen. She had a wild winter and arrived in the country in March, having quarrelled frantically with all her Baltimore relatives, and shocked them into fiery protest. A rather fast crowd had come out, who drank cocktails in limousines and were promiscuously condescending and patronizing toward older people, and Eleanor with an esprit that hinted strongly of the boulevards, led many innocents still redolent of St. Timothy's and Farmington, into paths of Bohemian naughtiness. When the story came to her uncle, a forgetful cavalier of a more hypocritical era, there was a scene, from which Eleanor emerged, subdued but rebellious and indignant, to seek haven with her grandfather who hovered in the country on the near side of senility. That's as far as her story went; she told him the rest herself, but that was later.

Often they swam and as Amory floated lazily in the water he shut his mind to all thoughts except those of hazy soap-bubble lands where the sun splattered through wind-drunk trees. How could any one possibly think or worry, or do anything except splash and dive and loll there on the edge of time while the flower months failed. Let the days move over—sadness and memory and pain recurred outside, and here, once more, before he went on to meet them he wanted to drift and be young.

There were days when Amory resented that life had changed from an even progress along a road stretching ever in sight, with the scenery merging and blending, into a succession of quick, unrelated scenes—two years of sweat and blood, that sudden absurd instinct for paternity that Rosalind had stirred; the half-sensual, half-neurotic quality of this autumn with Eleanor. He felt that it would take all time, more than he could ever spare, to glue these strange cumbersome pictures into the scrap-book of his life. It was all like a banquet where he sat for this half-hour of his youth and tried to enjoy brilliant epicurean courses.

Dimly he promised himself a time where all should be welded together. For months it seemed that he had alternated between being borne along a stream of love or fascination,

CHAPTER 3 Young Irony

or left in an eddy, and in the eddies he had not desired to think, rather to be picked up on a wave's top and swept along again.

"The despairing, dying autumn and our love—how well they harmonize!" said Eleanor sadly one day as they lay dripping by the water.

"The Indian summer of our hearts—" he ceased.

"Tell me," she said finally, "was she light or dark?"

"Light."

"Was she more beautiful than I am?"

"I don't know," said Amory shortly.

One night they walked while the moon rose and poured a great burden of glory over the garden until it seemed fairyland with Amory and Eleanor, dim phantasmal shapes, expressing eternal beauty in curious elfin love moods. Then they turned out of the moonlight into the trellised darkness of a vine-hung pagoda, where there were scents so plaintive as to be nearly musical.

"Light a match," she whispered. "I want to see you."

Scratch! Flare!

The night and the scarred trees were like scenery in a play, and to be there with Eleanor, shadowy and unreal, seemed somehow oddly familiar. Amory thought how it was only the past that ever seemed strange and unbelievable. The match went out.

"It's black as pitch."

"We're just voices now," murmured Eleanor, "little lonesome voices. Light another."

"That was my last match."

Suddenly he caught her in his arms.

"You are mine—you know you're mine!" he cried wildly... the moonlight twisted in through the vines and listened... the fireflies hung upon their whispers as if to win his glance from the glory of their eyes.

THE END OF SUMMER

"No wind is stirring in the grass; not one wind stirs... the water in the hidden pools, as glass, fronts the full moon and so inters the golden token in its icy mass," chanted Eleanor to the trees that skeletoned the body of the night. "Isn't it ghostly here? If you can hold your horse's feet up, let's cut through the woods and find the hidden pools."

"It's after one, and you'll get the devil," he objected, "and I don't know enough about horses to put one away in the pitch dark."

"Shut up, you old fool," she whispered irrelevantly, and, leaning over, she patted him lazily with her riding-crop. "You can leave your old plug in our stable and I'll send him over to-morrow."

"But my uncle has got to drive me to the station with this old plug at seven o'clock."

"Don't be a spoil-sport—remember, you have a tendency toward wavering that prevents you from being the entire light of my life."

155

Amory drew his horse up close beside, and, leaning toward her, grasped her hand.

"Say I am—quick, or I'll pull you over and make you ride behind me."

She looked up and smiled and shook her head excitedly.

"Oh, do!—or rather, don't! Why are all the exciting things so uncomfortable, like fighting and exploring and ski-ing in Canada? By the way, we're going to ride up Harper's Hill. I think that comes in our programme about five o'clock."

"You little devil," Amory growled. "You're going to make me stay up all night and sleep in the train like an immigrant all day to-morrow, going back to New York."

"Hush! some one's coming along the road—let's go! Whoo-ee-oop!" And with a shout that probably gave the belated traveller a series of shivers, she turned her horse into the woods and Amory followed slowly, as he had followed her all day for three weeks.

The summer was over, but he had spent the days in watching Eleanor, a graceful, facile Manfred, build herself intellectual and imaginative pyramids while she revelled in the artificialities of the temperamental teens and they wrote poetry at the dinner-table.

When Vanity kissed Vanity, a hundred happy Junes ago, he
pondered o'er her breathlessly, and, that all men might ever
know, he rhymed her eyes with life and death:

"Thru Time I'll save my love!" he said... yet Beauty
vanished with his breath, and, with her lovers, she was dead...

—Ever his wit and not her eyes, ever his art and not her hair:

"Who'd learn a trick in rhyme, be wise and pause before his
sonnet there"... So all my words, however true, might sing
you to a thousandth June, and no one ever know that you were
Beauty for an afternoon.

So he wrote one day, when he pondered how coldly we thought of the "Dark Lady of the Sonnets," and how little we remembered her as the great man wanted her remembered. For what Shakespeare must have desired, to have been able to write with such divine despair, was that the lady should live... and now we have no real interest in her.... The irony of it is that if he had cared more for the poem than for the lady the sonnet would be only obvious, imitative rhetoric and no one would ever have read it after twenty years....

This was the last night Amory ever saw Eleanor. He was leaving in the morning and they had agreed to take a long farewell trot by the cold moonlight. She wanted to talk, she said—perhaps the last time in her life that she could be rational (she meant pose with comfort). So they had turned into the woods and rode for half an hour with scarcely a word, except when she whispered "Damn!" at a bothersome branch—whispered it as no other girl was ever able to whisper it. Then they started up Harper's Hill, walking their tired horses.

CHAPTER 3 Young Irony

"Good Lord! It's quiet here!" whispered Eleanor; "much more lonesome than the woods."

"I hate woods," Amory said, shuddering. "Any kind of foliage or underbrush at night. Out here it's so broad and easy on the spirit."

"The long slope of a long hill."

"And the cold moon rolling moonlight down it."

"And thee and me, last and most important."

It was quiet that night—the straight road they followed up to the edge of the cliff knew few footsteps at any time. Only an occasional negro cabin, silver-gray in the rock-ribbed moonlight, broke the long line of bare ground; behind lay the black edge of the woods like a dark frosting on white cake, and ahead the sharp, high horizon. It was much colder—so cold that it settled on them and drove all the warm nights from their minds.

"The end of summer," said Eleanor softly. "Listen to the beat of our horses' hoofs—'tump-tump-tump-a-tump.' Have you ever been feverish and had all noises divide into 'tump-tump-tump' until you could swear eternity was divisible into so many tumps? That's the way I feel—old horses go tump-tump.... I guess that's the only thing that separates horses and clocks from us. Human beings can't go 'tump-tump-tump' without going crazy."

The breeze freshened and Eleanor pulled her cape around her and shivered.

"Are you very cold?" asked Amory.

"No, I'm thinking about myself—my black old inside self, the real one, with the fundamental honesty that keeps me from being absolutely wicked by making me realize my own sins."

They were riding up close by the cliff and Amory gazed over. Where the fall met the ground a hundred feet below, a black stream made a sharp line, broken by tiny glints in the swift water.

"Rotten, rotten old world," broke out Eleanor suddenly, "and the wretchedest thing of all is me—oh, why am I a girl? Why am I not a stupid—? Look at you; you're stupider than I am, not much, but some, and you can lope about and get bored and then lope somewhere else, and you can play around with girls without being involved in meshes of sentiment, and you can do anything and be justified—and here am I with the brains to do everything, yet tied to the sinking ship of future matrimony. If I were born a hundred years from now, well and good, but now what's in store for me—I have to marry, that goes without saying. Who? I'm too bright for most men, and yet I have to descend to their level and let them patronize my intellect in order to get their attention. Every year that I don't marry I've got less chance for a first-class man. At the best I can have my choice from one or two cities and, of course, I have to marry into a dinner-coat.

"Listen," she leaned close again, "I like clever men and good-looking men, and, of course, no one cares more for personality than I do. Oh, just one person in fifty has any glimmer of what sex is. I'm hipped on Freud and all that, but it's rotten that every bit of real

157

love in the world is ninety-nine per cent passion and one little soupcon of jealousy." She finished as suddenly as she began.

"Of course, you're right," Amory agreed. "It's a rather unpleasant overpowering force that's part of the machinery under everything. It's like an actor that lets you see his mechanics! Wait a minute till I think this out...."

He paused and tried to get a metaphor. They had turned the cliff and were riding along the road about fifty feet to the left.

"You see every one's got to have some cloak to throw around it. The mediocre intellects, Plato's second class, use the remnants of romantic chivalry diluted with Victorian sentiment—and we who consider ourselves the intellectuals cover it up by pretending that it's another side of us, has nothing to do with our shining brains; we pretend that the fact that we realize it is really absolving us from being a prey to it. But the truth is that sex is right in the middle of our purest abstractions, so close that it obscures vision.... I can kiss you now and will. ..." He leaned toward her in his saddle, but she drew away.

"I can't—I can't kiss you now—I'm more sensitive."

"You're more stupid then," he declared rather impatiently. "Intellect is no protection from sex any more than convention is..."

"What is?" she fired up. "The Catholic Church or the maxims of Confucius?"

Amory looked up, rather taken aback.

"That's your panacea, isn't it?" she cried. "Oh, you're just an old hypocrite, too. Thousands of scowling priests keeping the degenerate Italians and illiterate Irish repentant with gabble-gabble about the sixth and ninth commandments. It's just all cloaks, sentiment and spiritual rouge and panaceas. I'll tell you there is no God, not even a definite abstract goodness; so it's all got to be worked out for the individual by the individual here in high white foreheads like mine, and you're too much the prig to admit it." She let go her reins and shook her little fists at the stars.

"If there's a God let him strike me—strike me!"

"Talking about God again after the manner of atheists," Amory said sharply. His materialism, always a thin cloak, was torn to shreds by Eleanor's blasphemy.... She knew it and it angered him that she knew it.

"And like most intellectuals who don't find faith convenient," he continued coldly, "like Napoleon and Oscar Wilde and the rest of your type, you'll yell loudly for a priest on your death-bed."

Eleanor drew her horse up sharply and he reined in beside her.

"Will I?" she said in a queer voice that scared him. "Will I? Watch! I'm going over the cliff!" And before he could interfere she had turned and was riding breakneck for the end of the plateau.

He wheeled and started after her, his body like ice, his nerves in a vast clangor. There was no chance of stopping her. The moon was under a cloud and her horse would step blindly over. Then some ten feet from the edge of the cliff she gave a sudden shriek and flung herself sideways—plunged from her horse and, rolling over twice, landed in a pile of brush five feet from the edge. The horse went over with a frantic whinny. In a minute he was by Eleanor's side and saw that her eyes were open.

"Eleanor!" he cried.

She did not answer, but her lips moved and her eyes filled with sudden tears.

"Eleanor, are you hurt?"

"No; I don't think so," she said faintly, and then began weeping.

"My horse dead?"

"Good God—Yes!"

"Oh!" she wailed. "I thought I was going over. I didn't know—"

He helped her gently to her feet and boosted her onto his saddle. So they started homeward; Amory walking and she bent forward on the pommel, sobbing bitterly.

"I've got a crazy streak," she faltered, "twice before I've done things like that. When I was eleven mother went—went mad—stark raving crazy. We were in Vienna—"

All the way back she talked haltingly about herself, and Amory's love waned slowly with the moon. At her door they started from habit to kiss good night, but she could not run into his arms, nor were they stretched to meet her as in the week before. For a minute they stood there, hating each other with a bitter sadness. But as Amory had loved himself in Eleanor, so now what he hated was only a mirror. Their poses were strewn about the pale dawn like broken glass. The stars were long gone and there were left only the little sighing gusts of wind and the silences between... but naked souls are poor things ever, and soon he turned homeward and let new lights come in with the sun.

A POEM THAT ELEANOR SENT AMORY SEVERAL YEARS LATER

"Here, Earth born, over the lilt of the water,
  Lisping its music and bearing a burden of light,
 Bosoming day as a laughing and radiant daughter...
  Here we may whisper unheard, unafraid of the night.
 Walking alone... was it splendor, or what, we were bound with,
  Deep in the time when summer lets down her hair?
 Shadows we loved and the patterns they covered the ground with
  Tapestries, mystical, faint in the breathless air.

 That was the day... and the night for another story,
  Pale as a dream and shadowed with pencilled trees—
 Ghosts of the stars came by who had sought for glory,
  Whispered to us of peace in the plaintive breeze,
 Whispered of old dead faiths that the day had shattered,
  Youth the penny that bought delight of the moon;

That was the urge that we knew and the language that mattered
   That was the debt that we paid to the usurer June.

Here, deepest of dreams, by the waters that bring not
   Anything back of the past that we need not know,
What if the light is but sun and the little streams sing not,
   We are together, it seems... I have loved you so...
What did the last night hold, with the summer over,
   Drawing us back to the home in the changing glade?
What leered out of the dark in the ghostly clover?
   God!... till you stirred in your sleep... and were wild
   afraid...

Well... we have passed... we are chronicle now to the eerie.
   Curious metal from meteors that failed in the sky;
Earth-born the tireless is stretched by the water, quite weary,
   Close to this ununderstandable changeling that's I...
Fear is an echo we traced to Security's daughter;
   Now we are faces and voices... and less, too soon,
   Whispering half-love over the lilt of the water...
   Youth the penny that bought delight of the moon."

A POEM AMORY SENT TO ELEANOR AND WHICH HE CALLED "SUMMER STORM"

"Faint winds, and a song fading and leaves falling,
   Faint winds, and far away a fading laughter...
   And the rain and over the fields a voice calling...

Our gray blown cloud scurries and lifts above,
Slides on the sun and flutters there to waft her
Sisters on. The shadow of a dove
Falls on the cote, the trees are filled with wings;
And down the valley through the crying trees
The body of the darker storm flies; brings
With its new air the breath of sunken seas
And slender tenuous thunder...
            But I wait...
Wait for the mists and for the blacker rain—
Heavier winds that stir the veil of fate,

Happier winds that pile her hair;
>Again
They tear me, teach me, strew the heavy air
Upon me, winds that I know, and storm.

There was a summer every rain was rare;
There was a season every wind was warm....
And now you pass me in the mist... your hair
Rain-blown about you, damp lips curved once more
In that wild irony, that gay despair
That made you old when we have met before;
Wraith-like you drift on out before the rain,
Across the fields, blown with the stemless flowers,
With your old hopes, dead leaves and loves again—
Dim as a dream and wan with all old hours
(Whispers will creep into the growing dark...
Tumult will die over the trees)
>Now night
Tears from her wetted breast the splattered blouse
Of day, glides down the dreaming hills, tear-bright,
To cover with her hair the eerie green...
Love for the dusk... Love for the glistening after;
Quiet the trees to their last tops... serene...

Faint winds, and far away a fading laughter..."

CHAPTER 4 The Supercilious Sacrifice

Atlantic City. Amory paced the board walk at day's end, lulled by the everlasting surge of changing waves, smelling the half-mournful odor of the salt breeze. The sea, he thought, had treasured its memories deeper than the faithless land. It seemed still to whisper of Norse galleys ploughing the water world under raven-figured flags, of the British dreadnoughts, gray bulwarks of civilization steaming up through the fog of one dark July into the North Sea.

"Well—Amory Blaine!"

Amory looked down into the street below. A low racing car had drawn to a stop and a familiar cheerful face protruded from the driver's seat.

"Come on down, goopher!" cried Alec.

Amory called a greeting and descending a flight of wooden steps approached the car. He and Alec had been meeting intermittently, but the barrier of Rosalind lay always between them. He was sorry for this; he hated to lose Alec.

"Mr. Blaine, this is Miss Waterson, Miss Wayne, and Mr. Tully."

"How d'y do?"

"Amory," said Alec exuberantly, "if you'll jump in we'll take you to some secluded nook and give you a wee jolt of Bourbon."

Amory considered.

"That's an idea."

"Step in—move over, Jill, and Amory will smile very handsomely at you."

Amory squeezed into the back seat beside a gaudy, vermilion-lipped blonde.

"Hello, Doug Fairbanks," she said flippantly. "Walking for exercise or hunting for company?"

"I was counting the waves," replied Amory gravely. "I'm going in for statistics."

"Don't kid me, Doug."

When they reached an unfrequented side street Alec stopped the car among deep shadows.

"What you doing down here these cold days, Amory?" he demanded, as he produced a quart of Bourbon from under the fur rug.

Amory avoided the question. Indeed, he had had no definite reason for coming to the coast.

"Do you remember that party of ours, sophomore year?" he asked instead.

"Do I? When we slept in the pavilions up in Asbury Park—"

CHAPTER 4   The Supercilious Sacrifice

"Lord, Alec! It's hard to think that Jesse and Dick and Kerry are all three dead."

Alec shivered.

"Don't talk about it. These dreary fall days depress me enough."

Jill seemed to agree.

"Doug here is sorta gloomy anyways," she commented. "Tell him to drink deep—it's good and scarce these days."

"What I really want to ask you, Amory, is where you are—"

"Why, New York, I suppose—"

"I mean to-night, because if you haven't got a room yet you'd better help me out."

"Glad to."

"You see, Tully and I have two rooms with bath between at the Ranier, and he's got to go back to New York. I don't want to have to move. Question is, will you occupy one of the rooms?"

Amory was willing, if he could get in right away.

"You'll find the key in the office; the rooms are in my name."

Declining further locomotion or further stimulation, Amory left the car and sauntered back along the board walk to the hotel.

He was in an eddy again, a deep, lethargic gulf, without desire to work or write, love or dissipate. For the first time in his life he rather longed for death to roll over his generation, obliterating their petty fevers and struggles and exultations. His youth seemed never so vanished as now in the contrast between the utter loneliness of this visit and that riotous, joyful party of four years before. Things that had been the merest commonplaces of his life then, deep sleep, the sense of beauty around him, all desire, had flown away and the gaps they left were filled only with the great listlessness of his disillusion.

"To hold a man a woman has to appeal to the worst in him." This sentence was the thesis of most of his bad nights, of which he felt this was to be one. His mind had already started to play variations on the subject. Tireless passion, fierce jealousy, longing to possess and crush—these alone were left of all his love for Rosalind; these remained to him as payment for the loss of his youth—bitter calomel under the thin sugar of love's exaltation.

In his room he undressed and wrapping himself in blankets to keep out the chill October air drowsed in an armchair by the open window.

He remembered a poem he had read months before:

"Oh staunch old heart who toiled so long for me,
I waste my years sailing along the sea—"

Yet he had no sense of waste, no sense of the present hope that waste implied. He felt that life had rejected him.

"Rosalind! Rosalind!" He poured the words softly into the half-darkness until she seemed to permeate the room; the wet salt breeze filled his hair with moisture, the rim of a moon seared the sky and made the curtains dim and ghostly. He fell asleep.

When he awoke it was very late and quiet. The blanket had slipped partly off his shoulders and he touched his skin to find it damp and cold.

Then he became aware of a tense whispering not ten feet away.

He became rigid.

"Don't make a sound!" It was Alec's voice. "Jill—do you hear me?"

"Yes—" breathed very low, very frightened. They were in the bathroom.

Then his ears caught a louder sound from somewhere along the corridor outside. It was a mumbling of men's voices and a repeated muffled rapping. Amory threw off the blankets and moved close to the bathroom door.

"My God!" came the girl's voice again. "You'll have to let them in."

"Sh!"

Suddenly a steady, insistent knocking began at Amory's hall door and simultaneously out of the bathroom came Alec, followed by the vermilion-lipped girl. They were both clad in pajamas.

"Amory!" an anxious whisper.

"What's the trouble?"

"It's house detectives. My God, Amory—they're just looking for a test-case—"

"Well, better let them in."

"You don't understand. They can get me under the Mann Act."

The girl followed him slowly, a rather miserable, pathetic figure in the darkness.

Amory tried to plan quickly.

"You make a racket and let them in your room," he suggested anxiously, "and I'll get her out by this door."

"They're here too, though. They'll watch this door."

"Can't you give a wrong name?"

"No chance. I registered under my own name; besides, they'd trail the auto license number."

"Say you're married."

"Jill says one of the house detectives knows her."

The girl had stolen to the bed and tumbled upon it; lay there listening wretchedly to the knocking which had grown gradually to a pounding. Then came a man's voice, angry and imperative:

"Open up or we'll break the door in!"

In the silence when this voice ceased Amory realized that there were other things in the room besides people... over and around the figure crouched on the bed there hung an aura, gossamer as a moonbeam, tainted as stale, weak wine, yet a horror, diffusively brooding already over the three of them... and over by the window among the stirring curtains stood something else, featureless and indistinguishable, yet strangely familiar.... Simultaneously

CHAPTER 4 The Supercilious Sacrifice

two great cases presented themselves side by side to Amory; all that took place in his mind, then, occupied in actual time less than ten seconds.

The first fact that flashed radiantly on his comprehension was the great impersonality of sacrifice—he perceived that what we call love and hate, reward and punishment, had no more to do with it than the date of the month. He quickly recapitulated the story of a sacrifice he had heard of in college: a man had cheated in an examination; his roommate in a gust of sentiment had taken the entire blame—due to the shame of it the innocent one's entire future seemed shrouded in regret and failure, capped by the ingratitude of the real culprit. He had finally taken his own life—years afterward the facts had come out. At the time the story had both puzzled and worried Amory. Now he realized the truth; that sacrifice was no purchase of freedom. It was like a great elective office, it was like an inheritance of power—to certain people at certain times an essential luxury, carrying with it not a guarantee but a responsibility, not a security but an infinite risk. Its very momentum might drag him down to ruin—the passing of the emotional wave that made it possible might leave the one who made it high and dry forever on an island of despair.

... Amory knew that afterward Alec would secretly hate him for having done so much for him....

... All this was flung before Amory like an opened scroll, while ulterior to him and speculating upon him were those two breathless, listening forces: the gossamer aura that hung over and about the girl and that familiar thing by the window.

Sacrifice by its very nature was arrogant and impersonal; sacrifice should be eternally supercilious.

Weep not for me but for thy children.

That—thought Amory—would be somehow the way God would talk to me.

Amory felt a sudden surge of joy and then like a face in a motion-picture the aura over the bed faded out; the dynamic shadow by the window, that was as near as he could name it, remained for the fraction of a moment and then the breeze seemed to lift it swiftly out of the room. He clinched his hands in quick ecstatic excitement... the ten seconds were up....

"Do what I say, Alec—do what I say. Do you understand?"

Alec looked at him dumbly—his face a tableau of anguish.

"You have a family," continued Amory slowly. "You have a family and it's important that you should get out of this. Do you hear me?" He repeated clearly what he had said. "Do you hear me?"

"I hear you." The voice was curiously strained, the eyes never for a second left Amory's.

"Alec, you're going to lie down here. If any one comes in you act drunk. You do what I say—if you don't I'll probably kill you."

There was another moment while they stared at each other. Then Amory went briskly to the bureau and, taking his pocket-book, beckoned peremptorily to the girl. He heard one

165

word from Alec that sounded like "penitentiary," then he and Jill were in the bathroom with the door bolted behind them.

"You're here with me," he said sternly. "You've been with me all evening."

She nodded, gave a little half cry.

In a second he had the door of the other room open and three men entered. There was an immediate flood of electric light and he stood there blinking.

"You've been playing a little too dangerous a game, young man!"

Amory laughed.

"Well?"

The leader of the trio nodded authoritatively at a burly man in a check suit.

"All right, Olson."

"I got you, Mr. O'May," said Olson, nodding. The other two took a curious glance at their quarry and then withdrew, closing the door angrily behind them.

The burly man regarded Amory contemptuously.

"Didn't you ever hear of the Mann Act? Coming down here with her," he indicated the girl with his thumb, "with a New York license on your car—to a hotel like this." He shook his head implying that he had struggled over Amory but now gave him up.

"Well," said Amory rather impatiently, "what do you want us to do?"

"Get dressed, quick—and tell your friend not to make such a racket." Jill was sobbing noisily on the bed, but at these words she subsided sulkily and, gathering up her clothes, retired to the bathroom. As Amory slipped into Alec's B. V. D.'s he found that his attitude toward the situation was agreeably humorous. The aggrieved virtue of the burly man made him want to laugh.

"Anybody else here?" demanded Olson, trying to look keen and ferret-like.

"Fellow who had the rooms," said Amory carelessly. "He's drunk as an owl, though. Been in there asleep since six o'clock."

"I'll take a look at him presently."

"How did you find out?" asked Amory curiously.

"Night clerk saw you go up-stairs with this woman."

Amory nodded; Jill reappeared from the bathroom, completely if rather untidily arrayed.

"Now then," began Olson, producing a note-book, "I want your real names—no damn John Smith or Mary Brown."

"Wait a minute," said Amory quietly. "Just drop that big-bully stuff. We merely got caught, that's all."

Olson glared at him.

"Name?" he snapped.

Amory gave his name and New York address.

"And the lady?"

"Miss Jill—"

CHAPTER 4 The Supercilious Sacrifice

"Say," cried Olson indignantly, "just ease up on the nursery rhymes. What's your name? Sarah Murphy? Minnie Jackson?"

"Oh, my God!" cried the girl cupping her tear-stained face in her hands. "I don't want my mother to know. I don't want my mother to know."

"Come on now!"

"Shut up!" cried Amory at Olson.

An instant's pause.

"Stella Robbins," she faltered finally. "General Delivery, Rugway, New Hampshire."

Olson snapped his note-book shut and looked at them very ponderously.

"By rights the hotel could turn the evidence over to the police and you'd go to penitentiary, you would, for bringin' a girl from one State to 'nother f'r immoral purp'ses—" He paused to let the majesty of his words sink in. "But—the hotel is going to let you off."

"It doesn't want to get in the papers," cried Jill fiercely. "Let us off! Huh!"

A great lightness surrounded Amory. He realized that he was safe and only then did he appreciate the full enormity of what he might have incurred.

"However," continued Olson, "there's a protective association among the hotels. There's been too much of this stuff, and we got a 'rangement with the newspapers so that you get a little free publicity. Not the name of the hotel, but just a line sayin' that you had a little trouble in 'lantic City. See?"

"I see."

"You're gettin' off light—damn light—but—"

"Come on," said Amory briskly. "Let's get out of here. We don't need a valedictory."

Olson walked through the bathroom and took a cursory glance at Alec's still form. Then he extinguished the lights and motioned them to follow him. As they walked into the elevator Amory considered a piece of bravado—yielded finally. He reached out and tapped Olson on the arm.

"Would you mind taking off your hat? There's a lady in the elevator."

Olson's hat came off slowly. There was a rather embarrassing two minutes under the lights of the lobby while the night clerk and a few belated guests stared at them curiously; the loudly dressed girl with bent head, the handsome young man with his chin several points aloft; the inference was quite obvious. Then the chill outdoors—where the salt air was fresher and keener still with the first hints of morning.

"You can get one of those taxis and beat it," said Olson, pointing to the blurred outline of two machines whose drivers were presumably asleep inside.

"Good-by," said Olson. He reached in his pocket suggestively, but Amory snorted, and, taking the girl's arm, turned away.

"Where did you tell the driver to go?" she asked as they whirled along the dim street.

"The station."

167

"If that guy writes my mother—"

"He won't. Nobody'll ever know about this—except our friends and enemies."

Dawn was breaking over the sea.

"It's getting blue," she said.

"It does very well," agreed Amory critically, and then as an after-thought: "It's almost breakfast-time—do you want something to eat?"

"Food—" she said with a cheerful laugh. "Food is what queered the party. We ordered a big supper to be sent up to the room about two o'clock. Alec didn't give the waiter a tip, so I guess the little bastard snitched."

Jill's low spirits seemed to have gone faster than the scattering night. "Let me tell you," she said emphatically, "when you want to stage that sorta party stay away from liquor, and when you want to get tight stay away from bedrooms."

"I'll remember."

He tapped suddenly at the glass and they drew up at the door of an all-night restaurant.

"Is Alec a great friend of yours?" asked Jill as they perched themselves on high stools inside, and set their elbows on the dingy counter.

"He used to be. He probably won't want to be any more—and never understand why."

"It was sorta crazy you takin' all that blame. Is he pretty important? Kinda more important than you are?"

Amory laughed.

"That remains to be seen," he answered. "That's the question."

THE COLLAPSE OF SEVERAL PILLARS

Two days later back in New York Amory found in a newspaper what he had been searching for—a dozen lines which announced to whom it might concern that Mr. Amory Blaine, who "gave his address" as, etc., had been requested to leave his hotel in Atlantic City because of entertaining in his room a lady not his wife.

Then he started, and his fingers trembled, for directly above was a longer paragraph of which the first words were:

"Mr. and Mrs. Leland R. Connage are announcing the engagement of their daughter, Rosalind, to Mr. J. Dawson Ryder, of Hartford, Connecticut—"

He dropped the paper and lay down on his bed with a frightened, sinking sensation in the pit of his stomach. She was gone, definitely, finally gone. Until now he had half unconsciously cherished the hope deep in his heart that some day she would need him and send for him, cry that it had been a mistake, that her heart ached only for the pain she had caused him. Never again could he find even the sombre luxury of wanting her—not this Rosalind, harder, older—nor any beaten, broken woman that his imagination brought to the door of his forties—Amory had wanted her youth, the fresh radiance of her mind and body, the stuff that she was selling now once and for all. So far as he was concerned, young Rosalind was dead.

CHAPTER 4 The Supercilious Sacrifice

A day later came a crisp, terse letter from Mr. Barton in Chicago, which informed him that as three more street-car companies had gone into the hands of receivers he could expect for the present no further remittances. Last of all, on a dazed Sunday night, a telegram told him of Monsignor Darcy's sudden death in Philadelphia five days before.

He knew then what it was that he had perceived among the curtains of the room in Atlantic City.

CHAPTER 5

The Egotist Becomes a Personage

"A fathom deep in sleep I lie
 With old desires, restrained before,
To clamor lifeward with a cry,
 As dark flies out the greying door;
And so in quest of creeds to share
 I seek assertive day again...
But old monotony is there:
 Endless avenues of rain.

Oh, might I rise again! Might I
 Throw off the heat of that old wine,
See the new morning mass the sky
 With fairy towers, line on line;
Find each mirage in the high air
 A symbol, not a dream again...
But old monotony is there:
 Endless avenues of rain."

Under the glass portcullis of a theatre Amory stood, watching the first great drops of rain splatter down and flatten to dark stains on the sidewalk. The air became gray and opalescent; a solitary light suddenly outlined a window over the way; then another light; then a hundred more danced and glimmered into vision. Under his feet a thick, iron-studded skylight turned yellow; in the street the lamps of the taxi-cabs sent out glistening sheens along the already black pavement. The unwelcome November rain had perversely stolen the day's last hour and pawned it with that ancient fence, the night.

The silence of the theatre behind him ended with a curious snapping sound, followed by the heavy roaring of a rising crowd and the interlaced clatter of many voices. The matinee was over.

He stood aside, edged a little into the rain to let the throng pass. A small boy rushed out, sniffed in the damp, fresh air and turned up the collar of his coat; came three or four couples in a great hurry; came a further scattering of people whose eyes as they emerged glanced invariably, first at the wet street, then at the rain-filled air, finally at the dismal sky; last a dense, strolling mass that depressed him with its heavy odor compounded of the tobacco

CHAPTER 5 The Egotist Becomes a Personage

smell of the men and the fetid sensuousness of stale powder on women. After the thick crowd came another scattering; a stray half-dozen; a man on crutches; finally the rattling bang of folding seats inside announced that the ushers were at work.

New York seemed not so much awakening as turning over in its bed. Pallid men rushed by, pinching together their coat-collars; a great swarm of tired, magpie girls from a department-store crowded along with shrieks of strident laughter, three to an umbrella; a squad of marching policemen passed, already miraculously protected by oilskin capes.

The rain gave Amory a feeling of detachment, and the numerous unpleasant aspects of city life without money occurred to him in threatening procession. There was the ghastly, stinking crush of the subway—the car cards thrusting themselves at one, leering out like dull bores who grab your arm with another story; the querulous worry as to whether some one isn't leaning on you; a man deciding not to give his seat to a woman, hating her for it; the woman hating him for not doing it; at worst a squalid phantasmagoria of breath, and old cloth on human bodies and the smells of the food men ate—at best just people—too hot or too cold, tired, worried.

He pictured the rooms where these people lived—where the patterns of the blistered wall-papers were heavy reiterated sunflowers on green and yellow backgrounds, where there were tin bathtubs and gloomy hallways and verdureless, unnamable spaces in back of the buildings; where even love dressed as seduction—a sordid murder around the corner, illicit motherhood in the flat above. And always there was the economical stuffiness of indoor winter, and the long summers, nightmares of perspiration between sticky enveloping walls... dirty restaurants where careless, tired people helped themselves to sugar with their own used coffee-spoons, leaving hard brown deposits in the bowl.

It was not so bad where there were only men or else only women; it was when they were vilely herded that it all seemed so rotten. It was some shame that women gave off at having men see them tired and poor—it was some disgust that men had for women who were tired and poor. It was dirtier than any battle-field he had seen, harder to contemplate than any actual hardship moulded of mire and sweat and danger, it was an atmosphere wherein birth and marriage and death were loathsome, secret things.

He remembered one day in the subway when a delivery boy had brought in a great funeral wreath of fresh flowers, how the smell of it had suddenly cleared the air and given every one in the car a momentary glow.

"I detest poor people," thought Amory suddenly. "I hate them for being poor. Poverty may have been beautiful once, but it's rotten now. It's the ugliest thing in the world. It's essentially cleaner to be corrupt and rich than it is to be innocent and poor." He seemed to see again a figure whose significance had once impressed him—a well-dressed young man gazing from a club window on Fifth Avenue and saying something to his companion with a look of utter disgust. Probably, thought Amory, what he said was: "My God! Aren't people horrible!"

171

Never before in his life had Amory considered poor people. He thought cynically how completely he was lacking in all human sympathy. O. Henry had found in these people romance, pathos, love, hate—Amory saw only coarseness, physical filth, and stupidity. He made no self-accusations: never any more did he reproach himself for feelings that were natural and sincere. He accepted all his reactions as a part of him, unchangeable, unmoral. This problem of poverty transformed, magnified, attached to some grander, more dignified attitude might some day even be his problem; at present it roused only his profound distaste.

He walked over to Fifth Avenue, dodging the blind, black menace of umbrellas, and standing in front of Delmonico's hailed an auto-bus. Buttoning his coat closely around him he climbed to the roof, where he rode in solitary state through the thin, persistent rain, stung into alertness by the cool moisture perpetually reborn on his cheek. Somewhere in his mind a conversation began, rather resumed its place in his attention. It was composed not of two voices, but of one, which acted alike as questioner and answerer:

Question.—Well—what's the situation?

Answer.—That I have about twenty-four dollars to my name.

Q.—You have the Lake Geneva estate.

A.—But I intend to keep it.

Q.—Can you live?

A.—I can't imagine not being able to. People make money in books and I've found that I can always do the things that people do in books. Really they are the only things I can do.

Q.—Be definite.

A.—I don't know what I'll do—nor have I much curiosity. To-morrow I'm going to leave New York for good. It's a bad town unless you're on top of it.

Q.—Do you want a lot of money?

A.—No. I am merely afraid of being poor.

Q.—Very afraid?

A.—Just passively afraid.

Q.—Where are you drifting?

A.—Don't ask me!

Q.—Don't you care?

A.—Rather. I don't want to commit moral suicide.

Q.—Have you no interests left?

A.—None. I've no more virtue to lose. Just as a cooling pot gives off heat, so all through youth and adolescence we give off calories of virtue. That's what's called ingenuousness.

Q.—An interesting idea.

A.—That's why a "good man going wrong" attracts people. They stand around and literally warm themselves at the calories of virtue he gives off. Sarah makes an unsophisticated remark and the faces simper in delight—"How innocent the poor child is!"

CHAPTER 5 The Egotist Becomes a Personage

They're warming themselves at her virtue. But Sarah sees the simper and never makes that remark again. Only she feels a little colder after that.

Q.—All your calories gone?

A.—All of them. I'm beginning to warm myself at other people's virtue.

Q.—Are you corrupt?

A.—I think so. I'm not sure. I'm not sure about good and evil at all any more.

Q.—Is that a bad sign in itself?

A.—Not necessarily.

Q.—What would be the test of corruption?

A.—Becoming really insincere—calling myself "not such a bad fellow," thinking I regretted my lost youth when I only envy the delights of losing it. Youth is like having a big plate of candy. Sentimentalists think they want to be in the pure, simple state they were in before they ate the candy. They don't. They just want the fun of eating it all over again. The matron doesn't want to repeat her girlhood—she wants to repeat her honeymoon. I don't want to repeat my innocence. I want the pleasure of losing it again.

Q.—Where are you drifting?

This dialogue merged grotesquely into his mind's most familiar state—a grotesque blending of desires, worries, exterior impressions and physical reactions.

One Hundred and Twenty-seventh Street—or One Hundred and Thirty-seventh Street.... Two and three look alike—no, not much. Seat damp... are clothes absorbing wetness from seat, or seat absorbing dryness from clothes?... Sitting on wet substance gave appendicitis, so Froggy Parker's mother said. Well, he'd had it—I'll sue the steamboat company, Beatrice said, and my uncle has a quarter interest—did Beatrice go to heaven?... probably not—He represented Beatrice's immortality, also love-affairs of numerous dead men who surely had never thought of him... if it wasn't appendicitis, influenza maybe. What? One Hundred and Twentieth Street? That must have been One Hundred and Twelfth back there. One O Two instead of One Two Seven. Rosalind not like Beatrice, Eleanor like Beatrice, only wilder and brainier. Apartments along here expensive—probably hundred and fifty a month—maybe two hundred. Uncle had only paid hundred a month for whole great big house in Minneapolis. Question—were the stairs on the left or right as you came in? Anyway, in 12 Univee they were straight back and to the left. What a dirty river—want to go down there and see if it's dirty—French rivers all brown or black, so were Southern rivers. Twenty-four dollars meant four hundred and eighty doughnuts. He could live on it three months and sleep in the park. Wonder where Jill was—Jill Bayne, Fayne, Sayne—what the devil—neck hurts, darned uncomfortable seat. No desire to sleep with Jill, what could Alec see in her? Alec had a coarse taste in women. Own taste the best; Isabelle, Clara, Rosalind, Eleanor, were all-American. Eleanor would pitch, probably southpaw. Rosalind was outfield, wonderful hitter, Clara first base, maybe. Wonder what Humbird's body looked like now. If he himself hadn't been bayonet instructor he'd have gone up to line three months sooner,

173

probably been killed. Where's the darned bell—

The street numbers of Riverside Drive were obscured by the mist and dripping trees from anything but the swiftest scrutiny, but Amory had finally caught sight of one—One Hundred and Twenty-seventh Street. He got off and with no distinct destination followed a winding, descending sidewalk and came out facing the river, in particular a long pier and a partitioned litter of shipyards for miniature craft: small launches, canoes, rowboats, and catboats. He turned northward and followed the shore, jumped a small wire fence and found himself in a great disorderly yard adjoining a dock. The hulls of many boats in various stages of repair were around him; he smelled sawdust and paint and the scarcely distinguishable fiat odor of the Hudson. A man approached through the heavy gloom.

"Hello," said Amory.

"Got a pass?"

"No. Is this private?"

"This is the Hudson River Sporting and Yacht Club."

"Oh! I didn't know. I'm just resting."

"Well—" began the man dubiously.

"I'll go if you want me to."

The man made non-committal noises in his throat and passed on. Amory seated himself on an overturned boat and leaned forward thoughtfully until his chin rested in his hand.

"Misfortune is liable to make me a damn bad man," he said slowly.

IN THE DROOPING HOURS

While the rain drizzled on Amory looked futilely back at the stream of his life, all its glitterings and dirty shallows. To begin with, he was still afraid—not physically afraid any more, but afraid of people and prejudice and misery and monotony. Yet, deep in his bitter heart, he wondered if he was after all worse than this man or the next. He knew that he could sophisticate himself finally into saying that his own weakness was just the result of circumstances and environment; that often when he raged at himself as an egotist something would whisper ingratiatingly: "No. Genius!" That was one manifestation of fear, that voice which whispered that he could not be both great and good, that genius was the exact combination of those inexplicable grooves and twists in his mind, that any discipline would curb it to mediocrity. Probably more than any concrete vice or failing Amory despised his own personality—he loathed knowing that to-morrow and the thousand days after he would swell pompously at a compliment and sulk at an ill word like a third-rate musician or a first-class actor. He was ashamed of the fact that very simple and honest people usually distrusted him; that he had been cruel, often, to those who had sunk their personalities in him—several girls, and a man here and there through college, that he had been an evil influence on; people who had followed him here and there into mental adventures from which he alone rebounded unscathed.

Usually, on nights like this, for there had been many lately, he could escape from this

CHAPTER 5 The Egotist Becomes a Personage

consuming introspection by thinking of children and the infinite possibilities of children—he leaned and listened and he heard a startled baby awake in a house across the street and lend a tiny whimper to the still night. Quick as a flash he turned away, wondering with a touch of panic whether something in the brooding despair of his mood had made a darkness in its tiny soul. He shivered. What if some day the balance was overturned, and he became a thing that frightened children and crept into rooms in the dark, approached dim communion with those phantoms who whispered shadowy secrets to the mad of that dark continent upon the moon....

Amory smiled a bit.

"You're too much wrapped up in yourself," he heard some one say. And again—

"Get out and do some real work—"

"Stop worrying—"

He fancied a possible future comment of his own.

"Yes—I was perhaps an egotist in youth, but I soon found it made me morbid to think too much about myself."

Suddenly he felt an overwhelming desire to let himself go to the devil—not to go violently as a gentleman should, but to sink safely and sensuously out of sight. He pictured himself in an adobe house in Mexico, half-reclining on a rug-covered couch, his slender, artistic fingers closed on a cigarette while he listened to guitars strumming melancholy undertones to an age-old dirge of Castile and an olive-skinned, carmine-lipped girl caressed his hair. Here he might live a strange litany, delivered from right and wrong and from the hound of heaven and from every God (except the exotic Mexican one who was pretty slack himself and rather addicted to Oriental scents)—delivered from success and hope and poverty into that long chute of indulgence which led, after all, only to the artificial lake of death.

There were so many places where one might deteriorate pleasantly: Port Said, Shanghai, parts of Turkestan, Constantinople, the South Seas—all lands of sad, haunting music and many odors, where lust could be a mode and expression of life, where the shades of night skies and sunsets would seem to reflect only moods of passion: the colors of lips and poppies.

STILL WEEDING

Once he had been miraculously able to scent evil as a horse detects a broken bridge at night, but the man with the queer feet in Phoebe's room had diminished to the aura over Jill. His instinct perceived the fetidness of poverty, but no longer ferreted out the deeper evils in pride and sensuality.

There were no more wise men; there were no more heroes; Burne Holiday was sunk from sight as though he had never lived; Monsignor was dead. Amory had grown up to a thousand books, a thousand lies; he had listened eagerly to people who pretended to know, who knew nothing. The mystical reveries of saints that had once filled him with awe in the still hours of night, now vaguely repelled him. The Byrons and Brookes who had defied life from mountain tops were in the end but flaneurs and poseurs, at best mistaking the shadow of courage for the substance of wisdom. The pageantry of his disillusion took shape in a world-old procession of Prophets, Athenians, Martyrs, Saints, Scientists, Don Juans, Jesuits, Puritans, Fausts, Poets, Pacifists; like costumed alumni at a college reunion they streamed before him as their dreams, personalities, and creeds had in turn thrown colored lights on his soul; each had tried to express the glory of life and the tremendous significance of man; each had boasted of synchronizing what had gone before into his own rickety generalities; each had depended after all on the set stage and the convention of the theatre, which is that man in his hunger for faith will feed his mind with the nearest and most convenient food.

Women—of whom he had expected so much; whose beauty he had hoped to transmute into modes of art; whose unfathomable instincts, marvellously incoherent and inarticulate, he had thought to perpetuate in terms of experience—had become merely consecrations to their own posterity. Isabelle, Clara, Rosalind, Eleanor, were all removed by their very beauty, around which men had swarmed, from the possibility of contributing anything but a sick heart and a page of puzzled words to write.

Amory based his loss of faith in help from others on several sweeping syllogisms. Granted that his generation, however bruised and decimated from this Victorian war, were the heirs of progress. Waving aside petty differences of conclusions which, although they might occasionally cause the deaths of several millions of young men, might be explained away—supposing that after all Bernard Shaw and Bernhardi, Bonar Law and Bethmann-Hollweg were mutual heirs of progress if only in agreeing against the ducking of witches—waiving the antitheses and approaching individually these men who seemed to be the leaders, he was repelled by the discrepancies and contradictions in the men themselves.

There was, for example, Thornton Hancock, respected by half the intellectual world as an authority on life, a man who had verified and believed the code he lived by, an educator of educators, an adviser to Presidents—yet Amory knew that this man had, in his heart, leaned on the priest of another religion.

And Monsignor, upon whom a cardinal rested, had moments of strange and horrible insecurity—inexplicable in a religion that explained even disbelief in terms of its own faith: if you doubted the devil it was the devil that made you doubt him. Amory had seen Monsignor go to the houses of stolid philistines, read popular novels furiously, saturate himself in routine, to escape from that horror.

And this priest, a little wiser, somewhat purer, had been, Amory knew, not essentially older than he.

Amory was alone—he had escaped from a small enclosure into a great labyrinth. He was where Goethe was when he began "Faust"; he was where Conrad was when he wrote "Almayer's Folly."

Amory said to himself that there were essentially two sorts of people who through

CHAPTER 5   The Egotist Becomes a Personage

natural clarity or disillusion left the enclosure and sought the labyrinth. There were men like Wells and Plato, who had, half unconsciously, a strange, hidden orthodoxy, who would accept for themselves only what could be accepted for all men—incurable romanticists who never, for all their efforts, could enter the labyrinth as stark souls; there were on the other hand sword-like pioneering personalities, Samuel Butler, Renan, Voltaire, who progressed much slower, yet eventually much further, not in the direct pessimistic line of speculative philosophy but concerned in the eternal attempt to attach a positive value to life....

Amory stopped. He began for the first time in his life to have a strong distrust of all generalities and epigrams. They were too easy, too dangerous to the public mind. Yet all thought usually reached the public after thirty years in some such form: Benson and Chesterton had popularized Huysmans and Newman; Shaw had sugar-coated Nietzsche and Ibsen and Schopenhauer. The man in the street heard the conclusions of dead genius through some one else's clever paradoxes and didactic epigrams.

Life was a damned muddle... a football game with every one off-side and the referee gotten rid of—every one claiming the referee would have been on his side....

Progress was a labyrinth... people plunging blindly in and then rushing wildly back, shouting that they had found it... the invisible king—the elan vital—the principle of evolution... writing a book, starting a war, founding a school....

Amory, even had he not been a selfish man, would have started all inquiries with himself. He was his own best example—sitting in the rain, a human creature of sex and pride, foiled by chance and his own temperament of the balm of love and children, preserved to help in building up the living consciousness of the race.

In self-reproach and loneliness and disillusion he came to the entrance of the labyrinth.

Another dawn flung itself across the river, a belated taxi hurried along the street, its lamps still shining like burning eyes in a face white from a night's carouse. A melancholy siren sounded far down the river.

MONSIGNOR

Amory kept thinking how Monsignor would have enjoyed his own funeral. It was magnificently Catholic and liturgical. Bishop O'Neill sang solemn high mass and the cardinal gave the final absolutions. Thornton Hancock, Mrs. Lawrence, the British and Italian ambassadors, the papal delegate, and a host of friends and priests were there— yet the inexorable shears had cut through all these threads that Monsignor had gathered into his hands. To Amory it was a haunting grief to see him lying in his coffin, with closed hands upon his purple vestments. His face had not changed, and, as he never knew he was dying, it showed no pain or fear. It was Amory's dear old friend, his and the others'—for the church was full of people with daft, staring faces, the most exalted seeming the most stricken.

The cardinal, like an archangel in cope and mitre, sprinkled the holy water; the organ broke into sound; the choir began to sing the Requiem Eternam.

All these people grieved because they had to some extent depended upon Monsignor. Their grief was more than sentiment for the "crack in his voice or a certain break in his walk," as Wells put it. These people had leaned on Monsignor's faith, his way of finding cheer, of making religion a thing of lights and shadows, making all light and shadow merely aspects of God. People felt safe when he was near.

Of Amory's attempted sacrifice had been born merely the full realization of his disillusion, but of Monsignor's funeral was born the romantic elf who was to enter the labyrinth with him. He found something that he wanted, had always wanted and always would want—not to be admired, as he had feared; not to be loved, as he had made himself believe; but to be necessary to people, to be indispensable; he remembered the sense of security he had found in Burne.

Life opened up in one of its amazing bursts of radiance and Amory suddenly and permanently rejected an old epigram that had been playing listlessly in his mind: "Very few things matter and nothing matters very much."

On the contrary, Amory felt an immense desire to give people a sense of security.

THE BIG MAN WITH GOGGLES

On the day that Amory started on his walk to Princeton the sky was a colorless vault, cool, high and barren of the threat of rain. It was a gray day, that least fleshly of all weathers; a day of dreams and far hopes and clear visions. It was a day easily associated with those abstract truths and purities that dissolve in the sunshine or fade out in mocking laughter by the light of the moon. The trees and clouds were carved in classical severity; the sounds of the countryside had harmonized to a monotone, metallic as a trumpet, breathless as the Grecian urn.

The day had put Amory in such a contemplative mood that he caused much annoyance to several motorists who were forced to slow up considerably or else run him down. So engrossed in his thoughts was he that he was scarcely surprised at that strange phenomenon—cordiality manifested within fifty miles of Manhattan—when a passing car slowed down beside him and a voice hailed him. He looked up and saw a magnificent Locomobile in which sat two middle-aged men, one of them small and anxious looking, apparently an artificial growth on the other who was large and begoggled and imposing.

"Do you want a lift?" asked the apparently artificial growth, glancing from the corner of his eye at the imposing man as if for some habitual, silent corroboration.

"You bet I do. Thanks."

The chauffeur swung open the door, and, climbing in, Amory settled himself in the middle of the back seat. He took in his companions curiously. The chief characteristic of the big man seemed to be a great confidence in himself set off against a tremendous boredom with everything around him. That part of his face which protruded under the goggles was what is generally termed "strong"; rolls of not undignified fat had collected near his chin; somewhere above was a wide thin mouth and the rough model for a Roman nose, and, below, his shoulders collapsed without a struggle into the powerful bulk of his chest and belly. He was excellently and quietly dressed. Amory noticed that he was inclined to stare straight at the back of the chauffeur's head as if speculating steadily but hopelessly some baffling hirsute problem.

The smaller man was remarkable only for his complete submersion in the personality of the other. He was of that lower secretarial type who at forty have engraved upon their business cards: "Assistant to the President," and without a sigh consecrate the rest of their lives to second-hand mannerisms.

"Going far?" asked the smaller man in a pleasant disinterested way.

"Quite a stretch."

"Hiking for exercise?"

"No," responded Amory succinctly, "I'm walking because I can't afford to ride."

"Oh."

Then again:

"Are you looking for work? Because there's lots of work," he continued rather testily. "All this talk of lack of work. The West is especially short of labor." He expressed the West with a sweeping, lateral gesture. Amory nodded politely.

"Have you a trade?"

No—Amory had no trade.

"Clerk, eh?"

No—Amory was not a clerk.

"Whatever your line is," said the little man, seeming to agree wisely with something Amory had said, "now is the time of opportunity and business openings." He glanced again toward the big man, as a lawyer grilling a witness glances involuntarily at the jury.

Amory decided that he must say something and for the life of him could think of only one thing to say.

"Of course I want a great lot of money—"

The little man laughed mirthlessly but conscientiously.

"That's what every one wants nowadays, but they don't want to work for it."

"A very natural, healthy desire. Almost all normal people want to be rich without great effort—except the financiers in problem plays, who want to 'crash their way through.' Don't you want easy money?"

"Of course not," said the secretary indignantly.

"But," continued Amory disregarding him, "being very poor at present I am contemplating socialism as possibly my forte."

Both men glanced at him curiously.

"These bomb throwers—" The little man ceased as words lurched ponderously from the big man's chest.

"If I thought you were a bomb thrower I'd run you over to the Newark jail. That's what

I think of Socialists."

Amory laughed.

"What are you," asked the big man, "one of these parlor Bolsheviks, one of these idealists? I must say I fail to see the difference. The idealists loaf around and write the stuff that stirs up the poor immigrants."

"Well," said Amory, "if being an idealist is both safe and lucrative, I might try it."

"What's your difficulty? Lost your job?"

"Not exactly, but—well, call it that."

"What was it?"

"Writing copy for an advertising agency."

"Lots of money in advertising."

Amory smiled discreetly.

"Oh, I'll admit there's money in it eventually. Talent doesn't starve any more. Even art gets enough to eat these days. Artists draw your magazine covers, write your advertisements, hash out rag-time for your theatres. By the great commercializing of printing you've found a harmless, polite occupation for every genius who might have carved his own niche. But beware the artist who's an intellectual also. The artist who doesn't fit—the Rousseau, the Tolstoi, the Samuel Butler, the Amory Blaine—"

"Who's he?" demanded the little man suspiciously.

"Well," said Amory, "he's a—he's an intellectual personage not very well known at present."

The little man laughed his conscientious laugh, and stopped rather suddenly as Amory's burning eyes turned on him.

"What are you laughing at?"

"These intellectual people—"

"Do you know what it means?"

The little man's eyes twitched nervously.

"Why, it usually means—"

"It always means brainy and well-educated," interrupted Amory. "It means having an active knowledge of the race's experience." Amory decided to be very rude. He turned to the big man. "The young man," he indicated the secretary with his thumb, and said young man as one says bell-boy, with no implication of youth, "has the usual muddled connotation of all popular words."

"You object to the fact that capital controls printing?" said the big man, fixing him with his goggles.

"Yes—and I object to doing their mental work for them. It seemed to me that the root of all the business I saw around me consisted in overworking and underpaying a bunch of dubs who submitted to it."

"Here now," said the big man, "you'll have to admit that the laboring man is certainly

CHAPTER 5 The Egotist Becomes a Personage

highly paid—five and six hour days—it's ridiculous. You can't buy an honest day's work from a man in the trades-unions."

"You've brought it on yourselves," insisted Amory. "You people never make concessions until they're wrung out of you."

"What people?"

"Your class; the class I belonged to until recently; those who by inheritance or industry or brains or dishonesty have become the moneyed class."

"Do you imagine that if that road-mender over there had the money he'd be any more willing to give it up?"

"No, but what's that got to do with it?"

The older man considered.

"No, I'll admit it hasn't. It rather sounds as if it had though."

"In fact," continued Amory, "he'd be worse. The lower classes are narrower, less pleasant and personally more selfish—certainly more stupid. But all that has nothing to do with the question."

"Just exactly what is the question?"

Here Amory had to pause to consider exactly what the question was.

AMORY COINS A PHRASE

"When life gets hold of a brainy man of fair education," began Amory slowly, "that is, when he marries he becomes, nine times out of ten, a conservative as far as existing social conditions are concerned. He may be unselfish, kind-hearted, even just in his own way, but his first job is to provide and to hold fast. His wife shoos him on, from ten thousand a year to twenty thousand a year, on and on, in an enclosed treadmill that hasn't any windows. He's done! Life's got him! He's no help! He's a spiritually married man."

Amory paused and decided that it wasn't such a bad phrase.

"Some men," he continued, "escape the grip. Maybe their wives have no social ambitions; maybe they've hit a sentence or two in a 'dangerous book' that pleased them; maybe they started on the treadmill as I did and were knocked off. Anyway, they're the congressmen you can't bribe, the Presidents who aren't politicians, the writers, speakers, scientists, statesmen who aren't just popular grab-bags for a half-dozen women and children."

"He's the natural radical?"

"Yes," said Amory. "He may vary from the disillusioned critic like old Thornton Hancock, all the way to Trotsky. Now this spiritually unmarried man hasn't direct power, for unfortunately the spiritually married man, as a by product of his money chase, has garnered in the great newspaper, the popular magazine, the influential weekly—so that Mrs. Newspaper, Mrs. Magazine, Mrs. Weekly can have a better limousine than those oil people across the street or those cement people 'round the corner."

"Why not?"

"It makes wealthy men the keepers of the world's intellectual conscience and, of course, a man who has money under one set of social institutions quite naturally can't risk his family's happiness by letting the clamor for another appear in his newspaper."

"But it appears," said the big man.

"Where?—in the discredited mediums. Rotten cheap-papered weeklies."

"All right—go on."

"Well, my first point is that through a mixture of conditions of which the family is the first, there are these two sorts of brains. One sort takes human nature as it finds it, uses its timidity, its weakness, and its strength for its own ends. Opposed is the man who, being spiritually unmarried, continually seeks for new systems that will control or counteract human nature. His problem is harder. It is not life that's complicated, it's the struggle to guide and control life. That is his struggle. He is a part of progress—the spiritually married man is not."

The big man produced three big cigars, and proffered them on his huge palm. The little man took one, Amory shook his head and reached for a cigarette.

"Go on talking," said the big man. "I've been wanting to hear one of you fellows."

GOING FASTER

"Modern life," began Amory again, "changes no longer century by century, but year by year, ten times faster than it ever has before—populations doubling, civilizations unified more closely with other civilizations, economic interdependence, racial questions, and—we're dawdling along. My idea is that we've got to go very much faster." He slightly emphasized the last words and the chauffeur unconsciously increased the speed of the car. Amory and the big man laughed; the little man laughed, too, after a pause.

"Every child," said Amory, "should have an equal start. If his father can endow him with a good physique and his mother with some common sense in his early education, that should be his heritage. If the father can't give him a good physique, if the mother has spent in chasing men the years in which she should have been preparing herself to educate her children, so much the worse for the child. He shouldn't be artificially bolstered up with money, sent to these horrible tutoring schools, dragged through college... Every boy ought to have an equal start."

"All right," said the big man, his goggles indicating neither approval nor objection.

"Next I'd have a fair trial of government ownership of all industries."

"That's been proven a failure."

"No—it merely failed. If we had government ownership we'd have the best analytical business minds in the government working for something besides themselves. We'd have Mackays instead of Burlesons; we'd have Morgans in the Treasury Department; we'd have Hills running interstate commerce. We'd have the best lawyers in the Senate."

"They wouldn't give their best efforts for nothing. McAdoo—"

"No," said Amory, shaking his head. "Money isn't the only stimulus that brings out the best that's in a man, even in America."

"You said a while ago that it was."

"It is, right now. But if it were made illegal to have more than a certain amount the best men would all flock for the one other reward which attracts humanity—honor."

The big man made a sound that was very like boo.

"That's the silliest thing you've said yet."

"No, it isn't silly. It's quite plausible. If you'd gone to college you'd have been struck by the fact that the men there would work twice as hard for any one of a hundred petty honors as those other men did who were earning their way through."

"Kids—child's play!" scoffed his antagonist.

"Not by a darned sight—unless we're all children. Did you ever see a grown man when he's trying for a secret society—or a rising family whose name is up at some club? They'll jump when they hear the sound of the word. The idea that to make a man work you've got to hold gold in front of his eyes is a growth, not an axiom. We've done that for so long that we've forgotten there's any other way. We've made a world where that's necessary. Let me tell you"—Amory became emphatic—"if there were ten men insured against either wealth or starvation, and offered a green ribbon for five hours' work a day and a blue ribbon for ten hours' work a day, nine out of ten of them would be trying for the blue ribbon. That competitive instinct only wants a badge. If the size of their house is the badge they'll sweat their heads off for that. If it's only a blue ribbon, I damn near believe they'll work just as hard. They have in other ages."

"I don't agree with you."

"I know it," said Amory nodding sadly. "It doesn't matter any more though. I think these people are going to come and take what they want pretty soon."

A fierce hiss came from the little man.

"Machine-guns!"

"Ah, but you've taught them their use."

The big man shook his head.

"In this country there are enough property owners not to permit that sort of thing."

Amory wished he knew the statistics of property owners and non-property owners; he decided to change the subject.

But the big man was aroused.

"When you talk of 'taking things away,' you're on dangerous ground."

"How can they get it without taking it? For years people have been stalled off with promises. Socialism may not be progress, but the threat of the red flag is certainly the inspiring force of all reform. You've got to be sensational to get attention."

"Russia is your example of a beneficent violence, I suppose?"

"Quite possibly," admitted Amory. "Of course, it's overflowing just as the French Revolution did, but I've no doubt that it's really a great experiment and well worth while."

183

"Don't you believe in moderation?"

"You won't listen to the moderates, and it's almost too late. The truth is that the public has done one of those startling and amazing things that they do about once in a hundred years. They've seized an idea."

"What is it?"

"That however the brains and abilities of men may differ, their stomachs are essentially the same."

THE LITTLE MAN GETS HIS

"If you took all the money in the world," said the little man with much profundity, "and divided it up in equ—"

"Oh, shut up!" said Amory briskly and, paying no attention to the little man's enraged stare, he went on with his argument.

"The human stomach—" he began; but the big man interrupted rather impatiently.

"I'm letting you talk, you know," he said, "but please avoid stomachs. I've been feeling mine all day. Anyway, I don't agree with one-half you've said. Government ownership is the basis of your whole argument, and it's invariably a beehive of corruption. Men won't work for blue ribbons, that's all rot."

When he ceased the little man spoke up with a determined nod, as if resolved this time to have his say out.

"There are certain things which are human nature," he asserted with an owl-like look, "which always have been and always will be, which can't be changed."

Amory looked from the small man to the big man helplessly.

"Listen to that! That's what makes me discouraged with progress. Listen to that! I can name offhand over one hundred natural phenomena that have been changed by the will of man—a hundred instincts in man that have been wiped out or are now held in check by civilization. What this man here just said has been for thousands of years the last refuge of the associated mutton-heads of the world. It negates the efforts of every scientist, statesman, moralist, reformer, doctor, and philosopher that ever gave his life to humanity's service. It's a flat impeachment of all that's worth while in human nature. Every person over twenty-five years old who makes that statement in cold blood ought to be deprived of the franchise."

The little man leaned back against the seat, his face purple with rage. Amory continued, addressing his remarks to the big man.

"These quarter-educated, stale-minded men such as your friend here, who think they think, every question that comes up, you'll find his type in the usual ghastly muddle. One minute it's 'the brutality and inhumanity of these Prussians'—the next it's 'we ought to exterminate the whole German people.' They always believe that 'things are in a bad way now,' but they 'haven't any faith in these idealists.' One minute they call Wilson 'just a dreamer, not practical'—a year later they rail at him for making his dreams realities. They haven't clear logical ideas on one single subject except a sturdy, stolid opposition to all change. They don't think uneducated people should be highly paid, but they won't see that if they don't pay the uneducated people their children are going to be uneducated too, and we're going round and round in a circle. That—is the great middle class!"

The big man with a broad grin on his face leaned over and smiled at the little man.

"You're catching it pretty heavy, Garvin; how do you feel?"

The little man made an attempt to smile and act as if the whole matter were so ridiculous as to be beneath notice. But Amory was not through.

"The theory that people are fit to govern themselves rests on this man. If he can be educated to think clearly, concisely, and logically, freed of his habit of taking refuge in platitudes and prejudices and sentimentalisms, then I'm a militant Socialist. If he can't, then I don't think it matters much what happens to man or his systems, now or hereafter."

"I am both interested and amused," said the big man. "You are very young."

"Which may only mean that I have neither been corrupted nor made timid by contemporary experience. I possess the most valuable experience, the experience of the race, for in spite of going to college I've managed to pick up a good education."

"You talk glibly."

"It's not all rubbish," cried Amory passionately. "This is the first time in my life I've argued Socialism. It's the only panacea I know. I'm restless. My whole generation is restless. I'm sick of a system where the richest man gets the most beautiful girl if he wants her, where the artist without an income has to sell his talents to a button manufacturer. Even if I had no talents I'd not be content to work ten years, condemned either to celibacy or a furtive indulgence, to give some man's son an automobile."

"But, if you're not sure—"

"That doesn't matter," exclaimed Amory. "My position couldn't be worse. A social revolution might land me on top. Of course I'm selfish. It seems to me I've been a fish out of water in too many outworn systems. I was probably one of the two dozen men in my class at college who got a decent education; still they'd let any well-tutored flathead play football and I was ineligible, because some silly old men thought we should all profit by conic sections. I loathed the army. I loathed business. I'm in love with change and I've killed my conscience—"

"So you'll go along crying that we must go faster."

"That, at least, is true," Amory insisted. "Reform won't catch up to the needs of civilization unless it's made to. A laissez-faire policy is like spoiling a child by saying he'll turn out all right in the end. He will—if he's made to."

"But you don't believe all this Socialist patter you talk."

"I don't know. Until I talked to you I hadn't thought seriously about it. I wasn't sure of half of what I said."

"You puzzle me," said the big man, "but you're all alike. They say Bernard Shaw, in spite of his doctrines, is the most exacting of all dramatists about his royalties. To the last farthing."

"Well," said Amory, "I simply state that I'm a product of a versatile mind in a restless generation—with every reason to throw my mind and pen in with the radicals. Even if, deep in my heart, I thought we were all blind atoms in a world as limited as a stroke of a pendulum, I and my sort would struggle against tradition; try, at least, to displace old cants with new ones. I've thought I was right about life at various times, but faith is difficult. One thing I know. If living isn't a seeking for the grail it may be a damned amusing game."

For a minute neither spoke and then the big man asked:

"What was your university?"

"Princeton."

The big man became suddenly interested; the expression of his goggles altered slightly.

"I sent my son to Princeton."

"Did you?"

"Perhaps you knew him. His name was Jesse Ferrenby. He was killed last year in France."

"I knew him very well. In fact, he was one of my particular friends."

"He was—a—quite a fine boy. We were very close."

Amory began to perceive a resemblance between the father and the dead son and he told himself that there had been all along a sense of familiarity. Jesse Ferrenby, the man who in college had borne off the crown that he had aspired to. It was all so far away. What little boys they had been, working for blue ribbons—

The car slowed up at the entrance to a great estate, ringed around by a huge hedge and a tall iron fence.

"Won't you come in for lunch?"

Amory shook his head.

"Thank you, Mr. Ferrenby, but I've got to get on."

The big man held out his hand. Amory saw that the fact that he had known Jesse more than outweighed any disfavor he had created by his opinions. What ghosts were people with which to work! Even the little man insisted on shaking hands.

"Good-by!" shouted Mr. Ferrenby, as the car turned the corner and started up the drive. "Good luck to you and bad luck to your theories."

"Same to you, sir," cried Amory, smiling and waving his hand.

"OUT OF THE FIRE, OUT OF THE LITTLE ROOM"

Eight hours from Princeton Amory sat down by the Jersey roadside and looked at the frost-bitten country. Nature as a rather coarse phenomenon composed largely of flowers that, when closely inspected, appeared moth-eaten, and of ants that endlessly traversed blades of grass, was always disillusioning; nature represented by skies and waters and far horizons was more likable. Frost and the promise of winter thrilled him now, made him think of a wild battle between St. Regis and Groton, ages ago, seven years ago—and of

CHAPTER 5 The Egotist Becomes a Personage

an autumn day in France twelve months before when he had lain in tall grass, his platoon flattened down close around him, waiting to tap the shoulders of a Lewis gunner. He saw the two pictures together with somewhat the same primitive exaltation—two games he had played, differing in quality of acerbity, linked in a way that differed them from Rosalind or the subject of labyrinths which were, after all, the business of life.

"I am selfish," he thought.

"This is not a quality that will change when I 'see human suffering' or 'lose my parents' or 'help others.'

"This selfishness is not only part of me. It is the most living part.

"It is by somehow transcending rather than by avoiding that selfishness that I can bring poise and balance into my life.

"There is no virtue of unselfishness that I cannot use. I can make sacrifices, be charitable, give to a friend, endure for a friend, lay down my life for a friend—all because these things may be the best possible expression of myself; yet I have not one drop of the milk of human kindness."

The problem of evil had solidified for Amory into the problem of sex. He was beginning to identify evil with the strong phallic worship in Brooke and the early Wells. Inseparably linked with evil was beauty—beauty, still a constant rising tumult; soft in Eleanor's voice, in an old song at night, rioting deliriously through life like superimposed waterfalls, half rhythm, half darkness. Amory knew that every time he had reached toward it longingly it had leered out at him with the grotesque face of evil. Beauty of great art, beauty of all joy, most of all the beauty of women.

After all, it had too many associations with license and indulgence. Weak things were often beautiful, weak things were never good. And in this new loneness of his that had been selected for what greatness he might achieve, beauty must be relative or, itself a harmony, it would make only a discord.

In a sense this gradual renunciation of beauty was the second step after his disillusion had been made complete. He felt that he was leaving behind him his chance of being a certain type of artist. It seemed so much more important to be a certain sort of man.

His mind turned a corner suddenly and he found himself thinking of the Catholic Church. The idea was strong in him that there was a certain intrinsic lack in those to whom orthodox religion was necessary, and religion to Amory meant the Church of Rome. Quite conceivably it was an empty ritual but it was seemingly the only assimilative, traditionary bulwark against the decay of morals. Until the great mobs could be educated into a moral sense some one must cry: "Thou shalt not!" Yet any acceptance was, for the present, impossible. He wanted time and the absence of ulterior pressure. He wanted to keep the tree without ornaments, realize fully the direction and momentum of this new start.

The afternoon waned from the purging good of three o'clock to the golden beauty of four. Afterward he walked through the dull ache of a setting sun when even the clouds seemed bleeding and at twilight he came to a graveyard. There was a dusky, dreamy smell of flowers and the ghost of a new moon in the sky and shadows everywhere. On an impulse he considered trying to open the door of a rusty iron vault built into the side of a hill; a vault washed clean and covered with late-blooming, weepy watery-blue flowers that might have grown from dead eyes, sticky to the touch with a sickening odor.

Amory wanted to feel "William Dayfield, 1864."

He wondered that graves ever made people consider life in vain. Somehow he could find nothing hopeless in having lived. All the broken columns and clasped hands and doves and angels meant romances. He fancied that in a hundred years he would like having young people speculate as to whether his eyes were brown or blue, and he hoped quite passionately that his grave would have about it an air of many, many years ago. It seemed strange that out of a row of Union soldiers two or three made him think of dead loves and dead lovers, when they were exactly like the rest, even to the yellowish moss.

Long after midnight the towers and spires of Princeton were visible, with here and there a late-burning light—and suddenly out of the clear darkness the sound of bells. As an endless dream it went on; the spirit of the past brooding over a new generation, the chosen youth from the muddled, unchastened world, still fed romantically on the mistakes and half-forgotten dreams of dead statesmen and poets. Here was a new generation, shouting the old cries, learning the old creeds, through a revery of long days and nights; destined finally to go out into that dirty gray turmoil to follow love and pride; a new generation dedicated more than the last to the fear of poverty and the worship of success; grown up to find all Gods dead, all wars fought, all faiths in man shaken....

Amory, sorry for them, was still not sorry for himself—art, politics, religion, whatever his medium should be, he knew he was safe now, free from all hysteria—he could accept what was acceptable, roam, grow, rebel, sleep deep through many nights....

There was no God in his heart, he knew; his ideas were still in riot; there was ever the pain of memory; the regret for his lost youth—yet the waters of disillusion had left a deposit on his soul, responsibility and a love of life, the faint stirring of old ambitions and unrealized dreams. But—oh, Rosalind! Rosalind!...

"It's all a poor substitute at best," he said sadly.

And he could not tell why the struggle was worth while, why he had determined to use to the utmost himself and his heritage from the personalities he had passed....

He stretched out his arms to the crystalline, radiant sky.

"I know myself," he cried, "but that is all."

Appendix: Production notes for eBook edition 11

The primary feature of edition 11 is restoration of em-dashes which are missing from edition 10. (My favorite instance is "I won't belong" rather than "I won't be—long".)

CHAPTER 5   The Egotist Becomes a Personage

Characters which are 8-bit in the printed text were misrepresented in edition 10. Edition 10 had some end-of-paragraph problems. A handful of other minor errors are corrected.

Two volumes served as reference for edition 11: a 1960 reprint, and an undated reprint produced sometime after 1948. There are a number of differences between the volumes. Evidence suggests that the 1960 reprint has been somewhat "modernized", and that the undated reprint is a better match for the original 1920 printing. Therefore, when the volumes differ, edition 11 more closely follows the undated reprint.

In edition 11, underscores are used to denote words and phrases italicized for emphasis.

There is a section of text in book 2, chapter 3, beginning with "When Vanity kissed Vanity," which is referred to as "poetry" but is formatted as prose.

I considered, but decided against introducing an 8-bit version of edition 11, in large part because the bulk of the 8-bit usage (as found in the 1960 reprint) consists of words commonly used in their 7-bit form:

Aeschylus blase cafe debut debutante elan elite Encyclopaedia
matinee minutiae paean regime soupcon unaesthetic

Less-commonly-used 8-bit word forms in this book include:

anaemic bleme coeur manoeuvered mediaevalist tete-a-tete
and the name "Borge".

End of Project Gutenberg's This Side of Paradise, by F. Scott Fitzgerald

*** END OF THIS PROJECT GUTENBERG EBOOK THIS SIDE OF PARADISE ***

***** This file should be named 805-h htm or 805-h zip *****
This and all associated files of various formats will be found in:
http://www.gutenberg.org/8/0/805/

Produced by David Reed, Ken Reeder, and David Widger

Updated editions will replace the previous one--the old editions will be renamed.

Creating the works from public domain print editions means that no one owns a United States copyright in these works, so the Foundation (and you!) can copy and distribute it in the United States without permission and without paying copyright royalties. Special rules, set forth in the General Terms of Use part of this license, apply to copying and distributing Project Gutenberg-tm electronic works to

protect the PROJECT GUTENBERG-tm concept and trademark. Project
Gutenberg is a registered trademark, and may not be used if you
charge for the eBooks, unless you receive specific permission. If you
do not charge anything for copies of this eBook, complying with the
rules is very easy. You may use this eBook for nearly any purpose
such as creation of derivative works, reports, performances and
research. They may be modified and printed and given away--you may do
practically ANYTHING with public domain eBooks. Redistribution is
subject to the trademark license, especially commercial
redistribution.

*** START: FULL LICENSE ***

THE FULL PROJECT GUTENBERG LICENSE
PLEASE READ THIS BEFORE YOU DISTRIBUTE OR USE THIS WORK

To protect the Project Gutenberg-tm mission of promoting the free
distribution of electronic works, by using or distributing this work
(or any other work associated in any way with the phrase "Project
Gutenberg"), you agree to comply with all the terms of the Full Project
Gutenberg-tm License (available with this file or online at
http://gutenberg.org/license).

Section 1. General Terms of Use and Redistributing Project Gutenberg-tm
electronic works

1.A. By reading or using any part of this Project Gutenberg-tm
electronic work, you indicate that you have read, understand, agree to
and accept all the terms of this license and intellectual property
(trademark/copyright) agreement. If you do not agree to abide by all
the terms of this agreement, you must cease using and return or destroy
all copies of Project Gutenberg-tm electronic works in your possession.
If you paid a fee for obtaining a copy of or access to a Project
Gutenberg-tm electronic work and you do not agree to be bound by the
terms of this agreement, you may obtain a refund from the person or
entity to whom you paid the fee as set forth in paragraph 1.E.8.

1.B. "Project Gutenberg" is a registered trademark. It may only be
used on or associated in any way with an electronic work by people who

CHAPTER 5 The Egotist Becomes a Personage

agree to be bound by the terms of this agreement. There are a few things that you can do with most Project Gutenberg-tm electronic works even without complying with the full terms of this agreement. See paragraph 1.C below. There are a lot of things you can do with Project Gutenberg-tm electronic works if you follow the terms of this agreement and help preserve free future access to Project Gutenberg-tm electronic works. See paragraph 1.E below.

1.C. The Project Gutenberg Literary Archive Foundation ("the Foundation" or PGLAF), owns a compilation copyright in the collection of Project Gutenberg-tm electronic works. Nearly all the individual works in the collection are in the public domain in the United States. If an individual work is in the public domain in the United States and you are located in the United States, we do not claim a right to prevent you from copying, distributing, performing, displaying or creating derivative works based on the work as long as all references to Project Gutenberg are removed. Of course, we hope that you will support the Project Gutenberg-tm mission of promoting free access to electronic works by freely sharing Project Gutenberg-tm works in compliance with the terms of this agreement for keeping the Project Gutenberg-tm name associated with the work. You can easily comply with the terms of this agreement by keeping this work in the same format with its attached full Project Gutenberg-tm License when you share it without charge with others.

1.D. The copyright laws of the place where you are located also govern what you can do with this work. Copyright laws in most countries are in a constant state of change. If you are outside the United States, check the laws of your country in addition to the terms of this agreement before downloading, copying, displaying, performing, distributing or creating derivative works based on this work or any other Project Gutenberg-tm work. The Foundation makes no representations concerning the copyright status of any work in any country outside the United States.

1.E. Unless you have removed all references to Project Gutenberg:

1.E.1. The following sentence, with active links to, or other immediate access to, the full Project Gutenberg-tm License must appear prominently whenever any copy of a Project Gutenberg-tm work (any work on which the phrase "Project Gutenberg" appears, or with which the phrase "Project Gutenberg" is associated) is accessed, displayed, performed, viewed, copied or distributed:

This eBook is for the use of anyone anywhere at no cost and with almost no restrictions whatsoever. You may copy it, give it away or re-use it under the terms of the Project Gutenberg License included with this eBook or online at www.gutenberg.org

1.E.2. If an individual Project Gutenberg-tm electronic work is derived from the public domain (does not contain a notice indicating that it is posted with permission of the copyright holder), the work can be copied and distributed to anyone in the United States without paying any fees or charges. If you are redistributing or providing access to a work with the phrase "Project Gutenberg" associated with or appearing on the work, you must comply either with the requirements of paragraphs 1.E.1 through 1.E.7 or obtain permission for the use of the work and the Project Gutenberg-tm trademark as set forth in paragraphs 1.E.8 or 1.E.9.

1.E.3. If an individual Project Gutenberg-tm electronic work is posted with the permission of the copyright holder, your use and distribution must comply with both paragraphs 1.E.1 through 1.E.7 and any additional terms imposed by the copyright holder. Additional terms will be linked to the Project Gutenberg-tm License for all works posted with the permission of the copyright holder found at the beginning of this work.

1.E.4. Do not unlink or detach or remove the full Project Gutenberg-tm License terms from this work, or any files containing a part of this work or any other work associated with Project Gutenberg-tm.

1.E.5. Do not copy, display, perform, distribute or redistribute this electronic work, or any part of this electronic work, without prominently displaying the sentence set forth in paragraph 1.E.1 with active links or immediate access to the full terms of the Project Gutenberg-tm License.

1.E.6. You may convert to and distribute this work in any binary, compressed, marked up, nonproprietary or proprietary form, including any word processing or hypertext form. However, if you provide access to or distribute copies of a Project Gutenberg-tm work in a format other than "Plain Vanilla ASCII" or other format used in the official version posted on the official Project Gutenberg-tm web site (www.gutenberg.org), you must, at no additional cost, fee or expense to the user, provide a copy, a means of exporting a copy, or a means of obtaining a copy upon request, of the work in its original "Plain Vanilla ASCII" or other form. Any alternate format must include the full Project Gutenberg-tm License as specified in paragraph 1.E.1.

1.E.7. Do not charge a fee for access to, viewing, displaying, performing, copying or distributing any Project Gutenberg-tm works unless you comply with paragraph 1.E.8 or 1.E.9.

1.E.8. You may charge a reasonable fee for copies of or providing access to or distributing Project Gutenberg-tm electronic works provided that

- You pay a royalty fee of 20% of the gross profits you derive from the use of Project Gutenberg-tm works calculated using the method you already use to calculate your applicable taxes. The fee is owed to the owner of the Project Gutenberg-tm trademark, but he has agreed to donate royalties under this paragraph to the Project Gutenberg Literary Archive Foundation. Royalty payments must be paid within 60 days following each date on which you prepare (or are legally required to prepare) your periodic tax returns. Royalty payments should be clearly marked as such and sent to the Project Gutenberg Literary Archive Foundation at the address specified in Section 4, "Information about donations to the Project Gutenberg Literary Archive Foundation."

- You provide a full refund of any money paid by a user who notifies you in writing (or by e-mail) within 30 days of receipt that s/he does not agree to the terms of the full Project Gutenberg-tm License. You must require such a user to return or destroy all copies of the works possessed in a physical medium and discontinue all use of and all access to other copies of Project Gutenberg-tm works.

- You provide, in accordance with paragraph 1.F.3, a full refund of any
money paid for a work or a replacement copy, if a defect in the
electronic work is discovered and reported to you within 90 days
of receipt of the work.

- You comply with all other terms of this agreement for free
distribution of Project Gutenberg-tm works.

1.E.9. If you wish to charge a fee or distribute a Project Gutenberg-tm electronic work or group of works on different terms than are set forth in this agreement, you must obtain permission in writing from both the Project Gutenberg Literary Archive Foundation and Michael Hart, the owner of the Project Gutenberg-tm trademark. Contact the Foundation as set forth in Section 3 below.

1.F.

1.F.1. Project Gutenberg volunteers and employees expend considerable effort to identify, do copyright research on, transcribe and proofread public domain works in creating the Project Gutenberg-tm collection. Despite these efforts, Project Gutenberg-tm electronic works, and the medium on which they may be stored, may contain "Defects," such as, but not limited to, incomplete, inaccurate or corrupt data, transcription errors, a copyright or other intellectual property infringement, a defective or damaged disk or other medium, a computer virus, or computer codes that damage or cannot be read by your equipment.

1.F.2. LIMITED WARRANTY, DISCLAIMER OF DAMAGES - Except for the "Right of Replacement or Refund" described in paragraph 1.F.3, the Project Gutenberg Literary Archive Foundation, the owner of the Project Gutenberg-tm trademark, and any other party distributing a Project Gutenberg-tm electronic work under this agreement, disclaim all liability to you for damages, costs and expenses, including legal
fees. YOU AGREE THAT YOU HAVE NO REMEDIES FOR NEGLIGENCE, STRICT
LIABILITY, BREACH OF WARRANTY OR BREACH OF CONTRACT EXCEPT THOSE
PROVIDED IN PARAGRAPH F3. YOU AGREE THAT THE FOUNDATION, THE

TRADEMARK OWNER, AND ANY DISTRIBUTOR UNDER THIS AGREEMENT WILL NOT BE
LIABLE TO YOU FOR ACTUAL, DIRECT, INDIRECT, CONSEQUENTIAL, PUNITIVE OR
INCIDENTAL DAMAGES EVEN IF YOU GIVE NOTICE OF THE POSSIBILITY OF SUCH
DAMAGE.

1.F.3. LIMITED RIGHT OF REPLACEMENT OR REFUND - If you discover a defect in this electronic work within 90 days of receiving it, you can receive a refund of the money (if any) you paid for it by sending a written explanation to the person you received the work from. If you received the work on a physical medium, you must return the medium with your written explanation. The person or entity that provided you with the defective work may elect to provide a replacement copy in lieu of a refund. If you received the work electronically, the person or entity providing it to you may choose to give you a second opportunity to receive the work electronically in lieu of a refund. If the second copy is also defective, you may demand a refund in writing without further opportunities to fix the problem.

1.F.4. Except for the limited right of replacement or refund set forth in paragraph 1.F.3, this work is provided to you 'AS-IS' WITH NO OTHER WARRANTIES OF ANY KIND, EXPRESS OR IMPLIED, INCLUDING BUT NOT LIMITED TO
WARRANTIES OF MERCHANTIBILITY OR FITNESS FOR ANY PURPOSE.

1.F.5. Some states do not allow disclaimers of certain implied warranties or the exclusion or limitation of certain types of damages. If any disclaimer or limitation set forth in this agreement violates the law of the state applicable to this agreement, the agreement shall be interpreted to make the maximum disclaimer or limitation permitted by the applicable state law. The invalidity or unenforceability of any provision of this agreement shall not void the remaining provisions.

1.F.6. INDEMNITY - You agree to indemnify and hold the Foundation, the trademark owner, any agent or employee of the Foundation, anyone providing copies of Project Gutenberg-tm electronic works in accordance with this agreement, and any volunteers associated with the production, promotion and distribution of Project Gutenberg-tm electronic works, harmless from all liability, costs and expenses, including legal fees, that arise directly or indirectly from any of the following which you do or cause to occur: (a) distribution of this or any Project Gutenberg-tm work, (b) alteration, modification, or additions or deletions to any Project Gutenberg-tm work, and (c) any Defect you cause.

Section 2. Information about the Mission of Project Gutenberg-tm

Project Gutenberg-tm is synonymous with the free distribution of electronic works in formats readable by the widest variety of computers including obsolete, old, middle-aged and new computers. It exists because of the efforts of hundreds of volunteers and donations from people in all walks of life.

Volunteers and financial support to provide volunteers with the assistance they need, is critical to reaching Project Gutenberg-tm's goals and ensuring that the Project Gutenberg-tm collection will remain freely available for generations to come. In 2001, the Project Gutenberg Literary Archive Foundation was created to provide a secure and permanent future for Project Gutenberg-tm and future generations. To learn more about the Project Gutenberg Literary Archive Foundation and how your efforts and donations can help, see Sections 3 and 4 and the Foundation web page at http://www.pglaf.org.

Section 3. Information about the Project Gutenberg Literary Archive Foundation

The Project Gutenberg Literary Archive Foundation is a non profit 501(c)(3) educational corporation organized under the laws of the state of Mississippi and granted tax exempt status by the Internal Revenue Service. The Foundation's EIN or federal tax identification number is 64-6221541. Its 501(c)(3) letter is posted at http://pglaf.org/fundraising. Contributions to the Project Gutenberg Literary Archive Foundation are tax deductible to the full extent permitted by U.S. federal laws and your state's laws.

The Foundation's principal office is located at 4557 Melan Dr. S. Fairbanks, AK, 99712., but its volunteers and employees are scattered

CHAPTER 5 The Egotist Becomes a Personage

throughout numerous locations. Its business office is located at 809 North 1500 West, Salt Lake City, UT 84116, (801) 596-1887, email business@pglaf.org. Email contact links and up to date contact information can be found at the Foundation's web site and official page at http://pglaf.org

For additional contact information:
   Dr. Gregory B. Newby
   Chief Executive and Director
   gbnewby@pglaf.org

Section 4. Information about Donations to the Project Gutenberg Literary Archive Foundation

Project Gutenberg-tm depends upon and cannot survive without wide spread public support and donations to carry out its mission of increasing the number of public domain and licensed works that can be freely distributed in machine readable form accessible by the widest array of equipment including outdated equipment. Many small donations ($1 to $5,000) are particularly important to maintaining tax exempt status with the IRS.

The Foundation is committed to complying with the laws regulating charities and charitable donations in all 50 states of the United States. Compliance requirements are not uniform and it takes a considerable effort, much paperwork and many fees to meet and keep up with these requirements. We do not solicit donations in locations where we have not received written confirmation of compliance. To SEND DONATIONS or determine the status of compliance for any particular state visit http://pglaf.org

While we cannot and do not solicit contributions from states where we have not met the solicitation requirements, we know of no prohibition against accepting unsolicited donations from donors in such states who approach us with offers to donate.

International donations are gratefully accepted, but we cannot make any statements concerning tax treatment of donations received from outside the United States. U.S. laws alone swamp our small staff.

Please check the Project Gutenberg Web pages for current donation methods and addresses. Donations are accepted in a number of other ways including checks, online payments and credit card donations. To donate, please visit: http://pglaf.org/donate

Section 5. General Information About Project Gutenberg-tm electronic works.

Professor Michael S. Hart is the originator of the Project Gutenberg-tm concept of a library of electronic works that could be freely shared with anyone. For thirty years, he produced and distributed Project Gutenberg-tm eBooks with only a loose network of volunteer support.

Project Gutenberg-tm eBooks are often created from several printed editions, all of which are confirmed as Public Domain in the U.S. unless a copyright notice is included. Thus, we do not necessarily keep eBooks in compliance with any particular paper edition.

Most people start at our Web site which has the main PG search facility:

http://www.gutenberg.org

This Web site includes information about Project Gutenberg-tm, including how to make donations to the Project Gutenberg Literary Archive Foundation, how to help produce our new eBooks, and how to subscribe to our email newsletter to hear about new eBooks.

"It is not life that's complicated,
it's the struggle to guide and control life."